Twelve Short Novels

Twelve Short Novels

Ray J. Sherer

Harrisburg Area Community College

Holt, Rinehart and Winston

New York   Chicago   San Francisco   Atlanta   Dallas

Library of Congress Cataloging in Publication Data

Main entry under title:
Twelve short novels.

   CONTENTS: Melville, H. Bartleby the scrivener.—
Dostoevsky, F. Notes from underground.—James, H.
Daisy Miller. [etc.]
  Includes index.
   1. Fiction—Collections. I. Sherer, Ray.
PZ1.T918 [PN6014]   808.83'3   75-34327
ISBN 0-03-012151-5

Printed in the United States of America
0123 059 98765

Contents

Preface

These short novels are intended for college study, especially introductory courses in literature and composition. At least half of the fiction included is also suitable for humanities courses in western culture or other interdisciplinary courses in the history of ideas. The works by Melville, Dostoevsky, Tolstoy, Kafka, Wright, and Bellow all have the kind of historical and philosophical substantiveness that goes well beyond purely literary value. Substantiveness, in fact, has been the most important consideration in selecting these stories. Although all of them make claim to first-rate literary quality—some, of course, more than others—what they have in common even more importantly is a satisfying density of both surface and depth. Each is rich in technique, detail, and meaning; each invites in-depth discussion. Absent here, it is earnestly hoped, is that bane of the classroom inscribed on every instructor's private blacklist: the worthy story about which there is really little to say.

Study aids in *Twelve Short Novels* have been designed for versatile use. The introductory essay can be used as a concise glossary of literary concepts or as a starting point for classroom discussion of literary theory. Students in search of paper topics might also find the introduction's examples useful. Introductions to individual short novels deal in a direct way with central concerns of interpretation. They say much, but leave much more to be said, and while remaining within the bounds of critical responsibility, they are more than assertive enough to give rise to productive disagreement. For students limited to a single reading of any particular work, reading the introductions first will help to make that effort as efficient as possible. Conversely, the use of introductions as afterwords may be the better alternative for students who have become familiar with short novels by working with a few in class and wish to take on the challenge of subsequent reading unbiased by my opinions. Also available in this volume are more detailed biographies than are offered in any similar anthology. These in many cases provide biographical material directly relevant to the short novels, and beyond that they make possible an informed sympathy for the author and his time by conveying a sense of the drama, color, and total pattern of each author's life.

Ray Sherer

Harrisburg, Pennsylvania
October 1975

General Introduction

The short novel is not among the more easily defined forms of literature today. Most readers seem to know what short stories and novels are, but short novels have very little to offer in the way of definitive characteristics. The basic definition is in fact a rather unsatisfactory statistic: short novels are stories that, with occasional exceptions, fall in length between 12,000 and 40,000 words, or about thirty to one hundred pages. Because the distinctions between short novels and longer and shorter fiction forms are somewhat arbitrary, the same work can often be regarded as belonging to more than one category, depending on just how one looks at the question. Undoubtedly, only a portion of the many works considered as short novels today are the creation of authors who deliberately set out to write "a short novel." The rest are short stories that refused to end or novels that did happen to end in short-novel territory.

Although the short novel may not be easily distinguishable as a literary form, it has distinguished itself well as a form for exceptional literary achievement. For one thing, it incorporates some of the most attractive qualities of both longer and shorter fiction. As in the short story, language is characteristically used with exceptional care and economy. The short-story writer is under more pressure than the novelist to make every word count because he must accomplish everything the story is expected to do within a very limited space. He must set the scene, develop characters, provide complication, and bring the story to a meaningful conclusion in about as many pages as his reader is able to cover in one sitting. Partly because of their need for economy of language, short stories tend to use language "poetically." Words are made to enhance the story's significance not only through their surface dictionary meanings, but also by the subtler suggestions of their rhythms, ambiguities, sounds, and so forth. Short novels have even more reason than short stories for pushing language to its limits. While short stories are only expected to provide something like miniature pictures of life— "slices of life," as the saying goes—short novels generally share with their full-length counterparts the ambition of creating whole, self-contained worlds of fiction. Novel and short novel alike partake in a heady, conspicuously God-like creativity. They develop intricate environments, complex interactions among complex characters, and minute evolutions of individual fate. The novel may take eight hundred pages to do all that; the short novel must compress its fictional world into a tenth of the same space. It is no wonder that the best of short novels seem to crackle with a creative energy intense enough to have produced much longer works.

There is at least one other reason for the short novel's notable energy, compression, and precision: it is the ideal literary form for succinct philosophical statement. When a fiction writer wishes to present the essence of his own philosophical vision—and particularly when his vision is a somber one, as seems so often the case—he is likely to find that a short story is simply too short and that a full-length novel can obscure his philosophical theme with proliferation of plot and detail. The result is likely to be a short novel exceptionally precise in structure, intense in tone, and rich in meaning. It is likely, too, to be tragic or near-tragic in outcome. One might claim that the short novel is the primary form of literary tragedy in our own time, much as the tragic drama was for the classical Greeks. To survey the history of the short novel, or even the contents of this volume, is to encounter a tide of anguish, chaos, and death. Were it not for the particularly joyous creativity so evident in many of these stories, they could become grim fare indeed.

Aside from these considerations and potentially a few others, the interpretive skills demanded by short novels are practically the same as those relevant to fiction of any length. What follows is offered to help readers organize their interpretive skills. Concise explanations of literary concepts, and some clarification of the relationships among concepts, are grouped under five key headings—character, point of view, structure, symbolism, and tone.

Character

Revelation of character is the heart of fiction. A story may be first-rate despite a weak plot or sparse imagery, but unless it presents at least one character who is authentically human and who makes a forceful impact on the reader's imagination, its chances for genuinely high quality are slim. When we object that a character "just doesn't ring true" or "doesn't really come alive" we are in effect claiming that the character does not appeal in an authentic way to our inner sense of what makes people human, or that it fails to arouse a lively response in our imagination.

A well-drawn main character needs above all to possess a convincing sense of unity. Real people sometimes have only the most fragmentary of identities, yet there is always a specific core of self that makes each person a person, and the literary character must capture this quality.

In order for a story to succeed, its most important characters must also attain some kind of complexity, not necessarily in order to be "realistic," but in order to have enough human importance to be worth taking seriously. Usually, important characters gain complexity by being in the forefront of the story's action much of the time. Their depth is revealed by what they say and do, and by the reactions of other characters to them. Character is also revealed by relationships to setting or symbols, or to the tone of the work as a whole. *Epiphany* is a sophisticated method of characterization popularized by James Joyce. It means an insightful "showing forth" of personality through description of revealing gestures.

Very often it is easiest to respond favorably to characters who are presented sympathetically. As a literary term *sympathy* implies that the reader can identify with a character in a fairly extensive way; it also implies that the reader can accept the character's behavior even if that behavior contradicts laws or social customs. *Empathy* is a similar but importantly different term: it is an intuitive feeling of involvement with a character (or an entire fictive situation, for that matter) without the implication of moral approval. Empathy becomes especially important when the main character is not a *hero*—an attractive if perhaps flawed doer of good things—but an *anti-hero*. Anti-heroes are abundant in modern fiction, and certainly abundant in this volume. They compel the reader's empathy partly by their attractiveness, but more so by the opposite—by their fascinating immorality, their chilling perversity, their pathetic plight, or their absurdity. Probably all of these terms would apply to the main character of Dostoevsky's *Notes from Underground*. Anyone who reads Dostoevsky's short novel and enjoys it is likely to find himself sharing an uneasy empathy with the underground man. Despite his extraordinary unattractiveness, he compels empathy because Dostoevsky has made him intensely human.

Although characters seem to relate to one another in infinitely varied ways, nearly all of them can be classified into five key roles:

1. Main characters, whose actions take up most of the story's space and generate most of its interest;
2. Characters who constitute the goals sought by main characters (for example, the lover sought by the hero, or the criminal sought by the detective);
3. Those who help main characters attain their goals;
4. Those who oppose main characters in their struggle to attain goals, causing them to suffer or die;
5. Those who influence main characters incidentally.

Of course, many characters do not fit neatly into any single one of these roles, but instead play more than one role simultaneously or consecutively. Like any far-reaching system of literary categorization, these five designated "key" roles can be as useful for pointing out exceptions as for pointing out simple, clear examples. As a case in point one might consider Grete, the sister of the salesman-turned-beetle in Kafka's *The Metamorphosis*. She seems to function as goal, helper, and opponent; her shifting roles form an important part of the novel's ambiguity.

Point of View

Fiction is related through the eye and mind of an assumed personality which may be slightly different or sometimes very different from the writer's own. The assumed teller of the story is the narrator, and the narrator's relationship to the story itself is the *point of view*. Points of view can be divided into first and third person. A narrator who tells a story in the first person and participates in the story as well employs a *first-person participant* point of view. "I found my two officers waiting for me near the supper table," says Conrad's narrator in *The Secret Sharer*. A narrator who speaks in the first person but does not participate in the story is a *first-person observer*.

Third-person points of view are differentiated by the narrator's degree of *omniscience*. The narrator's personality is likely to be most similar to the author's if, like the author, he knows virtually everything going on in the story and can enter into the minds of most of the characters. This *omniscient point of view* differs from *selective omniscience*, which limits the narrator's vision and knowledge to that of just one or a few characters. When events are perceived through the mind of a particular character, perceptions are likely to be *impressionistic,* that is, somewhat distorted by the character's limited knowledge and emotional bias. In contrast, the *objective point of view* does not enter into characters' minds at all, but seeks to relate events more or less as if they had been recorded by cameras.

Obviously there are many engaging similarities between fiction-writing and movie-making. In fact, many modern novelists have been deeply influenced by film. Movie-making techniques can also be useful to keep in mind when considering point of view in its literal, physical aspect as *angle of vision*. Both before and after the advent of film, writers have used the prose equivalents of close-ups, distance shots, pan shots (moving the camera sideways on a fixed pivot), quick cuts (abrupt switches from one scene to another), still shots, and subjective shots (the scene as viewed through the eyes of one character).

Also considered as point of view are the several stock methods of story-telling: *narrative, dialogue, monologue,* and *stream-of-consciousness. Narrative* is simply what the narrator says in his own voice as story teller. *Dialogue* includes all that is spoken by characters to one another and placed in quotation marks. *Monologue,* rare in fiction, occurs when a character speaks at length without conversational response from others. *Stream-of-consciousness* has been a popular device in modern fiction for creating in-depth characterization directly. It allows the reader to hear thoughts, as it were, exactly as they occur in the mind of the character. In this way the writer is able to focus on the revealing semicoherence characteristic of most people's mental processes most of the time.

Structure

Fiction is composed of many parts which differ in type and size. For example, there are chapters, episodes, turning points, climaxes, interludes, sentences, phrases, and words. Questions of structure deal with relationships between parts, or between parts and the whole work. Some principles relevant to consideration of structure are size, contrast, likeness, repetition, order of sequence, and omission. Why, one might ask, does Tolstoy begin *The Death of Ivan Ilych* with the situation following Ivan's death, instead of presenting events chronologically, beginning with Ivan's early life and ending with his death and its consequences? Why does Thomas Mann make the events of Tonio Kröger's life so pointedly repetitive? Ultimately, the value of answering questions like these and perceiving fiction as a series of relationships among parts is the same as that of any worthwhile means of literary study—to gain a clearer understanding of the work's intentions, its merit, and its effects on readers.

Not surprisingly, time and space are as important in determining the structure of fiction as they are in giving shape to real life. Changes of scene from one place to another, or confinement to a single place, give fiction a particular sense of shape. The structuring effects of time are somewhat more complicated. Most stories are arranged as more or less chronological sequences of significant events. *Plot,* a major determinant of structure, can be defined in these same terms: plot is the chronological sequence of significant events in a story. The work may depart from strictly chronological sequence to reveal events which lie ahead, or more commonly, it may introduce relevant material from the past through *flashbacks. Pace* is the rate at which action moves forward. Fiction provides nearly unlimited opportunity for dramatic variations of pace. An entire generation may elapse within the space of a few words, or several paragraphs may be lavished on the significance of a few moments of fictional time.

The smallest structural elements are diction, sentence structure, and figures of speech. Taken together, these are primarily responsible for giving an author's writing the characteristic language pattern identifiable as *style.* Some writers, of course, have more distinct styles than others. But modern studies of language, some of them aided by computers, have shown that even minor writers tend to use all kinds of language patterns such as infinitives, adverb clauses, metaphors, and visual images in relatively consistent, characteristically personal ways. In effect, style, when examined closely enough, reveals a kind of linguistic fingerprint of the author.

Style often takes on meaning in itself, in relationship to the ideas being expressed in the story. A somewhat confusing sentence structure might be used to poke subtle fun at a somewhat confused character; a tense, anxious rhythm of words might reinforce a tense, anxious mood. Similarly, style can be used to suggest emotions or ideas purposefully at odds with those in the story, creating tension or irony.

Symbolism

A symbol by definition has at least two levels of meaning, and its various meanings are most often related to one another by similarity. Like all symbols, the fox in Lawrence's short novel has an apparent literal or "surface" meaning. The fox is simply an animal—sly, cunning, furry, a creature of the night, a predator who steals chickens. But to one woman in the novel, the fox becomes a symbol of passion and of the predatory male. To the predatory male who shoots the fox, the animal may also be symbolic, although less explicitly. To him the animal seems to represent something like natural vitality. The reader may find still other meanings in the fox. In each case the meanings of the symbol are based on similarities: the fox is *like* passion and vitality primarily because of its intense animal aliveness, and it is *like* the predatory male because of its similar behavior.

For a symbol to function truly as a symbol, its various meanings need to be perceived by someone. Lawrence's fox is perceived as symbolic by at least one character, and no doubt by Lawrence and most of his readers. Often, symbolic meanings are recognized only by the author and his readers, and many times the author himself remains unaware of them at first because he is too close to his own work to realize its full significance.

There are many kinds of literary symbols, and their functions differ considerably. Some images and acts have been used by many authors over the centuries to symbolize more or less the same things. These have in effect become *traditional symbols*. At least as far back as Homer's time, descents underground have symbolized encounter with radical evil or hell, so it is not surprising that Fred Daniels' retreat into the sewers in *The Man Who Lived Underground* has much the same meaning. Other symbols appeal more directly to the reader's intuition instead of relating to knowledge of traditional associations. Some stories have symbols whose meanings are merely incidental to that of the work as a whole. In other stories, symbolic meanings are central. In an *allegory*, the meanings of many symbols fit together in a precise way to express moral themes. *Expanding symbols* acquire increasingly complex meaning as the story unfolds. *Rituals* are symbolic acts that are repeated fairly regularly and with a sense of ceremonial importance. They are important in literature partly because they are extremely important in life. Probably since before the beginning of history, men have created rituals of work, play, and worship to overcome their anxieties and to strengthen cultural identity. Many writers—Lawrence, Mann, McCullers and Bellow among them—write with a studied consciousness that much of modern man's behavior is derived from, or can be related to, ritual patterns that originated thousands of years ago.

Related to ritual is the concept of "archetypal" symbolism made popular by the Swiss psychoanalyst and mythographer Carl Jung. He noticed that certain symbols seem to occur almost universally in the world's mythologies and in people's dreams. He then reasoned that the artist can evoke powerful depth-responses from his audience by presenting archetypal symbols in just the right way.

Tone

Tone in fiction is the combination of attitudes and emotions communicated by the author and narrator to the reader. Tone is partly determined by *mood,* the emotional situation of the tale itself. The mood of the conclusion of Carson McCullers' *The Ballad of the Sad Café,* where the hunchback dwarf and Marvin Macy ruthlessly destroy the café, is predominantly melancholy, bizarre, and perverse. But this mood is circumscribed by the tone of the novel, the larger consciousness and more sophisticated intentions of the author, who hints in various ways that the story as a whole should be perceived with something like mellow humor, a sense of detachment, and perhaps even a certain joy in the color and oddity of life's perversity. The many dimensions of tone and mood in the story are closely fused—often they all seem to come across at once—yet, each addresses itself to a different part of the reader's sensibility. The tonal effect is one of considerable emotional resonance and artistic subtlety.

Like the orchestrated sounds of a symphony, fiction presents itself as a complex sequence of emotional notes and chords. The hundreds of touches that create the tone of a story must be arranged with great precision. Tone may be supremely ambiguous if that is the author's intention, but if it is simply muddled it compromises the artistic excellence of fiction as badly as sour notes mar a symphony. And in much the same way that symphonic music gains from a wide variety of instrumental sounds, so the quality of fiction is heavily dependent on the writer's ability to work with a wide range of tones—from joy to despair, from straight-out emotion to convoluted irony, from classical health of spirit to the malaise of decadence.

Other concepts related to tone are *suggestiveness, foreshadowing, suspense, immediacy, esthetic distance,* and *irony. Suggestiveness* is the use of thought-provoking hints at possibilities relevant to the story but not expressly spelled out in it. This is one among a number of techniques that allow the reader to "read between the lines" intelligently. *Foreshadowing* refers to indications of what lies ahead. *Suspense* applies to fiction in its everyday sense as the anticipation about interesting questions which, one expects, will eventually be answered. In fiction the fates of empathic characters are the mainspring of suspense. But another key source of suspense is the pattern of momentary anticipations and fulfillments provided by style. By creating sophisticated patterns involving rhythm, metaphor, connotation, onomatopoeics (words or sentences that sound like what they mean), and other devices, the skillful writer can generate in his readers an eagerness to find not only the outcome of the plot, but the rewards provided, sentence by sentence, within the text.

Immediacy and *esthetic distance* are opposites. Immediacy implies that mood and tone are nearly the same, and that the writer presents the story in a forthrightly emotional way, without the "distancing" effects of attitudes like skepticism or comic irony. As in the example of Carson McCullers' story, esthetic distance creates differences between mood and tone, between the respective feelings of character, narrator, writer, and reader. The reader is made aware that the artistic process stands between the feelings within the work and his own responses to it. Some works seem to strive for a consistent sense of immediacy; this might be said of Katherine Porter's *Pale Horse, Pale Rider*. Other stories, like James's *Daisy Miller,* employ varying but substantial degrees of distance. Usually, though, writers combine both techniques in attempting to achieve as much versatility of tone as they can.

Maintenance of esthetic distance almost always demands the use of *irony*. Irony is one of the most difficult areas of fiction to deal with, partly because it occurs in so many forms. A highly condensed definition: irony is purposeful incongruity in tone, meaning, or outcome. When contrasting tones seem to be so at odds with each other that they have the effect of surprise, strangeness, or humor, the chances are that irony is at hand. The narrator of Kafka's *The Metamorphosis,* for example, creates irony by speaking of bizarre and horrifying events in a matter-of-fact, almost monotonous tone. Irony is produced by meaning more than by tone in the case of *dramatic irony,* when characters fail to perceive the implications of their own words or actions as fully as the reader can, and the contrast between the two perceptions is strong enough to be incongruous. The dramatic irony of entirely ignorant characters is usually funny; essentially, though, dramatic irony is serious in nature, because the actions of ignorant characters usually cause suffering either for themselves or others. *Satire* is a form of writing that combines the seriousness and humor of irony to dramatize the danger caused by specific people, institutions, or situations in a laughable way. Henry James satirizes the fastidious young man Winterbourne in saying that he had hurried to Rome "simply because of a certain sentimental impatience" —when in fact he has hurried to Rome because he cares more for Daisy Miller than he is willing to admit to himself. James's statement allows us to see through Winterbourne's dishonesty with himself, to chuckle at him, and to anticipate that he will probably suffer for his dishonesty, although not too seriously.

Lastly, the ironies created by incongruous outcomes are probably the least difficult of all to appreciate. Surprising turns of events, unexpected by character, reader, or both, often do a great deal to enhance the artistic tension of a well-written story. There is irony in Fred Daniels' murder by the same three policemen who had arrested him days before; in Tonio Kröger's midlife encounter with much the same alienation he had faced as a youth; in the way Adam Barclay dies of influenza without ever going to war. As grim as they may be, these ironies afford pleasure, not only because of their unexpectedness, but also because of the economy and subtlety with which they contribute to the meaning of fiction.

To summarize these elusive ideas, there are two hallmarks of irony in fiction: (1) the doubleness and contrast that create incongruity, and (2) a subjective response usually colored by surprise, ambivalence, or humor. The second concept is difficult to pin down, because it is subjective; maybe the best word to describe the relevant emotional response is the French term *frisson,* a sort of tingling of recognition in the brain. In every case, irony is distinguished by incongruity—between contrasting tones, between more and less informed perceptions of meaning, or between anticipated outcome and actual outcome.

1

HERMAN MELVILLE
Bartleby the Scrivener

One Sunday morning when the narrator of *Bartleby* stops at his office to idle away the time before church, the revelation that Bartleby actually lives there makes him realize for the first time the terrible loneliness and suffering of the scrivener. Inadvertently, he stumbles onto one of the principal truths of Bartleby's existence, "... Ah, happiness courts the light, so we deem the world is gay; but misery hides aloof, so we deem that misery there is none." At the heart of *Bartleby* is the paradox of happiness and misery in the manner of living which we call "civilization." Civilized man creates a structured, complex, and supposedly rational world. He creates walls, buildings, machines, laws, and prisons in order, if possible, to safeguard his prospects of uninterrupted happiness, especially against the whims of nature and other men. At a glance the scheme seems to work. Downtown streets are filled with the equivalent of the "bright silks and sparkling faces" Melville's narrator observes. Every so often, though, something happens to remind us that civilization conceals more human misery than it eliminates, and that man is still subject to the curse on Adam. Man must labor, suffer,

endure evil and irrationality, and die. Bartleby's sad fate is, among other things, a testimony to this truth.

Before and after his encounter with Bartleby, the narrator lives in the world where "happiness courts the light and misery hides aloof." He is considered to be "an eminently safe man," and he relishes doing "business among rich men's bonds and mortgages and title-deeds" in the "cool tranquillity of a snug retreat." It is no coincidence that his business is on Wall Street, the symbolic center of financial power, and that he plays an essential role in the accumulation of wealth by powerful men. Quite clearly, Melville is implying that his story will say something about the nature of wealth and power in America. Inside his law office, protected and happily imprisoned by Wall Street's walls, the lawyer devotes all his energies to the demands of profit. He looks with pride and amusement on his successful accommodation of the clerks' eccentricities. His sense of humor, it must be admitted, is entertaining. One cannot help but feel somewhat grateful to him for enlivening a story which might otherwise have been unbearably grim. His sense of humor, however, has a sinister way of masking the truth. The demands of endless copying have made a human wreck of the older clerk, and the same is already happening to the younger. The law office is not entirely the quaint and cheery place it seems to be. It is a place of real human destruction, and there is little doubt that Melville intended it to be representative of a vast system of commerce and labor where those at the bottom suffer endlessly, but unnoticed.

From his first encounter with Bartleby, the narrator feels a mysterious sympathy for him. Like most of us, he is fascinated by Bartleby's appearance of intense suffering. "I can see that figure now," he says in retrospect, "pallidly neat, pitiably respectable, incurably forlorn!" Bartleby appears to be a pliable worker. A man so respectable and so forlorn might be expected to conform to office routine and not cause trouble. Nevertheless he soon begins to rebel, replying to his employer's demands with his weak but resolute "I would prefer not to." To his own surprise, the lawyer continues to react with sympathy. "There was something about Bartleby that not only strangely disarmed me, but in a wonderful manner touched and disconcerted me." Why? Probably because Bartleby has begun to awaken in him an awareness of human suffering, without which he has long been imprisoned within his own superficial experience of life as safe and snug. Now his inward hunger for a more complete vision of humanity is called forth by Bartleby's anything but humorous torment. His sympathy for Bartleby becomes ambiguous. On the morning he discovers that Bartleby has been living in the office, his attitude undergoes a decided change. His pity reaches its greatest intensity, even to the point of threatening his mental balance. Too much pity for Bartleby, he concludes, is not only useless but perverse.

Despite his resolve to remain aloof from Bartleby, and subsequently to expel him from the office because of his complete refusal to cooperate, the narrator unwittingly finds himself identifying or being identified with the scrivener in several ways. He, and his employees as well, all find themselves using Bartleby's word "prefer" with unaccustomed frequency. Unwittingly, the narrator undergoes a series of experiences that mirror Bartleby's fate of guilt, expulsion, flight, and imprisonment.

Melville's deliberate pairing of the two men is significant. As two human beings who have entered into association with one another, they should share a mutual human identity based upon compassion and acceptance of suffering and guilt. But the narrator's compassion seems to fail, and Bartleby's acceptance of suffering is unnatural, so that the sharing between them becomes destructive. The narrator goes beyond the customs of his time in offering to help Bartleby, but does he ever really manifest a genuine charity adequate to save the scrivener? Bartleby too is far from blameless, although there is a strange nobleness in his resolve to die. Circumstantially, he might have chosen other-wise. His will to choose is a central question in the story. The narrator says of him, "it was his soul that suffered, and his soul I could not reach." Bartleby's will to die may come from a depth in himself that even he cannot reach.

More than that, the collective will of society seems to be complicit in his destruction. Melville's story, like several of the stories in this text, raises questions about the type of cultural pattern known to anthropology as "scapegoat" ritual. One person or one group is more or less arbitrarily chosen to suffer for the guilt or disorder experienced by the whole society. In Bartleby's case it was, after all, the collective disap-proval of the narrator's colleagues that necessitated Bartleby's imprisonment. And as the narrator had walked to his office the morning of Bartleby's supposed eviction, he had felt—mistakenly, but nonetheless significantly—that all Broadway was humming with speculation about Bartleby's fate. Beneath the narrator's mistaken impression lay a deeper truth. All of society *did* demand Bartleby's destruction, because society thereby fulfills its contradictory needs to partake in the irrationality of suffering and guilt, and at the same time to be rid of these burdens.

Bartleby
The Scrivener

I am a rather elderly man. The nature of my avocations for the last thirty years has brought me into more than ordinary contact with what would seem an interesting and somewhat singular set of men, of whom, as yet, nothing that I know of has ever been written—I mean the law-copyists, or scriveners. I have known very many of them, professionally and privately, and, if I pleased, could relate divers histories at which good-natured gentlemen might smile and sentimental souls might weep. But I waive the biographies of all other scriveners for a few passages in the life of Bartleby, who was a scrivener, the strangest I ever saw or heard of. While of other law-copyists I might write the complete life, of Bartleby nothing of that sort can be done. I believe that no materials exist for a full and satisfactory biography of this man. It is an irreparable loss to literature. Bartleby was one of those beings of whom nothing is ascertainable except from the original sources, and, in his case, those are very small. What my own astonished eyes saw of Bartleby, *that* is all I know of him, except, indeed, one vague report, which will appear in the sequel.

Ere introducing the scrivener as he first appeared to me, it is fit I make some mention of myself, my employees, my business, my chambers and general surroundings, because some such description is indispensable to an adequate understanding of the chief character about to be presented. *Imprimis:* I am a man who, from his youth upwards, has been filled with a profound conviction that the easiest way of life is the best. Hence, though I belong to a profession proverbially energetic and nervous even to turbulence at times, yet nothing of that sort have I ever suffered to invade my peace. I am one of those unambitious lawyers who never addresses a jury or in any way draws down public applause, but, in the cool tranquillity of a snug retreat, do a snug business among rich men's bonds, and mortgages, and title deeds. All who know me consider me an eminently *safe* man. The late John Jacob Astor, a personage little given to poetic enthusiasm, had no hesitation in pronouncing my first grand point to be prudence, my next, method. I do not speak it in vanity, but simply record the fact that I was not unemployed in my profession by the late John Jacob Astor, a name which, I admit, I love to repeat, for it hath a rounded and orbicular sound to it, and rings like unto bullion. I will freely add that I was not insensible to the late John Jacob Astor's good opinion.

Some time prior to the period at which this little history begins my avocations had been largely increased. The good old office, now extinct in the State of New York, of a Master in Chancery, had been conferred upon me. It was not a very arduous office, but very pleasantly remunerative. I seldom lose my temper, much more seldom indulge in dangerous indignation at wrongs and outrages, but I must be permitted to be rash here and declare that I consider the sudden and violent abrogation of the office of Master in Chancery, by the new Constitution, as a —— premature act, inasmuch as I had counted upon a life lease of the profits, whereas I only received those of a few short years. But this is by the way.

My chambers were upstairs at No. —— Wall Street. At one end they looked upon the white wall of the interior of a spacious skylight shaft, penetrating the building from top to bottom.

This view might have been considered rather tame than otherwise, deficient in what landscape painters call "life." But, if so, the view from the other end of my chambers offered at least a contrast, if nothing more. In that direction, my windows commanded an unobstructed view of a lofty brick wall, black by age and everlasting shade, which wall required no spyglass to bring out its lurking beauties, but, for the benefit of all nearsighted spectators, was pushed up to within ten feet of my windowpanes. Owing to the great height of the surrounding buildings, and my chambers' being on the second floor, the interval between this wall and mine not a little resembled a huge square cistern.

At the period just preceding the advent of Bartleby, I had two persons as copyists in my employment, and a promising lad as an office boy. First, Turkey; second, Nippers; third, Ginger Nut. These may seem names the like of which are not usually found in the Directory. In truth, they were nicknames, mutually conferred upon each other by my three clerks, and were deemed expressive of their respective persons or characters. Turkey was a short, pursy Englishman, of about my own age—that is, somewhere not far from sixty. In the morning, one might say, his face was of a fine florid hue, but after twelve o'clock, meridian—his dinner hour—it blazed like a grate full of Christmas coals; and continued blazing—but, as it were, with a gradual wane— till six o'clock, P.M., or thereabouts; after which I saw no more of the proprietor of the face, which, gaining its meridian with the sun, seemed to set with it, to rise, culminate, and decline the following day, with the like regularity and undiminished glory. There are many singular coin- cidences I have known in the course of my life, not the least among which was the fact, that, exactly when Turkey displayed his fullest beams from his red and radiant countenance, just then, too, at that critical moment, began the daily period when I considered his business capacities as seriously disturbed for the remainder of the twenty-four hours. Not that he was absolutely idle or averse to business then; far from it. The difficulty was, he was apt to be altogether too energetic. There was a strange, inflamed, flurried, flighty recklessness of activity about him. He would be incautious in dipping his pen into his ink- stand. All his blots upon my documents were dropped there after twelve o'clock, meridian. Indeed, not only would he be reckless and sadly given to making blots in the afternoon, but some days he went further and was rather noisy. At such times, too, his face flamed with augmented blazonry, as if cannel coal had been heaped on anthracite. He made an unpleasant racket with his chair; spilled his sandbox; in mending his pens, impatiently split them all to pieces and threw them on the floor in a sudden passion; stood up and leaned over his table, boxing his papers about in a most indecorous manner, very sad to behold in an elderly man like him. Nevertheless, as he was in many ways a most valuable person to me, and all the time before twelve o'clock, merid- ian, was the quickest, steadiest creature, too, accomplishing a great deal of work in a style not easily to be matched—for these reasons I was willing to overlook his eccentricities, though indeed, occasionally, I remonstrated with him. I did this very gently, however, because, though the civilest, nay, the blandest and most reverential of men in the morn- ing, yet, in the afternoon he was disposed, upon provocation, to be slightly rash with his tongue—in fact, insolent. Now, valuing his morn- ing services as I did, and resolved not to lose them—yet, at the same time, made uncomfortable by his inflamed ways after twelve o'clock— and being a man of peace, unwilling by my admonitions to call forth un- seemly retorts from him, I took upon me one Saturday noon (he was always worse on Saturdays) to hint to him, very kindly, that perhaps, now that he was growing old, it might be well to abridge his labors; in short, he need not come to my chambers after twelve o'clock, but, dinner over, had best go home to his lodgings and rest himself till tea- time. But no; he insisted upon his afternoon devotions. His countenance became intolerably fervid, as he oratorically assured me—gesticulating with a long ruler at the other end of the room—that if his services in the morning were useful, how indispensable, then, in the afternoon?

"With submission, sir," said Turkey, on this occasion, "I consider myself your right-hand man. In the morning I but marshal and deploy my columns, but in the afternoon I put myself at their head, and gallantly charge the foe, thus"—and he made a violent thrust with the ruler.

"But the blots, Turkey," intimated I.

"True; but, with submission, sir, behold these hairs! I am getting old. Surely, sir, a blot or two of a warm afternoon is not to be severely urged against gray hairs. Old age—even if it blot the page—is honorable. With submission, sir, we *both* are getting old."

This appeal to my fellow feeling was hardly to be resisted. At all events, I saw that go he would not. So I made up my mind to let him stay, resolving, nevertheless, to see to it that, during the afternoon, he had to do with my less important papers.

Nippers, the second on my list, was a whiskered, sallow, and upon the whole rather piratical-looking young man of about five and twenty. I always deemed him the victim of two evil powers—ambition and indigestion. The ambition was evinced by a certain impatience of the duties of a mere copyist, an unwarrantable usurpation of strictly professional affairs, such as the original drawing up of legal documents. The indigestion seemed betokened in an occasional nervous testiness and grinning irritability, causing the teeth to audibly grind together over mistakes committed in copying; unnecessary maledictions, hissed rather than spoken, in the heat of business; and especially by a continual discontent with the height of the table where he worked. Though of a very ingenious mechanical turn, Nippers could never get this table to suit him. He put chips under it, blocks of various sorts, bits of pasteboard, and at last went so far as to attempt an exquisite adjustment by final pieces of folded blotting paper. But no invention would answer. If, for the sake of easing his back, he brought the table lid at a sharp angle well up towards his chin, and wrote there like a man using the steep roof of a Dutch house for his desk, then he declared that it stopped the circulation in his arms. If now he lowered the table to his waistbands and stooped over it in writing, then there was a sore aching in his back. In short, the truth of the matter was Nippers knew not what he wanted. Or, if he wanted anything, it was to be rid of a scrivener's table altogether. Among the manifestations of his diseased ambition was a fondness he had for receiving visits from certain ambiguous-looking fellows in seedy coats, whom he called his clients. Indeed, I was aware that not only was he, at times, considerable of a ward politician, but he occasionally did a little business at the Justices' courts, and was not unknown on the steps of the Tombs. I have good reason to believe, however, that one individual who called upon him at my chambers, and who, with a grand air, he insisted was his client, was no other than a dun, and the alleged title deed, a bill. But, with all his failings, and the annoyances he caused me, Nippers, like his compatriot Turkey, was a very useful man to me; wrote a neat, swift hand; and, when he chose, was not deficient in a gentlemanly sort of deportment. Added to this, he always dressed in a gentlemanly sort of way, and so, incidentally, reflected credit upon my chambers. Whereas, with respect to Turkey, I had much ado to keep him from being a reproach to me. His clothes were apt to look oily, and smell of eating houses. He wore his pantaloons very loose and baggy in summer. His coats were execrable, his hat not to be handled. But while that hat was a thing of indifference to me, inasmuch as his natural civility and deference, as a dependent Englishman, always led him to doff it the moment he entered the room, yet his coat was another matter. Concerning his coats, I reasoned with him, but with no effect. The truth was, I suppose, that a man with so small an income could not afford to sport such a lustrous face and a lustrous coat at one and the same time. As Nippers once observed, Turkey's money went chiefly for red ink. One winter day, I presented Turkey with a highly respectable-looking coat of my own—a padded gray coat of a most comfortable warmth, and which buttoned straight up from the knee to the neck. I thought Turkey would appreciate the favor and abate his rashness and obstreperousness of afternoons. But no; I verily believe that buttoning himself up in so downy and blanketlike a coat had a pernicious effect upon him—upon the same principle that too much oats are bad for horses. In fact, precisely as a rash, restive horse is said to feel his oats, so Turkey felt his coat. It made him insolent. He was a man whom prosperity harmed.

Though, concerning the self-indulgent habits of Turkey, I had my own private surmises, yet, touching Nippers, I was well persuaded that, whatever might be his faults in other respects, he was, at least, a temperate young man. But indeed, nature herself seemed to have been his vintner, and, at his birth, charged him so thoroughly with an irritable, brandylike disposition that all subsequent potations were needless. When I consider how, amid the stillness of my chambers, Nippers would sometimes impatiently rise from his seat, and, stooping over his table, spread his arms wide apart, seize the whole desk, and move it, and jerk it, with a grim, grinding motion on the floor, as if the table were a perverse voluntary agent, intent on thwarting and vexing him, I plainly perceive that, for Nippers, brandy-and-water were altogether superfluous.

It was fortunate for me that, owing to its peculiar cause—indigestion —the irritability and consequent nervousness of Nippers were mainly observable in the morning, while in the afternoon he was comparatively mild. So that, Turkey's paroxysms only coming on about twelve o'clock, I never had to do with their eccentricities at one time. Their fits relieved each other, like guards. When Nippers's was on, Turkey's was off; and vice versa. This was a good natural arrangement, under the circumstances.

Ginger Nut, the third on my list, was a lad some twelve years old. His father was a carman, ambitious of seeing his son on the bench instead of a cart before he died. So he sent him to my office, as student at law, errand boy, cleaner and sweeper, at the rate of one dollar a week. He had a little desk to himself, but he did not use it much. Upon inspection, the drawer exhibited a great array of the shells of various sorts of nuts. Indeed, to this quick-witted youth, the whole noble science of the law was contained in a nutshell. Not the least among the employments of Ginger Nut, as well as one which he discharged with the most alacrity, was his duty as cake and apple purveyor for Turkey and Nippers. Copying law papers being proverbially a dry, husky sort of business, my two scriveners were fain to moisten their mouths very often with Spitzenbergs, to be had at the numerous stalls nigh the Custom House and Post Office. Also, they sent Ginger Nut very frequently for that peculiar cake—small, flat, round, and very spicy—after which he had been named by them. Of a cold morning, when business was but dull, Turkey would gobble up scores of these cakes, as if they were mere wafers—indeed, they sell them at the rate of six or eight for a penny—the scrape of his pen blending with the crunching of the crisp particles in his mouth. Of all the fiery afternoon blunders and flurried rashnesses of Turkey was his once moistening a ginger cake between his lips and clapping it on to a mortgage for a seal. I came within an ace of dismissing him then. But he mollified me by making an Oriental bow, and saying:

"With submission, sir, it was generous of me to find you in stationery on my own account."

Now my original business—that of a conveyancer and title hunter, and drawer-up of recondite documents of all sorts—was considerably increased by receiving the Master's office. There was now great work for scriveners. Not only must I push the clerks already with me, but I must have additional help.

In answer to my advertisement, a motionless young man one morning stood upon my office threshold, the door being open, for it was summer. I can see that figure now—pallidly neat, pitiably respectable, incurably forlorn! It was Bartleby.

After a few words touching his qualifications, I engaged him, glad to have among my corps of copyists a man of so singularly sedate an aspect, which I thought might operate beneficially upon the flighty temper of Turkey and the fiery one of Nippers.

I should have stated before that ground-glass folding doors divided my premises into two parts, one of which was occupied by my scriveners, the other by myself. According to my humor, I threw open these doors or closed them. I resolved to assign Bartleby a corner by the folding doors, but on my side of them, so as to have this quiet man within easy call, in case any trifling thing was to be done. I placed his desk close up to a small side window in that part of the room, a window which originally had afforded a lateral view of certain grimy back yards and bricks, but which, owing to subsequent erections, commanded at present no view at all, though it gave some light. Within three feet of the panes was a wall, and the light came down from far above, between two lofty buildings, as from a very small opening in a dome. Still further to a satisfactory arrangement, I procured a high green folding screen, which might entirely isolate Bartleby from my sight, though not remove him from my voice. And thus, in a manner, privacy and society were conjoined.

At first, Bartleby did an extraordinary quantity of writing. As if long famishing for something to copy, he seemed to gorge himself on my documents. There was no pause for digestion. He ran a day and night line, copying by sunlight and by candlelight. I should have been quite delighted with his application, had he been cheerfully industrious. But he wrote on silently, palely, mechanically.

It is, of course, an indispensable part of a scrivener's business to verify the accuracy of his copy, word by word. Where there are two or more scriveners in an office, they assist each other in this examination, one reading from the copy, the other holding the original. It is a very dull, wearisome, and lethargic affair. I can readily imagine that, to some sanguine temperaments, it would be altogether intolerable. For example, I cannot credit that the mettlesome poet, Byron, would have contentedly sat down with Bartleby to examine a law document of, say five hundred pages, closely written in a crimpy hand.

Now and then, in the haste of business, it had been my habit to assist in comparing some brief document myself, calling Turkey or Nippers for this purpose. One object I had in placing Bartleby so handy to me behind the screen was to avail myself of his services on such trivial occasions. It was on the third day, I think, of his being with me, and before any necessity had arisen for having his own writing examined, that, being much hurried to complete a small affair I had in hand, I abruptly called to Bartleby. In my haste and natural expectancy of instant compliance, I sat with my head bent over the original on my desk, and my right hand sideways, and somewhat nervously extended with the copy, so that, immediately upon emerging from his retreat, Bartleby might snatch it and proceed to business without the least delay.

In this very attitude did I sit when I called to him, rapidly stating what it was I wanted him to do—namely, to examine a small paper with me. Imagine my surprise, nay, my consternation, when, without moving from his privacy, Bartleby, in a singularly mild, firm voice, replied, "I would prefer not to."

I sat awhile in perfect silence, rallying my stunned faculties. Immediately it occurred to me that my ears had deceived me, or Bartleby had entirely misunderstood my meaning. I repeated my request in the clearest tone I could assume; but in quite as clear a one came the previous reply, "I would prefer not to."

"Prefer not to," echoed I, rising in high excitement, and crossing the room with a stride. "What do you mean? Are you moon-struck? I want you to help me compare this sheet here—take it," and I thrust it towards him.

"I would prefer not to," said he.

I looked at him steadfastly. His face was leanly composed; his gray eyes dimly calm. Not a wrinkle of agitation rippled him. Had there been the least uneasiness, anger, impatience or impertinence in his manner; in other words, had there been anything ordinarily human about him, doubtless I should have violently dismissed him from the premises. But as it was I should have as soon thought of turning my pale plaster-of-Paris bust of Cicero out of doors. I stood gazing at him awhile, as he went on with his own writing, and then reseated myself at my desk. This is very strange, thought I. What had one best do? But my business hurried me. I concluded to forget the matter for the present, reserving it for my future leisure. So calling Nippers from the other room, the paper was speedily examined.

A few days after this, Bartleby concluded four lengthy documents, being quadruplicates of a week's testimony taken before me in my High Court of Chancery. It became necessary to examine them. It was an important suit, and great accuracy was imperative. Having all things arranged, I called Turkey, Nippers and Ginger Nut, from the next room, meaning to place the four copies in the hands of my four clerks, while I should read from the original. Accordingly, Turkey, Nippers, and Ginger Nut had taken their seats in a row, each with his document in his hand, when I called to Bartleby to join this interesting group.

"Bartleby! quick, I am waiting."

I heard a slow scrape of his chair legs on the uncarpeted floor, and soon he appeared standing at the entrance of his hermitage.

"What is wanted?" said he, mildly.

"The copies, the copies," said I, hurriedly. "We are going to examine them. There"—and I held towards him the fourth quadruplicate.

"I would prefer not to," he said, and gently disappeared behind the screen.

For a few moments I was turned into a pillar of salt, standing at the head of my seated column of clerks. Recovering myself, I advanced towards the screen and demanded the reason for such extraordinary conduct.

"*Why* do you refuse?"

"I would prefer not to."

With any other man I should have flown outright into a dreadful passion, scorned all further words, and thrust him ignominiously from my presence. But there was something about Bartleby that not only strangely disarmed me, but, in a wonderful manner, touched and disconcerted me. I began to reason with him.

"These are your own copies we are about to examine. It is labor saving to you, because one examination will answer for your four papers. It is common usage. Every copyist is bound to help examine his copy. Is it not so? Will you not speak? Answer!"

"I prefer not to," he replied in a flutelike tone. It seemed to me that, while I had been addressing him, he carefully revolved every statement that I made; fully comprehended the meaning; could not gainsay the irresistible conclusion; but, at the same time, some paramount consideration prevailed with him to reply as he did.

"You are decided, then, not to comply with my request—a request made according to common usage and common sense?"

He briefly gave me to understand that on that point my judgment was sound. Yes: his decision was irreversible.

It is seldom the case that, when a man is browbeaten in some unprecedented and violently unreasonable way, he begins to stagger in his own plainest faith. He begins, as it were, vaguely to surmise that, wonderful as it may be, all the justice and all the reason is on the other side. Accordingly, if any disinterested persons are present, he turns to them for some reinforcement for his own faltering mind.

"Turkey," said I, "what do you think of this? Am I not right?"

"With submission, sir," said Turkey, in his blandest tone, "I think that you are."

"Nippers," said I, "what do *you* think of it?"

"I think I should kick him out of the office."

(The reader of nice perceptions, will here perceive that, it being morning, Turkey's answer is couched in polite and tranquil terms, but Nippers replies in ill-tempered ones. Or, to repeat a previous sentence, Nippers's ugly mood was on duty, and Turkey's off.)

"Ginger Nut," said I, willing to enlist the smallest suffrage in my behalf, "what do *you* think of it?"

"I think, sir, he's a little *luny*," replied Ginger Nut, with a grin.

"You hear what they say," said I, turning towards the screen, "come forth and do your duty."

But he vouchsafed no reply. I pondered a moment in sore perplexity. But once more business hurried me. I determined again to postpone the consideration of this dilemma to my future leisure. With a little trouble we made out to examine the papers without Bartleby, though at every page or two Turkey deferentially dropped his opinion that this proceeding was quite out of the common; while Nippers, twitching in his chair with a dyspeptic nervousness, ground out between his set teeth occasional hissing maledictions against the stubborn oaf behind the screen. And for his (Nippers's) part, this was the first and the last time he would do another man's business without pay.

Meanwhile Bartleby sat in his hermitage, oblivious to everything but his own peculiar business there.

Some days passed, the scrivener being employed upon another lengthy work. His late remarkable conduct led me to regard his ways narrowly. I observed that he never went to dinner; indeed, that he never went anywhere. As yet I had never, of my personal knowledge, known him to be outside of my office. He was a perpetual sentry in the corner. At about eleven o'clock, though, in the morning, I noticed that Ginger Nut would advance towards the opening in Bartleby's screen, as if silently beckoned thither by a gesture invisible to me where I sat. The boy would then leave the office jingling a few pence, and reappear with a handful of gingernuts, which he delivered in the hermitage, receiving two of the cakes for his trouble.

He lives, then, on gingernuts, thought I; never eats a dinner, properly speaking; he must be a vegetarian, then; but no, he never eats even vegetables, he eats nothing but gingernuts. My mind then ran on in reveries concerning the probable effects upon the human constitution of living entirely on gingernuts. Gingernuts are so called because they contain ginger as one of their peculiar constituents, and the final flavoring one. Now, what was ginger? A hot, spicy thing. Was Bartleby hot and spicy? Not at all. Ginger, then, had no effect upon Bartleby. Probably he preferred it should have none.

Nothing so aggravates an earnest person as a passive resistance. If the individual so resisted be of a not inhumane temper, and the resisting one perfectly harmless in his passivity, then, in the better moods of the former, he will endeavor charitably to construe to his imagination what proves impossible to be solved by his judgment. Even so, for the most part, I regarded Bartleby and his ways. Poor fellow! thought I, he means no mischief; it is plain he intends no insolence; his aspect sufficiently evinces that his eccentricities are involuntary. He is useful to me. I can get along with him. If I turn him away, the chances are he will fall in with some less indulgent employer, and then he will be rudely treated, and perhaps driven forth miserably to starve. Yes. Here I can cheaply purchase a delicious self-approval. To befriend Bartleby, to humor him in his strange willfulness, will cost me little or nothing, while I lay up in my soul what will eventually prove a sweet morsel for my conscience. But this mood was not invariable with me. The passiveness of Bartleby sometimes irritated me. I felt strangely goaded on to encounter him in new opposition—to elicit some angry spark from him answerable to my own. But, indeed, I might as well have essayed to strike fire with my knuckles against a bit of Windsor soap. But one afternoon the evil impulse in me mastered me, and the following little scene ensued:

"Bartleby," said I, "when those papers are all copied, I will compare them with you."

"I would prefer not to."

"How? Surely you do not mean to persist in that mulish vagary?"

No answer.

I threw open the folding doors near by, and, turning upon Turkey and Nippers, exclaimed:

"Bartleby a second time says he won't examine his papers. What do you think of it, Turkey?"

It was afternoon, be it remembered. Turkey sat glowing like a brass boiler, his bald head steaming, his hands reeling among his blotted papers.

"Think of it?" roared Turkey. "I think I'll just step behind his screen and black his eyes for him!"

So saying, Turkey rose to his feet and threw his arms into a pugilistic position. He was hurrying away to make good his promise when I detained him, alarmed at the effect of incautiously rousing Turkey's combativeness after dinner.

"Sit down, Turkey," said I, "and hear what Nippers has to say. What do you think of it, Nippers? Would I not be justified in immediately dismissing Bartleby?"

"Excuse me, that is for you to decide, sir. I think his conduct quite unusual, and indeed, unjust, as regards Turkey and myself. But it may only be a passing whim."

"Ah," exclaimed I, "you have strangely changed your mind, then— you speak very gently of him now."

"All beer," cried Turkey; "gentleness is effects of beer—Nippers and I dined together today. You see how gentle *I* am, sir. Shall I go and black his eyes?"

"You refer to Bartleby, I suppose. No, not today, Turkey," I replied; "pray, put up your fists."

I closed the doors and again advanced towards Bartleby. I felt additional incentives tempting me to my fate. I burned to be rebelled against again. I remembered that Bartleby never left the office.

"Bartleby," said I, "Ginger Nut is away; just step around to the Post Office, won't you? (it was but a three minutes' walk), and see if there is anything for me."

"I would prefer not to."

"You *will* not?"

"I *prefer* not."

I staggered to my desk and sat there in a deep study. My blind inveteracy returned. Was there any other thing in which I could procure myself to be ignominiously repulsed by this lean, penniless wight? —my hired clerk? What added thing is there, perfectly reasonable, that he will be sure to refuse to do?

"Bartleby!"

No answer.

"Bartleby," in a louder tone.

No answer.

"Bartleby," I roared.

Like a very ghost, agreeably to the laws of magical invocation, at the third summons he appeared at the entrance of his hermitage.

"Go to the next room, and tell Nippers to come to me."

"I prefer not to," he respectfully and slowly said, and mildly disappeared.

"Very good, Bartleby," said I, in a quiet sort of serenely severe self-possessed tone, intimating the unalterable purpose of some terrible retribution very close at hand. At the moment I half intended something of the kind. But upon the whole, as it was drawing towards my dinner hour, I thought it best to put on my hat and walk home for the day, suffering much from perplexity and distress of mind.

Shall I acknowledge it? The conclusion of this whole business was that it soon became a fixed fact of my chambers, that a pale young scrivener by the name of Bartleby had a desk there; that he copied for me at the usual rate of four cents a folio (one hundred words); but he was permanently exempt from examining the work done by him, that duty being transferred to Turkey and Nippers, out of compliment, doubtless, to their superior acuteness; moreover, said Bartleby was never, on any account, to be dispatched on the most trivial errand of any sort; and that even if entreated to take upon him such a matter, it was generally understood that he would "prefer not to"—in other words, that he would refuse point-blank.

As days passed on, I became considerably reconciled to Bartleby. His steadiness, his freedom from all dissipation, his incessant industry (except when he chose to throw himself into a standing reverie behind his screen), his great stillness, his unalterableness of demeanor under all circumstances, made him a valuable acquisition. One prime thing was this—*he was always there*—first in the morning, continually through the day, and the last at night. I had a singular confidence in his honesty. I felt my most precious papers perfectly safe in his hands. Sometimes, to be sure, I could not, for the very soul of me, avoid falling into sudden spasmodic passions with him. For it was exceeding difficult to bear in mind all the time those strange peculiarities, privileges, and unheard-of exemptions, forming the tacit stipulations on Bartleby's part under which he remained in my office. Now and then, in the eagerness of dispatching pressing business, I would inadvertently summon Bartleby, in a short, rapid tone, to put his finger, say, on the incipient tie of a bit of red tape with which I was about compressing some papers. Of course, from behind the screen the usual answer, "I prefer not to," was sure to come; and then, how could a human creature, with the common infirmities of our nature, refrain from bitterly exclaiming upon such perverseness—such unreasonableness. However, every added repulse of this sort which I received only tended to lessen the probability of my repeating the inadvertence.

Here it must be said that, according to the custom of most legal gentlemen occupying chambers in densely populated law buildings, there were several keys to my door. One was kept by a woman residing in the attic, which person weekly scrubbed and daily swept and dusted my apartments. Another was kept by Turkey for convenience' sake. The third I sometimes carried in my own pocket. The fourth I knew not who had.

Now, one Sunday morning I happened to go to Trinity Church, to hear a celebrated preacher, and finding myself rather early on the ground I thought I would walk round to my chambers for a while. Luckily I had my key with me, but upon applying it to the lock, I found it resisted by something inserted from the inside. Quite surprised, I called out, when to my consternation a key was turned from within, and, thrusting his lean visage at me, and holding the door ajar, the apparition of Bartleby appeared, in his shirt sleeves, and otherwise in a strangely tattered deshabille, saying quietly that he was sorry, but he was deeply engaged just then, and—preferred not admitting me at present. In a brief word or two, he moreover added, that perhaps I had better walk around the block two or three times, and by that time he would probably have concluded his affairs.

Now, the utterly unsurmised appearance of Bartleby, tenanting my law chambers of a Sunday morning, with his cadaverously gentlemanly *nonchalance,* yet withal firm and self-possessed, had such a strange effect upon me that incontinently I slunk away from my own door and did as desired. But not without sundry twinges of impotent rebellion against the mild effrontery of this unaccountable scrivener. Indeed, it was his wonderful mildness, chiefly, which not only disarmed me but unmanned me, as it were. For I consider that one, for the time, is sort of unmanned when he tranquilly permits his hired clerk to dictate to him and order him away from his own premises. Furthermore, I was full of uneasiness as to what Bartleby could possibly be doing in my office in his shirt sleeves, and in an otherwise dismantled condition, of a Sunday morning. Was anything amiss going on? Nay, that was out of the question. It was not to be thought of for a moment that Bartleby was an immoral person. But what could he be doing there?—copying? Nay again, whatever might be his eccentricities, Bartleby was an eminently decorous person. He would be the last man to sit down to his desk in any state approaching to nudity. Besides, it was Sunday; and there was something about Bartleby that forbade the supposition that he would by any secular occupation violate the proprieties of the day.

Nevertheless, my mind was not pacified, and, full of a restless curiosity, at last I returned to the door. Without hindrance I inserted my key, opened it, and entered. Bartleby was not to be seen. I looked round anxiously, peeped behind his screen, but it was very plain that he was gone. Upon more closely examining the place, I surmised that for an indefinite period Bartleby must have ate, dressed, and slept in my office, and that, too, without plate, mirror, or bed. The cushioned seat of a rickety old sofa in one corner bore that faint impress of a lean, reclining form. Rolled away under his desk I found a blanket; under the empty grate, a blacking box and brush; on a chair, a tin basin, with soap and a ragged towel; in a newspaper a few crumbs of gingernuts and a morsel of cheese. Yes, thought I, it is evident enough that Bartleby has been making his home here, keeping bachelor's hall all by himself. Immediately then the thought came sweeping across me, what miserable friendlessness and loneliness are here revealed. His poverty is great, but his solitude, how horrible! Think of it. Of a Sunday, Wall Street is deserted as Petra, and every night of every day it is an emptiness. This building, too, which of weekdays hums with industry and life, at nightfall echoes with sheer vacancy, and all through Sunday is forlorn. And here Bartleby makes his home, sole spectator of a solitude which he has seen all populous—a sort of innocent and transformed Marius brooding among the ruins of Carthage!

For the first time in my life a feeling of overpowering stinging melancholy seized me. Before, I had never experienced aught but a not unpleasing sadness. The bond of a common humanity now drew me irresistibly to gloom. A fraternal melancholy! For both I and Bartleby were sons of Adam. I remembered the bright silks and sparkling faces I had seen that day, in gala trim, swanlike sailing down the Mississippi of Broadway; and I contrasted them with the pallid copyist, and thought to myself, Ah, happiness courts the light, so we deem the world is gay, but misery hides aloof, so we deem that misery there is none. These sad fancyings—chimeras, doubtless, of a sick and silly brain—led on to other and more special thoughts, concerning the eccentricities of Bartleby. Presentiments of strange discoveries hovered round me. The scrivener's pale form appeared to me laid out, among uncaring strangers in its shivering winding sheet.

Suddenly I was attracted by Bartleby's closed desk, the key in open sight left in the lock.

I mean no mischief, seek the gratification of no heartless curiosity, thought I; besides, the desk is mine, and its contents, too, so I will make bold to look within. Everything was methodically arranged, the papers smoothly placed. The pigeonholes were deep, and, removing the files of documents, I groped into their recesses. Presently I felt something there, and dragged it out. It was an old bandanna handkerchief, heavy and knotted. I opened it, and saw it was a savings bank.

I now recalled all the quiet mysteries which I had noted in the man. I remembered that he never spoke but to answer; that, though at intervals he had considerable time to himself, yet I had never seen him reading—no, not even a newspaper; that for long periods he would stand looking out, at his pale window behind the screen, upon the dead brick wall; I was quite sure he never visited any refectory or eating house, while his pale face clearly indicated that he never drank beer like Turkey, or tea and coffee even, like other men; that he never went anywhere in particular that I could learn; never went out for a walk, unless, indeed, that was the case at present; that he had declined telling who he was, or whence he came, or whether he had any relatives in the world; that though so thin and pale, he never complained of ill health. And more than all I remembered a certain unconscious air of pallid—how shall I call it?—of pallid haughtiness, say, or rather an austere reserve about him, which had positively awed me into my tame compliance with his eccentricities, when I had feared to ask him to do the slightest incidental thing for me, even though I might know, from his long-continued motionlessness, that behind his screen he must be standing in one of those dead-wall reveries of his.

Revolving all these things, and coupling them with the recently discovered fact that he made my office his constant abiding place and home, and not forgetful of his morbid moodiness—revolving all these things, a prudential feeling began to steal over me. My first emotions had been those of purely melancholy and sincerest pity; but just in proportion as the forlornness of Bartleby grew and grew to my imagination, did that same melancholy merge into fear, that pity into repulsion. So true it is, and so terrible too, that up to a certain point the thought or sight of misery enlists our best affections; but, in certain special cases, beyond that point it does not. They err who would assert that invariably this is owing to the inherent selfishness of the human heart. It rather proceeds from a certain hopelessness of remedying excessive and organic ill. To a sensitive being, pity is not seldom pain. And when at last it is perceived that such pity cannot lead to effectual succor, common sense bids the soul be rid of it. What I saw that morning persuaded me that the scrivener was the victim of innate and incurable disorder. I might give alms to his body, but his body did not pain him—it was his soul that suffered, and his soul I could not reach.

I did not accomplish the purpose of going to Trinity Church that morning. Somehow, the things I had seen disqualified me for the time from churchgoing. I walked homeward, thinking what I would do with Bartleby. Finally, I resolved upon this—I would put certain calm questions to him the next morning, touching his history, etc., and if he declined to answer them openly and unreservedly (and I supposed he would prefer not), then to give him a twenty-dollar bill over and above whatever I might owe him, and tell him his services were no longer required; but that if in any other way I could assist him, I would be happy to do so, especially if he desired to return to his native place, wherever that might be, I would willingly help to defray the expenses. Moreover, if, after reaching home, he found himself at any time in want of aid, a letter from him would be sure of a reply.

The next morning came.

"Bartleby," said I, gently calling to him behind his screen.

No reply.

"Bartleby," said I, in a still gentler tone, "come here; I am not going to ask you to do anything you would prefer not to do—I simply wish to speak to you."

Upon this he noiselessly slid into view.

"Will you tell me, Bartleby, where you were born?"

"I would prefer not to."

"Will you tell me *anything* about yourself?"

"I would prefer not to."

"But what reasonable objection can you have to speak to me? I feel friendly towards you."

He did not look at me while I spoke, but kept his glance fixed upon my bust of Cicero, which, as I then sat, was directly behind me, some six inches above my head.

"What is your answer, Bartleby," said I, after waiting a considerable time for a reply, during which his countenance remained immovable, only there was the faintest conceivable tremor of the white attenuated mouth.

"At present I prefer to give no answer," he said, and retired into his hermitage.

It was rather weak in me I confess, but his manner, on this occasion, nettled me. Not only did there seem to lurk in it a certain calm disdain, but his perverseness seemed ungrateful, considering the undeniable good usage and indulgence he had received from me.

Again I sat ruminating what I should do. Mortified as I was at his behavior, and resolved as I had been to dismiss him when I entered my office, nevertheless I strangely felt something superstitious knocking at my heart, and forbidding me to carry out my purpose, and denouncing me for a villain if I dared to breathe one bitter word against this forlornest of mankind. At last, familiarly drawing my chair behind his screen, I sat down and said: "Bartleby, never mind, then, about revealing your history; but let me entreat you, as a friend, to comply as far as may be with the usages of this office. Say now, you will help to examine papers tomorrow or next day: in short, say now, that in a day or two you will begin to be a little reasonable:—say so, Bartleby."

"At present I would prefer not to be a little reasonable," was his mildly cadaverous reply.

Just then the folding doors opened and Nippers approached. He seemed suffering from an unusually bad night's rest, induced by severer indigestion than common. He overheard those final words of Bartleby.

"*Prefer not,* eh?" gritted Nippers—"I'd *prefer* him, if I were you, sir," addressing me—"I'd *prefer* him; I'd give him preferences, the stubborn mule! What is it, sir, pray, that he *prefers* not to do now?"

Bartleby moved not a limb.

"Mr. Nippers," said I, "I'd prefer that you would withdraw for the present."

Somehow, of late, I had got into the way of involuntarily using this word "prefer" upon all sorts of not exactly suitable occasions. And I trembled to think that my contact with the scrivener had already and seriously affected me in a mental way. And what further and deeper aberration might it not yet produce? This apprehension had not been without efficacy in determining me to summary measures.

As Nippers, looking very sour and sulky, was departing, Turkey blandly and deferentially approached.

"With submission, sir," said he, "yesterday I was thinking about Bartleby here, and I think that if he would but prefer to take a quart of good ale every day, it would do much towards mending him, and enabling him to assist in examining his papers."

"So you have got the word, too," said I, slightly excited.

"With submission, what word, sir?" asked Turkey, respectfully crowding himself into the contracted space behind the screen, and by so doing making me jostle the scrivener. "What word, sir?"

"I would prefer to be left alone here," said Bartleby, as if offended at being mobbed in his privacy.

"*That's* the word, Turkey," said I—"*that's* it."

"Oh, *prefer?* oh yes—queer word. I never use it myself. But, sir, as I was saying, if he would but prefer——"

"Turkey," interrupted I, "you will please withdraw."

"Oh certainly, sir, if you prefer that I should."

As he opened the folding door to retire, Nippers at his desk caught a glimpse of me, and asked whether I would prefer to have a certain paper copied on blue paper or white. He did not in the least roguishly accent the word prefer. It was plain that it involuntarily rolled from his tongue. I thought to myself, surely I must get rid of a demented man, who already has in some degree turned the tongues, if not the heads, of myself and clerks. But I thought it prudent not to break the dismission at once.

The next day I noticed that Bartleby did nothing but stand at his window in his dead-wall reverie. Upon asking him why he did not write, he said that he had decided upon doing no more writing.

"Why, how now? what next?" exclaimed I, "do no more writing?"

"No more."

"And what is the reason?"

"Do you not see the reason for yourself?" he indifferently replied.

I looked steadfastly at him, and perceived that his eyes looked dull and glazed. Instantly it occurred to me that his unexampled diligence in copying by his dim window for the first few weeks of his stay with me might have temporarily impaired his vision.

I was touched. I said something in condolence with him. I hinted that of course he did wisely in abstaining from writing for a while; and urged him to embrace that opportunity of taking wholesome exercise in the open air. This, however, he did not do. A few days after this, my other clerks being absent, and being in a great hurry to dispatch certain letters by the mail, I thought that, having nothing else earthly to do, Bartleby would surely be less inflexible than usual, and carry these letters to the Post Office. But he blankly declined. So, much to my inconvenience, I went myself.

Still added days went by. Whether Bartleby's eyes improved or not, I could not say. To all appearance, I thought they did. But when I asked him if they did, he vouchsafed no answer. At all events, he would do no copying. At last, in reply to my urgings, he informed me that he had permanently given up copying.

"What!" exclaimed I; "suppose your eyes should get entirely well —better than ever before—would you not copy then?"

"I have given up copying," he answered, and slid aside.

He remained as ever, a fixture in my chamber. Nay—if that were possible—he became still more of a fixture than before. What was to be done? He would do nothing in the office; why should he stay there? In plain fact, he had now become a millstone to me, not only useless as a necklace, but afflictive to bear. Yet I was sorry for him. I speak less than truth when I say that, on his own account, he occasioned me uneasiness. If he would but have named a single relative or friend, I would instantly have written and urged their taking the poor fellow away to some convenient retreat. But he seemed alone, absolutely alone in the universe. A bit of wreck in the mid-Atlantic. At length, necessities connected with my business tyrannized over all other considerations. Decently as I could, I told Bartleby that in six days' time he must unconditionally leave the office. I warned him to take measures, in the interval, for procuring some other abode. I offered to assist him in this endeavor, if he himself would but take the first step towards a removal. "And when you finally quit me, Bartleby," added I, "I shall see that you go not away entirely unprovided. Six days from this hour, remember."

At the expiration of that period, I peeped behind the screen, and lo! Bartleby was there.

I buttoned up my coat, balanced myself, advanced slowly towards him, touched his shoulder, and said, "The time has come; you must quit this place; I am sorry for you; here is money; but you must go."

"I would prefer not," he replied, with his back still towards me.

"You *must.*"

He remained silent.

Now I had an unbounded confidence in this man's common honesty. He had frequently restored to me six-pences and shillings carelessly dropped upon the floor, for I am apt to be very reckless in such shirt-button affairs. The proceeding, then, which followed will not be deemed extraordinary.

"Bartleby," said I, "I owe you twelve dollars on account; here are thirty-two; the odd twenty are yours—Will you take it?" and I handed the bills towards him.

But he made no motion.

"I will leave them here, then," putting them under a weight on the table. Then taking my hat and cane and going to the door, I tranquilly turned and added—"After you have removed your things from these offices, Bartleby, you will of course lock the door—since everyone is now gone for the day but you—and if you please, slip your key underneath the mat, so that I may have it in the morning. I shall not see you again; so good-bye to you. If, hereafter, in your new place of abode, I can be of any service to you, do not fail to advise me by letter. Good-bye, Bartleby, and fare you well."

But he answered not a word; like the last column of some ruined temple, he remained standing mute and solitary in the middle of the otherwise deserted room.

As I walked home in a pensive mood, my vanity got the better of my pity. I could not but highly plume myself on my masterly management in getting rid of Bartleby. Masterly I call it, and such it must appear to any dispassionate thinker. The beauty of my procedure seemed to consist in its perfect quietness. There was no vulgar bullying, no bravado of any sort, no choleric hectoring and striding to and fro across the apartment, jerking out vehement commands for Bartleby to bundle himself off with his beggarly traps. Nothing of the kind. Without loudly bidding Bartleby depart—as an inferior genius might have done—I *assumed* the ground that depart he must, and upon that assumption built all I had to say. The more I thought over my procedure, the more I was charmed with it. Nevertheless, next morning, upon awakening, I had my doubts—I had somehow slept off the fumes of vanity. One of the coolest and wisest hours a man has is just after he awakes in the morning. My procedure seemed as sagacious as ever—but only in theory. How it would prove in practice—there was the rub. It was truly a beautiful thought to have assumed Bartleby's departure; but, after all, that assumption was simply my own, and none of Bartleby's. The great point was, not whether I had assumed that he would quit me, but whether he would prefer so to do. He was more a man of preferences than assumptions.

After breakfast, I walked downtown, arguing the probabilities pro and con. One moment I thought it would prove a miserable failure, and Bartleby would be found all alive at my office as usual; the next moment it seemed certain that I should find his chair empty. And so I kept veering about. At the corner of Broadway and Canal Street, I saw quite an excited group of people standing in earnest conversation.

"I'll take odds he doesn't," said a voice as I passed.

"Doesn't go?—done!" said I, "put up your money.'

I was instinctively putting my hand in my pocket to produce my own, when I remembered that this was an election day. The words I had overheard bore no reference to Bartleby but to the success or non-success of some candidate for the mayoralty. In my intent frame of mind, I had, as it were, imagined that all Broadway shared in my excitement, and were debating the same question with me. I passed on, very thankful that the uproar of the street screened my momentary absent-mindedness.

As I had intended, I was earlier than usual at my office door. I stood listening for a moment. All was still. He must be gone. I tried the knob. The door was locked. Yes, my procedure had worked to a charm; he indeed must be vanished. Yet a certain melancholy mixed with this: I was almost sorry for my brilliant success. I was fumbling under the door mat for the key, which Bartleby was to have left there for me, when accidentally my knee knocked against a panel, producing a summoning sound, and in response a voice came to me from within —"Not yet; I am occupied."

It was Bartleby.

I was thunderstruck. For an instant I stood like the man who, pipe in mouth, was killed one cloudless afternoon long ago in Virginia by summer lightning; at his own warm open window he was killed, and remained leaning out there upon the dreamy afternoon, till someone touched him, when he fell.

"Not gone!" I murmured at last. But again obeying that wondrous ascendancy which the inscrutable scrivener had over me, and from which ascendancy, for all my chafing, I could not completely escape, I slowly went downstairs and out into the street, and while walking round the block considered what I should next do in this unheard-of perplexity. Turn the man out by an actual thrusting I could not; to drive him away by calling him hard names would not do; calling in the police was an unpleasant idea; and yet, permit him to enjoy his cadaverous triumph over me—this, too, I could not think of. What was to be done? or, if nothing could be done, was there anything further that I could *assume* in the matter? Yes, as before I had prospectively assumed that Bartleby would depart, so now I might retrospectively assume that departed he was. In the legitimate carrying out of this assumption I might enter my office in a great hurry, and, pretending not to see Bartleby at all, walk straight against him as if he were air. Such a proceeding would in a singular degree have the appearance of a home thrust. It was hardly possible that Bartleby could withstand such an application of the doctrine of assumptions. But upon second thoughts the success of the plan seemed rather dubious. I resolved to argue the matter over with him again.

"Bartleby," said I, entering the office, with a quietly severe expression, "I am seriously displeased. I am pained, Bartleby. I had thought better of you. I had imagined you of such a gentlemanly organization that in any delicate dilemma a slight hint would suffice—in short, an assumption. But it appears I am deceived. Why," I added, unaffectedly starting, "you have not even touched that money yet," pointing to it, just where I had left it the evening previous.

He answered nothing.

"Will you, or will you not, quit me?" I now demanded in a sudden passion, advancing close to him.

"I would prefer *not* to quit you," he replied, gently emphasizing the *not*.

"What earthly right have you to stay here? Do you pay any rent? Do you pay my taxes? Or is this property yours?"

He answered nothing.

"Are you ready to go on and write now? Are your eyes recovered? Could you copy a small paper for me this morning? or help examine a few lines? or step round to the Post Office? In a word, will you do anything at all to give a coloring to your refusal to depart the premises?"

He silently retired into his hermitage.

I was now in such a state of nervous resentment that I thought it but prudent to check myself at present from further demonstrations. Bartleby and I were alone. I remembered the tragedy of the unfortunate Adams and the still more unfortunate Colt in the solitary office of the latter; and how poor Colt, being dreadfully incensed by Adams, and imprudently permitting himself to get wildly excited, was at unawares hurried into his fatal act—an act which certainly no man could possibly deplore more than the actor himself. Often it had occurred to me in my ponderings upon the subject that had that altercation taken place in the public street, or at a private residence, it would not have terminated as it did. It was the circumstance of being alone in a solitary office, upstairs, of a building entirely unhallowed by humanizing domestic associations—an uncarpeted office, doubtless, of a dusty, haggard sort of appearance—this it must have been which greatly helped to enhance the irritable desperation of the hapless Colt.

But when this old Adam of resentment rose in me and tempted me concerning Bartleby, I grappled him and threw him. How? Why, simply by recalling the divine injunction: "A new commandment give I unto you, that ye love one another." Yes, this it was that saved me. Aside from higher considerations, charity often operates as a vastly wise and prudent principle—a great safeguard to its possessor. Men have committed murder for jealousy's sake, and anger's sake, and hatred's sake, and selfishness' sake, and spiritual pride's sake; but no man that ever I heard of ever committed a diabolical murder for sweet charity's sake. Mere self-interest, then, if no better motive can be enlisted, should, especially with high-tempered men, prompt all beings to charity and philanthropy. At any rate, upon the occasion in question, I strove to drown my exasperated feelings towards the scrivener by benevolently construing his conduct. Poor fellow, poor fellow! thought I, he don't mean anything, and besides, he has seen hard times, and ought to be indulged.

I endeavored, also, immediately to occupy myself, and at the same time to comfort my despondency. I tried to fancy that in the course of the morning, at such time as might prove agreeable to him, Bartleby, of his own free accord, would emerge from his hermitage and take up some decided line of march in the direction of the door. But no. Half-past twelve o'clock came; Turkey began to glow in the face, overturn his inkstand, and become generally obstreperous; Nippers abated down into quietude and courtesy; Ginger Nut munched his noon apple; and Bartleby remained standing at his window in one of his profoundest dead-wall reveries. Will it be credited? Ought I to acknowledge it? That afternoon I left the office without saying one further word to him.

Some days now passed during which, at leisure intervals, I looked a little into "Edwards on the Will," and "Priestley on Necessity." Under the circumstances, those books induced a salutary feeling. Gradually I slid into the persuasion that these troubles of mine touching the scrivener had been all predestinated from eternity, and Bartleby was billeted upon me for some mysterious purpose of an all-wise Providence, which it was not for a mere mortal like me to fathom. Yes, Bartleby, stay there behind your screen, thought I; I shall persecute you no more; you are harmless and noiseless as any of these old chairs; in short, I never feel so private as when I know you are here. At last I see it, I feel it; I penetrate to the predestinated purposes of my life. I am content. Others may have loftier parts to enact, but my mission in this world, Bartleby, is to furnish you with office room for such period as you may see fit to remain.

I believe that this wise and blessed frame of mind would have continued with me had it not been for the unsolicited and uncharitable remarks obtruded upon me by my professional friends who visited the rooms. But thus it often is that the constant friction of illiberal minds wears out at last the best resolves of the more generous. Though, to be sure, when I reflected upon it it was not strange that people entering my office should be struck by the peculiar aspect of the unaccountable

Bartleby, and so be tempted to throw out some sinister observations concerning him. Sometimes an attorney having business with me, and calling at my office, and finding no one but the scrivener there, would undertake to obtain some sort of precise information from him touching my whereabouts; but without heeding his idle talk, Bartleby would remain standing immovable in the middle of the room. So, after contemplating him in that position for a time, the attorney would depart no wiser than he came.

Also, when a reference was going on, and the room full of lawyers and witnesses, and business driving fast, some deeply-occupied legal gentleman present, seeing Bartleby wholly unemployed, would request him to run round to his (the legal gentleman's) office and fetch some papers for him. Thereupon Bartleby would tranquilly decline, and yet remain idle as before. Then the lawyer would give a great stare, and turn to me. And what could I say? At last I was made aware that all through the circle of my professional acquaintance a whisper of wonder was running round, having reference to the strange creature I kept at my office. This worried me very much. And as the idea came upon me of his possibly turning out a long-lived man, and keep occupying my chambers, and denying my authority; and perplexing my visitors; and scandalizing my professional reputation; and casting a general gloom over the premises; keeping soul and body together to the last upon his savings (for doubtless he spent but half a dime a day), and in the end perhaps outlive me, and claim possession of my office by right of his perpetual occupancy—as all these dark anticipations crowded upon me more and more, and my friends continually intruded their relentless remarks upon the apparition in my room, a great change was wrought in me. I resolved to gather all my faculties together and forever rid me of this intolerable incubus.

Ere revolving any complicated project, however, adapted to this end, I first simply suggested to Bartleby the propriety of his permanent departure. In a calm and serious tone, I commended the idea to his careful and mature consideration. But, having taken three days to meditate upon it, he apprised me that his original determination remained the same; in short, that he still preferred to abide with me.

What shall I do? I now said to myself, buttoning up my coat to the last button. What shall I do? what ought I to do? what does conscience say I *should* do with this man, or, rather, ghost. Rid myself of him, I must; go, he shall. But how? You will not thrust him, the poor, pale, passive mortal—you will not thrust such a helpless creature out of your door? you will not dishonor yourself by such cruelty? No, I will not, I cannot do that. Rather would I let him live and die here, and then mason up his remains in the wall. What, then, will you do? For all your coaxing, he will not budge. Bribes he leaves under your own paperweight on your table; in short, it is quite plain that he prefers to cling to you.

Then something severe, something unusual, must be done. What! surely you will not have him collared by a constable, and commit his innocent pallor to the common jail? And upon what ground could you procure such a thing to be done?—a vagrant, is he? What! he a vagrant, a wanderer, who refuses to budge? It is because he will *not* be a vagrant, then, that you seek to count him *as* a vagrant. That is too absurd. No visible means of support: there I have him. Wrong again: for indubitably he *does* support himself, and that is the only unanswerable proof that any man can show of his possessing the means so to do. No more, then. Since he will not quit me, I must quit him. I will change my offices; I will move elsewhere, and give him fair notice that if I find him on my new premises I will then proceed against him as a common trespasser.

Acting accordingly, next day I thus addressed him: "I find these chambers too far from the City Hall; the air is unwholesome. In a word, I propose to remove my offices next week, and shall no longer require your services. I tell you this now, in order that you may seek another place."

He made no reply, and nothing more was said.

On the appointed day I engaged carts and men, proceeded to my chambers, and, having but little furniture, everything was removed in a few hours. Throughout, the scrivener remained standing behind the screen, which I directed to be removed the last thing. It was withdrawn; and, being folded up like a huge folio, left him the motionless occupant of a naked room. I stood in the entry watching him a moment, while something from within me upbraided me.

I re-entered, with my hand in my pocket—and—and my heart in my mouth.

"Good-bye, Bartleby; I am going—good-bye; and God some way bless you; and take that," slipping something in his hand. But it dropped upon the floor, and then—strange to say—I tore myself from him whom I had so longed to be rid of.

Established in my new quarters, for a day or two I kept the door locked, and started at every footfall in the passages. When I returned to my rooms after any little absence, I would pause at the threshold for an instant and attentively listen ere applying my key. But these fears were needless. Bartleby never came nigh me.

I thought all was going well, when a perturbed-looking stranger visited me, inquiring whether I was the person who had recently occupied rooms at No. — Wall Street.

Full of forebodings, I replied that I was.

"Then, sir," said the stranger, who proved a lawyer, "you are responsible for the man you left there. He refuses to do any copying; he refuses to do anything; he says he prefers not to; and he refuses to quit the premises."

"I am very sorry, sir," said I, with assumed tranquillity, but an inward tremor, "but, really, the man you allude to is nothing to me—he is no relation or apprentice of mine, that you should hold me responsible for him."

"In mercy's name, who is he?"

"I certainly cannot inform you. I know nothing about him. Formerly I employed him as a copyist; but he has done nothing for me now for some time past."

"I shall settle him, then—good morning, sir."

Several days passed, and I heard nothing more; and, though I often felt a charitable prompting to call at the place and see poor Bartleby, yet a certain squeamishness, of I know not what, withheld me.

All is over with him, by this time, thought I at last, when, through another week, no further intelligence reached me. But, coming to my room the day after, I found several persons waiting at my door in a high state of nervous excitement.

"That's the man—here he comes," cried the foremost one, whom I recognized as the lawyer who had previously called upon me alone.

"You must take him away, sir, at once," cried a portly person among them, advancing upon me, and whom I knew to be the landlord of No. — Wall Street. "These gentlemen, my tenants, cannot stand it any longer; Mr. B——," pointing to the lawyer, "has turned him out of his room, and he now persists in haunting the building generally, sitting upon the banisters of the stairs by day, and sleeping in the entry by night. Everybody is concerned; clients are leaving the offices; some fears are entertained of a mob; something you must do, and that without delay."

Aghast at this torrent, I fell back before it, and would fain have locked myself in my new quarters. In vain I persisted that Bartleby was nothing to me—no more than to anyone else. In vain—I was the last person known to have anything to do with him, and they held me to the terrible account. Fearful, then, of being exposed in the papers (as one person present obscurely threatened), I considered the matter, and at length said that if the lawyer would give me a confidential interview with the scrivener, in his (the lawyer's) own room, I would, that afternoon, strive my best to rid them of the nuisance they complained of.

Going upstairs to my old haunt, there was Bartleby silently sitting upon the banister at the landing.

"What are you doing here, Bartleby?" said I.

"Sitting upon the banister," he mildly replied.

I motioned him into the lawyer's room, who then left us.

"Bartleby," said I, "are you aware that you are the cause of great tribulation to me, by persisting in occupying the entry after being dismissed from the office?"

No answer.

"Now one of two things must take place. Either you must do something, or something must be done to you. Now what sort of business would you like to engage in? Would you like to re-engage in copying for someone?"

"No; I would prefer not to make any change."

"Would you like a clerkship in a dry-goods store?"

"There is too much confinement about that. No, I would not like a clerkship; but I am not particular."

"Too much confinement," I cried; "why you keep yourself confined all the time!"

"I would prefer not to take a clerkship," he rejoined, as if to settle that little item at once.

"How would a bartender's business suit you? There is no trying of the eyesight in that."

"I would not like it at all; though, as I said before, I am not particular."

His unwonted wordiness inspirited me. I returned to the charge.

"Well, then, would you like to travel through the country collecting bills for the merchants? That would improve your health."

"No, I would prefer to be doing something else."

"How, then, would going as a companion to Europe, to entertain some young gentleman with your conversation—how would that suit you?"

"Not at all. It does not strike me that there is anything definite about that. I like to be stationary. But I am not particular."

"Stationary you shall be, then," I cried, now losing all patience, and, for the first time in all my exasperating connection with him, fairly flying into a passion. "If you do not go away from these premises before night, I shall feel bound—indeed, I *am* bound—to—to—to quit the premises myself!" I rather absurdly concluded, knowing not with what possible threat to try to frighten his immobility into compliance. Despairing of all further efforts, I was precipitately leaving him, when a final thought occurred to me—one which had not been wholly unindulged before.

"Bartleby," said I, in the kindest tone I could assume under such exciting circumstances, "will you go home with me now—not to my office, but my dwelling—and remain there till we can conclude upon some convenient arrangement for you at our leisure? Come, let us start now, right away."

"No; at present I would prefer not to make any change at all."

I answered nothing, but, effectually dodging everyone by the suddenness and rapidity of my flight, rushed from the building, ran up Wall Street towards Broadway, and, jumping into the first omnibus, was soon removed from pursuit. As soon as tranquillity returned, I distinctly perceived that I had now done all that I possibly could, both in respect to the demands of the landlord and his tenants, and with regard to my own desire and sense of duty, to benefit Bartleby, and shield him from rude persecution. I now strove to be entirely carefree and quiescent, and my conscience justified me in the attempt, though, indeed, it was not so successful as I could have wished. So fearful was I of being again hunted out by the incensed landlord and his exasperated tenants that, surrendering my business to Nippers for a few days, I drove about the upper part of the town and through the suburbs in my rockaway; crossed over to Jersey City and Hoboken, and paid fugitive visits to Manhattan-ville and Astoria. In fact, I almost lived in my rockaway for the time.

When again I entered my office, lo, a note from the landlord lay upon the desk. I opened it with trembling hands. It informed me that the writer had sent to the police, and had Bartleby removed to the Tombs as a vagrant. Moreover, since I knew more about him than anyone else, he wished me to appear at that place and make a suitable statement of the facts. These tidings had a conflicting effect upon me. At first I was indignant, but at last almost approved. The landlord's energetic, summary disposition had led him to adopt a procedure which I do not think I would have decided upon myself; and yet, as a last resort, under such peculiar circumstances, it seemed the only plan.

As I afterwards learned, the poor scrivener, when told that he must be conducted to the Tombs, offered not the slightest obstacle, but, in his pale, unmoving way, silently acquiesced.

Some of the compassionate and curious bystanders joined the party, and, headed by one of the constables arm in arm with Bartleby, the silent procession filed its way through all the noise, and heat, and joy of the roaring thoroughfares at noon.

The same day I received the note, I went to the Tombs, or, to speak more properly, the Halls of Justice. Seeking the right officer, I stated the purpose of my call, and was informed that the individual I described was indeed within. I then assured the functionary that Bartleby was a perfectly honest man, and greatly to be compassionated, however un-accountably eccentric. I narrated all I knew, and closed by suggesting the idea of letting him remain in as indulgent confinement as possible till something less harsh might be done—though, indeed, I hardly knew what. At all events, if nothing else could be decided upon, the alms-house must receive him. I then begged to have an interview.

Being under no disgraceful charge, and quite serene and harmless in all his ways, they had permitted him freely to wander about the prison, and, especially, in the inclosed grass-platted yards thereof. And so I found him there, standing all alone in the quietest of the yards, his face towards a high wall, while all around, from the narrow slits of the jail windows, I thought I saw peering out upon him the eyes of mur-derers and thieves.

"Bartleby!"

"I know you," he said, without looking round—"and I want nothing to say to you."

"It was not I that brought you here, Bartleby," said I, keenly pained at his implied suspicion. "And, to you, this should not be so vile a place. Nothing reproachful attaches to you by being here. And see, it is not so sad a place as one might think. Look, there is the sky, and here is the grass."

"I know where I am," he replied, but would say nothing more, and so I left him.

As I entered the corridor again, a broad meatlike man in an apron accosted me, and, jerking his thumb over his shoulder, said—"Is that your friend?"

"Yes."

"Does he want to starve? If he does, let him live on the prison fare, that's all."

"Who are you?" asked I, not knowing what to make of such an unofficially speaking person in such a place.

"I am the grubman. Such gentlemen as have friends here hire me to provide them with something good to eat."

"Is this so?" said I, turning to the turnkey.

He said it was.

"Well, then," said I, slipping some silver into the grubman's hands (for so they called him), "I want you to give particular attention to my friend there; let him have the best dinner you can get. And you must be as polite to him as possible."

"Introduce me, will you?" said the grubman, looking at me with an expression which seemed to say he was all impatience for an opportunity to give a specimen of his breeding.

Thinking it would prove of benefit to the scrivener, I acquiesced, and, asking the grubman his name, went up with him to Bartleby.

"Bartleby, this is a friend; you will find him very useful to you."

"Your sarvant, sir, your sarvant," said the grubman, making a low salutation behind his apron. "Hope you find it pleasant here, sir; nice grounds—cool apartments—hope you'll stay with us some time—try to make it agreeable. What will you have for dinner today?"

"I prefer not to dine today," said Bartleby, turning away. "It would disagree with me; I am unused to dinners." So saying, he slowly moved to the other side of the inclosure and took up a position fronting the dead-wall.

"How's this?" said the grubman, addressing me with a stare of astonishment. "He's odd, ain't he?"

"I think he is a little deranged," said I, sadly.

"Deranged? deranged is it? Well, now, upon my word, I thought that friend of yourn was a gentleman forger; they are always pale and genteel-like, them forgers. I can't help pity 'em—can't help it, sir. Did you know Monroe Edwards?" he added, touchingly, and paused. Then, laying his hand piteously on my shoulder, sighed, "he died of consumption at Sing-Sing. So you weren't acquainted with Monroe?"

"No, I was never socially acquainted with any forgers. But I cannot stop longer. Look to my friend yonder. You will not lose by it. I will see you again."

Some few days after this, I again obtained admission to the Tombs, and went through the corridors in quest of Bartleby; but without finding him.

"I saw him coming from his cell not long ago," said a turnkey, "maybe he's gone to loiter in the yards."

So I went in that direction.

"Are you looking for the silent man?" said another turnkey, passing me. "Yonder he lies—sleeping in the yard there. 'Tis not twenty minutes since I saw him lie down."

The yard was entirely quiet. It was not accessible to the common prisoners. The surrounding walls, of amazing thickness, kept off all sounds behind them. The Egyptian character of the masonry weighed upon me with its gloom. But a soft imprisoned turf grew underfoot. The heart of the eternal pyramids, it seemed, wherein, by some strange magic, through the clefts, grass-seed, dropped by birds, had sprung.

Strangely huddled at the base of the wall, his knees drawn up and lying on his side, his head touching the cold stones, I saw the wasted Bartleby. But nothing stirred. I paused, then went close up to him, stooped over, and saw that his dim eyes were open; otherwise he seemed profoundly sleeping. Something prompted me to touch him. I felt his hand, when a tingling shiver ran up my arm and down my spine to my feet.

The round face of the grubman peered upon me now. "His dinner is ready. Won't he dine today, either? Or does he live without dining?"

"Lives without dining," said I, and closed the eyes.

"Eh!—He's asleep, ain't he?"

"With kings and counselors," murmured I.

There would seem little need for proceeding further in this history. Imagination will readily supply the meager recital of poor Bartleby's interment. But, ere parting with the reader, let me say that if this little narrative has sufficiently interested him to awaken curiosity as to who Bartleby was, and what manner of life he led prior to the present narrator's making his acquaintance, I can only reply that in such curiosity I fully share, but am wholly unable to gratify it. Yet here I hardly know whether I should divulge one little item of rumor which came to my ear a few months after the scrivener's decease. Upon what basis it rested, I could never ascertain, and hence how true it is I cannot now tell. But, inasmuch as this vague report has not been without a certain suggestive interest to me, however sad, it may prove the same with some others, and so I will briefly mention it. The report was this: that Bartleby had been a subordinate clerk in the Dead Letter

Office at Washington, from which he had been suddenly removed by a change in the administration. When I think over this rumor, hardly can I express the emotions which seize me. Dead letters! does it not sound like dead men? Conceive a man by nature and misfortune prone to a pallid hopelessness, can any business seem more fitted to heighten it than that of continually handling these dead letters, and assorting them for the flames? For by the cartload they are annually burned. Sometimes from out the folded paper the pale clerk takes a ring—the finger it was meant for, perhaps, molders in the grave; a bank note sent in swiftest charity—he whom it would relieve nor eats nor hungers any more; pardon for those who died despairing; hope for those who died unhoping; good tidings for those who died stifled by unrelieved calamities. On errands of life, these letters speed to death.

Ah, Bartleby! Ah, humanity!

2

FEDOR DOSTOEVSKY
Notes from Underground

Dostoevsky's title provides a good starting point for considering what *Notes from Underground* is about. The narrator, the underground man, writes just what the title states, a set of "notes." He claims that his purpose is therapeutic. He writes as an "experiment" to try to be "even with oneself . . . perfectly open, and not take fright at the whole truth." He hopes thereby that "if I write it down I should get rid of it." But because of the extraordinary perverseness of his character, his writing also functions as a means of self-incrimination and self-abuse.

"The underground" of the narrator suggests his total alienation from the world around him. He is as far removed from all genuine human contact as if he were literally buried beneath the earth in a state of living death. Also, he writes from "the underground" in the sense that his conscious, voluntary behavior is submerged in the irrationality of his unconscious. Traditional concepts of psychology can provide only very limited explanation of the elusive underground man, but the familiar psychoanalytic terms "conscious," "unconscious," and "repression" are especially useful in this case. The unconscious, metaphorically conceived as being below consciousness, is the part of personality of which man has no normal awareness. It brims with forgotten bad memories and illicit psychological drives which must be repressed—pushed down into unawareness—because they would cause unpleasant feelings and unacceptable behavior if allowed to surface. Considered strictly from this point of view, the underground man is a study in the failure of repression. Nearly everything he does or thinks is poisoned by unconscious impulses, especially by his immense self-hatred, so that in effect his life is buried by the subterranean chaos of his own personality.

There is still another, equally important meaning of "the underground"—the massive, subtle hidden psychological forces which comprise the underground or unconscious of entire civilizations. Although the underground man may at first seem to many readers like no other human being, his personality is in fact a brilliant parody of the dark psychological realities of western man's "modern" spirit. The underground man's isolation, his revolving-door identity, his self-consciousness and self-hatred, his helpless cynicism, his whole existence as part of a godless and unredeemed society, all mirror themes dominant in western art and history since the mid-nineteenth century. Like the eighteenth-century Enlightenment and other similarly wide-scale historical phenomena, the modern spirit has taken shape in many different ways, times, and places. Nevertheless its onset has been well documented, and *Notes from Underground* itself has gained the stature of a historical document because it is one of the most prophetic and lucid insights into the modern spirit. Paradoxically, the underground man's wretchedness and his uncanny power as a prophet stem from the same psychological condition. His unwilling intimacy with his own unconscious creates a dark meeting ground between the latent realities of self and culture, and burdens him with repressed mental powers which possess a shrewdness more profound than that of conscious intellect.

Part I is a sprawling, convoluted statement. Its complexity is compounded by an apparent lack of structure, so that its implications virtually spin off in every direction. But this is a studied appearance of formlessness, and beneath it, Dostoevsky's work is purposefully structured. In general, the underground man's thoughts move from description of his private dilemma to related philosophical and political concerns: the "laws of nature," consciousness, will, irrationality, suffering, freedom, and the prospect of a utopian society where all human impulses are controlled. He attacks the idea of a perfect and controlled society, a notion much discussed by Russian intellectuals at that time. He dreads the prospect that advancing human knowledge may indeed master all the "laws of nature" and thereby make complete behavioral control a reality. His arguments are compelling. Human will, he asserts, must be "a manifestation of the whole life . . . including reason and all the impulses." Irrational impulses—"caprice" as he calls them—are essential to the preservation of individuality, and suffering is the sole origin of consciousness. By doing away with suffering as well as all irrational impulses, the utopian state would destroy the integrity of human will, obliterate genuine individuality, and lead to the atrophy of consciousness.

One of the most fascinating ironies of *Notes from Underground* is that the narrator, who suffers miserably from irrationality and an excess of consciousness, is driven by his underground wisdom to the realization that consciousness, irrationality, and suffering are somehow essential to the value of human life.

The relationship between the two parts of this novel seems open to question. Either one could stand alone as a remarkable literary work. Part II, among other things, lends the vividness of literary dramatization to the relatively abstract philosophical presentation of Part I. The underground man at last assumes full dimensions as a person, and his human reality illuminates his earlier statements in retrospect. His successive encounters with the officer, with his school acquaintances, and with Liza become increasingly more complex and personal. Each episode reveals in a more incisive way the degree to which his being is dominated by misery. His anguish is transcendent: its energy and intensity point to realities beyond the merely psychological. To Dostoevsky there is a terrible necessity for such suffering. Man must suffer inwardly—in a manner at least somewhat like that of the underground man—in order to find Christ and be redeemed. In the earliest version of the work, Dostoevsky in fact allowed the underground man to realize that his salvation lay in Christ, but he later deleted that ending in order to confront his narrator with the heightened suffering of an indeterminate future.

Notes from Underground
A NOVEL

Part I · Underground

I

I am a sick man. . . . I am a spiteful man. I am an unattractive man. I believe my liver is diseased. However, I know nothing at all about my disease, and do not know for certain what ails me. I don't consult a doctor for it, and never have, though I have a respect for medicine and doctors. Besides, I am extremely superstitious, sufficiently so to respect medicine, anyway (I am well-educated enough not to be superstitious, but I am superstitious). No, I refuse to consult a doctor from spite. That you probably will not understand. Well, I understand it, though. Of course, I can't explain who it is precisely that I am mortifying in this case by my spite: I am perfectly well aware

The author of the diary and the diary itself are, of course, imaginary. Nevertheless it is clear that such persons as the writer of these notes not only may, but positively must, exist in our society, when we consider the circumstances in the midst of which our society is formed. I have tried to expose to the view of the public more distinctly than is commonly done, one of the characters of the recent past. He is one of the representatives of a generation still living. In this fragment, entitled "Underground," this person introduces himself and his views, and, as it were, tries to explain the causes owing to which he has made his appearance and was bound to make his appearance in our midst. In the second fragment there are added the actual notes of this person concerning certain events in his life. [AUTHOR'S NOTE.]

Reprinted with permission of Macmillan Publishing Co., Inc. from WHITE NIGHTS AND OTHER STORIES by F. Dostoevsky, translated by Constance Garnett. Printed in Great Britain.

that I cannot "pay out" the doctors by not consulting them; I know better than any one that by all this I am only injuring myself and no one else. But still, if I don't consult a doctor it is from spite. My liver is bad, well—let it get worse!

I have been going on like that for a long time—twenty years. Now I am forty. I used to be in the government service, but am no longer. I was a spiteful official. I was rude and took pleasure in being so. I did not take bribes, you see, so I was bound to find a recompense in that, at least. (A poor jest, but I will not scratch it out. I wrote it thinking it would sound very witty; but now that I have seen myself that I only wanted to show off in a despicable way, I will not scratch it out on purpose!)

When petitioners used to come for information to the table at which I sat, I used to grind my teeth at them, and felt intense enjoyment when I succeeded in making anybody unhappy. I almost always did succeed. For the most part they were all timid people—of course, they were petitioners. But of the uppish ones there was one officer in particular I could not endure. He simply would not be humble, and clanked his sword in a disgusting way. I carried on a feud with him for eighteen months over that sword. At last I got the better of him. He left off clanking it. That happened in my youth, though.

But do you know, gentlemen, what was the chief point about my spite? Why, the whole point, the real sting of it lay in the fact that continually, even in the moment of the acutest spleen, I was inwardly conscious with shame that I was not only not a spiteful but not even an embittered man, that I was simply scaring sparrows at random and amusing myself by it. I might foam at the mouth, but bring me a doll to play with, give me a cup of tea with sugar in it, and maybe I should be appeased. I might even be genuinely touched, though probably I should grind my teeth at myself afterwards and lie awake at night with shame for months after. That was my way.

I was lying when I said just now that I was a spiteful official. I was lying from spite. I was simply amusing myself with the petitioners and with the officer, and in reality I never could become spiteful. I was conscious every moment in myself of many, very many elements absolutely opposite to that. I felt them positively swarming in me, these opposite elements. I knew that they had been swarming in me all my life and craving some outlet from me, but I would not let them, would not let them, purposely would not let them come out. They tormented me till I was ashamed: they drove me to convulsions and—sickened me, at last, how they sickened me! Now, are not you fancying, gentlemen, that I am expressing remorse for something now, that I am asking your forgiveness for something? I am sure you are fancying that. . . . However, I assure you I do not care if you are. . . .

It was not only that I could not become spiteful, I did not know how to become anything: neither spiteful nor kind, neither a rascal nor an honest man, neither a hero nor an insect. Now, I am living out my life in my corner, taunting myself with the spiteful and useless consolation that an intelligent man cannot become anything seriously, and it is only the fool who becomes anything. Yes, a man in the nineteenth century must and morally ought to be pre-eminently a characterless creature; a man of character, an active man is pre-eminently a limited creature. That is my conviction of forty years. I am forty years old now, and you know forty years is a whole lifetime; you know it is extreme old age. To live longer than forty years is bad manners, is vulgar, immoral. Who does live beyond forty? Answer that, sincerely and honestly. I will tell you who do: fools and worthless fellows. I tell all old men that to their face, all these venerable old men, all these silver-haired and reverend seniors! I tell the whole world that to its face! I have a right to say so, for I shall go on living to sixty myself. To seventy! To eighty! . . . Stay, let me take breath. . . .

You imagine no doubt, gentlemen, that I want to amuse you. You are mistaken in that, too. I am by no means such a mirthful person as you imagine, or as you may imagine; however, irritated by all this babble (and I feel that you are irritated) you think fit to ask me who am I—then my answer is, I am a collegiate assessor. I was in the service that I might have something to eat (and solely for that reason), and when last year a distant relation left me six thousand roubles in his will I immediately retired from the service and settled down in my corner. I used to live in this corner before, but now I have settled down in it. My room is a wretched, horrid one in the outskirts of the town. My servant is an old country-woman, ill-natured from stupidity, and, moreover, there is always a nasty smell about her. I am told that the Petersburg climate is bad for me, and that with my small means it is very expensive to live in Petersburg. I know all that better than all these sage and experienced counsellors and monitors. . . . But I am remaining in Petersburg; I am not going away from Petersburg! I am not going away because . . . ech! Why, it is absolutely no matter whether I am going away or not going away.

But what can a decent man speak of with most pleasure?

Answer: Of himself.

Well, so I will talk about myself.

II

I want now to tell you, gentlemen, whether you care to hear it or not, why I could not even become an insect. I tell you solemnly, that I have many times tried to become an insect. But I was not equal even to that. I swear, gentlemen, that to be too conscious is an illness—a real thoroughgoing illness. For man's everyday needs, it would have been

quite enough to have the ordinary human consciousness, that is, half
of a quarter of the amount which falls to the lot of a cultivated man of
our unhappy nineteenth century, especially one who has the fatal ill-
luck to inhabit Petersburg, the most theoretical and intentional town on
the whole terrestrial globe. (There are intentional and unintentional
towns.) It would have been quite enough, for instance, to have the
consciousness by which all so-called direct persons and men of action
live. I bet you think I am writing all this from affectation, to be witty
at the expense of men of action; and what is more, that from ill-bred
affectation, I am clanking a sword like my officer. But, gentlemen,
whoever can pride himself on his diseases and even swagger over
them?

Though, after all, every one does do that; people do pride themselves
on their diseases, and I do, may be, more than any one. We will not dispute it; my contention was absurd. But yet I am firmly persuaded that a
great deal of consciousness, every sort of consciousness, in fact, is a disease. I stick to that. Let us leave that, too, for a minute. Tell me this:
why does it happen that at the very, yes, at the very moments when I
am most capable of feeling every refinement of all that is "good and beautiful," as they used to say at one time, it would, as though of design,
happen to me not only to feel but to do such ugly things, such that . . .
Well, in short, actions that all, perhaps, commit; but which, as though
purposely, occurred to me at the very time when I was most conscious
that they ought not to be committed. The more conscious I was of
goodness and of all that was "good and beautiful," the more deeply
I sank into my mire and the more ready I was to sink in it altogether.
But the chief point was that all this was, as it were, not accidental in
me, but as though it were bound to be so. It was as though it were my
most normal condition, and not in the least disease or depravity, so
that at last all desire in me to struggle against this depravity passed. It
ended by my almost believing (perhaps actually believing) that this
was perhaps my normal condition. But at first, in the beginning, what
agonies I endured in that struggle! I did not believe it was the same
with other people, and all my life I hid this fact about myself as a
secret. I was ashamed (even now, perhaps, I am ashamed): I got to
the point of feeling a sort of secret abnormal, despicable enjoyment in
returning home to my corner on some disgusting Petersburg night,
acutely conscious that that day I had committed a loathsome action again,
that what was done could never be undone, and secretly, inwardly gnawing, gnawing at myself for it, tearing and consuming myself till at last
the bitterness turned into a sort of shameful accursed sweetness, and
at last—into positive real enjoyment! Yes, into enjoyment, into enjoyment! I insist upon that. I have spoken of this because I keep wanting
to know for a fact whether other people feel such enjoyment. I will

explain: the enjoyment was just from the too intense consciousness of one's own degradation; it was from feeling oneself that one had reached the last barrier, that it was horrible, but that it could not be otherwise; that there was no escape for you; that you never could become a different man; that even if time and faith were still left you to change into something different you would most likely not wish to change; or if you did wish to, even then you would do nothing; because perhaps in reality there was nothing for you to change into.

And the worst of it was, and the root of it all, that it was all in accord with the normal fundamental laws of over-acute consciousness, and with the inertia that was the direct result of those laws, and that consequently one was not only unable to change but could do absolutely nothing. Thus it would follow, as the result of acute consciousness, that one is not to blame in being a scoundrel; as though that were any consolation to the scoundrel once he has come to realize that he actually is a scoundrel. But enough. . . . Ech, I have talked a lot of nonsense, but what have I explained? How is enjoyment in this to be explained? But I will explain it. I will get to the bottom of it! That is why I have taken up my pen. . . .

I, for instance, have a great deal of *amour propre*. I am as suspicious and prone to take offence as a humpback or a dwarf. But upon my word I sometimes have had moments when if I had happened to be slapped in the face I should, perhaps, have been positively glad of it. I say, in earnest, that I should probably have been able to discover even in that a peculiar sort of enjoyment—the enjoyment, of course, of despair; but in despair there are the most intense enjoyments, especially when one is very acutely conscious of the hopelessness of one's position. And when one is slapped in the face—why then the consciousness of being rubbed into a pulp would positively overwhelm one. The worst of it is, look at it which way one will, it still turns out that I was always the most to blame in everything. And what is most humiliating of all, to blame for no fault of my own but, so to say, through the laws of nature. In the first place, to blame because I am cleverer than any of the people surrounding me. (I have always considered myself cleverer than any of the people surrounding me, and sometimes, would you believe it, have been positively ashamed of it. At any rate, I have all my life, as it were, turned my eyes away and never could look people straight in the face.) To blame, finally, because even if I had had magnanimity, I should only have had more suffering from the sense of its uselessness. I should certainly have never been able to do anything from being magnanimous—neither to forgive, for my assailant would perhaps have slapped me from the laws of nature, and one cannot forgive the laws of nature; nor to forget, for even if it were owing to the laws of nature, it is insulting all the same. Finally, even if I had wanted to be anything but magnanimous, had desired on the contrary to revenge myself on my assailant, I could not have revenged myself on any one for anything because I should certainly never have made up my mind to do anything, even if I had been able to. Why should I not have made up my mind? About that in particular I want to say a few words.

III

With people who know how to revenge themselves and to stand up for themselves in general, how is it done? Why, when they are possessed, let us suppose, by the feeling of revenge, then for the time there is nothing else but that feeling left in their whole being. Such a gentleman simply dashes straight for his object like an infuriated bull with its horns down, and nothing but a wall will stop him. (By the way: facing the wall, such gentlemen—that is, the "direct" persons and men of action—are genuinely nonplussed. For them a wall is not an evasion, as for us people who think and consequently do nothing; it is not an excuse for turning aside, an excuse for which we are always very glad, though we scarcely believe in it ourselves, as a rule. No, they are nonplussed in all sincerity. The wall has for them something tranquillizing, morally soothing, final—maybe even something mysterious . . . but of the wall later.)

Well, such a direct person I regard as the real normal man, as his tender mother nature wished to see him when she graciously brought him into being on the earth. I envy such a man till I am green in the face. He is stupid. I am not disputing that, but perhaps the normal man should be stupid, how do you know? Perhaps it is very beautiful, in fact. And I am the more persuaded of that suspicion, if one can call it so, by the fact that if you take, for instance, the antithesis of the normal man, that is, the man of acute consciousness, who has come, of course, not out of the lap of nature but out of a retort (this is almost mysticism, gentlemen, but I suspect this, too), this retort-made man is sometimes so nonplussed in the presence of his antithesis that with all his exaggerated consciousness he genuinely thinks of himself as a mouse and not a man. It may be an acutely conscious mouse, yet it is a mouse, while the other is a man, and therefore, et caetera, et caetera. And the worst of it is, he himself, his very own self, looks on himself as a mouse; no one asks him to do so; and that is an important point. Now let us look at this mouse in action. Let us suppose, for instance, that it feels insulted, too (and it almost always does feel insulted), and wants to revenge itself, too. There may even be a greater accumulation of spite in it than in *l'homme de la nature et de la vérité*. The base and nasty desire to vent that spite on its assailant rankles perhaps even more nastily in it than in *l'homme de la nature et de la vérité*. For through his innate stupidity the latter looks upon his revenge as justice pure and simple;

while in consequence of his acute consciousness the mouse does not believe in the justice of it. To come at last to the deed itself, to the very act of revenge. Apart from the one fundamental nastiness the luckless mouse succeeds in creating around it so many other nastinesses in the form of doubts and questions, adds to the one question so many unsettled questions that there inevitably works up around it a sort of fatal brew, a stinking mess, made up of its doubts, emotions, and of the contempt spat upon it by the direct men of action who stand solemnly about it as judges and arbitrators, laughing at it till their healthy sides ache. Of course the only thing left for it is to dismiss all that with a wave of its paw, and, with a smile of assumed contempt in which it does not even itself believe, creep ignominiously into its mouse-hole. There in its nasty, stinking, underground home our insulted, crushed and ridiculed mouse promptly becomes absorbed in cold, malignant and, above all, everlasting spite. For forty years together it will remember its injury down to the smallest, most ignominious details, and every time will add, of itself, details still more ignominious, spitefully teasing and tormenting itself with its own imagination. It will itself be ashamed of its imaginings, but yet it will recall it all, it will go over and over every detail, it will invent unheard of things against itself, pretending that those things might happen, and will forgive nothing. Maybe it will begin to revenge itself, too, but, as it were, piecemeal, in trivial ways, from behind the stove, incognito, without believing either in its own right to vengeance, or in the success of its revenge, knowing that from all its efforts at revenge it will suffer a hundred times more than he on whom it revenges itself, while he, I daresay, will not even scratch himself. On its deathbed it will recall it all over again, with interest accumulated over all the years and. . . .

But it is just in that cold, abominable half despair, half belief, in that conscious burying oneself alive for grief in the underworld for forty years, in that acutely recognized and yet partly doubtful hopelessness of one's position, in that hell of unsatisfied desires turned inward, in that fever of oscillations, of resolutions determined for ever and repented of again a minute later—that the savour of that strange enjoyment of which I have spoken lies. It is so subtle, so difficult of analysis, that persons who are a little limited, or even simply persons of strong nerves, will not understand a single atom of it. "Possibly," you will add on your own account with a grin, "people will not understand it either who have never received a slap in the face," and in that way you will politely hint to me that I, too, perhaps, have had the experience of a slap in the face in my life, and so I speak as one who knows. I bet that you are thinking that. But set your minds at rest, gentlemen, I have not received a slap in the face, though it is absolutely a matter of indifference to me what you may think about it. Possibly, I even regret, myself, that I have given so few slaps in the face during my life. But enough . . . not another word on that subject of such extreme interest to you.

I will continue calmly concerning persons with strong nerves who do not understand a certain refinement of enjoyment. Though in certain circumstances these gentlemen bellow their loudest like bulls, though this, let us suppose, does them the greatest credit, yet, as I have said already, confronted with the impossible they subside at once. The impossible means the stone wall! What stone wall? Why, of course, the laws of nature, the deductions of natural science, mathematics. As soon as they prove to you, for instance, that you are descended from a monkey, then it is no use scowling, accept it for a fact. When they prove to you that in reality one drop of your own fat must be dearer to you than a hundred thousand of your fellow-creatures, and that this conclusion is the final solution of all so-called virtues and duties and all such prejudices and fancies, then you have just to accept it, there is no help for it, for twice two is a law of mathematics. Just try refuting it.

"Upon my word," they will shout at you, "it is no use protesting: it is a case of twice two makes four! Nature does not ask your permission, she has nothing to do wth your wishes, and whether you like her laws or dislike them, you are bound to accept her as she is, and consequently all her conclusions. A wall, you see, is a wall . . . and so on, and so on."

"Merciful Heavens! but what do I care for the laws of nature and arithmetic, when, for some reason, I dislike those laws and the fact that twice two makes four? Of course I cannot break through the wall by battering my head against it if I really have not the strength to knock it down, but I am not going to be reconciled to it simply because it is a stone wall and I have not the strength.

As though such a stone wall really were a consolation, and really did contain some word of conciliation, simply because it is as true as twice two makes four. Oh, absurdity of absurdities! How much better it is to understand it all, to recognize it all, all the impossibilities and the stone wall; not to be reconciled to one of those impossibilities and stone walls if it disgusts you to be reconciled to it; by the way of the most inevitable, logical combinations to reach the most revolting conclusions on the everlasting theme, that even for the stone wall you are yourself somehow to blame, though again it is as clear as day you are not to blame in the least, and therefore grinding your teeth in silent impotence to sink into luxurious inertia, brooding on the fact that there is no one even for you to feel vindictive against, that you have not, and perhaps never will have, an object for your spite, that it is a sleight of hand, a bit of juggling, a cardsharper's trick, that it is simply a mess, no knowing what and no knowing who, but in spite of all these uncertainties and jugglings, still there is an ache in you, and the more you do not know, the worse the ache.

IV

"Ha, ha, ha! You will be finding enjoyment in toothache next," you cry, with a laugh.

"Well? Even in toothache there is enjoyment," I answer. I had toothache for a whole month and I know there is. In that case, of course, people are not spiteful in silence, but moan; but they are not candid moans, they are malignant moans, and the malignancy is the whole point. The enjoyment of the sufferer finds expression in those moans; if he did not feel enjoyment in them he would not moan. It is a good example, gentlemen, and I will develop it. Those moans express in the first place all the aimlessness of your pain, which is so humiliating to your consciousness; the whole legal system of nature on which you spit disdainfully, of course, but from which you suffer all the same while she does not. They express the consciousness that you have no enemy to punish, but that you have pain; the consciousness that in spite of all possible Vagenheims you are in complete slavery to your teeth; that if some one wishes it, your teeth will leave off aching, and if he does not, they will go on aching another three months; and that finally if you are still contumacious and still protest, all that is left you for your own gratification is to thrash yourself or beat your wall with your fist as hard as you can, and absolutely nothing more. Well, these mortal insults, these jeers on the part of some one unknown, end at last in an enjoyment which sometimes reaches the highest degree of voluptuousness. I ask you, gentlemen, listen sometimes to the moans of an educated man of the nineteenth century suffering from toothache, on the second or third day of the attack, when he is beginning to moan, not as he moaned on the first day, that is, not simply because he has toothache, not just as any coarse peasant, but as a man affected by progress and European civilization, a man who is "divorced from the soil and the national elements," as they express it nowadays. His moans become nasty, disgustingly malignant, and go on for whole days and nights. And of course he knows himself that he is doing himself no sort of good with his moans; he knows better than any one that he is only lacerating and harassing himself and others for nothing; he knows that even the audience before whom he is making his efforts, and his whole family, listen to him with loathing, do not put a ha'porth of faith in him, and inwardly understand that he might moan differently, more simply, without trills and flourishes, and that he is only amusing himself like that from ill-humour, from malignancy. Well, in all these recognitions and disgraces it is that there lies a voluptuous pleasure. As though he would say: "I am worrying you, I am lacerating your hearts, I am keeping every one in the house awake. Well, stay awake then, you, too, feel every minute that I have toothache. I am not a hero to you now, as I tried to seem before, but simply a nasty person, an impostor. Well, so be it, then! I am very glad that you see through me. It is nasty for you to hear my despicable moans: well, let it be nasty; here I will let you have a nastier flourish in a minute. . . ." You do not understand even now, gentlemen? No, it seems our development and our consciousness must go further to understand all the intricacies of this pleasure. You laugh? Delighted. My jests, gentlemen, are of course in bad taste, jerky, involved, lacking self-confidence. But of course that is because I do not respect myself. Can a man of perception respect himself at all?

V

Come, can a man who attempts to find enjoyment in the very feeling of his own degradation possibly have a spark of respect for himself? I am not saying this now from any mawkish kind of remorse. And, indeed, I could never endure saying, "Forgive me, Papa, I won't do it again," not because I am incapable of saying that—on the contrary, perhaps just because I have been too capable of it, and in what a way, too! As though of design I used to get into trouble in cases when I was not to blame in any way. That was the nastiest part of it. At the same time I was genuinely touched and penitent, I used to shed tears and, of course, deceived myself, though I was not acting in the least and there was a sick feeling in my heart at the time. . . . For that one could not blame even the laws of nature, though the laws of nature have continually all my life offended me more than anything. It is loathsome to remember it all, but it was loathsome even then. Of course, a minute or so later I would realize wrathfully that it was all a lie, a revolting lie, an affected lie, that is, all this penitence, this emotion, these vows of reform. You will ask why did I worry myself with such antics: answer, because it was very dull to sit with one's hands folded, and so one began cutting capers. That is really it. Observe yourselves more carefully, gentlemen, then you will understand that it is so. I invented adventures for myself and made up a life, so as at least to live in some way. How many times it has happened to me—well, for instance, to take offence simply on purpose, for nothing; and one knows oneself, of course, that one is offended at nothing, that one is putting it on, but yet one brings oneself, at last, to the point of being really offended. All my life I have had an impulse to play such pranks, so that in the end I could not control it in myself. Another time, twice, in fact, I tried hard to be in love. I suffered, too, gentlemen, I assure you. In the depth of my heart there was no faith in my suffering, only a faint stir of mockery, but yet I did suffer, and in the real, orthodox way; I was jealous, beside myself . . . and it was all from *ennui,* gentlemen, all from *ennui;* inertia overcame me. You know the direct, legitimate fruit of consciousness is inertia, that is, conscious sitting-with-the-hands-folded. I have referred to this already. I repeat, I repeat with emphasis: all "direct" persons and men of action are active just because they are stupid and limited. How explain that? I will tell you: in consequence of their limitation they take immediate and secondary causes for primary ones, and in that way persuade themselves more quickly and easily than other people do that they have found an infallible foundation for their activity, and their minds are at ease and you know that is the chief thing. To begin to act, you know, you must first have your mind completely at ease and no trace of doubt left in it. Why, how am I, for example, to set my mind at rest? Where are the primary causes on which I am to build? Where are my foundations? Where am I to get them from? I exercise myself in reflection, and consequently with me every primary cause at once draws after itself another still more primary, and so on to infinity. That is just the essence of every sort of consciousness and reflection. It must be a case of the laws of nature again. What is the result of it in the end? Why, just the same. Remember I spoke just now of vengeance. (I am sure you did not take it in.) I said that a man revenges himself because he sees justice in it. Therefore he has found a primary cause, that is, justice. And so he is at rest on all sides, and consequently he carries out his revenge calmly and successfully, being persuaded that he is doing a just and honest thing. But I see no justice in it, I find no sort of virtue in it either, and consequently if I attempt to revenge myself, it is only out of spite. Spite, of course, might overcome everything, all my doubts, and so might serve quite successfully in place of a primary cause, precisely because it is not a cause. But what is to be done if I have not even spite (I began with that just now, you know). In consequence again of those accursed laws of consciousness, anger in me is subject to chemical disintegration. You look into it, the object flies off into air, your reasons evaporate, the criminal is not to be found, the wrong becomes not a wrong but a phantom, something like the toothache, for which no one is to blame, and consequently there is only the same outlet left again—that is, to beat the wall as hard as you can. So you give it up with a wave of the hand because you have not found a fundamental cause. And try letting yourself be carried away by your feelings, blindly, without reflection, without a primary cause, repelling consciousness at least for a time; hate or love, if only not to sit with your hands folded. The day after to-morrow, at the latest, you will begin despising yourself for having knowingly deceived yourself. Result: a soap-bubble and inertia. Oh, gentlemen, do you know, perhaps I consider myself an intelligent man, only because all my life I have been able neither to begin nor to finish anything. Granted I am a babbler, a harmless vexatious babbler, like all of us. But what is to be done if the direct and sole vocation of every intelligent man is babble, that is, the intentional pouring of water through a sieve?

VI

Oh, if I had done nothing simply from laziness! Heavens, how I should
have respected myself, then. I should have respected myself because I
should at least have been capable of being lazy; there would at least
have been one quality, as it were, positive in me, in which I could have
believed myself. Question: What is he? Answer: A sluggard; how very
pleasant it would have been to hear that of oneself! It would mean that
I was positively defined, it would mean that there was something to say
about me. "Sluggard"—why, it is a calling and vocation, it is a career. Do
not jest, it is so. I should then be a member of the best club by right, and
should find my occupation in continually respecting myself. I knew a
gentleman who prided himself all his life on being a connoisseur of
Lafitte. He considered this as his positive virtue, and never doubted himself. He died, not simply with a tranquil, but with a triumphant, conscience, and he was quite right, too. Then I should have chosen a career
for myself, I should have been a sluggard and a glutton, not a simple one,
but, for instance, one with sympathies for everything good and beautiful.
How do you like that? I have long had visions of it. That "good and beautiful" weighs heavily on my mind at forty. But that is at forty; then—
oh, then it would have been different! I should have found for myself a
form of activity in keeping with it, to be precise, drinking to the health
of everything "good and beautiful." I should have snatched at every opportunity to drop a tear into my glass and then to drain it to all that is
"good and beautiful." I should then have turned everything into the
good and the beautiful; in the nastiest, unquestionable trash, I should
have sought out the good and the beautiful. I should have exuded tears
like a wet sponge. An artist, for instance, paints a picture worthy of Gué.
At once I drink to the health of the artist who painted the picture worthy
of Gué, because I love all that is "good and beautiful." An author has
written *As you will*: at once I drink to the health of "any one you will"
because I love all that is "good and beautiful."

I should claim respect for doing so. I should persecute any one who
would not show me respect. I should live at ease, I should die with
dignity, why, it is charming, perfectly charming! And what a good round
belly I should have grown, what a treble chin I should have established, what a ruby nose I should have coloured for myself, so that every
one would have said, looking at me: "Here is an asset! Here is something real and solid!" And, say what you like, it is very agreeable to hear
such remarks about oneself in this negative age.

VII

But these are all golden dreams. Oh, tell me, who was it first announced,
who was it first proclaimed, that man only does nasty things because he
does not know his own interests; and that if he were enlightened, if his

eyes were opened to his real normal interests, man would at once cease to do nasty things, would at once become good and noble because, being enlightened and understanding his real advantage, he would see his own advantage in the good and nothing else, and we all know that not one man can, consciously, act against his own interests, consequently, so to say, through necessity, he would begin doing good? Oh, the babe! Oh, the pure, innocent child! Why, in the first place, when in all these thousands of years has there been a time when man has. acted only from his own interest? What is to be done with the millions of facts that bear witness that men, *consciously*, that is, fully understanding their real interests, have left them in the background and have rushed headlong on another path, to meet peril and danger, compelled to this course by nobody and by nothing, but, as it were, simply disliking the beaten track, and have obstinately, wilfully, struck out another difficult, absurd way, seeking it almost in the darkness. So, I suppose, this obstinacy and perversity were pleasanter to them than any advantage. . . . Advantage! What is advantage? And will you take it upon yourself to define with perfect accuracy in what the advantage of man consists? And what if it so happens that a man's advantage, *sometimes,* not only may, but even must, consist in his desiring in certain cases what is harmful to himself and not advantageous? And if so, if there can be such a case, the whole principle falls into dust. What do you think—are there such cases? You laugh; laugh away, gentlemen, but only answer me: have man's advantages been reckoned up with perfect certainty? Are there not some which not only have not been included but cannot possibly be included under any classification? You see, you gentlemen have, to the best of my knowledge, taken your whole register of human advantages from the averages of statistical figures and politico-economical formulas. Your advantages are prosperity, wealth, freedom, peace—and so on, and so on. So that the man who should, for instance, go openly and knowingly in opposition to all that list would, to your thinking, and indeed mine, too, of course, be an obscurantist or an absolute madman: would not he? But, you know, this is what is surprising: why does it so happen that all these statisticians, sages and lovers of humanity, when they reckon up human advantages invariably leave out one? They don't even take it into their reckoning in the form in which it should be taken, and the whole reckoning depends upon that. It would be no great matter, they would simply have to take it, this advantage, and add it to the list. But the trouble is, that this strange advantage does not fall under any classification and is not in place in any list. I have a friend for instance . . . Ech! gentlemen, but of course he is your friend, too; and indeed there is no one, no one, to whom he is not a friend! When he prepares for any undertaking this gentleman immediately explains to you, elegantly and clearly, exactly how he must act in accordance with the laws of reason and truth. What is more, he will talk to you with excitement and passion of the true normal interests of man; with irony he will upbraid the shortsighted fools who do not understand their own interests, nor the true significance of virtue; and, within a quarter of an hour, without any sudden outside provocation, but simply through something inside him which is stronger than all his interests, he will go off on quite a different tack—that is, act in direct opposition to what he has just been saying about himself, in opposition to the laws of reason, in opposition to his own advantage, in fact in opposition to everything. . . . I warn you that my friend is a compound personality, and therefore it is difficult to blame him as an individual. The fact is, gentlemen, it seems there must really exist something that is dearer to almost every man than his greatest advantages, or (not to be illogical) there is a most advantageous advantage (the very one omitted of which we spoke just now) which is more important and more advantageous than all other advantages, for the sake of which a man if necessary is ready to act in opposition to all laws; that is, in opposition to reason, honour, peace, prosperity—in fact, in opposition to all those excellent and useful things if only he can attain that fundamental, most advantageous advantage which is dearer to him than all. "Yes, but it's advantage all the same" you will retort. But excuse me, I'll make the point clear, and it is not a case of playing upon words. What matters is, that this advantage is remarkable from the very fact that it breaks down all our classifications, and continually shatters every system constructed by lovers of mankind for the benefit of mankind. In fact, it upsets everything. But before I mention this advantage to you, I want to compromise myself personally, and therefore I boldly declare that all these fine systems, all these theories for explaining to mankind their real normal interests, in order that inevitably striving to pursue these interests they may at once become good and noble—are, in my opinion, so far, mere logical exercises! Yes, logical exercises. Why, to maintain this theory of the regeneration of mankind by means of the pursuit of his own advantage is to my mind almost the same thing as . . . as to affirm, for instance, following Buckle, that through civilization mankind becomes softer, and consequently less bloodthirsty and less fitted for warfare. Logically it does seem to follow from his arguments. But man has such a predilection for systems and abstract deductions that he is ready to distort the truth intentionally, he is ready to deny the evidence of his senses only to justify his logic. I take this example because it is the most glaring instance of it. Only look about you: blood is being spilt in streams, and in the merriest way, as though it were champagne. Take the whole of the nineteenth century in which Buckle lived. Take Napoleon—the Great and also the present one. Take North America—the eternal union. Take the farce of Schleswig-Holstein. . . . And what is it that civilization softens in us? The only gain of civilization for mankind is the greater capacity for variety of sensations—and absolutely nothing more. And through the development of this many-sidedness man may come to finding enjoyment in bloodshed. In fact, this has already happened to him. Have you noticed that it is the most civilized gentlemen who have been the subtlest slaughterers, to whom the Attilas and Stenka Razins could not hold a candle, and if they are not so conspicuous as the Attilas and Stenka Razins it is simply because they are so often met with, are so ordinary and have become so familiar to us. In any case civilization has made mankind if not more bloodthirsty, at least more vilely, more loathsomely bloodthirsty. In old days he saw justice in bloodshed and with his conscience at peace exterminated those he thought proper. Now we do think bloodshed abominable and yet we engage in this abomination, and with more energy than ever. Which is worse? Decide that for yourselves. They say that Cleopatra (excuse an instance from Roman history) was fond of sticking gold pins into her slave-girls' breasts and derived gratification from their screams and writhings. You will say that that was in the comparatively barbarous times; that these are barbarous times too, because also, comparatively speaking, pins are stuck in even now; that though man has now learned to see more clearly than in barbarous ages, he is still far from having learnt to act as reason and science would dictate. But yet you are fully convinced that he will be sure to learn when he gets rid of certain old bad habits, and when common sense and science have completely re-educated human nature and turned it in a normal direction. You are confident that then man will cease from *intentional* error and will, so to say, be compelled not to want to set his will against his normal interests. That is not all; then, you say, science itself will teach man (though to my mind it's a superfluous luxury) that he never has really had any caprice or will of his own, and that he himself is something of the nature of a piano-key or the stop of an organ, and that there are, besides, things called the laws of nature; so that everything he does is not done by his willing it, but is done of itself, by the laws of nature. Consequently we have only to discover these laws of nature, and man will no longer have to answer for his actions and life will become exceedingly easy for him. All human actions will then, of course, be tabulated according to these laws, mathematically, like tables of logarithms up to 108,000, and entered in an index; or, better still, there would be published certain edifying works of the nature of encyclopaedic lexicons, in which everything will be so clearly calculated and explained that there will be no more incidents or adventures in the world.

Then—this is all what you say—new economic relations will be established, all ready-made and worked out with mathematical exactitude, so that every possible question will vanish in the twinkling of an eye, simply because every possible answer to it will be provided. Then the "Palace of Crystal" will be built. Then. . . . In fact, those will be halcyon days. Of course there is no guaranteeing (this is my comment) that it will not be, for instance, frightfully dull then (for what will one have to do when everything will be calculated and tabulated), but on the other hand everything will be extraordinarily rational. Of course boredom may lead you to anything. It is boredom sets one sticking golden pins into people, but all that would not matter. What is bad (this is my comment again) is that I dare say people will be thankful for the gold pins then. Man is stupid, you know, phenomenally stupid; or rather he is not at all stupid, but he is so ungrateful that you could not find another like him in all creation. I, for instance, would not be in the least surprised if all of a sudden, *à propos* of nothing, in the midst of general prosperity a gentleman with an ignoble, or rather with a reactionary and ironical, countenance were to arise and, putting his arms akimbo, say to us all: "I say, gentlemen, hadn't we better kick over the whole show and scatter rationalism to the winds, simply to send these logarithms to the devil, and to enable us to live once more at our own sweet foolish will!" That again would not matter, but what is annoying is that he would be sure to find followers—such is the nature of man. And all that for the most foolish reason, which, one would think, was hardly worth mentioning: that is, that man everywhere and at all times, whoever he may be, has preferred to act as he chose and not in the least as his reason and advantage dictated. And one may choose what is contrary to one's own interests, and sometimes one *positively ought* (that is my idea). One's own free unfettered choice, one's own caprice, however wild it may be, one's own fancy worked up at times to frenzy—is that very "most advantageous advantage" which we have overlooked, which comes under no classification and against which all systems and theories are continually being shattered to atoms. And how do these wiseacres know that man wants a normal, a virtuous choice? What has made them conceive that man must want a rationally advantageous choice? What man wants is simply *independent* choice, whatever that independence may cost and wherever it may lead. And choice, of course, the devil only knows what choice.

VIII

"Ha! ha! ha! But you know there is no such thing as choice in reality, say what you like," you will interpose with a chuckle. "Science has succeeded in so far analysing man that we know already that choice and what is called freedom of will is nothing else than—"

Stay, gentlemen, I meant to begin with that myself. I confess, I was rather frightened. I was just going to say that the devil only knows what choice depends on, and that perhaps that was a very good thing, but I remembered the teaching of science . . . and pulled myself up. And here you have begun upon it. Indeed, if there really is some day discovered a formula for all our desires and caprices—that is, an explanation of what they depend upon, by what laws they arise, how they develop, what they are aiming at in one case and in another and so on, that is a real mathematical formula—then, most likely, man will at once cease to feel desire, indeed, he will be certain to. For who would want to choose by rule? Besides, he will at once be transformed from a human being into an organ-stop or something of the sort; for what is a man without desires, without free will and without choice, if not a stop in an organ? What do you think? Let us reckon the chances—can such a thing happen or not?

"H'm!" you decide. "Our choice is usually mistaken from a false view of our advantage. We sometimes choose absolute nonsense because in our foolishness we see in that nonsense the easiest means for attaining a supposed advantage. But when all that is explained and worked out on paper (which is perfectly possible, for it is contemptible and sense-less to suppose that some laws of nature man will never under-stand), then certainly so-called desires will no longer exist. For if a desire should come into conflict with reason we shall then reason and not desire, because it will be impossible retaining our reason to be *senseless* in our desires, and in that way knowingly act against reason and desire to injure ourselves. And as all choice and reasoning can be really calculated—because there will some day be discovered the laws of our so-called free will—so, joking apart, there may one day be some-thing like a table constructed of them, so that we really shall choose in accordance with it. If, for instance, some day they calculate and prove to me that I made a long nose at some one because I could not help mak-ing a long nose at him and that I had to do it in that particular way, what *freedom* is left me, especially if I am a learned man and have taken my degree somewhere? Then I should be able to calculate my whole life for thirty years beforehand. In short, if this could be arranged there would be nothing left for us to do; anyway, we should have to under-stand that. And, in fact, we ought unwearyingly to repeat to ourselves that at such and such a time and in such and such circumstances nature does not ask our leave; that we have got to take her as she is and not fashion her to suit our fancy, and if we really aspire to formulas and tables of rules, and well, even . . . to the chemical retort, there's no help for it, we must accept the retort too, or else it will be accepted with-out our consent. . . ."

Yes, but here I come to a stop! Gentlemen, you must excuse me for being over-philosophical: it's the result of forty years underground! Allow me to indulge my fancy. You see, gentlemen, reason is an ex-cellent thing, there's no disputing that, but reason is nothing but reason and satisfies only the rational side of man's nature, while will is a mani-festation of the whole life, that is, of the whole human life including reason and all the impulses. And although our life, in this manifestation of it, is often worthless, yet it is life and not simply extracting square roots. Here I, for instance, quite naturally want to live, in order to satisfy all my capacities for life, and not simply my capacity for reasoning, that is, not simply one twentieth of my capacity for life. What does reason know? Reason only knows what it has succeeded in learning (some things, perhaps, it will never learn; this is a poor comfort, but why not say so frankly?) and human nature acts as a whole, with everything that is in it, consciously or unconsciously, and, even if it goes wrong, it lives. I suspect, gentlemen, that you are looking at me with compassion; you tell me again that an enlightened and developed man, such, in short, as the future man will be, cannot consciously desire anything disadvantageous to himself, that that can be proved mathematically. I thoroughly agree, it can—by mathematics. But I repeat for the hundredth time, there is one case, one only, when man may consciously, purposely, desire what is injurious to himself, what is stupid, very stupid—simply in order to have the right to desire for himself even what is very stupid and not to be bound by an obligation to desire only what is sensible. Of course, this very stupid thing, this caprice of ours, may be in reality, gentlemen, more advantageous for us than anything else on earth, especially in certain cases. And in particular it may be more advantageous than any advantage even when it does us obvious harm, and contradicts the soundest conclusions of our reason concerning our advantage —for in any circumstances it preserves for us what is most precious and most important—that is, our personality, our individuality. Some, you see, maintain that this really is the most precious thing for mankind; choice can, of course, if it chooses, be in agreement with reason; and especially if this be not abused but kept within bounds. It is profitable and sometimes even praiseworthy. But very often, and even most often, choice is utterly and stubbornly opposed to reason . . . and . . . and . . . do you know that that, too, is profitable, sometimes even praiseworthy? Gentlemen, let us suppose that man is not stupid. (Indeed one cannot refuse to suppose that, if only from the one consideration, that, if man is stupid, then who is wise?) But if he is not stupid, he is monstrously ungrateful! Phenomenally ungrateful. In fact, I believe that the best definition of man is the ungrateful biped. But that is not all, that is not his worst defect; his worst defect is his perpetual moral obliquity, perpetual—from the days of the Flood to the Schleswig-Holstein period. Moral obliquity and consequently lack of good sense; for it has long been accepted that lack of good sense is due to no other cause than moral obliquity. Put it to the test and cast your eyes upon the history of mankind. What will you see? Is it a grand spectacle? Grand, if you like. Take the Colossus of Rhodes, for instance, that's worth something. With good reason Mr. Anaevsky testifies of it that some say that it is the work of man's hands, while others maintain that it has been created by nature herself. Is it many-coloured? May be it is many-coloured, too: if one takes the dress uniforms, military and civilian, of all peoples in all ages —that alone is worth something, and if you take the undress uniforms you will never get to the end of it; no historian would be equal to the job. Is it monotonous? Maybe it's monotonous too: it's fighting and fighting; they are fighting now, they fought first and they fought last—you will admit, that it is almost too monotonous. In short, one may say anything about the history of the world—anything that might enter the most disordered imagination. The only thing one can't say is that it's rational. The very word sticks in one's throat. And, indeed, this is the odd thing that is continually happening: there are continually turning up in life moral and rational persons, sages and lovers of humanity who make it their object to live all their lives as morally and rationally as possible, to be, so to speak, a light to their neighbours simply in order to show them that it is possible to live morally and rationally in this world. And yet we all know that those very people sooner or later have been false to themselves, playing some queer trick, often a most unseemly one. Now I ask you: what can be expected of man since he is a being endowed with such strange qualities? Shower upon him every earthly blessing, drown him in a sea of happiness, so that nothing but bubbles of bliss can be seen on the surface; give him economic prosperity, such that he should have nothing else to do but sleep, eat cakes and busy himself with the continuation of his species, and even then out of sheer ingratitude, sheer spite, man would play you some nasty trick. He would even risk his cakes and would deliberately desire the most fatal rubbish, the most uneconomical absurdity, simply to introduce into all this positive good sense his fatal fantastic element. It is just his fantastic dreams, his vulgar folly that he will desire to retain, simply in order to prove to himself—as though that were so necessary—that men still are men and not the keys of a piano, which the laws of nature threaten to control so completely that soon one will be able to desire nothing but by the calendar. And that is not all: even if man really were nothing but a piano-key, even if this were proved to him by natural science and mathematics, even then he would not become reasonable, but would purposely do something perverse out of simple ingratitude, simply to gain his point. And if he does not find means he will contrive destruction and chaos, will contrive sufferings of all sorts, only to gain his point! He will launch a curse upon the world, and as only man can curse (it is his privilege, the primary distinction between him and other animals), may be by his curse alone he will attain his object—that is, convince himself that he is a man and not a piano-key! If you say that all this, too, can be calculated and tabulated—chaos and darkness and curses, so that the mere possibility of calculating it all beforehand would stop it all, and reason would reassert itself, then man would purposely go mad in order to be rid of reason and gain his point! I believe in it, I answer for it, for the whole work of man really seems to consist in nothing but proving to himself every minute that he is a man and not a piano-key! It may be at the cost of his skin, it may be by cannibalism! And this being so, can one help being tempted to rejoice that it has not yet come off, and that desire still depends on something we don't know?

You will scream at me (that is, if you condescend to do so) that no one is touching my free will, that all they are concerned with is that my will should of itself, of its own free will, coincide with my own normal interests, with the laws of nature and arithmetic.

Good Heavens, gentlemen, what sort of free will is left when we come to tabulation and arithmetic, when it will all be a case of twice two make four? Twice two makes four without my will. As if free will meant that!

IX

Gentlemen, I am joking, and I know myself that my jokes are not brilliant, but you know one can't take everything as a joke. I am, perhaps, jesting against the grain. Gentlemen, I am tormented by questions; answer them for me. You, for instance, want to cure men of their old habits and reform their will in accordance with science and good sense. But how do you know, not only that it is possible, but also that it is *desirable*, to reform man in that way? And what leads you to the conclusion that man's inclinations *need* reforming? In short, how do you know that such a reformation will be a benefit to man? And to go to the root of the matter, why are you so positively convinced that not to act against his real normal interests guaranteed by the conclusions of reason and arithmetic is certainly always advantageous for man and must always be a law for mankind? So far, you know, this is only your supposition. It may be the law of logic, but not the law of humanity. You think, gentlemen, perhaps that I am mad? Allow me to defend myself. I agree that man is pre-eminently a creative animal, predestined to strive consciously for an object and to engage in engineering—that is, incessantly and eternally to make new roads, *wherever they may lead*. But the reason why he wants sometimes to go off at a tangent may just be that he is *predestined* to make the road, and perhaps, too, that however stupid the "direct" practical man may be, the thought sometimes will occur to him that the road almost always does lead *somewhere*, and that the destination it leads to is less important than the process of making it, and that the chief thing is to save the well-conducted child from despising engineering, and so giving way to the fatal idleness, which, as we all know, is the mother of all the vices. Man likes to make roads and to create, that is a fact beyond dispute. But why has he such a passionate love for destruction and chaos also? Tell me that! But on that point I want to say a couple of words myself. May it not be that he loves chaos and destruction (there can be no disputing that he does sometimes love it) because he is instinctively afraid of attaining his object and completing the edifice he is constructing? Who knows, perhaps he only loves that edifice from a distance, and is by no means in love with it at close quarters; perhaps he only loves building it and does not want to live in it, but will leave it, when completed, for the use of *les animaux domes-*

tiques—such as the ants, the sheep, and so on. Now the ants have quite a different taste. They have a marvellous edifice of that pattern which endures for ever—the ant-heap.

With the ant-heap the respectable race of ants began and with the ant-heap they will probably end, which does the greatest credit to their perseverance and good sense. But man is a frivolous and incongruous creature, and perhaps, like a chess player, loves the process of the game, not the end of it. And who knows (there is no saying with certainty), perhaps the only goal on earth to which mankind is striving lies in this incessant process of attaining, in other words, in life itself, and not in the thing to be attained, which must always be expressed as a formula, as positive as twice two makes four, and such positiveness is not life, gentlemen, but is the beginning of death. Anyway, man has always been afraid of this mathematical certainty, and I am afraid of it now. Granted that man does nothing but seek that mathematical certainty, he traverses oceans, sacrifices his life in the quest, but to succeed, really to find it, he dreads, I assure you. He feels that when he has found it there will be nothing for him to look for. When workmen have finished their work they do at least receive their pay, they go to the tavern, then they are taken to the police-station—and there is occupation for a week. But where can man go? Anyway, one can observe a certain awkwardness about him when he has attained such objects. He loves the process of attaining, but does not quite like to have attained, and that, of course, is very absurd. In fact, man is a comical creature; there seems to be a kind of jest in it all. But yet mathematical certainty is, after all, something insufferable. Twice two makes four seems to me simply a piece of insolence. Twice two makes four is a pert coxcomb who stands with arms akimbo barring your path and spitting. I admit that twice two makes four is an excellent thing, but if we are to give everything its due, twice two makes five is sometimes a very charming thing too.

And why are you so firmly, so triumphantly, convinced that only the normal and the positive—in other words, only what is conducive to welfare—is for the advantage of man? Is not reason in error as regards advantage? Does not man, perhaps, love something besides well-being? Perhaps he is just as fond of suffering? Perhaps suffering is just as great a benefit to him as well-being? Man is sometimes extraordinarily, passionately, in love with suffering, and that is a fact. There is no need to appeal to universal history to prove that; only ask yourself, if you are a man and have lived at all. As far as my personal opinion is concerned, to care only for well-being seems to me positively ill-bred. Whether it's good or bad, it is sometimes very pleasant, too, to smash things. I hold no brief for suffering nor for well-being either. I am standing for . . . my caprice, and for its being guaranteed to me when necessary. Suffering would be out of place in vaudevilles, for instance; I know that. In the "Palace of Crystal" it is unthinkable; suffering means doubt, negation, and what would be the good of a "palace of crystal" if there could be any doubt about it? And yet I think man will never renounce real suffering, that is, destruction and chaos. Why, suffering is the sole origin of consciousness. Though I did lay it down at the beginning that consciousness is the greatest misfortune for man, yet I know man prizes it and would not give it up for any satisfaction. Consciousness, for instance, is infinitely superior to twice two makes four. Once you have mathematical certainty there is nothing left to do or to understand. There will be nothing left but to bottle up your five senses and plunge into contemplation. While if you stick to consciousness, even though the same result is attained, you can at least flog yourself at times, and that will, at any rate, liven you up. Reactionary as it is, corporal punishment is better than nothing.

X

You believe in a palace of crystal that can never be destroyed—a palace at which one will not be able to put out one's tongue or make a long nose on the sly. And perhaps that is just why I am afraid of this edifice, that it is of crystal and can never be destroyed and that one cannot put one's tongue out at it even on the sly.

You see, if it were not a palace, but a hen-house, I might creep into it to avoid getting wet, and yet I would not call the hen-house a palace out of gratitude to it for keeping me dry. You laugh and say that in such circumstances a hen-house is as good as a mansion. Yes, I answer, if one had to live simply to keep out of the rain.

But what is to be done if I have taken it into my head that that is not the only object in life, and that if one must live one had better live in a mansion. That is my choice, my desire. You will only eradicate it when you have changed my preference. Well, do change it, allure me with something else, give me another ideal. But meanwhile I will not take a hen-house for a mansion. The palace of crystal may be an idle dream, it may be that it is inconsistent with the laws of nature and that I have invented it only through my own stupidity, through the old-fashioned irrational habits of my generation. But what does it matter to me that it is inconsistent? That makes no difference since it exists in my desires, or rather exists as long as my desires exist. Perhaps you are laughing again? Laugh away; I will put up with any mockery rather than pretend that I am satisfied when I am hungry. I know, anyway, that I will not be put off with a compromise, with a recurring zero, simply because it is consistent with the laws of nature and actually exists. I will not accept as the crown of my desires a block of buildings with tenements for the poor on a lease of a thousand years, and perhaps with a signboard of a dentist hanging out. Destroy my desires, eradicate my ideals, show me something better, and I will follow you. You will say, perhaps, that it is not worth your trouble; but in that case I can give you the same answer. We are discussing things seriously; but if you won't deign to give me your attention, I will drop your acquaintance. I can retreat into my underground hole.

But while I am alive and have desires I would rather my hand were withered off than bring one brick to such a building! Don't remind me that I have just rejected that palace of crystal for the sole reason that one cannot put out one's tongue at it. I did not say because I am so fond of putting my tongue out. Perhaps the thing I resented was, that of all your edifices there has not been one at which one could not put out one's tongue. On the contrary, I would let my tongue be cut off out of gratitude if things could be so arranged that I should lose all desire to put it out. It is not my fault that things cannot be so arranged, and that one must be satisfied with model flats. Then why am I made with such desires? Can I have been constructed simply in order to come to the conclusion that all my construction is a cheat? Can this be my whole purpose? I do not believe it.

But do you know what: I am convinced that we underground folk ought to be kept on a curb. Though we may sit forty years underground without speaking, when we do come out into the light of day and break out we talk and talk and talk. . . .

XI

The long and the short of it is, gentlemen, that it is better to do nothing! Better conscious inertia! And so hurrah for underground! Though I have said that I envy the normal man to the last drop of my bile, yet I should not care to be in his place such as he is now (though I shall not cease envying him). No, no; anyway the underground life is more advantageous. There, at any rate, one can . . . Oh, but even now I am lying! I am lying because I know myself that it is not underground that is better, but something different, quite different, for which I am thirsting, but which I cannot find! Damn underground!

I will tell you another thing that would be better, and that is, if I myself believed in anything of what I have just written. I swear to you, gentlemen, there is not one thing, not one word of what I have written that I really believe. That is, I believe it, perhaps, but at the same time I feel and suspect that I am lying like a cobbler.

"Then why have you written all this?" you will say to me. "I ought to put you underground for forty years without anything to do and then come to you in your cellar, to find out what stage you have reached! How can a man be left with nothing to do for forty years?"

"Isn't that shameful, isn't that humiliating?" you will say, perhaps, wagging your heads contemptuously. "You thirst for life and try to settle the problems of life by a logical tangle. And how persistent, how insolent are your sallies, and at the same time what a scare you are in! You talk nonsense and are pleased with it; you say impudent things and are in continual alarm and apologizing for them. You declare that you are afraid of nothing and at the same time try to ingratiate yourself in our good opinion. You declare that you are gnashing your teeth and at the same time you try to be witty so as to amuse us. You know that your witticisms are not witty, but you are evidently well satisfied with their literary value. You may, perhaps, have really suffered, but you have no respect for your own suffering. You may have sincerity, but you have no modesty; out of the pettiest vanity you expose your sincerity to publicity and ignominy. You doubtlessly mean to say something, but hide your last word through fear, because you have not the resolution to utter it, and only have a cowardly impudence. You boast of consciousness, but you are not sure of your ground, for though your mind works, yet your heart is darkened and corrupt, and you cannot have a full, genuine consciousness without a pure heart. And how intrusive you are, how you insist and grimace! Lies, lies, lies!"

Of course I have myself made up all the things you say. That, too, is from underground. I have been for forty years listening to you through a crack under the floor. I have invented them myself, there was nothing else I could invent. It is no wonder that I have learned it by heart and it has taken a literary form. . . .

But can you really be so credulous as to think that I will print all this and give it to you to read too? And another problem: why do I call you "gentlemen," why do I address you as though you really were my readers? Such confessions as I intend to make are never printed nor given to other people to read. Anyway, I am not strong-minded enough for that, and I don't see why I should be. But you see a fancy has occurred to me and I want to realize it at all costs. Let me explain.

Every man has reminiscences which he would not tell to every one, but only to his friends. He has other matters in his mind which he would not reveal even to his friends, but only to himself, and that in secret. But there are other things which a man is afraid to tell even to himself, and every decent man has a number of such things stored away in his mind. The more decent he is, the greater the number of such things in his mind. Anyway, I have only lately determined to remember some of my early adventures. Till now I have always avoided them, even with a certain uneasiness. Now, when I am not only recalling them, but have actually decided to write an account of them, I want to try the experiment whether one can, even with oneself, be perfectly open and not take fright at the whole truth. I will observe, in parenthesis, that Heine says that a true autobiography is almost an impossibility, and that man is bound to lie about himself. He considers that Rousseau certainly told lies about himself in his confessions, and even intentionally lied, out of vanity. I am convinced that Heine is right; I quite understand how sometimes one may, out of sheer vanity, attribute regular crimes to oneself, and indeed I can very well conceive that kind of vanity. But Heine judged of people who made their confessions to the public. I write only for myself, and I wish to declare once and for all that if I write as though I were addressing readers, that is simply because it is easier for me to write in that form. It is a form, an empty form—I shall never have readers. I have made this plain already. . . .

I don't wish to be hampered by any restrictions in the compilation of my notes. I shall not attempt any system or method. I will jot things down as I remember them.

But here, perhaps, some one will catch at the word and ask me: if you really don't reckon on readers, why do you make such compacts with yourself—and on paper too—that is, that you won't attempt any system or method, that you jot things down as you remember them, and so on, and so on? Why are you explaining? Why do you apologize?

Well, there it is, I answer.

There is a whole psychology in all this, though. Perhaps it is simply that I am a coward. And perhaps that I purposely imagine an audience before me in order that I may be more dignified while I write. There are perhaps thousands of reasons. Again, what is my object precisely in writing? If it is not for the benefit of the public why should I not simply recall these incidents in my own mind without putting them on paper?

Quite so; but yet it is more imposing on paper. There is something more impressive in it; I shall be better able to criticize myself and improve my style. Besides, I shall perhaps obtain actual relief from writing. To-day, for instance, I am particularly oppressed by one memory of a distant past. It came back vividly to my mind a few days ago, and has remained haunting me like an annoying tune that one cannot get rid of. And yet I must get rid of it somehow. I have hundreds of such reminiscences; but at times some one stands out from the hundred and oppresses me. For some reasons I believe that if I write it down I should get rid of it. Why not try?

Besides, I am bored, and I never have anything to do. Writing will be a sort of work. They say work makes man kind-hearted and honest. Well, here is a chance for me, anyway.

Snow is falling to-day, yellow and dingy. It fell yesterday, too, and a few days ago. I fancy it is the wet snow that has reminded me of that incident which I cannot shake off now. And so let it be a story *à propos* of the falling snow.

Part II · À Propos of the Wet Snow

When from dark error's subjugation
My words of passionate exhortation
  Had wrenched thy fainting spirit free;
And writhing prone in thine affliction

Thou didst recall with malediction
   The vice that had encompassed thee:
And when thy slumbering conscience, fretting
   By recollection's torturing flame,
Thou didst reveal the hideous setting
   Of thy life's current ere I came:
When suddenly I saw thee sicken,
   And weeping, hide thine anguished face,
Revolted, maddened, horror-stricken,
   At memories of foul disgrace.
                NEKRASOV (*translated by Juliet Soskice*)

I

At that time I was only twenty-four. My life was even then gloomy, ill-regulated, and as solitary as that of a savage. I made friends with no one and positively avoided talking, and buried myself more and more in my hole. At work in the office I never looked at any one, and I was perfectly well aware that my companions looked upon me, not only as a queer fellow, but even looked upon me—I always fancied this—with a sort of loathing. I sometimes wondered why it was that nobody except me fancied that he was looked upon with aversion? One of the clerks had a most repulsive, pock-marked face, which looked positively villainous. I believe I should not have dared to look at any one with such an unsightly countenance. Another had such a very dirty old uniform that there was an unpleasant odour in his proximity. Yet not one of these gentlemen showed the slightest self-consciousness—either about their clothes or their countenance or their character in any way. Neither of them ever imagined that they were looked at with repulsion; if they had imagined it they would not have minded—so long as their superiors did not look at them in that way. It is clear to me now that, owing to my unbounded vanity and to the high standard I set for myself, I often looked at myself with furious discontent, which verged on loathing, and so I inwardly attributed the same feeling to every one. I hated my face, for instance: I thought it disgusting, and even suspected that there was something base in my expression, and so every day when I turned up at the office I tried to behave as independently as possible, and to assume a lofty expression, so that I might not be suspected of being abject. "My face may be ugly," I thought, "but let it be lofty, expressive, and, above all, *extremely* intelligent." But I was positively and painfully certain that it was impossible for my countenance ever to express those qualities. And what was worst of all, I thought it actually stupid looking, and I would have been quite satisfied if I could have looked intelligent. In fact, I would even have put up with looking base if, at the same time, my face could have been thought strikingly intelligent.

Of course, I hated my fellow clerks one and all, and I despised them all, yet at the same time I was, as it were, afraid of them. In fact, it happened at times that I thought more highly of them than of myself. It somehow happened quite suddenly that I alternated between despising them and thinking them superior to myself. A cultivated and decent man cannot be vain without setting a fearfully high standard for himself, and without despising and almost hating himself at certain moments. But whether I despised them or thought them superior I dropped my eyes almost every time I met any one. I even made experiments whether I could face so and so's looking at me, and I was always the first to drop my eyes. This worried me to distraction. I had a sickly dread, too, of being ridiculous, and so had a slavish passion for the conventional in everything external. I loved to fall into the common rut, and had a wholehearted terror of any kind of eccentricity in myself. But how could I live up to it? I was morbidly sensitive, as a man of our age should be. They were all stupid, and as like one another as so many sheep. Perhaps I was the only one in the office who fancied that I was a coward and a slave, and I fancied it just because I was more highly developed. But it was not only that I fancied it, it really was so. I was a coward and a slave. I say this without the slightest embarrassment. Every decent man of our age must be a coward and a slave. That is his normal condition. Of that I am firmly persuaded. He is made and constructed to that very end. And not only at the present time owing to some casual circumstances, but always, at all times, a decent man is bound to be a coward and a slave. It is the law of nature for all decent people all over the earth. If any one of them happens to be valiant about something, he need not be comforted nor carried away by that; he would show the white feather just the same before something else. That is how it invariably and inevitably ends. Only donkeys and mules are valiant, and they only till they are pushed up to the wall. It is not worth while to pay attention to them for they really are of no consequence.

Another circumstance, too, worried me in those days: that there was no one like me and I was unlike any one else. "I am alone and they are *every one*," I thought—and pondered.

From that it is evident that I was still a youngster.

The very opposite sometimes happened. It was loathsome sometimes to go to the office; things reached such a point that I often came home ill. But all at once, *à propos* of nothing, there would come a phase of scepticism and indifference (everything happened in phases to me), and I would laugh myself at my intolerance and fastidiousness, I would reproach myself with being *romantic*. At one time I was unwilling to speak to any one, while at other times I would not only talk, but go to the length of contemplating making friends with them. All my fastidiousness would suddenly, for no rhyme or reason, vanish. Who knows, perhaps I never had really had it, and it had simply been affected, and got out of books. I have not decided that question even now. Once I quite made friends with them, visited their homes, played prefer- ence, drank vodka, talked of promotions. . . . But here let me make a digression.

We Russians, speaking generally, have never had those foolish tran- scendental "romantics"—German, and still more French—on whom noth- ing produces any effect; if there were an earthquake, if all France perished at the barricades, they would still be the same, they would not even have the decency to affect a change, but would still go on singing their transcendental songs to the hour of their death, because they are fools. We, in Russia, have no fools; that is well known. That is what dis- tinguishes us from foreign lands. Consequently these transcendental natures are not found amongst us in their pure form. The idea that they are is due to our "realistic" journalists and critics of that day, always on the look out for Kostanzhoglos and Uncle Pyotr Ivanitchs and foolishly accepting them as our ideal; they have slandered our romantics, taking them for the same transcendental sort as in Germany or France. On the contrary, the characteristics of our "romantics" are absolutely and directly opposed to the transcendental European type, and no European standard can be applied to them. (Allow me to make use of this word "romantic" —an old-fashioned and much respected word which has done good serv- ice and is familiar to all.) The characteristics of our romantic are to un- derstand everything, *to see everything and to see it often incom- parably more clearly than our most realistic minds see it;* to refuse to accept anyone or anything, but at the same time not to despise anything; to give way, to yield, from policy; never to lose sight of a useful practical object (such as rent-free quarters at the government expense, pen- sions, decorations), to keep their eye on that object through all the enthusiasms and volumes of lyrical poems, and at the same time to pre- serve "the good and the beautiful" inviolate within them to the hour of their death, and to preserve themselves also, incidentally, like some precious jewel wrapped in cotton wool if only for the benefit of "the good and the beautiful." Our "romantic" is a man of great breadth and the greatest rogue of all our rogues, I assure you. . . . I can assure you from experience, indeed. Of course, that is, if he is intelligent. But what am I saying! The romantic is always intelligent, and I only meant to observe that although we have had foolish romantics they don't count, and they were only so because in the flower of their youth they degen- erated into Germans, and to preserve their precious jewel more com- fortably, settled somewhere out there—by preference in Weimar or the Black Forest.

I, for instance, genuinely despised my official work and did not openly abuse it simply because I was in it myself and got a salary for it. Anyway, take note, I did not openly abuse it. Our romantic would rather go out of his mind—a thing, however, which very rarely happens—than take to open abuse, unless he had some other career in view; and he is never kicked out. At most, they would take him to the lunatic asylum as "the King of Spain" if he should go very mad. But it is only the thin, fair people who go out of their minds in Russia. Innumerable "romantics" attain later in life to considerable rank in the service. Their many-sidedness is remarkable! And what a faculty they have for the most contradictory sensations! I was comforted by this thought even in those days, and I am of the same opinion now. That is why there are so many "broad natures" among us who never lose their ideal even in the depths of degradation; and though they never stir a finger for their ideal, though they are arrant thieves and knaves, yet they tearfully cherish their first ideal and are extraordinarily honest at heart. Yes, it is only among us that the most incorrigible rogue can be absolutely and loftily honest at heart without in the least ceasing to be a rogue. I repeat, our romantics, frequently, become such accomplished rascals (I use the term "rascals" affectionately), suddenly display such a sense of reality and practical knowledge that their bewildered superiors and the public generally can only ejaculate in amazement.

Their many-sidedness is really amazing, and goodness knows what it may develop into later on, and what the future has in store for us. It is not a poor material! I do not say this from any foolish or boastful patri-otism. But I feel sure that you are again imagining that I am joking. Or perhaps it's just the contrary, and you are convinced that I really think so. Anyway, gentlemen, I shall welcome both views as an honour and a special favour. And do forgive my digression.

I did not, of course, maintain friendly relations with my comrades and soon was at loggerheads with them, and in my youth and inexperience I even gave up bowing to them, as though I had cut off all relations. That, however, only happened to me once. As a rule, I was always alone.

In the first place I spent most of my time at home, reading. I tried to stifle all that was continually seething within me by means of external impressions. And the only external means I had was reading. Reading, of course, was a great help—exciting me, giving me pleasure and pain. But at times it bored me fearfully. One longed for movement in spite of everything, and I plunged all at once into dark, underground, loath-some vice of the pettiest kind. My wretched passions were acute, smart-ing, from my continual, sickly irritability. I had hysterical impulses, with tears and convulsions. I had no resource except reading, that is, there was nothing in my surroundings which I could respect and which at-tracted me. I was overwhelmed with depression, too; I had an hysteri-cal craving for incongruity and for contrast, and so I took to vice. I have not said all this to justify myself. . . . But, no! I am lying. I did want to justify myself. I make that little observation for my own benefit, gentle-men. I don't want to lie. I vowed to myself I would not.

And so, furtively, timidly, in solitude, at night, I indulged in filthy vice, with a feeling of shame which never deserted me, even at the most loathsome moments, and which at such moments nearly made me curse. Already even then I had my underground world in my soul. I was fearfully afraid of being seen, of being met, of being recognized. I visited various obscure haunts.

One night as I was passing a tavern I saw through a lighted window some gentlemen fighting with billiard cues, and saw one of them thrown out of the window. At other times I should have felt very much disgusted, but I was in such a mood at the time, that I actually envied the gentleman thrown out of the window—and I envied him so much that I even went into the tavern and into the billiard-room. "Perhaps," I thought, "I'll have a fight, too, and they'll throw me out of the window."

I was not drunk—but what is one to do—depression will drive a man to such a pitch of hysteria? But nothing happened. It seemed that I was not even equal to being thrown out of the window and I went away without having my fight.

An officer put me in my place from the first moment.

I was standing by the billiard-table and in my ignorance blocking up the way, and he wanted to pass; he took me by the shoulders and without a word—without a warning or explanation—moved me from where I was standing to another spot and passed by as though he had not noticed me. I could have forgiven blows, but I could not forgive his having moved me without noticing me.

Devil knows what I would have given for a real regular quarrel—a more decent, a more *literary* one, so to speak. I had been treated like a fly. This officer was over six foot, while I was a spindly little fellow. But the quarrel was in my hands. I had only to protest and I certainly would have been thrown out of the window. But I changed my mind and preferred to beat a resentful retreat.

I went out of the tavern straight home, confused and troubled, and the next night I went out again with the same lewd intentions, still more furtively, abjectly and miserably than before, as it were, with tears in my eyes—but still I did go out again. Don't imagine, though, it was cowardice made me slink away from the officer: I never have been a coward at heart, though I have always been a coward in action. Don't be in a hurry to laugh—I assure you I can explain it all.

Oh, if only that officer had been one of the sort who would consent to fight a duel! But no, he was one of those gentlemen (alas, long extinct!) who preferred fighting with cues or, like Gogol's Lieutenant Pirogov, appealing to the police. They did not fight duels and would have thought a duel with a civilian like me an utterly unseemly procedure in any case—and they looked upon the duel altogether as something impossible, something free-thinking and French. But they were quite ready to bully, especially when they were over six foot.

I did not slink away through cowardice, but through an unbounded vanity. I was afraid not of his six foot, nor of getting a sound thrashing and being thrown out of the window; I should have had physical courage, enough, I assure you; but I had not the moral courage. What I was afraid of was that every one present, from the insolent marker down to the lowest little stinking, pimply clerk in a greasy collar, would jeer at me and fail to understand when I began to protest and to address them in literary language. For of the point of honour—not of honour, but of the point of honour (*point d'honneur*)—one cannot speak among us except in literary language. You can't allude to the "point of honour" in ordinary language. I was fully convinced (the sense of reality, in spite of all my romanticism!) that they would all simply split their sides with laughter, and that the officer would not simply beat me, that is, without insulting me, but would certainly prod me in the back with his knee, kick me round the billiard-table, and only then perhaps have pity and drop me out of the window.

Of course, this trivial incident could not with me end in that. I often met that officer afterwards in the street and noticed him very carefully. I am not quite sure whether he recognized me, I imagine not; I judge from certain signs. But I—I stared at him with spite and hatred and so it went on . . . for several years! My resentment grew even deeper with years. At first I began making stealthy inquiries about this officer. It was difficult for me to do so, for I knew no one. But one day I heard some one shout his surname in the street as I was following him at a distance, as though I were tied to him—and so I learnt his surname. Another time I followed him to his flat, and for ten kopecks learned from the porter where he lived, on which storey, whether he lived alone or with others, and so on—in fact, everything one could learn from a porter. One morning, though I had never tried my hand with the pen, it suddenly occurred to me to write a satire on this officer in the form of a novel which would unmask his villainy. I wrote the novel with relish. I did unmask his villainy, I even exaggerated it; at first I so altered his surname that it could easily be recognized, but on second thoughts I changed it, and sent the story to the *Otetchestvenniya Zapiski*. But at that time such attacks were not the fashion and my story was not printed. That was a great vexation to me.

Sometimes I was positively choked with resentment. At last I determined to challenge my enemy to a duel. I composed a splendid, charming letter to him, imploring him to apologize to me, and hinting rather plainly at a duel in case of refusal. The letter was so composed that if the officer had had the least understanding of the good and the beautiful he would certainly have flung himself on my neck and have offered me his friendship. And how fine that would have been! How we should have got on together! "He could have shielded me with his higher rank, while I could have improved his mind with my culture, and, well . . . my ideas, and all sorts of things might have happened." Only fancy, this was two years after his insult to me, and my challenge would have been a ridiculous anachronism, in spite of all the ingenuity of my letter in disguising and explaining away the anachronism. But, thank God (to this day I thank the Almighty with tears in my eyes), I did not send the letter to him. Cold shivers run down my back when I think of what might have happened if I had sent it.

And all at once I revenged myself in the simplest way, by a stroke of genius! A brilliant thought suddenly dawned upon me. Sometimes on holidays I used to stroll along the sunny side of the Nevsky about four o'clock in the afternoon. Though it was hardly a stroll so much as a series of innumerable miseries, humiliations and resentments; but no doubt that was just what I wanted. I used to wriggle along in a most unseemly fashion, like an eel, continually moving aside to make way for generals, for officers of the guards and the hussars, or for ladies. At such minutes there used to be a convulsive twinge at my heart, and I used to feel hot all down my back at the mere thought of the wretchedness of my attire, of the wretchedness and abjectness of my little scurrying figure. This was a regular martyrdom, a continual, intolerable humiliation at the thought, which passed into an incessant and direct sensation, that I was a mere fly in the eyes of all this world, a nasty, disgusting fly— more intelligent, more highly developed, more refined in feeling than any of them, of course—but a fly that was continually making way for every one, insulted and injured by every one. Why I inflicted this torture upon myself, why I went to the Nevsky, I don't know. I felt simply drawn there at every possible opportunity.

Already then I began to experience a rush of the enjoyment of which I spoke in the first chapter. After my affair with the officer I felt even more drawn there than before: it was on the Nevsky that I met him most frequently, there I could admire him. He, too, went there chiefly on holidays. He, too, turned out of his path for generals and persons of high rank, and he, too, wriggled between them like an eel; but people like me, or even better dressed than me, he simply walked over; he made straight for them as though there was nothing but empty space before him, and never, under any circumstances, turned aside. I gloated over my resentment watching him and . . . always resentfully made way for him. It exasperated me that even in the street I could not be on an even footing with him.

"Why must you invariably be the first to move aside?" I kept asking myself in hysterical rage, waking up sometimes at three o'clock in the morning. "Why is it you and not he? There's no regulation about it; there's no written law. Let the making way be equal as it usually is when refined people meet: he moves half-way and you move half-way; you pass with mutual respect."

But that never happened, and I always moved aside, while he did not even notice my making way for him. And lo and behold a bright idea dawned upon me! "What," I thought, "if I meet him and don't move on one side? What if I don't move aside on purpose, even if I knock up against him? How would that be?" This audacious idea took such a hold on me that it gave me no peace. I was dreaming of it continually, horribly, and I purposely went more frequently to the Nevsky in order to picture more vividly how I should do it when I did do it. I was delighted. This intention seemed to me more and more practical and possible.

"Of course I shall not really push him," I thought, already more good-natured in my joy. "I will simply not turn aside, will run up against him, not very violently, but just shouldering each other—just as much as decency permits. I will push against him just as much as he pushes against me." At last I made up my mind completely. But my preparations took a great deal of time. To begin with, when I carried out my plan I should need to be looking rather more decent, and so I had to think of my get-up. "In case of emergency, if, for instance, there were any sort of public scandal (and the public there is of the most *recherché*: the Countess walks there; Prince D. walks there; all the literary world is there), I must be well dressed; that inspires respect and of itself puts us on an equal footing in the eyes of society."

With this object I asked for some of my salary in advance, and bought at Tchurkin's a pair of black gloves and a decent hat. Black gloves seemed to me both more dignified and *bon ton* than the lemon-coloured ones which I had contemplated at first. "The colour is too gaudy, it looks as though one were trying to be conspicuous," and I did not take the lemon-coloured ones. I had got ready long beforehand a good shirt, with white bone studs; my overcoat was the only thing that held me back. The coat in itself was a very good one, it kept me warm; but it was wadded and it had a raccoon collar which was the height of vulgarity. I had to change the collar at any sacrifice, and to have a beaver one like an officer's. For this purpose I began visiting the Gostiny Dvor and after several attempts I pitched upon a piece of cheap German beaver. Though these German beavers soon grow shabby and look wretched, yet at first they look exceedingly well, and I only needed it for one occasion. I asked the price; even so, it was too expensive. After thinking it over thoroughly I decided to sell my raccoon collar. The rest of the money—a considerable sum for me, I decided to borrow from Anton Antonitch Syetotchkin, my immediate superior, an unassuming person, though grave and judicious. He never lent money to any one, but I had, on entering the service, been specially recommended to him by an important personage who had got me my berth. I was horribly worried. To borrow from Anton Antonitch seemed to me monstrous and shameful. I did not sleep for two or three nights. Indeed, I did not sleep well at that time, I was in a fever; I had a vague sinking at my heart or else a sudden throbbing, throbbing, throbbing! Anton Antonitch was surprised at first, then he frowned, then he reflected, and did after all lend me the money,

receiving from me a written authorization to take from my salary a fortnight later the sum that he had lent me.

In this way everything was at last ready. The handsome beaver replaced the mean-looking raccoon, and I began by degrees to get to
work. It would never have done to act off-hand, at random; the plan had
to be carried out skilfully, by degrees. But I must confess that after
many efforts I began to despair: we simply could not run into each other.
I made every preparation, I was quite determined—it seemed as though
we should run into one another directly—and before I knew what I was
doing I had stepped aside for him again and he had passed without
noticing me. I even prayed as I approached him that God would grant
me determination. One time I had made up my mind thoroughly, but it
ended in my stumbling and falling at his feet because at the very last
instant when I was six inches from him my courage failed me. He very
calmly stepped over me, while I flew on one side like a ball. That night
I was ill again, feverish and delirious.

And suddenly it ended most happily. The night before I had made
up my mind not to carry out my fatal plan and to abandon it all, and with
that object I went to the Nevsky for the last time, just to see how I
would abandon it all. Suddenly, three paces from my enemy, I unexpectedly made up my mind—I closed my eyes, and we ran full tilt,
shoulder to shoulder, against one another! I did not budge an inch and
passed him on a perfectly equal footing! He did not even look round
and pretended not to notice it; but he was only pretending, I am convinced of that. I am convinced of that to this day! Of course, I got the
worst of it, he was stronger, but that was not the point. The point was
that I had attained my object, I had kept up my dignity, I had not yielded
a step, and had put myself publicly on an equal social footing with him. I
returned home feeling that I was fully avenged for everything. I was
delighted. I was triumphant and sang Italian arias. Of course, I will not
describe to you what happened to me three days later; if you have read
my first chapter you can guess that for yourself. The officer was afterwards transferred; I have not seen him now for fourteen years. What is
the dear fellow doing now? Whom is he walking over?

II

But the period of my dissipation would end and I always felt very sick
afterwards. It was followed by remorse—I tried to drive it away: I felt
too sick. By degrees, however, I grew used to that too. I grew used to
everything, or rather I voluntarily resigned myself to enduring it. But I
had a means of escape that reconciled everything—that was to find
refuge in "the good and the beautiful," in dreams, of course. I was a
terrible dreamer, I would dream for three months on end, tucked away
in my corner, and you may believe me that at those moments I had
no resemblance to the gentleman who, in the perturbation of his

chicken heart, put a collar of German beaver on his great coat. I suddenly became a hero. I would not have admitted my six-foot lieutenant
even if he had called on me. I could not even picture him before me
then. What my dreams were and how I could satisfy myself with them
—it is hard to say now, but at the time I was satisfied with them. Though,
indeed, even now, I am to some extent satisfied with them. Dreams
were particularly sweet and vivid after a spell of dissipation; they came
with remorse and with tears, with curses and transports. There were
moments of such positive intoxication, of such happiness, that there was
not the faintest trace of irony within me, on my honour. I had faith, hope,
love. I believed blindly at such times that by some miracle, by some
external circumstance, all this would suddenly open out, expand; that
suddenly a vista of suitable activity—beneficent, good, and, above all,
ready made (what sort of activity I had no idea, but the great thing was
that it should be all ready for me)—would rise up before me—and I
should come out into the light of day, almost riding a white horse and
crowned with laurel. Anything but the foremost place I could not conceive for myself, and for that very reason I quite contentedly occupied
the lowest in reality. Either to be a hero or to grovel in the mud—there
was nothing between. That was my ruin, for when I was in the mud I
comforted myself with the thought that at other times I was a hero, and
the hero was a cloak for the mud: for an ordinary man it was shameful
to defile himself, but a hero was too lofty to be utterly defiled, and so he
might defile himself. It is worth noting that these attacks of the "good
and the beautiful" visited me even during the period of dissipation and
just at the times when I was touching the bottom. They came in separate
spurts, as though reminding me of themselves, but did not banish the
dissipation by their appearance. On the contrary, they seemed to add
a zest to it by contrast, and were only sufficiently present to serve as an
appetizing sauce. That sauce was made up of contradictions and sufferings, of agonizing inward analysis, and all these pangs and pin-pricks
gave a certain piquancy, even a significance to my dissipation—in fact,
completely answered the purpose of an appetizing sauce. There was a
certain depth of meaning in it. And I could hardly have resigned myself
to the simple, vulgar, direct debauchery of a clerk and have endured all
the filthiness of it. What could have allured me about it then and have
drawn me at night into the street? No, I had a lofty way of getting out
of it all.

And what loving-kindness, oh Lord, what loving-kindness I felt at
times in those dreams of mine! in those "flights into the good and the
beautiful"; though it was fantastic love, though it was never applied to
anything human in reality, yet there was so much of this love that one
did not feel afterwards even the impulse to apply it in reality; that
would have been superfluous. Everything, however, passed satisfactorily
by a lazy and fascinating transition into the sphere of art, that is, into the

beautiful forms of life, lying ready, largely stolen from the poets and novelists and adapted to all sorts of needs and uses. I, for instance, was triumphant over every one; every one, of course, was in dust and ashes, and was forced spontaneously to recognize my superiority, and I forgave them all. I was a poet and a grand gentleman, I fell in love; I came in for countless millions and immediately devoted them to humanity, and at the same time I confessed before all the people my shameful deeds, which, of course, were not merely shameful, but had in them much that was "good and beautiful!" something in the Manfred style. Every one would kiss me and weep (what idiots they would be if they did not), while I should go barefoot and hungry preaching new ideas and fighting a victorious Austerlitz against the obscurantists. Then the band would play a march, an amnesty would be declared, the Pope would agree to retire from Rome to Brazil; then there would be a ball for the whole of Italy at the Villa Borghese on the shores of the Lake of Como, the Lake of Como being for that purpose transferred to the neighbourhood of Rome; then would come a scene in the bushes, and so on, and so on—as though you did not know all about it! You will say that it is vulgar and contemptible to drag all this into public after all the tears and transports which I have myself confessed. But why is it contemptible? Can you imagine that I am ashamed of it all, and that it was stupider than anything in your life, gentlemen? And I can assure you that some of these fancies were by no means badly composed. . . . It did not all happen on the shores of Lake Como. And yet you are right—it really is vulgar and contemptible. And most contemptible of all it is that now I am attempting to justify myself to you. And even more contemptible than that is my making this remark now. But that's enough, or there will be no end to it: each step will be more contemptible than the last. . . .

I could never stand more than three months of dreaming at a time without feeling an irresistible desire to plunge into society. To plunge into society meant to visit my superior at the office, Anton Antonitch Syetotchkin. He was the only permanent acquaintance I have had in my life, and wonder at the fact myself now. But I only went to see him when that phase came over me, and when my dreams had reached such a point of bliss that it became essential at once to embrace my fellows and all mankind; and for that purpose I needed, at least, one human being, actually existing. I had to call on Anton Antonitch, however, on Tuesday —his at-home day; so I had always to time my passionate desire to embrace humanity so that it might fall on a Tuesday.

This Anton Antonitch lived on the fourth storey in a house in Five Corners, in four low-pitched rooms, one smaller than the other, of a particularly frugal and sallow appearance. He had two daughters and their aunt, who used to pour out the tea. Of the daughters one was thirteen and another fourteen, they both had snub noses, and I was awfully

shy of them because they were always whispering and giggling together. The master of the house usually sat in his study on a leather
couch in front of the table with some grey-headed gentleman, usually a
colleague from our office or some other department. I never saw more
than two or three visitors there, always the same. They talked about the
excise duty, about business in the senate, about salaries, about promotions, about His Excellency, and the best means of pleasing him, and so
on. I had the patience to sit like a fool beside these people for four
hours at a stretch, listening to them without knowing what to say to them
or venturing to say a word. I became stupified, several times I felt myself perspiring, I was overcome by a sort of paralysis; but this was pleasant and good for me. On returning home I deferred for a time my desire to embrace all mankind.

I had, however, one other acquaintance of a sort, Simonov, who was an
old schoolfellow. I had a number of schoolfellows, indeed, in Petersburg, but I did not associate with them and had even given up nodding
to them in the street. I believe I had transferred into the department I
was in simply to avoid their company and to cut off all connection with
my hateful childhood. Curses on that school and all those terrible years
of penal servitude! In short, I parted from my schoolfellows as soon as
I got out into the world. There were two or three left to whom I
nodded in the street. One of them was Simonov, who had been in no
way distinguished at school, was of a quiet and equable disposition; but
I discovered in him a certain independence of character and even honesty.
I don't even suppose that he was particularly stupid. I had at one time
spent some rather soulful moments with him, but these had not lasted
long and had somehow been suddenly clouded over. He was evidently
uncomfortable at these reminiscences, and was, I fancy, always afraid
that I might take up the same tone again. I suspected that he had an
aversion for me, but still I went on going to see him, not being quite
certain of it.

And so on one occasion, unable to endure my solitude and knowing
that as it was Thursday Anton Antonitch's door would be closed, I
thought of Simonov. Climbing up to his fourth storey I was thinking that
the man disliked me and that it was a mistake to go and see him. But
as it always happened that such reflections impelled me, as though purposely, to put myself into a false position, I went in. It was almost a
year since I had last seen Simonov.

III

I found two of my old schoolfellows with him. They seemed to be
discussing an important matter. All of them took scarcely any notice
of my entrance, which was strange, for I had not met them for years.
Evidently they looked upon me as something on the level of a common
fly. I had not been treated like that even at school, though they all

hated me. I knew, of course, that they must despise me now for my lack of success in the service, and for my having let myself sink so low, going about badly dressed and so on—which seemed to them a sign of my incapacity and insignificance. But I had not expected such contempt. Simonov was positively surprised at my turning up. Even in the old days he had always seemed surprised at my coming. All this disconcerted me: I sat down, feeling rather miserable, and began listening to what they were saying.

They were engaged in warm and earnest conversation about a farewell dinner which they wanted to arrange for the next day to a comrade of theirs called Zverkov, an officer in the army, who was going away to a distant province. This Zverkov had been all the time at school with me too. I had begun to hate him particularly in the upper forms. In the lower forms he had simply been a pretty, playful boy whom everybody liked. I had hated him, however, even in the lower forms, just because he was a pretty and playful boy. He was always bad at his lessons and got worse and worse as he went on; however, he left with a good certificate, as he had powerful interest. During his last year at school he came in for an estate of two hundred serfs, and as almost all of us were poor he took up a swaggering tone among us. He was vulgar in the extreme, but at the same time he was a good-natured fellow, even in his swaggering. In spite of superficial, fantastic and sham notions of honour and dignity, all but very few of us positively grovelled before Zverkov, and the more so the more he swaggered. And it was not from any interested motive that they grovelled, but simply because he had been favoured by the gifts of nature. Moreover, it was, as it were, an accepted idea among us that Zverkov was a specialist in regard to tact and the social graces. This last fact particularly infuriated me. I hated the abrupt self-confident tone of his voice, his admiration of his own witticisms, which were often frightfully stupid, though he was bold in his language; I hated his handsome but stupid face (for which I would, however, have gladly exchanged my intelligent one), and the free-and-easy military manners in fashion in the "'forties." I hated the way in which he used to talk of his future conquests of women (he did not venture to begin his attack upon women until he had the epaulettes of an officer, and was looking forward to them with impatience), and boasted of the duels he would constantly be fighting. I remember how I, invariably so taciturn, suddenly fastened upon Zverkov, when one day talking at a leisure moment with his schoolfellows of his future relations with the fair sex, and growing as sportive as a puppy in the sun, he all at once declared that he would not leave a single village girl on his estate unnoticed, that that was his *droit de seigneur,* and that if the peasants dared to protest he would have them all flogged and double the tax on them, the bearded rascals. Our servile rabble applauded, but I attacked him, not from compassion for the girls and their fathers, but simply because they were applauding such an insect. I got the better of him on that occasion, but though Zverkov was stupid he was lively and impudent, and so laughed it off, and in such a way that my victory was not really complete: the laugh was on his side. He got the better of me on several occasions afterwards, but without malice, jestingly, casually. I remained angrily and contemptuously silent and would not answer him. When we left school he made advances to me; I did not rebuff them, for I was flattered, but we soon parted and quite naturally. Afterwards I heard of his barrack-room success as a lieutenant, and of the fast life he was leading. Then there came other rumours—of his successes in the service. By then he had taken to cutting me in the street, and I suspected that he was afraid of compromising himself by greeting a personage as insignificant as me. I saw him once in the theatre, in the third tier of boxes. By then he was wearing shoulder-straps. He was twisting and twirling about, ingratiating himself with the daughters of an ancient General. In three years he had gone off considerably, though he was still rather handsome and adroit. One could see that by the time he was thirty he would be corpulent. So it was to this Zverkov that my schoolfellows were going to give a dinner on his departure. They had kept up with him for those three years, though privately they did not consider themselves on an equal footing with him, I am convinced of that.

Of Simonov's two visitors, one was Ferfitchkin, a Russianized German—a little fellow with the face of a monkey, a blockhead who was always deriding every one, a very bitter enemy of mine from our days in the lower forms—a vulgar, impudent, swaggering fellow, who affected a most sensitive feeling of personal honour, though, of course, he was a wretched little coward at heart. He was one of those worshippers of Zverkov who made up to the latter from interested motives, and often borrowed money from him. Simonov's other visitor, Trudolyubov, was a person in no way remarkable—a tall young fellow, in the army, with a cold face, fairly honest, though he worshipped success of every sort, and was only capable of thinking of promotion. He was some sort of distant relation of Zverkov's, and this, foolish as it seems, gave him a certain importance among us. He always thought me of no consequence whatever; his behaviour to me, though not quite courteous, was tolerable.

"Well, with seven roubles each," said Trudolyubov, "twenty-one roubles between the three of us, we ought to be able to get a good dinner. Zverkov, of course, won't pay."

"Of course not, since we are inviting him," Simonov decided.

"Can you imagine," Ferfitchkin interrupted hotly and conceitedly, like some insolent flunkey boasting of his master the General's decorations, "can you imagine that Zverkov will let us pay alone? He will accept from delicacy, but he will order half a dozen bottles of champagne."

"Do we want half a dozen for the four of us?" observed Trudol-yubov, taking notice only to the half dozen.

"So the three of us, with Zverkov for the fourth, twenty-one rou-bles, at the Hôtel de Paris at five o'clock to-morrow," Simonov, who had been asked to make the arrangements, concluded finally.

"How twenty-one roubles?" I asked in some agitation, with a show of being offended; "if you count me it will not be twenty-one, but twenty-eight roubles."

It seemed to me that to invite myself so suddenly and unexpectedly would be positively graceful, and that they would all be conquered at once and would look at me with respect.

"Do you want to join, too?" Simonov observed, with no appearance of pleasure, seeming to avoid looking at me. He knew me through and through.

It infuriated me that he knew me so thoroughly.

"Why not? I am an old schoolfellow of his, too, I believe, and I must own I feel hurt that you have left me out," I said, boiling over again.

"And where were we to find you?" Ferfitchkin put in roughly.

"You never were on good terms with Zverkov," Trudolyubov added, frowning.

But I had already clutched at the idea and would not give it up.

"It seems to me that no one has a right to form an opinion upon that," I retorted in a shaking voice, as though something tremendous had hap-pened. "Perhaps that is just my reason for wishing it now, that I have not always been on good terms with him."

"Oh, there's no making you out . . . with these refinements," Trudol-yubov jeered.

"We'll put your name down," Simonov decided, addressing me. "To-morrow at five o'clock at the Hôtel de Paris."

"What about the money?" Ferfitchkin began in an undertone, indicat-ing me to Simonov, but he broke off, for even Simonov was embar-rassed.

"That will do," said Trudolyubov, getting up. "If he wants to come so much, let him."

"But it's a private thing, between us friends," Ferfitchkin said crossly, as he, too, picked up his hat. "It's not an official gathering."

"We do not want at all, perhaps . . ."

They went away. Fertfitchkin did not greet me in any way as he went out, Trudolyubov barely nodded. Simonov, with whom I was left *tête-à-tête,* was in a state of vexation and perplexity, and looked at me queerly. He did not sit down and did not ask me to.

"H'm . . . yes . . . to-morrow, then. Will you pay your subscription now? I just ask so as to know," he muttered in embarrassment.

I flushed crimson, and as I did so I remembered that I had owed

Simonov fifteen roubles for ages—which I had, indeed, never forgotten, though I had not paid it.

"You will understand, Simonov, that I could have no idea when I came here ... I am very much vexed that I have forgotten. ..."

"All right, all right, that doesn't matter. You can pay to-morrow after the dinner. I simply wanted to know. ... Please don't ..."

He broke off and began pacing the room still more vexed. As he walked he began to stamp with his heels.

"Am I keeping you?" I asked, after two minutes of silence.

"Oh!" he said, starting, "that is—to be truthful—yes. I have to go and see some one . . . not far from here," he added in an apologetic voice, somewhat abashed.

"My goodness, why didn't you say so?" I cried, seizing my cap, with an astonishingly free-and-easy air, which was the last thing I should have expected of myself.

"It's close by . . . not two paces away," Simonov repeated, accompanying me to the front door with a fussy air which did not suit him at all. "So five o'clock, punctually, to-morrow," he called down the stairs after me. He was very glad to get rid of me. I was in a fury.

"What possessed me, what possessed me to force myself upon them?" I wondered, grinding my teeth as I strode along the street, "for a scoundrel, a pig like that Zverkov! Of course, I had better not go; of course, I must just snap my fingers at them. I am not bound in any way. I'll send Simonov a note by to-morrow's post. ..."

But what made me furious was that I knew for certain that I should go, that I should make a point of going; and the more tactless, the more unseemly my going would be, the more certainly I would go.

And there was a positive obstacle to my going: I had no money. All I had was nine roubles, I had to give seven of that to my servant, Apollon, for his monthly wages. That was all I paid him—he had to keep himself.

Not to pay him was impossible, considering his character. But I will talk about that fellow, about that plague of mine, another time.

However, I knew I should go and should not pay him his wages.

That night I had the most hideous dreams. No wonder; all the evening I had been oppressed by memories of my miserable days at school, and I could not shake them off. I was sent to the school by distant relations, upon whom I was dependent and of whom I have heard nothing since—they sent me there a forlorn, silent boy, already crushed by their reproaches, already troubled by doubt, and looking with savage distrust at every one. My schoolfellows met me with spiteful and merciless jibes because I was not like any of them. But I could not endure their taunts; I could not give in to them with the ignoble readiness with which they gave in to one another. I hated them from the first, and shut myself away from every one in timid, wounded and disproportionate pride. Their coarseness revolted me. They laughed cynically at my face, at my clumsy figure; and yet what stupid faces they had themselves. In our school the boys' faces seemed in a special way to degenerate and grow stupider. How many fine-looking boys came to us! In a few years they became repulsive. Even at sixteen I wondered at them morosely; even then I was struck by the pettiness of their thoughts, the stupidity of their pursuits, their games, their conversations. They had no understanding of such essential things, they took no interest in such striking, impressive subjects, that I could not help considering them inferior to myself. It was not wounded vanity that drove me to it, and for God's sake do not thrust upon me your hackneyed remarks, repeated to nausea, that "I was only a dreamer," while they even then had an understanding of life. They understood nothing, they had no idea of real life, and I swear that that was what made me most indignant with them. On the contrary, the most obvious, striking reality they accepted with fantastic stupidity and even at that time were accustomed to respect success. Everything that was just, but oppressed and looked down upon, they laughed at heartlessly and shamefully. They took rank for intelligence; even at sixteen they were already talking about a snug berth. Of course, a great deal of it was due to their stupidity, to the bad examples with which they had always been surrounded in their childhood and boyhood. They were monstrously depraved. Of course a great deal of that, too, was superficial and an assumption of cynicism; of course there were glimpses of youth and freshness even in their depravity; but even that freshness was not attractive, and showed itself in a certain rakishness. I hated them horribly, though perhaps I was worse than any of them. They repaid me in the same way, and did not conceal their aversion for me. But by then I did not desire their affection: on the contrary I continually longed for their humiliation. To escape from their derision I purposely began to make all the progress I could with my studies and forced my way to the very top. This impressed them. Moreover, they all began by degrees to grasp that I had already read books none of them could read, and understood things (not forming part of our school curriculum) of which they had not even heard. They took a savage and sarcastic view of it, but were morally impressed, especially as the teachers began to notice me on those grounds. The mockery ceased, but the hostility remained, and cold and strained relations became permanent between us. In the end I could not put up with it: with years a craving for society, for friends, developed in me. I attempted to get on friendly terms with some of my schoolfellows; but somehow or other my intimacy with them was always strained and soon ended of itself. Once, indeed, I did have a friend. But I was already a tyrant at heart; I wanted to exercise unbounded sway over him; I tried to instil into him a contempt for his surroundings; I required of him a disdainful and complete break with those surroundings. I frightened him with my passionate affection; I reduced him to tears, to hysterics. He was a simple and devoted soul; but when he devoted himself to me entirely I began to hate him immediately and repulsed him—as though all I needed him for was to win a victory over him, to subjugate him and nothing else. But I could not subjugate all of them; my friend was not at all like them either, he was, in fact, a rare exception. The first thing I did on leaving school was to give up the special job for which I had been destined so as to break all ties, to curse my past and shake the dust from off my feet. . . . And goodness knows why, after all that, I should go trudging off to Simonov's!

Early next morning I roused myself and jumped out of bed with excitement, as though it were all about to happen at once. But I believed that some radical change in my life was coming, and would inevitably come that day. Owing to its rarity, perhaps, any external event, however trivial, always made me feel as though some radical change in my life were at hand. I went to the office, however, as usual, but sneaked away home two hours earlier to get ready. The great thing, I thought, is not to be the first to arrive, or they will think I am overjoyed at coming. But there were thousands of such great points to consider, and they all agitated and overwhelmed me. I polished my boots a second time with my own hands; nothing in the world would have induced Apollon to clean them twice a day, as he considered that it was more than his duties required of him. I stole the brushes to clean them from the passage, being careful he should not detect it, for fear of his contempt. Then I minutely examined my clothes and thought that everything looked old, worn and threadbare. I had let myself get too slovenly. My uniform, perhaps, was tidy, but I could not go out to dinner in my uniform. The worst of it was that on the knee of my trousers was a big yellow stain. I had a foreboding that that stain would deprive me of nine-tenths of my personal dignity. I knew, too, that it was very poor to think so. "But this is no time for thinking: now I am in for the real thing," I thought, and my heart sank. I knew, too, perfectly well even then, that I was monstrously exaggerating the facts. But how could I help it? I could not control myself and was already shaking with fever. With despair I pictured to myself how coldly and disdainfully that "scoundrel" Zverkov would meet me; with what dull-witted, invincible contempt the blockhead Trudolyubov would look at me; with what impudent rudeness the insect Ferfitchkin would snigger at me in order to curry favour with Zverkov; how completely Simonov would take it all in, and how he would despise me for the abjectness of my vanity and lack of spirit—and, worst of all, how paltry, *unliterary*, commonplace it would all be. Of course, the best thing would be not to go at all. But that was most impossible of all: if I feel impelled to do anything, I seem to be pitchforked into it. I should have jeered at myself ever afterwards: "So you funked it, you funked it, you funked the *real thing!*" On the contrary, I passionately longed to show all that "rabble" that I was by no means such a spiritless creature as I seemed to myself. What is more, even in the acutest paroxysm of this cowardly fever, I dreamed of getting the upper hand, of dominating them, carrying them away, making them like me—if only for my "elevation of thought and unmistakable wit." They would abandon Zverkov, he would sit on one side, silent and ashamed, while I should crush him. Then, perhaps, we would be reconciled and drink to our everlasting friendship; but what was most bitter and most humiliating for me was that I knew even then, knew fully and for certain, that I needed nothing of all this really, that I did not really want to crush, to subdue, to attract them, and that I did not care a straw really for the result, even if I did achieve it. Oh, how I prayed for the day to pass quickly! In unutterable anguish I went to the window, opened the movable pane and looked out into the troubled darkness of the thickly falling wet snow. At last my wretched little clock hissed out five. I seized my hat and, trying not to look at Apollon, who had been all day expecting his month's wages, but in his foolishness was unwilling to be the first to speak about it, I slipt between him and the door and jumping into a high-class sledge, on which I spent my last half rouble, I drove up in grand style to the Hôtel de Paris.

IV

I had been certain the day before that I should be the first to arrive. But it was not a question of being the first to arrive. Not only were they not there, but I had difficulty in finding our room. The table was not laid even. What did it mean? After a good many questions I elicited from the waiters that the dinner had been ordered not for five, but for six o'clock. This was confirmed at the buffet too. I felt really ashamed to go on questioning them. It was only twenty-five minutes past five. If they changed the dinner hour they ought at least to have let me know— that is what the post is for, and not to have put me in an absurd position in my own eyes and . . . and even before the waiters. I sat down; the servant began laying the table; I felt even more humiliated when he was present. Towards six o'clock they brought in candles, though there were lamps burning in the room. It had not occurred to the waiter, however, to bring them in at once when I arrived. In the next room two gloomy, angry-looking persons were eating their dinners in silence at two different tables. There was a great deal of noise, even shouting, in a room further away; one could hear the laughter of a crowd of people, and nasty little shrieks in French: there were ladies at the dinner. It was sickening, in fact. I rarely passed more unpleasant moments, so much so that when they did arrive all together punctually at six I was overjoyed to see them, as though they were my deliverers, and even forgot that it was incumbent upon me to show resentment.

Zverkov walked in at the head of them; evidently he was the leading spirit. He and all of them were laughing; but, seeing me, Zverkov drew himself up a little, walked up to me deliberately with a slight, rather jaunty bend from the waist. He shook hands with me in a friendly, but not over-friendly, fashion, with a sort of circumspect courtesy like that of a General, as though in giving me his hand he were warding off something. I had imagined, on the contrary, that on coming in he would at once break into his habitual thin, shrill laugh and fall to making his insipid jokes and witticisms. I had been preparing for them ever since the previous day, but I had not expected such condescension, such high-official courtesy. So, then, he felt himself ineffably superior to me in every respect! If he only meant to insult me by that high-official tone, it would not matter, I thought—I could pay him back for it one way or another. But what if, in reality, without the least desire to be offensive, that sheepshead had a notion in earnest that he was superior to me and could only look at me in a patronizing way? The very supposition made me gasp.

"I was surprised to hear of your desire to join us," he began, lisping and drawling, which was something new. "You and I seem to have seen nothing of one another. You fight shy of us. You shouldn't. We are not such terrible people as you think. Well, anyway, I am glad to renew our acquaintance."

And he turned carelessly to put down his hat on the window.

"Have you been waiting long?" Trudolyubov inquired.

"I arrived at five o'clock as you told me yesterday," I answered aloud, with an irritability that threatened an explosion.

"Didn't you let him know that we had changed the hour?" said Trudolyubov to Simonov.

"No, I didn't. I forgot," the latter replied, with no sign of regret, and without even apologizing to me he went off to order the *hors d'oeuvres*.

"So you've been here a whole hour? Oh, poor fellow!" Zverkov cried ironically, for to his notions this was bound to be extremely funny. That rascal Ferfitchkin followed with his nasty little snigger like a puppy yapping. My position struck him, too, as exquisitely ludicrous and embarrassing.

"It isn't funny at all!" I cried to Ferfitchkin, more and more irritated. "It wasn't my fault, but other people's. They neglected to let me know. It was . . . it was . . . it was simply absurd."

"It's not only absurd, but something else as well," muttered Trudolyubov, naïvely taking my part. "You are not hard enough upon it. It was simply rudeness—unintentional, of course. And how could Simonov . . . h'm!"

"If a trick like that had been played on me," observed Ferfitchkin, "I should . . ."

"But you should have ordered something for yourself," Zverkov interrupted, "or simply asked for dinner without waiting for us."

"You will allow that I might have done that without your permission," I rapped out. "If I waited, it was . . ."

"Let us sit down, gentlemen," cried Simonov, coming in. "Everything is ready; I can answer for the champagne; it is capitally frozen. . . . You see, I did not know your address, where was I to look for you?" He suddenly turned to me, but again he seemed to avoid looking at me. Evidently he had something against me. It must have been what happened yesterday.

All sat down; I did the same, It was a round table. Trudolyubov was on my left, Simonov on my right. Zverkov was sitting opposite, Ferfitchkin next to him, between him and Trudolyubov.

"Tell me, are you . . . in a government office?" Zverkov went on attending to me. Seeing that I was embarrassed he seriously thought that he ought to be friendly to me, and, so to speak, cheer me up.

"Does he want me to throw a bottle at his head?" I thought, in a fury. In my novel surroundings I was unnaturally ready to be irritated.

"In the N—— office," I answered jerkily, with my eyes on my plate.

"And ha-ave you a go-od berth? I say, what ma-a-de you leave your original job?"

"What ma-a-de me was that I wanted to leave my original job," I drawled more than he, hardly able to control myself. Ferfitchkin went off into a guffaw. Simonov looked at me ironically. Trudolyubov left off eating and began looking at me with curiosity.

Zverkov winced, but he tried not to notice it.

"And the remuneration?"

"What remuneration?"

"I mean, your sa-a-lary?"

"Why are you cross-examining me?" However, I told him at once what my salary was. I turned horribly red.

"It is not very handsome," Zverkov observed majestically.

"Yes, you can't afford to dine at cafés on that," Ferfitchkin added insolently.

"To my thinking it's very poor," Trudolyubov observed gravely.

"And how thin you have grown! How you have changed!" added Zverkov with a shade of venom in his voice, scanning me and my attire with a sort of insolent compassion.

"Oh, spare his blushes," cried Ferfitchkin, sniggering.

"My dear sir, allow me to tell you I am not blushing," I broke out at last; "do you hear? I am dining here, at this café, at my own expense, not at other people's—note that, Mr. Ferfitchkin."

"Wha-at? Isn't every one here dining at his own expense? You would seem to be . . ." Ferfitchkin flew out at me, turning as red as a lobster, and looking me in the face with fury.

"Tha-at," I answered, feeling I had gone too far, "and I imagine it would be better to talk of something more intelligent."

"You intend to show off your intelligence, I suppose?"

"Don't disturb yourself, that would be quite out of place here."

"Why are you clacking away like that, my good sir, eh? Have you gone out of your wits in your office?"

"Enough, gentlemen, enough!" Zverkov cried, authoritatively.

"How stupid it is!" muttered Simonov.

"It really is stupid. We have met here, a company of friends, for a farewell dinner to a comrade and you carry on an altercation," said Trudolyubov, rudely addressing himself to me alone. "You invited yourself to join us, so don't disturb the general harmony."

"Enough, enough!" cried Zverkov. "Give over, gentlemen, it's out of place. Better let me tell you how I nearly got married the day before yesterday. . . ."

And then followed a burlesque narrative of how this gentleman had almost been married two days before. There was not a word about the marriage, however, but the story was adorned with generals, colonels and kammer-junkers, while Zverkov almost took the lead among them. It was greeted with approving laughter; Ferfitchkin positively squealed.

No one paid any attention to me, and I sat crushed and humiliated.

"Good Heavens, these are not the people for me!" I thought. "And what a fool I have made of myself before them! I let Ferfitchkin go too far, though. The brutes imagine they are doing me an honour in letting me sit down with them. They don't understand that it's an honour to them and not to me! I've grown thinner! My clothes! Oh, damn my trousers! Zverkov noticed the yellow stain on the knee as soon as he came in. . . . But what's the use! I must get up at once, this very minute, take my hat and simply go without a word . . . with contempt! And to-morrow I can send a challenge. The scoundrels! As though I cared about the seven roubles. They may think . . . Damn it! I don't care about the seven roubles. I'll go this minute!"

Of course I remained. I drank sherry and Lafitte by the glassful in my discomfiture. Being unaccustomed to it, I was quickly affected. My annoyance increased as the wine went to my head. I longed all at once to insult them all in a most flagrant manner and then go away. To seize the moment and show what I could do, so that they would say, "He's clever, though he is absurd," and . . . and . . . in fact, damn them all!

I scanned them all insolently with my drowsy eyes. But they seemed to have forgotten me altogether. They were noisy, vociferous, cheerful. Zverkov was talking all the time. I began listening. Zverkov was talking of some exuberant lady whom he had at last led on to declaring her love (of course, he was lying like a horse), and how he had been helped in this affair by an intimate friend of his, a Prince Kolya, an officer in the hussars, who had three thousand serfs.

"And yet this Kolya, who has three thousand serfs, has not put in an appearance here to-night to see you off," I cut in suddenly.

For a minute every one was silent. "You are drunk already." Trudolyubov deigned to notice me at last, glancing contemptuously in my direction. Zverkov, without a word, examined me as though I were an insect. I dropped my eyes. Simonov made haste to fill up the glasses with champagne.

Trudolyubov raised his glass, as did every one else but me.

"Your health and good luck on the journey!" he cried to Zverkov. "To old times, to our future, hurrah!"

They all tossed off their glasses, and crowded round Zverkov to kiss him. I did not move; my full glass stood untouched before me.

"Why, aren't you going to drink it?" roared Trudolyubov, losing patience and turning menacingly to me.

"I want to make a speech separately, on my own account . . . and then I'll drink it, Mr. Trudolyubov."

"Spiteful brute!" muttered Simonov. I drew myself up in my chair and feverishly seized my glass, prepared for something extraordinary, though I did not know myself precisely what I was going to say.

"*Silence!*" cried Ferfitchkin. "Now for a display of wit!"

Zverkov waited very gravely, knowing what was coming.

"Mr. Lieutenant Zverkov," I began, "let me tell you that I hate phrases, phrasemongers and men in corsets . . . that's the first point, and there is a second one to follow it."

There was a general stir.

"The second point is: I hate ribaldry and ribald talkers. Especially ribald talkers! The third point: I love justice, truth and honesty." I went on almost mechanically, for I was beginning to shiver with horror myself and had no idea how I came to be talking like this. "I love thought, Monsieur Zverkov; I love true comradeship, on an equal footing and not . . . H'm . . . I love . . . But, however, why not? I will drink your health, too, Mr. Zverkov! Seduce the Circassian girls, shoot the enemies of the fatherland and . . . and . . . to your health, Monsieur Zverkov!"

Zverkov got up from his seat, bowed to me and said:

"I am very much obliged to you." He was frightfully offended and turned pale.

"Damn the fellow!" roared Trudolyubov, bringing his fist down on the table.

"Well, he wants a punch in the face for that," squealed Ferfitchkin.

"We ought to turn him out," muttered Simonov.

"Not a word, gentlemen, not a movement!" cried Zverkov solemnly, checking the general indignation. "I thank you all, but I can show him for myself how much value I attach to his words."

"Mr. Ferfitchkin, you will give me satisfaction to-morrow for your words just now!" I said aloud, turning with dignity to Ferfitchkin.

"A duel, you mean? Certainly," he answered. But probably I was so ridiculous as I challenged him and it was so out of keeping with my appearance that everyone, including Ferfitchkin, was prostrate with laughter.

"Yes, let him alone, of course! He is quite drunk," Trudolyubov said with disgust.

"I shall never forgive myself for letting him join us," Simonov muttered again.

"Now is the time to throw a bottle at their heads," I thought to myself. I picked up the bottle . . . and filled my glass. . . . "No, I'd better sit on to the end," I went on thinking; "you would be pleased, my friends, if I went away. Nothing will induce me to go. I'll go on sitting here and drinking to the end, on purpose, as a sign that I don't think you of the slightest consequence. I will go on sitting and drinking, because this is a public-house and I paid my entrance money. I'll sit here and drink, for I look upon you as so many pawns, as inanimate pawns. I'll sit here and drink . . . and sing if I want to, yes, sing, for I have the right to . . . to sing . . . h'm!"

But I did not sing. I simply tried not to look at any of them. I assumed most unconcerned attitudes and waited with impatience for them to speak *first*. But alas, they did not address me! And oh, how I wished, how I wished at that moment to be reconciled to them! It struck eight, at last nine. They moved from the table to the sofa. Zverkov stretched himself on a lounge and put one foot on a round table. Wine was brought there. He did, as a fact, order three bottles on his own account. I, of course, was not invited to join them. They all sat round him on the sofa. They listened to him, almost with reverence. It was evident that they were fond of him. "What for? What for?" I wondered. From time to time they were moved to drunken enthusiasm and kissed each other. They talked of the Caucasus, of the nature of true passion, of snug berths in the service, of the income of an hussar called Podharzhevsky, whom none of them knew personally, and rejoiced in the largeness of it, of the extraordinary grace and beauty of a Princess D., whom none of them had ever seen; then it came to Shakespeare's being immortal.

I smiled contemptuously and walked up and down the other side of the room, opposite the sofa, from the table to the stove and back again. I tried my very utmost to show them that I could do without them, and yet I purposely made a noise with my boots, thumping with my heels. But it was all in vain. They paid no attention. I had the patience to walk up and down in front of them from eight o'clock till eleven, in the same place, from the table to the stove and back again. "I walk up and down to please myself and no one can prevent me." The waiter who came into the room stopped, from time to time, to look at me. I was somewhat giddy from turning round so often; at moments it seemed to me that I was in delirium. During those three hours I was three times soaked with sweat and dry again. At times, with an intense, acute pang I was stabbed to the heart by the thought that ten years, twenty years, forty years would pass, and that even in forty years I would remember with loathing and humiliation those filthiest, most ludicrous, and most awful moments of my life. No one could have gone out of his way to degrade himself more shamelessly, and I fully realized it, fully, and yet I went on pacing up and down from the table to the stove. "Oh, if you only knew what thoughts and feelings I am capable of, how cultured I am!" I thought at moments, mentally addressing the sofa on which my enemies were sitting. But my enemies behaved as though I were not in the room. Once—only once—they turned towards me, just when Zverkov was talking about Shakespeare, and I suddenly gave a contemptuous laugh. I laughed in such an affected and disgusting way that they all at once broke off their conversation, and silently and gravely for two minutes watched me walking up and down from the table to the stove, *taking no notice of them.* But nothing came of it: they said nothing, and two minutes later they ceased to notice me again. It struck eleven.

"Friends," cried Zverkov getting up from the sofa, "let us all be off now, *there!*"

"Of course, of course," the others assented. I turned sharply to Zverkov. I was so harassed, so exhausted, that I would have cut my throat to put an end to it. I was in a fever; my hair, soaked with perspiration, stuck to my forehead and temples.

"Zverkov, I beg your pardon," I said abruptly and resolutely. "Ferfitchkin, yours too, and every one's, every one's: I have insulted you all!"

"Aha! A duel is not in your line, old man," Ferfitchkin hissed venomously.

It sent a sharp pang to my heart.

"No, it's not the duel I am afraid of, Ferfitchkin! I am ready to fight you to-morrow, after we are reconciled. I insist upon it, in fact, and you cannot refuse. I want to show you that I am not afraid of a duel. You shall fire first and I shall fire into the air."

"He is comforting himself," said Simonov.

"He's simply raving," said Trudolyubov.

"But let us pass. Why are you barring our way? What do you want?"

Zverkov answered disdainfully.

They were all flushed: their eyes were bright: they had been drinking heavily.

"I ask for your friendship, Zverkov; I insulted you, but . . ."

"Insulted? *You* insulted *me?* Understand, sir, that you never, under any circumstances, could possibly insult *me."*

"And that's enough for you. Out of the way!" concluded Trudolyubov.

"Olympia is mine, friends, that's agreed!" cried Zverkov.

"We won't dispute your right, we won't dispute your right," the others answered, laughing.

I stood as though spat upon. The party went noisily out of the room. Trudolyubov struck up some stupid song. Simonov remained behind for a moment to tip the waiters. I suddenly went up to him.

"Simonov! give me six roubles!" I said, with desperate resolution.

He looked at me in extreme amazement, with vacant eyes. He, too, was drunk.

"You don't mean you are coming with us?"

"Yes."

"I've no money," he snapped out, and with a scornful laugh he went out of the room.

I clutched at his overcoat. It was a nightmare.

"Simonov, I saw you had money. Why do you refuse me? Am I a scoundrel? Beware of refusing me: if you knew, if you knew why I am asking! My whole future, my whole plans depend upon it!"

Simonov pulled out the money and almost flung it at me.

"Take it, if you have no sense of shame!" he pronounced pitilessly, and ran to overtake them.

I was left for a moment alone. Disorder, the remains of dinner, a broken wine-glass on the floor, spilt wine, cigarette ends, fumes of drink and delirium in my brain, an agonizing misery in my heart and finally the waiter, who had seen and heard all and was looking inquisitively into my face.

"I am going there!" I cried. "Either they shall all go down on their knees to beg for my friendship, or I will give Zverkov a slap in the face!"

V

"So this is it, this is it at last—contact with real life," I muttered as I ran headlong downstairs. "This is very different from the Pope's leaving Rome and going to Brazil, very different from the ball on Lake Como!"

"You are a scoundrel," a thought flashed through my mind, "if you laugh at this now."

"No matter!" I cried, answering myself. "Now everything is lost!"

There was no trace to be seen of them, but that made no difference
—I knew where they had gone.

At the steps was standing a solitary night sledge-driver in a rough
peasant coat, powdered over with the still falling, wet, and as it were
warm, snow. It was hot and steamy. The little shaggy piebald horse was
also covered with snow and coughing, I remember that very well. I made
a rush for the roughly made sledge; but as soon as I raised my foot to get
into it, the recollection of how Simonov had just given me six roubles
seemed to double me up and I tumbled into the sledge like a sack.

"No, I must do a great deal to make up for all that," I cried. "But I
will make up for it or perish on the spot this very night. Start!"

We set off. There was a perfect whirl in my head.

"They won't go down on their knees to beg for my friendship. That
is a mirage, cheap mirage, revolting, romantic and fantastical—that's
another ball on Lake Como. And so I am bound to slap Zverkov's face!
It is my duty to. And so it is settled; I am flying to give him a slap in
the face. Hurry up!"

The driver tugged at the reins.

"As soon as I go in I'll give it to him. Ought I before giving him
the slap to say a few words by way of preface? No. I'll simply go in and
give it to him. They will all be sitting in the drawing-room, and he with
Olympia on the sofa. That damned Olympia! She laughed at my looks
on one occasion and refused me. I'll pull Olympia's hair, pull Zverkov's
ears! No, better one ear, and pull him by it round the room. Maybe they
will all begin beating me and will kick me out. That's most likely,
indeed. No matter! Anyway, I shall first slap him; the initiative will
be mine; and by the laws of honour that is everything: he will be
branded and cannot wipe off the slap by any blows, by nothing but a
duel. He will be forced to fight. And let them beat me now. Let
them, the ungrateful wretches! Trudolyubov will beat me hardest, he
is so strong; Ferfitchkin will be sure to catch hold sideways and tug
at my hair. But no matter, no matter! That's what I am going for. The
blockheads will be forced at last to see the tragedy of it all! When they
drag me to the door I shall call out to them that in reality they are not
worth my little finger. Get on, driver, get on!" I cried to the driver.
He started and flicked his whip, I shouted so savagely.

"We shall fight at daybreak, that's a settled thing. I've done with the
office. Ferfitchkin made a joke about it just now. But where can I get
pistols? Nonsense! I'll get my salary in advance and buy them. And
powder, and bullets? That's the second's business. And how can it all
be done by daybreak? And where am I to get a second? I have no
friends. Nonsense!" I cried, lashing myself up more and more. "It's
of no consequence! the first person I meet in the street is bound to be
my second, just as he would be bound to pull a drowning man out of

water. The most eccentric things may happen. Even if I were to ask the director himself to be my second to-morrow, he would be bound to consent, if only from a feeling of chivalry, and to keep the secret! Anton Antonitch. . . ."

The fact is, that at that very minute the disgusting absurdity of my plan and the other side of the question was clearer and more vivid to my imagination than it could be to any one on earth. But . . .

"Get on, driver, get on, you rascal, get on!"

"Ugh, sir!" said the son of toil.

Cold shivers suddenly ran down me. Wouldn't it be better . . . to go straight home? My God, my God! Why did I invite myself to this dinner yesterday? But no, it's impossible. And my walking up and down for three hours from the table to the stove? No, they, they and no one else must pay for my walking up and down! They must wipe out this dishonour! Drive on!

And what if they give me into custody? They won't dare! They'll be afraid of the scandal. And what if Zverkov is so contemptuous that he refuses to fight a duel! He is sure to; but in that case I'll show them . . . I will turn up at the posting station when he is setting off to-morrow, I'll catch him by the leg, I'll pull off his coat when he gets into the carriage. I'll get my teeth into his hand, I'll bite him. "See what lengths you can drive a desperate man to!" He may hit me on the head and they may belabour me from behind. I will shout to the assembled multitude: "Look at this young puppy who is driving off to captivate the Circassian girls after letting me spit in his face!"

Of course, after that everything will be over! The office will have vanished off the face of the earth. I shall be arrested, I shall be tried, I shall be dismissed from the service, thrown in prison, sent to Siberia. Never mind! In fifteen years when they let me out of prison I will trudge off to him, a beggar, in rags. I shall find him in some provincial town. He will be married and happy. He will have a grown-up daughter. . . . I shall say to him: "Look, monster, at my hollow cheeks and my rags! I've lost everything—my career, my happiness, art, science, *the woman I loved,* and all through you. Here are pistols. I have come to discharge my pistol and . . . and I . . . forgive you. Then I shall fire into the air and he will hear nothing more of me. . . ."

I was actually on the point of tears, though I knew perfectly well at that moment that all this was out of Pushkin's *Silvio* and Lermontov's *Masquerade.* And all at once I felt horribly ashamed, so ashamed that I stopped the horse, got out of the sledge, and stood still in the snow in the middle of the street. The driver gazed at me, sighing and astonished.

What was I to do? I could not go on there—it was evidently stupid, and I could not leave things as they were, because that would seem as though . . . Heavens, how could I leave things! And after such insults! "No!" I cried, throwing myself into the sledge again. "It is ordained! It is fate! Drive on, drive on!"

And in my impatience I punched the sledge-driver on the back of the neck.

"What are you up to? What are you hitting me for?" the peasant shouted, but he whipped up his nag so that it began kicking.

The wet snow was falling in big flakes; I unbuttoned myself, regardless of it. I forgot everything else, for I had finally decided on the slap, and felt with horror that it was going to happen *now, at once,* and that *no force could stop it.* The deserted street lamps gleamed sullenly in the snowy darkness like torches at a funeral. The snow drifted under my great-coat, under my coat, under my cravat, and melted there. I did not wrap myself up—all was lost, anyway.

At last we arrived. I jumped out, almost unconscious, ran up the steps and began knocking and kicking at the door. I felt fearfully weak, particularly in my legs and my knees. The door was opened quickly as though they knew I was coming. As a fact, Simonov had warned them that perhaps another gentleman would arrive, and this was a place in which one had to give notice and to observe certain precautions. It was one of those "millinery establishments" which were abolished by the police a good time ago. By day it really was a shop; but at night, if one had an introduction, one might visit it for other purposes.

I walked rapidly through the dark shop into the familiar drawing-room, where there was only one candle burning, and stood still in amazement: there was no one there. "Where are they?" I asked somebody. But by now, of course, they had separated. Before me was standing a person with a stupid smile, the "madam" herself, who had seen me before. A minute later a door opened and another person came in.

Taking no notice of anything I strode about the room, and, I believe, I talked to myself. I felt as though I had been saved from death and was conscious of this, joyfully, all over: I should have given that slap, I should certainly, certainly have given it! But now they were not here and . . . everything had vanished and changed! I looked round. I could not realize my condition yet. I looked mechanically at the girl who had come in: and had a glimpse of a fresh, young, rather pale face, with straight, dark eyebrows, and with grave, as it were wondering, eyes that attracted me at once; I should have hated her if she had been smiling. I began looking at her more intently and, as it were, with effort. I had not fully collected my thoughts. There was something simple and good-natured in her face, but something strangely grave. I am sure that this stood in her way here, and no one of those fools had noticed her. She could not, however, have been called a beauty, though she was tall, strong-looking, and well built. She was very simply dressed. Something loathsome stirred within me. I went straight up to her.

I chanced to look into the glass. My harassed face struck me as revolting in the extreme, pale, angry, abject, with dishevelled hair. "No matter, I am glad of it," I thought; "I am glad that I shall seem repulsive to her; I like that."

VI

. . . Somewhere behind a screen a clock began wheezing, as though oppressed by something, as though some one were strangling it. After an unnaturally prolonged wheezing there followed a shrill, nasty, and as it were unexpectedly rapid, chime—as though some one were suddenly jumping forward. It struck two. I woke up, though I had indeed not been asleep but lying half conscious.

It was almost completely dark in the narrow, cramped, low-pitched room, cumbered up with an enormous wardrobe and piles of cardboard boxes and all sorts of frippery and litter. The candle end that had been burning on the table was going out and gave a faint flicker from time to time. In a few minutes there would be complete darkness.

I was not long in coming to myself; everything came back to my mind at once, without an effort, as though it had been in ambush to pounce upon me again. And, indeed, even while I was unconscious a point seemed continually to remain in my memory unforgotten, and round it my dreams moved drearily. But strange to say, everything that had happened to me in that day seemed to me now, on waking, to be in the far, far away past, as though I had long, long ago lived all that down.

My head was full of fumes. Something seemed to be hovering over me, rousing me, exciting me, and making me restless. Misery and spite seemed surging up in me again and seeking an outlet. Suddenly I saw beside me two wide open eyes scrutinizing me curiously and persistently. The look in those eyes were coldly detached, sullen, as it were utterly remote; it weighed upon me.

A grim idea came into my brain and passed all over my body, as a horrible sensation, such as one feels when one goes into a damp and mouldy cellar. There was something unnatural in those two eyes, beginning to look at me only now. I recalled, too, that during those two hours I had not said a single word to this creature, and had, in fact, considered it utterly superfluous; in fact, the silence had for some reason gratified me. Now I suddenly realized vividly the hideous idea —revolting as a spider—of vice, which, without love, grossly and shamelessly begins with that in which true love finds its consummation. For a long time we gazed at each other like that, but she did not drop her eyes before mine and her expression did not change, so that at last I felt uncomfortable.

"What is your name?" I asked abruptly, to put an end to it.

"Liza," she answered almost in a whisper, but somehow far from graciously, and she turned her eyes away.

I was silent.

"What weather! The snow . . . it's disgusting!" I said, almost to myself, putting my arm under my head despondently, and gazing at the ceiling.

She made no answer. This was horrible.

"Have you always lived in Petersburg?" I asked a minute later, almost angrily, turning my head slightly towards her.

"No."

"Where do you come from?"

"From Riga," she answered reluctantly.

"Are you a German?"

"No, Russian."

"Have you been here long?"

"Where?"

"In this house?"

"A fortnight."

She spoke more and more jerkily. The candle went out; I could no longer distinguish her face.

"Have you a father and mother?"

"Yes . . . no . . . I have."

"Where are they?"

"There . . . in Riga."

"What are they?"

"Oh, nothing."

"Nothing? Why, what class are they?"

"Tradespeople."

"Have you always lived with them?"

"Yes."

"How old are you?"

"Twenty."

"Why did you leave them?"

"Oh, for no reason."

That answer meant "Let me alone; I feel sick, sad."

We were silent.

God knows why I did not go away. I felt myself more and more sick and dreary. The images of the previous day began of themselves, apart from my will, flitting through my memory in confusion. I suddenly recalled something I had seen that morning when, full of anxious thoughts, I was hurrying to the office.

"I saw them carrying a coffin out yesterday and they nearly dropped it," I suddenly said aloud, not that I desired to open the conversation, but as it were by accident.

"A coffin?"

"Yes, in the Haymarket; they were bringing it up out of a cellar."

"From a cellar?"

"Not from a cellar, but from a basement. Oh, you know . . . down below . . . from a house of ill-fame. It was filthy all round . . . Egg-shells, litter . . . a stench. It was loathsome."

Silence.

"A nasty day to be buried," I began, simply to avoid being silent.

"Nasty, in what way?"

"The snow, the wet." (I yawned.)

"It makes no difference," she said suddenly, after a brief silence.

"No, it's horrid." (I yawned again.) "The gravediggers must have sworn at getting drenched by the snow. And there must have been water in the grave."

"Why water in the grave?" she asked, with a sort of curiosity, but speaking even more harshly and abruptly than before.

I suddenly began to feel provoked.

"Why, there must have been water at the bottom a foot deep. You can't dig a dry grave in Volkovo Cemetery."

"Why?"

"Why? Why, the place is waterlogged. It's a regular marsh. So they bury them in water. I've seen it myself . . . many times."

(I had never seen it once, indeed, I had never been in Volkovo, and had only heard stories of it.)

"Do you mean to say, you don't mind how you die?"

"But why should I die?" she answered, as though defending herself.

"Why, some day you will die, and you will die just the same as that dead woman. She was . . . a girl like you. She died of consumption."

"A wench would have died in hospital. . . ." (She knows all about it already: she said "wench," not "girl.")

"She was in debt to her madam," I retorted, more and more provoked by the discussion; "and went on earning money for her up to the end, though she was in consumption. Some sledge-drivers standing by were talking about her to some soldiers and telling them so. No doubt they knew her. They were laughing. They were going to meet in a pot-house to drink to her memory."

A great deal of this was my invention. Silence followed, profound silence. She did not stir.

"And is it better to die in a hospital?"

"Isn't it just the same? Besides, why should I die?" she added irritably.

"If not now, a little later."

"Why a little later?"

"Why, indeed? Now you are young, pretty, fresh, you fetch a high price. But after another year of this life you will be very different—you will go off."

"In a year?"

"Anyway, in a year you will be worth less," I continued malignantly. "You will go from here to something lower, another house; a year later—to a third, lower and lower, and in seven years you will come to a basement in the Haymarket. That will be if you were lucky. But it would be much worse if you got some disease, consumption, say . . . and caught a chill, or something or other. It's not easy to get over an illness in your way of life. If you catch anything you may not get rid of it. And so you would die."

"Oh, well, then I shall die," she answered, quite vindictively, and she made a quick movement.

"But one is sorry."

"Sorry for whom?"

"Sorry for life."

Silence.

"Have you been engaged to be married? Eh?"

"What's that to you?"

"Oh, I am not cross-examining you. It's nothing to me. Why are you so cross? Of course you may have had your own troubles. What is it to me? It's simply that I felt sorry."

"Sorry for whom?"

"Sorry for you."

"No need," she whispered hardly audibly, and again made a faint movement.

That incensed me at once. What! I was so gentle with her, and she . . .

"Why, do you think that you are on the right path?"

"I don't think anything."

"That's what's wrong, that you don't think. Realize it while there is still time. There still is time. You are still young, good-looking; you might love, be married, be happy. . . ."

"Not all married women are happy," she snapped out in the rude abrupt tone she had used at first.

"Not all, of course, but anyway it is much better than the life here. Infinitely better. Besides, with love one can live even without happiness. Even in sorrow life is sweet; life is sweet, however one lives. But here what is there but . . . foulness? Phew!"

I turned away with disgust; I was no longer reasoning coldly. I began to feel myself what I was saying and warmed to the subject. I was already longing to expound the cherished ideas I had brooded over in my corner. Something suddenly flared up in me. An object had appeared before me.

"Never mind my being here, I am not an example for you. I am, perhaps, worse than you are. I was drunk when I came here, though," I hastened, however, to say in self-defence. "Besides, a man is no example for a woman. It's a different thing. I may degrade and defile myself, but I am not any one's slave. I come and go, and that's an end of it. I shake it off, and I am a different man. But you are a slave from the start. Yes, a slave! You give up everything, your whole freedom. If you want to break your chains afterwards, you won't be able to: you will be more and more fast in the snares. It is an accursed bondage. I know it. I won't speak of anything else, maybe you won't understand, but tell me: no doubt you are in debt to your madam? There, you see," I added, though she made no answer, but only listened in silence, entirely absorbed, "that's a bondage for you! You will never buy your freedom. They will see to that. It's like selling your soul to the devil. . . . And besides . . . perhaps I, too, am just as unlucky—how do you know—and wallow in the mud on purpose, out of misery? You know, men take to drink from grief; well, maybe I am here from grief. Come, tell me, what is there good here? Here you and I . . . came together . . . just now and did not say one word to one another all the time, and it was only afterwards you began staring at me like a wild creature, and I at you. Is that loving? Is that how one human being should meet another? It's hideous, that's what it is!"

"Yes!" she assented sharply and hurriedly.

I was positively astounded by the promptitude of this "Yes." So the same thought may have been straying through her mind when she was staring at me just before. So she, too, was capable of certain thoughts? "Damn it all, this was interesting, this was a point of likeness!" I thought, almost rubbing my hands. And indeed it's easy to turn a young soul like that!

It was the exercise of my power that attracted me most.

She turned her head nearer to me, and it seemed to me in the darkness that she propped herself on her arm. Perhaps she was scrutinizing me. How I regretted that I could not see her eyes. I heard her deep breathing.

"Why have you come here?" I asked her, with a note of authority already in my voice.

"Oh, I don't know."

"But how nice it would be to be living in your father's house! It's warm and free; you have a home of your own."

"But what if it's worse than this?"

"I must take the right tone," flashed through my mind. "I may not get far with sentimentality." But it was only a momentary thought. I swear she really did interest me. Besides, I was exhausted and moody. And cunning so easily goes hand-in-hand with feeling.

"Who denies it!" I hastened to answer. "Anything may happen. I am convinced that some one has wronged you, and that you are more sinned against than sinning. Of course, I know nothing of your story, but it's not likely a girl like you has come here of her own inclination. . . ."

"A girl like me?" she whispered, hardly audibly; but I heard it.

Damn it all, I was flattering her. That was horrid. But perhaps it was a good thing. . . . She was silent.

"See, Liza, I will tell you about myself. If I had had a home from childhood, I shouldn't be what I am now. I often think that. However bad it may be at home, anyway they are your father and mother, and not enemies, strangers. Once a year at least they'll show their love of you. Anyway, you know you are at home. I grew up without a home; and perhaps that's why I've turned so . . . unfeeling."

I waited again. "Perhaps she doesn't understand," I thought, "and, indeed, it is absurd—it's moralizing."

"If I were a father and had a daughter, I believe I should love my daughter more than my sons, really," I began indirectly, as though talking of something else, to distract her attention. I must confess I blushed.

"Why so?" she asked.

Ah! so she was listening!

"I don't know, Liza. I knew a father who was a stern, austere man, but used to go down on his knees to his daughter, used to kiss her hands, her feet, he couldn't make enough of her, really. When she danced at parties he used to stand for five hours at a stretch, gazing at her. He was mad over her: I understand that! She would fall asleep tired at night, and he would wake to kiss her in her sleep and make the sign of the cross over her. He would go about in a dirty old coat, he was stingy to every one else, but would spend his last penny for her, giving her expensive presents, and it was his greatest delight when she was pleased with what he gave her. Fathers always love their daughters more than the mothers do. Some girls live happily at home! And I believe I should never let my daughters marry."

"What next?" she said, with a faint smile.

"I should be jealous, I really should. To think that she should kiss any one else! That she should love a stranger more than her father! It's painful to imagine it. Of course, that's all nonsense, of course every father would be reasonable at last. But I believe before I should let her marry, I should worry myself to death; I should find fault with her suitors. But I should end by letting her marry whom she herself loved. The one whom the daughter loves always seems the worst to the father, you know. That is always so. So many family troubles come from that."

"Some are glad to sell their daughters, rather than marrying them honourably."

Ah, so that was it!

"Such a thing, Liza, happens in those accursed families in which there is neither love nor God," I retorted warmly, "and where there is no love, there is no sense either. There are such families, it's true, but I am not speaking of them. You must have seen wickedness in your own family, if you talk like that. Truly, you must have been unlucky. H'm! . . . that sort of thing mostly comes about through poverty."

"And is it any better with the gentry? Even among the poor, honest people live happily."

"H'm . . . yes. Perhaps. Another thing, Liza, man is fond of reckoning up his troubles, but does not count his joys. If he counted them up as he ought, he would see that every lot has enough happiness provided for it. And what if all goes well with the family, if the blessing of God is upon it, if the husband is a good one, loves you, cherishes you, never leaves you! There is happiness in such a family! Even sometimes there is happiness in the midst of sorrow; and indeed sorrow is everywhere. If you marry *you will find out for yourself*. But think of the first years of married life with one you love: what happiness, what happiness there sometimes is in it! And indeed it's the ordinary thing. In those early days even quarrels with one's husband end happily. Some women get up quarrels with their husbands just because they love them. Indeed, I knew a woman like that: she seemed to say that because she loved him, she would torment him and make him feel it. You know that you may torment a man on purpose through love. Women are particularly given to that, thinking to themselves 'I will love him so, I will make so much of him afterwards, that it's no sin to torment him a little now.' And all in the house rejoice in the sight of you, and you are happy and gay and peaceful and honourable. . . . Then there are some women who are jealous. If he went off anywhere—I knew one such a woman, she couldn't restrain herself, but would jump up at night and run off on the sly to find out where he was, whether he was with some other woman. That's a pity. And the woman knows herself it's wrong, and her heart fails her and she suffers, but she loves— it's all through love. And how sweet it is to make it up after quarrels, to own herself in the wrong or to forgive him! And they are both so happy all at once—as though they had met anew, been married over again; as though their love had begun afresh. And no one, no one should know what passes between husband and wife if they love one another. And whatever quarrels there may be between them they ought not to call in their own mother to judge between them and tell tales of one another. They are their own judges. Love is a holy mystery and ought to be hidden from all other eyes, whatever happens. That makes it holier and better. They respect one another more, amd much is built on respect. And if once there has been love, if they have been married for love, why should love pass away? Surely one can keep it! It is rare that one cannot keep it. And if the husband is kind and straightforward, why should not love last? The first phrase of married love will pass, it is true, but then there will come a love that is better still. Then there will be the union of souls they will have everything in common, there will be no secrets between them. And once they have children, the most difficult times will seem to them happy, so long as there is love and courage. Even toil will be a joy, you may deny yourself bread for your children and even that will be a joy. They will love you for it afterwards; so you are laying by for your future. As the children grow up you feel that you are an example, a support for them; that even after you die your children will always keep your thoughts and feelings, because they have received them from you, they will take on your semblance and likeness. So you see this is a great duty. How can it fail to draw the father and mother nearer? People say it's a trial to have children. Who says that? It is heavenly happiness! Are you fond of little children, Liza? I am awfully fond of them. You know—a little rosy baby boy at your bosom, and what husband's heart is not touched, seeing his wife nursing his child! A plump little rosy baby, sprawling and snuggling, chubby little hands and feet, clean tiny little nails, so tiny that it makes one laugh to look at them; eyes that look as if they understand everything. And while it sucks it clutches at your bosom with its little hand, plays. When its father comes up, the child tears itself away from the bosom, flings itself back, looks at its father, laughs, as though it were fearfully funny and falls to sucking again. Or it will bite its mother's breast when its little teeth are coming, while it looks sideways at her with its little eyes as though to say, 'Look, I am biting!' Is not all that happiness when they are the three together, husband, wife and child? One can forgive a great deal for the sake of such moments. Yes, Liza, one must first learn to live oneself before one blames others!"

"It's by pictures, pictures like that one must get at you," I thought to myself, though I did speak with real feeling, and all at once I flushed crimson. "What if she were suddenly to burst out laughing, what should I do then?" That idea drove me to fury. Towards the end of my speech I really was excited, and now my vanity was somehow wounded. The silence continued. I almost nudged her.

"Why are you—" she began and stopped. But I understood: there was a quiver of something different in her voice, not abrupt, harsh and unyielding as before, but something soft and shamefaced, so shamefaced that I suddenly felt ashamed and guilty.

"What?" I asked, with tender curiosity.

"Why, you . . ."

"What?"

"Why, you . . . speak somehow like a book," she said, and again there was a note of irony in her voice.

That remark sent a pang to my heart. It was not what I was expecting.

I did not understand that she was hiding her feelings under irony, that this is usually the last refuge of modest and chaste-souled people when the privacy of their soul is coarsely and intrusively invaded, and that their pride makes them refuse to surrender till the last moment and shrink from giving expression to their feelings before you. I ought to have guessed the truth from the timidity with which she had repeatedly approached her sarcasm, only bringing herself to utter it at last with an effort. But I did not guess, and an evil feeling took possession of me.

"Wait a bit!" I thought.

VII

"Oh, hush, Liza! How can you talk about being like a book, when it makes even me, an outsider, feel sick? Though I don't look at it as an outsider, for, indeed, it touches me to the heart. . . . Is it possible, is it possible that you do not feel sick at being here yourself? Evidently habit does wonders! God knows what habit can do with any one. Can you seriously think that you will never grow old, that you will always be good-looking, and that they will keep you here for ever and ever? I say nothing of the loathsomeness of the life here. . . . Though let me tell you this about it—about your present life, I mean; here though you are young now, attractive, nice, with soul and feeling, yet you know as soon as I came to myself just now I felt at once sick at being here with you! One can only come here when one is drunk. But if you were anywhere else, living as good people live, I should perhaps be more than attracted by you, should fall in love with you, should be glad of a look from you, let alone a word; I should hang about your door, should go down on my knees to you, should look upon you as my betrothed and think it an honour to be allowed to. I should not dare to have an impure thought about you. But here, you see, I know that I have only to whistle and you have to come with me whether you like it or not. I don't consult your wishes, but you mine. The lowest labourer hires himself as a workman, but he doesn't make a slave of himself altogether; besides, he knows that he will be free again presently. But when are you free? Only think what you are giving up here. What is it you are making a slave of? It is your soul, together with your body; you are selling your soul which you have no right to dispose of! You give your love to be outraged by every drunkard! Love! But that's everything, you know, it's a priceless diamond, it's a maiden's treasure, love—why, a man would be ready to give his soul, to face death to gain that love. But how much is your love worth now? You are sold, all of you, body and soul, and there is no need to strive for love when you can have everything without love. And you know there is no greater insult to a girl than that, do you understand? To be sure, I have heard that they comfort you, poor fools, they let you have lovers of your own here. But you know that's simply a farce, that's simply a sham, it's just laughing at you, and you are taken in by it! Why, do you suppose he really loves you, that lover of yours? I don't believe it. How can he love you when he knows you may be called away from him any minute? He would be a low fellow if he did! Will he have a grain of respect for you? What have you in common with him? He laughs at you and robs you—that is all his love amounts to! You are lucky if he does not beat you. Very likely he does beat you, too. Ask him, if you have got one, whether he will marry you. He will laugh in your face, if he doesn't spit in it or give you a blow—though maybe he is not worth a bad halfpenny himself. And for what have you ruined your life, if you come to think of it? For the coffee they give you to drink and the plentiful meals? But with what object are they feeding you up? An honest girl couldn't swallow the food, for she would know what she was being fed for. You are in debt here, and, of course, you will always be in debt, and you will go on in debt to the end, till the visitors here begin to scorn you. And that will soon happen, don't rely upon your youth—all that flies by express train here, you know. You will be kicked out. And not simply kicked out; long before that she'll begin nagging at you, scolding you, abusing you, as though you had not sacrificed your health for her, had not thrown away your youth and your soul for her benefit, but as though you had ruined her, beggared her, robbed her. And don't expect any one to take your part: the others, your companions, will attack you, too, to win her favour, for all are in slavery here, and have lost all conscience and pity here long ago. They have become utterly vile, and nothing on earth is viler, more loathsome, and more insulting than their abuse. And you are laying down everything here, unconditionally, youth and health and beauty and hope, and at twenty-two you will look like a woman of five-and-thirty, and you will be lucky if you are not diseased, pray to God for that! No doubt you are thinking now that you have a gay time and no work to do! Yet there is no work harder or more dreadful in the world or ever has been. One would think that the heart alone would be worn out with tears. And you won't dare to say a word, not half a word when they drive you away from here; you will go away as though you were to blame. You will change to another house, then to a third, then somewhere else, till you come down at last to the Haymarket. There you will be beaten at every turn; that is good manners there, the visitors don't know how to be friendly without beating you. You don't believe that it is so hateful there? Go and look for yourself some time, you can see with your own eyes. Once, one New Year's Day, I saw a woman at a door. They had turned her out as a joke, to give her a taste of the frost because she had been crying so much, and they shut the door behind her. At nine o'clock in the morning she was already quite drunk, dishevelled, half-naked, covered with bruises, her face was powdered, but she had a black eye, blood was trickling from her nose and her teeth; some cabman had just given her a drubbing. She was sitting on the stone steps, a salt fish of some sort was in her hand; she was crying, wailing something about her luck and beating with the fish on the steps, and cabmen and drunken soldiers were crowding in the doorway taunting her. You don't believe that you will ever be like that? I should be sorry to believe it, too, but how do you know; maybe ten years, eight years ago that very woman with the salt fish came here fresh as a cherub, innocent, pure, knowing no evil, blushing at every word. Perhaps she was like you, proud, ready to take offence, not like the others; perhaps she looked like a queen, and knew what happiness was in store for the man who should love her and whom she should love. Do you see how it ended? And what if at that very minute when she was beating on the filthy steps with that fish, drunken and dishevelled—what if at that very minute she recalled the pure early days in her father's house, when she used to go to school and the neighbour's son watched for her on the way, declaring that he would love her as long as he lived, that he would devote his life to her, and when they vowed to love one another for ever and be married as soon as they were grown up! No, Liza, it would be happy for you if you were to die soon of consumption in some corner, in some cellar like that woman just now. In the hospital, do you say? You will be lucky if they take you, but what if you are still of use to the madam here? Consumption is a queer disease, it is not like fever. The patient goes on hoping till the last minute and says he is all right. He deludes himself. And that just suits your madam. Don't doubt it, that's how it is; you have sold your soul, and what is more you owe money, so you daren't say a word. But when you are dying, all will abandon you, all will turn away from you, for then there will be nothing to get from you. What's more, they will reproach you for cumbering the place, for being so long over dying. However you beg you won't get a drink of water without abuse: 'Whenever are you going off, you nasty hussy, you won't let us sleep with your moaning, you make the gentlemen sick.' That's true, I have heard such things said myself. They will thrust you dying into the filthiest corner in the cellar—in the damp and darkness; what will your thoughts be, lying there alone? When you die, strange hands will lay you out, with grumbling and impatience; no one will bless you, no one will sigh for you, they only want to get rid of you as soon as may be; they will buy a coffin, take you to the grave as they did that poor woman to-day and celebrate your memory at the tavern. In the grave sleet, filth, wet snow—no need to put themselves out for you—'Let her down, Vanuha; it's just like her luck —even here, she is head-foremost, the hussy. Shorten the cord, you rascal.' 'It's all right as it is.' 'All right, is it? Why, she's on her side! She was a fellow-creature, after all! But, never mind, throw the earth on her.' And they won't care to waste much time quarrelling over you.

They will scatter the wet blue clay as quick as they can and go off to the tavern . . . and there your memory on earth will end; other women have children to go to their graves, fathers, husbands. While for you neither tear, nor sigh, nor remembrance; no one in the whole world will ever come to you, your name will vanish from the face of the earth—as though you had never existed, never been born at all! Nothing but filth and mud, however you knock at your coffin lid at night, when the dead arise, however you cry: 'Let me out, kind people, to live in the light of day! My life was no life at all; my life has been thrown away like a dish-clout; it was drunk away in the tavern at the Haymarket; let me out, kind people, to live in the world again.' "

And I worked myself up to such a pitch that I began to have a lump in my throat myself, and . . . and all at once I stopped, sat up in dismay, and bending over apprehensively, began to listen with a beating heart. I had reason to be troubled.

I had felt for some time that I was turning her soul upside down and rending her heart, and—and the more I was convinced of it, the more eagerly I desired to gain my object as quickly and as effectually as possible. It was the exercise of my skill that carried me away; yet it was not merely sport. . . .

I knew I was speaking stiffly, artificially, even bookishly, in fact, I could not speak except "like a book." But that did not trouble me: I knew, I felt that I should be understood and that this very bookishness might be an assistance. But now, having attained my effect, I was suddenly panic-stricken. Never before had I witnessed such despair! She was lying on her face, thrusting her face into the pillow and clutching it in both hands. Her heart was being torn. Her youthful body was shuddering all over as though in convulsions. Suppressed sobs rent her bosom and suddenly burst out in weeping and wailing, then she pressed closer into the pillow: she did not want any one here, not a living soul, to know of her anguish and her tears. She bit the pillow, bit her hand till it bled (I saw that afterwards), or thrusting her fingers into her dishevelled hair, seemed rigid with the effort of restraint, holding her breath and clenching her teeth. I began saying something, begging her to calm herself, but felt that I did not dare; and all at once, in a sort of cold shiver, almost in terror, began fumbling in the dark, trying hurriedly to get dressed to go. It was dark: though I tried my best I could not finish dressing quickly. Suddenly I felt a box of matches and a candlestick with a whole candle in it. As soon as the room was lighted up, Liza sprang up, sat up in bed, and with a contorted face, with a half insane smile, looked at me almost senselessly. I sat down beside her and took her hands; she came to herself, made an impulsive movement towards me, would have caught hold of me, but did not dare, and slowly bowed her head before me.

"Liza, my dear, I was wrong . . . forgive me, my dear," I began, but she squeezed my hand in her fingers so tightly that I felt I was saying the wrong thing and stopped.

"This is my address, Liza, come to me."

"I will come," she answered resolutely, her head still bowed.

"But now I am going, good-bye . . . till we meet again."

I got up; she, too, stood up and suddenly flushed all over, gave a shudder, snatched up a shawl that was lying on a chair and muffled herself in it to her chin. As she did this she gave another sickly smile, blushed and looked at me strangely. I felt wretched; I was in haste to get away—to disappear.

"Wait a minute," she said suddenly, in the passage just at the doorway, stopping me with her hand on my overcoat. She put down the candle in hot haste and ran off; evidently she had thought of something or wanted to show me something. As she ran away she flushed, her eyes shone, and there was a smile on her lips—what was the meaning of it? Against my will I waited: she came back a minute later with an expression that seemed to ask forgiveness for something. In fact, it was not the same face, not the same look as the evening before: sullen, mistrustful and obstinate. Her eyes now were imploring, soft, and at the same time trustful, caressing, timid. The expression with which children look at people they are very fond of, of whom they are asking a favour. Her eyes were a light hazel, they were lovely eyes, full of life, and capable of expressing love as well as sullen hatred.

Making no explanation, as though I, as a sort of higher being, must understand everything without explanations, she held out a piece of paper to me. Her whole face was positively beaming at that instant with naïve, almost childish, triumph. I unfolded it. It was a letter to her from a medical student or some one of that sort—a very high-flown and flowery, but extremely respectful, love-letter. I don't recall the words now, but I remember well that through the high-flown phrases there was apparent a genuine feeling, which cannot be feigned. When I had finished reading it I met her glowing, questioning, and childishly impatient eyes fixed upon me. She fastened her eyes upon my face and waited impatiently for what I should say. In a few words, hurriedly, but with a sort of joy and pride, she explained to me that she had been to a dance somewhere in a private house, a family of "very nice people, *who knew nothing,* absolutely nothing, for she had only come here so lately and it had all happened . . . and she hadn't made up her mind to stay and was certainly going away as soon as she had paid her debt . . ." and at that party there had been the student who had danced with her all the evening. He had talked to her, and it turned out that he had known her in old days at Riga when he was a child, they had played together, but a very long time ago—and he knew her parents, but *about this* he knew nothing, nothing whatever and had no suspicion! And the day after the dance (three days ago) he had sent her that letter through the friend with whom she had gone to the party . . . and . . . well, that was all.

She dropped her shining eyes with a sort of bashfulness as she finished.

The poor girl was keeping that student's letter as a precious treasure, and had run to fetch it, her only treasure, because she did not want me to go away without knowing that she, too, was honestly and genuinely loved; that she, too, was addressed respectfully. No doubt that letter was destined to lie in her box and lead to nothing. But none the less, I am certain that she would keep it all her life as a precious treasure, as her pride and justification, and now at such a minute she had thought of that letter and brought it with naïve pride to raise herself in my eyes that I might see, that I, too, might think well of her. I said nothing, pressed her hand and went out. I so longed to get away. . . . I walked all the way home, in spite of the fact that the melting snow was still falling in heavy flakes. I was exhausted, shattered, in bewilderment. But behind the bewilderment the truth was already gleaming. The loathsome truth.

VIII

It was some time, however, before I consented to recognize that truth. Waking up in the morning after some hours of heavy, leaden sleep, and immediately realizing all that had happened on the previous day, I was positively amazed at my last night's *sentimentality* with Liza, at all those "outcries of horror and pity." "To think of having such an attack of womanish hysteria, pah!" I concluded. And what did I thrust my address upon her for? What if she comes? Let her come, though; it doesn't matter. . . . But *obviously,* that was not now the chief and the most important matter: I had to make haste and at all costs save my reputation in the eyes of Zverkov and Simonov as quickly as possible; that was the chief business. And I was so taken up that morning that I actually forgot all about Liza.

First of all I had at once to repay what I had borrowed the day before from Simonov. I resolved on a desperate measure: to borrow fifteen roubles straight off from Anton Antonitch. As luck would have it he was in the best of humours that morning, and gave it to me at once, on the first asking. I was so delighted at this that, as I signed the I O U with a swaggering air, I told him casually that the night before "I had been keeping it up with some friends at the Hôtel de Paris; we were giving a farewell party to a comrade, in fact, I might say a friend of my childhood, and you know—a desperate rake, fearfully spoilt—of course, he belongs to a good family, and has considerable means, a brilliant career; he is witty, charming, a regular Lovelace, you understand; we drank an extra 'half-dozen' and . . ."

And it went off all right; all this was uttered very easily, unconstrainedly and complacently.

On reaching home I promptly wrote to Simonov.

To this hour I am lost in admiration when I recall the truly gentle-manly, good-humoured, candid tone of my letter. With tact and good breeding, and, above all, entirely without superfluous words, I blamed myself for all that had happened. I defended myself, "if I really may be allowed to defend myself," by alleging that being utterly unaccustomed to wine, I had been intoxicated with the first glass, which I said I had drunk before they arrived, while I was waiting for them at the Hôtel de Paris between five and six o'clock. I begged Simonov's pardon espe-cially; I asked him to convey my explanations to all the others, especially to Zverkov, whom "I seemed to remember as though in a dream" I had insulted. I added that I would have called upon all of them myself, but my head ached, and besides I had not the face to. I was par-ticularly pleased with a certain lightness, almost carelessness (strictly within the bounds of politeness, however), which was apparent in my style, and better than any possible arguments, gave them at once to un-derstand that I took rather an independent view of "all that unpleasant-ness last night"; that I was by no means so utterly crushed as you, my friends, probably imagine; but on the contrary, looked upon it as a gen-tleman serenely respecting himself should look upon it. "On a young hero's past no censure is cast!"

"There is actually an aristocratic playfulness about it!" I thought ad-miringly, as I read over the letter. And it's all because I am an intellec-tual and cultivated man! Another man in my place would not have known how to extricate himself, but here I have got out of it and am as jolly as ever again, and all because I am "a cultivated and educated man of our day." And, indeed, perhaps, everything was due to the wine yes-terday. H'm! . . . no, it was not the wine. I did not drink anything at all between five and six when I was waiting for them. I had lied to Simonov; I had lied shamelessly; and indeed I wasn't ashamed now. . . . Hang it all though, the great thing was that I was rid of it.

I put six roubles in the letter, sealed it up, and asked Apollon to take it to Simonov. When he learned that there was money in the letter, Apollon became more respectful and agreed to take it. Towards eve-ning I went out for a walk. My head was still aching and giddy after yesterday. But as evening came on and the twilight grew denser, my impressions and, following them, my thoughts, grew more and more dif-ferent and confused. Something was not dead within me, in the depths of my heart and conscience it would not die, and it showed itself in acute de-pression. For the most part I jostled my way through the most crowded business streets, along Myeshtchansky Street, along Sadovy Street and in Yusupov Garden. I always liked particularly sauntering along these streets in the dusk, just when there were crowds of working people of all sorts going home from their daily work, with faces looking cross with anxiety. What I liked was just that cheap bustle, that bare prose. On this occasion the jostling of the streets irritated me more than ever. I could not make out what was wrong with me, I could not find the clue, something seemed rising up continually in my soul, painfully, and refusing to be appeased. I returned home completely upset, it was just as though some crime were lying on my conscience.

The thought that Liza was coming worried me continually. It seemed queer to me that of all my recollections of yesterday this tormented me, as it were, especially, as it were, quite separately. Everything else I had quite succeeded in forgetting by the evening; I dismissed it all and was still perfectly satisfied with my letter to Simonov. But on this point I was not satisfied at all. It was as though I were worried only by Liza. "What if she comes," I thought incessantly, "well, it doesn't matter, let her come! H'm! it's horrid that she should see, for instance, how I live. Yesterday I seemed such a hero to her, while now, h'm! It's horrid, though, that I have let myself go so, the room looks like a beggar's. And I brought myself to go out to dinner in such a suit! And my American leather sofa with the stuffing sticking out. And my dressing-gown, which will not cover me, such tatters, and she will see all this and she will see Apollon. That beast is certain to insult her. He will fasten upon her in order to be rude to me. And I, of course, shall be panic-stricken as usual, I shall begin bowing and scraping before her and pulling my dressing-gown round me, I shall begin smiling, telling lies. Oh, the beastliness! And it isn't the beastliness of it that matters most! There is something more important, more loathsome, viler! Yes, viler! And to put on that dishonest lying mask again!" . . .

When I reached that thought I fired up all at once.

"Why dishonest? How dishonest? I was speaking sincerely last night. I remember there was real feeling in me, too. What I wanted was to excite an honourable feeling in her. . . . Her crying was a good thing, it will have a good effect."

Yet I could not feel at ease. All that evening, even when I had come back home, even after nine o'clock, when I calculated that Liza could not possibly come, she still haunted me, and what was worse, she came back to my mind always in the same position. One moment out of all that had happened last night stood vividly before my imagination; the moment when I struck a match and saw her pale, distorted face, with its look of torture. And what a pitiful, what an unnatural, what a distorted smile she had at that moment! But I did not know then, that fifteen years later I should still in my imagination see Liza, always with the pitiful, distorted, inappropriate smile which was on her face at that minute.

Next day I was ready again to look upon it all as nonsense, due to overexcited nerves, and, above all, as *exaggerated*. I was always conscious of that weak point of mine, and sometimes very much afraid of it. "I exaggerate everything, that is where I go wrong," I repeated to myself every hour. But, however, "Liza will very likely come all the same," was the refrain with which all my reflections ended. I was so uneasy that I sometimes flew into a fury: "She'll come, she is certain to come!" I cried, running about the room, "if not to-day, she will come to-morrow; she'll find me out! The damnable romanticism of these pure hearts! Oh, the vileness—oh, the silliness—oh, the stupidity of these 'wretched sentimental souls!' Why, how fail to understand? How could one fail to understand? . . ."

But at this point I stopped short, and in great confusion, indeed.

And how few, how few words, I thought, in passing, were needed; how little of the idyllic (and affectedly, bookishly, artificially idyllic too) had sufficed to turn a whole human life at once according to my will. That's virginity, to be sure! Freshness of soil!

At times a thought occurred to me, to go to her, "to tell her all," and beg her not to come to me. But this thought stirred such wrath in me that I believed I should have crushed that "damned" Liza if she had chanced to be near me at the time. I should have insulted her, have spat at her, have turned her out, have struck her!

One day passed, however, another and another; she did not come and I began to grow calmer. I felt particularly bold and cheerful after nine o'clock, I even sometimes began dreaming, and rather sweetly: I, for instance, became the salvation of Liza, simply through her coming to me and my talking to her. . . . I develop her, educate her. Finally, I notice that she loves me, loves me passionately. I pretend not to understand (I don't know, however, why I pretend, just for effect, perhaps). At last all confusion, transfigured, trembling and sobbing, she flings herself at my feet and says that I am her saviour, and that she loves me better than anything in the world. I am amazed, but . . . "Liza," I say, "can you imagine that I have not noticed your love, I saw it all, I divined it, but I did not dare to approach you first, because I had an influence over you and was afraid that you would force yourself, from gratitude, to respond to my love, would try to rouse in your heart a feeling which was perhaps absent, and I did not wish that . . . because it would be tyranny . . . it would be indelicate (in short, I launch off at that point into European, inexplicably lofty subtleties à la George Sand), but now, now you are mine, you are my creation, you are pure, you are good, you are my noble wife.

> Into my house come bold and free,
> Its rightful mistress there to be."

Then we begin living together, go abroad and so on, and so on. In fact, in the end it seemed vulgar to me myself, and I began putting out my tongue at myself.

Besides, they won't let her out, "the hussy!" I thought. They don't let them go out very readily, especially in the evening (for some reason I fancied she would come in the evening, and at seven o'clock precisely). Though she did say she was not altogether a slave there yet, and had certain rights; so, h'm! Damn it all, she will come, she is sure to come!

It was a good thing, in fact, that Apollon distracted my attention at that time by his rudeness. He drove me beyond all patience! He was the bane of my life, the curse laid upon me by Providence. We had been squabbling continually for years, and I hated him. My God, how I hated him! I believe I had never hated any one in my life as I hated him, especially at some moments. He was an elderly, dignified man, who worked part of his time as a tailor. But for some unknown reason he despised me beyond all measure, and looked down upon me insufferably. Though, indeed, he looked down upon every one. Simply to glance at that flaxen, smoothly brushed head, at the tuft of hair he combed up on his forehead and oiled with sunflower oil, at that dignified mouth, compressed into the shape of the letter V, made one feel one was confronting a man who never doubted of himself. He was a pedant, to the most extreme point, the greatest pedant I had met on earth, and with that had a vanity only befitting Alexander of Macedon. He was in love with every button on his coat, every nail on his fingers—absolutely in love with them, and he looked it! In his behaviour to me he was a perfect tyrant, he spoke very little to me, and if he chanced to glance at me he gave me a firm, majestically self-confident and invariably ironical look that drove me sometimes to fury. He did his work with the air of doing me the greatest favour. Though he did scarcely anything for me, and did not, indeed, consider himself bound to do anything. There could be no doubt that he looked upon me as the greatest fool on earth, and that "he did not get rid of me" was simply that he could get wages from me every month. He consented to do nothing for me for seven roubles a month. Many sins should be forgiven me for what I suffered from him. My hatred reached such a point that sometimes his very step almost threw me into convulsions. What I loathed particularly was his lisp. His tongue must have been a little too long or something of that sort, for he continually lisped, and seemed to be very proud of it, imagining that it greatly added to his dignity. He spoke in a slow, measured tone, with his hands behind his back and his eyes fixed on the ground. He maddened me particularly when he read aloud the psalms to himself behind his partition. Many a battle I waged over that reading! But he was awfully fond of reading aloud in the evenings, in a slow, even sing-song voice, as though over the dead. It is interesting that that is how he has ended: he hires himself out to read the psalms over the dead, and at the same time he kills rats and makes blacking. But at that time I could not get rid of him, it was as though he were chemically combined with my existence. Besides, nothing would have induced him to consent to leave me. I could not live in furnished lodgings: my lodging was my private solitude, my shell, my cave, in which I concealed myself from all mankind, and Apollon seemed to me, for some reason, an integral part of that flat, and for seven years I could not turn him away.

To be two or three days behind with his wages, for instance, was impossible. He would have made such a fuss, I should not have known where to hide my head. But I was so exasperated with every one during those days, that I made up my mind for some reason and with some object to *punish* Apollon and not to pay him for a fortnight the wages that were owing him. I had for a long time—for the last two years—been intending to do this, simply in order to teach him not to give himself airs with me, and to show him that if I liked I could withhold his wages. I purposed to say nothing to him about it, and was purposely silent indeed, in order to score off his pride and force himself to be the first to speak of his wages. Then I would take the seven roubles out of a drawer, show him I have the money put aside on purpose, but that I won't, I won't, I simply won't pay him his wages, I won't just because that is "what I wish," because "I am master, and it is for me to decide," because he has been disrespectful, because he has been rude; but if he were to ask respectfully I might be softened and give it to him, otherwise he might wait another fortnight, another three weeks, a whole month.

But angry as I was, yet he got the better of me. I could not hold out for four days. He began as he always did begin in such cases, for there had been such cases already, there had been attempts (and it may be observed I knew all this beforehand, I knew his nasty tactics by heart). He would begin by fixing upon me an exceedingly severe stare, keeping it up for several minutes at a time, particularly on meeting me or seeing me out of the house. If I held out and pretended not to notice these stares, he would, still in silence, proceed to further tortures. All at once, *à propos* of nothing, he would walk softly and smoothly into my room, when I was pacing up and down or reading, stand at the door, one hand behind his back and one foot behind the other, and fix upon me a stare more than severe, utterly contemptuous. If I suddenly asked him what he wanted, he would make me no answer, but continue staring at me persistently for some seconds, then, with a peculiar compression of his lips and a most significant air, deliberately turn round and deliberately go back to his room. Two hours later he would come out again and again present himself before me in the same way. It had happened that in my fury I did not even ask him what he wanted, but simply raised my head sharply and imperiously and began staring back at him. So we stared at one another for two minutes; at last he turned with deliberation and dignity and went back again for two hours.

If I were still not brought to reason by all this, but persisted in my revolt, he would suddenly begin sighing while he looked at me, long, deep sighs as though measuring by them the depths of my moral degradation, and, of course, it ended at last by his triumphing completely: I raged and shouted, but still was forced to do what he wanted.

This time the usual staring manoeuvres had scarcely begun when I lost my temper and flew at him in a fury. I was irritated beyond endurance apart from him.

"Stay," I cried, in a frenzy, as he was slowly and silently turning, with one hand behind his back, to go to his room, "stay! Come back, come back, I tell you!" and I must have bawled so unnaturally, that he turned round and even looked at me with some wonder. However, he persisted in saying nothing, and that infuriated me.

"How dare you come and look at me like that without being sent for? Answer!"

After looking at me calmly for half a minute, he began turning round again.

"Stay!" I roared, running up to him, "don't stir! There. Answer, now: what did you come in to look at?"

"If you have any order to give me it's my duty to carry it out," he answered, after another silent pause, with a slow, measured lisp, raising his eyebrows and calmly twisting his head from one side to another, all this with exasperating composure.

"That's not what I am asking you about, you torturer!" I shouted, turning crimson with anger. "I'll tell you why you came here myself: you see, I don't give you your wages, you are so proud you don't want to bow down and ask for it, and so you come to punish me with your stupid stares, to worry me and you have no sus . . . pic . . . ion how stupid it is— stupid, stupid, stupid, stupid!" . . .

He would have turned round again without a word, but I seized him.

"Listen," I shouted to him. "Here's the money, do you see, here it is" (I took it out of the table drawer); "here's the seven roubles complete, but you are not going to have it, you . . . are . . . not . . . going . . . to . . . have it until you come respectfully with bowed head to beg my pardon. Do you hear?"

"That cannot be," he answered, with the most unnatural self-confidence.

"It shall be so," I said, "I give you my word of honour, it shall be!"

"And there's nothing for me to beg your pardon for," he went on, as though he had not noticed my exclamations at all. "Why, besides, you called me a 'torturer,' for which I can summon you at the police-station at any time for insulting behaviour."

"Go, summon me," I roared, "go at once, this very minute, this very second! You are a torturer all the same! a torturer!"

But he merely looked at me, then turned, and regardless of my loud calls to him, he walked to his room with an even step and without looking round.

"If it had not been for Liza nothing of this would have happened," I decided inwardly. Then, after waiting a minute, I went myself behind his screen with a dignified and solemn air, though my heart was beating slowly and violently.

"Apollon," I said quietly and emphatically, though I was breathless, "go at once without a minute's delay and fetch the police-officer."

He had meanwhile settled himself at his table, put on his spectacles and taken up some sewing. But, hearing my order, he burst into a guffaw.

"At once, go this minute! Go on, or else you can't imagine what will happen."

"You are certainly out of your mind," he observed, without even raising his head, lisping as deliberately as ever and threading his needle. "Whoever heard of a man sending for the police against himself? And as for being frightened—you are upsetting yourself about nothing, for nothing will come of it."

"Go!" I shrieked, clutching him by the shoulder. I felt I should strike him in a minute.

But I did not notice the door from the passage softly and slowly open at that instant and a figure come in, stop short, and begin staring at us in perplexity. I glanced, nearly swooned with shame, and rushed back to my room. There, clutching at my hair with both hands, I leaned my head against the wall and stood motionless in that position.

Two minutes later I heard Apollon's deliberate footsteps. "There is some woman asking for you," he said, looking at me with peculiar severity. Then he stood aside and let in Liza. He would not go away, but stared at us sarcastically.

"Go away, go away," I commanded in desperation. At that moment my clock began whirring and wheezing and struck seven.

IX

Into my house come bold and free,
Its rightful mistress there to be.

I stood before her crushed, crestfallen, revoltingly confused, and I believe I smiled as I did my utmost to wrap myself in the skirts of my ragged wadded dressing-gown—exactly as I had imagined the scene not long before in a fit of depression. After standing over us for a couple of minutes Apollon went away, but that did not make me more at ease. What made it worse was that she, too, was overwhelmed with confusion, more so, in fact, than I should have expected. At the sight of me, of course.

"Sit down," I said mechanically, moving a chair up to the table, and I sat down on the sofa. She obediently sat down at once and gazed at me open-eyed, evidently expecting something from me at once. This naïveté of expectation drove me to fury, but I restrained myself.

She ought to have tried not to notice, as though everything had been as usual, while instead of that, she . . . and I dimly felt that I should make her pay dearly for *all this*.

"You have found me in a strange position, Liza," I began, stammering and knowing that this was the wrong way to begin. "No, no, don't imagine anything," I cried, seeing that she had suddenly flushed. "I am not ashamed of my poverty. . . . On the contrary I look with pride on my poverty. I am poor but honourable. . . . One can be poor and honourable," I muttered. "However . . . would you like tea?" . . .

"No," she was beginning.

"Wait a minute."

I leapt up and ran to Apollon. I had to get out of the room somehow.

"Apollon," I whispered in feverish haste, flinging down before him the seven roubles which had remained all the time in my clenched fist, "here are your wages, you see I give them to you; but for that you must come to my rescue: bring me tea and a dozen rusks from the restaurant. If you won't go, you'll make me a miserable man! You don't know what this woman is. . . . This is—everything! You may be imagining something. . . . But you don't know what that woman is!" . . .

Apollon, who had already sat down to his work and put on his spectacles again, at first glanced askance at the money without speaking or putting down his needle; then, without paying the slightest attention to me or making any answer he went on busying himself with his needle, which he had not yet threaded. I waited before him for three minutes with my arms crossed *à la Napoléon.* My temples were moist with sweat. I was pale, I felt it. But, thank God, he must have been moved to pity, looking at me. Having threaded his needle he deliberately got up from his seat, deliberately moved back his chair, deliberately took off his spectacles, deliberately counted the money, and finally asking me over his shoulder: "Shall I get a whole portion?" deliberately walked out of the room. As I was going back to Liza, the thought occurred to me on the way: shouldn't I run away just as I was in my dressing-gown, no matter where, and then let happen what would?

I sat down again. She looked at me uneasily. For some minutes we were silent.

"I will kill him," I shouted suddenly, striking the table with my fist so that the ink spurted out of the inkstand.

"What are you saying!" she cried, starting.

"I will kill him! kill him!" I shrieked, suddenly striking the table in absolute frenzy, and at the same time fully understanding how stupid it was to be in such a frenzy. "You don't know, Liza, what that torturer is to me. He is my torturer. . . . He has gone now to fetch some rusks; he . . ."

And suddenly I burst into tears. It was an hysterical attack. How ashamed I felt in the midst of my sobs; but still I could not restrain them.

She was frightened.

"What is the matter? What is wrong?" she cried, fussing about me.

"Water, give me water, over there!" I muttered in a faint voice, though I was inwardly conscious that I could have got on very well without water and without muttering in a faint voice. But I was, what is called, *putting it on,* to save appearances, though the attack was a genuine one.

She gave me water, looking at me in bewilderment. At that moment Apollon brought in the tea. It suddenly seemed to me that this commonplace, prosaic tea was horribly undignified and paltry after all that had happened, and I blushed crimson. Liza looked at Apollon with positive alarm. He went out without a glance at either of us.

"Liza, do you despise me?" I asked, looking at her fixedly, trembling with impatience to know what she was thinking.

She was confused, and did not know what to answer.

"Drink your tea," I said to her angrily. I was angry with myself, but, of course, it was she who would have to pay for it. A horrible spite against her suddenly surged up in my heart; I believe I could have killed her. To revenge myself on her I swore inwardly not to say a word to her all the time. "She is the cause of it all," I thought.

Our silence lasted for five minutes. The tea stood on the table; we did not touch it. I had got to the point of purposely refraining from beginning in order to embarrass her further; it was awkward for her to begin alone. Several times she glanced at me with mournful perplexity. I was obstinately silent. I was, of course, myself the chief sufferer, because I was fully conscious of the disgusting meanness of my spiteful stupidity, and yet at the same time I could not restrain myself.

"I want to . . . get away . . . from there altogether," she began, to break the silence in some way, but, poor girl, that was just what she ought not to have spoken about at such a stupid moment to a man so stupid as I was. My heart positively ached with pity for her tactless and unnecessary straightforwardness. But something hideous at once stifled all compassion in me; it even provoked me to greater venom. I did not care what happened. Another five minutes passed.

"Perhaps I am in your way," she began timidly, hardly audibly, and was getting up.

But as soon as I saw this first impulse of wounded dignity I positively trembled with spite, and at once burst out.

"Why have you come to me, tell me that, please?" I began, gasping for breath and regardless of logical connection in my words. I longed to have it all out at once, at one burst; I did not even trouble how to begin. "Why have you come? Answer, answer," I cried, hardly knowing what I was doing. "I'll tell you, my good girl, why you have come. You've come because I talked sentimental stuff to you then. So now you are soft as butter and longing for fine sentiments again. So you may as well know that I was laughing at you then. And I am laughing at you now. Why are you shuddering? Yes, I was laughing at you! I had been insulted just before, at dinner, by the fellows who came that evening before me. I came to you, meaning to thrash one of them, an officer; but I didn't succeed, I didn't find him; I had to avenge the insult on some one to get back my own again; you turned up, I vented my spleen on

you and laughed at you. I had been humiliated, so I wanted to humili-
atc; I had been treated like a rag, so I wanted to show my power. . . .
That's what it was, and you imagined I had come there on purpose to
save you. Yes? You imagined that? You imagined that?"

I knew that she would perhaps be muddled and not take it all in
exactly, but I knew, too, that she would grasp the gist of it, very well indeed. And so, indeed, she did. She turned white as a handkerchief,
tried to say something, and her lips worked painfully; but she sank on a
chair as though she had been felled by an axe. And all the time afterwards she listened to me with her lips parted and her eyes wide open,
shuddering with awful terror. The cynicism, the cynicism of my words
overwhelmed her. . . .

"Save you!" I went on, jumping up from my chair and running up
and down the room before her. "Save you from what? But perhaps I
am worse than you myself. Why didn't you throw it in my teeth when I
was giving you that sermon: 'But what did you come here yourself for?
was it to read us a sermon?' Power, power was what I wanted then,
sport was what I wanted, I wanted to wring out your tears, your humiliation, your hysteria—that was what I wanted then! Of course, I couldn't
keep it up then, because I am a wretched creature, I was frightened,
and, the devil knows why, gave you my address in my folly. Afterwards,
before I got home, I was cursing and swearing at you because of that
address, I hated you already because of the lies I had told you. Because
I only like playing with words, only dreaming, but, do you know, what I
really want is that you should all go to hell. That is what I want. I want
peace; yes, I'd sell the whole world for a farthing, straight off, so long
as I was left in peace. Is the world to go to pot, or am I to go without
my tea? I say that the world may go to pot for me so long as I always
get my tea. Did you know that, or not? Well, anyway, I know that I
am a blackguard, a scoundrel, an egoist, a sluggard. Here I have been
shuddering for the last three days at the thought of your coming. And
so you know what has worried me particularly for these three days? That
I posed as such a hero to you, and now you would see me in a wretched
torn dressing-gown, beggarly, loathsome. I told you just now that I was
not ashamed of my poverty; so you may as well know that I am
ashamed of it; I am more ashamed of it than of anything, more afraid of
it than of being found out if I were a thief, because I am as vain as
though I had been skinned and the very air blowing on me hurt. Surely
by now you must realize that I shall never forgive you for having found
me in this wretched dressing gown, just as I was flying at Apollon like a
spiteful cur. The saviour, the former hero, was ·flying like a mangy,
unkempt sheep-dog at his lackey, and the lackey was jeering at him!
And I shall never forgive you for the tears I could not help shedding
before you just now, like some silly woman put to shame! And for what
I am confessing to you now, I shall never forgive *you* either! Yes—

you must answer for it all because you turned up like this, because I am a blackguard, because I am the nastiest, stupidest, absurdest and most envious of all the worms on earth, who are not a bit better than I am, but, the devil knows why, are never put to confusion; while I shall always be insulted by every louse, that is my doom! And what is it to me that you don't understand a word of this! And what do I care, what do I care about you, and whether you go to ruin there or not? Do you understand? How I shall hate you now after saying this, for having been here and listening. Why, it's not once in a lifetime a man speaks out like this, and then it is in hysterics! . . . What more do you want? Why do you still stand confronting me, after all this? Why are you worrying me? Why don't you go?"

But at this point a strange thing happened. I was so accustomed to think and imagine everything from books, and to picture everything in the world to myself just as I had made it up in my dreams beforehand, that I could not all at once take in this strange circumstance. What happened was this: Liza, insulted and crushed by me, understood a great deal more than I imagined. She understood from all this what a woman understands first of all, if she feels genuine love, that is, that I was myself unhappy.

The frightened and wounded expression on her face was followed first by a look of sorrowful perplexity. When I began calling myself a scoundrel and a blackguard and my tears flowed (the tirade was accompanied throughout by tears) her whole face worked convulsively. She was on the point of getting up and stopping me; when I finished she took no notice of my shouting: "Why are you here, why don't you go away?" but realized only that it must have been very bitter to me to say all this. Besides, she was so crushed, poor girl; she considered herself infinitely beneath me; how could she feel anger or resentment? She suddenly leapt up from her chair with an irresistible impulse and held out her hands, yearning towards me, though still timid and not daring to stir. . . . At this point there was a revulsion in my heart, too. Then she suddenly rushed to me, threw her arms round me and burst into tears. I, too, could not restrain myself, and sobbed as I never had before.

"They won't let me . . . I can't be good!" I managed to articulate; then I went to the sofa, fell on it face downwards, and sobbed on it for a quarter of an hour in genuine hysterics. She came close to me, put her arms round me and stayed motionless in that position. But the trouble was that the hysterics could not go on for ever, and (I am writing the loathsome truth) lying face downwards on the sofa with my face thrust into my nasty leather pillow, I began by degrees to be aware of a faraway, involuntary but irresistible feeling that it would be awkward now for me to raise my head and look Liza straight in the face. Why was I ashamed? I don't know, but I was ashamed. The thought, too, came into my overwrought brain that our parts now were completely changed, that she was now the heroine, while I was just such a crushed and humiliated creature as she had been before me that night—four days before. . . . And all this came into my mind during the minutes I was lying on my face on the sofa.

My God! surely I was not envious of her then.

I don't know, to this day I cannot decide, and at the time, of course, I was still less able to understand what I was feeling than now. I cannot get on without domineering and tyrannizing over some one, but . . . there is no explaining anything by reasoning and so it is useless to reason.

I conquered myself, however, and raised my head; I had to do so sooner or later . . . and I am convinced to this day that it was just because I was ashamed to look at her that another feeling was suddenly kindled and flamed up in my heart . . . a feeling of mastery and possession. My eyes gleamed with passion, and I gripped her hands tightly. How I hated her and how I was drawn to her at that minute! The one feeling intensified the other. It was almost like an act of vengeance. At first there was a look of amazement, even of terror on her face, but only for one instant. She warmly and rapturously embraced me.

X

A quarter of an hour later I was rushing up and down the room in frenzied impatience, from minute to minute I went up to the screen and peeped through the crack at Liza. She was sitting on the ground with her head leaning against the bed, and must have been crying. But she did not go away, and that irritated me. This time she understood it all. I had insulted her finally, but . . . there's no need to describe it. She realized that my outburst of passion had been simply revenge, a fresh humiliation, and that to my earlier, almost causeless hatred was added now a *personal hatred,* born of envy. . . . Though I do not maintain positively that she understood all this distinctly; but she certainly did fully understand that I was a despicable man, and what was worse, incapable of loving her.

I know I shall be told that this is incredible—but it is incredible to be as spiteful and stupid as I was; it may be added that it was strange I should not love her, or at any rate, appreciate her love. Why is it strange? In the first place, by then I was incapable of love, for I repeat, with me loving meant tyrannizing and showing my moral superiority. I have never in my life been able to imagine any other sort of love, and have nowadays come to the point of sometimes thinking that love really consists in the right—freely given by the beloved object—to tyrannize over her.

Even in my underground dreams I did not imagine love except as a struggle. I began it always with hatred and ended it with moral subjugation, and afterwards I never knew what to do with the subjugated object. And what is there to wonder at in that, since I had succeeded in so corrupting myself, since I was so out of touch with "real life" as to have actually thought of reproaching her, and putting her to shame for having come to me to hear "fine sentiments"; and did not even guess that she had come not to hear fine sentiments, but to love me, because to a woman all reformation, all salvation from any sort of ruin, and all moral renewal is included in love and can only show itself in that form.

I did not hate her so much, however, when I was running about the room and peeping through the crack in the screen. I was only insufferably oppressed by her being here. I wanted her to disappear. I wanted "peace," to be left alone in my underground world. Real life oppressed me with its novelty so much that I could hardly breathe.

But several minutes passed and she still remained, without stirring, as though she were unconscious. I had the shamelessness to tap softly at the screen as though to remind her. . . . She started, sprang up, and flew to seek her kerchief, her hat, her coat, as though making her escape from me. . . . Two minutes later she came from behind the screen and looked with heavy eyes at me. I gave a spiteful grin, which was forced, however, to *keep up appearances,* and I turned away from her eyes.

"Good-bye," she said, going towards the door.

I ran up to her, seized her hand, opened it, thrust something in it and closed it again. Then I turned at once and dashed away in haste to the other corner of the room to avoid seeing, anyway. . . .

I did mean a moment since to tell a lie—to write that I did this accidentally, not knowing what I was doing through foolishness, through losing my head. But I don't want to lie, and so I will say straight out that I opened her hand and put the money in it . . . from spite. It came into my head to do this while I was running up and down the room and she was sitting behind the screen. But this I can say for certain: though I did that cruel thing purposely, it was not an impulse from the heart, but came from my evil brain. This cruelty was so affected, so purposely made up, so completely a product of the brain, of books, that I could not even keep it up a minute—first I dashed away to avoid seeing her, and then in shame and despair rushed after Liza. I opened the door in the passage and began listening.

"Liza! Liza!" I cried on the stairs, but in a low voice, not boldly.

There was no answer, but I fancied I heard her footsteps, lower down on the stairs.

"Liza!" I cried, more loudly.

No answer. But at that minute I heard the stiff outer glass door open heavily with a creak and slam violently, the sound echoed up the stairs.

She had gone. I went back to my room in hesitation. I felt horribly oppressed.

I stood still at the table, beside the chair on which she had sat and looked aimlessly before me. A minute passed, suddenly I started;

straight before me on the table I saw . . . In short, I saw a crumpled blue five-rouble note, the one I had thrust into her hand a minute before. It was the same note; it could be no other, there was no other in the flat. So she had managed to fling it from her hand on the table at the moment when I had dashed into the further corner.

Well! I might have expected that she would do that. Might I have expected it? No, I was such an egoist, I was so lacking in respect for my fellow-creatures that I could not even imagine she would do so. I could not endure it. A minute later I flew like a madman to dress, flinging on what I could at random and ran headlong after her. She could not have got two hundred paces away when I ran out into the street.

It was a still night and the snow was coming down in masses and falling almost perpendicularly, covering the pavement and the empty street as though with a pillow. There was no one in the street, no sound was to be heard. The street lamps gave a disconsolate and useless glimmer. I ran two hundred paces to the cross-roads and stopped short.

Where had she gone? And why was I running after her?

Why? To fall down before her, to sob with remorse, to kiss her feet, to entreat her forgiveness! I longed for that, my whole breast was being rent to pieces, and never, never shall I recall that minute with indifference. But—what for? I thought. Should I not begin to hate her, perhaps, even to-morrow, just because I had kissed her feet to-day? Should I give her happiness? Had I not recognized that day, for the hundredth time, what I was worth? Should I not torture her?

I stood in the snow, gazing into the troubled darkness and pondered this.

"And will it not be better?" I mused fantastically, afterwards at home, stifling the living pang of my heart with fantastic dreams. "Will it not be better that she should keep the resentment of the insult for ever? Resentment—why, it is purification; it is a most stinging and painful consciousness! To-morrow I should have defiled her soul and have exhausted her heart, while now the feeling of insult will never die in her heart, and however loathsome the filth awaiting her—the feeling of insult will elevate and purify her . . . by hatred . . . h'm! . . . perhaps, too, by forgiveness . . . Will all that make things easier for her though? . . ."

And, indeed, I will ask on my own account here, an idle question: which is better—cheap happiness or exalted sufferings? Well, which is better?

So I dreamed as I sat at home that evening, almost dead with the pain in my soul. Never had I endured such suffering and remorse, yet could there have been the faintest doubt when I ran out from my lodging that I should turn back half-way? I never met Liza again and I have heard nothing of her. I will add, too, that I remained for a long time afterwards pleased with the phrase about the benefit from resentment and hatred in spite of the fact that I almost fell ill from misery.

Even now, so many years later, all this is somehow a very evil memory. I have many evil memories now, but . . . hadn't I better end my "Notes" here? I believe I made a mistake in beginning to write them, anyway I have felt ashamed all the time I've been writing this story; so it's hardly literature so much as a corrective punishment. Why, to tell long stories, showing how I have spoiled my life through morally rotting in my corner, through lack of fitting environment, through divorce from real life, and rankling spite in my underground world, would certainly not be interesting; a novel needs a hero, and all the traits for an anti-hero are *expressly* gathered together here, and what matters most, it all produces an unpleasant impression, for we are all divorced from life, we are all cripples, every one of us, more or less. We are so divorced from it that we feel at once a sort of loathing for real life, and so cannot bear to be reminded of it. Why, we have come almost to looking upon real life as an effort, almost as hard work, and we are all privately agreed that it is better in books. And why do we fuss and fume sometimes? Why are we perverse and ask for something else? We don't know what ourselves. It would be the worse for us if our petulant prayers were answered. Come, try, give any one of us, for instance, a little more independence, untie our hands, widen the spheres of our activity, relax the control and we . . . yes, I assure you . . . we should be begging to be under control again at once. I know that you will very likely be angry with me for that, and will begin shouting and stamping. Speak for yourself, you will say, and for your miseries in your underground holes, and don't dare to say all of us—excuse me, gentlemen, I am not justifying myself with that "all of us." As for what concerns me in particular I have only in my life carried to an extreme what you have not dared to carry half-way, and what's more, you have taken your cowardice for good sense, and have found comfort in deceiving yourselves. So that perhaps, after all, there is more life in me than in you. Look into it more carefully! Why, we don't even know what living means now, what it is, and what it is called! Leave us alone without books and we shall be lost and in confusion at once. We shall not know what to join on to, what to cling to, what to love and what to hate, what to respect and what to despise. We are oppressed at being men—men with a real individual body and blood, we are ashamed of it, we think it a disgrace and try to contrive to be some sort of impossible generalized man. We are still-born, and for generations past have been begotten, not by living fathers, and that suits us better and better. We are developing a taste for it. Soon we shall contrive to be born somehow from an idea. But enough; I don't want to write more from "Underground."

[*The notes of this paradoxalist do not end here, however. He could not refrain from going on with them, but it seems to us that we may stop here.*]

3

HENRY JAMES
Daisy Miller

The publication of *Daisy Miller* in 1878 touched off a vocal and curiously two-sided response by the reading public. In America, James's friend William Dean Howells wrote, "There has been vast discussion in which nobody felt very deeply, and everybody talked very loudly. The thing went so far that society almost divided itself into Daisy Millerites and anti-Daisy Millerites." The controversy did not center on the literary merit of what James had written, for the story was almost universally acknowledged as an extremely interesting one. The controversy concerned Daisy herself and her fittingness as a representative of "the American girl." On both sides of the Atlantic Daisy Miller became something of a culture heroine. Her name became a catch phrase, and for a time "Daisy Miller hats" appeared in millinery shops. Many felt, however, that James's portrait of Daisy was an unconscionable slur on the American girl. *The New York Times* claimed in June of 1879, "There are many ladies in and around New York today who feel very indignant with Mr. James for his portrait of Daisy Miller, and declare it is shameful to give for-

eigners so untrue a portrait of an American girl."

In part, the notoriety of *Daisy Miller* was fostered by the temper of the times. Even before the story appeared, the American girl touring Europe had become a recognized type and a focus of interest. The decades before the turn of the century were expansive ones in America. Businessmen who were amassing fortunes in places like New York, Chicago, or Schenectady often sent their idle daughters and wives to sample the old-world curiosities of Europe. James captured the type perfectly in Daisy: pretty, imperious, nonchalant, and above all, vivacious and quite ignorant of the tradition-bound strictures of European life. Abroad, these young women created an unsettling contrast. In the Europe of 1878 there was already a vague groundswell of feeling that things were in need of change. The privileges of the aristocracy, the materialism of the bourgeoisie, and the harsh demands of new industrialism were among the contributing causes. Many literary works testified to this feeling. Significantly, Ibsen's *A Doll's House,* a widely read play dramatizing a

Norwegian woman's resolt against middle-class conventionality, appeared within a year of *Daisy Miller*. The liberation of women was not a clearly recognized idea throughout Europe at this time, but during the following two decades women—especially the literary image of women—became a symbol of the desire of both sexes to overcome cultural repression of various kinds. Against this background, lively, irrepressible young women of Daisy Miller's type stood out with particular brilliance. One scholar has even suggested that Henry James's desire to study the American girl in this revealing context was a major reason for his move to Europe.

Today, most readers can find little sympathy for the qualms of the "anti-Daisy Millerites" of 1879. On behalf of those who became genuinely upset at Daisy's flirtatious ways, it should be mentioned that conventions of dating were much more strict a century ago. Important, too, is the Italian setting of Daisy's indiscretions. Even today, among many conservative Italians, dating is surprisingly restricted and chaperons and early curfews are commonplace. There can be little doubt, though, that James himself was on Daisy's side. He portrays her exceptional vivacity and charm as truly admirable qualities. More importantly, he portrays her as a person of real integrity. Unlike Winterbourne, Daisy knows who she is, she knows what she wants, and she shows honesty and courage in defining her freedom of action to those who try to restrict her. She defines her intentions bluntly to Mrs.

Walker, for example, in a scene which delightfully satirizes Winterbourne's prissy alliance of respectability with that old lady. Daisy is also quite clear in expressing her early affection for Winterbourne, and it is only after encountering his puzzling diffidence that she becomes coy and conceals her affection by spending more and more time with her Italian friend, Giovanelli.

The satiric perceptions of Daisy are generally rendered from Winterbourne's point of view, but Winterbourne himself is frequently the target of James's deliberate ridicule. James reveals him as a young man who is victimized by ignorance of himself and, to a certain extent, by dishonesty with himself. What he really wants from Daisy, it seems, is not love but some form of revelation that will enable him to explain and somehow possess her bewildering feminine spirit. Of course, he never really succeeds. Ignorant of his own inner motives, he is condemned to remain ignorant of Daisy's.

If Daisy is guilty of anything, it is probably her failure to dismiss Winterbourne from her mind entirely. Her final motives in the story pose some interesting questions. Was she really in love with him, as her final message suggested? Or was her message a gesture of coquettish pride, intended to hurt and haunt a man who she knew all too well was immune to feminine charms? In any case, James apparently intends that Winterbourne's deliberate coldness towards her is somehow a cause of her death. Winterbourne's rebuff of Daisy when he discovers her touring the Colosseum with Giovanelli coincides with her contraction of malaria. Significantly, Winterbourne is convinced at this moment that he has finally objectified Daisy with the right formula.

The scene of Daisy's funeral reveals the extent of the evil which has worked towards her death. Giovanelli at last makes clear his shocking cynicism when questioned by Winterbourne. His confession—which Winterbourne accepts with strange passiveness—reveals that Daisy has been the victim of considerably more than just Winterbourne's confused motives. The scene in the Colosseum involved a personal encounter among three people, but it should be remembered that the same place is also symbolic of public martyrdom. Daisy's death is the result of complex social forces, including the hypocrisy of the American-Roman clique, possibly the long absence of her father, certainly the incompetence of her mother.

At the same time, Giovanelli's confession to Winterbourne reveals that Daisy was truly no disreputable woman. She was, rather, "the most innocent" of women, and Daisy's actions seem to provide reason for interpreting the meaning of Giovanelli's phrase as chaste, not naïve. Again, Winterbourne's formula is shattered, and the enigma of Daisy Miller is reborn in his troubled soul, even as the "April daisies" push up through the cemetery sod.

Daisy Miller

1

Les Trois Couronnes

At the little town of Vevay, in Switzerland, there is a particularly comfortable hotel. There are, indeed, many hotels; for the entertainment of tourists is the business of the place, which, as many travellers will remember, is seated upon the edge of a remarkably blue lake—a lake that it behooves every tourist to visit. The shore of the lake presents an unbroken array of establishments of this order, of every category, from the "grand hotel" of the newest fashion, with a chalk-white front, a hundred balconies, and a dozen flags flying from its roof, to the little Swiss *pension* of an elder day, with its name inscribed in German-looking lettering upon a pink or yellow wall, and an awkward summer-house in the angle of the garden. One of the hotels at Vevay, however, is famous, even classical, being distinguished from any of its upstart neighbors by an air both of luxury and of maturity. In this region, in the month of June, American travellers are extremely numerous; it may be said, indeed, that Vevay assumes at this period some of the characteristics of an American watering-place. There are sights and sounds which evoke a vision, an echo, of Newport and Saratoga. There is a flitting hither and thither of "stylish" young girls, a rustling of muslin flounces, a rattle of dance-music in the morning hours, a sound of high-pitched voices at all times. You receive an impression of these things at the excellent inn of the Trois Couronnes, and are transported in fancy to the Ocean House or to Congress Hall. But at the Trois Couronnes, it must be added, there are other features that are much at variance with these suggestions: neat German waiters, who look like secretaries of legation, Russian princesses sitting in the garden; little Polish boys walking about, held by the hand, with their governors; a view of the sunny crest of the Dent du Midi and the picturesque towers of the Castle of Chillon.

I hardly know whether it was the analogies or the differences that were uppermost in the mind of a young American, who, two or three years ago, sat in the garden of the Trois Couronnes, looking about him, rather idly, at some of the graceful objects I have mentioned. It was a beautiful summer morning, and in whatever fashion the young American looked at things they must have seemed to him charming. He had come from Geneva the day before by the little steamer to see his aunt, who was staying at the hotel—Geneva having been for a long time his place of residence. But his aunt had a headache—his aunt had almost always a headache—and now she was shut up in her room, smelling camphor, so that he was at liberty to wander about. He was some seven-and-twenty years of age. When his friends spoke of him, they usually said that he "was at Geneva studying"; when his enemies spoke of him, they said—but, after all, he had no enemies; he was an extremely amiable fellow, and universally liked. What I should say, is, simply, that when certain persons spoke of him they affirmed that the reason of his spending so much time at Geneva was that he was extremely devoted to a lady who lived there—a foreign lady—a person older than himself. Very few Americans—indeed, I think none —had ever seen this lady, about whom there were some singular stories. But Winterbourne had an old attachment for the little metropolis of Calvinism; he had been put to school there as a boy, and he had afterwards gone to college there—circumstances which had led to his forming a great many youthful friendships. Many of these he had kept, and they were a source of great satisfaction to him.

After knocking at his aunt's door, and learning that she was indisposed, he had taken a walk about the town, and then he had come in to his breakfast. He had now finished his breakfast; but he was drinking a small cup of coffee, which had been served to him on a little table in the garden by one of the waiters who looked like an attaché. At last he finished his coffee and lit a cigarette. Presently a small boy came walking along the path—an urchin of nine or ten. The child, who was diminutive for his years, had an aged expression of countenance: a pale complexion, and sharp little features. He was dressed in knickerbockers, with red stockings, which displayed his poor little spindle-shanks; he also wore a brilliant red cravat. He carried in his hand a long alpenstock, the sharp point of which he thrust into everything that he approached—the flower-beds, the garden-benches, the trains of the ladies' dresses. In front of Winterbourne he paused, looking at him with a pair of bright, penetrating little eyes.

"Will you give me a lump of sugar?" he asked, in a sharp, hard little voice—a voice immature, and yet, somehow, not young.

Winterbourne glanced at the small table near him, on which his coffee-service rested, and saw that several morsels of sugar remained. "Yes, you may take one," he answered; "but I don't think sugar is good for little boys."

This little boy stepped forward and carefully selected three of the coveted fragments, two of which he buried in the pocket of his knicker bockers, depositing the other as promptly in another place. He poked his alpenstock, lance-fashion, into Winterbourne's bench, and tried to crack the lump of sugar with his teeth.

"Oh, blazes; it's har-r-d!" he exclaimed, pronouncing the adjective in a peculiar manner.

Winterbourne had immediately perceived that he might have the honor of claiming him as a fellow-countryman. "Take care you don't hurt your teeth," he said, paternally.

"I haven't got any teeth to hurt. They have all come out. I have only got seven teeth. My mother counted them last night, and one came out right afterwards. She said she'd slap me if any more came out. I can't help it. It's this old Europe. It's the climate that makes them come out. In America they didn't come out. It's these hotels."

Winterbourne was much amused. "If you eat three lumps of sugar, your mother will certainly slap you," he said.

"She's got to give me some candy, then," rejoined his young inter-locutor. "I can't get any candy here—any American candy. American candy's the best candy."

"And are American little boys the best little boys?" asked Winter-bourne.

"I don't know. I'm an American boy," said the child.

"I see you are one of the best!" laughed Winterbourne.

"Are you an American man?" pursued this vivacious infant. And then, on Winterbourne's affirmative reply—"American men are the best!" he declared.

His companion thanked him for the compliment; and the child, who had now got astride his alpenstock, stood looking about him, while he attacked a second lump of sugar. Winterbourne wondered if he himself had been like this in his infancy, for he had been brought to Europe at about this age.

"Here comes my sister!" cried the child, in a moment. "She's an American girl."

Winterbourne looked along the path and saw a beautiful young lady advancing. "American girls are the best girls!" he said, cheerfully, to his young companion.

"My sister ain't the best!" the child declared. "She's always blowing at me."

"I imagine that is your fault, not hers," said Winterbourne. The young lady meanwhile had drawn near. She was dressed in white mus-lin, with a hundred frills and flounces, and knots of pale-colored ribbon.

She was bareheaded; but she balanced in her hand a large parasol, with a deep border of embroidery; and she was strikingly, admirably pretty. "How pretty they are!" thought Winterbourne, straightening himself in his seat, as if he were prepared to rise.

The young lady paused in front of his bench, near the parapet of the garden, which overlooked the lake. The little boy had now converted his alpenstock into a vaulting-pole, by the aid of which he was springing about in the gravel, and kicking it up a little.

"Randolph," said the young lady, "what *are* you doing?"

"I'm going up the Alps," replied Randolph. "This is the way!" And he gave another little jump, scattering the pebbles about Winterbourne's ears.

"That's the way they come down," said Winterbourne.

"He's an American man!" cried Randolph, in his hard little voice.

The young lady gave no heed to this announcement, but looked straight at her brother. "Well, I guess you had better be quiet," she simply observed.

It seemed to Winterbourne that he had been in a manner presented. He got up and stepped slowly towards the young girl, throwing away his cigarette. "This little boy and I have made acquaintance," he said, with great civility. In Geneva, as he had been perfectly aware, a young man was not at liberty to speak to a young unmarried lady except under certain rarely occurring conditions; but here at Vevay, what conditions could be better than these?—a pretty American girl coming and standing in front of you in a garden. This pretty American girl, however, on hearing Winterbourne's observation, simply glanced at him; she then turned her head and looked over the parapet, at the lake and the opposite mountain. He wondered whether he had gone too far; but he decided that he must advance farther, rather than retreat. While he was thinking of something else to say, the young lady turned to the little boy again.

"I should like to know where you got that pole?" she said.

"I bought it," responded Randolph.

"You don't mean to say you're going to take it to Italy?"

"Yes, I am going to take it to Italy," the child declared.

The young girl glanced over the front of her dress, and smoothed out a knot or two of ribbon. Then she rested her eyes upon the prospect again. "Well, I guess you had better leave it somewhere," she said, after a moment.

"Are you going to Italy?" Winterbourne inquired, in a tone of great respect.

The young lady glanced at him again. "Yes, sir," she replied. And she said nothing more.

"Are you—a—going over the Simplon?" Winterbourne pursued, a little embarrassed.

"I don't know," she said. "I suppose it's some mountain. Randolph, what mountain are we going over?"

"Going where?" the child demanded.

"To Italy," Winterbourne explained.

"I don't know," said Randolph. "I don't want to go to Italy. I want to go to America."

"Oh, Italy is a beautiful place!" rejoined the young man.

"Can you get candy there?" Randolph loudly inquired.

"I hope not," said his sister. "I guess you have had enough candy, and mother thinks so, too."

"I haven't had any for ever so long—for a hundred weeks!" cried the boy, still jumping about.

The young lady inspected her flounces and smoothed her ribbons again, and Winterbourne presently risked an observation upon the beauty of the view. He was ceasing to be embarrassed, for he had begun to perceive that she was not in the least embarrassed herself. There had not been the slightest alteration in her charming complexion; she was evidently neither offended nor fluttered. If she looked another way when he spoke to her, and seemed not particularly to hear him, this was simply her habit, her manner. Yet, as he talked a little more, and pointed out some of the objects of interest in the view, with which she appeared quite unacquainted, she gradually gave him more of the benefit of her glance; and then he saw that this glance was perfectly direct and unshrinking. It was not, however, what would have been called an immodest glance, for the young girl's eyes were singularly honest and fresh. They were wonderfully pretty eyes; and, indeed, Winterbourne had not seen for a long time anything prettier than his fair countrywoman's various features—her complexion, her nose, her ears, her teeth. He had a great relish for feminine beauty; he was addicted to observing and analyzing it; and as regards this young lady's face he made several observations. It was not at all insipid, but it was not exactly expressive; and though it was eminently delicate, Winterbourne mentally accused it—very forgivingly—of a want of finish. He thought it very possible that Master Randolph's sister was a coquette; he was sure she had a spirit of her own; but in her bright, sweet, superficial little visage there was no mockery, no irony. Before long it became obvious that she was much disposed towards conversation. She told him that they were going to Rome for the winter—she and her mother and Randolph. She asked him if he was a "real American"; she shouldn't have taken him for one; he seemed more like a German—this was said after a little hesitation—especially when he spoke. Winterbourne, laughing, answered that he had met Germans who spoke like Americans; but that he had not, so far as he remembered, met an American who spoke like a German. Then he asked her if she should not be more comfortable in sitting upon the bench which he had just quitted. She answered that she liked standing up and walking about; but she presently sat down. She told him she was from New York State—"if you know where that is." Winterbourne learned more about her by catching hold of her small, slippery brother, and making him stand a few minutes by his side.

"Tell me your name, my boy," he said.

"Randolph C. Miller," said the boy, sharply. "And I'll tell you her name"; and he levelled his alpenstock at his sister.

"You had better wait till you are asked!" said this young lady, calmly.

"I should like very much to know your name," said Winterbourne.

"Her name is Daisy Miller!" cried the child. "But that isn't her real name; that isn't her name on her cards."

"It's a pity you haven't got one of my cards!" said Miss Miller.

"Her real name is Annie P. Miller," the boy went on.

"Ask him *his* name," said his sister, indicating Winterbourne.

But on this point Randolph seemed perfectly indifferent; he continued to supply information with regard to his own family. "My father's name is Ezra B. Miller," he announced. "My father ain't in Europe; my father's in a better place than Europe."

Winterbourne imagined for a moment that this was the manner in which the child had been taught to intimate that Mr. Miller had been removed to the sphere of celestial rewards. But Randolph immediately added, "My father's in Schenectady. He's got a big business. My father's rich, you bet!"

"Well!" ejaculated Miss Miller, lowering her parasol and looking at the embroidered border. Winterbourne presently released the child, who departed, dragging his alpenstock along the path. "He doesn't like Europe," said the young girl. "He wants to go back."

"To Schenectady, you mean?"

"Yes; he wants to go right home. He hasn't got any boys here. There is one boy here, but he always goes round with a teacher; they won't let him play."

"And your brother hasn't any teacher?" Winterbourne inquired.

"Mother thought of getting him one to travel round with us. There was a lady told her of a very good teacher; an American lady—perhaps you know her—Mrs. Sanders. I think she came from Boston. She told her of this teacher, and we thought of getting him to travel round with us. But Randolph said he didn't want a teacher travelling round with us. He said he wouldn't have lessons when he was in the cars. And we *are* in the cars about half the time. There was an English lady we met in the cars—I think her name was Miss Featherstone; perhaps you know her. She wanted to know why I didn't give Randolph lessons—

give him 'instructions,' she called it. I guess he could give me more instruction that I could give him. He's very smart."

"Yes," said Winterbourne; "he seems very smart."

"Mother's going to get a teacher for him as soon as we get to Italy. Can you get good teachers in Italy?"

"Very good, I should think," said Winterbourne.

"Or else she's going to find some school. He ought to learn some more. He's only nine. He's going to college." And in this way Miss Miller continued to converse upon the affairs of her family, and upon other topics. She sat there with her extremely pretty hands, ornamented with very brilliant rings, folded in her lap, and with her pretty eyes now resting upon those of Winterbourne, now wandering over the garden, the people who passed by, and the beautiful view. She talked to Winterbourne as if she had known him a long time. He found it very pleasant. It was many years since he had heard a young girl talk so much. It might have been said of this unknown young lady, who had come and sat down beside him upon a bench, that she chattered. She was very quiet; she sat in a charming, tranquil attitude, but her lips and her eyes were constantly moving. She had a soft, slender, agreeable voice, and her tone was decidedly sociable. She gave Winterbourne a history of her movements and intentions, and those of her mother and brother, in Europe, and enumerated, in particular, the various hotels at which they had stopped. "That English lady in the cars," she said—"Miss Featherstone—asked me if we didn't all live in hotels in America. I told her I had never been in so many hotels in my life as since I came to Europe. I have never seen so many —it's nothing but hotels." But Miss Miller did not make this remark with a querulous accent; she appeared to be in the best humor with everything. She declared that the hotels were very good, when once you got used to their ways, and that Europe was perfectly sweet. She was not disappointed—not a bit. Perhaps it was because she had heard so much about it before. She had ever so many intimate friends that had been there ever so many times. And then she had ever so many dresses and things from Paris. Whenever she put on a Paris dress she felt as if she were in Europe.

"It was a kind of a wishing-cap," said Winterbourne.

"Yes," said Miss Miller, without examining this analogy; "it always made me wish I was here. But I needn't have done that for dresses. I am sure they send all the pretty ones to America; you see the most frightful things here. The only thing I don't like," she proceeded, "is the society. There isn't any society; or, if there is, I don't know where it keeps itself. Do you? I suppose there is some society somewhere, but I haven't seen anything of it. I'm very fond of society, and I have always had a great deal of it. I don't mean only in Schenectady, but in New York. I used to go to New York every winter. In New York I had lots of society. Last winter I had seventeen dinners given me; and three of them were by gentlemen," added Daisy Miller. "I have more friends in New York than in Schenectady—more gentlemen friends; and more young lady friends, too," she resumed in a moment. She paused again for an instant; she was looking at Winterbourne with all her prettiness in her lively eyes, and in her light, slightly monotonous smile. "I have always had," she said, "a great deal of gentlemen's society."

Poor Winterbourne was amused, perplexed, and decidedly charmed. He had never yet heard a young girl express herself in just this fashion—never, at least, save in cases where to say such things seemed a kind of demonstrative evidence of a certain laxity of deportment. And yet was he to accuse Miss Daisy Miller of actual or potential *inconduite,* as they said at Geneva? He felt that he had lived at Geneva so long that he had lost a good deal; he had become dishabituated to the American tone. Never, indeed, since he had grown old enough to appreciate things had he encountered a young American girl of so pronounced a type as this. Certainly she was very charming, but how deucedly sociable! Was she simply a pretty girl from New York State? Were they all like that, the pretty girls who had a good deal of gentlemen's society? Or was she also a designing, an audacious, an unscrupulous young person? Winterbourne had lost his instinct in this matter, and his reason could not help him. Miss Daisy Miller looked extremely innocent. Some people had told him that, after all, American girls were exceedingly innocent; and others had told him that, after all, they were not. He was inclined to think Miss Daisy Miller was a flirt—a pretty American flirt. He had never, as yet, had any relations with young ladies of this category. He had known, here in Europe, two or three women—persons older than Miss Daisy Miller, and provided, for respectability's sake, with husbands—who were great coquettes—dangerous, terrible women, with whom one's relations were liable to take a serious turn. But this young girl was not a coquette in that sense; she was very unsophisticated; she was only a pretty American flirt. Winterbourne was almost grateful for having found the formula that applied to Miss Daisy Miller. He leaned back in his seat; he remarked to himself that she had the most charming nose he had ever seen; he wondered what were the regular conditions and limitations of one's intercourse with a pretty American flirt. It presently became apparent that he was on the way to learn.

"Have you been to that old castle?" asked the young girl, pointing with her parasol to the far-gleaming walls of the Château de Chillon.

"Yes, formerly, more than once," said Winterbourne. "You, too, I suppose, have seen it?"

"No; we haven't been there. I want to go there dreadfully. Of course I mean to go there. I wouldn't go away from here without having seen that old castle."

"It's a very pretty excursion," said Winterbourne, "and very easy to make. You can drive or go by the little steamer."

"You can go in the cars," said Miss Miller.

"Yes; you can go in the cars," Winterbourne assented.

"Our courier says they take you right up to the castle," the young girl continued. "We were going last week; but my mother gave out. She suffers dreadfully from dyspepsia. She said she couldn't go. Randolph wouldn't go, either; he say he doesn't think much of old castles. But I guess we'll go this week, if we can get Randolph."

"Your brother is not interested in ancient monuments?" Winterbourne inquired, smiling.

"He says he don't care much about old castles. He's only nine. He wants to stay at the hotel. Mother's afraid to leave him alone, and the courier won't stay with him; so we haven't been to many places. But it will be too bad if we don't go up there." And Miss Miller pointed again at the Château de Chillon.

"I should think it might be arranged," said Winterbourne. "Couldn't you get some one to stay for the afternoon with Randolph?"

Miss Miller looked at him a moment, and then very placidly, "I wish *you* would stay with him!" she said.

Winterbourne hesitated a moment. "I should much rather go to Chillon with you."

"With me?" asked the young girl, with the same placidity.

She didn't rise, blushing, as a young girl at Geneva would have done; and yet Winterbourne, conscious that he had been very bold, thought it possible that she was offended. "With your mother," he answered, very respectfully.

But it seemed that both his audacity and his respect were lost upon Miss Daisy Miller. "I guess my mother won't go, after all," she said. "She don't like to ride round in the afternoon. But did you really mean what you said just now, that you would like to go up there?"

"Most earnestly," Winterbourne declared.

"Then we may arrange it. If mother will stay with Randolph, I guess Eugenio will."

"Eugenio?" the young man inquired.

"Eugenio's our courier. He doesn't like to stay with Randolph; he's the most fastidious man I ever saw. But he's a splendid courier. I guess he'll stay at home with Randolph if mother does, and then we can go to the castle."

Winterbourne reflected for an instant as lucidly as possible—"we" could only mean Miss Daisy Miller and himself. This programme seemed almost too agreeable for credence; he felt as if he ought to kiss the young lady's hand. Possibly he would have done so, and quite spoiled the project; but at this moment another person, presumably Eugenio, appeared. A tall, handsome man, with superb whiskers, wearing a velvet morning-coat and a brilliant watch-chain, approached Miss Miller, looking sharply at her companion. "Oh, Eugenio!" said Miss Miller, with the friendliest accent.

Eugenio had looked at Winterbourne from head to foot; he now bowed gravely to the young lady. "I have the honor to inform mademoiselle that luncheon is upon the table."

Miss Miller slowly rose. "See here, Eugenio!" she said; "I'm going to that old castle, anyway."

"To the Château de Chillon, mademoiselle?" the courier inquired. "Mademoiselle has made arrangements?" he added, in a tone which struck Winterbourne as very impertinent.

Eugenio's tone apparently threw, even to Miss Miller's own apprehension, a slightly ironical light upon the young girl's situation. She turned to Winterbourne, blushing a little—a very little. "You won't back out?" she said.

"I shall not be happy till we go!" he protested.

"And you are staying in this hotel?" she went on. "And you are really an American?"

The courier stood looking at Winterbourne offensively. The young man, at least, thought his manner of looking an offence to Miss Miller; it conveyed an imputation that she "picked up" acquaintances. "I shall have the honor of presenting to you a person who will tell you all about me," he said, smiling, and referring to his aunt.

"Oh, well, we'll go some day," said Miss Miller. And she gave him a smile and turned away. She put up her parasol and walked back to the inn beside Eugenio. Winterbourne stood looking after her; and as she moved away, drawing her muslin furbelows over the gravel, said to himself that she had the *tournure* of a princess.

He had, however, engaged to do more than proved feasible, in promising to present his aunt, Mrs. Costello, to Miss Daisy Miller. As soon as the former lady had got better of her headache he waited upon her in her apartment; and, after the proper inquiries in regard to her health, he asked her if she had observed in the hotel an American family—a mamma, a daughter, and a little boy.

"And a courier?" said Mrs. Costello. "Oh yes, I have observed them. Seen them—heard them—and kept out of their way." Mrs. Costello was a widow with a fortune; a person of much distinction, who frequently intimated that, if she were not so dreadfully liable to sick-headaches, she would probably have left a deeper impress upon her time. She had a long, pale face, a high nose, and a great deal of very striking white hair, which she wore in large puffs and *rouleaux* over the top of her head. She had two sons married in New York, and another who was now in Europe. This young man was amusing himself at Hombourg; and though he was on his travels, was rarely perceived to visit any particular city at the moment selected by his mother for her own appearance there. Her nephew, who had come up to Vevay expressly to see her, was therefore more attentive than those who, as she said, were nearer to her. He had imbibed at Geneva the idea that one must always be attentive to one's aunt. Mrs. Costello had not seen him for many years, and she was greatly pleased with him, manifesting her approbation by initiating him into many of the secrets of that social sway which, as she gave him to understand, she exerted in the American capital. She admitted that she was very exclusive; but, if he were acquainted with New York, he would see that one had to be. And her picture of the minutely hierarchical constitution of the society of that city, which she presented to him in many different lights, was, to Winterbourne's imagination, almost oppressively striking.

He immediately perceived, from her tone, that Miss Daisy Miller's place in the social scale was low. "I am afraid you don't approve of them," he said.

"They are very common," Mrs. Costello declared. "They are the sort of Americans that one does one's duty by not—not accepting."

"Ah, you don't accept them?" said the young man.

"I can't, my dear Frederick. I would if I could, but I can't."

"The young girl is very pretty," said Winterbourne, in a moment.

"Of course she's pretty. But she is very common."

"I see what you mean, of course," said Winterbourne, after another pause.

"She has that charming look that they all have," his aunt resumed. "I can't think where they pick it up; and she dresses in perfection—no, you don't know how well she dresses. I can't think where they get their taste."

"But, my dear aunt, she is not, after all, a Comanche savage."

"She is a young lady," said Mrs. Costello, "who has an intimacy with her mamma's courier."

"An intimacy with the courier?" the young man demanded.

"Oh, the mother is just as bad! They treat the courier like a familiar friend—like a gentleman. I shouldn't wonder if he dines with them. Very likely they have never seen a man with such good manners, such fine clothes, so like a gentleman. He probably corresponds to the young lady's idea of a count. He sits with them in the garden in the evening. I think he smokes."

Winterbourne listened with interest to these disclosures; they helped him to make up his mind about Miss Daisy. Evidently she was rather wild.

"Well," he said, "I am not a courier, and yet she was very charming to me."

"You had better have said at first," said Mrs. Costello, with dignity, "that you had made her acquaintance."

"We simply met in the garden, and we talked a bit."

"*Tout bonnement!* And pray what did you say?"

"I said I should take the liberty of introducing her to my admirable aunt."

"I am much obliged to you."

"It was to guarantee my respectability," said Winterbourne.

"And pray who is to guarantee hers?"

"Ah, you are cruel," said the young man. "She's a very nice young girl."

"You don't say that as if you believed it," Mrs. Costello observed.

"She is completely uncultivated," Winterbourne went on. "But she is wonderfully pretty, and, in short, she is very nice. To prove that I believe it, I am going to take her to the Château de Chillon."

"You two are going off there together? I should say it proved just the contrary. How long had you known her, may I ask, when this interesting project was formed? You haven't been twenty-four hours in the house."

"I had known her half an hour!" said Winterbourne, smiling.

"Dear me!" cried Mrs. Costello. "What a dreadful girl!"

Her nephew was silent for some moments. "You really think, then," he began, earnestly, and with a desire for trustworthy information—"you really think that—" But he paused again.

"Think what, sir?" said his aunt.

"That she is the sort of young lady who expects a man, sooner or later, to carry her off?"

"I haven't the least idea what such young ladies expect a man to do. But I really think that you had better not meddle with little American girls that are uncultivated, as you call them. You have lived too long out of the country. You will be sure to make some great mistake. You are too innocent."

"My dear aunt, I am not so innocent," said Winterbourne, smiling and curling his mustache.

"You are too guilty, then!"

Winterbourne continued to curl his mustache, meditatively. "You won't let the poor girl know you, then?" he asked at last.

"Is it literally true that she is going to the Château de Chillon with you?"

"I think that she fully intends it."

"Then, my dear Frederick," said Mrs. Costello, "I must decline the honor of her acquaintance. I am an old woman, but I am not too old, thank Heaven, to be shocked!"

"But don't they all do these things—the young girls in America?" Winterbourne inquired.

Mrs. Costello stared a moment. "I should like to see my granddaughters do them!" she declared, grimly.

This seemed to throw some light upon the matter, for Winterbourne remembered to have heard that his pretty cousins in New York were "tremendous flirts." If, therefore, Miss Daisy Miller exceeded the liberal margin allowed to these young ladies, it was probable that anything might be expected of her. Winterbourne was impatient to see her again, and he was vexed with himself that, by instinct, he should not appreciate her justly.

Though he was impatient to see her, he hardly knew what he should say to her about his aunt's refusal to become acquainted with her; but he discovered, promptly enough, that with Miss Daisy Miller there was no great need of walking on tiptoe. He found her that evening in the garden, wandering about in the warm starlight like an indolent sylph, and swinging to and fro the largest fan he had ever beheld. It was ten o'clock. He had just dined with his aunt, had been sitting with her since dinner, and had just taken leave of her till the morrow. Miss Daisy Miller seemed very glad to see him; she declared it was the longest evening she had ever passed.

"Have you been all alone?" he asked.

"I have been walking round with mother. But mother gets tired walking round," she answered.

"Has she gone to bed?"

"No; she doesn't like to go to bed," said the young girl. "She doesn't sleep—not three hours. She says she doesn't know how she lives. She's dreadfully nervous. I guess she sleeps more than she thinks. She's gone somewhere after Randolph; she wants to try to get him to go to bed. He doesn't like to go to bed."

"Let us hope she will persuade him," observed Winterbourne.

"She will talk to him all she can; but he doesn't like her to talk to him," said Miss Daisy, opening her fan. "She's going to try to get Eugenio to talk to him. But he isn't afraid of Eugenio. Eugenio's a splendid courier, but he can't make much impression on Randolph! I don't believe he'll go to bed before eleven." It appeared that Randolph's vigil was in fact triumphantly prolonged, for Winterbourne strolled about with the young girl for some time without meeting her mother. "I have been looking round for that lady you want to introduce me to," his companion resumed. "She's your aunt." Then, on Winterbourne's admitting the fact, and expressing some curiosity as to how she had learned it, she said she had heard all about Mrs. Costello from the chambermaid. She was very quiet, and very *comme il faut;* she wore white puffs; she spoke to no one, and she never dined at the *table d'hôte*. Every two days she had a headache. "I think that's a lovely description, headache and all!" said Miss Daisy, chattering along in her thin, gay voice. "I want to know her ever so much. I know just what *your* aunt would be; I know I should like her. She would be very exclusive. I like a lady to be exclusive; I'm dying to be exclusive myself. Well, we *are* exclusive, mother and I. We don't speak to every one—or they don't speak to us. I suppose it's about the same thing. Anyway, I shall be ever so glad to know your aunt."

Winterbourne was embarrassed. "She would be most happy," he said; "but I am afraid those headaches will interfere."

The young girl looked at him through the dusk. "But I suppose she doesn't have a headache every day," she said, sympathetically.

Winterbourne was silent a moment. "She tells me she does," he answered at last, not knowing what to say.

Miss Daisy Miller stopped, and stood looking at him. Her prettiness was still visible in the darkness; she was opening and closing her enormous fan. "She doesn't want to know me!" she said, suddenly. "Why don't you say so? You needn't be afraid. I'm not afraid!" And she gave a little laugh.

Winterbourne fancied there was a tremor in her voice; he was touched, shocked, mortified by it. "My dear young lady," he protested, "she knows no one. It's her wretched health."

The young girl walked on a few steps, laughing still. "You needn't be afraid," she repeated. "Why should she want to know me?" Then she paused again; she was close to the parapet of the garden, and in front of her was the starlit lake. There was a vague sheen upon its surface, and in the distance were dimly-seen mountain forms. Daisy Miller looked out upon the mysterious prospect, and then she gave another little laugh. "Gracious! she *is* exclusive!" she said. Winterbourne wondered whether she was seriously wounded, and for a moment almost wished that her sense of injury might be such as to make it becoming in him to attempt to reassure and comfort her. He had a pleasant sense that she would be very approachable for consolatory purposes. He felt then, for the instant, quite ready to sacrifice his aunt, conversationally; to admit that she was a proud, rude woman, and to declare that they needn't mind her. But before he had time to commit himself to this perilous mixture of gallantry and impiety, the young lady, resuming her walk, gave an exclamation in quite another tone. "Well, here's mother! I guess she hasn't got Randolph to go to bed." The figure of a lady appeared, at a distance, very indistinct in the darkness, and advancing with a slow and wavering movement. Suddenly it seemed to pause.

"Are you sure it is your mother? Can you distinguish her in this thick dusk?" Winterbourne asked.

"Well!" cried Miss Daisy Miller, with a laugh; "I guess I know my own mother. And when she has got on my shawl, too! She is always wearing my things."

The lady in question, ceasing to advance, hovered vaguely about the spot at which she had checked her steps.

"I am afraid your mother doesn't see you," said Winterbourne. "Or perhaps," he added, thinking, with Miss Miller, the joke permissible— "perhaps she feels guilty about your shawl."

"Oh, it's a fearful old thing!" the young girl replied, serenely. "I told her she could wear it. She won't come here, because she sees you."

"Ah, then," said Winterbourne, "I had better leave you."

"Oh, no; come on!" urged Miss Daisy Miller.

"I'm afraid your mother doesn't approve of my walking with you."

Miss Miller gave him a serious glance. "It isn't for me; it's for you— that is, it's for *her*. Well, I don't know who it's for! But mother doesn't like any of my gentlemen friends. She's right down timid. She always makes a fuss if I introduce a gentleman. But I *do* introduce them—almost always. If I didn't introduce my gentlemen friends to mother," the young girl added, in her little soft, flat monotone, "I shouldn't think it was natural."

"To introduce me," said Winterbourne, "you must know my name." And he proceeded to pronounce it to her.

"Oh, dear, I can't say all that!" said his companion with a laugh. But by this time they had come up to Mrs. Miller, who, as they drew near, walked to the parapet of the garden and leaned upon it, looking intently at the lake, and turning her back to them. "Mother!" said the young girl, in a tone of decision. Upon this the elder lady turned round. "Mr. Winterbourne," said Miss Daisy Miller, introducing the young man very frankly and prettily. "Common," she was, as Mrs. Costello had pronounced her; yet it was a wonder to Winterbourne that, with her commonness, she had a singularly delicate grace.

Her mother was a small, spare, light person, with a wandering eye, a very exiguous nose, and a large forehead, decorated with a certain amount of thin, much-frizzled hair. Like her daughter, Mrs. Miller was dressed with extreme elegance; she had enormous diamonds in her ears. So far as Winterbourne could observe, she gave him no greeting —she certainly was not looking at him. Daisy was near her, pulling her shawl straight. "What are you doing, poking round here?" this young lady inquired, but by no means with that harshness of accent which her choice of words may imply.

"I don't know," said her mother, turning toward the lake again.

"I shouldn't think you'd want that shawl!" Daisy exclaimed.

"Well, I do!" her mother answered, with a little laugh.

"Did you get Randolph to go to bed?" asked the young girl.

"No; I couldn't induce him," said Mrs. Miller, very gently. "He wants to talk to the waiter. He likes to talk to that waiter."

"I was telling Mr. Winterbourne," the young girl went on; and to the young man's ear her tone might have indicated that she had been uttering his name all her life.

"Oh yes!" said Winterbourne; "I have the pleasure of knowing your son."

Randolph's mamma was silent; she turned her attention to the lake. But at last she spoke. "Well, I don't see how he lives!"

"Anyhow, it isn't so bad as it was at Dover," said Daisy Miller.

"And what occurred at Dover?" Winterbourne asked.

"He wouldn't go to bed at all. I guess he sat up all night in the public parlor. He wasn't in bed at twelve o'clock; I know that."

"It was half-past twelve," declared Mrs. Miller, with mild emphasis.

"Does he sleep much during the day?" Winterbourne demanded.

"I guess he doesn't sleep much," Daisy rejoined.

"I wish he would!" said her mother. "It seems as if he couldn't."

"I think he's real tiresome," Daisy pursued.

Then for some moments there was silence. "Well, Daisy Miller," said the elder lady, presently, "I shouldn't think you'd want to talk against your own brother!"

"Well, he *is* tiresome, mother," said Daisy, quite without the asperity of a retort.

"He's only nine," urged Mrs. Miller.

"Well, he wouldn't go to that castle," said the young girl. "I'm going there with Mr. Winterbourne."

To this announcement, very placidly made, Daisy's mamma offered no response. Winterbourne took for granted that she deeply disapproved of the projected excursion; but he said to himself that she was a simple, easily-managed person, and that a few deferential protestations would take the edge from her displeasure. "Yes," he began; "your daughter has kindly allowed me the honor of being her guide."

Mrs. Miller's wandering eyes attached themselves, with a sort of appealing air, to Daisy, who, however, strolled a few steps farther, gently humming to herself. "I presume you will go in the cars," said her mother.

"Yes, or in the boat," said Winterbourne.

"Well, of course, I don't know," Mrs. Miller rejoined. "I have never been to that castle."

"It is a pity you shouldn't go," said Winterbourne, beginning to feel reassured as to her opposition. And yet he was quite prepared to find that, as a matter of course, she meant to accompany her daughter.

"We've been thinking ever so much about going," she pursued; "but it seems as if we couldn't. Of course Daisy, she wants to go round. But there's a lady here—I don't know her name—she says she shouldn't

think we'd want to go to see castles *here;* she should think we'd want
to wait till we got to Italy. It seems as if there would be so many there,"
continued Mrs. Miller, with an air of increasing confidence. "Of course
we only want to see the principal ones. We visited several in England,"
she presently added.

"Ah, yes! in England there are beautiful castles," said Winterbourne.
"But Chillon, here, is very well worth seeing."

"Well, if Daisy feels up to it—" said Mrs. Miller, in a tone im-
pregnated with a sense of the magnitude of the enterprise. "It seems
as if there was nothing she wouldn't undertake."

"Oh, I think she'll enjoy it!" Winterbourne declared. And he desired more and more to make it a certainty that he was to have the
privilege of the tête-à-tête with the young lady, who was still strolling
along in front of them, softly vocalizing. "You are not disposed, madam," he inquired, "to undertake it yourself?"

Daisy's mother looked at him an instant askance, and then walked forward in silence. Then—"I guess she had better go alone," she said,
simply. Winterbourne observed to himself that this was a very different type of maternity from that of the vigilant matrons who massed
themselves in the fore-front of social intercourse in the dark old city
at the other end of the lake. But his meditations were interrupted by
hearing his name very distinctly pronounced by Mrs. Miller's unprotected daughter.

"Mr. Winterbourne!" murmured Daisy.

"Mademoiselle!" said the young man.

"Don't you want to take me out in a boat?"

"At present?" he asked.

"Of course!" said Daisy.

"Well, Annie Miller!" exclaimed her mother.

"I beg you, madam, to let her go," said Winterbourne, ardently;
for he had never yet enjoyed the sensation of guiding through the
summer starlight a skiff freighted with a fresh and beautiful young
girl.

"I shouldn't think she'd want to," said her mother. "I should think
she'd rather go indoors."

"I'm sure Mr. Winterbourne wants to take me," Daisy declared.
"He's so awfully devoted!"

"I will row you over to Chillon in the starlight."

"I don't believe it!" said Daisy.

"Well!" ejaculated the elder lady again.

"You haven't spoken to me for half an hour," her daughter went
on.

"I have been having some very pleasant conversation with your
mother," said Winterbourne.

"Well, I want you to take me out in a boat!" Daisy repeated. They had all stopped, and she had turned round and was looking at Winterbourne. Her face wore a charming smile, her pretty eyes were gleaming, she was swinging her great fan about. No; it's impossible to be prettier than that, thought Winterbourne.

"There are half a dozen boats moored at the landing-place," he said, pointing to certain steps which descended from the garden to the lake. "If you will do me the honor to accept my arm, we will go and select one of them."

Daisy stood there smiling; she threw back her head and gave a little light laugh. "I like a gentleman to be formal!" she declared.

"I assure you it's a formal offer."

"I was bound I would make you say something," Daisy went on.

"You see, it's not very difficult," said Winterbourne. "But I am afraid you are chaffing me."

"I think not, sir," remarked Mrs. Miller, very gently.

"Do, then, let me give you a row," he said to the young girl.

"It's quite lovely, the way you say that!" cried Daisy.

"It will be still more lovely to do it."

"Yes, it would be lovely!" said Daisy. But she made no movement to accompany him; she only stood there laughing.

"I should think you had better find out what time it is," interposed her mother.

"It is eleven o'clock, madam," said a voice, with a foreign accent, out of the neighboring darkness; and Winterbourne, turning, perceived the florid personage who was in attendance upon the two ladies. He had apparently just approached.

"Oh, Eugenio," said Daisy, "I am going out in a boat!"

Eugenio bowed. "At eleven o'clock, mademoiselle?"

"I am going with Mr. Winterbourne—this very minute."

"Do tell her she can't," said Mrs. Miller to the courier.

"I think you had better not go out in a boat, mademoiselle," Eugenio declared.

Winterbourne wished to Heaven this pretty girl were not so familiar with her courier; but he said nothing.

"I suppose you don't think it's proper!" Daisy exclaimed. "Eugenio doesn't think anything's proper."

"I am at your service," said Winterbourne.

"Does mademoiselle propose to go alone?" asked Eugenio of Mrs. Miller.

"Oh, no; with this gentleman!" answered Daisy's mamma.

The courier looked for a moment at Winterbourne—the latter thought he was smiling—and then, solemnly, with a bow, "As mademoiselle pleases!" he said.

"Oh, I hoped you would make a fuss!" said Daisy. "I don't care to go now."

"I myself shall make a fuss if you don't go," said Winterbourne.

"That's all I want—a little fuss!" And the young girl began to laugh again.

"Mr. Randolph has gone to bed!" the courier announced, frigidly.

"Oh, Daisy; now we can go!" said Mrs. Miller.

Daisy turned away from Winterbourne, looking at him, smiling, and fanning herself. "Good-night," she said; "I hope you are disappointed, or disgusted, or something!"

He looked at her, taking the hand she offered him. "I am puzzled," he answered.

"Well, I hope it won't keep you awake!" she said, very smartly; and, under the escort of the privileged Eugenio, the two ladies passed towards the house.

Winterbourne stood looking after them; he was indeed puzzled. He lingered beside the lake for a quarter of an hour, turning over the mystery of the young girl's sudden familiarities and caprices. But the only very definite conclusion he came to was that he should enjoy deucedly "going off" with her somewhere.

Two days afterwards he went off with her to the Castle of Chillon. He waited for her in the large hall of the hotel, where the couriers, the servants, the foreign tourists, were lounging about and staring. It was not the place he should have chosen, but she had appointed it. She came tripping down-stairs, buttoning her long gloves, squeezing her folded parasol against her pretty figure, dressed in the perfection of a soberly elegant travelling costume. Winterbourne was a man of imagination and, as our ancestors used to say, sensibility; as he looked at her dress and—on the great staircase—her little rapid, confiding step, he felt as if there were something romantic going forward. He could have believed he was going to elope with her. He passed out with her among all the idle people that assembled there; they were all looking at her very hard; she had begun to chatter as soon as she joined him. Winterbourne's preference had been that they should be conveyed to Chillon in a carriage; but she expressed a lively wish to go in the little steamer; she declared that she had a passion for steamboats. There was always such a lovely breeze upon the water, and you saw such lots of people. The sail was not long, but Winterbourne's companion found time to say a great many things. To the young man himself their little excursion was so much of an escapade—an adventure —that, even allowing for her habitual sense of freedom, he had some expectation of seeing her regard it in the same way. But it must be confessed that, in this particular, he was disappointed. Daisy Miller was extremely animated, she was in charming spirits; but she was apparently not at all excited; she was not fluttered; she avoided neither his eyes nor those of any one else; she blushed neither when she looked at him nor when she felt that people were looking at her. People continued to look at her a great deal, and Winterbourne took much satisfaction in his pretty companion's distinguished air. He had been a little afraid that she would talk loud, laugh overmuch, and even, perhaps, desire to move about the boat a good deal. But he quite forgot his fears; he sat smiling, with his eyes upon her face, while, without moving from her place, she delivered herself of a great number of original reflections. It was the most charming garrulity he had ever heard. He had assented to the idea that she was "common"; but was she so, after all, or was he simply getting used to her commonness? Her conversation was chiefly of what metaphysicians term the objective cast; but every now and then it took a subjective turn.

"What on *earth* are you so grave about?" she suddenly demanded, fixing her agreeable eyes upon Winterbourne's.

"Am I grave?" he asked. "I had an idea I was grinning from ear to ear."

"You look as if you were taking me to a funeral. If that's a grin, your ears are very near together."

"Should you like me to dance a hornpipe on the deck?"

"Pray do, and I'll carry round your hat. It will pay the expenses of our journey."

"I never was better pleased in my life," murmured Winterbourne.

She looked at him a moment, and then burst into a little laugh. "I like to make you say those things! You're a queer mixture!"

In the castle, after they had landed, the subjective element decidedly prevailed. Daisy tripped about the vaulted chambers, rustled her skirts in the corkscrew staircases, flirted back with a pretty little cry and a shudder from the edge of the *oubliettes*, and turned a singularly well-shaped ear to everything that Winterbourne told her about the place. But he saw that she cared very little for feudal antiquities, and that the dusky traditions of Chillon made but a slight impression upon her. They had the good-fortune to have been able to walk about without other companionship than that of the custodian; and Winterbourne arranged with this functionary—that they should not be hurried—that they should linger and pause wherever they chose. The custodian interpreted the bargain generously—Winterbourne, on his side, had been generous—and ended by leaving them quite to themselves. Miss Miller's observations were not remarkable for logical consistency; for anything she wanted to say she was sure to find a pretext. She found a great many pretexts in the rugged embrasures of Chillon for asking Winterbourne sudden questions about himself—his family, his previous history, his tastes, his habits, his intentions—and for supplying information upon corresponding points in her own personality. Of her own tastes, habits, and intentions Miss Miller was prepared to give the most definite, and, indeed, the most favorable account.

"Well, I hope you know enough!" she said to her companion, after he had told her the history of the unhappy Bonnivard. "I never saw a man that knew so much!" The history of Bonnivard had evidently, as they say, gone into one ear and out of the other. But Daisy went on to say that she wished Winterbourne would travel with them, and "go round" with them; they might know something, in that case. "Don't you want to come and teach Randolph?" she asked. Winterbourne said that nothing could possibly please him so much, but that he had unfortunately other occupations. "Other occupations? I don't believe it!" said Miss Daisy. "What do you mean? You are not in business." The young man admitted that he was not in business; but he had engagements which, even within a day or two, would force him to go back to Geneva. "Oh, bother!" she said; "I don't believe it!" and she began to talk about something else. But a few moments later, when he was pointing out to her the pretty design of an antique fireplace, she broke out irrelevantly, "You don't mean to say you are going back to Geneva?"

"It is a melancholy fact that I shall have to return tomorrow."

"Well, Mr. Winterbourne," said Daisy, "I think you're horrid!"

"Oh, don't say such dreadful things!" said Winterbourne—"just at the last!"

"The last!" cried the young girl; "I call it the first. I have half a mind to leave you here and go straight back to the hotel alone." And for the next ten minutes she did nothing but call him horrid. Poor Winterbourne was fairly bewildered; no young lady had as yet done him the honor to be so agitated by the announcement of his movements. His companion, after this, ceased to pay any attention to the curiosities of Chillon or the beauties of the lake; she opened fire upon the mysterious charmer of Geneva, whom she appeared to have instantly taken it for granted that he was hurrying back to see. How did Miss Daisy Miller know that there was a charmer in Geneva? Winterbourne, who denied the existence of such a person, was quite unable to discover; and he was divided between amazement at the rapidity of her induction and amusement at the frankness of her *persiflage*. She seemed to him, in all this, an extraordinary mixture of innocence and crudity. "Does she never allow you more than three days at a time?" asked Daisy, ironically. "Doesn't she give you a vacation in summer? There is no one so hard worked but they can get leave to go off somewhere at this season. I suppose, if you stay another day, she'll come after you in the boat. Do wait over till Friday, and I will go down to the landing to see her arrive!" Winterbourne began to think he had been wrong to feel disappointed in the temper in which the young lady had embarked. If he had missed the personal accent, the personal accent was now making its appearance. It sounded very distinctly, at last, in her telling him she would stop "teasing" him if he would promise her solemnly to come down to Rome in the winter.

"That's not a difficult promise to make," said Winterbourne. "My aunt has taken an apartment in Rome for the winter, and has already asked me to come and see her."

"I don't want you to come for your aunt," said Daisy; "I want you to come for me." And this was the only allusion that the young man was ever to hear her make to his invidious kinswoman. He declared that, at any rate, he would certainly come. After this Daisy stopped teasing. Winterbourne took a carriage, and they drove back to Vevay in the dusk. The young girl was very quiet.

In the evening Winterbourne mentioned to Mrs. Costello that he had spent the afternoon at Chillon with Miss Daisy Miller.

"The Americans—of the courier?" asked this lady.

"Ah, happily," said Winterbourne, "the courier stayed at home."

"She went with you all alone?"

"All alone."

Mrs. Costello sniffed a little at her smelling-bottle. "And that," she exclaimed, "is the young person whom you wanted me to know!"

2

Rome

Winterbourne, who had returned to Geneva the day after his excursion to Chillon, went to Rome towards the end of January. His aunt had been established there for several weeks, and he had received a couple of letters from her. "Those people you were so devoted to last summer at Vevay have turned up here, courier and all," she wrote. "They seem to have made several acquaintances, but the courier continues to be the most *intime*. The young lady, however, is also very intimate with some third-rate Italians, with whom she rackets about in a way that makes much talk. Bring me that pretty novel of Cherbuliez's—*Paule Méré*—and don't come later than the 23rd."

In the natural course of events, Winterbourne, on arriving in Rome, would presently have ascertained Mrs. Miller's address at the American banker's, and have gone to pay his compliments to Miss Daisy. "After what happened at Vevay, I think I may certainly call upon them," he said to Mrs. Costello.

"If, after what happens—at Vevay and everywhere—you desire to keep up the acquaintance, you are very welcome. Of course a man may know every one. Men are welcome to the privilege!"

"Pray, what is it that happens—here, for instance?" Winterbourne demanded.

"The girl goes about alone with her foreigners. As to what happens further, you must apply elsewhere for information. She has picked up half a dozen of the regular Roman fortune-hunters, and she takes them about to people's houses. When she comes to a party she brings with her a gentleman with a good deal of manner and a wonderful mustache."

"And where is the mother?"

"I haven't the least idea. They are very dreadful people."

Winterbourne meditated a moment. "They are very ignorant—very innocent only. Depend upon it they are not bad."

"They are hopelessly vulgar," said Mrs. Costello. "Whether or no being hopelessly vulgar is being 'bad' is a question for the metaphysicians. They are bad enough to dislike, at any rate; and for this short life that is quite enough."

The news that Daisy Miller was surrounded by half a dozen wonderful mustaches checked Winterbourne's impulse to go straightway to see her. He had, perhaps, not definitely flattered himself that he had made an ineffaceable impression upon her heart, but he was annoyed at hearing of a state of affairs so little in harmony with an image that had lately flitted in and out of his own meditations; the image of a very pretty girl looking out of an old Roman window and asking herself urgently when Mr. Winterbourne would arrive. If, however, he determined to wait a little before reminding Miss Miller of his claims to her consideration, he went very soon to call upon two or three other friends. One of these friends was an American lady who had spent several winters at Geneva, where she had placed her children at school. She was a very accomplished woman, and she lived in the Via Gregoriana. Winterbourne found her in a little crimson drawing-room on a third floor; the room was filled with southern sunshine. He had not been there ten minutes when the servant came in, announcing "Madame Mila!" This announcement was presently followed by the entrance of little Randolph Miller, who stopped in the middle of the room and stood staring at Winterbourne. An instant later his pretty sister crossed the threshold; and then, after a considerable interval, Mrs. Miller slowly advanced.

"I know you!" said Randolph.

"I'm sure you know a great many things," exclaimed Winterbourne, taking him by the hand. "How is your education coming on?"

Daisy was exchanging greetings very prettily with her hostess; but when she heard Winterbourne's voice she quickly turned her head. "Well, I declare!" she said.

"I told you I should come, you know," Winterbourne rejoined, smiling.

"Well, I didn't believe it," said Miss Daisy.

"I am much obliged to you," laughed the young man.

"You might have come to see me!" said Daisy.

"I arrived only yesterday."

"I don't believe that!" the young girl declared.

Winterbourne turned with a protesting smile to her mother; but this lady evaded his glance, and, seating herself, fixed her eyes upon her son. "We've got a bigger place than this," said Randolph. "It's all gold on the walls."

Mrs. Miller turned uneasily in her chair. "I told you if I were to bring you, you would say something!" she murmured.

"I told *you!*" Randolph exclaimed. "I tell *you,* sir!" he added, jocosely, giving Winterbourne a thump on the knee. "It *is* bigger, too!"

Daisy had entered upon a lively conversation with her hostess, and Winterbourne judged it becoming to address a few words to her mother. "I hope you have been well since we parted at Vevay," he said.

Mrs. Miller now certainly looked at him—at his chin. "Not very well, sir," she answered.

"She's got the dyspepsia," said Randolph. "I've got it, too. Father's got it. I've got it most!"

This announcement, instead of embarrassing Mrs. Miller, seemed to relieve her. "I suffer from the liver," she said. "I think it's this climate; it's less bracing than Schenectady, especially in the winter season. I don't know whether you know we reside at Schenectady. I was saying to Daisy that I certainly hadn't found any one like Dr. Davis, and I didn't believe I should. Oh, at Schenectady he stands first; they think everything of him. He has so much to do, and yet there was nothing he wouldn't do for me. He said he never saw anything like my dyspepsia, but he was bound to cure it. I'm sure there was nothing he wouldn't try. He was just going to try something new when we came off. Mr. Miller wanted Daisy to see Europe for herself. But I wrote to Mr. Miller that it seems as if I couldn't get on without Dr. Davis. At Schenectady he stands at the very top; and there's a great deal of sickness there, too. It affects my sleep."

Winterbourne had a good deal of pathological gossip with Dr. Davis's patient, during which Daisy chatted unremittingly to her own companion. The young man asked Mrs. Miller how she was pleased with Rome. "Well, I must say I am disappointed," she answered. "We had heard so much about it; I suppose we had heard too much. But we couldn't help that. We had been led to expect something different."

"Ah, wait a little, and you will become very fond of it," said Winterbourne.

"I hate it worse and worse every day!" cried Randolph.

"You are like the infant Hannibal," said Winterbourne.

"No, I ain't!" Randolph declared, at a venture.

"You are not much like an infant," said his mother. "But we have seen places," she resumed, "that I should put a long way before Rome." And in reply to Winterbourne's interrogation, "There's Zürich," she concluded, "I think Zürich is lovely; and we hadn't heard half so much about it."

"The best place we've seen is the City of Richmond" said Randolph.

"He means the ship," his mother explained. "We crossed in that ship. Randolph had a good time on the *City of Richmond."*

"It's the best place I've seen," the child repeated. "Only it was turned the wrong way."

"Well, we've got to turn the right way some time," said Mrs. Miller, with a little laugh. Winterbourne expressed the hope that her daughter at least found some gratification in Rome, and she declared that Daisy was quite carried away. "It's on account of the society—the society's splendid. She goes round everywhere; she has made a great number of acquaintances. Of course she goes round more than I do. I must say they have been very sociable; they have taken her right in. And then she knows a great many gentlemen. Oh, she thinks there's nothing like Rome. Of course, it's a great deal pleasanter for a young lady if she knows plenty of gentlemen."

By this time Daisy had turned her attention again to Winterbourne. "I've been telling Mrs. Walker how mean you were!" the young girl announced.

"And what is the evidence you have offered?" asked Winterbourne, rather annoyed at Miss Miller's want of appreciation of the zeal of an admirer who on his way down to Rome had stopped neither at Bologna nor at Florence, simply because of a certain sentimental impatience. He remembered that a cynical compatriot had once told him that American women—the pretty ones, and this gave a largeness to the axiom— were at once the most exacting in the world and the least endowed with a sense of indebtedness.

"Why, you were awfully mean at Vevay," said Dasiy. 'You wouldn't do anything. You wouldn't stay there when I asked you."

"My dearest young lady," cried Winterbourne, with eloquence, "have I come all the way to Rome to encounter your reproaches?"

"Just hear him say that!" said Daisy to her hostess, giving a twist to a bow on this lady's dress. "Did you ever hear anything so quaint?"

"So quaint, my dear?" murmured Mrs. Walker, in the tone of a partisan of Winterbourne.

"Well, I don't know," said Daisy, fingering Mrs. Walker's ribbons. "Mrs. Walker, I want to tell you something."

"Mother-r," interposed Randolph, with his rough ends to his words, "I tell you you've got to go. Eugenio'll raise—something!"

"I'm not afraid of Eugenio," said Daisy, with a toss of her head. "Look here, Mrs. Walker," she went on, "you know I'm coming to your party."

"I am delighted to hear it."

"I've got a lovely dress!"

"I am very sure of that."

"But I want to ask a favor—permission to bring a friend."

"I shall be happy to see any of your friends," said Mrs. Walker, turning with a smile to Mrs. Miller.

"Oh, they are not my friends," answered Daisy's mamma, smiling shyly, in her own fashion. "I never spoke to them."

"It's an intimate friend of mine—Mr. Giovanelli," said Daisy, without a tremor in her clear little voice, or a shadow on her brilliant little face.

Mrs. Walker was silent a moment; she gave a rapid glance at Winterbourne. "I shall be glad to see Mr. Giovanelli," she then said.

"He's an Italian," Daisy pursued with the prettiest serenity. "He's a great friend of mine; he's the handsomest man in the world—except Mr. Winterbourne! He knows plenty of Italians, but he wants to know some Americans. He thinks ever so much of Americans. He's tremendously clever. He's perfectly lovely!"

It was settled that this brilliant personage should be brought to Mrs. Walker's party, and then Mrs. Miller prepared to take her leave. "I guess we'll go back to the hotel," she said.

"You may go back to the hotel, mother, but I'm going to take a walk," said Daisy.

"She's going to walk with Mr. Giovanelli," Randolph proclaimed.

"I am going to the Pincio," said Daisy, smiling.

"Alone, my dear—at this hour?" Mrs. Walker asked. The afternoon was drawing to a close—it was the hour for the throng of carriages and of contemplative pedestrians. "I don't think it's safe, my dear," said Mrs. Walker.

"Neither do I," subjoined Mrs. Miller. "You'll get the fever, as sure as you live. Remember what Dr. Davis told you!"

"Give her some medicine before she goes," said Randolph.

The company had risen to its feet; Daisy, still showing her pretty teeth, bent over and kissed her hostess. "Mrs. Walker, you are too perfect," she said. "I'm not going alone; I am going to meet a friend."

"Your friend won't keep you from getting the fever," Mrs. Miller observed.

"Is it Mr. Giovanelli?" asked the hostess.

Winterbourne was watching the young girl; at this question his attention quickened. She stood there smiling and smoothing her bonnet ribbons; she glanced at Winterbourne. Then, while she glanced and smiled, she answered, without a shade of hesitation, "Mr. Giovanelli—the beautiful Giovanelli."

"My dear young friend," said Mrs. Walker, taking her hand, pleadingly, "don't walk off to the Pincio at this unhealthy hour to meet a beautiful Italian."

"Well, he speaks English," said Mrs. Miller.

"Gracious me!" Daisy exclaimed, "I don't want to do anything improper. There's an easy way to settle it." She continued to glance at Winterbourne. "The Pincio is only a hundred yards distant; and if Mr. Winterbourne were as polite as he pretends, he would offer to walk with me!"

Winterbourne's politeness hastened to affirm itself, and the young girl gave him gracious leave to accompany her. They passed down-stairs before her mother, and at the door Winterbourne perceived Mrs. Miller's carriage drawn up, with the ornamental courier whose acquaintance he had made at Vevay, seated within. "Good-bye, Eugenio!" cried Daisy; "I'm going to take a walk." The distance from the Via Gregoriana to the other end of the Pincian Hill is, in fact, rapidly traversed. As the day was splendid, however, and the concourse of vehicles, walkers, and loungers numerous, the young Americans found their progress much delayed. This fact was highly agreeable to Winterbourne, in spite of his consciousness of his singular situation. The slow-moving, idly-gazing Roman crowd bestowed much attention upon the extremely pretty young foreign lady who was passing through it upon his arm; and he wondered what on earth had been in Daisy's mind when she proposed to expose herself, unattended, to its appreciation. His own mission, to her sense, apparently, was to consign her to the hands of Mr. Giovanelli; but Winterbourne, at once annoyed and gratified, resolved that he would do no such thing.

"Why haven't you been to see me?" asked Daisy. "You can't get out of that."

"I have had the honor of telling you that I have only just stepped out of the train."

"You must have stayed in the train a good while after it stopped!" cried the young girl, with her little laugh. "I suppose you were asleep. You have had time to go to see Mrs. Walker."

"I knew Mrs. Walker—" Winterbourne began to explain.

"I know where you knew her. You knew her at Geneva. She told me so. Well, you knew me at Vevay. That's just as good. So you ought to have come." She asked him no other questions than this; she began to prattle about her own affairs. "We've got splendid rooms at the hotel; Eugenio says they're the best rooms in Rome. We are going to stay all winter, if we don't die of the fever; and I guess we'll stay then. It's a great deal nicer than I thought; I thought it would be fearfully quiet; I was sure it would be awfully poky. I was sure we should be going round all the time with one of those dreadful old men that explain about the pictures and things. But we only had about a week of that, and now I'm enjoying myself. I know ever so many people, and they are all so charming. The society's extremely select. There are all kinds—English and Germans and Italians. I think I like the English best. I like their style of conversation. But there are some lovely Americans. I never saw anything so hospitable. There's something or other every day. There's not much dancing; but I must say I never thought dancing was everything. I was always fond of conversation. I guess I shall have plenty at Mrs. Walker's, her rooms are so small." When they had passed the gate of the Pincian Gardens, Miss Miller began to wonder where Mr. Giovanelli might be. "We had better go straight to that place in front," she said, "where you look at the view."

"I certainly shall not help you to find him," Winterbourne declared.

"Then I shall find him without you," said Miss Daisy.

She burst into her little laugh. "Are you afraid you'll get lost—or run over? But there's Giovanelli, leaning against that tree. He's staring at the women in the carriages; did you ever see anything so cool?"

Winterbourne perceived at some distance a little man standing with folded arms nursing his cane. He had a handsome face, an artfully poised hat, a glass in one eye, and a nosegay in his buttonhole. Winterbourne looked at him a moment, and then said, "Do you mean to speak to that man?"

"Do I mean to speak to him? Why, you don't suppose I mean to communicate by signs?"

"Pray understand, then," said Winterbourne, "that I intend to remain with you."

Daisy stopped and looked at him, without a sign of troubled consciousness in her face; with nothing but the presence of her charming eyes and her happy dimples. "Well, she's a cool one!" thought the young man.

"I don't like the way you say that," said Daisy. "It's too imperious."

"I beg your pardon if I say it wrong. The main point is to give you an idea of my meaning."

The young girl looked at him more gravely, but with eyes that were prettier than ever. "I have never allowed a gentleman to dictate to me, or to interfere with anything I do."

"I think you have made a mistake," said Winterbourne. "You should sometimes listen to a gentleman—the right one."

Daisy began to laugh again. "I do nothing but listen to gentlemen!" she exclaimed. "Tell me if Mr. Giovanelli is the right one."

The gentleman with the nosegay in his bosom had now perceived our two friends, and was approaching the young girl with obsequious rapidity. He bowed to Winterbourne as well as to the latter's companion; he had a brilliant smile, an intelligent eye; Winterbourne thought him not a bad-looking fellow. But he nevertheless said to Daisy, "No, he's not the right one."

Daisy evidently had a natural talent for performing introductions; she mentioned the name of each of her companions to the other. She strolled along with one of them on each side of her; Mr. Giovanelli, who spoke English very cleverly—Winterbourne afterwards learned that he had practised the idiom upon a great many American heiresses—addressed to her a great deal of very polite nonsense; he was extremely urbane, and the young American, who said nothing, reflected upon that profundity of Italian cleverness which enables people to appear more gracious in proportion as they are more acutely disappointed. Giovanelli, of course, had counted upon something more intimate; he had not bargained for a party of three. But he kept his temper in a manner which suggested far-stretching intentions. Winterbourne flattered himself that he had taken his measure. "He is not a gentleman," said the young American; "he is only a clever imitation of one. He is a music-master, or a penny-a-liner, or a third-rate artist. D—n his good looks!" Mr. Giovanelli had certainly a very pretty face; but Winterbourne felt a superior indignation at his own lovely fellow-countrywoman's not knowing the difference between a spurious gentleman and a real one. Giovanelli chattered and jested, and made himself wonderfully agreeable. It was true that, if he was an imitation, the imitation was brilliant. "Nevertheless," Winterbourne said to himself, "a nice girl ought to know!" And then he came back to the question whether this was, in fact, a nice girl. Would a nice girl, even allowing for her being a little American flirt, make a rendezvous with a presumably low-lived foreigner? The rendezvous in this case, indeed, had been in broad daylight, and in the most crowded corner of Rome; but was it not impossible to regard the choice of these circumstances as a proof of extreme cynicism? Singular though it may seem, Winterbourne was vexed that the young girl, in joining her *amoroso,* should not appear more impatient of his own company, and he was vexed because of his inclination. It was impossible to regard her as a perfectly well-conducted young lady; she was wanting in a certain indispensable delicacy. It would therefore simplify matters greatly to be able to treat her as the object of one of those sentiments which are called by romancers "lawless passions." That she should seem to wish to get rid of him would help him to think more lightly of her, and to be able to think more lightly of her would make her much less perplexing. But Daisy, on this occasion, continued to present herself as an inscrutable combination of audacity and innocence.

She had been walking some quarter of an hour, attended by her two cavaliers, and responding in a tone of very childish gayety, as it seemed to Winterbourne, to the pretty speeches of Mr. Giovanelli, when a carriage that had detached itself from the revolving train drew up beside the path. At the same moment Winterbourne perceived that his friend Mrs. Walker—the lady whose house he had lately left—was seated in the vehicle, and was beckoning to him. Leaving Miss Miller's side, he hastened to obey her summons. Mrs. Walker was flushed; she wore an excited air. "It is really too dreadful," she said. "That girl must not do this sort of thing. She must not walk here with you two men. Fifty people have noticed her."

Winterbourne raised his eyebrows. "I think it's a pity to make too much fuss about it."

"It's a pity to let the girl ruin herself."

"She is very innocent," said Winterbourne.

"She's very crazy!" cried Mrs. Walker. "Did you ever see anything so imbecile as her mother? After you had all left me just now I could not sit still for thinking of it. It seemed too pitiful not even to attempt to save her. I ordered the carriage and put on my bonnet, and came here as quickly as possible. Thank Heaven I have found you!"

"What do you propose to do with us?" asked Winterbourne, smiling.

"To ask her to get in, to drive her about here for half an hour, so that the world may see that she is not running absolutely wild, and then to take her safely home."

"I don't think it's a very happy thought," said Winterbourne; "but you can try."

Mrs. Walker tried. The young man went in pursuit of Miss Miller, who had simply nodded and smiled at his interlocutor in the carriage, and had gone her way with her companion. Daisy, on learning that Mrs. Walker wished to speak to her, retracted her steps with a perfect good grace and with Mr. Giovanelli at her side. She declared that she was delighted to have a chance to present this gentleman to Mrs. Walker. She immediately achieved the introduction, and declared that she had never in her life seen anything so lovely as Mrs. Walker's carriage-rug.

"I am glad you admire it," said this lady, smiling sweetly. "Will you get in and let me put it over you?"

"Oh no, thank you," said Daisy. "I shall admire it much more as I see you driving round with it."

"Do get in and drive with me!" said Mrs. Walker.

"That would be charming, but it's so enchanting just as I am!" and Daisy gave a brilliant glance at the gentlemen on either side of her.

"It may be enchanting, dear child, but it is not the custom here," urged Mrs. Walker, leaning forward in her victoria, with her hands devoutly clasped.

"Well, it ought to be, then!" said Daisy. "If I didn't walk I should expire."

"You should walk with your mother, dear," cried the lady from Geneva, losing patience.

"With my mother, dear!" exclaimed the young girl. Winterbourne saw that she scented interference. "My mother never walked ten steps in her life. And then, you know," she added, with a laugh, "I am more than five years old."

"You are old enough to be more reasonable. You are old enough, dear Miss Miller, to be talked about."

Daisy looked at Mrs. Walker, smiling intensely. "Talked about? What do you mean?"

"Come into my carriage, and I will tell you."

Daisy turned her quickened glance again from one of the gentlemen beside her to the other. Mr. Giovanelli was bowing to and fro, rubbing down his gloves and laughing very agreeably; Winterbourne thought it a most unpleasant scene. "I don't think I want to know what you mean," said Daisy, presently. "I don't think I should like it."

Winterbourne wished that Mrs. Walker would tuck in her carriage-rug and drive away; but this lady did not enjoy being defied, as she afterwards told him. "Should you prefer being thought a very reckless girl?" she demanded.

"Gracious!" exclaimed Daisy. She looked again at Mr. Giovanelli, then she turned to Winterbourne. There was a little pink flush in her cheek; she was tremendously pretty. "Does Mr. Winterbourne think," she asked slowly, smiling, throwing back her head and glancing at him from head to foot, "that, to save my reputation, I ought to get into the carriage?"

Winterbourne colored; for an instant he hesitated greatly. It seemed so strange to hear her speak that way of her "reputation." But he himself, in fact, must speak in accordance with gallantry. The finest gallantry here was simply to tell her the truth, and the truth for Winterbourne—as the few indications I have been able to give have made him known to the reader—was that Daisy Miller should have taken Mrs. Walker's advice. He looked at her exquisite prettiness, and then said, very gently, "I think you should get into the carriage."

Daisy gave a violent laugh. "I never heard anything so stiff! If this is improper, Mrs. Walker," she pursued, "then I am all improper, and you must give me up. Good-bye; I hope you'll have a lovely ride!" and, with Mr. Giovanelli, who made a triumphantly obsequious salute, she turned away.

Mrs. Walker sat looking after her, and there were tears in Mrs. Walker's eyes. "Get in here, sir," she said to Winterbourne, indicating the place beside her. The young man answered that he felt bound to accompany Miss Miller; whereupon Mrs. Walker declared that if he refused her this favor she would never speak to him again. She was evidently in earnest. Winterbourne overtook Daisy and her companion, and, offering the young girl his hand, told her that Mrs. Walker had made an imperious claim upon his society. He expected that in answer she would say something rather free, something to commit herself still further to that "recklessness" from which Mrs. Walker had so charitably endeavored to dissuade her. But she only shook his hand, hardly looking at him; while Mr. Giovanelli bade him farewell with a too emphatic flourish of the hat.

Winterbourne was not in the best possible humor as he took his seat in Mrs. Walker's victoria. "That was not clever of you," he said, candidly, while the vehicle mingled again with the throng of carriages.

"In such a case," his companion answered, "I don't wish to be clever; I wish to be *earnest!*"

"Well, your earnestness has only offended her and put her off."

"It has happened very well," said Mrs. Walker. "If she is so perfectly determined to compromise herself, the sooner one knows it the better; one can act accordingly."

"I suspect she meant no harm," Winterbourne rejoined.

"So I thought a month ago. But she has been going too far."

"What has she been doing?"

"Everything that is not done here. Flirting with any man she could pick up; sitting in corners with mysterious Italians; dancing all the evening with the same partners; receiving visits at eleven o'clock at night. Her mother goes away when visitors come."

"But her brother," said Winterbourne, laughing, "sits up till midnight."

"He must be edified by what he sees. I'm told that at their hotel every one is talking about her, and that a smile goes round among all the servants when a gentleman comes and asks for Miss Miller."

"The servants be hanged!" said Winterbourne, angrily. "The poor girl's only fault," he presently added, "is that she is very uncultivated."

"She is naturally indelicate," Mrs. Walker declared. "Take that example this morning. How long had you know her at Vevay?"

"A couple of days."

"Fancy, then, her making it a personal matter that you should have left the place?"

Winterbourne was silent for some moments; then he said, "I suspect, Mrs. Walker, that you and I have lived too long at Geneva!" And he added a request that she should inform him with what particular design she had made him enter the carriage.

"I wished to beg you to cease your relations with Miss Miller—not to flirt with her—to give her no further opportunity to expose herself—to let her alone, in short."

"I'm afraid I can't do that," said Winterbourne. "I like her extremely."

"All the more reason that you shouldn't help her to make a scandal."

"There shall be nothing scandalous in my attentions to her."

"There certainly will be in the way she takes them. But I have said what I had on my conscience," Mrs. Walker pursued. "If you wish to rejoin the young lady I will put you down. Here, by-the-way, you have a chance."

The carriage was traversing that part of the Pincian Garden that overhangs the wall of Rome and overlooks the beautiful Villa Borghese. It is bordered by a large parapet, near which there are several seats. One of the seats at a distance was occupied by a gentleman and a lady, towards which Mrs. Walker gave a toss of her head. At the same moment these persons rose and walked towards the parapet. Winterbourne had asked the coachman to stop; he now descended from the carriage. His companion looked at him a moment in silence; then, while he raised his hat, she drove majestically away. Winterbourne stood there; he had turned his eyes towards Daisy and her cavalier. They evidently saw no one; they were too deeply occupied with each other. When they reached the low garden-wall they stood a moment looking off at the great flat-topped pine-clusters of the Villa Borghese; then Giovanelli seated himself familiarly upon the broad ledge of the wall. The western sun in the opposite sky sent out a brilliant shaft through a couple of cloud-bars, whereupon Daisy's companion took her parasol out of her hands and opened it. She came a little nearer, and he held the parasol over her; then, still holding it, he let it rest upon her shoulder, so that both of their heads were hidden from Winterbourne. This young man lingered a moment, then he began to walk. But he walked—not towards the couple with the parasol—towards the residence of his aunt, Mrs. Costello.

He flattered himself on the following day that there was no smiling among the servants when he, at least, asked for Mrs. Miller at her hotel. This lady and her daughter, however, were not at home; and on the next day after, repeating his visit, Winterbourne again had the misfortune not to find them. Mrs. Walker's party took place on the evening of the third day, and, in spite of the frigidity of his last interview with the hostess, Winterbourne was among the guests. Mrs. Walker was one of those American ladies who, while residing abroad, make a point, in their own phrase, of studying European society; and she had on this occasion collected several specimens of her diversely-born fellow-mortals to serve, as it were, as text-books. When Winterbourne arrived, Daisy Miller was not there, but in a few moments he saw her mother come in alone, very shyly and ruefully. Mrs. Miller's hair above her exposed-looking temples was more frizzled than ever. As she approached Mrs. Walker, Winterbourne also drew near.

"You see I've come all alone," said poor Mrs. Miller. "I'm so frightened I don't know what to do. It's the first time I've ever been to a party alone, especially in this country. I wanted to bring Randolph, or Eugenio, or some one, but Daisy just pushed me off by myself. I ain't used to going round alone."

"And does not your daughter intend to favor us with her society?" demanded Mrs. Walker, impressively.

"Well, Daisy's all dressed," said Mrs. Miller, with that accent of the dispassionate, if not of the philosophic, historian with which she always recorded incidents of her daughter's career. "She got dressed on purpose before dinner. But she's got a friend of hers there; that gentleman—the Italian—that she wanted to bring. They've got going at the piano; it seems as if they couldn't leave off. Mr. Giovanelli sings splendidly. But I guess they'll come before very long," concluded Mrs. Miller, hopefully.

"I'm sorry she should come in that way," said Mrs. Walker.

"Well, I told her that there was no use in her getting dressed before dinner if she was going to wait three hours," responded Daisy's mamma. "I didn't see the use of her putting on such a dress as that to sit around with Mr. Giovanelli."

"This is most horrible!" said Mrs. Walker, turning away and addressing herself to Winterbourne. *"Elle s'affiche.* It's her revenge for my having ventured to remonstrate with her. When she comes I shall not speak to her."

Daisy came after eleven o'clock; but she was not, on such an occasion, a young lady to wait to be spoken to. She rustled forward in radiant loveliness, smiling and chattering, carrying a large bouquet, and attended by Mr. Giovanelli. Every one stopped talking, and turned and looked at her. She came straight to Mrs. Walker. "I'm afraid you thought I never was coming, so I sent mother off to tell you. I wanted to make Mr. Giovanelli practise some things before he came; you know he sings beautifully, and I want you to ask him to sing. This is Mr. Giovanelli; you know I introduced him to you; he's got the most lovely voice, and he knows the most charming set of songs. I made him go over them this evening on purpose; we had the greatest time at the hotel." Of all this Daisy delivered herself with the sweetest, brightest audibleness, looking now at her hostess and now round the room, while she gave a series of little pats round her shoulders to the edges of her dress. "Is there any one I know?" she asked.

"I think every one knows you!" said Mrs. Walker, pregnantly, and she gave a very cursory greeting to Mr. Giovanelli. This gentleman bore himself gallantly. He smiled and bowed, and showed his white teeth; he curled his mustaches and rolled his eyes, and performed all the proper functions of a handsome Italian at an evening party. He sang very prettily half a dozen songs, though Mrs. Walker afterwards declared that she had been quite unable to find out who asked him. It was apparently not Daisy who had given him his orders. Daisy sat at a distance from the piano; and though she had publicly, as it were, professed a high admiration for his singing, talked, not inaudibly, while it was going on.

"It's a pity these rooms are so small; we can't dance," she said to Winterbourne, as if she had seen him five minutes before.

"I am not sorry we can't dance," Winterbourne answered; "I don't dance."

"Of course you don't dance; you're too stiff," said Miss Daisy. "I hope you enjoyed your drive with Mrs. Walker."

"No, I didn't enjoy it; I preferred walking with you."

"We paired off; that was much better," said Daisy. "But did you ever hear anything so cool as Mrs. Walker's wanting me to get into her carriage and drop poor Mr. Giovanelli, and under the pretext that it was proper? People have different ideas! It would have been most unkind; he had been talking about that walk for ten days."

"He should not have talked about it at all," said Winterbourne; "he would never have proposed to a young lady of this country to walk about the streets with him."

"About the streets?" cried Daisy, with her pretty stare. "Where, then, would he have proposed to her to walk? The Pincio is not the streets, either; and I, thank goodness, am not a young lady of this country. The young ladies of this country have a dreadfully poky time of it, so far as I can learn; I don't see why I should change my habits for *them.*"

"I am afraid your habits are those of a flirt," said Winterbourne, gravely.

"Of course they are," she cried, giving him her little smiling stare again. "I'm a fearful, frightful flirt! Did you ever hear of a nice girl that was not? But I suppose you will tell me now that I am not a nice girl."

"You're a very nice girl; but I wish you would flirt with me, and me only," said Winterbourne.

"Ah! thank you—thank you very much; you are the last man I should think of flirting with. As I have had the pleasure of informing you, you are too stiff."

"You say that too often," said Winterbourne.

Daisy gave a delighted laugh. "If I could have the sweet hope of making you angry, I should say it again."

"Don't do that; when I am angry I'm stiffer than ever. But if you won't flirt with me, do cease, at least, to flirt with your friend at the piano; they don't understand that sort of thing here."

"I thought they understood nothing else!" exclaimed Daisy.

"Not in young unmarried women."

"It seems to me much more proper in young unmarried women than in old married ones," Daisy declared.

"Well," said Winterbourne, "when you deal with natives you must go by the custom of the place. Flirting is a purely American custom; it doesn't exist here. So when you show yourself in public with Mr. Giovanelli, and without your mother—"

"Gracious! poor mother!" interposed Daisy.

"Though you may be flirting, Mr. Giovanelli is not; he means something else."

"He isn't preaching, at any rate," said Daisy, with vivacity. "And if you want very much to know, we are too good friends for that; we are very intimate friends."

"Ah!" rejoined Winterbourne, "if you are in love with each other, it is another affair."

She had allowed him up to this point to talk so frankly that he had no expectation of shocking her by this ejaculation; but she immediately got up, blushing visibly, and leaving him to exclaim mentally that little American flirts were the queerest creatures in the world. "Mr. Giovanelli, at least," she said, giving her interlocutor a single glance, "never says such very disagreeable things to me."

Winterbourne was bewildered; he stood staring. Mr. Giovanelli had finished singing. He left the piano and came over to Daisy. "Won't you come into the other room and have some tea?" he asked, bending before her with his ornamental smile.

Daisy turned to Winterbourne, beginning to smile again. He was still more perplexed, for this inconsequent smile made nothing clear, though it seemed to prove, indeed, that she had a sweetness and softness that reverted instinctively to the pardon of offences. "It has never occurred to Mr. Winterbourne to offer me any tea," she said, with her little tormenting manner.

"I have offered you advice," Winterbourne rejoined.

"I prefer weak tea!" cried Daisy, and she went off with the brilliant Giovanelli. She sat with him in the adjoining room, in the embrasure of the window, for the rest of the evening. There was an interesting performance at the piano, but neither of these young people gave heed to it. When Daisy came to take leave of Mrs. Walker, this lady conscientiously repaired the weakness of which she had been guilty at the moment of the young girl's arrival. She turned her back straight upon Miss Miller, and left her to depart with what grace she might. Winterbourne was standing near the door; he saw it all. Daisy turned very pale, and looked at her mother; but Mrs. Miller was humbly unconscious of any violation of the usual social forms. She appeared, indeed, to have felt an incongruous impulse to draw attention to her own striking observance of them. "Good-night, Mrs. Walker," she said; "we've had a beautiful evening. You see, if I let Daisy come to parties without me, I don't want her to go away without me." Daisy turned away, looking with a pale, grave face at the circle near the door; Winterbourne saw that, for the first moment, she was too much shocked and puzzled even for indignation. He on his side was greatly touched.

"That was very cruel," he said to Mrs. Walker.

"She never enters my drawing-room again!" replied his hostess.

Since Winterbourne was not to meet her in Mrs. Walker's drawing-room, he went as often as possible to Mrs. Miller's hotel. The ladies were rarely at home; but when he found them the devoted Giovanelli was always present. Very often the brilliant little Roman was in the drawing-room with Daisy alone, Mrs. Miller being apparently constantly of the opinion that discretion is the better part of surveillance. Winterbourne noted, at first with surprise, that Daisy on these occasions was never embarrassed or annoyed by his own entrance; but he very presently began to feel that she had no more surprises for him; the unexpected in her behavior was the only thing to expect. She showed no displeasure at her tête-à-tête with Giovanelli being interrupted; she could chatter as freshly and freely with two gentlemen as with one; there was always, in her conversation, the same odd mixture of audacity and puerility. Winterbourne remarked to himself that if she was seriously interested in Giovanelli, it was very singular that she should not take more trouble to preserve the sanctity of their interviews; and he liked her the more for her innocent-looking indifference and her apparently inexhaustible good-humor. He could hardly have said why, but she seemed to him a girl who would never be jealous. At the risk of exciting a somewhat derisive smile on the reader's part, I may affirm that with regard to the women who had hitherto interested him, it very often seemed to Winterbourne among the possibilities that, given certain contingencies, he should be afraid—literally afraid—of these ladies; he had a pleasant sense that he should never be afraid of Daisy Miller. It must be added that this sentiment was not altogether flattering to Daisy; it was part of his conviction, or rather of his apprehension, that she would prove a very light young person.

But she was evidently very much interested in Giovanelli. She looked at him whenever he spoke; she was perpetually telling him to do this and to do that; she was constantly "chaffing" and abusing him. She appeared completely to have forgotten that Winterbourne had said anything to displease her at Mrs. Walker's little party. One Sunday afternoon, having gone to St. Peter's with his aunt, Winterbourne perceived Daisy strolling about the great church in company with the inevitable Giovanelli. Presently he pointed out the young girl and her cavalier to Mrs. Costello. This lady looked at them a moment through her eyeglass, and then she said,

"That's what makes you so pensive in these days, eh?"

"I had not the least idea I was pensive," said the young man.

"You are very much preoccupied; you are thinking of something."

"And what is it," he asked, "that you accuse me of thinking of?"

"Oh that young lady's—Miss Baker's, Miss Chandler's—what's her name?—Miss Miller's intrigue with that little barber's block."

"Do you call it an intrigue," Winterbourne asked—"an affair that goes on with such peculiar publicity?"

"That's their folly," said Mrs. Costello; "it's not their merit."

"No," rejoined Winterbourne, with something of that pensiveness to which his aunt had alluded. "I don't believe that there is anything to be called an intrigue."

"I have heard a dozen people speak of it; they say she is quite carried away by him."

"They're certainly very intimate," said Winterbourne.

Mrs. Costello inspected the young couple again with her optical instrument. "He is very handsome. One easily sees how it is. She thinks
him the most elegant man in the world—the finest gentleman. She has
never seen anything like him; he is better, even, than the courier. It
was the courier, probably, who introduced him; and if he succeeds in
marrying the young lady, the courier will come in for a magnificent
commission."

"I don't believe she thinks of marrying him," said Winterbourne,
"and I don't believe he hopes to marry her."

"You may be very sure she thinks of nothing. She goes on from day
to day, from hour to hour, as they did in the Golden Age. I can imagine
nothing more vulgar. And at the same time," added Mrs. Costello,
"depend upon it that she may tell you any moment that she is 'engaged.' "

"I think that is more than Giovanelli expects," said Winterbourne.

"Who is Giovanelli?"

"The little Italian. I have asked questions about him, and learned
something. He is apparently a perfectly respectable little man. I believe he is, in a small way, a *cavaliere avvocato*. But he doesn't move in
what are called the first circles. I think it is really not absolutely impossible that the courier introduced him. He is evidently immensely
charmed with Miss Miller. If she thinks him the finest gentleman in the
world, he, on his side, has never found himself in personal contact with
such splendor, such opulence, such expensiveness, as this young lady's.
And then she must seem to him wonderfully pretty and interesting. I
rather doubt that he dreams of marrying her. That must appear to him
too impossible a piece of luck. He has nothing but his handsome face
to offer, and there is a substantial Mr. Miller in that mysterious land
of dollars. Giovanelli knows that he hasn't a title to offer. If he were
only a count or a *marchese!* He must wonder at his luck, at the way they
have taken him up."

"He accounts for it by his handsome face, and thinks Miss Miller a
young lady *qui se passe ses fantaisies!*" said Mrs. Costello.

"It is very true," Winterbourne pursued, "that Daisy and her
mamma have not yet risen to that stage of—what shall I call it?—of culture, at which the idea of catching a count or a *marchese* begins. I believe that they are intellectually incapable of that conception."

"Ah! but the *avvocato* can't believe it," said Mrs. Costello.

Of the observation excited by Daisy's "intrigue," Winterbourne gathered that day at St. Peter's sufficient evidence. A dozen of the American colonists in Rome came to talk with Mrs. Costello, who sat on a little
portable stool at the base of one of the great pilasters. The vesper
service was going forward in splendid chants and organ-tones in the
adjacent choir, and meanwhile, between Mrs. Costello and her friends,
there was a great deal said about poor little Miss Miller's going really

"too far." Winterbourne was not pleased with what he heard; but when, coming out upon the great steps of the church, he saw Daisy, who had emerged before him, get into an open cab with her accomplice and roll away through the cynical streets of Rome, he could not deny to himself that she was going very far indeed. He felt very sorry for her—not exactly that he believed that she had completely lost her head, but because it was painful to hear so much that was pretty and undefended and natural assigned to a vulgar place among the categories of disorder. He made an attempt after this to give a hint to Mrs. Miller. He met one day in the Corso a friend, a tourist like himself, who had just come out of the Doria Palace, where he had been walking through the beautiful gallery. His friend talked for a moment about the superb portrait of Innocent X., by Velasquez, which hangs in one of the cabinets of the palace, and then said, "And in the same cabinet, by-the-way, I had the pleasure of contemplating a picture of a different kind—that pretty American girl whom you pointed out to me last week." In answer to Winterbourne's inquiries, his friend narrated that the pretty American girl—prettier than ever—was seated with a companion in the secluded nook in which the great papal portrait was enshrined.

"Who was her companion?" asked Winterbourne.

"A little Italian with a bouquet in his button-hole. The girl is delightfully pretty; but I thought I understood from you the other day that she was a young lady *du meilleur monde.*"

"So she is!" answered Winterbourne; and having assured himself that his informant had seen Daisy and her companion but five minutes before, he jumped into a cab and went to call on Mrs. Miller. She was at home; but she apologized to him for receiving him in Daisy's absence.

"She's gone out somewhere with Mr. Giovanelli," said Mrs. Miller. "She's always going round with Mr. Giovanelli."

"I have noticed that they are very intimate," Winterbourne observed.

"Oh, it seems as if they couldn't live without each other!" said Mrs. Miller. "Well, he's a real gentleman, anyhow. I keep telling Daisy she's engaged!"

"And what does Daisy say?"

"Oh, she says she isn't engaged. But she might as well be!" this impartial parent resumed; "she goes on as if she was. But I've made Mr. Giovanelli promise to tell me, if *she* doesn't. I should want to write to Mr. Miller about it—shouldn't you?"

Winterbourne replied that he certainly should; and the state of mind of Daisy's mamma struck him as so unprecedented in the annals of parental vigilance that he gave up as utterly irrelevant the attempt to place her upon her guard.

After this Daisy was never at home, and Winterbourne ceased to meet her at the house of their common acquaintances, because, as he perceived, these shrewd people had quite made up their minds that

she was going too far. They ceased to invite her; and they intimated that
they desired to express to observant Europeans the great truth that,
though Miss Daisy Miller was a young American lady, her behavior
was not representative—was regarded by her compatriots as abnormal.
Winterbourne wondered how she felt about all the cold shoulders that
were turned towards her, and sometimes it annoyed him to suspect that
she did not feel at all. He said to himself that she was too light and
childish, too uncultivated and unreasoning, too provincial, to have reflected upon her ostracism, or even to have perceived it. Then at other
moments he believed that she carried about in her elegant and irresponsible little organism a defiant, passionate, perfectly observant consciousness of the impression she produced. He asked himself whether Daisy's
defiance came from the consciousness of innocence, or from her being,
essentially, a young person of the reckless class. It must be admitted
that holding one's self to a belief in Daisy's "innocence" came to seem
to Winterbourne more and more a matter of fine-spun gallantry. As I
have already had occasion to relate, he was angry at finding himself reduced to chopping logic about this young lady; he was vexed at his
want of instinctive certitude as to how far her eccentricities were
generic, national, and how far they were personal. From either view of
them he had somehow missed her, and now it was too late. She was
"carried away" by Mr. Giovanelli.

A few days after his brief interview with her mother, he encountered her in that beautiful abode of flowering desolation known as the
Palace of the Caesars. The early Roman spring had filled the air with
bloom and perfume, and the rugged surface of the Palatine was muffled
with tender verdure. Daisy was strolling along the top of one of those
great mounds of ruin that are embanked with mossy marble and paved
with monumental inscriptions. It seemed to him that Rome had never
been so lovely as just then. He stood looking off at the enchanting harmony of line and color that remotely encircles the city, inhaling the
softly humid odors, and feeling the freshness of the year and the antiq-
uity of the place reaffirm themselves in mysterious interfusion. It
seemed to him, also, that Daisy had never looked so pretty; but this had
been an observation of his whenever he met her. Giovanelli was at
her side, and Giovanelli, too, wore an aspect of even unwonted brilliancy.

"Well," said Daisy, "I should think you would be lonesome!"

"Lonesome?" asked Winterbourne.

"You are always going round by yourself. Can't you get any one to
walk with you?"

"I am not so fortunate," said Winterbourne, "as your companion."

Giovanelli, from the first, had treated Winterbourne with distinguished politeness. He listened with a deferential air to his remarks;
he laughed punctiliously at his pleasantries; he seemed disposed to
testify to his belief that Winterbourne was a superior young man. He

carried himself in no degree like a jealous wooer; he had obviously a great deal of tact; he had no objection to your expecting a little humility of him. It even seemed to Winterbourne at times that Giovanelli would find a certain mental relief in being able to have a private understanding with him—to say to him, as an intelligent man, that, bless you, he knew how extraordinary was this young lady, and didn't flatter himself with delusive—or, at least, *too* delusive—hopes of matrimony and dollars. On this occasion he strolled away from his companion to pluck a sprig of almond-blossom, which he carefully arranged in his button-hole.

"I know why you say that," said Daisy, watching Giovanelli. "Because you think I go round too much with *him*." And she nodded at her attendant.

"Every one thinks so—if you care to know," said Winterbourne.

"Of course I care to know!" Daisy exclaimed, seriously. "But I don't believe it. They are only pretending to be shocked. They don't really care a straw what I do. Besides, I don't go round so much."

"I think you will find they do care. They will show it disagreeably."

Daisy looked at him a moment. "How disagreeably?"

"Haven't you noticed anything?" Winterbourne asked.

"I have noticed you. But I noticed you were as stiff as an umbrella the first time I saw you."

"You will find I am not so stiff as several others," said Winterbourne, smiling.

"How shall I find it?"

"By going to see the others."

"What will they do to me?"

"They will give you the cold shoulder. Do you know what that means?"

Daisy was looking at him intently; she began to color.

"Do you mean as Mrs. Walker did the other night?"

"Exactly!" said Winterbourne.

She looked away at Giovanelli, who was decorating himself with his almond-blossom. Then, looking back at Winterbourne, "I shouldn't think you would let people be so unkind!" she said.

"How can I help it?" he asked.

"I should think you would say something."

"I did say something"; and he paused a moment. "I say that your mother tells me that she believes you are engaged."

"Well, she does," said Daisy, very simply.

Winterbourne began to laugh. "And does Randolph believe it?" he asked.

"I guess Randolph doesn't believe anything," said Daisy. Randolph's scepticism excited Winterbourne to further hilarity, and he observed that Giovanelli was coming back to them. Daisy, observing it too, addressed herself again to her countryman. "Since you have mentioned it," she said, "I *am* engaged." . . . Winterbourne looked at her; he had stopped laughing. "You don't believe it!" she added.

He was silent a moment; and then, "Yes, I believe it," he said.

"Oh, no, you don't!" she answered. "Well, then—I am not!"

The young girl and her cicerone were on their way to the gate of the enclosure, so that Winterbourne, who had but lately entered, presently took leave of them. A week afterwards he went to dine at a beautiful villa on the Caelian Hill, and, on arriving, dismissed his hired vehicle. The evening was charming, and he promised himself the satisfaction of walking home beneath the Arch of Constantine and past the vaguely-lighted monuments of the Forum. There was a waning moon in the sky, and her radiance was not brilliant, but she was veiled in a thin cloud-curtain which seemed to diffuse and equalize it. When, on his return from the villa (it was eleven o'clock), Winterbourne approached the dusky circle of the Colosseum, it occurred to him, as a lover of the picturesque, that the interior, in the pale moonshine, would be well worth a glance. He turned aside and walked to one of the empty arches, near which, as he observed, an open carriage—one of the little Roman street-cabs—was stationed. Then he passed in, among the cavernous shadows of the great structure, and emerged upon the clear and silent arena. The place had never seemed to him more impressive. One-half of the gigantic circus was in deep shade, the other was sleeping in the luminous dusk. As he stood there he began to murmur Byron's famous lines, out of "Manfred"; but before he had finished his quotation he remembered that if nocturnal meditations in the Colosseum are recommended by the poets, they are deprecated by the doctors. The historic atmosphere was there, certainly; but the historic atmosphere, scientifically considered, was no better than a villainous miasma. Winterbourne walked to the middle of the arena, to take a more general glance, intending thereafter to make a hasty retreat. The great cross in the centre was covered with shadow; it was only as he drew near it that he made it out distinctly. Then he saw that two persons were stationed upon the low steps which formed its base. One of these was a woman, seated; her companion was standing in front of her.

Presently the sound of the woman's voice came to him distinctly in the warm night air: "Well, he looks at us as one of the old lions or tigers may have looked at the Christian martyrs!" These were the words he heard in the familiar accent of Miss Daisy Miller.

"Let us hope he is not very hungry," responded the ingenious Giovanelli. "He will have to take me first; you will serve for dessert!"

Winterbourne stopped, with a sort of horror, and, it must be added, with a sort of relief. It was as if a sudden illumination had been flashed upon the ambiguity of Daisy's behavior, and the riddle had become easy to read. She was a young lady whom a gentleman need no longer be at pains to respect. He stood there looking at her—looking at her companion, and not reflecting that though he saw them vaguely, he himself must have been more brightly visible. He felt angry with himself that he had bothered so much about the right way of regarding Miss Daisy Miller. Then, as he was going to advance again, he checked himself; not from the fear that he was doing her injustice, but from the sense of the danger of appearing unbecomingly exhilarated by this sudden revulsion from cautious criticism. He turned away towards the entrance of the place, but, as he did so, he heard Daisy speak again.

"Why, it was Mr. Winterbourne! He saw me, and he cuts me!"

What a clever little reprobate she was, and how smartly she played at injured innocence! But he wouldn't cut her. Winterbourne came forward again, and went towards the great cross. Daisy had got up; Giovanelli lifted his hat. Winterbourne had now begun to think simply of the craziness, from a sanitary point of view, of a delicate young girl lounging away the evening in this nest of malaria. What if she *were* a clever little reprobate? that was no reason for her dying of the *perniciosa*. "How long have you been here?" he asked, almost brutally.

Daisy, lovely in the flattering moonlight, looked at him a moment. Then—"All the evening," she answered, gently. . . . "I never saw anything so pretty."

"I am afraid," said Winterbourne, "that you will not think Roman fever very pretty. This is the way people catch it. I wonder," he added, turning to Giovanelli, "that you, a native Roman, should countenance such a terrible indiscretion."

"Ah," said the handsome native, "for myself I am not afraid."

"Neither am I—for you! I am speaking for this young lady."

Giovanelli lifted his well-shaped eyebrows and showed his brilliant teeth. But he took Winterbourne's rebuke with docility. "I told the signorina it was a grave indiscretion; but when was the signorina ever prudent?"

"I never was sick, and I don't mean to be!" the signorina declared. "I don't look like much, but I'm healthy! I was bound to see the Colosseum by moonlight; I shouldn't have wanted to go home without that; and we have had the most beautiful time, haven't we, Mr. Giovanelli? If there has been any danger, Eugenio can give me some pills. He has got some splendid pills."

"I should advise you," said Winterbourne, "to drive home as fast as possible and take one!"

"What you say is very wise," Giovanelli rejoined. "I will go and make sure the carriage is at hand." And he went forward rapidly.

Daisy followed with Winterbourne. He kept looking at her; she seemed not in the least embarrassed. Winterbourne said nothing; Daisy chattered about the beauty of the place. "Well, I *have* seen the Colosseum by moonlight!" she exclaimed. "That's one good thing." Then, noticing Winterbourne's silence, she asked him why he didn't speak. He made no answer; he only began to laugh. They passed under one of the dark archways; Giovanelli was in front with the carriage. Here Daisy stopped a moment, looking at the young American. *"Did* you believe I was engaged the other day?" she asked.

"It doesn't matter what I believed the other day," said Winterbourne, still laughing.

"Well, what do you believe now?"

"I believe that it makes very little difference whether you are engaged or not!"

He felt the young girl's pretty eyes fixed upon him through the thick gloom of the archway; she was apparently going to answer. But Giovanelli hurried her forward. "Quick! quick!" he said; "if we get in by midnight we are quite safe."

Daisy took her seat in the carriage, and the fortunate Italian placed himself beside her. "Don't forget Eugenio's pills!" said Winterbourne, as he lifted his hat.

"I don't care," said Daisy, in a little strange tone, "whether I have Roman fever or not!" Upon this the cab-driver cracked his whip, and they rolled away over the desultory patches of the antique pavement.

Winterbourne, to do him justice, as it were, mentioned to no one that he had encountered Miss Miller, at midnight, in the Colosseum with a gentleman; but, nevertheless, a couple of days later, the fact of her having been there under these circumstances was known to every member of the little American circle, and commented accordingly. Winterbourne reflected that they had of course known it at the hotel, and, that, after Daisy's return there had been an exchange of remarks between the porter and the cab-driver. But the young man was conscious, at the same moment, that it had ceased to be a matter of serious regret to him that the little American flirt should be "talked about" by low-minded menials. These people, a day or two later, had serious information to give: the little American flirt was alarmingly ill. Winterbourne, when the rumor came to him, immediately went to the hotel for more news. He found that two or three charitable friends had preceded him, and that they were being entertained in Mrs. Miller's salon by Randolph.

"It's going round at night," said Randolph—"that's what made her sick. She's always going round at night. I shouldn't think she'd want to, it's so plaguy dark. You can't see anything here at night, except when there's a moon! In America there's always a moon!" Mrs. Miller was invisible; she was now, at least, giving her daughter the advantage of her society. It was evident that Daisy was dangerously ill.

Winterbourne went often to ask for news of her, and once he saw Mrs. Miller, who, though deeply alarmed, was, rather to his surprise, perfectly composed, and, as it appeared, a most efficient and judicious nurse. She talked a good deal about Dr. Davis, but Winterbourne paid her the compliment of saying to himself that she was not, after all, such a monstrous goose. "Daisy spoke of you the other day," she said to him. "Half the time she doesn't know what she's saying, but that time I think she did. She gave me a message. She told me to tell you—she told me to tell you that she never was engaged to that handsome Italian. I am sure I am very glad. Mr. Giovanelli hasn't been near us since she was taken ill. I thought he was so much of a gentleman; but I don't call that very polite! A lady told me that he was afraid I was angry with him for taking Daisy round at night. Well, so I am; but I suppose he knows I'm a lady. I would scorn to scold him. Anyway, she says she's not engaged. I don't know why she wanted you to know; but she said to me three times, 'Mind you tell Mr. Winterbourne.' And then she told me to ask if you remembered the time you went to that castle in Switzerland. But I said I wouldn't give any such messages as that. Only, if she is not engaged, I'm sure I'm glad to know it."

But, as Winterbourne had said, it mattered very little. A week after this the poor girl died; it had been a terrible case of the fever. Daisy's grave was in the little Protestant cemetery, in an angle of the wall of imperial Rome, beneath the cypresses and the thick spring-flowers. Winterbourne stood there beside it, with a number of other mourners —a number larger than the scandal excited by the young lady's career would have led you to expect. Near him stood Giovanelli, who came nearer still before Winterbourne turned away. Giovanelli was very pale: on this occasion he had no flower in his button-hole; he seemed to wish to say something. At last he said, "She was the most beautiful young lady I ever saw, and the most amiable"; and then he added in a moment, "and she was the most innocent."

Winterbourne looked at him, and presently repeated his words, "And the most innocent?"

"The most innocent!"

Winterbourne felt sore and angry. "Why, the devil," he asked, "did you take her to that fatal place?"

Mr. Giovanelli's urbanity was apparently imperturbable. He looked on the ground a moment, and then he said, "For myself I had no fear; and she wanted to go."

"That was no reason!" Winterbourne declared.

The subtle Roman again dropped his eyes. "If she had lived, I should have got nothing. She would never have married me, I am sure."

"She would never have married you?"

"For a moment I hoped so. But no. I am sure."

Winterbourne listened to him: he stood staring at the raw protuberance among the April daisies. When he turned away again, Mr. Giovanelli with his light, slow step, had retired.

Winterbourne almost immediately left Rome; but the following summer he again met his aunt, Mrs. Costello, at Vevay. Mrs. Costello was fond of Vevay. In the interval Winterbourne had often thought of Daisy Miller and her mystifying manners. One day he spoke of her to his aunt—said it was on his conscience that he had done her injustice.

"I am sure I don't know," said Mrs. Costello. "How did your injustice affect her?"

"She sent me a message before her death which I didn't understand at the time; but I have understood it since. She would have appreciated one's esteem."

"Is that a modest way," asked Mrs. Costello, "of saying that she would have reciprocated one's affection?"

Winterbourne offered no answer to this question; but he presently said, "You were right in that remark that you made last summer. I was booked to make a mistake. I have lived too long in foreign parts."

Nevertheless, he went back to live at Geneva, whence there continue to come the most contradictory accounts of his motives of sojourn: a report that he is "studying" hard—an intimation that he is much interested in a very clever foreign lady.

4

LEO TOLSTOY
The Death of Ivan Ilych

"Ivan Ilych's life had been most simple and most ordinary and therefore most terrible," states Tolstoy. *The Death of Ivan Ilych* is an illumination of this paradox.

In the events following immediately upon Ivan's death there is much that is quite ordinary, as well as the first intimations of something most terrible. The opening tone of the story is anticlimactic. Ivan Ilych is dead, but the rest of the world goes on altogether well without him. His former colleagues, ordinary men like himself, greet the news of his death with a moment of conventional sorrow before turning their thoughts to the more pleasing idea of the likely promotions necessitated by the new vacancy. To all those who hear it, the news of Ivan's death inspires "the complacent feeling that 'it is he who is dead and not I.'" At his funeral his colleagues put on faces of mock gravity while shielding themselves from the depressing situation with whispered plans for a card game to follow immediately afterwards. Ivan's wife reveals that she too has her mind on her own interests. She draws the embarrassed Peter Ivanovich into the back room and pumps him for advice on ways to extract from the government as much money as possible for her husband's death.

With these opening scenes Tolstoy introduces the world of Ivan Ilych. Interestingly, perhaps frighteningly, it is our own world. Its people are neither saintly nor wicked, but ordinary. They have a healthy regard for their own interests, and they naturally prefer things to be pleasant and convivial rather than morbid. As innocent as these attitudes may be, Tolstoy saw in them an inhuman and unregenerate way of life.

The evils of Ivan's life are of many kinds. Some are obvious. But most are so ordinary and so closely allied to what is decent and even admirable that one feels inclined to side with Ivan Ilych against the author's gathering scorn. Ivan is, after all, a likable man: "He was neither as cold and formal as his elder brother nor as wild as the younger, but was a happy mean between them—an intelligent, polished, lively, and agreeable man."

Tolstoy portrays Ivan Ilych as the kind of man whose enormous desire to savor the sweetness of life amounts to a kind of lust. The thrill of pleasure he finds in a good evening of bridge, and almost as innocently, his self-conscious relish of his power over others as a judge—these point the way towards the socially acceptable but potentially° ruthless self-seeking which Tolstoy saw at the heart of materialistic society. Probably no one, including Tolstoy, would wish to condemn the likes of Ivan Ilych as a human monstrosity for the pleasure he takes in a mere game of cards. As always, his actions are simply those of a shrewd man determined to live life to best advantage. Yet, his card playing can justly be considered as an expression of his whole existence. His pleasure at cards expresses the values of an entire society where each person seeks a maximum of pleasure as his life's goal and where the disturbing realities of human suffering are not allowed to intrude upon pleasure.

Ivan's feverish preparation of his new house is yet another expression of his total self-interest, and Tolstoy makes clear the irony that the fateful bump he suffers while hanging drapes is a symbol of all the evil in his life. The sickness initiated by his injury, like this evil, is hidden, odious, and unnameable. He comes to realize that sickness is poisoning his cherished pleasure in much the same way that hypocrisy has poisoned his existence almost from the start. All his life he has fled from the unpleasantness of suffering, but in the end he does nothing but suffer. The physical reality of death is vivid throughout the last half of the story. Ivan Ilych suffers, and we are made to suffer with him as he progresses from alarm to resentment to self-pity, panic, and despair. His

torments are so relentless that one is tempted to complain—before being silenced by the knife-point of Tolstoy's irony—that *The Death of Ivan Ilych* really contains too much suffering and is an unpleasant short novel.

Readers have often remarked that the energetic directness of Tolstoy's style seems to make literary technique transparent, so that his novels seem to *be* life itself. Actually, his writing employs a wide range of deliberate literary techniques. Tolstoy masterfully structures *The Death of Ivan Ilych* by beginning with the events following Ivan's death to establish a retrospective point of view and then going back over Ivan's entire life, ultimately to unfold a *complete* life story. One of the most remarkable characteristics of his writing is his warm yet elaborate use of detail to bring the inner world of character alive. Even his description of Ivan's corpse is alive with intensity and meaning: "The dead man lay, as dead men always lie, in a specially heavy way, his rigid limbs sunk on the pillow. His yellow waxen brow with bald patches over his sunken temples was thrust up in a way peculiar to the dead, the protruding nose seeming to press on the upper lip." Such descriptions seem to possess a more than real realism. Tolstoy described in his diaries how he deliberately sought to write in a way that would dispel the customary laziness of human perception, so that in his work familiar things might once again be experienced as strange, vital, and meaningful.

Also extremely important in *The*

Death of Ivan Ilych is Tolstoy's use of irony. His ironies run the full range from broad and humorous to scarcely perceptible. There is obvious and ironic humor in Peter Ivanovich's interview with Praskovya Fëdorovna. Peter Ivanovich is made to sit on an upholstered footstool, the springs of which bounce and creak rebelliously beneath him, adding a comic physical emphasis to all that is absurd, persistent, and unseemly in the entire conversation. Tolstoy also imparts the doubleness of irony to what seem the most innocent of details. He tops off the description of Ivan's leave-taking from his first position as a magistrate with: "they had a group-photograph taken and presented him with a silver cigarette-case, and he set off to his new post." These briskly rendered details capture the *just so* perfectness of Ivan's early life, and the matter-of-factness with which he accepted it—truths which add painfully to the horror of his last days.

The Death
of Ivan Ilych

I

During an interval in the Melvinski
trial in the large building of the Law Courts, the members and public
prosecutor met in Ivan Egorovich Shebek's private room, where the
conversation turned on the celebrated Krasovski case. Fëdor Vasilievich
warmly maintained that it was not subject to their jurisdiction, Ivan
Egorovich maintained the contrary, while Peter Ivanovich, not having
entered into the discussion at the start, took no part in it but looked
through the *Gazette* which had just been handed in.

"Gentlemen," he said, "Ivan Ilych has died!"

"You don't say so!"

"Here, read it yourself," replied Peter Ivanovich, handing Fëdor
Vasilievich the paper still damp from the press. Surrounded by a black
border were the words: "Praskovya Fëdorovna Goloviná, with profound
sorrow, informs relatives and friends of the demise of her beloved
husband Ivan Ilych Golovin, Member of the Court of Justice, which occurred on February the 4th of this year 1882. The funeral will take
place on Friday at one o'clock in the afternoon."

Ivan Ilych had been a colleague of the gentlemen present and was
liked by them all. He had been ill for some weeks with an illness said
to be incurable. His post had been kept open for him, but there had

From THE DEATH OF IVAN ILYCH AND OTHER STORIES by Leo Tolstoy, translated by Louise and Aylmer Maude and published by Oxford University Press.

been conjectures that in case of his death Alexeev might receive his appointment, and that either Vinnikov or Shtabel would succeed Alexeev. So on receiving the news of Ivan Ilych's death the first thought of each of the gentlemen in that private room was of the changes and promotions it might occasion among themselves or their acquaintances.

"I shall be sure to get Shtabel's place or Vinnikov's," thought Fëdor Vasilievich. "I was promised that long ago, and the promotion means an extra eight hundred rubles a year for me besides the allowance."

"Now I must apply for my brother-in-law's transfer from Kaluga," thought Peter Ivanovich. "My wife will be very glad, and then she won't be able to say that I never do anything for her relations."

"I thought he would never leave his bed again," said Peter Ivanovich aloud. "It's very sad."

"But what really was the matter with him?"

"The doctors couldn't say—at least they could, but each of them said something different. When last I saw him I thought he was getting better."

"And I haven't been to see him since the holidays. I always meant to go."

"Had he any property?"

"I think his wife had a little—but something quite trifling."

"We shall have to go to see her, but they live so terribly far away."

"Far away from you, you mean. Everything's far away from your place."

"You see, he never can forgive my living on the other side of the river," said Peter Ivanovich, smiling at Shebek. Then, still talking of the distances between different parts of the city, they returned to the Court.

Besides considerations as to the possible transfers and promotions likely to result from Ivan Ilych's death, the mere fact of the death of a near acquaintance aroused, as usual, in all who heard of it the complacent feeling that, "it is he who is dead and not I."

Each one thought or felt, "Well, he's dead but I'm alive!" But the more intimate of Ivan Ilych's acquaintances, his so-called friends, could not help thinking also that they would now have to fulfil the very tiresome demands of propriety by attending the funeral service and paying a visit of condolence to the widow.

Fëdor Vasilievich and Peter Ivanovich had been his nearest acquaintances. Peter Ivanovich had studied law with Ivan Ilych and had considered himself to be under obligations to him.

Having told his wife at dinner-time of Ivan Ilych's death and of his conjecture that it might be possible to get her brother transferred to their circuit, Peter Ivanovich sacrificed his usual nap, put on his evening clothes, and drove to Ivan Ilych's house.

At the entrance stood a carriage and two cabs. Leaning against the wall in the hall downstairs near the cloak-stand was a coffin-lid covered with cloth of gold, ornamented with gold cord and tassels, that had been polished up with metal powder. Two ladies in black were taking off their fur cloaks. Peter Ivanovich recognized one of them as Ivan Ilych's sister, but the other was a stranger to him. His colleague Schwartz was just coming downstairs, but on seeing Peter Ivanovich enter he stopped and winked at him, as if to say: "Ivan Ilych has made a mess of things—not like you and me."

Schwartz's face with his Piccadilly whiskers and his slim figure in evening dress had as usual an air of elegant solemnity which contrasted with the playfulness of his character and had a special piquancy here, or so it seemed to Peter Ivanovich.

Peter Ivanovich allowed the ladies to precede him and slowly followed them upstairs. Schwartz did not come down but remained where he was, and Peter Ivanovich understood that he wanted to arrange where they should play bridge that evening. The ladies went upstairs to the widow's room, and Schwartz with seriously compressed lips but a playful look in his eyes, indicated by a twist of his eyebrows the room to the right where the body lay.

Peter Ivanovich, like everyone else on such occasions, entered feeling uncertain what he would have to do. All he knew was that at such times it is always safe to cross oneself. But he was not quite sure whether one should make obeisances while doing so. He therefore adopted a middle course. On entering the room he began crossing himself and made a slight movement resembling a bow. At the same time, as far as the motion of his head and arm allowed, he surveyed the room. Two young men—apparently nephews, one of whom was a high-school pupil—were leaving the room, crossing themselves as they did so. An old woman was standing motionless, and a lady with strangely arched eyebrows was saying something to her in a whisper. A vigorous, resolute Church Reader, in a frock-coat, was reading something in a loud voice with an expression that precluded any contradiction. The butler's assistant, Gerasim, stepping lightly in front of Peter Ivanovich, was strewing something on the floor. Noticing this, Peter Ivanovich was immediately aware of a faint odour of a decomposing body.

The last time he had called on Ivan Ilych, Peter Ivanovich had seen Gerasim in the study. Ivan Ilych had been particularly fond of him and he was performing the duty of a sick nurse.

Peter Ivanovich continued to make the sign of the cross, slightly inclining his head in an intermediate direction between the coffin, the Reader, and the icons on the table in a corner of the room. Afterwards, when it seemed to him that this movement of his arm in crossing himself had gone on too long, he stopped and began to look at the corpse.

The dead man lay, as dead men always lie, in a specially heavy way, his rigid limbs sunk in the soft cushions of the coffin, with the head forever bowed on the pillow. His yellow waxen brow with bald patches over his sunken temples was thrust up in the way peculiar to the dead, the protruding nose seeming to press on the upper lip. He was much changed and had grown even thinner since Peter Ivanovich had last seen him, but, as is always the case with the dead, his face was handsomer and above all more dignified than when he was alive. The expression on the face said that what was necessary had been accomplished, and accomplished rightly. Besides this there was in that expression a reproach and a warning to the living. This warning seemed to Peter Ivanovich out of place, or at least not applicable to him. He felt a certain discomfort and so he hurriedly crossed himself once more and turned and went out of the door—too hurriedly and too regardless of propriety, as he himself was aware.

Schwartz was waiting for him in the adjoining room with legs spread wide apart and both hands toying with his top-hat behind his back. The mere sight of that playful, well-groomed, and elegant figure refreshed Peter Ivanovich. He felt that Schwartz was above all these happenings and would not surrender to any depressing influences. His very look said that this incident of a church service for Ivan Ilych could not be a sufficient reason for infringing the order of the session—in other words, that it would certainly not prevent his unwrapping a new pack of cards and shuffling them that evening while a footman placed four fresh candles on the table: in fact, that there was no reason for supposing that this incident would hinder their spending the evening agreeably. Indeed he said this in a whisper as Peter Ivanovich passed him, proposing that they should meet for a game at Fëdor Vasilievich's. But apparently Peter Ivanovich was not destined to play bridge that evening. Praskovya Fëdorovna (a short, fat woman who despite all efforts to the contrary had continued to broaden steadily from her shoulders downwards and who had the same extraordinarily arched eyebrows as the lady who had been standing by the coffin), dressed all in black, her head covered with lace, came out of her own room with some other ladies, conducted them to the room where the dead body lay, and said: "The service will begin immediately. Please go in."

Schwartz, making an indefinite bow, stood still, evidently neither accepting nor declining this invitation. Praskovya Fëdorovna, recognizing Peter Ivanovich, sighed, went close up to him, took his hand, and said: "I know you were a true friend of Ivan Ilych . . ." and looked at him awaiting some suitable response. And Peter Ivanovich knew that, just as it had been the right thing to cross himself in that room, so what he had to do here was to press her hand, sigh, and say, "Believe me. . . ." So he did all this and as he did it felt that the desired result had been achieved: that both he and she were touched.

"Come with me. I want to speak to you before it begins," said the widow. "Give me your arm."

Peter Ivanovich gave her his arm and they went to the inner rooms, passing Schwartz, who winked at Peter Ivanovich compassionately.

"That does for our bridge! Don't object if we find another player Perhaps you can cut in when you do escape," said his playful look.

Peter Ivanovich sighed still more deeply and despondently, and Praskovya Fëdorovna pressed his arm gratefully. When they reached the drawing-room, upholstered in pink cretonne and lighted by a dim lamp, they sat down at the table—she on a sofa and Peter Ivanovich on a low pouffe, the springs of which yielded spasmodically under his weight. Praskovya Fëdorovna had been on the point of warning him to take another seat, but felt that such a warning was out of keeping with her present condition and so changed her mind. As he sat down on the pouffe Peter Ivanovich recalled how Ivan Ilych had arranged this room and had consulted him regarding this pink cretonne with green leaves. The whole room was full of furniture and knick-knacks, and on her way to the sofa the lace of the widow's black shawl caught on the carved edge of the table. Peter Ivanovich rose to detach it, and the springs of the pouffe, relieved of his weight, rose also and gave him a push. The widow began detaching her shawl herself, and Peter Ivanovich again sat down, suppressing the rebellious springs of the pouffe under him. But the widow had not quite freed herself and Peter Ivanovich got up again, and again the pouffe rebelled and even creaked. When this was all over she took out a clean cambric handkerchief and began to weep. The episode with the shawl and the struggle with the pouffe had cooled Peter Ivanovich's emotions and he sat there with a sullen look on his face. This awkward situation was interrupted by Sokolov, Ivan Ilych's butler, who came to report that the plot in the cemetery that Praskovya Fëdorovna had chosen would cost two hundred rubles. She stopped weeping and, looking at Peter Ivanovich with the air of a victim, remarked in French that it was very hard for her. Peter Ivanovich made a silent gesture signifying his full conviction that it must indeed be so.

"Please smoke," she said in a magnanimous yet crushed voice, and turned to discuss with Sokolov the price of the plot for the grave.

Peter Ivanovich while lighting his cigarette heard her inquiring very circumstantially into the prices of different plots in the cemetery and finally decide which she would take. When that was done she gave instructions about engaging the choir. Sokolov then left the room.

"I look after everything myself," she told Peter Ivanovich, shifting the albums that lay on the table; and noticing that the table was endangered by his cigarette-ash, she immediately passed him an ashtray, saying as she did so: "I consider it an affectation to say that my grief prevents my attending to practical affairs. On the contrary, if anything can —I won't say console me, but—distract me, it is seeing to everything concerning him." She again took out her handkerchief as if preparing to cry, but suddenly, as if mastering her feeling, she shook herself and began to speak calmly. "But there is something I want to talk to you about."

Peter Ivanovich bowed, keeping control of the springs of the pouffe, which immediately began quivering under him.

"He suffered terribly the last few days."

"Did he?" said Peter Ivanovich.

"Oh, terribly! He screamed unceasingly, not for minutes but for hours. For the last three days he screamed incessantly. It was unendurable. I cannot understand how I bore it; you could hear him three rooms off. Oh, what I have suffered!"

"Is it possible that he was conscious all that time?" asked Peter Ivanovich.

"Yes," she whispered. "To the last moment. He took leave of us a quarter of an hour before he died, and asked us to take Volodya away."

The thought of the sufferings of this man he had known so intimately, first as a merry little boy, then as a school-mate, and later as a grown-up colleague, suddenly struck Peter Ivanovich with horror, despite an unpleasant consciousness of his own and this woman's dissimulation. He again saw that brow, and that nose pressing down on the lip, and felt afraid for himself.

"Three days of frightful suffering and then death! Why, that might suddenly, at any time, happen to me," he thought, and for a moment felt terrified. But—he did not himself know how—the customary reflection at once occurred to him that this had happened to Ivan Ilych and not to him, and that it should not and could not happen to him, and that to think that it could would be yielding to depression which he ought not to do, as Schwartz's expression plainly showed. After which reflection Peter Ivanovich felt reassured, and began to ask with interest about the details of Ivan Ilych's death, as though death was an accident natural to Ivan Ilych but certainly not to himself.

After many details of the really dreadful physical sufferings Ivan Ilych had endured (which details he learnt only from the effect those sufferings had produced on Praskovya Fëdorovna's nerves) the widow apparently found it necessary to get to business.

"Oh, Peter Ivanovich, how hard it is! How terribly, terribly hard!" and she again began to weep.

Peter Ivanovich sighed and waited for her to finish blowing her nose. When she had done so he said, "Believe me . . ." and she again began talking and brought out what was evidently her chief concern with him —namely, to question him as to how she could obtain a grant of money from the government on the occasion of her husband's death. She made it appear that she was asking Peter Ivanovich's advice about her pension, but he soon saw that she already knew about that to the minutest detail, more even than he did himself. She knew how much could be got out of the government in consequence of her husband's death, but wanted to find out whether she could not possibly extract something more. Peter Ivanovich tried to think of some means of doing so, but after reflecting for a while and, out of propriety, condemning the government for its niggardliness, he said he thought that nothing more could be got. Then she sighed and evidently began to devise means of getting rid of her visitor. Noticing this, he put out his cigarette, rose, pressed her hand, and went out into the anteroom.

In the dining-room where the clock stood that Ivan Ilych had liked so much and had bought at an antique shop, Peter Ivanovich met a priest and a few acquaintances who had come to attend the service, and he recognized Ivan Ilych's daughter, a handsome young woman. She was in black and her slim figure appeared slimmer than ever. She had a gloomy, determined, almost angry expression, and bowed to Peter Ivanovich as though he were in some way to blame. Behind her, with the same offended look, stood a wealthy young man, an examining magistrate, whom Peter Ivanovich also knew and who was her fiancé, as he had heard. He bowed mournfully to them and was about to pass into the death-chamber, when from under the stairs appeared the figure of Ivan Ilych's schoolboy son, who was extremely like his father. He seemed a little Ivan Ilych, such as Peter Ivanovich remembered when they studied law together. His tear-stained eyes had in them the look that is seen in the eyes of boys of thirteen or fourteen who are not pure-minded. When he saw Peter Ivanovich he scowled morosely and shame-facedly. Peter Ivanovich nodded to him and entered the death-chamber. The service began: candles, groans, incense, tears, and sobs. Peter Ivanovich stood looking gloomily down at his feet. He did not look once at the dead man, did not yield to any depressing influence, and was one of the first to leave the room. There was no one in the anteroom, but Gerasim darted out of the dead man's room, rummaged with his strong hands among the fur coats to find Peter Ivanovich's, and helped him on with it.

"Well, friend Gerasim," said Peter Ivanovich, so as to say something. "It's a sad affair, isn't it?"

"It's God's will. We shall all come to it some day," said Gerasim, displaying his teeth—the even, white teeth of a healthy peasant—and, like a man in the thick of urgent work, he briskly opened the front door, called the coachman, helped Peter Ivanovich into the sledge, and sprang back to the porch as if in readiness for what he had to do next.

Peter Ivanovich found the fresh air particularly pleasant after the smell of incense, the dead body, and carbolic acid.

"Where to, sir?" asked the coachman.

"It's not too late even now. . . . I'll call round on Fëdor Vasilievich."

He accordingly drove there and found them just finishing the first rubber, so that it was quite convenient for him to cut in.

II

Ivan Ilych's life had been most simple and most ordinary and therefore most terrible.

He had been a member of the Court of Justice, and died at the age of forty-five. His father had been an official who after serving in various ministries and departments in Petersburg had made the sort of career which brings men to positions from which by reason of their long service they cannot be dismissed, though they are obviously unfit to hold any responsible position, and for whom therefore posts are specially created, which though fictitious carry salaries of from six to ten thousand rubles that are not fictitious, and in receipt of which they live on to a great age.

Such was the Privy Councillor and superfluous member of various superfluous institutions, Ilya Epimovich Golovin.

He had three sons, of whom Ivan Ilych was the second. The eldest son was following in his father's footsteps only in another department, and was already approaching that stage in the service at which a similar sinecure would be reached. The third son was a failure. He had ruined his prospects in a number of positions and was now serving in the rail-way department. His father and brothers, and still more their wives, not merely disliked meeting him, but avoided remembering his existence unless compelled to do so. His sister had married Baron Greff, a Petersburg official of her father's type. Ivan Ilych was *le phénix de la famille* as people said. He was neither as cold and formal as his elder brother nor as wild as the younger, but was a happy mean between them —an intelligent, polished, lively, and agreeable man. He had studied with his younger brother at the School of Law, but the latter had failed to complete the course and was expelled when he was in the fifth class. Ivan Ilych finished the course well. Even when he was at the School of Law he was just what he remained for the rest of his life: a capable, cheerful, good-natured, and sociable man, though strict in the fulfilment of what he considered to be his duty: and he considered his duty to be what was so considered by those in authority. Neither as a boy nor as a man was he a toady, but from early youth was by nature attracted to people of high station as a fly is drawn to the light, assimilating their ways and views of life and establishing friendly relations with them. All the enthusiasms of childhood and youth passed without leaving much trace on him; he succumbed to sensuality, to vanity, and latterly among the highest classes to liberalism, but always within limits which his instinct unfailingly indicated to him as correct.

At school he had done things which had formerly seemed to him very horrid and made him feel disgusted with himself when he did them;

but when later on he saw that such actions were done by people of good position and that they did not regard them as wrong, he was able not exactly to regard them as right, but to forget about them entirely or not be at all troubled at remembering them.

Having graduated from the School of Law and qualified for the tenth rank of the civil service, and having received money from his father for his equipment, Ivan Ilych ordered himself clothes at Scharmer's, the fashionable tailor, hung a medallion inscribed *respice finem* on his watch-chain, took leave of his professor and the prince who was patron of the school, had a farewell dinner with his comrades at Donon's first-class restaurant, and with his new and fashionable portmanteau, linen, clothes, shaving and other toilet appliances, and a travelling rug all purchased at the best shops, he set off for one of the provinces where, through his father's influence, he had been attached to the Governor as an official for special service.

In the province Ivan Ilych soon arranged as easy and agreeable a position for himself as he had had at the School of Law. He performed his official tasks, made his career, and at the same time amused himself pleasantly and decorously. Occasionally he paid official visits to country districts, where he behaved with dignity both to his superiors and inferiors, and performed the duties entrusted to him, which related chiefly to the sectarians, with an exactness and incorruptible honesty of which he could not but feel proud.

In official matters, despite his youth and taste for frivolous gaiety, he was exceedingly reserved, punctilious, and even severe; but in society he was often amusing and witty, and always good-natured, correct in his manner, and *bon enfant,* as the Governor and his wife—with whom he was like one of the family—used to say of him.

In the province he had an affair with a lady who made advances to the elegant young lawyer, and there was also a milliner; and there were carousals with aides-de-camp who visited the district, and after-supper visits to a certain outlying street of doubtful reputation; and there was too some obsequiousness to his chief and even to his chief's wife, but all this was done with such a tone of good breeding that no hard names could be applied to it. It all came under the heading of the French saying: *"Il faut que jeunesse se passe."* It was all done with clean hands, in clean linen, with French phrases, and above all among people of the best society and consequently with the approval of people of rank.

So Ivan Ilych served for five years and then came a change in his official life. The new and reformed judicial institutions were introduced, and new men were needed. Ivan Ilych became such a new man. He was offered the post of examining magistrate, and he accepted it though the post was in another province and obliged him to give up the connexions he had formed and to make new ones. His friends met to give him a send-off; they had a group-photograph taken and presented him with a silver cigarette-case, and he set off to his new post.

As examining magistrate Ivan Ilych was just as *comme il faut* and decorous a man, inspiring general respect and capable of separating his official duties from his private life, as he had been when acting as an official on special service. His duties now as examining magistrate were far more interesting and attractive than before. In his former position it had been pleasant to wear an undress uniform made by Scharmer, and to pass through the crowd of petitioners and officials who were timorously awaiting an audience with the Governor, and who envied him as with free and easy gait he went straight into his chief's private room to have a cup of tea and a cigarette with him. But not many people had been directly dependent on him—only police officials and the sectarians when he went on special missions—and he liked to treat them politely, almost as comrades, as if he were letting them feel that he who had the power to crush them was treating them in this simple, friendly way. There were then but few such people. But now, as an examining magistrate, Ivan Ilych felt that everyone without exception, even the most important and self-satisfied, was in his power, and that he need only write a few words on a sheet of paper with a certain heading, and this or that important, self-satisfied person would be brought before him in the role of an accused person or a witness, and if he did not choose to allow him to sit down, would have to stand before him and answer his questions. Ivan Ilych never abused his power; he tried on the contrary to soften its expression, but the consciousness of it and of the possibility of softening its effect, supplied the chief interest and attraction of his office. In his work itself, especially in his examinations, he very soon acquired a method of eliminating all considerations irrelevant to the legal aspect of the case, and reducing even the most complicated case to a form in which it would be presented on paper only in its externals, completely excluding his personal opinion of the matter, while above all observing every prescribed formality. The work was new and Ivan Ilych was one of the first men to apply the new Code of 1864.

On taking up the post of examining magistrate in a new town, he made new acquaintances and connexions, placed himself on a new footing, and assumed a somewhat different tone. He took up an attitude of rather dignified aloofness towards the provincial authorities, but picked out the best circle of legal gentlemen and wealthy gentry living in the town and assumed a tone of slight dissatisfaction with the government, of moderate liberalism, and of enlightened citizenship. At the same time, without at all altering the elegance of his toilet, he ceased shaving his chin and allowed his beard to grow as it pleased.

Ivan Ilych settled down very pleasantly in this new town. The society there, which inclined towards opposition to the Governor, was friendly, his salary was larger, and he began to play *vint,* which he found added not a little to the pleasure of life, for he had a capacity for cards, played good-humouredly, and calculated rapidly and astutely, so that he usually won.

After living there for two years he met his future wife, Praskovya Fëdorovna Mikhel, who was the most attractive, clever, and brilliant girl of the set in which he moved, and among other amusements and relaxations from his labours as examining magistrate, Ivan Ilych established light and playful relations with her.

While he had been an official on special service he had been accustomed to dance, but now as an examining magistrate it was exceptional for him to do so. If he danced now, he did it as if to show that though he served under the reformed order of things, and had reached the fifth official rank, yet when it came to dancing he could do it better than most people. So at the end of an evening he sometimes danced with Praskovya Fëdorovna, and it was chiefly during these dances that he captivated her. She fell in love with him. Ivan Ilych had at first no definite intention of marrying, but when the girl fell in love with him he said to himself: "Really, why shouldn't I marry?"

Praskovya Fëdorovna came of a good family, was not bad-looking, and had some little property. Ivan Ilych might have aspired to a more brilliant match, but even this was good. He had his salary, and she, he hoped, would have an equal income. She was well connected, and was a sweet, pretty, and thoroughly correct young woman. To say that Ivan Ilych married because he fell in love with Praskovya Fëdorovna and found that she sympathized with his views of life would be as incorrect as to say that he married because his social circle approved of the match. He was swayed by both these considerations: the marriage gave him personal satisfaction, and at the same time it was considered the right thing by the most highly placed of his associates.

So Ivan Ilych got married.

The preparations for marriage and the beginning of married life, with its conjugal caresses, the new furniture, new crockery, and new linen, were very pleasant until his wife became pregnant—so that Ivan Ilych had begun to think that marriage would not impair the easy, agreeable, gay, and always decorous character of his life, approved of by society and regarded by himself as natural, but would even improve it. But from the first months of his wife's pregnancy, something new, unpleasant, depressing, and unseemly, and from which there was no way of escape, unexpectedly showed itself.

His wife, without any reason—*de gaieté de coeur* as Ivan Ilych expressed it to himself—began to disturb the pleasure and propriety of their life. She began to be jealous without any cause, expected him to devote his whole attention to her, found fault with everything, and made coarse and ill-mannered scenes.

At first Ivan Ilych hoped to escape from the unpleasantness of this state of affairs by the same easy and decorous relation to life that had served him heretofore: he tried to ignore his wife's disagreeable moods, continued to live in his usual easy and pleasant way, invited friends to his house for a game of cards, and also tried going out to his club or spending his evenings with friends. But one day his wife began upbraiding him so vigorously, using such coarse words, and continued to abuse him every time he did not fulfil her demands, so resolutely and with such evident determination not to give way till he submitted—that is, till he stayed at home and was bored just as she was—that he became alarmed. He now realized that matrimony—at any rate with Praskovya Fëdorovna—was not always conducive to the pleasures and amenities of life, but on the contrary often infringed both comfort and propriety, and that he must therefore entrench himself against such infringement. And Ivan Ilych began to seek for means of doing so. His official duties were the one thing that imposed upon Praskovya Fëdorovna, and by means of his official work and the duties attached to it he began struggling with his wife to secure his own independence.

With the birth of their child, the attempts to feed it and the various failures in doing so, and with the real and imaginary illnesses of mother and child, in which Ivan Ilych's sympathy was demanded but about which he understood nothing, the need of securing for himself an existence outside his family life became still more imperative.

As his wife grew more irritable and exacting and Ivan Ilych transferred the centre of gravity of his life more and more to his official work, so did he grow to like his work better and become more ambitious than before.

Very soon, within a year of his wedding, Ivan Ilych had realized that marriage, though it may add some comforts to life, is in fact a very intricate and difficult affair towards which in order to perform one's duty, that is, to lead a decorous life approved of by society, one must adopt a definite attitude just as toward's one's official duties.

And Ivan Ilych evolved such an attitude towards married life. He only required of it those conveniences—dinner at home, housewife, and bed—which it could give him, and above all that propriety of external forms required by public opinion. For the rest he looked for light-hearted pleasure and propriety, and was very thankful when he found them, but if he met with antagonism and querulousness he at once retired into his separate fenced-off world of official duties, where he found satisfaction.

Ivan Ilych was esteemed a good official, and after three years was made Assistant Public Prosecutor. His new duties, their importance, the possibility of indicting and imprisoning anyone he chose, the publicity his speeches received, and the success he had in all these things, made his work still more attractive.

More children came. His wife became more and more querulous and ill-tempered, but the attitude Ivan Ilych had adopted towards his home life rendered him almost impervious to her grumbling.

After seven years' service in that town he was transferred to another province as Public Prosecutor. They moved, but were short of money and his wife did not like the place they moved to. Though the salary was higher the cost of living was greater, besides which two of their children died and family life became still more unpleasant for him.

Praskovya Fëdorovna blamed her husband for every inconvenience they encountered in their new home. Most of the conversations be· tween husband and wife, especially as to the children's education, led to topics which recalled former disputes, and those disputes were apt to flare up again at any moment. There remained only those rare periods of amorousness which still came to them at times but did not last long. These were islets at which they anchored for a while and then again set out upon that ocean of veiled hostility which showed itself in their aloofness from one another. This aloofness might have grieved Ivan Ilych had he considered that it ought not to exist, but he now regarded the position as normal, and even made it the goal at which he aimed in family life. His aim was to free himself more and more from those unpleasantnesses and to give them a semblance of harmlessness and propriety. He attained this by spending less and less time with his family, and when obliged to be at home he tried to safeguard his position by the presence of outsiders. The chief thing however was that he had his official duties. The whole interest of his life now centred in the official world and that interest absorbed him. The consciousness of his power, being able to ruin anybody he wished to ruin, the importance, even the external dignity of his entry into court, or meetings with his subordinates, his success with superiors and inferiors, and above all his masterly handling of cases, of which he was conscious—all this gave him pleasure and filled his life, to-gether with chats with his colleagues, dinners, and bridge. So that on the whole Ivan Ilych's life continued to flow as he considered it should do—pleasantly and properly.

So things continued for another seven years. His eldest daughter was already sixteen, another child had died, and only one son was left, a schoolboy and a subject of dissension. Ivan Ilych wanted to put him in the School of Law, but to spite him Praskovya Fëdorovna entered him at the High School. The daughter had been educated at home and had turned out well: the boy did not learn badly either.

III

So Ivan Ilych lived for seventeen years after his marriage. He was already a Public Prosecutor of long standing, and had declined several proposed transfers while awaiting a more desirable post, when an un·

anticipated and unpleasant occurrence quite upset the peaceful course of his life. He was expecting to be offered the post of presiding judge in a University town, but Happe somehow came to the front and obtained the appointment instead. Ivan Ilych became irritable, reproached Happe, and quarrelled both with him and with his immediate superiors—who became colder to him and again passed him over when other appointments were made.

This was in 1880, the hardest year of Ivan Ilych's life. It was then that it became evident on the one hand that his salary was insufficient for them to live on, and on the other that he had been forgotten, and not only this, but that what was for him the greatest and most cruel injustice appeared to others a quite ordinary occurrence. Even his father did not consider it his duty to help him. Ivan Ilych felt himself abandoned by everyone, and that they regarded his position with a salary of 3,500 rubles as quite normal and even fortunate. He alone knew that with the consciousness of the injustices done him, with his wife's incessant nagging, and with the debts he had contracted by living beyond his means, his position was far from normal.

In order to save money that summer he obtained leave of absence and went with his wife to live in the country at her brother's place.

In the country, without his work, he experienced *ennui* for the first time in his life, and not only *ennui* but intolerable depression, and he decided that it was impossible to go on living like that, and that it was necessary to take energetic measures.

Having passed a sleepless night pacing up and down the veranda, he decided to go to Petersburg and bestir himself, in order to punish those who had failed to appreciate him and to get transferred to another ministry.

Next day, despite many protests from his wife and her brother, he started for Petersburg with the sole object of obtaining a post with a salary of five thousand rubles a year. He was no longer bent on any particular department, or tendency, or kind of activity. All he now wanted was an appointment to another post with a salary of five thousand rubles, either in the administration, in the banks, with the railways, in one of the Empress Marya's Institutions, or even in the customs—but it had to carry with it a salary of five thousand rubles and be in a ministry other than that in which they had failed to appreciate him.

And this quest of Ivan Ilych's was crowned with remarkable and unexpected success. At Kursk an acquaintance of his, F. I. Ilyin, got into the first-class carriage, sat down beside Ivan Ilych, and told him of a telegram just received by the Governor of Kursk announcing that a change was about to take place in the ministry: Peter Ivanovich was to be superseded by Ivan Semënovich.

The proposed change, apart from its significance for Russia, had a special significance for Ivan Ilych, because by bringing forward a new man, Peter Petrovich, and consequently his friend Zachar Ivanovich, it was highly favourable for Ivan Ilych, since Zachar Ivanovich was a friend and colleague of his.

In Moscow this news was confirmed, and on reaching Petersburg Ivan Ilych found Zachar Ivanovich and received a definite promise of an appointment in his former department of Justice.

A week later he telegraphed to his wife: "Zachar in Miller's place. I shall receive appointment on presentation of report."

Thanks to this change of personnel, Ivan Ilych had unexpectedly obtained an appointment in his former ministry which placed him two stages above his former colleagues besides giving him five thousand rubles salary and three thousand five hundred rubles for expenses connected with his removal. All his ill humour towards his former enemies and the whole department vanished, and Ivan Ilych was completely happy.

He returned to the country more cheerful and contented than he had been for a long time. Praskovya Fëdorovna also cheered up and a truce was arranged between them. Ivan Ilych told of how he had been fêted by everybody in Petersburg, how all those who had been his enemies were put to shame and now fawned on him, how envious they were of his appointment, and how much everybody in Petersburg had liked him.

Praskovya Fëdorovna listened to all this and appeared to believe it. She did not contradict anything, but only made plans for their life in the town to which they were going. Ivan Ilych saw with delight that these plans were his plans, that he and his wife agreed, and that, after a stumble, his life was regaining its due and natural character of pleasant lightheartedness and decorum.

Ivan Ilych had come back for a short time only, for he had to take up his new duties on the 10th of September. Moreover, he needed time to settle into the new place, to move all his belongings from the province, and to buy and order many additional things: in a word, to make such arrangements as he had resolved on, which were almost exactly what Praskovya Fëdorovna too had decided on.

Now that everything had happened so fortunately, and that he and his wife were at one in their aims and moreover saw so little of one another, they got on together better than they had done since the first years of marriage. Ivan Ilych had thought of taking his family away with him at once, but the insistence of his wife's brother and her sister-in-law, who had suddenly become particularly amiable and friendly to him and his family, induced him to depart alone.

So he departed, and the cheerful state of mind induced by his success and by the harmony between his wife and himself, the one intensifying the other, did not leave him. He found a delightful house, just the thing both he and his wife had dreamt of. Spacious, lofty reception rooms in the old style, a convenient and dignified study, rooms for his wife and daughter, a study for his son—it might have been specially built for them. Ivan Ilych himself superintended the arrangements, chose the wallpapers, supplemented the furniture (preferably with antiques which he considered particularly *comme il faut*), and supervised the upholstering. Everything progressed and progressed and approached the ideal he had set himself: even when things were only half completed they exceeded his expectations. He saw what a refined and elegant character, free from vulgarity, it would all have when it was ready. On falling asleep he pictured to himself how the reception-room would look. Looking at the yet unfinished drawing-room he could see the fireplace, the screen, the what-not, the little chairs dotted here and there, the dishes and plates on the walls, and the bronzes, as they would be when everything was in place. He was pleased by the thought of how his wife and daughter, who shared his taste in this matter, would be impressed by it. They were certainly not expecting as much. He had been particularly successful in finding, and buying cheaply, antiques which gave a particularly aristocratic character to the whole place. But in his letters he intentionally understated everything in order to be able to surprise them. All this so absorbed him that his new duties—though he liked his official work—interested him less than he had expected. Sometimes he even had moments of absentmindedness during the Court Sessions, and would consider whether he should have straight or curved cornices for his curtains. He was so interested in it all that he often did things himself, rearranging the furniture, or rehanging the curtains. Once when mounting a stepladder to show the upholsterer, who did not understand, how he wanted the hangings draped, he made a false step and slipped, but being a strong and agile man he clung on and only knocked his side against the knob of the window frame. The bruised place was painful but the pain soon passed, and he felt particularly bright and well just then. He wrote: "I feel fifteen years younger." He thought he would have everything ready by September, but it dragged on till mid-October. But the result was charming not only in his eyes but to everyone who saw it.

In reality it was just what is usually seen in the houses of people of moderate means who want to appear rich, and therefore succeed only in resembling others like themselves: there were damasks, dark wood, plants, rugs, and dull and polished bronzes—all the things people of a certain class have in order to resemble other people of that class. His house was so like the others that it would never have been noticed, but to him it all seemed to be quite exceptional. He was very happy when he met his family at the station and brought them to the newly furnished house all lit up, where a footman in a white tie opened the door into the hall decorated with plants, and when they went on into the drawing-room and the study uttering exclamations of delight. He conducted them everywhere, drank in their praises eagerly, and beamed with pleasure. At tea that evening, when Praskovya Fëdorovna among other things asked him about his fall, he laughed and showed them how he had gone flying and had frightened the upholsterer.

"It's a good thing I'm a bit of an athlete. Another man might have been killed, but I merely knocked myself, just here; it hurts when it's touched, but it's passing off already—it's only a bruise."

So they began living in their new home—in which, as always happens, when they got thoroughly settled in they found they were just one room short—and with the increased income, which as always was just a little (some five hundred rubles) too little, but it was all very nice.

Things went particularly well at first, before everything was finally arranged and while something had still to be done: this thing bought, that thing ordered, another thing moved, and something else adjusted. Though there were some disputes between husband and wife, they were both so well satisfied and had so much to do that it all passed off without any serious quarrels. When nothing was left to arrange it became rather dull and something seemed to be lacking, but they were then making acquaintances, forming habits, and life was growing fuller.

Ivan Ilych spent his mornings at the law courts and came home to dinner, and at first he was generally in a good humor, though he occasionally became irritable just on account of his house. (Every spot on the tablecloth or the upholstery, and every broken window-blind string, irritated him. He had devoted so much trouble to arranging it all that every disturbance of it distressed him.) But on the whole his life ran its course as he believed life should do: easily, pleasantly, and decorously.

He got up at nine, drank his coffee, read the paper, and then put on his undress uniform and went to the law courts. There the harness in which he worked had already been stretched to fit him and he donned it without a hitch: petitioners, inquiries at the chancery, the chancery itself, and the sittings public and administrative. In all this the thing was to exclude everything fresh and vital, which always disturbs the regular course of official business, and to admit only official relations with people, and then only on official grounds. A man would come, for instance, wanting some information. Ivan Ilych, as one in whose sphere the matter did not lie, would have nothing to do with him: but if the man had some business with him in his official capacity, something that could be expressed on officially stamped paper, he would do everything, positively everything he could within the limits of such relations, and in doing so would maintain the semblance of friendly human relations, that is, would observe the courtesies of life. As soon as the official relations ended, so did everything else. Ivan Ilych possessed this capacity to separate his real life from the official side of affairs and not mix the two, in the highest degree, and by long practice and natural aptitude had brought it to such a pitch that sometimes, in the manner of a virtuoso, he would even allow himself to let the human and official relations mingle. He let himself do this just because he felt that he could at any time he chose resume the strictly official attitude again and drop the human relation. And he did it all easily, pleasantly, correctly, and even artistically. In the intervals between the sessions he smoked, drank tea, chatted a little about politics, a little about general topics, a little about cards, but most of all about official appointments. Tired, but with the feelings of a virtuoso—one of the first violins who has played his part in an orchestra with precision—he would return home to find that his wife and daughter had been out paying calls, or had a visitor, and that his son had been to school, had done his homework with his tutor, and was duly learning what is taught at High Schools. Everything was as it should be. After dinner, if they had no visitors, Ivan Ilych sometimes read a book that was being much discussed at the time, and in the evening settled down to work, that is, read official papers, compared the depositions of witnesses, and noted paragraphs of the Code applying to them. This was neither dull nor amusing. It was dull when he might have been playing bridge, but if no bridge was available it was at any rate better than doing nothing or sitting with his wife. Ivan Ilych's chief pleasure was giving little dinners to which he invited men and women of good social position, and just as his drawing-room resembled all other drawing-rooms so did his enjoyable little parties resemble all other such parties.

Once they even gave a dance. Ivan Ilych enjoyed it and everything went off well, except that it led to a violent quarrel with his wife about the cakes and sweets. Praskovya Fëdorovna had made her own plans, but Ivan Ilych insisted on getting everything from an expensive confectioner and ordered too many cakes, and the quarrel occurred because some of those cakes were left over and the confectioner's bill came to forty-five rubles. It was a great and disagreeable quarrel. Praskovya Fëdorovna called him "a fool and an imbecile," and he clutched at his head and made angry allusions to divorce.

But the dance itself had been enjoyable. The best people were there, and Ivan Ilych had danced with Princess Trufonova, a sister of the distinguished founder of the Society "Bear my Burden."

The pleasures connected with his work were pleasures of ambition; his social pleasures were those of vanity; but Ivan Ilych's greatest pleasure was playing bridge. He acknowledged that whatever disagreeable incident happened in his life, the pleasure that beamed like a ray of light above everything else was to sit down to bridge with good players, not noisy partners, and of course to four-handed bridge (with five players it was annoying to have to stand out, though one pretended not to mind), to play a clever and serious game (when the cards allowed it), and then to have supper and drink a glass of wine. After a game of bridge, especially if he had won a little (to win a large sum was unpleasant), Ivan Ilych went to bed in specially good humour.

So they lived. They formed a circle of acquaintances among the best people and were visited by people of importance and by young folk. In their views as to their acquaintances, husband, wife, and daughter were entirely agreed, and tacitly and unanimously kept at arm's length and shook off the various shabby friends and relations who, with much show of affection, gushed into the drawing-room with its Japanese plates on the walls. Soon these shabby friends ceased to obtrude themselves and only the best people remained in the Golovins' set.

Young men made up to Lisa, and Petrishchev, an examining magistrate and Dmitri Ivanovich Petrishchev's son and sole heir, began to be so attentive to her that Ivan Ilych had already spoken to Praskovya Fëdorovna about it, and considered whether they should not arrange a party for them, or get up some private theatricals.

So they lived, and all went well, without change, and life flowed pleasantly.

IV

They were all in good health. It could not be called ill health if Ivan Ilych sometimes said that he had a queer taste in his mouth and felt some discomfort in his left side.

But this discomfort increased and, though not exactly painful, grew into a sense of pressure in his side accompanied by ill humour. And his irritability became worse and worse and began to mar the agreeable, easy, and correct life that had established itself in the Golovin family. Quarrels between husband and wife became more and more frequent, and soon the ease and amenity disappeared and even the decorum was barely maintained. Scenes again became frequent, and very few of those islets remained on which husband and wife could meet without an explosion. Praskovya Fëdorovna now had good reason to say that her husband's temper was trying. With characteristic exaggeration she said he had always had a dreadful temper, and that it had needed all her good nature to put up with it for twenty years. It was true that now the quarrels were started by him. His bursts of temper always came just before dinner, often just as he began to eat his soup. Sometimes he noticed that a plate or dish was chipped, or the food was not right, or his son put his elbow on the table, or his daughter's hair was not done as he liked it, and for all this he blamed Praskovya Fëdorovna. At first she retorted and said disagreeable things to him, but once or twice he fell into such a rage at the beginning of dinner that she realized it was due to some physical derangement brought on by taking food, and so she restrained herself and did not answer, but only hurried to get the dinner over. She regarded this self-restraint as highly praiseworthy. Having come to the conclusion that her husband had a dreadful temper and made her life miserable, she began to feel sorry for herself, and the more she pitied herself the more she hated her husband. She began to wish he would die; yet she did not want him to die because then his salary would cease. And this irritated her against him still more. She considered herself dreadfully unhappy just because not even his death could save her, and though she concealed her exasperation, that hidden exasperation of hers increased his irritation also.

After one scene in which Ivan Ilych had been particularly unfair and after which he had said in explanation that he certainly was irritable but that it was due to his not being well, she said that if he was ill it should be attended to, and insisted on his going to see a celebrated doctor.

He went. Everything took place as he had expected and as it always does. There was the usual waiting and the important air assumed by the doctor, with which he was so familiar (resembling that which he himself assumed in court), and the sounding and listening, and the questions which called for answers that were foregone conclusions and were evidently unnecessary, and the look of importance which implied that "if only you put yourself in our hands we will arrange everything —we know indubitably how it has to be done, always in the same way for everybody alike." It was all just as it was in the law courts. The doctor put on just the same air towards him as he himself put on towards an accused person.

The doctor said that so-and-so indicated that there was so-and-so inside the patient, but if the investigation of so-and-so did not confirm this, then he must assume that and that. If he assumed that and that, then . . . and so on. To Ivan Ilych only one question was important: was his case serious or not? But the doctor ignored that inappropriate question. From his point of view it was not the one under consideration, the real question was to decide between a floating kidney, chronic catarrh, or appendicitis. It was not a question of Ivan Ilych's life or death, but one between a floating kidney and appendicitis. And that question the doctor solved brilliantly, as it seemed to Ivan Ilych, in favour of the appendix, with the reservation that should an examination of the urine give fresh indications the matter would be reconsidered. All this was just what Ivan Ilych had himself brilliantly accomplished a thousand times in dealing with men on trial. The doctor summed up just as brilliantly, looking over his spectacles triumphantly and even gaily at the accused. From the doctor's summing up Ivan Ilych concluded that things were bad, but that for the doctor, and perhaps for everybody else, it was a matter of indifference, though for him it was bad. And this conclusion struck him painfully, arousing in him a great feeling of pity for himself and of bitterness towards the doctor's indifference to a matter of such importance.

He said nothing of this, but rose, placed the doctor's fee on the table, and remarked with a sigh: "We sick people probably often put inappropriate questions. But tell me, in general, is this complaint dangerous, or not? . . ."

The doctor looked at him sternly over his spectacles with one eye, as if to say: "Prisoner, if you will not keep to the questions put to you, I shall be obliged to have you removed from the court."

"I have already told you what I consider necessary and proper. The analysis may show something more." And the doctor bowed.

Ivan Ilych went out slowly, seated himself disconsolately in his sledge, and drove home. All the way home he was going over what the doctor had said, trying to translate those complicated, obscure, scientific phrases into plain language and find in them an answer to the question: "Is my condition bad? Is it very bad? Or is there as yet nothing much wrong?" And it seemed to him that the meaning of what the doctor had said was that it was very bad. Everything in the streets seemed depressing. The cabmen, the houses, the passers-by, and the shops, were dismal. His ache, this dull gnawing ache that never ceased for a moment, seemed to have acquired a new and more serious significance from the doctor's dubious remarks. Ivan Ilych now watched it with a new and oppressive feeling.

He reached home and began to tell his wife about it. She listened, but in the middle of his account his daughter came in with her hat on, ready to go out with her mother. She sat down reluctantly to listen to this tedious story, but could not stand it long, and her mother too did not hear him to the end.

"Well, I am very glad," she said. "Mind now to take your medicine regularly. Give me the prescription and I'll send Gerasim to the chemist's." And she went to get ready to go out.

While she was in the room Ivan Ilych had hardly taken time to breathe, but he sighed deeply when she left it.

"Well," he thought, "perhaps it isn't so bad after all."

He began taking his medicine and following the doctor's directions, which had been altered after the examination of the urine. But then it happened that there was a contradiction between the indications drawn from the examination of the urine and the symptoms that showed themselves. It turned out that what was happening differed from what the doctor had told him, and that he had either forgotten, or blundered, or hidden something from him. He could not, however, be blamed for that, and Ivan Ilych still obeyed his orders implicitly and at first derived some comfort from doing so.

From the time of his visit to the doctor, Ivan Ilych's chief occupation was the exact fulfilment of the doctor's instructions regarding hygiene and the taking of medicine, and the observation of his pain and his excretions. His chief interests came to be people's ailments and people's health. When sickness, deaths, or recoveries were mentioned in his presence, especially when the illness resembled his own, he listened with agitation which he tried to hide, asked questions, and applied what he heard to his own case.

The pain did not grow less, but Ivan Ilych made efforts to force himself to think he was better. And he could do this so long as nothing agitated him. But as soon as he had any unpleasantness with his wife, any lack of success in his official work, or held bad cards at bridge, he was at once acutely sensible of his disease. He had formerly borne such mischances, hoping soon to adjust what was wrong, to master it and attain success, or make a grand slam. But now every mischance upset him and plunged him into despair. He would say to himself: "There now, just as I was beginning to get better and the medicine had begun to take effect, comes this accursed misfortune, or unpleasantness. . . ." And he was furious with the mishap, or with the people who were causing the unpleasantness and killing him, for he felt that this fury was killing him but could not restrain it. One would have thought that it should have been clear to him that this exasperation with circumstances and people aggravated his illness, and that he ought therefore to ignore unpleasant occurrences. But he drew the very opposite conclusion: he said that he needed peace, and he watched for everything that might disturb it and became irritable at the slightest infringement of it. His condition was rendered worse by the fact that he read medical books and consulted doctors. The progress of his disease was so gradual that he could deceive himself when comparing one day with another—the difference was so slight. But when he consulted the doctors it seemed to him that he was getting worse, and even very rapidly. Yet despite this he was continually consulting them.

That month he went to see another celebrity, who told him almost the same as the first had done but put his questions rather differently, and the interview with this celebrity only increased Ivan Ilych's doubts and fears. A friend of a friend of his, a very good doctor, diagnosed his illness again quite differently from the others, and though he predicted recovery, his questions and suppositions bewildered Ivan Ilych still more and increased his doubts. A homoeopathist diagnosed the disease in yet another way, and prescribed medicine which Ivan Ilych took secretly for a week. But after a week, not feeling any improvement and having lost confidence both in the former doctor's treatment and in this one's, he became still more despondent. One day a lady acquaintance mentioned a cure effected by a wonder-working icon. Ivan Ilych caught himself listening attentively and beginning to believe that it had occurred. This incident alarmed him. "Has my mind really weakened to such an extent?" he asked himself. "Nonsense! It's all rubbish. I mustn't give way to nervous fears but having chosen a doctor must keep strictly to his treatment. That is what I will do. Now it's all settled. I won't think about it, but will follow the treatment seriously till summer, and then we shall see. From now there must be no more of this wavering!" This was easy to say but impossible to carry out. The pain in his side oppressed him and seemed to grow worse and more incessant, while the taste in his mouth grew stranger and stranger. It seemed to him that his breath had a disgusting smell, and he was conscious of a loss of appetite and strength. There was no deceiving himself: something terrible, new, and more important than anything before in his life, was taking place within him of which he alone was aware. Those about him did not understand or would not understand it, but thought everything in the world was going on as usual. That tormented Ivan Ilych more than anything. He saw that his household, especially his wife and daughter who were in a perfect whirl of visiting, did not understand anything of it and were annoyed that he was so depressed and so exacting, as if he were to blame for it. Though they tried to disguise it he saw that he was an obstacle in their path, and that his wife had adopted a definite line in regard to his illness and kept to it regardless of anything he said or did. Her attitude was this: "You know," she would say to her friends, "Ivan Ilych can't do as other people do, and keep to the treatment prescribed for him. One day he'll take his drops and keep strictly to his diet and go to bed in good time, but the next day unless I watch him he'll suddenly forget his medicine, eat sturgeon—which is forbidden —and sit up playing cards till one o'clock in the morning."

"Oh, come, when was that?" Ivan Ilych would ask in vexation. "Only once at Peter Ivanovich's."

"And yesterday with Shebek."

"Well, even if I hadn't stayed up, this pain would have kept me awake."

"Be that as it may you'll never get well like that, but will always make us wretched."

Praskovya Fëdorovna's attitude to Ivan Ilych's illness, as she expressed it both to others and to him, was that it was his own fault and was another of the annoyances he caused her. Ivan Ilych felt that this opinion escaped her involuntarily—but that did not make it easier for him.

At the law courts too, Ivan Ilych noticed, or thought he noticed, a strange attitude towards himself. It sometimes seemed to him that people were watching him inquisitively as a man whose place might soon be vacant. Then again, his friends would suddenly begin to chaff him in a friendly way about his low spirits, as if the awful, horrible, and unheard-of thing that was going on within him, incessantly gnawing at him and irresistibly drawing him away, was a very agreeable subject for jests. Schwartz in particular irritated him by his jocularity, vivacity, and *savoir-faire,* which reminded him of what he himself had been ten years ago.

Friends came to make up a set and they sat down to cards. They dealt, bending the new cards to soften them, and he sorted the diamonds in his hand and found he had seven. His partner said "No trumps" and supported him with two diamonds. What more could be wished for? It ought to be jolly and lively. They would make a grand slam. But suddenly Ivan Ilych was conscious of that gnawing pain, that taste in his mouth, and it seemed ridiculous that in such circumstances he should be pleased to make a grand slam.

He looked at his partner Mikhail Mikhaylovich, who rapped the table with his strong hand and instead of snatching up the tricks pushed the cards courteously and indulgently towards Ivan Ilych that he might have the pleasure of gathering them up without the trouble of stretching out his hand for them. "Does he think I am too weak to stretch out my arm?" thought Ivan Ilych, and forgetting what he was doing he over-trumped his partner, missing the grand slam by three tricks. And what was most awful of all was that he saw how upset Mikhail Mikhaylovich was about it but did not himself care. And it was dreadful to realize why he did not care.

They all saw that he was suffering, and said: "We can stop if you are tired. Take a rest." Lie down? No, he was not at all tired, and he finished the rubber. All were gloomy and silent. Ivan Ilych felt that he had diffused this gloom over them and could not dispel it. They had supper and went away, and Ivan Ilych was left alone with the consciousness that his life was poisoned and was poisoning the lives of others, and that this poison did not weaken but penetrated more and more deeply into his whole being.

With this consciousness, and with physical pain besides the terror, he must go to bed, often to lie awake the greater part of the night. Next morning he had to get up again, dress, go to the law courts, speak, and write; or if he did not go out, spend at home those twenty-four hours a day each of which was a torture. And he had to live thus all alone on the brink of an abyss, with no one who understood or pitied him.

V

So one month passed and then another. Just before the New Year his brother-in-law came to town and stayed at their house. Ivan Ilych was at the law courts and Praskovya Fëdorovna had gone shopping. When Ivan Ilych came home and entered his study he found his brother-in-law there—a healthy, florid man—unpacking his portmanteau himself. He raised his head on hearing Ivan Ilych's footsteps and looked up at him for a moment without a word. That stare told Ivan Ilych everything. His brother-in-law opened his mouth to utter an exclamation of surprise but checked himself, and that action confirmed it all.

"I have changed, eh?"

"Yes, there is a change."

And after that, try as he would to get his brother-in-law to return to the subjects of his looks, the latter would say nothing about it. Praskovya Fëdorovna came home and her brother went out to her. Ivan Ilych locked the door and began to examine himself in the glass, first full face, then in profile. He took up a portrait of himself taken with his wife, and compared it with what he saw in the glass. The change in him was immense. Then he bared his arms to the elbow, looked at them, drew the sleeves down again, sat down on an ottoman, and grew blacker than night.

"No, no, this won't do!" he said to himself, and jumped up, went to the table, took up some law papers, and began to read them, but could not continue. He unlocked the door and went into the reception-room. The door leading to the drawing-room was shut. He approached it on tiptoe and listened.

"No, you are exaggerating!" Praskovya Fëdorovna was saying.

"Exaggerating! Don't you see it? Why, he's a dead man! Look at his eyes—there's no light in them. But what is it that is wrong with him?"

"No one knows. Nikolaevich said something, but I don't know what. And Leshchetitsky said quite the contrary. . . ."

Ivan Ilych walked away, went to his own room, lay down, and began musing: "The kidney, a floating kidney." He recalled all the doctors had told him of how it detached itself and swayed about. And by an effort of imagination he tried to catch that kidney and arrest it and support it. So little was needed for this, it seemed to him. "No, I'll go to see Peter Ivanovich again." He rang, ordered the carriage, and got ready to go.

"Where are you going, Jean?" asked his wife, with a specially sad and exceptionally kind look.

This exceptionally kind look irritated him. He looked morosely at her.

"I must go to see Peter Ivanovich."

He went to see Peter Ivanovich, and together they went to see his friend, the doctor. He was in, and Ivan Ilych had a long talk with him.

Reviewing the anatomical and physiological details of what in the doctor's opinion was going on inside him, he understood it all.

There was something, a small thing, in the vermiform appendix. It might all come right. Only stimulate the energy of one organ and check the activity of another, then absorption would take place and everything would come right. He got home rather late for dinner, ate his dinner, and conversed cheerfuly, but could not for a long time bring himself to go to work in his room. At last, however, he went to his study and did what was necessary, but the consciousness that he had put something aside—an important, intimate matter which he would revert to when his work was done—never left him. When he had finished his work he remembered that this intimate matter was the thought of his vermiform appendix. But he did not give himself up to it, and went to the drawing-room for tea. There were callers there, including the examining magistrate who was a desirable match for his daughter, and they were conversing, playing the piano, and singing. Ivan Ilych, as Praskovya Fëdorovna remarked, spent that evening more cheerfully then usual, but he never for a moment forgot that he had postponed the important matter of the appendix. At eleven o'clock he said good-night and went to his bedroom. Since his illness he had slept alone in a small room next to his study. He undressed and took up a novel by Zola, but instead of reading it he fell into thought, and in his imagination that desired improvement in the vermiform appendix occurred. There was the absorption and evacuation and the re-establishment of normal activity. "Yes, that's it!" he said to himself. "One need only assist nature, that's all." He remembered his medicine, rose, took it, and lay down on his back watching for the beneficent action of the medicine and for it to lessen the pain. "I need only take it regularly and avoid all injurious influences. I am already feeling better, much better." He began touching his side: it was not painful to the touch. "There, I really don't feel it. It's much better already." He put out the light and turned on his side. . . . "The appendix is getting better, absorption is occurring." Suddenly he felt the old, familiar, dull, gnawing pain, stubborn and serious. There was the same familiar loathsome taste in his mouth. His heart sank and he felt dazed. "My God! My God!" he muttered. "Again, again! and it will never cease." And suddenly the matter presented itself in a quite different aspect. "Vermiform appendix! Kidney!" he said to himself. "It's not a question of appendix or kidney, but of life and . . . death. Yes, life was there and now it is going, going and I cannot stop it. Yes. Why deceive myself? Isn't it obvious to everyone but me that I'm dying, and that it's only a question of weeks, days . . . it may happen this moment. There was light and now there is darkness. I was here and now I'm going there! Where?" A chill came over him, his breathing ceased, and he felt only the throbbing of his heart.

"When I am not, what will there be? There will be nothing. Then where shall I be when I am no more? Can this be dying? No, I don't want to!" He jumped up and tried to light the candle, felt for it with trembling hands, dropped candle and candlestick on the floor, and fell back on his pillow.

"What's the use? It makes no difference," he said to himself, staring with wide-open eyes into the darkness. "Death. Yes, death. And none of them know or wish to know it, and they have no pity for me. Now they are playing." (He heard through the door the distant sound of a song and its accompaniment.) "It's all the same to them, but they will die too! Fools! I first, and they later, but it will be the same for them. And now they are merry . . . the beasts!"

Anger choked him and he was agonizingly, unbearably miserable. "It is impossible that all men have been doomed to suffer this awful horror!" He raised himself.

"Something must be wrong. I must calm myself—must think it all over from the beginning." And he again began thinking. "Yes, the beginning of my illness: I knocked my side, but I was still quite well that day and the next. It hurt a little, then rather more. I saw the doctors, then followed despondency and anguish, more doctors, and I drew nearer to the abyss. My strength grew less and I kept coming nearer and nearer, and now I have wasted away and there is no light in my eyes. I think of the appendix—but this is death! I think of mending the appendix, and all the while here is death! Can it really be death?" Again terror seized him and he gasped for breath. He leant down and began feeling for the matches, pressing with his elbow on the stand beside the bed. It was in his way and hurt him, he grew furious with it, pressed on it still harder, and upset it. Breathless and in despair, he fell on his back, expecting death to come immediately.

Meanwhile the visitors were leaving. Praskovya Fëdorovna was seeing them off. She heard something fall and came in.

"What has happened?"

"Nothing. I knocked it over accidentally."

She went out and returned with a candle. He lay there panting heavily, like a man who has run a thousand yards, and stared upwards at her with a fixed look.

"What is it, Jean?"

"No . . . o . . . thing. I upset it." ("Why speak of it? She won't understand," he thought.)

And in truth she did not understand. She picked up the stand, lit his candle, and hurried away to see another visitor off. When she came back he still lay on his back, looking upwards.

"What is it? Do you feel worse?"

"Yes."

She shook her head and sat down.

"Do you know, Jean, I think we must ask Leshchetitsky to come and see you here."

This meant calling in the famous specialist, regardless of expense. He smiled malignantly and said "No." She remained a little longer and then went up to him and kissed his forehead.

While she was kissing him he hated her from the bottom of his soul and with difficulty refrained from pushing her away.

"Good-night. Please God you'll sleep."

"Yes."

VI

Ivan Ilych saw that he was dying, and he was in continual despair.

In the depth of his heart he knew he was dying, but not only was he not accustomed to the thought, he simply did not and could not grasp it.

The syllogism he had learnt from Kiezewetter's Logic: "Caius is a man, men are mortal, therefore Caius is mortal," had always seemed to him correct as applied to Caius, but certainly not as applied to himself. That Caius—man in the abstract—was mortal, was perfectly correct, but he was not Caius, not an abstract man, but a creature quite, quite separate from all others. He had been little Vanya, with a mamma and a papa, with Mitya and Volodya, with the toys, a coachman and a nurse, afterwards with Katenka and with all the joys, griefs, and delights of childhood, boyhood, and youth. What did Caius know of the smell of that striped leather ball Vanya had been so fond of? Had Caius kissed his mother's hand like that, and did the silk of her dress rustle so for Caius? Had he rioted like that at school when the pastry was bad? Had Caius been in love like that? Could Caius preside at a session as he did? "Caius really was mortal, and it was right for him to die; but for me, little Vanya, Ivan Ilych, with all my thoughts and emotions, it's altogether a different matter. It cannot be that I ought to die. That would be too terrible."

Such was his feeling.

"If I had to die like Caius I should have known it was so. An inner voice would have told me so, but there was nothing of the sort in me and I and all my friends felt that our case was quite different from that of Caius. And now here it is!" he said to himself. "It can't be. It's impossible! But here it is. How is this? How is one to understand it?"

He could not understand it, and tried to drive this false, incorrect, morbid thought away and to replace it by other proper and healthy thoughts. But that thought, and not the thought only but the reality itself, seemed to come and confront him.

And to replace that thought he called up a succession of others, hoping to find in them some support. He tried to get back into the former current of thoughts that had once screened the thought of death from him. But strange to say, all that had formerly shut off, hidden, and destroyed his consciousness of death, no longer had that effect. Ivan Ilych now spent most of his time in attempting to re-establish that old current. He would say to himself: "I will take up my duties again—after all I used to live by them." And banishing all doubts he would go to the law courts, enter into conversation with his colleagues, and sit carelessly as was his wont, scanning the crowd with a thoughtful look and leaning both his emaciated arms on the arms of his oak chair;

bending over as usual to a colleague and drawing his papers nearer he would interchange whispers with him, and then suddenly raising his eyes and sitting erect would pronounce certain words and open the proceedings. But suddenly in the midst of those proceedings the pain in his side, regardless of the stage the proceedings had reached, would begin its own gnawing work. Ivan Ilych would turn his attention to it and try to drive the thought of it away, but without success. *It* would come and stand before him and look at him, and he would be petrified and the light would die out of his eyes, and he would again begin asking himself, whether *It* alone was true. And his colleagues and subordinates would see with surprise and distress that he, the brilliant and subtle judge, was becoming confused and making mistakes. He would shake himself, try to pull himself together, manage somehow to bring the sitting to a close, and return home with the sorrowful consciousness that his judicial labours could not as formerly hide from him what he wanted them to hide, and could not deliver him from *It*. And what was worst of all was that *It* drew his attention to itself not in order to make him take some action but only that he should look at *It*, look it straight in the face: look at it and, without doing anything, suffer inexpressibly.

And to save himself from this condition Ivan Ilych looked for consolations—new screens—and new screens were found and for a while seemed to save him, but then they immediately fell to pieces or rather became transparent, as if *It* penetrated them and nothing could veil *It*.

In these latter days he would go into the drawing-room he had arranged—that drawing-room where he had fallen and for the sake of which (how bitterly ridiculous it seemed) he had sacrificed his life —for he knew that his illness originated with that knock. He would enter and see that something had scratched the polished table. He would look for the cause of this and find that it was the bronze ornamentation of an album, that had got bent. He would take up the expensive album which he had lovingly arranged, and feel vexed with his daughter and her friends for their untidiness—for the album was torn here and there and some of the photographs turned upside down. He would put it carefully in order and bend the ornamentation back into position. Then it would occur to him to place all those things in another corner of the room, near the plants. He could call the footman, but his daughter or wife would come to help him. They would not agree, and his wife would contradict him, and he would dispute and grow angry. But that was all right, for then he did not think about. *It*. *It* was invisible.

But then, when he was moving something himself, his wife would say: "Let the servants do it. You will hurt yourself again." And suddenly *It* would flash through the screen and he would see it. It was just a flash, and he hoped it would disappear, but he would involuntarily pay attention to his side. "It sits there as before, gnawing just the same!" And he could no longer forget *It*, but could distinctly see it looking at him from behind the flowers. "What is it all for?"

"It really is so! I lost my life over that curtain as I might have done when storming a fort. Is that possible? How terrible and how stupid. It can't be true! It can't, but it is."

He would go to his study, lie down, and again be alone with *It:* face to face with *It*. And nothing could be done with *It* except to look at it and shudder.

VII

How it happened it is impossible to say because it came about step by step, unnoticed, but in the third month of Ivan Ilych's illness, his wife, his daughter, his son, his acquaintances, the doctors, the servants, and above all he himself, were aware that the whole interest he had for other people was whether he would soon vacate his place, and at last release the living from the discomfort caused by his presence and be himself released from his sufferings.

He slept less and less. He was given opium and hypodermic injections of morphine, but this did not relieve him. The dull depression he experienced in a somnolent condition at first gave him a little relief, but only as something new, afterwards it became as distressing as the pain itself or even more so.

Special foods were prepared for him by the doctors' orders, but all those foods became increasingly distasteful and disgusting to him.

For his excretions also special arrangements had to be made, and this was a torment to him every time—a torment from the uncleanliness, the unseemliness, and the smell, and from knowing that another person had to take part in it.

But just through this most unpleasant matter, Ivan Ilych obtained comfort. Gerasim, the butler's young assistant, always came in to carry the things out. Gerasim was a clean, fresh peasant lad, grown stout on town food and always cheerful and bright. At first the sight of him, in his clean Russian peasant costume, engaged on that disgusting task embarrassed Ivan Ilych.

Once when he got up from the commode too weak to draw up his trousers, he dropped into a soft armchair and looked with horror at his bare, enfeebled thighs with the muscles so sharply marked on them.

Gerasim with a firm light tread, his heavy boots emitting a pleasant smell of tar and fresh winter air, came in wearing a clean Hessian apron, the sleeves of his print shirt tucked up over his strong, bare young arms; and refraining from looking at his sick master out of consideration for his feelings, and restraining the joy of life that beamed from his face, he went up to the commode.

"Gerasim!" said Ivan Ilych in a weak voice.

Gerasim started, evidently afraid he might have committed some blunder, and with a rapid movement turned his fresh, kind, simple young face which just showed the first downy signs of a beard.

"Yes, sir?"

"That must be very unpleasant for you. You must forgive me. I am helpless."

"Oh, why, sir," and Gerasim's eyes beamed and he showed his glistening white teeth, "what's a little trouble? It's a case of illness with you, sir."

And his deft strong hands did their accustomed task, and he went out of the room stepping lightly. Five minutes later he as lightly returned.

Ivan Ilych was still sitting in the same position in the armchair.

"Gerasim," he said when the latter had replaced the freshly-washed utensil. "Please come here and help me." Gerasim went up to him. "Lift me up. It is hard for me to get up, and I have sent Dmitri away."

Gerasim went up to him, grasped his master with his strong arms deftly but gently, in the same way that he stepped—lifted him, supported him with one hand, and with the other drew up his trousers and would have set him down again, but Ivan Ilych asked to be led to the sofa. Gerasim, without an effort and without apparent pressure, led him, almost lifting him, to the sofa and placed him on it.

"Thank you. How easily and well you do it all!"

Gerasim smiled again and turned to leave the room. But Ivan Ilych felt his presence such a comfort that he did not want to let him go.

"One thing more, please move up that chair. No, the other one— under my feet. It is easier for me when my feet are raised."

Gerasim brought the chair, set it down gently in place, and raised Ivan Ilych's legs on to it. It seemed to Ivan Ilych that he felt better while Gerasim was holding up his legs.

"It's better when my legs are higher," he said. "Place that cushion under them."

Gerasim did so. He again lifted the legs and placed them, and again Ivan Ilych felt better while Gerasim held his legs. When he set them down Ivan Ilych fancied he felt worse.

"Gerasim," he said. "Are you busy now?"

"Not at all, sir," said Gerasim, who had learnt from the townsfolk how to speak to gentlefolk.

"What have you still to do?"

"What have I to do? I've done everything except chopping the logs for tomorrow."

"Then hold my legs up a bit higher, can you?"

"Of course I can. Why not?" And Gerasim raised his master's legs higher and Ivan Ilych thought that in that position he did not feel any pain at all.

"And how about the logs?"

"Don't trouble about that, sir. There's plenty of time."

Ivan Ilych told Gerasim to sit down and hold his legs, and began to talk to him. And strange to say it seemed to him that he felt better while Gerasim held his legs up.

After that Ivan Ilych would sometimes call Gerasim and get him to hold his legs on his shoulders, and he liked talking to him. Gerasim did it all easily, willingly, simply, and with a good nature that touched Ivan Ilych. Health, strength, and vitality in other people were offensive to him, but Gerasim's strength and vitality did not mortify but soothed him.

What tormented Ivan Ilych most was the deception, the lie, which for some reason they all accepted, that he was not dying but was simply ill, and that he only need keep quiet and undergo a treatment and then something very good would result. He however knew that do what they would nothing would come of it, only still more agonizing suffering and death. This deception tortured him—their not wishing to admit what they all knew and what he knew, but wanting to lie to him concerning his terrible condition, and wishing and forcing him to participate in that lie. Those lies—lies enacted over him on the eve of his death and destined to degrade this awful, solemn act to the level of their visitings, their curtains, their sturgeon for dinner—were a terrible agony for Ivan Ilych. And strangely enough, many times when they were going through their antics over him he had been within a hairbreadth of calling out to them: "Stop lying! You know and I know that I am dying. Then at least stop lying about it!" But he had never had the spirit to do it. The awful, terrible act of his dying was, he could see, reduced by those about him to the level of a casual, unpleasant, and almost indecorous incident (as if someone entered a drawing-room diffusing an unpleasant odour) and this was done by that very decorum which he had served all his life long. He saw that no one felt for him, because no one even wished to grasp his position. Only Gerasim recognized it and pitied him. And so Ivan Ilych felt at ease only with him. He felt comforted when Gerasim supported his legs (sometimes all night long) and refused to go to bed, saying: "Don't you worry, Ivan Ilych. I'll get sleep enough later on," or when he suddenly became familiar and exclaimed: "If you weren't sick it would be another matter, but as it is, why should I grudge a little trouble?" Gerasim alone did not lie; everything showed that he alone understood the facts of the case and did not consider it necessary to disguise them, but simply felt sorry for his emaciated and enfeebled master. Once when Ivan Ilych was sending him away he even said straight out. "We shall all of us die, so why should I grudge a little trouble?"—expressing the fact that he did not think his work burdensome, because he was doing it for a dying man and hoped someone would do the same for him when his time came.

Apart from this lying, or because of it, what most tormented Ivan Ilych was that no one pitied him as he wished to be pitied. At certain moments after prolonged suffering he wished most of all (though he would have been ashamed to confess it) for someone to pity him as a sick child is pitied. He longed to be petted and comforted. He knew he was an important functionary, that he had a beard turning grey, and that therefore what he longed for was impossible, but still he longed for it. And in Gerasim's attitude towards him there was something akin to what he wished for, and so that attitude comforted him. Ivan Ilych wanted to weep, wanted to be petted and cried over, and then his colleague Shebek would come, and instead of weeping and being petted, Ivan Ilych would assume a serious, severe, and profound air, and by force of habit would express his opinion on a decision of the Court of Cassation and would stubbornly insist on that view. This falsity around him and within him did more than anything else to poison his last days.

VIII

It was morning. He knew it was morning because Gerasim had gone, and Peter the footman had come and put out the candles, drawn back one of the curtains, and begun quietly to tidy up. Whether it was morning or evening, Friday or Sunday, made no difference, it was all just the same: the gnawing, unmitigated, agonizing pain, never ceasing for an instant, the consciousness of life inexorably waning but not yet extinguished, the approach of that ever dreaded and hateful Death which was the only reality, and always the same falsity. What were days, weeks, hours, in such a case?

"Will you have some tea, sir?"

"He wants things to be regular, and wishes the gentlefolk to drink tea in the morning," thought Ivan Ilych, and only said "No."

"Wouldn't you like to move onto the sofa, sir?"

"He wants to tidy up the room, and I'm in the way. I am uncleanliness and disorder," he thought, and said only:

"No, leave me alone."

The man went on bustling about. Ivan Ilych stretched out his hand. Peter came up, ready to help.

"What is it, sir?"

"My watch."

Peter took the watch which was close at hand and gave it to his master.

"Half-past eight. Are they up?"

"No, sir, except Vladimir Ivanovich" (the son) "who has gone to

school. Praskovya Fëdorovna ordered me to wake her if you asked for
her. Shall I do so?"

"No, there's no need to." "Perhaps I'd better have some tea," he
thought, and added aloud: "Yes, bring me some tea."

Peter went to the door, but Ivan Ilych dreaded being left alone.
"How can I keep him here? Oh yes, my medicine." "Peter, give me
my medicine." "Why not? Perhaps it may still do me some good." He
took a spoonful and swallowed it. "No, it won't help. It's all tomfoolery,
all deception," he decided as soon as he became aware of the familiar,
sickly, hopeless taste. "No, I can't believe in it any longer. But the pain,
why this pain? If it would only cease just for a moment!" And he
moaned. Peter turned towards him. "It's all right. Go and fetch me some
tea."

Peter went out. Left alone Ivan Ilych groaned not so much with pain,
terrible though that was, as from mental anguish. Always and for ever the
same, always these endless days and nights. If only it would come quicker!
If only *what* would come quicker? Death, darkness? . . . No, no! Anything
rather than death!

When Peter returned with the tea on a tray, Ivan Ilych stared at him for a
time in perplexity, not realizing who and what he was. Peter was disconcerted by that look and his embarrassment brought Ivan Ilych to himself.

"Oh, tea! All right, put it down. Only help me to wash and put on a
clean shirt."

And Ivan Ilych began to wash. With pauses for rest, he washed his
hands and then his face, cleaned his teeth, brushed his hair, and looked in
the glass. He was terrified by what he saw, especially by the limp way in
which his hair clung to his pallid forehead.

While his shirt was being changed he knew that he would be still more
frightened at the sight of his body, so he avoided looking at it. Finally
he was ready. He drew on a dressing-gown, wrapped himself in a plaid,
and sat down in the armchair to take his tea. For a moment he felt refreshed, but soon as he began to drink the tea he was again aware of the
same taste, and the pain also returned. He finished it with an effort, and
then lay down stretching out his legs, and dismissed Peter.

Always the same. Now a spark of hope flashes up, then a sea of despair
rages, and always pain; always pain, always despair, and always the same.
When alone he had a dreadful and distressing desire to call someone, but
he knew beforehand that with others present it would be still worse. "Another dose of morphine—to lose consciousness. I will tell him, the doctor,
that he must think of something else. It's impossible, impossible, to go on
like this."

An hour and another pass like that. But now there is a ring at the door
bell. Perhaps it's the doctor? It is. He comes in fresh, hearty, plump, and
cheerful, with that look on his face that seems to say: "There now, you're

in a panic about something, but we'll arrange it all for you directly!" The doctor knows this expression is out of place here, but he has put it on once for all and can't take it off—like a man who has put on a frock-coat in the morning to pay a round of calls.

The doctor rubs his hands vigorously and reassuringly.

"Brr! How cold it is! There's such a sharp frost; just let me warm myself!" he says, as if it were only a matter of waiting till he was warm, and then he would put everything right.

"Well now, how are you?"

Ivan Ilych feels that the doctor would like to say: "Well, how are our affairs?" but that even he feels that this would not do, and says instead: "What sort of a night have you had?"

Ivan Ilych looks at him as much as to say: "Are you really never ashamed of lying?" But the doctor does not wish to understand this question, and Ivan Ilych says: "Just as terrible as ever. The pain never leaves me and never subsides. If only something . . ."

"Yes, you sick people are always like that. . . . There, now I think I am warm enough. Even Praskovya Fëdorovna, who is so particular, could find no fault with my temperature. Well, now I can say good-morning," and the doctor presses his patient's hand.

Then, dropping his former playfulness, he begins with a most serious face to examine the patient, feeling his pulse and taking his temperature, and then begins the sounding and auscultation.

Ivan Ilych knows quite well and definitely that all this is nonsense and pure deception, but when the doctor, getting down on his knee, leans over him, putting his ear first higher then lower, and performs various gymnastic movements over him with a significant expression on his face, Ivan Ilych submits to it all as he used to submit to the speeches of the lawyers, though he knew very well that they were all lying and why they were lying.

The doctor, kneeling on the sofa, is still sounding him when Praskovya Fëdorovna's silk dress rustles at the door and she is heard scolding Peter for not having let her know of the doctor's arrival.

She comes in, kisses her husband, and at once proceeds to prove that she has been up a long time already, and only owing to a misunderstanding failed to be there when the doctor arrived.

Ivan Ilych looks at her, scans her all over, sets against her the whiteness and plumpness and cleanness of her hands and neck, the gloss of her hair, and the sparkle of her vivacious eyes. He hates her with his whole soul. And the thrill of hatred he feels for her makes him suffer from her touch.

Her attitude towards him and his disease is still the same. Just as the doctor had adopted a certain relation to his patient which he could not abandon, so had she formed one towards him—that he was not doing something he ought to do and was himself to blame, and that she reproached him lovingly for this—and she could not now change that attitude.

"You see he doesn't listen to me and doesn't take his medicine at the proper time. And above all he lies in a position that is no doubt bad for him—with his legs up."

She described how he made Gerasim hold his legs up.

The doctor smiled with a contemptuous affability that said: "What's to be done? These sick people do have foolish fancies of that kind, but we must forgive them."

When the examination was over the doctor looked at his watch, and then Praskovya Fëdorovna announced to Ivan Ilych that it was of course as he pleased, but she had sent today for a celebrated specialist who would examine him and have a consultation with Michael Danilovich (their regular doctor).

"Please don't raise any objections. I am doing this for my own sake," she said ironically, letting it be felt that she was doing it all for his sake and only said this to leave no right to refuse. He remained silent, knitting his brows. He felt that he was so surrounded and involved in a mesh of falsity that it was hard to unravel anything.

Everything she did for him was entirely for her own sake, and she told him she was doing for herself what she actually was doing for herself, as if that was so incredible that he must understand the opposite.

At half-past eleven the celebrated specialist arrived. Again the sounding began and the significant conversations in his presence and in another room, about the kidneys and the appendix, and the questions and answers, with such an air of importance that again, instead of the real question of life and death which now alone confronted him, the question arose of the kidney and appendix which were not behaving as they ought to and would now be attacked by Michael Danilovich and the specialist and forced to amend their ways.

The celebrated specialist took leave of him with a serious though not hopeless look, and in reply to the timid question Ivan Ilych, with eyes glistening with fear and hope, put to him as to whether there was a chance of recovery, said that he could not vouch for it but there was a possibility. The look of hope with which Ivan Ilych watched the doctor out was so pathetic that Praskovya Fëdorovna, seeing it, even wept as she left the room to hand the doctor his fee.

The gleam of hope kindled by the doctor's encouragement did not last long. The same room, the same pictures, curtains, wallpaper, medicine bottles, were all there, and the same aching suffering body, and Ivan Ilych began to moan. They gave him a subcutaneous injection and he sank into oblivion.

It was twilight when he came to. They brought him his dinner and he swallowed some beef tea with difficulty, and then everything was the same again and night was coming on.

After dinner, at seven o'clock, Praskovya Fëdorovna came into the room in evening dress, her full bosom pushed up by her corset, and with traces of powder on her face. She had reminded him in the morning that they were going to the theatre. Sarah Bernhardt was visiting the town and they had a box, which he had insisted on their taking. Now he had forgotten about it and her toilet offended him, but he concealed his vexation when he remembered that he had himself insisted on their securing a box and going because it would be an instructive and aesthetic pleasure for the children.

Praskovya Fëdorovna came in, self-satisfied but yet with a rather guilty air. She sat down and asked how he was, but, as he saw, only for the sake of asking and not in order to learn about it, knowing that there was nothing to learn—and then went on to what she really wanted to say: that she would not on any account have gone but that the box had been taken and Helen and their daughter were going, as well as Petrishchev (the examining magistrate, their daughter's fiancé), and that it was out of the question to let them go alone; but that she would have much preferred to sit with him for a while; and he must be sure to follow the doctor's orders while she was away.

"Oh, and Fëdor Petrovich" (the fiancé) "would like to come in. May he? And Lisa?"

"All right."

Their daughter came in in full evening dress, her fresh young flesh exposed (making a show of that very flesh which in his own case caused so much suffering), strong, healthy, evidently in love, and impatient with illness, suffering, and death, because they interfered with her happiness.

Fëdor Petrovich came in too, in evening dress, his hair curled *à la Capoul,* a tight stiff collar round his long sinewy neck, an enormous white shirt-front, and narrow black trousers tightly stretched over his strong thighs. He had one white glove tightly drawn on, and was holding his opera hat in his hand.

Following him the schoolboy crept in unnoticed, in a new uniform, poor little fellow, and wearing gloves. Terribly dark shadows showed under his eyes, the meaning of which Ivan Ilych knew well.

His son had always seemed pathetic to him, and now it was dreadful to see the boy's frightened look of pity. It seemed to Ivan Ilych that Vasya was the only one besides Gerasim who understood and pitied him.

They all sat down and again asked how he was. A silence followed. Lisa asked her mother about the opera-glasses, and there was an altercation between mother and daughter as to who had taken them and where they had been put. This occasioned some unpleasantness.

Fëdor Petrovich inquired of Ivan Ilych whether he had ever seen Sarah Bernhardt. Ivan Ilych did not at first catch the question, but then replied: "No, have you seen her before?"

"Yes, in *Adrienne Lecouvreur.*"

Praskovya Fëdorovna mentioned some rôles in which Sarah Bernhardt was particularly good. Her daughter disagreed. Conversation sprang up as to the elegance and realism of her acting—the sort of conversation that is always repeated and is always the same.

In the midst of the conversation Fëdor Petrovich glanced at Ivan Ilych and became silent. The others also looked at him and grew silent. Ivan Ilych was staring with glittering eyes straight before him, evidently indignant with them. This had to be rectified, but it was impossible to do so. The silence had to be broken, but for a time no one dared to break it and they all became afraid that the conventional deception would suddenly become obvious and the truth become plain to all. Lisa was the first to pluck up courage and break that silence, but by trying to hide what everybody was feeling, she betrayed it.

"Well, if we are going it's time to start," she said, looking at her watch, a present from her father, and with a faint and significant smile at Fëdor Petrovich relating to something known only to them. She got up with a rustle of her dress.

They all rose, said good-night, and went away.

When they had gone it seemed to Ivan Ilych that he felt better; the falsity had gone with them. But the pain remained—that same pain and that same fear that made everything monotonously alike, nothing harder and nothing easier. Everything was worse.

Again minute followed minute and hour followed hour. Everything remained the same and there was no cessation. And the inevitable end of it all became more and more terrible.

"Yes, send Gerasim here," he replied to a question Peter asked.

IX

His wife returned late at night. She came in on tiptoe, but he heard her, opened his eyes, and made haste to close them again. She wished to send Gerasim away and to sit with him herself, but he opened his eyes and said: "No, go away."

"Are you in great pain?"

"Always the same."

"Take some opium."

He agreed and took some. She went away.

Till about three in the morning he was in a state of stupefied misery. It seemed to him that he and his pain were being thrust into a narrow, deep black sack, but though they were pushed further and further in they could not be pushed to the bottom. And this, terrible enough in itself, was accompanied by suffering. He was frightened yet wanted to fall through the sack, he struggled but yet co-operated. And suddenly he broke through, fell, and regained consciousness. Gerasim was sitting at the foot of the bed dozing quietly and patiently, while he himself lay with his emaciated stockinged legs resting on Gerasim's shoulders; the same shaded candle was there and the same unceasing pain.

"Go away, Gerasim," he whispered.

"It's all right, sir. I'll stay a while."

"No. Go away."

He removed his legs from Gerasim's shoulders, turned sideways onto his arm, and felt sorry for himself. He only waited till Gerasim had gone into the next room and then restrained himself no longer but wept like a child. He wept on account of his helplessness, his terrible loneliness, the cruelty of man, the cruelty of God, and the absence of God.

"Why hast Thou done all this? Why hast Thou brought me here? Why, why dost Thou torment me so terribly?"

He did not expect an answer and yet wept because there was no answer and could be none. The pain again grew more acute, but he did not stir and did not call. He said to himself: "Go on! Strike me! But what is it for? What have I done to Thee? What is it for?"

Then he grew quiet and not only ceased weeping but even held his breath and became all attention. It was as though he were listening not to an audible voice but to the voice of his soul, to the current of thoughts arising within him.

"What is it you want?" was the first clear conception capable of expression in words, that he heard.

"What do you want? What do you want?" he repeated to himself.

"What do I want? To live and not to suffer," he answered.

And again he listened with such concentrated attention that even his pain did not distract him.

"To live? How?" asked his inner voice.

"Why, to live as I used to—well and pleasantly."

"As you lived before, well and pleasantly?" the voice repeated.

And in imagination he began to recall the best moments of his pleasant life. But strange to say none of those best moments of his pleasant life now seemed at all what they had then seemed—none of them except the first recollections of childhood. There, in childhood, there had been something really pleasant with which it would be possible to live if it could return. But the child who had experienced that happiness existed no longer, it was like a reminiscence of somebody else.

As soon as the period began which had produced the present Ivan Ilych, all that had then seemed joys now melted before his sight and turned into something trivial and often nasty.

And the further he departed from childhood and the nearer he came to the present the more worthless and doubtful were the joys. This began with the School of Law. A little that was really good was still found there—there was lightheartedness, friendship, and hope. But in the upper classes there had already been fewer of such good moments. Then during the first years of his official career, when he was in the service of the Governor, some pleasant moments again occurred; they were the memories of love for a woman. Then all became confused and there was still less of what was good; later on again there was still less that was good, and the further he went the less there was. His marriage, a mere accident, then the disenchantment that followed it, his wife's bad breath and the sensuality and hypocrisy: then that deadly official life and those preoccupations about money, a year of it, and two, and ten, and twenty, and always the same thing. And the longer it lasted the more deadly it became. "It is as if I had been going downhill while I imagined I was going up. And that is really what it was. I was going up in public opinion, but to the same extent life was ebbing away from me. And now it is all done and there is only death."

"Then what does it mean? Why? It can't be that life is so senseless and horrible. But if it really has been so horrible and senseless, why must I die and die in agony? There is something wrong!"

"Maybe I did not live as I ought to have done," it suddenly occurred to him. "But how could that be, when I did everything properly?" he replied, and immediately dismissed from his mind this, the sole solution of all the riddles of life and death, as something quite impossible.

"Then what do you want now? To live? Live how? Live as you lived in the law courts when the usher proclaimed 'The judge is coming!' The judge is coming, the judge!" he repeated to himself. "Here he is, the judge. But I am not guilty!" he exclaimed angrily. "What is it for?" And he ceased crying, but turning his face to the wall continued to ponder on the same question: Why, and for what purpose, is there all this horror? But however much he pondered he found no answer. And whenever the thought occurred to him, as it often did, that it all resulted from his not having lived as he ought to have done, he at once recalled the correctness of his whole life and dismissed so strange an idea.

X

Another fortnight passed. Ivan Ilych now no longer left his sofa. He would not lie in bed but lay on the sofa, facing the wall nearly all the time. He suffered ever the same unceasing agonies and in his loneliness pondered always on the same insoluble question: "What is this? Can it be that it is Death?" And the inner voice answered: "Yes, it is Death."

"Why these sufferings?" And the voice answered, "For no reason—they just are so." Beyond and besides this there was nothing.

From the very beginning of his illness, ever since he had first been to see the doctor, Ivan Ilych's life had been divided between two contrary and alternating moods: now it was despair and the expectation of this uncomprehended and terrible death, and now hope and an intently interested observation of the functioning of his organs. Now before his eyes there was only a kidney or an intestine that temporarily evaded its duty, and now only that incomprehensible and dreadful death from which it was impossible to escape.

These two states of mind had alternated from the very beginning of his illness, but the further it progressed the more doubtful and fantastic became the conception of the kidney, and the more real the sense of impending death.

He had but to call to mind what he had been three months before and what he was now, to call to mind with what regularity he had been going downhill, for every possibility of hope to be shattered.

Latterly during that loneliness in which he found himself as he lay facing the back of the sofa, a loneliness in the midst of a populous town and surrounded by numerous acquaintances and relations but that yet could not have been more complete anywhere—either at the bottom of the sea or under the earth—during that terrible loneliness Ivan Ilych had lived only in memories of the past. Pictures of his past rose before him one after another. They always began with what was nearest in time and then went back to what was most remote—to his childhood—and rested there. If he thought of the stewed prunes that had been offered him that day, his mind went back to the raw shrivelled French plums of his childhood, their peculiar flavour and the flow of saliva when he sucked their stones, and along with the memory of that taste came a whole series of memories of those days: his nurse, his brother, and their toys. "No, I mustn't think of that. . . . It is too painful," Ivan Ilych said to himself, and brought himself back to the present—to the button on the back of the sofa and the creases in its morocco. "Morocco is expensive, but it does not wear well: there had been a quarrel about it. It was a different kind of quarrel and a different kind of morocco that time when we tore father's portfolio and were punished, and mamma brought us some tarts. . . ." And again his thoughts dwelt on his childhood, and again it was painful and he tried to banish them and fix his mind on something else.

Then again together with that chain of memories another series passed through his mind—of how his illness had progressed and grown worse. There also the further back he looked the more life there had been. There had been more of what was good in life and more of life itself. The two merged together. "Just as the pain went on getting worse and worse, so my life grew worse and worse," he thought. "There is one bright spot there at the back, at the beginning of life, and afterwards all becomes blacker and blacker and proceeds more and more rapidly—in inverse ratio to the square of the distance from death," thought Ivan Ilych. And the example of a stone falling downwards with increasing velocity entered his mind. Life, a series of increasing sufferings, flies further and further towards its end—the most terrible suffering. "I am flying. . . ." He shuddered, shifted himself, and tried to resist, but was already aware that resistance was impossible, and again, with eyes weary of gazing but unable to cease seeing what was before them, he stared at the back of the sofa and waited—awaiting that dreadful fall and shock and destruction.

"Resistence is impossible!" he said to himself. "If I could only understand what it is all for! But that too is impossible. An explanation would be possible if it could be said that I have not lived as I ought to. But it is impossible to say that," and he remembered all the legality, correctitude, and propriety of his life. "That at any rate can certainly not be admitted," he thought, and his lips smiled ironically as if someone could see that smile and be taken in by it. "There is no explanation! Agony, death . . . What for?"

XI

Another two weeks went by in this way and during that fortnight an event occurred that Ivan Ilych and his wife had desired. Petrishchev formally proposed. It happened in the evening. The next day Praskovya Fëdorovna came into her husband's room considering how best to inform him of it, but that very night there had been a fresh change for the worse in his condition. She found him still lying on the sofa but in a different position. He lay on his back, groaning and staring fixedly straight in front of him.

She began to remind him of his medicines, but he turned his eyes towards her with such a look that she did not finish what she was saying; so great an animosity, to her in particular, did that look express.

"For Christ's sake let me die in peace!" he said.

She would have gone away, but just then their daughter came in and went up to say good morning. He looked at her as he had done at his wife, and in reply to her inquiry about his health said dryly that he would soon free them all of himself. They were both silent and after sitting with him for a while went away.

"Is it our fault?" Lisa said to her mother. "It's as if we were to blame! I am sorry for papa, but why should we be tortured?"

The doctor came at his usual time. Ivan Ilych answered "Yes" and "No," never taking his angry eyes from him, and at last said: "You know you can do nothing for me, so leave me alone."

"We can ease your sufferings."

"You can't even do that. Let me be."

The doctor went into the drawing-room and told Praskovya Fëdorovna that the case was very serious and that the only resource left was opium to allay her husband's sufferings, which must be terrible.

It was true, as the doctor said, that Ivan Ilych's sufferings were terrible, but worse than the physical sufferings were his mental sufferings, which were his chief torture.

His mental sufferings were due to the fact that that night, as he looked at Gerasim's sleepy, good-natured face with its prominent cheekbones, the question suddenly occurred to him: "What if my whole life has really been wrong?"

It occurred to him that what had appeared perfectly impossible before, namely that he had not spent his life as he should have done, might after all be true. It occurred to him that his scarcely perceptible attempts to struggle against what was considered good by the most highly placed people, those scarcely noticeable impulses which he had immediately suppressed, might have been the real thing, and all the rest false. And his professional duties and the whole arrangement of his life and of his family, and all his social and official interests, might all have been false. He tried to defend all those things to himself and suddenly felt the weakness of what he was defending. There was nothing to defend.

"But if that is so," he said to himself, "and I am leaving this life with the consciousness that I have lost all that was given me and it is impossible to rectify it—what then?"

He lay on his back and began to pass his life in review in quite a new way. In the morning when he saw first his footman, then his wife, then his daughter, and then the doctor, their every word and movement confirmed to him the awful truth that had been revealed to him during the night. In them he saw himself—all that for which he had lived—and saw clearly that it was not real at all, but a terrible and huge deception which had hidden both life and death. This consciousness intensified his physical suffering tenfold. He groaned and tossed about, and pulled at his clothing which choked and stifled him. And he hated them on that account.

He was given a large dose of opium and became unconscious, but at noon his sufferings began again. He drove everybody away and tossed from side to side.

His wife came to him and said:

"Jean, my dear, do this for me. It can't do any harm and often helps. Healthy people often do it."

He opened his eyes wide.

"What? Take communion? Why? It's unnecessary! However . . ."

She began to cry.

"Yes, do, my dear. I'll send for our priest. He is such a nice man."

"All right. Very well," he muttered.

When the priest came and heard his confession, Ivan Ilych was softened and seemed to feel a relief from his doubts and consequently from his sufferings, and for a moment there came a ray of hope. He again began to think of the vermiform appendix and the possibility of correcting it. He received the sacrament with tears in his eyes.

When they laid him down again afterwards he felt a moment's ease, and the hope that he might live awoke in him again. He began to think of the operation that had been suggested to him. "To live! I want to live!" he said to himself.

His wife came in to congratulate him after his communion, and when uttering the usual conventional words she added:

"You feel better, don't you?"

Without looking at her he said "Yes."

Her dress, her figure, the expression of her face, the tone of her voice, all revealed the same thing. "This is wrong, it is not as it should be. All you have lived for and still live for is falsehood and deception, hiding life and death from you." And as soon as he admitted that thought, his hatred and his agonizing physical suffering again sprang up, and with that suffering a consciousness of the unavoidable, approaching end. And to this was added a new sensation of grinding shooting pain and a feeling of suffocation.

The expression of his face when he uttered that "yes" was dreadful. Having uttered it, he looked her straight in the eyes, turned on his face with a rapidity extraordinary in his weak state and shouted:

"Go away! Go away and leave me alone!"

XII

From that moment the screaming began that continued for three days, and was so terrible that one could not hear it through two closed doors without horror. At the moment he answered his wife he realized that he was lost, that there was no return, that the end had come, the very end, and his doubts were still unsolved and remained doubts.

"Oh! Oh! Oh!" he cried in various intonations. He had begun by screaming "I won't!" and continued screaming on the letter O.

For three whole days, during which time did not exist for him, he struggled in that black sack into which he was being thrust by an invisible, resistless force. He struggled as a man condemned to death struggles in the hands of the executioner, knowing that he cannot save himself. And every moment he felt that despite all his efforts he was drawing nearer and nearer to what terrified him. He felt that his agony was due to his being thrust into that black hole and still more to his not being able to get right into it. He was hindered from getting into it by his conviction that his life had been a good one. That very justification of his life held him fast and prevented his moving forward, and it caused him most torment of all.

Suddenly some force struck him in the chest and side, making it still harder to breathe, and he fell through the hole and there at the bottom was a light. What had happened to him was like the sensation one sometimes experiences in a railway carriage when one thinks one is going backwards while one is really going forwards and suddenly becomes aware of the real direction.

"Yes, it was all not the right thing," he said to himself, "but that's no matter. It can be done. But what *is* the right thing?" he asked himself, and suddenly grew quiet.

This occurred at the end of the third day, two hours before his death. Just then his schoolboy son had crept softly in and gone up to the bedside. The dying man was still screaming desperately and waving his arms. His hand fell on the boy's head, and the boy caught it, pressed it to his lips, and began to cry.

At that very moment Ivan Ilych fell through and caught sight of the light, and it was revealed to him that though his life had not been what it should have been, this could still be rectified. He asked himself, "What *is* the right thing?" and grew still, listening. Then he felt that someone was kissing his hand. He opened his eyes, looked at his son, and felt sorry for him. His wife came up to him and he glanced at her. She was gazing at him open-mouthed, with undried tears on her nose and cheek and a despairing look on her face. He felt sorry for her too.

"Yes, I am making them wretched," he thought. "They are sorry, but it will be better for them when I die." He wished to say this but had not the strength to utter it. "Besides, why speak? I must act," he thought. With a look at his wife he indicated his son and said: "Take him away . . . sorry for him . . . sorry for you too. . . ." He tried to add, "Forgive me," but said "forgo" and waved his hand, knowing that He whose understanding mattered would understand.

And suddenly it grew clear to him that what had been oppressing him and would not leave him was all dropping away at once from two sides, from ten sides, and from all sides. He was sorry for them, he must act so as not to hurt them: release them and free himself from these sufferings. "How good and how simple!" he thought. "And the pain?" he asked himself. "What has become of it? Where are you, pain?"

He turned his attention to it.

"Yes, here it is. Well, what of it? Let the pain be."

"And death . . . where is it?"

He sought his former accustomed fear of death and did not find it. "Where is it? What death?" There was no fear because there was no death.

In place of death there was light.

"So that's what it is!" he suddenly exclaimed aloud. "What joy!"

To him all this happened in a single instant, and the meaning of that instant did not change. For those present his agony continued for another two hours. Something rattled in his throat, his emaciated body twitched, then the gasping and rattle became less and less frequent.

"It is finished!" said someone near him.

He heard these words and repeated them in his soul.

"Death is finished," he said to himself. "It is no more!"

"He drew in a breath, stopped in the midst of ∙a sigh, stretched out, and died.

5

THOMAS MANN
Tonio Kröger

"Craftsmanlike" is a word often used to describe the fiction of Thomas Mann. His work reflects the kinds of concern one associates with the cabinetmaker or stone mason, particularly deliberateness, painstaking elaboration, and attention to structural relationship among parts. It is no wonder that nearly everything in his writing—and most importantly, characterization—evinces such a satisfying sense of carefully constructed psychological contours. Mann also reveals the craftsman's love for his material and for the process of creating substantial, enduring works worthy of respect.

In *Tonio Kröger* his craftsmanship, his love of his art, and his quest for literary respectability are not only characteristics of style and tone, but also main themes. More than in any other fiction he wrote, he turned to the circumstances of his own life for the material of this short novel. Even a quick glance over the facts of his life (see p. 618) reveals the extent of autobiographical reference in Tonio's parentage, character, and artistic philosophy. The autobiographical flavor of *Tonio Kröger* adds to its exceptional tone of personal warmth, as well as its special kind of self-consciousness. Because Tonio's artistic sensibility is much like Mann's, the story acquires a double framework of self-consciousness; the artist writes self-consciously about the acutely self-conscious perceptions of the artistic character. This sort of introspection is not often successfully employed in fiction, and it has been the ruin of many a second-rate novelist. But instead of deviating into morbidness or cynicism, the redoubled consciousness of *Tonio Kröger* strikes through to the genuine universality of great art: each image and scene reverberates with the heightened tension of the symbolic meaning intuited by the artist-as-character. Moreover, Mann reveals that self-conciousness actually makes the artist a symbolic representative of mankind, even though it is the very quality which most alienates the artist from society. If the Hamlet-like Tonio thinks, feels, and suffers more than ordinary people, there is still more of humanity in him for that reason. But does the artist's increased consciousness lead to a more valuable or viable way of life either for himself or others? These disturbing questions are also important themes of *Tonio Kröger*.

Two quietly dramatized sequences typify the psychological scars of Tonio's youth. Bewildered by a sweet-sad knowledge of life far beyond his years, he idealizes sturdy, popular Hans Hansen. To a certain extent, Tonio confuses his love for Hans with his desire to partake in Hans's greater ability to live life fully. He is wounded when Hans is unable to return his ardor with anything more than casual affection. When Tonio falls in love around the age of sixteen, it is of course with a female counterpart of Hans, "blond Inge Holm." He is so distracted by love that he mistakenly joins in the ladies' quadrille during dancing class—a scene made delightfully absurd by the eccentric Herr Knaak. The occasion is anything but delightful to Tonio, who is once again stricken with the intuition that he will never be permitted to join in the dance of life with those who are spontaneous, vital, and ordinary.

Background setting plays an important role in these scenes. The drama and symbolism of Tonio's experiences are accentuated by the gabled, spired, and fountained quaintness of ancient Lübeck. To him it is a father-dominated place: venerable, perfect in its North European way, and alive with masculine virtues of commerce and respectability. A great part of the charm of this novel is its distinctively European quality, and almost like a tourist, like a stranger in his own land, Tonio instinctively scrutinizes everything around him, including architectural details, clothing, gestures, even distinctive language sounds, for clues to his own cultural identity.

By moving south to Bavarian Munich, Tonio symbolically rejects this way of life and embraces a life of passion and art, which he associates with his mother. Tonio is already an accomplished author and nearing middle age when he visits Lisabeta Ivanovna. His discourse to her on art is worth taking seriously, both for itself and for the way its themes unify the story by reaching back through events of the first half and anticipating those of the second. Nevertheless, his words sound rather academic and stiff. As almost always, Mann's technique is subtly ironic. Here he gently mocks Tonio for being pompous, when in reality Tonio is trying passionately to communicate the truth of his convictions to one of the very few people who might understand him.

Searching for the meaning of his own life, Tonio returns to the place of his birth. By its very nature the act of returning to an ancestral home evokes powerful emotions, and Mann's genius is evident in the way he suggests the passions warring in Tonio's soul as he relives the events of his youth in memory. To Tonio, each revisited scene is like a symbol in some dream code, and at night he dreams furiously. Memories of his father's disapproval are never far from his mind. His brief encounter with the Lübeck police is a symbolic warning that the time is forever past when he might have assumed the identity of a genuine, respectable bourgeois like his father.

Still farther north, in the region of Hamlet's legendary castle in Denmark, the lovely Danish beaches and meadows enable Tonio to put aside the cares of art. He begins to feel something of the strength and spontaneity of spirit that others find in social community. But again, patterns of return and repetition emerge: there is another Hans, another Inge, and another dance. Once again Tonio is the outsider, looking in on life and wishing he were part of it. Mann intensifies the meaning of these repeated patterns by repeating key lines and phrases with subtle variation, a technique made famous in nineteenth-century Europe by the opera composer Richard Wagner. The effect in *Tonio Kröger* is a distinctively musical one. Like musical notes, Mann's repeated phrases create harmonies of emotional resonance.

One traditional formula for short fiction demands that by the end of the story the main character must undergo substantial change as a result of conflict. Tonio Kröger certainly undergoes conflict, and he changes by growing from a difficult childhood to manhood and fame. But the crucial conflicts that face him throughout the story—conflicts between art and life, mother and father, south and north—these remain unresolved in the end. The real change in Tonio, implied in his concluding letter to Lisabeta, is his decision not to change and not to resolve his conflicts.

Tonio Kröger

The winter sun, poor ghost of itself, hung milky and wan behind layers of cloud above the huddled roofs of the town. In the gabled streets it was wet and windy and there came in gusts a sort of soft hail, not ice, not snow.

School was out. The hosts of the released streamed over the paved court and out at the wrought-iron gate, where they broke up and hastened off right and left. Elder pupils held their books in a strap high on the left shoulder and rowed, right arm against the wind, towards dinner. Small people trotted gaily off, splashing the slush with their feet, the tools of learning rattling amain in their walrus-skin satchels. But one and all pulled off their caps and cast down their eyes in awe before the Olympian hat and ambrosial beard of a master moving homewards with measured stride. . . .

"Ah, there you are at last, Hans," said Tonio Kröger. He had been waiting a long time in the street and went up with a smile to the friend he saw coming out of the gate in talk with other boys and about to go off with them. . . . "What?" said Hans, and looked at Tonio. "Right-oh! We'll take a little walk, then."

Tonio said nothing and his eyes were clouded. Did Hans forget, had he only just remembered that they were to take a walk together today? And he himself had looked forward to it with almost incessant joy.

"Well, good-bye, fellows," said Hans Hansen to his comrades. "I'm taking a walk with Kröger." And the two turned to their left, while the others sauntered off in the opposite direction.

Hans and Tonio had time to take a walk after school because in neither of their families was dinner served before four o'clock. Their fathers were prominent business men, who held public office and were of consequence in the town. Hans's people had owned for some generations the big wood-yards down by the river, where powerful machine-saws hissed and spat and cut up timber; while Tonio was the son of Consul Kröger, whose grain-sacks with the firm name in great black letters you might see any day driven through the streets; his large, old ancestral home was the finest house in all the town. The two friends had to keep taking off their hats to their many acquaintances; some folk did not even wait for the fourteen-year-old lads to speak first, as by rights they should.

Both of them carried their satchels across their shoulders and both were well and warmly dressed: Hans in a short sailor jacket, with the wide blue collar of his sailor suit turned out over shoulders and back, and Tonio in a belted grey overcoat. Hans wore a Danish sailor cap with black ribbons, beneath which streamed a shock of straw-coloured hair. He was uncommonly handsome and well built, broad in the shoulders and narrow in the hips, with keen, far-apart, steel-blue eyes; while beneath Tonio's round fur cap was a brunette face with the finely chiselled features of the south; the dark eyes, with delicate shadows and too heavy lids, looked dreamily and a little timorously on the world. Tonio's walk was idle and uneven, whereas the other's slim legs in their black stockings moved with an elastic, rhythmic tread.

Tonio did not speak. He suffered. His rather oblique brows were drawn together in a frown, his lips were rounded to whistle, he gazed into space with his head on one side. Posture and manner were habitual.

Suddenly Hans shoved his arm into Tonio's, with a sideways look—he knew very well what the trouble was. And Tonio, though he was silent for the next few steps, felt his heart soften.

"I hadn't forgotten, you see, Tonio," Hans said, gazing at the pavement, "I only thought it wouldn't come off today because it was so wet and windy. But I don't mind that at all, and it's jolly of you to have waited. I thought you had gone home, and I was cross. . . ."

Everything in Tonio leaped and jumped for joy at the words.

"All right; let's go over the wall," he said with a quaver in his voice. "Over the Millwall and the Holstenwall, and I'll go as far as your house with you, Hans. Then I'll have to walk back alone, but that doesn't matter; next time you can go round my way."

At bottom he was not really convinced by what Hans said; he quite knew the other attached less importance to this walk than he did himself. Yet he saw Hans was sorry for his remissness and willing to be put in a position to ask pardon, a pardon that Tonio was far indeed from withholding.

The truth was, Tonio loved Hans Hansen, and had already suffered much on his account. He who loves the more is the inferior and must suffer; in this hard and simple fact his fourteen-year-old soul had already been instructed by life; and he was so organized that he received such experiences consciously, wrote them down as it were inwardly, and even, in a certain way, took pleasure in them, though without ever letting them mould his conduct, indeed, or drawing any practical advantage from them. Being what he was, he found this knowledge far more important and far more interesting than the sort they made him learn in schools; yes, during his lesson hours in the vaulted Gothic classrooms he was mainly occupied in feeling his way about among these intuitions of his and penetrating them. The process gave him the same kind of satisfaction as that he felt when he moved about in his room with his violin—for he played the violin—and made the tones, brought out as softly as ever he knew how, mingle with the plashing of the fountain that leaped and danced down there in the garden beneath the branches of the old walnut tree.

The fountain, the old walnut tree, his fiddle, and away in the distance the North Sea, within sound of whose summer murmurings he spent his holidays—these were the things he loved, within these he enfolded his spirit, among these things his inner life took its course. And they were all things whose names were effective in verse and occurred pretty frequently in the lines Tonio Kröger sometimes wrote.

The fact that he had a note-book full of such things, written by himself, leaked out through his own carelessness and injured him no little with the masters as well as among his fellows. On the one hand, Consul Kröger's son found their attitude both cheap and silly, and despised his schoolmates and his masters as well, and in his turn (with extraordinary penetration) saw through and disliked their personal weaknesses and bad breeding. But then, on the other hand, he himself felt his verse-making extravagant and out of place and to a certain extent agreed with those who considered it an unpleasing occupation. But that did not enable him to leave off.

As he wasted his time at home, was slow and absent-minded at school, and always had bad marks from the masters, he was in the habit of bringing home pitifully poor reports, which troubled and angered his father, a tall, fastidiously dressed man, with thoughtful blue eyes, and always a wild flower in his buttonhole. But for his mother, she cared nothing about the reports—Tonio's beautiful black-haired mother, whose name was Consuelo, and who was so absolutely different from the other ladies in the town, because father had brought her long ago from some place far down on the map.

Tonio loved his dark, fiery mother, who played the piano and mandolin so wonderfully, and he was glad his doubtful standing among men did not distress her. Though at the same time he found his father's annoyance a more dignified and respectable attitude and despite his scoldings understood him very well, whereas his mother's blithe indifference always seemed just a little wanton. His thoughts at times would run something like this: "It is true enough that I am what I am and will not and cannot alter: heedless, self-willed, with my mind on things nobody else thinks of. And so it is right they should scold and punish me and not smother things all up with kisses and music. After all, we are not gypsies living in a green wagon; we're respectable people, the family of Consul Kröger." And not seldom he would think: "Why is it I am different, why do I fight everything, why am I at odds with the masters and like a stranger among the other boys? The good scholars, and the solid majority—they don't find the masters funny, they don't write verses, their thoughts are all about things that people do think about and can talk about out loud. How regular and comfortable they must feel, knowing that everybody knows just where they stand! It must be nice! But what is the matter with me, and what will be the end of it all?"

These thoughts about himself and his relation to life played an important part in Tonio's love for Hans Hansen. He loved him in the first place because he was handsome; but in the next because he was in every respect his own opposite and foil. Hans Hansen was a capital scholar, and a jolly chap to boot, who was head at drill, rode and swam to perfection, and lived in the sunshine of popularity. The masters were almost tender with him, they called him Hans and were partial to him in every way; the other pupils curried favour with him; even grown people stopped him on the street, twitched the shock of hair beneath his Danish sailor cap, and said: "Ah, here you are, Hans Hansen, with your pretty blond hair! Still head of the school? Remember me to your father and mother, that's a fine lad!"

Such was Hans Hansen; and ever since Tonio Kröger had known him, from the very minute he set eyes on him, he had burned inwardly with a heavy, envious longing. "Who else has blue eyes like yours, or lives in such friendliness and harmony with all the world? You are always spending your time with some right and proper occupation. When you have done your prep you take your riding-lesson, or make things with a fret-saw; even in the holidays, at the seashore, you row and sail and swim all the time, while I wander off somewhere and lie down in the sand and stare at the strange and mysterious changes that whisk over the face of the sea. And all that is why your eyes are so clear. To be like you . . ."

He made no attempt to be like Hans Hansen, and perhaps hardly even seriously wanted to. What he did ardently, painfully want was that just as he was, Hans Hansen should love him; and he wooed Hans Hansen in his own way, deeply, lingeringly, devotedly, with a melancholy that gnawed and burned more terribly than all the sudden passion one might have expected from his exotic looks.

And he wooed not in vain. Hans respected Tonio's superior power of putting certain difficult matters into words; moreover, he felt the lively presence of an uncommonly strong and tender feeling for himself; he was grateful for it, and his response gave Tonio much happiness—though also many pangs of jealousy and disillusion over his futile efforts to establish a communion of spirit between them. For the queer thing was that Tonio, who after all envied Hans Hansen for being what he was, still kept on trying to draw him over to his own side; though of course he could succeed in this at most only at moments and superficially. . . .

"I have just been reading something so wonderful and splendid . . ." he said. They were walking and eating together out of a bag of fruit toffees they had bought at Iverson's sweet-shop in Mill Street for ten pfennigs. "You must read it, Hans, it is Schiller's *Don Carlos* . . . I'll lend it you if you like. . . ."

"Oh, no," said Hans Hansen, "you needn't, Tonio, that's not anything for me. I'll stick to my horse books. There are wonderful cuts in them, let me tell you. I'll show them to you when you come to see me. They are instantaneous photography—the horse in motion; you can see him trot and canter and jump, in all positions, that you never can get to see in life, because they happen so fast. . . ."

"In all positions?" asked Tonio politely. "Yes, that must be great. But about *Don Carlos*—it is beyond anything you could possibly dream of. There are places in it that are so lovely they make you jump . . . as though it were an explosion—"

"An explosion?" asked Hans Hansen. "What sort of an explosion?"

"For instance, the place where the king has been crying because the marquis betrayed him . . . but the marquis did it only out of love for the prince, you see, he sacrifices himself for his sake. And the word comes out of the cabinet into the antechamber that the king has been weeping. 'Weeping? The king been weeping?' All the courtiers are fearfully upset, it goes through and through you, for the king has always been so frightfully stiff and stern. But it is so easy to understand why he cried, and I feel sorrier for him than for the prince and the marquis put together. He is always so alone, nobody loves him, and then he thinks he has found one man, and then *he* betrays him. . . ."

Hans Hensen looked sideways into Tonio's face, and something in it must have won him to the subject, for suddenly he shoved his arm once more into Tonio's and said:

"How had he betrayed him, Tonio?"

Tonio went on.

"Well," he said, "you see all the letters for Brabant and Flanders—"

"There comes Irwin Immerthal," said Hans.

Tonio stopped talking. If only the earth would open and swallow Immerthal up! "Why does he have to come disturbing us? If he only doesn't go with us all the way and talk about the riding-lessons!" For Irwin Immerthal had riding-lessons too. He was the son of the bank president and lived close by, outside the city wall. He had already been home and left his bag, and now he walked towards them through the avenue. His legs were crooked and his eyes like slits.

" 'lo, Immerthal," said Hans. "I'm taking a little walk with Kröger. . . ."

"I have to go into town on an errand," said Immerthal. "But I'll walk a little way with you. Are those fruit toffees you've got? Thanks, I'll have a couple. Tomorrow we have our next lesson, Hans." He meant the riding-lesson.

"What larks!" said Hans. "I'm going to get the leather gaiters for a present, because I was top lately in our papers."

"You don't take riding-lessons, I suppose, Kröger?" asked Immerthal, and his eyes were only two gleaming cracks.

"No . . ." answered Tonio, uncertainly.

"You ought to ask your father," Hans Hansen remarked, "so you could have lessons too, Kröger."

"Yes . . ." said Tonio. He spoke hastily and without interest; his throat had suddenly contracted, because Hans had called him by his last name. Hans seemed conscious of it too, for he said by way of explanation: "I call you Kröger because your first name is so crazy. Don't mind my saying so, I can't do with it all. Tonio—why, what sort of name is that? Though of course I know it's not your fault in the least."

"No, they probably called you that because it sounds so foreign and sort of something special," said Immerthal, obviously with intent to say just the right thing.

Tonio's mouth twitched. He pulled himself together and said:

"Yes, it's a silly name—Lord knows I'd rather be called Heinrich or Wilhelm. It's all because I'm named after my mother's brother Antonio. She comes from down there, you know. . . ."

There he stopped and let the others have their say about horses and saddles. Hans had taken Immerthal's arm; he talked with a fluency that *Don Carlos* could never have roused in him. . . . Tonio felt a mounting desire to weep pricking his nose from time to time; he had hard work to control the trembling of his lips.

Hans could not stand his name—what was to be done? He himself was called Hans, and Immerthal was called Irwin; two good, sound, familiar names, offensive to nobody. And Tonio was foreign and queer. Yes, there was always something queer about him, whether he would or no, and he was alone, the regular and usual would none of him; although after all he was no gypsy in a green wagon, but the son of Consul Kröger, a member of the Kröger family. But why did Hans call him Tonio as long as they were alone and then feel ashamed as soon as anybody else was by? Just now he had won him over, they had been close together, he was sure. "How had he betrayed him, Tonio?" Hans asked, and took his arm. But he had breathed easier directly Immerthal came up, he had dropped him like a shot, even gratuitously taunted him with his outlandish name. How it hurt to have to see through all this! . . . Hans Hansen did like him a little, when they were alone, that he knew. But let a third person come, he was ashamed, and offered up his friend. And again he was alone. He thought of King Philip. The king had wept. . . .

"Goodness, I have to go," said Irwin Immerthal. "Good-bye, and thanks for the toffee." He jumped upon a bench that stood by the way, ran along it with his crooked legs, jumped down, and trotted off.

"I like Immerthal," said Hans, with emphasis. He had a spoilt and arbitrary way of announcing his likes and dislikes, as though graciously pleased to confer them like an order on this person and that. . . . He went on talking about the riding-lessons where he had left off. Anyhow, it was not very much farther to his house; the walk over the walls was not a long one. They held their caps and bent their heads before the strong, damp wind that rattled and groaned in the leafless trees. And Hans Hansen went on talking, Tonio throwing in a forced yes or no from time to time. Hans talked eagerly, had taken his arm again; but the contact gave Tonio no pleasure. The nearness was only apparent, not real; it meant nothing. . . .

They struck away from the walls close to the station, where they saw a train puff busily past, idly counted the coaches, and waved to the man who was perched on top of the last one bundled in a leather coat. They stopped in front of the Hansen villa on the Lindenplatz, and Hans went into detail about what fun it was to stand on the bottom rail of the garden gate and let it swing on its cracking hinges. After that they said good-bye.

"I must go in now," said Hans. "Good-bye, Tonio. Next time I'll take you home, see if I don't."

"Good-bye, Hans," said Tonio. "It was a nice walk."

They put out their hands, all wet and rusty from the garden gate. But as Hans looked into Tonio's eyes, he bethought himself, a look of remorse came over his charming face.

"And I'll read *Don Carlos* pretty soon, too," he said quickly. "That bit about the king in his cabinet must be nuts." Then he took his bag under his arm and ran off through the front garden. Before he disappeared he turned and nodded once more.

And Tonio went off as though on wings. The wind was at his back; but it was not the wind alone that bore him along so lightly.

Hans would read *Don Carlos,* and then they would have something to talk about, and neither Irwin Immerthal nor another could join in. How well they understood each other! Perhaps—who knew?—some day he might even get Hans to write poetry! . . . No, no, that he did not ask. Hans must not become like Tonio, he must stop just as he was, so strong and bright, everybody loved him as he was, and Tonio most of all. But it would do him no harm to read *Don Carlos.* . . . Tonio passed under the squat old city gate, along by the harbour, and up the steep, wet, windy, gabled street to his parents' house. His heart beat richly: longing was awake in it, and a gentle envy; a faint contempt, and no little innocent bliss.

Ingeborg Holm, blonde little Inge, the daughter of Dr. Holm, who lived on Market Square opposite the tall old Gothic fountain with its manifold spires—she it was Tonio Kröger loved when he was sixteen years old.

Strange how things came about! He had seen her a thousand times; then one evening he saw her again; saw her in a certain light, talking with a friend in a certain saucy way, laughing and tossing her head; saw her lift her arm and smooth her back hair with her schoolgirl hand, that was by no means particularly fine or slender, in such a way that the thin white sleeve slipped down from her elbow; heard her speak a word or two, a quite indifferent phrase, but with a certain intonation, with a warm ring in her voice; and his heart throbbed with ecstasy, far stronger than that he had once felt when he looked at Hans Hansen long ago, when he was still a little, stupid boy.

That evening he carried away her picture in his eye: the thick blond plait, the longish, laughing blue eyes, the saddle of pale freckles across the nose. He could not go to sleep for hearing that ring in her voice; he tried in a whisper to imitate the tone in which she had uttered the commonplace phrase, and felt a shiver run through and through him. He knew by experience that this was love. And he was accurately aware that love would surely bring him much pain, affliction, and sadness, that it would certainly destroy his peace, filling his heart to overflowing with melodies which would be no good to him because he would never have the time or tranquillity to give them permanent form. Yet he received this love with joy, surrendered himself to it, and cherished it with all the strength of his being; for he knew that love made one vital and rich, and he longed to be vital and rich, far more than he did to work tranquilly on anything to give it permanent form.

Tonio Kröger fell in love with merry Ingeborg Holm in Frau Consul Hustede's drawing-room on the evening when it was emptied of furniture for the weekly dancing-class. It was a private class, attended only by members of the first families; it met by turns in the various parental houses to receive instruction from Knaak, the dancing-master, who came from Hamburg expressly for the purpose.

François Knaak was his name, and what a man he was! *"J'ai l'honneur de me vous représenter,"* he would say, *"mon nom est Knaak. . . .* This is not said during the bowing, but after you have finished and are standing up straight again. In a low voice, but distinctly. Of course one does not need to introduce oneself in French every day in the week, but if you can do it correctly and faultlessly in French you are not likely to make a mistake when you do it in German." How marvellously the silky black frock-coat fitted his chubby hips! His trouser-legs fell down in soft folds upon his patent-leather pumps with their wide satin bows, and his brown eyes glanced about him with languid pleasure in their own beauty.

All this excess of self-confidence and good form was positively overpowering. He went trippingly—and nobody tripped like him, so elastically, so weavingly, rockingly, royally—up to the mistress of the house, made a bow, waited for a hand to be put forth. This vouchsafed, he gave murmurous voice to his gratitude, stepped buoyantly back, turned on his left foot, swiftly drawing the right one backwards on its toe-tip, and moved away, with his hips shaking.

When you took leave of a company you must go backwards out at the door; when you fetched a chair, you were not to shove it along the floor or clutch it by one leg; but gently, by the back, and set it down without a sound. When you stood, you were not to fold your hands on your tummy or seek with your tongue the corners of your mouth. If you did, Herr Knaak had a way of showing you how it looked that filled you with disgust for that particular gesture all the rest of your life.

This was deportment. As for dancing, Herr Knaak was, if possible, even more of a master at that. The salon was emptied of furniture and lighted by a gas-chandelier in the middle of the ceiling and candles on the mantelshelf. The floor was strewn with talc, and the pupils stood about in a dumb semicircle. But in the next room, behind the portières, mothers and aunts sat on plush-upholstered chairs and watched Herr Knaak through their lorgnettes, as in little springs and hops, curtsying slightly, the hem of his frock-coat held up on each side by two fingers, he demonstrated the single steps of the mazurka. When he wanted to dazzle his audience completely he would suddenly and unexpectedly spring from the ground, whirling his two legs about each other with bewildering swiftness in the air, as it were trilling with them, and then, with a subdued bump, which nevertheless shook everything within him to its depths, return to earth.

"What an unmentionable monkey!" thought Tonio Kröger to himself. But he saw the absorbed smile on jolly little Inge's face as she followed Herr Knaak's movements; and that, though not that alone, roused in him something like admiration of all this wonderfully controlled corporeality. How tranquil, how imperturbable was Herr Knaak's gaze! His eyes did not plumb the depth of things to the place where life becomes complex and melancholy; they knew nothing save that they were beautiful brown eyes. But that was just why his bearing was so proud. To be able to walk like that, one must be stupid; then one was loved, then one was lovable. He could so well understand how it was that Inge, blonde, sweet little Inge, looked at Herr Knaak as she did. But would never a girl look at him like that?

Oh, yes, there would, and did. For instance, Magdalena Vermehren, Attorney Vermehren's daughter, with the gentle mouth and the great, dark, brilliant eyes, so serious and adoring. She often fell down in the dance; but when it was "ladies' choice" she came up to him; she knew he wrote verses and twice she had asked him to show them to her. She often sat at a distance, with drooping head, and gazed at him. He did not care. It was Inge he loved, blonde, jolly Inge, who most assuredly despised him for his poetic effusions . . . he looked at her, looked at her narrow blue eyes full of fun and mockery, and felt an envious longing; to be shut away from her like this, to be forever strange—he felt it in his breast, like a heavy, burning weight.

"First couple *en avant,*" said Herr Knaak; and no words can tell how marvellously he pronounced the nasal. They were to practise the quadrille, and to Tonio Kröger's profound alarm he found himself in the same set with Inge Holm. He avoided her where he could, yet somehow was forever near her; kept his eyes away from her person and yet found his gaze ever on her. There she came, tripping up hand-in-hand with red-headed Ferdinand Matthiessen; she flung back her braid, drew a deep breath, and took her place opposite Tonio. Herr Heinzelmann, at the piano, laid bony hands upon the keys, Herr Knaak waved his arm, the quadrille began.

She moved to and fro before his eyes, forwards and back, pacing and swinging; he seemed to catch a fragrance from her hair or the folds of her thin white frock, and his eyes grew sadder and sadder. "I love you, dear, sweet Inge," he said to himself, and put into his words all the pain he felt to see her so intent upon the dance with not a thought of him. Some lines of an exquisite poem by Storm came into his mind: "I would sleep, but thou must dance." It seemed against all sense, and most depressing, that he must be dancing when he was in love. . . .

"First couple *en avant,*" said Herr Knaak; it was the next figure. *"Compliment! Moulinet des dames! Tour de main!"* and he swallowed the silent *e* in the *"de,"* with quite indescribable ease and grace.

"Second couple *en avant!*" This was Tonio Kröger and his partner. *"Compliment!"* And Tonio Kröger bowed. *"Moulinet des dames!"* And Tonio Kröger, with bent head and gloomy brows, laid his hand on those of the four ladies, on Ingeborg Holm's hand, and danced the *moulinet.*

Roundabout rose a tittering and laughing. Herr Knaak took a ballet pose conventionally expressive of horror. "Oh, dear! Oh, dear!" he cried. "Stop! Stop! Kröger among the ladies! *En arrière,* Fräulein Kröger, step back, *fi donc!* Everybody else understood it but you. Shoo! Get out! Get away!" He drew out his yellow silk handkerchief and flapped Tonio Kröger back to his place.

Everyone laughed, the girls and the boys and the ladies beyond the portières; Herr Knaak had made something too utterly funny out of the little episode, it was as amusing as a play. But Herr Heinzelmann at the piano sat and waited, with a dry, business-like air, for a sign to go on; he was hardened against Herr Knaak's effects.

Then the quadrille went on. And the intermission followed. The parlourmaid came clinking in with a tray of wine-jelly glasses, the cook followed in her wake with a load of plum-cake. But Tonio Kröger stole away. He stole out into the corridor and stood there, his hands behind his back, in front of a window with the blind down. He never thought that one could not see through the blind and that it was absurd to stand there as though one were looking out.

For he was looking within, into himself, the theatre of so much pain and longing. Why, why was he here? Why was he not sitting by the window in his own room, reading Storm's *Immensee* and lifting his eyes to the twilight garden outside, where the old walnut tree moaned? That was the place for him! Others might dance, others bend their fresh and lively minds upon the pleasure in hand! . . . But no, no, after all, his place was here, where he could feel near Inge even although he stood lonely and aloof, seeking to distinguish the warm notes of her voice amid the buzzing, clattering, and laughter within. Oh, lovely Inge, blonde Inge of the narrow, laughing blue eyes! So lovely and laughing as you are one can only be if one does not read *Immensee* and never tries to write things like it. And that was just the tragedy!

Ah, she *must* come! She *must* notice where he had gone, must feel how he suffered! She must slip out to him, even pity must bring her, to lay her hand on his shoulder and say: "Do come back to us, ah, don't be sad—I love you, Tonio." He listened behind him and waited in frantic suspense. But not in the least. Such things did not happen on this earth.

Had she laughed at him too like all the others? Yes, she had, however gladly he would have denied it for both their sakes. And yet it was only because he had been so taken up with her that he had danced the *moulinet des dames*. Suppose he had—what did that matter? Had not a magazine accepted a poem of his a little while ago—even though the magazine had failed before his poem could be printed? The day was coming when he would be famous, when they would print everything he wrote; and *then* he would see if that made any impression on Inge Holm! No, it would make no impression at all; that was just it. Magdalena Vermehren, who was always falling down in the dances, yes, she would be impressed. But never Ingeborg Holm, never blue-eyed, laughing Inge. So what was the good of it?

Tonio Kröger's heart contracted painfully at the thought. To feel stirring within you the wonderful and melancholy play of strange forces and to be aware that those others you yearn for are blithely inaccessible to all that moves you—what a pain is this! And yet! He stood there aloof and alone, staring hopelessly at a drawn blind and making, in his distraction, as though he could look out. But yet he was happy. For he lived. His heart was full; hotly and sadly it beat for thee, Ingeborg Holm, and his soul embraced thy blonde, simple, pert, commonplace little personality in blissful self-abnegation.

Often after that he stood thus, with burning cheeks, in lonely corners, whither the sound of music, the tinkling of glasses and fragrance of flowers came but faintly, and tried to distinguish the ringing tones of thy voice amid the distant happy din; stood suffering for thee—and still was happy! Often it angered him to think that he might talk with Magdalena Vermehren, who always fell down in the dance. She understood him, she laughed or was serious in the right places; while Inge the fair, let him sit never so near her, seemed remote and estranged, his speech not being her speech. And still—he was happy. For happiness, he told himself, is not in being loved—which is a satisfaction of the vanity and mingled with disgust. Happiness is in loving, and perhaps in snatching fugitive little approaches to the beloved object. And he took inward note of this thought, wrote it down in his mind; followed out all its implications and felt it to the depths of his soul.

"Faithfulness," thought Tonio Kröger. "Yes, I will be faithful, I will love thee, Ingeborg, as long as I live!" He said this in the honesty of his intentions. And yet a still small voice whispered misgivings in his ear: after all, he had forgotten Hans Hansen utterly, even though he saw him every day! And the hateful, the pitiable fact was that this still, small, rather spiteful voice was right: time passed and the day came when Tonio Kröger was no longer so unconditionally ready as once he had been to die for the lively Inge, because he felt in himself desires and powers to accomplish in his own way a host of wonderful things in this world.

And he circled with watchful eye the sacrificial altar, where flickered the pure, chaste flame of his love; knelt before it and tended and cherished it in every way, because he so wanted to be faithful. And in a little while, unobservably, without sensation or stir, it went out after all.

But Tonio Kröger still stood before the cold altar, full of regret and dismay at the fact that faithfulness was impossible upon this earth. Then he shrugged his shoulders and went his way.

He went the way that go he must, a little idly, a little irregularly, whistling to himself, gazing into space with his head on one side; and if he went wrong it was because for some people there is no such thing as a right way. Asked what in the world he meant to become, he gave various answers, for he was used to say (and had even already written it) that he bore within himself the possibility of a thousand ways of life, together with the private conviction that they were all sheer impossibilities.

Even before he left the narrow streets of his native city, the threads that bound him to it had gently loosened. The old Kröger family gradually declined, and some people quite rightly considered Tonio Kröger's own existence and way of life as one of the signs of decay. His father's mother, the head of the family, had died, and not long after his own father followed, the tall, thoughtful, carefully dressed gentleman with the field-flower in his buttonhole. The great Kröger house, with all its stately tradition, came up for sale, and the firm was dissolved. Tonio's mother, his beautiful, fiery mother, who played the piano and mandolin so wonderfully and to whom nothing mattered at all, she married again after a year's time; married a musician, moreover, a virtuoso with an Italian name, and went away with him into remote blue distances. Tonio Kröger found this a little irregular, but who was he to call her to order, who wrote poetry himself and could not even give an answer when asked what he meant to do in life?

And so he left his native town and its tortuous, gabled streets with the damp wind whistling through them; left the fountain in the garden and the ancient walnut tree, familiar friends of his youth; left the sea too, that he loved so much, and felt no pain to go. For he was grown up and sensible and had come to realize how things stood with him; he looked down on the lowly and vulgar life he had led so long in these surroundings.

He surrendered utterly to the power that to him seemed the highest on earth, to whose service he felt called, which promised him elevation and honours: the power of intellect, the power of the Word, that lords it with a smile over the unconscious and inarticulate. To this power he surrendered with all the passion of youth, and it rewarded him with all it had to give, taking from him inexorably, in return, all that it is wont to take.

It sharpened his eyes and made him see through the large words which puff out the bosoms of mankind; it opened for him men's souls and his own, made him clairvoyant, showed him the inwardness of the world and the ultimate behind men's words and deeds. And all that he saw could be put in two words: the comedy and the tragedy of life.

And then, with knowledge, its torment and its arrogance, came solitude; because he could not endure the blithe and innocent with their darkened understanding, while they in turn were troubled by the sign on his brow. But his love of the word kept growing sweeter and sweeter, and his love of form; for he used to say (and had already said it in writing) that knowledge of the soul would unfailingly make us melancholy if the pleasures of expression did not keep us alert and of good cheer.

He lived in large cities and in the south, promising himself a luxuriant ripening of his art by southern suns; perhaps it was the blood of his mother's race that drew him thither. But his heart being dead and loveless, he fell into adventures of the flesh, descended into the depths of lust and searing sin, and suffering unspeakably thereby. It might have been his father in him, that tall, thoughtful, fastidiously dressed man with the wild flower in his buttonhole, that made him suffer so down there in the south; now and again he would feel a faint, yearning memory of a certain joy that was of the soul; once it had been his own, but now, in all his joys, he could not find it again.

Then he would be seized with disgust and hatred of the senses; pant after purity and seemly peace, while still he breathed the air of art, the tepid, sweet air of permanent spring, heavy with fragrance where it breeds and brews and burgeons in the mysterious bliss of creation. So for all result he was flung to and fro forever between two crass extremes: between icy intellect and scorching sense, and what with his pangs of conscience led an exhausting life, rare, extraordinary, excessive, which at bottom he, Tonio Kröger, despised. "What a labyrinth!" he sometimes thought. "How could I possibly have got into all these fantastic adventures? As though I had a wagonful of travelling gypsies for my ancestors!"

But as his health suffered from these excesses, so his artistry was sharpened; it grew fastidious, precious, *raffiné*, morbidly sensitive in questions of tact and taste, rasped by the banal. His first appearance in print elicited much applause; there was joy among the elect, for it was a good and workmanlike performance, full of humour and acquaintance with pain. In no long time his name—the same by which his masters had reproached him, the same he had signed to his earliest verses on the walnut tree and the fountain and the sea, those syllables compact of the north and the south, that good middle-class name with the exotic twist to it—became a synonym for excellence; for the painful thoroughness of the experiences he had gone through, combined with a tenacious ambition and a persistent industry, joined battle with the irritable fastidiousness of his taste and under grinding torments issued in work of a quality quite uncommon.

He worked, not like a man who works that he may live; but as one who is bent on doing nothing but work; having no regard for himself as a human being but only as a creator; moving about grey and unobtrusive among his fellows like an actor without his make-up, who counts for nothing as soon as he stops representing something else. He worked withdrawn out of sight and sound of the small fry, for whom he felt nothing but contempt, because to them a talent was a social asset like another; who, whether they were poor or not, went about ostentatiously shabby or else flaunted startling cravats, all the time taking jolly good care to amuse themselves, to be artistic and charming without the smallest notion of the fact that good work only comes out under pressure of a bad life; that he who lives does not work; that one must die to life in order to be utterly a creator.

"Shall I disturb you?" asked Tonio Kröger on the threshold of the atelier. He held his hat in his hand and bowed with some ceremony, although Lisabeta Ivanovna was a good friend of his, to whom he told all his troubles.

"Mercy on you, Tonio Kröger! Don't be so formal," answered she, with her lilting intonation. "Everybody knows you were taught good manners in your nursery." She transferred her brush to her left hand, that held the palette, reached him her right, and looked him in the face, smiling and shaking her head.

"Yes, but you are working," he said. "Let's see. Oh, you've been getting on," and he looked at the colour-sketches leaning against chairs at both sides of the easel and from them to the large canvas covered with a square linen mesh, where the first patches of colour were beginning to appear among the confused and schematic lines of the charcoal sketch.

This was in Munich, in a back building in Schellingstrasse, several storeys up. Beyond the wide window facing the north were blue sky, sunshine, birds twittering; the young sweet breath of spring streaming through an open pane mingled with the smells of paint and fixative. The afternoon light, bright golden, flooded the spacious emptiness of the atelier; it made no secret of the bad flooring or the rough table under the window, covered with little bottles, tubes, and brushes; it illumined the unframed studies on the unpapered walls, the torn silk screen that shut off a charmingly furnished little living-corner near the door; it shone upon the inchoate work on the easel, upon the artist and the poet there before it.

She was about the same age as himself—slightly past thirty. She sat there on a low stool, in her dark-blue apron, and leant her chin in her hand. Her brown hair, compactly dressed, already a little grey at the sides, was parted in the middle and waved over the temples, framing a sensitive, sympathetic, dark-skinned face, which was Slavic in its facial structure, with flat nose, strongly accentuated cheek-bones, and little bright black eyes. She sat there measuring her work with her head on one side and her eyes screwed up; her features were drawn with a look of misgiving, almost of vexation.

He stood beside her, his right hand on his hip, with the other furiously twirling his brown moustache. His dress, reserved in cut and a soothing shade of grey, was punctilious and dignified to the last degree. He was whistling softly to himself, in the way he had, and his slanting brows were gathered in a frown. The dark-brown hair was parted with severe correctness, but the laboured forehead beneath showed a nervous twitching, and the chiselled southern features were sharpened as though they had been gone over again with a graver's tool. And yet the mouth—how gently curved it was, the chin how softly formed! . . . After a little he drew his hand across his brow and eyes and turned away.

"I ought not to have come," he said.

"And why not, Tonio Kröger?"

"I've just got up from my desk, Lisabeta, and inside my head it looks just the way it does on this canvas. A scaffolding, a faint first draft smeared with corrections and a few splotches of colour; yes, and I came up here and see the same thing. And the same conflict and contradiction in the air," he went on, sniffing, "that has been torturing me at home. It's extraordinary. If you are possessed by an idea, you find it expressed everywhere, you even *smell* it. Fixative and the breath of spring; art and—what? Don't say nature, Lisabeta, 'nature' isn't exhausting. Ah, no, I ought to have gone for a walk, though it's doubtful if it would have made me feel better. Five minutes ago, not far from here, I met a man I know, Adalbert, the novelist. 'God damn the spring!' says he in the aggressive way he has. 'It is and always has been the most ghastly time of the year. Can you get hold of a single sensible idea, Kröger? Can you sit still and work out even the smallest effect, when your blood tickles till it's positively indecent and you are teased by a whole host of irrelevant sensations that when you look at them turn out to be unworkable trash? For my part, I am going to a café. A café is neutral territory, the change of the seasons doesn't affect it; it represents, so to speak, the detached and elevated sphere of the literary man, in which one is only capable of refined ideas.' And he went into the café . . . and perhaps I ought to have gone with him.''

Lisabeta was highly entertained.

"I like that, Tonio Kröger. That part about the indecent tickling is good. And he is right too, in a way, for spring is really not very conducive to work. But now listen. Spring or no spring, I will just finish this little place —work out this little effect, as your friend Adalbert would say. Then we'll go into the 'salon' and have tea, and you can talk yourself out, for I can perfectly well see you are too full for utterance. Will you just compose yourself somewhere—on that chest, for instance, if you are not afraid for your aristocratic garments—"

"Oh, leave my clothes alone, Lisabeta Ivanovna! Do you want me to go about in a ragged velveteen jacket or a red waistcoat? Every artist is as bohemian as the deuce, inside! Let him at least wear proper clothes and behave outwardly like a respectable being. No, I am not too full for utterance," he said as he watched her mixing her paints. "I've told you, it is only that I have a problem and a conflict, that sticks in my mind and disturbs me at my work. . . . Yes, what was it we were just saying? We were talking about Adalbert, the novelist, that stout and forthright man. 'Spring is the most ghastly time of the year,' says he, and goes into a café. A man has to know what he needs, eh? Well, you see he's not the only one; the spring makes me nervous, too; I get dazed with the triflingness and sacredness of the memories and feelings it evokes; only that I don't succeed in looking down on it; for the truth is it makes me ashamed; I quail before its sheer naturalness and triumphant youth. And I don't know whether I should envy Adalbert or despise him for his ignorance. . . .

"Yes, it is true; spring is a bad time for work; and why? Because we are feeling too much. Nobody but a beginner imagines that he who creates must feel. Every real and genuine artist smiles at such naïve blunders as that. A melancholy enough smile, perhaps, but still a smile. For what an artist talks about is never the main point; it is the raw material, in and for itself indifferent, out of which, with bland and serene mastery, he creates the work of art. If you care too much about what you have to say, if your heart is too much in it, you can be pretty sure of making a mess. You get pathetic, you wax sentimental; something dull and doddering, without roots or outlines, with no sense of humour—something tiresome and banal grows under your hand, and you get nothing out of it but apathy in your audience and disappointment and misery in yourself. For so it is, Lisabeta; feeling, warm, heartfelt feeling, is always banal and futile; only the irritations and icy ecstasies of the artist's corrupted nervous system are artistic. The artist must be unhuman, extra-human; he must stand in a queer aloof relationship to our humanity; only so is he in a position, I ought to say only so would he be tempted, to represent it, to present it, to portray it to good effect. The very gift of style, of form and expression, is nothing else than this cool and fastidious attitude towards humanity; you might say there has to be this impoverishment and devastation as a preliminary condition. For sound natural feeling, say what you like, has no taste. It is all up with the artist as soon as he becomes a man and begins to feel. Adalbert knows that; that's why he betook himself to the café, the neutral territory—God help him!"

"Yes, God help him, Batuschka," said Lisabeta, as she washed her hands in a tin basin. "You don't need to follow his example."

"No, Lisabeta, I am not going to; and the only reason is that I am now and again in a position to feel a little ashamed of the springtime of my art. You see sometimes I get letters from strangers, full of praise and thanks and admiration from people whose feelings I have touched. I read them and feel touched myself at these warm if ungainly emotions I have called up; a sort of pity steals over me at this naïve enthusiasm; and I positively blush at the thought of how these good people would freeze up if they were to get a look behind the scenes. What they, in their innocence, cannot comprehend is that a properly constituted, healthy, decent man never writes, acts, or composes—all of which does not hinder me from using his admiration for my genius to goad myself on; nor from taking it in deadly earnest and aping the airs of a great man. Oh, don't talk to me, Lisabeta. I tell you I am sick to death of depicting humanity without having any part or lot in it. . . . Is an artist a male, anyhow? Ask the females! It seems to me we artists are all of us something like those unsexed papal singers . . . we sing like angels; but—"

"Shame on you, Tonio Kröger. But come to tea. The water is just on the boil, and here are some *papyros*. You were talking about singing soprano, do go on. But really you ought to be ashamed of yourself. If I did not know your passionate devotion to your calling and how proud you are of it—"

"Don't talk about 'calling,' Lisabeta Ivanovna. Literature is not a calling, it is a curse, believe me! When does one begin to feel the curse? Early, horribly early. At a time when one ought by rights still to be living in peace and harmony with God and the world. It begins by your feeling yourself set apart, in a curious sort of opposition to the nice, regular people; there is a gulf of ironic sensibility, of knowledge, scepticism, disagreement between you and the others; it grows deeper and deeper, you realize that you are alone; and from then on any *rapprochement* is simply hopeless! What a fate! That is, if you still have enough heart, enough warmth of affections, to feel how frightful it is! . . . Your self-consciousness is kindled, because you among thousands feel the sign on your brow and know that everyone else sees it. I once knew an actor, a man of genius, who had to struggle with a morbid self-consciousness and instability. When he had no rôle to play, nothing to represent, this man, consummate artist but impoverished human being, was overcome by an exaggerated consciousness of his ego. A genuine artist—not one who has taken up art as a profession like another, but artist foreordained and damned—you can pick out, without boasting very sharp perceptions, out of a group of men. The sense of being set apart and not belonging, of being known and observed, something both regal and incongruous shows in his face. You might see something of the same sort on the features of a prince walking through a crowd in ordinary clothes. But no civilian clothes are any good here, Lisabeta. You can disguise yourself, you can dress up like an attaché or a lieutenant of the guard on leave; you hardly need to give a glance or speak a word before everyone knows you are not a human being, but something else: something queer, different, inimical.

"But what is it, to be an artist? Nothing shows up the general human dislike of thinking, and man's innate craving to be comfortable, better than his attitude to this question. When these worthy people are affected by a work of art, they say humbly that that sort of thing is a 'gift.' And because in their innocence they assume that beautiful and uplifting results must have beautiful and uplifting causes, they never dream that the 'gift' in question is a very dubious affair and rests upon extremely sinister foundations. Everybody knows that artists are 'sensitive' and easily wounded; just as everybody knows that ordinary people, with a normal bump of self-confidence, are not. Now you see, Lisabeta, I cherish at the bottom of my soul all the scorn and suspicion of the artist gentry—translated into terms of the intellectual—that my upright old forbears there on the Baltic would have felt for any juggler or mountebank that entered their houses. Listen to this. I know a banker, grey-haired business man, who has a gift for writing stories. He employs this gift in his idle hours, and some of his stories are of the first rank. But despite—I say despite—this excellent gift his withers are by no means unwrung: on the contrary, he has had to serve a prison sentence, on anything but trifling grounds. Yes, it was actually first *in prison* that he became conscious of his gift, and his experiences as a convict are the main theme in all his works. One might be rash enough to conclude that a man has to be at home in some kind of jail in order to become a poet. But can you escape the suspicion that the source and essence of his being an artist had less to do with his life in prison than they had with the reasons that *brought him there?* A banker who writes—that is a rarity, isn't it? But a banker who isn't a criminal, who is irreproachably respectable, and yet writes—he doesn't exist. Yes, you are laughing, and yet I am more than half serious. No problem, none in the world, is more tormenting than this of the artist and his human aspect. Take the most miraculous case of all, take the most typical and therefore the most powerful of artists, take such a morbid and profoundly equivocal work as *Tristan and Isolde,* and look at the effect it has on a healthy young man of thoroughly normal feelings. Exaltation, encouragement, warm, downright enthusiasm, perhaps incitement to 'artistic' creation of his own. Poor young dilettante! In us artists it looks fundamentally different from what he wots of, his 'warm heart' and 'honest enthusiasm.' I've seen women and youths go mad over artists . . . and I *knew* about them . . . ! The origin, the accompanying phenomena, and the conditions of the artist life—good Lord, what I haven't observed about them, over and over!"

"Observed, Tonio Kröger? If I may ask, only 'observed'?"

He was silent, knitting his oblique brown brows and whistling softly to himself.

"Let me have your cup, Tonio. The tea is weak. And take another cigarette. Now, you perfectly know that you are looking at things as they do not necessarily have to be looked at. . . ."

"That is Horatio's answer, dear Lisabeta. ' 'Twere to consider too curiously, to consider so.' "

"I mean, Tonio Kröger, that one can consider them just exactly as well from another side. I am only a silly painting female, and if I can contradict you at all, if I can defend your own profession a little against you, it is not by saying anything new, but simply by reminding you of some things you very well know yourself: of the purifying and healing influence of letters, the subduing of the passions by knowledge and eloquence; literature as the guide to understanding, forgiveness, and love, the redeeming power of the word, literary art as the noblest manifestation of the human mind, the poet as the most highly developed of human beings, the poet as saint. Is it to consider things not curiously enough, to consider them so?"

"You may talk like that, Lisabeta Ivanovna, you have a perfect right. And with reference to Russian literature, and the words of your poets, one can really worship them; they really come close to being that elevated literature you are talking about. But I am not ignoring your objections, they are part of the things I have in my mind today. . . . Look at me, Lisabeta. I don't look any too cheerful, do I? A little old and tired and pinched, eh? Well, now to come back to the 'knowledge.' Can't you imagine a man, born orthodox, mild-mannered, well-meaning, a bit sentimental, just simply over-stimulated by his psychological clairvoyance, and going to the dogs? Not to let the sadness of the world unman you; to read, mark, learn, and put to account even the most torturing things and to be of perpetual good cheer, in the sublime consciousness of moral superiority over the horrible invention of existence—yes, thank you! But despite all the joys of expression once in a while the thing gets on your nerves. *'Tout comprendre c'est tout pardonner.'* I don't know about that. There is something I call being sick of kowledge, Lisabeta; when it is enough for you to see through a thing in order to be sick to death of it, and not in the least in a forgiving mood. Such was the case of Hamlet the Dane, that typical literary man. He knew what it meant to be called to knowledge without being born to it. To see things clear, if even through your tears, to recognize, notice, observe— and have to put it all down with a smile, at the very moment when hands

are clinging, and lips meeting, and the human gaze is blinded with feeling
—it is infamous, Lisabeta, it is indecent, outrageous—but what good does
it do to be outraged?

"Then another and no less charming side of the thing, of course, is your
ennui, your indifferent and ironic attitude towards truth. It is a fact that
there is no society in the world so dumb and hopeless as a circle of literary
people who are hounded to death as it is. All knowledge is old and tedious
to them. Utter some truth that it gave you considerable youthful joy to con-
quer and possess—and they will all chortle at you for your naïveté. Oh,
yes, Lisabeta, literature is a wearing job. In human society, I do assure you,
a reserved and sceptical man can be taken for stupid, whereas he is really
only arrogant and perhaps lacks courage. So much for 'knowledge.' Now
for the 'Word.' It isn't so much a matter of the 'redeeming power' as it is
of putting your emotions on ice and serving them up chilled! Honestly,
don't you think there's a good deal of cool cheek in the prompt and superficial way a writer can get rid of his feelings by turning them into literature? If your heart is too full, if you are overpowered with the emotions of
some sweet or exalted moment—nothing simpler! Go to the literary man,
he will put it all straight for you instanter. He will analyse and formulate
your affair, label it and express it and discuss it and polish it off and make
you indifferent to it for time and eternity—and not charge you a farthing.
You will go home quite relieved, cooled off, enlightened; and wonder what
it was all about and why you were so mightily moved. And will you ser-
ously enter the lists in behalf of this vain and frigid charlatan? What is
uttered, so runs this *credo,* is finished and done with. If the whole world
could be expressed, it would be saved, finished and done. . . . Well and
good. But I am not a nihilist—"

"You are not a—" said Lisabeta. . . . She was lifting a teaspoonful of
tea to her mouth and paused in the act to stare at him.

"Come, come, Lisabeta, what's the matter? I say I am not a nihilist, with
respect, that is, to lively feeling. You see, the literary man does not understand that life may go on living, unashamed, even after it has been
expressed and therewith finished. No matter how much it has been
redeemed by becoming literature, it keeps right on sinning—for all action
is sin in the mind's eye—

"I'm nearly done, Lisabeta. Please listen. I love life—this is an admission. I present it to you, you may have it. I have never made it to anyone
else. People say—people have even written and printed—that I hate life, or
fear or despise or abominate it. I liked to hear this, it has always flattered
me; but that does not make it true. I love life. You smile; and I know why,
Lisabeta. But I implore you not to take what I am saying for literature.
Don't think of Caesar Borgia or any drunken philosophy that has him for a
standard-bearer. He is nothing to me, your Caesar Borgia. I have no opinion
of him, and I shall never comprehend how one can honour the extraordinary and daemonic as an ideal. No, life as the eternal antinomy of mind and

art does not represent itself to us as a vision of savage greatness and ruthless beauty; we who are set apart and different do not conceive it as, like us,
unusual; it is the normal, respectable, and admirable that is the kingdom of
our longing: life, in all its seductive banality! That man is very far from
being an artist, my dear, whose last and deepest enthusiasm is the *raffiné*,
the eccentric and satanic; who does not know a longing for the innocent,
the simple, and the living, for a little friendship, devotion, familiar human
happiness—the gnawing, surreptitious hankering, Lisabeta, for the bliss of
the commonplace. . . .

"A genuine human friend. Believe me, I should be proud and happy to
possess a friend among men. But up to now all the friends I have had have
been daemons, kobolds, impious monsters, and spectres dumb with excess of
knowledge—that is to say, literary men.

"I may be standing upon some platform, in some hall in front of people
who have come to listen to me. And I find myself looking round among
my hearers, I catch myself secretly peering about the auditorium, and all
the while I am thinking who it is that has come here to listen to me, whose
grateful applause is in my ears, with whom my art is making me one. . . . I
do not find what I seek, Lisabeta, I find the herd. The same old community, the same old gathering of early Christians, so to speak: people with
fine souls in uncouth bodies, people who are always falling down in the
dance, if you know what I mean; the kind to whom poetry serves as a sort
of mild revenge on life. Always and only the poor and suffering, never any
of the others, the blue-eyed ones, Lisabeta—they do not need mind. . . .

"And, after all, would it not be a lamentable lack of logic to want it otherwise? It is against all sense to love life and yet bend all the powers you
have to draw it over to your own side, to the side of finesse and melancholy
and the whole sickly aristocracy of letters. The kingdom of art increases
and that of health and innocence declines on this earth. What there is left
of it ought to be carefully preserved; one ought not to tempt people to read
poetry who would much rather read books about the instantaneous photography of horses.

"For, after all, what more pitiable sight is there than life led astray by
art? We artists have a consummate contempt for the dilettante, the man
who is leading a living life and yet thinks he can be an artist too if he gets
the chance. I am speaking from personal experience, I do assure you. Suppose I am in a company in a good house, with eating and drinking going
on, and plenty of conversation and good feeling: I am glad and grateful to
be able to lose myself among good regular people for a while. Then all of a
sudden—I am thinking of something that actually happened—an officer
gets up, a lieutenant, a stout, good-looking chap, whom I could never have
believed guilty of any conduct unbecoming his uniform, and actually in
good set terms asks the company's permission to read some verses of his
own composition. Everybody looks disconcerted, they laugh and tell him to
go on, and he takes them at their word and reads from a sheet of paper he

has up to now been hiding in his coat-tail pocket—something about love and music, as deeply felt as it is inept. But I ask you: a lieutenant! A man of the world! He surely did not need to. . . . Well, the inevitable result is long faces, silence, a little artificial applause, everybody thoroughly uncomfortable. The first sensation I am conscious of is guilt—I feel partly responsible for the disturbance this rash youth has brought upon the company; and no wonder, for I, as a member of the same guild, am a target for some of the unfriendly glances. But next minute I realize something else: this man for whom just now I felt the greatest respect has suddenly sunk in my eyes. I feel a benevolent pity. Along with some other brave and good-natured gentlemen I go up and speak to him. 'Congratulations, Herr Lieutenant,' I say, 'that is a very pretty talent you have. It was charming.' And I am within an ace of clapping him on the shoulder. But is that the way one is supposed to feel towards a lieutenant—benevolent? . . . It was his own fault. There he stood, suffering embarrassment for the mistake of thinking that one may pluck a single leaf from the laurel tree of art without paying for it with his life. No, there I go with my colleague, the convict banker—but don't you find, Lisabeta, that I have quite a Hamlet-like flow of oratory today?"

"Are you done, Tonio Kröger?"

"No. But there won't be any more."

"And quite enough too. Are you expecting a reply?"

"Have you one ready?"

"I should say. I have listened to you faithfully, Tonio, from beginning to end, and I will give you the answer to everything you have said this afternoon and the solution of the problem that has been upsetting you. Now: the solution is that you, as you sit there, are, quite simply, a bourgeois."

"Am I?" he asked a little crestfallen.

"Yes, that hits you hard, it must. So I will soften the judgment just a little. You are a bourgeois on the wrong path, a bourgeois *manqué*."

Silence. Then he got up resolutely and took his hat and stick.

"Thank you, Lisabeta Ivanovna; now I can go home in peace. I am expressed."

Towards autumn Tonio Kröger said to Lisabeta Ivanovna:

"Well, Lisabeta, I think I'll be off. I need a change of air. I must get away, out into the open."

"Well, well, well, little Father! Does it please your Highness to go down to Italy again?"

"Oh, get along with your Italy, Lisabeta. I'm fed up with Italy, I spew it out of my mouth. It's a long time since I imagined I could belong down there. Art, eh? Blue-velvet sky, ardent wine, the sweets of sensuality. In short, I don't want it—I decline with thanks. The whole *bellezza* business makes me nervous. All those frightfully animated people down there with their black animal-like eyes; I don't like them either. These Romance peoples have no soul in their eyes. No, I'm going to take a trip to Denmark."

"To Denmark?"

"Yes. I'm quite sanguine of the results. I happen never to have been there, though I lived all my youth so close to it. Still I have always known and loved the country. I suppose I must have this northern tendency from my father, for my mother was really more for the *bellezza*, in so far, that is, as she cared very much one way or the other. But just take the books that are written up there, that clean, meaty, whimsical Scandinavian literature. Lisabeta, there's nothing like it, I love it. Or take the Scandinavian meals, those incomparable meals, which can only be digested in strong sea air (I don't know whether I can digest them in any sort of air); I know them from my home too, because we ate that way up there. Take even the names, the given names that people rejoice in up north; we have a good many of them in my part of the country too: Ingeborg, for instance, isn't it the purest poetry—like a harp-tone? And then the sea—up there it's the Baltic! . . . In a word, I am going, Lisabeta, I want to see the Baltic again and read the books and hear the names on their native heath; I want to stand on the terrace at Kronberg, where the ghost appeared to Hamlet, bringing despair and death to that poor, noble-souled youth. . . ."

"How are you going, Tonio, if I may ask? What route are you taking?"

"The usual one," he said, shrugging his shoulders, and blushed perceptibly. "Yes, I shall touch my—my point of departure, Lisabeta, after thirteen years, and that may turn out rather funny."

She smiled.

"That is what I wanted to hear, Tonio Kröger. Well, be off, then, in God's name. Be sure to write to me, do you hear? I shall expect a letter full of your experiences in—Denmark."

And Tonio Kröger travelled north. He travelled in comfort (for he was wont to say that anyone who suffered inwardly more than other people had a right to a little outward ease); and he did not stay until the towers of the little town he had left rose up in the grey air. Among them he made a short and singular stay.

The dreary afternoon was merging into evening when the train pulled into the narrow, reeking shed, so marvellously familiar. The volumes of thick smoke rolled up to the dirty glass roof and wreathed to and fro there in long tatters, just as they had, long ago, on the day when Tonio Kröger, with nothing but derision in his heart, had left his native town.—He arranged to have his luggage sent to his hotel and walked out of the station.

There were the cabs, those enormously high, enormously wide black cabs drawn by two horses, standing in a rank. He did not take one, he only looked at them, as he looked at everything: the narrow gables, and the pointed towers peering above the roofs close at hand; the plump, fair, easy-going populace, with their broad yet rapid speech. And a nervous laugh mounted in him mysteriously akin to a sob.—He walked on, slowly, with the damp wind constantly in his face, across the bridge, with the mythological statues on the railings, and some distance along the harbour.

Good Lord, how tiny and close it all seemed! The comical little gabled streets were climbing up just as of yore from the port to the town! And on the ruffled waters the smoke-stacks and masts of the ships dipped gently in the wind and twilight. Should he go up that next street, leading, he knew, to a certain house? No, tomorrow. He was too sleepy. His head was heavy from the journey, and slow, vague trains of thought passed through his mind.

Sometimes in the past thirteen years, when he was suffering from indigestion, he had dreamed of being back home in the echoing old house in the steep, narrow street. His father had been there too, and reproached him bitterly for his dissolute manner of life, and this, each time, he had found quite as it should be. And now the present refused to distinguish itself in any way from one of those tantalizing dream-fabrications in which the dreamer asks himself if this be delusion or reality and is driven to decide for the latter, only to wake up after all in the end. . . . He paced through the half-empty streets with his head inclined against the wind, moving as though in his sleep in the direction of the hotel, the first hotel in the town, where he meant to sleep. A bow-legged man, with a pole at the end of which burned a tiny fire, walked before him with a rolling, seafaring gait and lighted the gas-lamps.

What was at the bottom of this? What was it burning darkly beneath the ashes of his fatigue, refusing to burst out into a clear blaze? Hush, hush, only no talk. Only don't make words! He would have liked to go on so, for a long time, in the wind, through the dusky, dreamily familiar streets—but everything was so little and close together here. You reached your goal at once.

In the upper town there were arc-lamps, just lighted. There was the hotel with the two black lions in front of it; he had been afraid of them as a child. And there they were, still looking at each other as though they were about to sneeze; only they seemed to have grown much smaller. Tonio Kröger passed between them into the hotel.

As he came on foot, he was received with no great ceremony. There was a porter, and a lordly gentleman dressed in black, to do the honours; the latter, shoving back his cuffs with his little fingers, measured him from the crown of his head to the soles of his boots, obviously with intent to place him, to assign him to his proper category socially and hierarchically speaking and then mete out the suitable degree of courtesy. He seemed not to come to any clear decision and compromised on a moderate display of politeness. A mild-mannered waiter with yellow-white side-whiskers, in a dress suit shiny with age, and rosettes on his soundless shoes, led him up two flights into a clean old room furnished in patriarchal style. Its windows gave on a twilit view of courts and gables, very mediaeval and picturesque, with the fantastic bulk of the old church close by. Tonio Kröger stood awhile before this window; then he sat down on the wide sofa, crossed his arms, drew down his brows, and whistled to himself.

Lights were brought and his luggage came up. The mild-mannered waiter laid the hotel register on the table, and Tonio Kröger, his head on one side, scrawled something on it that might be taken for a name, a station, and a place of origin. Then he ordered supper and went on gazing into space from his sofa-corner. When it stood before him he let it wait long untouched, then took a few bites and walked up and down an hour in his room, stopping from time to time and closing his eyes. Then he very slowly undressed and went to bed. He slept long and had curiously confused and ardent dreams.

It was broad day when he woke. Hastily he recalled where he was and got up to draw the curtains; the pale-blue sky, already with a hint of autumn, was streaked with frayed and tattered cloud; still, above his native city the sun was shining.

He spent more care than usual upon his toilette, washed and shaved and made himself fresh and immaculate as though about to call upon some smart family where a well-dressed and flawless appearance was *de rigueur;* and while occupied in this wise he listened to the anxious beating of his heart.

How bright it was outside! He would have liked better a twilight air like yesterday's, instead of passing through the streets in the broad sunlight, under everybody's eye. Would he meet people he knew, be stopped and questioned and have to submit to be asked how he had spent the last thirteen years? No, thank goodness, he was known to nobody here; even if anybody remembered him, it was unlikely he would be recognized—for certainly he had changed in the meantime! He surveyed himself in the glass and felt a sudden sense of security behind his mask, behind his work-worn face, that was older than his years. . . . He sent for breakfast, and after that he went out; he passed under the disdainful eye of the porter and the gentleman in black, through the vestibule and between the two lions, and so into the street.

Where was he going? He scarcely knew. It was the same as yesterday. Hardly was he in the midst of this long-familiar scene, this stately conglomeration of gables, turrets, arcades, and fountains, hardly did he feel once more the wind in his face, that strong current wafting a faint and pungent aroma from far-off dreams, when the same mistiness laid itself like a veil about his senses. . . . The muscles of his face relaxed, and he looked at men and things with a look grown suddenly calm. Perhaps right there, on the street corner, he might wake up after all. . . .

Where was he going? It seemed to him the direction he took had a connection with his sad and strangely rueful dreams of the night. . . . He went to Market Square, under the vaulted arches of the Rathaus, where the butchers were weighing out their wares red-handed, where the tall old Gothic fountain stood with its manifold spires. He paused in front of a house, a plain narrow building, like many another, with a fretted baroque gable; stood there lost in contemplation. He read the plate on the door, his eyes rested a little while on each of the windows. Then slowly he turned away.

Where did he go? Towards home. But he took a roundabout way outside the walls—for he had plenty of time. He went over the Millwall and over the Holstenwall, clutching his hat, for the wind was rushing and moaning through the trees. He left the wall near the station, where he saw a train puffing busily past, idly counted the coaches, and looked after the man who sat perched upon the last. In the Lindenplatz he stopped at one of the pretty villas, peered long into the garden and up at the windows, lastly conceived the idea of swinging the gate to and fro upon its hinges till it creaked. Then he looked awhile at his moist, rust-stained hand and went on, went through the squat old gate, along the harbour, and up the steep, windy street to his parents' house.

It stood aloof from its neighbors, its gable towering above them; grey and sombre, as it had stood these three hundred years; and Tonio Kröger read the pious, half-illegible motto above the entrance. Then he drew a long breath and went in.

His heart gave a throb of fear, lest his father might come out of one of the doors on the ground floor, in his office coat, with the pen behind his ear, and take him to task for his excesses. He would have found the reproach quite in order; but he got past unchidden. The inner door was ajar, which appeared to him reprehensible though at the same time he felt as one does in certain broken dreams, where obstacles melt away of themselves, and one presses onward in marvellous favour with fortune. The wide entry, paved with great square flags, echoed to his tread. Opposite the silent kitchen was the curious projecting structure, of rough boards, but cleanly varnished, that had been the servants' quarters. It was quite high up and could only be reached by a sort of ladder from the entry. But the great cupboards and carven presses were gone. The son of the house climbed the majestic staircase, with his hand on the white-enamelled, fret-work balustrade. At each step he lifted his hand, and put it down again with the next as though testing whether he could call back his ancient familiarity with the stout old railing. . . . But at the landing of the entresol he stopped. For on the entrance door was a white plate; and on it in black letters he read: "Public Library."

"Public Library?" thought Tonio Kröger. What were either literature or the public doing here? He knocked . . . heard a "come in," and obeying it with gloomy suspense gazed upon a scene of most unhappy alteration.

The storey was three rooms deep, and all the doors stood open. The walls were covered nearly all the way up with long rows of books in uniform bindings, standing in dark-coloured bookcases. In each room a poor creature of a man sat writing behind a sort of counter. The farthest two just turned their heads, but the nearest got up in haste and, leaning with both hands on the table, stuck out his head, pursed his lips, lifted his brows, and looked at the visitor with eagerly blinking eyes.

"I beg pardon," said Tonio Kröger without turning his eyes from the book-shelves. "I am a stranger here, seeing the sights. So this is your Public Library? May I examine your collection a little?"

"Certainly, with pleasure," said the official, blinking still more violently. "It is open to everybody. . . . Pray look about you. Should you care for a catalogue?"

"No, thanks," answered Tonio Kröger, "I shall soon find my way about." And he began to move slowly along the walls, with the appearance of studying the rows of books. After a while he took down a volume, opened it, and posted himself at the window.

This was the breakfast-room. They had eaten here in the morning instead of in the big dining-room upstairs, with its white statues of gods and goddesses standing out against the blue walls. . . . Beyond there had been a bedroom, where his father's mother had died—only after a long struggle, old as she was, for she had been of a pleasure-loving nature and clung to life. And his father too had drawn his last breath in the same room; that tall, correct, slightly melancholy and pensive gentleman with the wild flower in his buttonhole. . . . Tonio had sat at the foot of his death-bed, quite given over to unutterable feelings of love and grief. His mother had knelt at the bedside, his lovely, fiery mother, dissolved in hot tears, and after that she had withdrawn with her artist into the far blue south. . . . And beyond still, the small third-room, likewise full of books and presided over by a shabby man—that had been for years on end his own. Thither he had come after school and a walk—like today's; against that wall his table had stood with the drawer where he had kept his first clumsy, heartfelt attempts at verse. . . . The walnut tree . . . a pang went through him. He gave a sidewise glance out at the window. The garden lay desolate, but there stood the old walnut tree where it used to stand, groaning and creaking heavily in the wind. And Tonio Kröger let his gaze fall upon the book he had in his hands, an excellent piece of work, and very familiar. He followed the black lines of print, the paragraphs, the flow of words that flowed with so much art, mounting in the ardour of creation to a certain climax and effect and then as artfully breaking off.

"Yes, that was well done," he said; put back the book and turned away. Then he saw that the functionary still stood bolt-upright, blinking with a mingled expression of zeal and misgiving. "A capital collection, I see," said Tonio Kröger. "I have already quite a good idea of it. Much obliged to you. Good-bye." He went out; but it was a poor exit, and he felt sure the official would stand there perturbed and blinking for several minutes.

He felt no desire for further researches. He had been home. Strangers were living upstairs in the large rooms behind the pillared hall; the top of the stairs was shut off by a glass door which used not to be there, and on the door was a plate. He went away, down the steps, across the echoing corridor, and left his parental home. He sought a restaurant, sat down in a corner, and brooded over a heavy, greasy meal. Then he returned to his hotel.

"I am leaving," he said to the fine gentleman in black. "This afternoon." And he asked for his bill, and for a carriage to take him down to the harbour where he should take the boat for Copenhagen. Then he went up to his room and sat there stiff and still, with his cheek on his hand, looking down on the table before him with absent eyes. Later he paid his bill and packed his things. At the appointed hour the carriage was announced and Tonio Kröger went down in travel array.

At the foot of the stairs the gentleman in black was waiting.

"Beg pardon," he said shoving back his cuffs with his little fingers. . . . "Beg pardon, but we must detain you just a moment. Herr Seehaase, the proprietor, would like to exchange a few words with you. A matter of form. . . . He is back there. . . . If you will have the goodness to step this way. . . . It is *only* Herr Seehaase, the proprietor."

And he ushered Tonio Kröger into the background of the vestibule. . . . There, in fact, stood Herr Seehaase. Tonio Kröger recognized him from old time. He was small, fat, and bow-legged. His shaven side-whisker was white, but he wore the same old low-cut dress coat and little velvet cap embroidered in green. He was not alone. Beside him, at a little high desk fastened into the wall, stood a policeman in a helmet, his gloved right hand resting on a document in coloured inks; he turned towards Tonio Kröger with his honest, soldierly face as though he expected Tonio to sink into the earth at his glance.

Tonio Kröger looked at the two and confined himself to waiting.

"You came from Munich?" the policeman asked at length in a heavy, good-natured voice.

Tonio Kröger said he had.

"You are going to Copenhagen?"

"Yes, I am on the way to a Danish seashore resort."

"Seashore resort? Well, you must produce your papers," said the policeman. He uttered the last word with great satisfaction.

"Papers . . .?" He had no papers. He drew out his pocketbook and looked into it; but aside from notes there was nothing there but some proof-sheets of a story which he had taken along to finish reading. He hated relations with officials and had never got himself a passport. . . .

"I am sorry," he said, "but I don't travel with papers."

"Ah!" said the policeman. "And what might be your name?"

Tonio replied.

"Is that a fact?" asked the policeman, suddenly erect, and expanding his nostrils as wide as he could. . . .

"Yes, that is a fact," answered Tonio Kröger.

"And what are you, anyhow?"

Tonio Kröger gulped and gave the name of his trade in a firm voice. Herr Seehaase lifted his head and looked him curiously in the face.

"H'm," said the policeman. "And you give out that you are not identical with an individdle named"—he said "individdle" and then, referring to his document in coloured inks, spelled out an involved, fantastic name which mingled all the sounds of all the races—Tonio Kröger forgot it next minute—"of unknown parentage and unspecified means," he went on, "wanted by the Munich police for various shady transactions, and probably in flight towards Denmark?"

"Yes, I give out all that, and more," said Tonio Kröger, wriggling his shoulders. The gesture made a certain impression.

"What? Oh, yes, of course," said the policeman. "You say you can't show any papers—"

Herr Seehaase threw himself into the breach.

"It is only a formality," he said pacifically, "nothing else. You must bear in mind the official is only doing his duty. If you could only identify yourself somehow—some document. . . ."

They were all silent. Should he make an end of the business, by revealing to Herr Seehaase that he was no swindler without specified means, no gypsy in a green wagon, but the son of the late Consul Kröger, a member of the Kröger family? No, he felt no desire to do that. After all, were not these guardians of civic order within their right? He even agreed with them—up to a point. He shrugged his shoulders and kept quiet.

"What have you got, then?" asked the policeman. "In your portfoly, I mean?"

"Here? Nothing. Just a proof-sheet," answered Tonio Kröger.

"Proof-sheet? What's that? Let's see it."

And Tonio Kröger handed over his work. The policeman spread it out on the shelf and began reading. Herr Seehaase drew up and shared it with him. Tonio Kröger looked over their shoulders to see what they read. It was a good moment, a little effect he had worked out to a perfection. He had a sense of self-satisfaction.

"You see," he said, "there is my name. I wrote it, and it is going to be published, you understand."

"All right, that will answer," said Herr Seehaase with decision, gathered up the sheets and gave them back. "That will have to answer, Petersen," he repeated crisply, shutting his eyes and shaking his head as though to see and hear no more. "We must not keep the gentleman any longer. The carriage is waiting. I implore you to pardon the little inconvenience, sir. The officer has only done his duty, but I told him at once he was on the wrong track. . . ."

"Indeed!" thought Tonio Kröger.

The officer seemed still to have his doubts; he muttered something else about individdle and document. But Herr Seehaase, overflowing with regrets, led his guest through the vestibule, accompanied him past the two lions to the carriage, and himself, with many respectful bows, closed the door upon him. And then the funny, high, wide old cab rolled and rattled and bumped down the steep, narrow street to the quay.

And such was the manner of Tonio Kröger's visit to his ancestral home.

Night fell and the moon swam up with silver gleam as Tonio Kröger's boat reached the open sea. He stood at the prow wrapped in his cloak against a mounting wind, and looked beneath into the dark going and coming of the waves as they hovered and swayed and came on, to meet with a clap and shoot erratically away in a bright gush of foam.

He was lulled in a mood of still enchantment. The episode at the hotel, their wanting to arrest him for a swindler in his own home, had cast him down a little, even although he found it quite in order—in a certain way. But after he came on board he had watched, as he used to do as a boy with his father, the lading of goods into the deep bowels of the boat, amid shouts of mingled Danish and Plattdeutsch; not only boxes and bales, but also a Bengal tiger and a polar bear were lowered in cages with stout iron bars. They had probably come from Hamburg and were destined for a Danish menagerie. He had enjoyed these distractions. And as the boat glided along between flat river-banks he quite forgot Officer Petersen's inquisition; while all the rest—his sweet, sad, rueful dreams of the night before, the walk he had taken, the walnut tree—had welled up again in his soul. The sea opened out and he saw in the distance the beach where he as a lad had been let to listen to the ocean's summer dreams; saw the flashing of the lighthouse tower and the lights of the Kurhaus where he and his parents had lived. . . . The Baltic! He bent his head to the strong salt wind; it came sweeping on, it enfolded him, made him faintly giddy and a little deaf; and in that mild confusion of the senses all memory of evil, of anguish and error, effort and exertion of the will, sank away into joyous oblivion and were gone. The roaring, foaming, flapping, and slapping all about him came to his ears like the groan and rustle of an old walnut tree, the creaking of a garden gate. . . . More and more the darkness came on.

"The stars! Oh, by Lord, look at the stars!" a voice suddenly said, with a heavy singsong accent that seemed to come out of the inside of a tun. He recognized it. It belonged to a young man with red-blond hair who had been Tonio Kröger's neighbour at dinner in the salon. His dress was very simple, his eyes were red, and he had the moist and chilly look of a person who has just bathed. With nervous and self-conscious movements he had taken unto himself an astonishing quantity of lobster omelet. Now he leaned on the rail beside Tonio Kröger and looked up at the skies, holding his chin between thumb and forefinger. Beyond a doubt he was in one of those rare and festal and edifying moods that cause the barriers between man and man to fall; when the heart opens even to the stranger, and the mouth utters that which otherwise it would blush to speak. . . .

"Look, by dear sir, just look at the stars. There they stahd and glitter; by goodness, the whole sky is full of theb! And I ask you, when you stahd ahd look up at theb, ahd realize that bany of theb are a huddred tibes larger thad the earth, how does it bake you feel? Yes, we have idvehted the telegraph and the telephode and all the triuphs of our bodern tibes. But whed we look up there, after all we have to recogdize and uhderstad that we are worbs, biserable worbs, ahd dothing else. Ab I right, sir, or ab I wrog? Yes, we are worbs," he answered himself, and nodded meekly and abjectly in the direction of the firmament.

"Ah, no, he has no literature in his belly," thought Tonio Kröger. And he recalled something he had lately read, an essay by a famous French writer on cosmological and psychological philosophies, a very delightful *causerie.*

He made some sort of reply to the young man's feeling remarks, and they went on talking, leaning over the rail, and looking into the night with its movement and fitful lights. The young man, it seemed, was a Hamburg merchant on his holiday.

"Y'ought to travel to Copedhagen on the boat, thigks I, and so here I ab, and so far it's been fide. But they shouldn't have given us the lobster obelet, sir, for it's going to be storby—the captain said so hibself—and that's do joke with indigestible food like that in your stobach. . . ."

Tonio Kröger listened to all this engaging artlessness and was privately drawn to it.

"Yes," he said, "all the food up here is too heavy. It makes one lazy and melancholy."

"Belancholy?" repeated the young man, and looked at him, taken aback. Then he asked, suddenly: "You are a stradger up here, sir?"

"Yes, I come from a long way off," answered Tonio Kröger vaguely, waving his arm.

"But you're right," said the youth; "Lord kdows you are right about the belancholy. I am dearly always belancholy, but specially on evedings like this when there are stars in the sky." And he supported his chin again with thumb and forefinger.

"Surely this man writes verses," thought Tonio Kröger; "business man's verses, full of deep feeling and singlemindedness."

Evening drew on. The wind had grown so violent as to prevent them from talking. So they thought they would sleep a bit, and wished each other good-night.

Tonio Kröger stretched himself out on the narrow cabin bed, but he found no repose. The strong wind with its sharp tang had power to rouse him; he was strangely restless with sweet anticipations. Also he was violently sick with the motion of the ship as she glided down a steep mountain of wave and her screw vibrated as in agony, free of the water. He put on all his clothes again and went up to the deck.

Clouds raced across the moon. The sea danced. It did not come on in full-bodied, regular waves; but far out in the pale and flickering light the water was lashed, torn, and tumbled; leaped upward like great licking flames; hung in jagged and fantastic shapes above dizzy abysses, where the foam seemed to be tossed by the playful strength of colossal arms and flung upward in all directions. The ship had a heavy passage; she lurched and stamped and groaned through the welter; and far down in her bowels the tiger and the polar bear voiced their acute discomfort. A man in an oilskin, with the hood drawn over his head and a lantern strapped to his chest, went straddling painfully up and down the deck. And at the stern, leaning far out, stood the young man from Hamburg suffering the worst. "Lord!" he said, in a hollow, quavering voice, when he saw Tonio Kröger. "Look at the uproar of the elebents, sir!" But he could say no more—he was obliged to turn hastily away.

Tonio Kröger clutched at a taut rope and looked abroad into the arrogance of the elements. His exultation outvied storm and wave; within himself he chanted a song to the sea, instinct with love of her: "O thou wild friend of my youth, Once more I behold thee—" But it go no further, he did not finish it. It was not fated to receive a final form nor in tranquillity to be welded to a perfect whole. For his heart was too full. . . .

Long he stood; then stretched himself out on a bench by the pilot-house and looked up at the sky, where stars were flickering. He even slept a little. And when the cold foam splashed his face it seemed in his half-dreams like a caress.

Perpendicular chalk-cliffs, ghostly in the moonlight, came in sight. They were nearing the island of Möen. Then sleep came again, broken by salty showers of spray that bit into his face and made it stiff. . . . When he really roused, it was broad day, fresh and palest grey, and the sea had gone down. At breakfast he saw the young man from Hamburg again, who blushed rosy-red for shame of the poetic indiscretions he had been betrayed into by the dark, ruffled up his little red-blond moustache with all five fingers, and called out a brisk and soldierly good-morning—after that he studiously avoided him.

And Tonio Kröger landed in Denmark. He arrived in Copenhagen, gave tips to everybody who laid claim to them, took a room at a hotel, and roamed the city for three days with an open guide-book and the air of an intelligent foreigner bent on improving his mind. He looked at the king's New Market and the "Horse" in the middle of it, gazed respectfully up the columns of the Frauenkirch, stood long before Thorwaldsen's noble and beautiful statuary, climbed the round tower, visited castles, and spent two lively evenings in the Tivoli. But all this was not exactly what he saw.

The doors of the houses—so like those in his native town, with open-work gables of baroque shape—bore names known to him of old; names that had a tender and precious quality, and withal in their syllables an accent of plaintive reproach, of a repining after the lost and gone. He walked, he gazed, drawing deep, lingering draughts of moist sea air; and everywhere he saw eyes as blue, hair as blond, faces as familiar, as those that had visited his rueful dreams the night he had spent in his native town. There in the open street it befell him that a glance, a ringing word, a sudden laugh would pierce him to his marrow.

He could not stand the bustling city for long. A restlessness, half memory and half hope, half foolish and half sweet, possessed him; he was moved to drop this rôle of ardently inquiring tourist and lie somewhere, quite quietly, on a beach. So he took ship once more and travelled under a cloudy sky, over a black water, northwards along the coast of Seeland towards Helsingör. Thence he drove, at once, by carriage, for three-quarters of an hour, along and above the sea, reaching at length his ultimate goal, the little white "bath-hotel" with green blinds. It stood surrounded by a settlement of cottages, and its shingled turret tower looked out on the beach and the Swedish coast. Here he left the carriage, took possession of the light room they had ready for him, filled shelves and presses with his kit, and prepared to stop awhile.

It was well on in September; not many guests were left in Aalsgaard. Meals were served on the ground floor, in the great beamed dining-room, whose lofty windows led out upon the veranda and the sea. The landlady presided, an elderly spinster with white hair and faded eyes, a faint colour in her cheek and a feeble twittering voice. She was forever arranging her red hands to look well upon the table-cloth. There was a short-necked old gentleman, quite blue in the face, with a grey sailor beard; a fish-dealer he was, from the capital, and strong at the German. He seemed entirely congested and inclined to apoplexy; breathed in short gasps, kept putting his beringed first finger to one nostril, and snorting violently to get a passage of air through the other. Notwithstanding, he addressed himself constantly to the whisky-bottle, which stood at his place at luncheon and dinner, and breakfast as well. Besides him the company consisted only of three tall American youths with their governor or tutor, who kept adjusting his glasses in unbroken silence. All day long he played football with his charges, who had narrow, taciturn faces and reddish-yellow hair parted in the middle. "Please pass the *wurst*," said one. "That's not *wurst*, it's *schinken*," said the other, and this was the extent of their conversation, as the rest of the time they sat there dumb, drinking hot water.

Tonio Kröger could have wished himself no better table-companions. He revelled in the peace and quiet, listened to the Danish palatals, the clear and the clouded vowels in which the fish-dealer and the landlady desultorily conversed; modestly exchanged views with the fish-dealer on the state of the barometer, and then left the table to go through the veranda and onto the beach once more, where he had already spent long, long morning hours.

Sometimes it was still and summery there. The sea lay idle and smooth, in stripes of blue and russet and bottle-green, played all across with glittering silvery lights. The seaweed shrivelled in the sun and the jelly-fish lay steaming. There was a faintly stagnant smell and a whiff of tar from the fishing-boat against which Tonio Kröger leaned, so standing that he had before his eyes not the Swedish coast but the open horizon, and in his face the pure, fresh breath of the softly breathing sea.

Then grey, stormy days would come. The waves lowered their heads like bulls and charged against the beach; they ran and ramped high up the sands and left them strewn with shining wet sea-grass, driftwood, and mussels. All abroad beneath an overcast sky extended ranges of billows, and between them foaming valleys palely green; but above the spot where the sun hung behind the cloud a patch like white velvet lay on the sea.

Tonio Kröger stood wrapped in wind and tumult, sunk in the continual dull, drowsy uproar that he loved. When he turned away it seemed suddenly warm and silent all about him. But he was never unconscious of the sea at his back; it called, it lured, it beckoned him. And he smiled.

He went landward, by lonely meadow-paths, and was swallowed up in the beech-groves that clothed the rolling landscape near and far. Here he sat down on the moss, against a tree, and gazed at the strip of water he could see between the trunks. Sometimes the sound of surf came on the wind—a noise like boards collapsing at a distance. And from the tree-tops over his head a cawing—hoarse, desolate, forlorn. He held a book on his knee, but did not read a line. He enjoyed profound forgetfulness, hovered disembodied above space and time; only now and again his heart would contract with a fugitive pain, a stab of longing and regret, into whose origin he was too lazy to inquire.

Thus passed some days. He could not have said how many and had no desire to know. But then came one on which something happened; happened while the sun stood in the sky and people were about; and Tonio Kröger, even, felt no vast surprise.

The very opening of the day had been rare and festal. Tonio Kröger woke early and suddenly from his sleep, with a vague and exquisite alarm; he seemed to be looking at a miracle, a magic illumination. His room had a glass door and balcony facing the sound; a thin white gauze curtain divided it into living- and sleeping-quarters, both hung with delicate tinted paper and furnished with an airy good taste that gave them a sunny and friendly look. But now to his sleep drunken eyes it lay bathed in a serene and roseate light, an unearthly brightness that gilded walls and furniture and turned the gauze curtain to radiant pink cloud. Tonio Kröger did not at once understand. Not until he stood at the glass door and looked out did he realize that this was the sunrise.

For several days there had been clouds and rain; but now the sky was like a piece of pale-blue silk, spanned shimmering above sea and land, and shot with light from red and golden clouds. The sun's disk rose in splendour from a crisply glittering sea that seemed to quiver and burn beneath it. So began the day. In a joyous daze Tonio Kröger flung on his clothes, and breakfasting in the veranda before everybody else, swam from the little wooden bathhouse some distance out into the sound, then walked for an hour along the beach. When he came back, several omnibuses were before the door, and from the dining-room he could see people in the parlour next door where the piano was, in the veranda, and on the terrace in front; quantities of people sitting at little tables enjoying beer and sandwiches amid lively discourse. There were whole families; there were old and young, there were even a few children.

At second breakfast—the table was heavily laden with cold viands, roast, pickled, and smoked—Tonio Kröger inquired what was going on.

"Guests," said the fish-dealer. "Tourists and ball-guests from Helsingör. Lord help us, we shall get no sleep this night! There will be dancing and music, and I fear me it will keep up till late. It is a family reunion, a sort of celebration and excursion combined; they all subscribe to it and take advantage of the good weather. They came by boat and bus and they are having breakfast. After that they go on with their drive, but at night they will all come back for a dance here in the hall. Yes, damn it, you'll see we shan't get a wink of sleep."

"Oh, it will be a pleasant change," said Tonio Kröger.

After that there was nothing more said for some time. The landlady arranged her red fingers on the cloth, the fish-dealer blew through his nostril, the Americans drank hot water and made long faces.

Then all at once a thing came to pass: *Hans Hansen and Ingeborg Holm walked through the room.*

Tonio Kröger, pleasantly fatigued after his swim and rapid walk, was leaning back in his chair and eating smoked salmon on toast; he sat facing the veranda and the ocean. All at once the door opened and the two entered hand-in-hand—calmly and unhurried. Ingeborg, blonde Inge, was dressed just as she used to be at Herr Knaak's dancing-class. The light flowered frock reached down to her ankles and it had a tulle fichu draped with a pointed opening that left her soft throat free. Her hat hung by its ribbons over her arm. She, perhaps, was a little more grown up than she used to be, and her wonderful plait of hair was wound round her head; but Hans Hansen was the same as ever. He wore his sailor overcoat with gilt buttons, and his wide blue sailor collar lay across his shoulders and back; the sailor cap with its short ribbons he was dangling carelessly in his hand. Ingeborg's narrow eyes were turned away; perhaps she felt shy before the company at table. But Hans Hansen turned his head straight towards them, and measured one after another defiantly with his steel-blue eyes; challengingly, with a sort of contempt. He even dropped Ingeborg's hand and swung his cap harder than ever, to show what manner of man he was. Thus the two, against the silent, blue-dyed sea, measured the length of the room and passed through the opposite door into the parlour.

This was at half past eleven in the morning. While the guests of the house were still at table the company in the veranda broke up and went away by the side door. No one else came into the dining-room. The guests could hear them laughing and joking as they got into the omnibuses, which rumbled away one by one. . . . "So they are coming back?" asked Tonio Kröger.

"That they are," said the fish-dealer. "More's the pity. They have ordered music, let me tell you—and my room is right above the dining-room."

"Oh, well, it's a pleasant change," repeated Tonio Kröger. Then he got up and went away.

That day he spent as he had the others, on the beach and in the wood, holding a book on his knee and blinking in the sun. He had but one thought; they were coming back to have a dance in the hall, the fish-dealer had promised they would; and he did nothing but be glad of this, with a sweet and timorous gladness such as he had not felt through all these long dead years. Once he happened, by some chance association, to think of his friend Adalbert, the novelist, the man who had known what he wanted and betaken himself to the café to get away from the spring. Tonio Kröger shrugged his shoulders at the thought of him.

Luncheon was served earlier than usual, also supper, which they ate in the parlour because the dining-room was being got ready for the ball, and the whole house flung in disorder for the occasion. It grew dark; Tonio Kröger sitting in his room heard on the road and in the house the sounds of approaching festivity. The picknickers were coming back; from Helsingör, by bicycle and carriage, new guests were arriving; a fiddle and a nasal clarinet might be heard practising down in the dining-room. Everything promised a brilliant ball. . . .

Now the little orchestra struck up a march; he could hear the notes, faint but lively. The dancing opened with a polonaise. Tonio Kröger sat for a while and listened. But when he heard the march-time go over into a waltz he got up and slipped noiselessly out of his room.

From his corridor it was possible to go by the side stairs to the side entrance of the hotel and thence to the veranda without passing through a room. He took this route, softly and stealthily as though on forbidden paths, feeling along through the dark, relentlessly drawn by this stupid jigging music, that now came up to him loud and clear.

The veranda was empty and dim, but the glass door stood open into the hall, where shone two large oil lamps, furnished with bright reflectors. Thither he stole on soft feet; and his skin prickled with the thievish pleasure of standing unseen in the dark and spying on the dancers there in the brightly lighted room. Quickly and eagerly he glanced about for the two whom he sought. . . .

Even though the ball was only half an hour old, the merriment seemed in full swing; however, the guests had come hither already warm and merry, after a whole day of carefree, happy companionship. By bending forward a little, Tonio Kröger could see into the parlour from where he was. Several old gentlemen sat there smoking, drinking, and playing cards; others were with their wives on the plush-upholstered chairs in the foreground watching the dance. They sat with their knees apart and their hands resting on them, puffing out their cheeks with a prosperous air; the mothers, with bonnets perched on their parted hair, with their hands folded over their stomachs and their heads on one side, gazed into the whirl of dancers. A platform had been erected on the long side of the hall, and on it the musicians were doing their utmost. There was even a trumpet, that blew with a certain caution, as though afraid of its own voice, and yet after all kept breaking and cracking. Couples were dipping and circling about, others walked arm-in-arm up and down the room. No one wore ballroom clothes; they were dressed as for an outing in the summertime: the men in countrified suits which were obviously their Sunday wear; the girls in light-coloured frocks with bunches of field-flowers in their bodices. Even a few children were there, dancing with each other in their own way, even after the music stopped. There was a long-legged man in a coat with a little swallow-tail, a provincial lion with an eye-glass and frizzed hair, a post-office clerk or some such thing; he was like a comic figure stepped bodily out of a Danish novel; and he seemed to be the leader and manager of the ball. He was everywhere at once, bustling, perspiring, officious, utterly absorbed; setting down his feet, in shiny, pointed military half-boots, in a very artificial and involved manner, toes first; waving his arms to issue an order, clapping his hands for the music to begin; here, there, and everywhere, and glancing over his shoulder in pride at his great bow of office, the streamers of which fluttered grandly in his rear.

Yes, there they were, those two, who had gone by Tonio Kröger in the broad light of day; he saw them again—with a joyful start he recognized them almost at the same moment. Here was Hans Hansen by the door, quite close; his legs apart, a little bent over, he was eating with circumspection a large piece of sponge-cake, holding his hand cupwise under his chin to catch the crumbs. And there by the wall sat Ingeborg Holm, Inge the fair; the post-office clerk was just mincing up to her with an exaggerated bow and asking her to dance. He laid one hand on his back and gracefully shoved the other into his bosom. But she was shaking her head in token that she was a little out of breath and must rest awhile, whereat the post-office clerk sat down by her side.

Tonio Kröger looked at them both, these two for whom he had in time past suffered love—at Hans and Ingeborg. They were Hans and Ingeborg not so much by virtue of individual traits and similarity of costume as by similarity of race and type. This was the blond, fair-haired breed of the steel-blue eyes, which stood to him for the pure, the blithe, the untroubled in life; for a virginal aloofness that was at once both simple and full of pride. . . . He looked at them. Hans Hansen was standing there in his sailor suit, lively and well built as ever, broad in the shoulders and narrow in the hips; Ingeborg was laughing and tossing her head in a certain high-spirited way she had; she carried her hand, a schoolgirl hand, not at all slender, not at all particularly aristocratic, to the back of her head in a certain manner so that the thin sleeve fell away from her elbow—and suddenly such a pang of home-sickness shook his breast that involuntarily he drew farther back into the darkness lest someone might see his features twitch.

"Had I forgotten you?" he asked. "No, never. Not thee, Hans, not thee, Inge the fair! It was always you I worked for; when I heard applause I always stole a look to see if you were there. . . . Did you read *Don Carlos*, Hans Hansen, as you promised me at the garden gate? No, don't read it! I do not ask it any more. What have you to do with a king who weeps for loneliness? You must not cloud your clear eyes or make them dreamy and dim by peering into melancholy poetry. . . . To be like you! To begin again, to grow up like you, regular like you, simple and normal and cheerful, in conformity and understanding with God and man, beloved of the innocent and happy. To take you, Ingeborg Holm, to wife, and have a son like you, Hans Hansen—to live free from the curse of knowledge and the torment of creation, live and praise God in blessed mediocrity! Begin again? But it would do no good. It would turn out the same—everything would turn out the same as it did before. For some go of necessity astray, because for them there is no such thing as a right path."

The music ceased; there was a pause in which refreshments were handed round. The post-office assistant tripped about in person with a trayful of herring salad and served the ladies; but before Ingeborg Holm he even went down on one knee as he passed her the dish, and she blushed for pleasure.

But now those within began to be aware of a spectator behind the glass door; some of the flushed and pretty faces turned to measure him with hostile glances; but he stood his ground. Ingeborg and Hans looked at him too, at almost the same time, both with that utter indifference in their eyes that looks so like contempt. And he was conscious too of a gaze resting on him from a different quarter; turned his head and met with his own the eyes that had sought him out. A girl stood not far off, with a fine, pale little face—he had already noticed her. She had not danced much, she had few partners, and he had seen her sitting there against the wall, her lips closed in a bitter line. She was standing alone now too; her dress was a thin light stuff, like the others, but beneath the transparent frock her shoulders showed angular and poor, and the thin neck was thrust down so deep between those meagre shoulders that as she stood there motionless she might almost be thought a little deformed. She was holding her hands in their thin mitts across her flat breast, with the finger-tips touching; her head was dropped, yet she was looking up at Tonio Kröger with black swimming eyes. He turned away. . . .

Here, quite close to him, were Ingeborg and Hans. He had sat down beside her—she was perhaps his sister—and they ate and drank together surrounded by other rosy-cheeked folk; they chattered and made merry, called to each other in ringing voices, and laughed aloud. Why could he not go up and speak to them? Make some trivial remark to him or her, to which they might at least answer with a smile? It would make him happy —he longed to do it; he would go back more satisfied to his room if he might feel he had established a little contact with them. He thought out what he might say; but he had not the courage to say it. Yes, this too was just as it had been: they would not understand him, they would listen like strangers to anything he was able to say. For their speech was not his speech.

It seemed the dance was about to begin again. The leader developed a comprehensive activity. He dashed hither and thither, adjuring everybody to get partners; helped the waiters to push chairs and glasses out of the way, gave orders to the musicians, even took some awkward people by the shoulders and shoved them aside. . . . What was coming? They formed squares of four couples each. . . . A frightful memory brought the colour to Tonio Kröger's cheeks. They were forming for a quadrille.

The music struck up, the couples bowed and crossed over. The leader called off; he called off—Heaven save us—in French! And pronounced the nasals with great distinction. Ingeborg Holm danced close by, in the set nearest the glass door. She moved to and fro before him, forwards and back, pacing and turning; he caught a waft from her hair or the thin stuff of her frock, and it made him close his eyes with the old, familiar feeling, the fragrance and bitter-sweet enchantment he had faintly felt in all these days, that now filled him utterly with irresistible sweetness. And what was the feeling? Longing, tenderness? Envy? Self-contempt? . . . *Moulinet des dames!* "Did you laugh, Ingeborg the blonde, did you laugh at me when I disgraced myself by dancing the *moulinet?* And would you still laugh today even after I have become something like a famous man? Yes, that you would, and you would be right to laugh. Even if I in my own person had written the nine symphonies and *The World as Will and Idea* and painted the Last Judgment, you would still be eternally right to laugh. . . ." As he looked at her he thought of a line of verse once so familiar to him, now long forgotten: "I would sleep, but thou must dance." How well he knew it, that melancholy northern mood it evoked—its heavy inarticulateness. To sleep. . . . To long to be allowed to live the life of simple feeling, to rest sweetly and passively in feeling alone, without compulsion to act and achieve—and yet to be forced to dance, dance the cruel and perilous sword-dance of art; without even being allowed to forget the melancholy conflict within oneself; to be forced to dance, the while one loved. . . .

A sudden wild extravagance had come over the scene. The sets had broken up, the quadrille was being succeeded by a galop, and all the couples were leaping and gliding about. They flew past Tonio Kröger to a maddeningly quick tempo, crossing, advancing, retreating, with quick, breathless laughter. A couple came rushing and circling towards Tonio Kröger; the girl had a pale, refined face and lean, high shoulders. Suddenly, directly in front of him, they tripped and slipped and stumbled. . . . The pale girl fell, so hard and violently it almost looked dangerous; and her partner with her. He must have hurt himself badly, for he quite forgot her, and, half-rising, began to rub his knee and grimace; while she, quite dazed, it seemed, still lay on the floor. Then Tonio Kröger came forward, took her gently by the arms, and lifted her up. She looked dazed, bewildered, wretched; then suddenly her delicate face flushed pink.

"*Tak, O, mange tak!*" she said, and gazed up at him with dark, swimming eyes.

"You should not dance any more, Fräulein," he said gently. Once more he looked round at *them*, at Ingeborg and Hans, and then he went out, left the ball and the veranda and returned to his own room.

He was exhausted with jealousy, worn out with the gaiety in which he had had no part. Just the same, just the same as it had always been. Always with burning cheeks he had stood in his dark corner and suffered for you, you blond, you living, you happy ones! And then quite simply gone away. Somebody *must* come now! Ingeborg *must* notice he had gone, must slip after him, lay a hand on his shoulder and say: "Come back and be happy. I love you!" But she came not at all. No, such things did not happen. Yes, all was as it had been, and he too was happy, just as he had been. For his heart was alive. But between that past and this present what had happened to make him become that which he now was? Icy desolation, solitude: mind, and art, forsooth!

He undressed, lay down, put out the light. Two names he whispered into his pillow, the few chaste northern syllables that meant for him his true and native way of love, of longing and happiness; that meant to him life and home, meant simple and heartfelt feeling. He looked back on the years that had passed. He thought of the dreamy adventures of the senses, nerves, and mind in which he had been involved; saw himself eaten up with intellect and introspection, ravaged and paralysed by insight, half worn out by the fevers and frosts of creation, helpless and in anguish of conscience between two extremes, flung to and fro between austerity and lust; *raffiné*, impoverished, exhausted by frigid and artificially heightened ecstasies; erring, forsaken, martyred, and ill—and sobbed with nostalgia and remorse.

Here in his room it was still and dark. But from below life's lulling, trivial waltz-rhythm came faintly to his ears.

Tonio Kröger sat up in the north, composing his promised letter to his friend Lisabeta Ivanovna.

"Dear Lisabeta down there in Arcady, whither I shall shortly return," he wrote: "Here is something like a letter, but it will probably disappoint you, for I mean to keep it rather general. Not that I have nothing to tell; for indeed, in my way, I have had experiences; for instance, in my native town they were even going to arrest me . . . but of that by word of mouth. Sometimes now I have days when I would rather state things in general terms than go on telling stories.

"You probably still remember, Lisabeta, that you called me a *bourgeois*, a *bourgeois manqué?* You called me that in an hour when, led on by other confessions I had previously let slip, I confessed to you my love of life, or what I call life. I ask myself if you were aware how very close you came to the truth, how much my love of 'life' is one and the same thing as my being a *bourgeois*. This journey of mine has given me much occasion to ponder the subject.

"My father, you know, had the temperament of the north: solid, reflective, puritanically correct, with a tendency to melancholia. My mother, of indeterminate foreign blood, was beautiful, sensuous, naïve, passionate, and careless at once, and, I think, irregular by instinct. The mixture was no doubt extraordinary and bore with it extraordinary dangers. The issue of it, a *bourgeois* who strayed off into art, a bohemian who feels nostalgic yearnings for respectability, an artist with a bad conscience. For surely it is my *bourgeois* conscience makes me see in the artist life, in all irregularity and all genius, something profoundly suspect, profoundly disreputable; that fills me with this lovelorn *faiblesse* for the simple and good, the comfortably normal, the average unendowed respectable human being.

"I stand between two worlds. I am at home in neither, and I suffer in consequence. You artists call me a *bourgeois*, and the *bourgeois* try to arrest me. . . . I don't know which makes me feel worse. The *bourgeois* are stupid; but you adorers of the beautiful, who call me phlegmatic and without aspirations, you ought to realize that there is a way of being an artist that goes so deep and is so much a matter of origins and destinies that no longing seems to it sweeter and more worth knowing than longing after the bliss of the commonplace.

"I admire those proud, cold beings who adventure upon the paths of great and daemonic beauty and 'despise mankind'; but I do not envy them. For if anything is capable of making a poet of a literary man, it is my *bourgeois* love of the human, the living and usual. It is the source of all warmth, goodness, and humour; I even almost think it is itself that love of which it stands written that one may speak with the tongues of men and of angels and yet having it not is as sounding brass and tinkling cymbals.

"The work I have so far done is nothing or not much—as good as nothing. I will do better, Lisabeta—this is a promise. As I write, the sea whispers to me and I close my eyes. I am looking into a world unborn and formless, that needs to be ordered and shaped; I see into a whirl of shadows of human figures who beckon to me to weave spells to redeem them:

tragic and laughable figures and some that are both together—and to these I am drawn. But my deepest and secretest love belongs to the blond and blue-eyed, the fair and living, the happy, lovely, and commonplace.

"Do not chide this love, Lisabeta; it is good and fruitful. There is longing in it, and a gentle envy; a touch of contempt and no little innocent bliss."

6

JOSEPH CONRAD
The Secret Sharer

The Secret Sharer is an exceptionally fine short novel—and an exceptionally difficult one—mostly because of the elusive relationship between its surface action and its symbolic meaning. The surface of the story is quite simple and can easily be read as a familiar type of sea-adventure. A young sailing-ship captain, hard pressed by the tensions of his first command, secretly takes on board a fugitive seaman named Leggatt. The captain is faced with a moral dilemma when he learns that Leggatt has killed another seaman, under mitigating circumstances, on another ship. Should he turn the fugitive over to the law, or help him escape? Although there are several tense episodes, this is an uncomplicated tale, made vivid by the reality of its moral questions, by its manly earnestness, and by Conrad's rare talent for dramatizing life at sea.

But there is obviously a great deal more to the work than that. *The Secret Sharer* presents itself, even through the inevitable confusions of a first reading, as a painstakingly symbolic story which conceals further meaning beneath obvious details. The sea, for example, is an obvious and important image in the story. Psychologists agree that the sea is a universal symbol of the unconscious. Leggatt is repeatedly associated with the sea. He is under water when first and last seen, and also when he commits his crucial act of murder. In his role as the "double" or "secret sharer" of the captain, Leggatt represents more or less the captain's unconscious. The story as a whole dramatizes the captain's confrontation with the hidden depths of his own personality, externalized in the form of his relationship with Leggatt. By linking Leggatt's apparent crime and guilt with the captain's personality, Conrad suggests that even the most civilized of men harbor potentially destructive passions. Just as importantly, Conrad dramatizes the psychological realities that Freud was evolving, at nearly the same time, in his essays on psychoanalysis: human personality is not unitary, but made up of different mental systems which sometimes work at cross purposes to one another. Human well-being requires complex, harmonious interplay among mental systems.

These are the outlines of symbolic meaning in *The Secret Sharer*, but in fact, no single, simple interpretive formula seems adequate. The work is iridescent. At its core is the supremely ambiguous relationship between the captain and Leggatt. Leggatt at some points seems, literally, to *be* part of the captain's personality. At other moments he seems by turns to *represent,* or *act as a reflection of,* or merely *evoke a response from* the captain's hidden self. With each shift in the nature of this "psychological doubling" the reality of the entire story shifts. It is tempting to explain Leggatt's role as a double by dismissing him as hallucination, a dream-twin produced by the captain's imagination. Nevertheless he is quite real, and far from being a literal twin, he is, the captain admits, "not a bit like me."

Although Leggatt is no figment of the imagination, his role as a double is intensified by the captain's intense imagination and self-awareness. The captain is a very sensitive and perceptive young man. His self-awareness has been heightened by his own doubts about his leadership, by his alienation from the crew, and by the romantic flavor of the challenge ahead in an exotic part of the world. Moreover, his position as skipper of an English ship is a prominent one. The story is set at the time when English sea power, military and mercantile, had made England the most powerful nation in the world. The captain's role is a symbolic expression of English competence, duty, and power, and because he is an intelligent, conscientious upper-middle-class Englishman, a "Conway boy," he cannot help but know it. He also knows

that failure in the performance of his duty on this first command would effectively end his career as a seaman. In short, he is under the kind of pressure that could make the identity of almost any man begin to blur.

Duality has everything to do with *The Secret Sharer* as a work of fiction, not only because the captain is "dual" during the presence of his other self, but also because of the story's purposefully double emotional atmosphere. The captain reacts to his situation with opposite emotions. He experiences intense mental anguish, but at the same time, a rare sense of well-being. The narrator remarks about the first feeling: "all the time the dual working of my mind distracted me almost to the point of insanity. . . . It was very much like being mad, only worse, because one was aware of it." The same duality that leads to the point of insanity also creates a mellow, dreamlike intimacy between the two men. Their below-decks conversations are heavy with the atmosphere and imagery of sleep—darkness, quiet, the sleeping suit Leggatt wears, and the protective enclosure of the captain's room. Their face-to-face encounters have the intensity of profound introspection and the heightened consciousness of self totally present to self. Despite their mutual fears, they share a spiritual intimacy which seems to reaffirm in each of them a tenacious will to survive. Psychologically, the sense of well-being they experience is related to commonly shared human fantasies of encountering one's own twin. Such fantasies usually involve a working out of destructive inner tensions through encounter with oneself envisioned in the literal form of the twin. The universal need for self-encounter helps explain the pattern of dream-like intimacy, urgency, and finally, fulfillment in *The Secret Sharer*.

In the end, the captain finds himself confronted by the riddle of his own psyche, and Leggatt's, transformed into external circumstances. With a precision that few modern writers have achieved, Conrad exemplifies an ancient theme: a man's fate is his own soul writ large. In the drama of redemption and near-destruction which ends *The Secret Sharer*, the process of psychological doubling reaches its greatest complexity. In order to save themselves, both men confront the necessity to destroy; in the moment of crisis, each acts from an inner passion that transcends conventional distinctions of right and wrong. Leg-

gatt's "crime," it must be noted, had been an ambiguously destructive and redemptive act. "The same strung-up force which had given twenty-four men a chance, at least, for their lives, had, in a sort of recoil, crushed an unworthy mutinous existence." In a very real way, the captain recapitulates Leggatt's act of murder by choosing to steer the ship through the unknown shoal waters off Koh-ring. The captain's act of "standing in" could be regarded as totally irrational. Foolishly, one might say, he risks all—his ship, his crew, his own life and Leggatt's. However, it is the inner drama of his own creative–destructive spirit that demands this act.

But the moment of greatest crisis is yet to come. In its resolution, though, the captain and his secret sharer endure the encounter of self with self, and each is made whole by it.

The Secret Sharer

AN EPISODE FROM THE COAST

I

On my right hand there were lines of fishing-stakes resembling a mysterious system of half-submerged bamboo fences, incomprehensible in its division of the domain of tropical fishes, and crazy of aspect as if abandoned for ever by some nomad tribe of fishermen now gone to the other end of the ocean; for there was no sign of human habitation as far as the eye could reach. To the left a group of barren islets, suggesting ruins of stone walls, towers, and blockhouses, had its foundations set in a blue sea that itself looked solid, so still and stable did it lie below my feet; even the track of light from the westering sun shone smoothly, without that animated glitter which tells of an imperceptible ripple. And when I turned my head to take a parting glance at the tug which had just left us anchored outside the bar, I saw the straight line of the flat shore joined to the stable sea, edge to edge, with a perfect and unmarked closeness, in one levelled floor half brown, half blue under the enormous dome of the sky. Corresponding in their insignificance to the

Reprinted from Joseph Conrad: 'TWIXT LAND AND SEA TALES by permission of J. M. Dent & Sons, Ltd., and the Trustees of the Joseph Conrad Estate.

islets of the sea, two small clumps of trees, one on each side of the only fault in the impeccable joint, marked the mouth of the river Meinam we had just left on the first preparatory stage of our homeward journey; and, far back on the inland level, a larger and loftier mass, the grove surrounding the great Paknam pagoda, was the only thing on which the eye could rest from the vain task of exploring the monotonous sweep of the horizon. Here and there gleams as of a few scattered pieces of silver marked the windings of the great river; and on the nearest of them, just within the bar, the tug steaming right into the land became lost to my sight, hull and funnel and masts, as though the impassive earth had swallowed her up without an effort, without a tremor. My eye followed the light cloud of her smoke, now here, now there, above the plain, according to the devious curves of the stream, but always fainter and farther away, till I lost it at last behind the mitre-shaped hill of the great pagoda. And then I was left alone with my ship, anchored at the head of the Gulf of Siam.

She floated at the starting-point of a long journey, very still in an immense stillness, the shadows of her spars flung far to the eastward by the setting sun. At that moment I was alone on her decks. There was not a sound in her—and around us nothing moved, nothing lived, not a canoe on the water, not a bird in the air, not a cloud in the sky. In this breathless pause at the threshold of a long passage we seemed to be measuring our fitness for a long and arduous enterprise, the appointed task of both our existences to be carried out, far from all human eyes, with only sky and sea for spectators and for judges.

There must have been some glare in the air to interfere with one's sight, because it was only just before the sun left us that my roaming eyes made out beyond the highest ridge of the principal islet of the group something which did away with the solemnity of perfect solitude. The tide of darkness flowed on swiftly; and with tropical suddenness a swarm of stars came out above the shadowy earth, while I lingered yet, my hand resting lightly on my ship's rail as if on the shoulder of a trusted friend. But, with all that multitude of celestial bodies staring down at one, the comfort of quiet communion with her was gone for good. And there were also disturbing sounds by this time—voices, footsteps forward; the steward flitted along the main-deck, a busily ministering spirit; a hand-bell tinkled urgently under the poop-deck. . . .

I found my two officers waiting for me near the supper table, in the lighted cuddy. We sat down at once, and as I helped the chief mate, I said:

"Are you aware that there is a ship anchored inside the islands? I saw her mastheads above the ridge as the sun went down."

He raised sharply his simple face, overcharged by a terrible growth of whisker, and emitted his usual ejaculations: "Bless my soul, sir! You don't say so!"

My second mate was a round-cheeked, silent young man, grave beyond his years, I thought; but as our eyes happened to meet I detected a slight quiver on his lips. I looked down at once. It was not my part to encourage sneering on board my ship. It must be said, too, that I knew very little of my officers. In consequence of certain events of no particular significance, except to myself, I had been appointed to the command only a fortnight before. Neither did I know much of the hands forward. All these people had been together for eighteen months or so, and my position was that of the only stranger on board. I mention this because it has some bearing on what is to follow. But what I felt most was my being a stranger to the ship; and if all the truth must be told, I was somewhat of a stranger to myself. The youngest man on board (barring the second mate), and untried as yet by a position of the fullest responsibility, I was willing to take the adequacy of the others for granted. They had simply to be equal to their tasks; but I wondered how far I should turn out faithful to that ideal conception of one's own personality every man sets up for himself secretly.

Meantime the chief mate, with an almost visible effect of collaboration on the part of his round eyes and frightful whiskers, was trying to evolve a theory of the anchored ship. His dominant trait was to take all things into earnest consideration. He was of a painstaking turn of mind. As he used to say, he "liked to account to himself" for practically everything that came in his way, down to a miserable scorpion he had found in his cabin a week before. The why and the wherefore of that scorpion—how it got on board and came to select his room rather than the pantry (which was a dark place and more what a scorpion would be partial to), and how on earth it managed to drown itself in the inkwell of his writing-desk—had exercised him infinitely. The ship within the islands was much more easily accounted for; and just as we were about to rise from table he made his pronouncement. She was, he doubted not, a ship from home lately arrived. Probably she drew too much water to cross the bar except at the top of spring tides. Therefore she went into that natural harbour to wait for a few days in preference to remaining in an open roadstead.

"That's so," confirmed the second mate, suddenly, in his slightly hoarse voice. "She draws over twenty feet. She's the Liverpool ship *Sephora* with a cargo of coal. Hundred and twenty-three days from Cardiff."

We looked at him in surprise.

"The tugboat skipper told me when he came on board for your letters, sir," explained the young man. "He expects to take her up the river the day after to-morrow."

After thus overwhelming us with the extent of his information he slipped out of the cabin. The mate observed regretfully that he "could not account for that young fellow's whims." What prevented him telling us all about it at once, he wanted to know.

I detained him as he was making a move. For the last two days the crew had had plenty of hard work, and the night before they had very little sleep. I felt painfully that I—a stranger—was doing something unusual when I directed him to let all hands turn in without setting an anchor-watch. I proposed to keep on deck myself till one o'clock or thereabouts. I would get the second mate to relieve me at that hour.

"He will turn out the cook and the steward at four," I concluded, "and then give you a call. Of course at the slightest sign of any sort of wind we'll have the hands up and make a start at once."

He concealed his astonishment. "Very well, sir." Outside the cuddy he put his head in the second mate's door to inform him of my unheard-of caprice to take a five hours' anchor-watch on myself. I heard the other raise his voice incredulously—"What? The Captain himself?" Then a few more murmurs, a door closed, then another. A few moments later I went on deck.

My strangeness, which had made me sleepless, had prompted that unconventional arrangement, as if I had expected in those solitary hours of the night to get on terms with the ship of which I knew nothing, manned by men of whom I knew very little more. Fast alongside a wharf, littered like any ship in port with a tangle of unrelated things, invaded by unrelated shore people, I had hardly seen her yet properly. Now, as she lay cleared for sea, the stretch of her main-deck seemed to me very fine under the stars. Very fine, very roomy for her size, and very inviting. I descended the poop and paced the waist, my mind picturing to myself the coming passage through the Malay Archipelago, down the Indian Ocean, and up the Atlantic. All its phases were familiar enough to me, every characteristic, all the alternatives which were likely to face me on the high seas—everything! . . . except the novel responsibility of command. But I took heart from the reasonable thought that the ship was like other ships, the men like other men, and that the sea was not likely to keep any special surprises expressly for my discomfiture.

Arrived at that comforting conclusion, I bethought myself of a cigar and went below to get it. All was still down there. Everybody at the after end of the ship was sleeping profoundly. I came out again on the quarter-deck, agreeably at ease in my sleeping-suit on that warm breathless night, barefooted, a glowing cigar in my teeth, and, going forward, I was met by the profound silence of the fore end of the ship. Only as I passed the door of the forecastle I heard a deep, quiet, trustful sigh of some sleeper inside. And suddenly I rejoiced in the great security of the sea as compared with the unrest of the land, in my choice of that untempted life presenting no disquieting problems, invested with an elementary moral beauty by the absolute straightforwardness of its appeal and by the singleness of its purpose.

The riding-light in the fore-rigging burned with a clear, untroubled, as if symbolic, flame, confident and bright in the mysterious shades of the night. Passing on my way aft along the other side of the ship, I observed that the rope side-ladder, put over, no doubt, for the master of the tug when he came to fetch away our letters, had not been hauled in as it should have been. I became annoyed at this, for exactitude in small matters is the very soul of discipline. Then I reflected that I had myself peremptorily dismissed my officers from duty, and by my own act had prevented the anchor-watch being formally set and things properly attended to. I asked myself whether it was wise ever to interfere with the established routine duties even from the kindest of motives. My action might have made me appear eccentric. Goodness only knew how that absurdly whiskered mate would "account" for my conduct, and what the whole ship thought of that informality of their new captain. I was vexed with myself.

Not from compunction certainly, but, as it were mechanically, I proceeded to get the ladder in myself. Now a side-ladder of that sort is a light affair and comes in easily, yet my vigorous tug, which should have brought it flying on board, merely recoiled upon my body in a totally unexpected jerk. What the devil! . . . I was so astounded by the immovableness of that ladder that I remained stock-still, trying to account for it to myself like that imbecile mate of mine. In the end, of course, I put my head over the rail.

The side of the ship made an opaque belt of shadow on the darkling glassy shimmer of the sea. But I saw at once something elongated and pale floating very close to the ladder. Before I could form a guess a faint flash of phosphorescent light, which seemed to issue suddenly from the naked body of a man, flickered in the sleeping water with the elusive, silent play of summer lightning in a night sky. With a gasp I saw revealed to my stare a pair of feet, the long legs, a broad livid back immersed right up to the neck in a greenish cadaverous glow. One hand, awash, clutched the bottom rung of the ladder. He was complete but for the head. A headless corpse! The cigar dropped out of my gaping mouth with a tiny plop and a short hiss quite audible in the absolute stillness of all things under heaven. At that I suppose he raised up his face, a dimly pale oval in the shadow of the ship's side. But even then I could only barely make out down there the shape of his black-haired head. However, it was enough for the horrid, frost-bound sensation which had gripped me about the chest to pass off. The moment of vain exclamations was past, too. I only climbed on the spare spar and leaned over the rail as far as I could, to bring my eyes nearer to that mystery floating alongside.

As he hung by the ladder, like a resting swimmer, the sea-lightning played about his limbs at every stir; and he appeared in it ghastly, silvery, fish-like. He remained as mute as a fish, too. He made no motion to get out of the water, either. It was inconceivable that he should not attempt to come on board, and strangely troubling to suspect that perhaps he did not want to. And my first words were prompted by just that troubled incertitude.

"What's the matter?" I asked in my ordinary tone, speaking down to the face upturned exactly under mine.

"Cramp," it answered, no louder. Then slightly anxious, "I say, no need to call any one."

"I was not going to," I said.

"Are you alone on deck?"

"Yes."

I had somehow the impression that he was on the point of letting go the ladder to swim away beyond my ken—mysterious as he came. But, for the moment, this being appearing as if he had risen from the bottom of the sea (it was certainly the nearest land to the ship) wanted only to know the time. I told him. And he, down there, tentatively:

"I suppose your captain's turned in?"

"I am sure he isn't," I said.

He seemed to struggle with himself, for I heard something like the low, bitter murmur of doubt. "What's the good?" His next words came out with a hesitating effort.

"Look here, my man. Could you call him out quietly?"

I thought the time had come to declare myself.

"*I* am the captain."

I heard a "By Jove!" whispered at the level of the water. The phosphorescence flashed in the swirl of the water all about his limbs, his other hand seized the ladder.

"My name's Leggatt."

The voice was calm and resolute. A good voice. The self-possession of that man had somehow induced a corresponding state in myself. It was very quietly that I remarked:

"You must be a good swimmer."

"Yes. I've been in the water practically since nine o'clock. The question for me now is whether I am to let go this ladder and go on swimming till I sink from exhaustion, or—to come on board here."

I felt this as no mere formula of desperate speech, but a real alternative in the view of a strong soul. I should have gathered from this that he was young; indeed, it is only the young who are ever confronted by such clear issues. But at the time it was pure intuition on my part. A mysterious communication was established already between us two—in the face of that silent, darkened tropical sea. I was young, too; young enough to make no comment. The man in the water began suddenly to climb up the ladder, and I hastened away from the rail to fetch some clothes.

Before entering the cabin I stood still, listening in the lobby at the foot of the stairs. A faint snore came through the closed door of the chief mate's room. The second mate's door was on the hook, but the darkness in there was absolutely soundless. He, too, was young and could sleep like a stone. Remained the steward, but he was not likely to wake up before he was called. I got a sleeping-suit out of my room and, coming back on deck, saw the naked man from the sea sitting on the main-hatch, glimmering white in the darkness, his elbows on his knees and his head in his hands. In a moment he had concealed his damp body in a sleeping-suit of the same grey-stripe pattern as the one I was wearing and followed me like my double on the poop. Together we moved right aft, barefooted, silent.

"What is it?" I asked in a deadened voice, taking the lighted lamp out of the binnacle, and raising it to his face.

"An ugly business."

He had rather regular features; a good mouth; light eyes under somewhat heavy, dark eyebrows; a smooth, square forehead; no growth on his cheeks; a small, brown moustache, and a well-shaped, round chin. His expression was concentrated, meditative, under the inspecting light of the lamp I held up to his face; such as a man thinking hard in solitude might wear. My sleeping-suit was just right for his size. A well-knit young fellow of twenty-five at most. He caught his lower lip with the edge of white, even teeth.

"Yes," I said, replacing the lamp in the binnacle. The warm, heavy tropical night closed upon his head again.

"There's a ship over there," he murmured.

"Yes, I know. The *Sephora*. Did you know of us?"

"Hadn't the slighest idea. I am the mate of her—" He paused and corrected himself. "I should say I *was*."

"Aha! Something wrong?"

"Yes. Very wrong indeed. I've killed a man."

"What do you mean? Just now?"

"No, on the passage. Weeks ago. Thirty-nine south. When I say man—"

"Fit of temper," I suggested confidently.

The shadowy, dark head, like mine, seemed to nod imperceptibly above the ghostly grey of my sleeping-suit. It was, in the night, as though I had been faced by my own reflection in the depths of a sombre and immense mirror.

"A pretty thing to have to own up to for a Conway boy," murmured my double, distinctly.

"You're a Conway boy?"

"I am," he said, as if startled. Then, slowly . . . "Perhaps you too—"

It was so; but being a couple of years older I had left before he joined. After a quick interchange of dates a silence fell; and I thought suddenly of my absurd mate with his terrific whiskers and the "Bless my soul—you don't say so" type of intellect. My double gave me an inkling of his thoughts by saying: "My father's a parson in Norfolk. Do you see me before a judge and jury on that charge? For myself I can't see the necessity. There are fellows that an angel from heaven— And I am not that. He was one of those creatures that are just simmering all the time with a silly sort of wickedness. Miserable devils that have no business to live at all. He wouldn't do his duty and wouldn't let anybody else do theirs. But what's the good of talking! You know well enough the sort of ill-conditioned snarling cur—"

He appealed to me as if our experiences had been as identical as our clothes. And I knew well enough the pestiferous danger of such a character where there are no means of legal repression. And I knew well enough also that my double there was no homicidal ruffian. I did not think of asking him for details, and he told me the story roughly in brusque, disconnected sentences. I needed no more. I saw it all going on as though I were myself inside that other sleeping suit.

"It happened while we were setting a reefed foresail, at dusk. Reefed foresail! You understand the sort of weather. The only sail we had left to keep the ship running; so you may guess what it had been like for days. Anxious sort of job, that. He gave me some of his cursed insolence at the sheet. I tell you I was overdone with this terrific weather that seemed to have no end to it. Terrific, I tell you—and a deep ship. I believe the fellow himself was half crazed with funk. It was no time for gentlemanly reproof, so I turned round and felled him like an ox. He up and at me. We closed just as an awful sea made for the ship. All hands saw it coming and took to the rigging, but I had him by the throat, and went on shaking him like a rat, the men above us yelling, 'Look out! Look out!' Then a crash as if the sky had fallen on my head. They say that for over ten minutes hardly anything was to be seen of the ship—just the three masts and a bit of the forecastle head and of the poop all awash driving along in a smother of foam. It was a miracle that they found us, jammed together behind the forebits. It's clear that I meant business, because I was holding him by the throat still when they picked us up. He was black in the face. It was too much for them. It seems they rushed us aft together, gripped as we were, screaming 'Murder!' like a lot of lunatics, and broke into the cuddy. And the ship running for her life, touch and go all the time, any minute her last in a sea fit to turn your hair grey only a-looking at it. I understand that the skipper, too, started raving like the rest of them. The man had been deprived of sleep for more than a week, and to have this sprung on him at the height of a furious gale nearly drove him out of his mind. I wonder they didn't fling me overboard after getting the carcass of their precious ship-mate out of my fingers. They had rather a job to separate us, I've been told. A sufficiently fierce story to make an old judge and a respectable jury sit up a bit. The first thing I heard when I came to myself was the maddening howling of that endless gale, and on that the voice of the old man. He was hanging on to my bunk, staring into my face out of his sou'wester.

"'Mr. Leggatt, you have killed a man. You can act no longer as chief mate of this ship.'"

His care to subdue his voice made it sound monotonous. He rested a hand on the end of the skylight to steady himself with, and all that time did not stir a limb, so far as I could see. "Nice little tale for a quiet tea-party," he concluded in the same tone.

One of my hands, too, rested on the end of the skylight; neither did I stir a limb, so far as I knew. We stood less than a foot from each other. It occurred to me that if old "Bless my soul—you don't say so" were to put his head up the companion and catch sight of us, he would think he was seeing double, or imagine himself come upon a scene of weird witchcraft; the strange captain having a quiet confabulation by the wheel with his own grey ghost. I became very much concerned to prevent anything of the sort. I heard the other's soothing undertone.

"My father's a parson in Norfolk," it said. Evidently he had forgotten he had told me this important fact before. Truly a nice little tale.

"You had better slip down into my stateroom now," I said, moving off stealthily. My double followed my movements; our bare feet made no sound; I let him in, closed the door with care, and, after giving a call to the second mate, returned on deck for my relief.

"Not much sign of any wind yet," I remarked when he approached.

"No, sir. Not much," he assented, sleepily, in his hoarse voice, with just enough deference, no more, and barely suppressing a yawn.

"Well, that's all you have to look out for. You have got your orders."

"Yes, sir."

I paced a turn or two on the poop and saw him take up his position face forward with his elbow in the ratlines of the mizzen-rigging before I went below. The mate's faint snoring was still going on peacefully. The cuddy lamp was burning over the table on which stood a vase with flowers, a polite attention from the ship's provision merchant—the last flowers we should see for the next three months at the very least. Two bunches of bananas hung from the beam symmetrically, one on each side of the rudder-casing. Everything was as before in the ship—except that two of her captain's sleeping-suits were simultaneously in use, one motionless in the cuddy, the other keeping very still in the captain's stateroom.

It must be explained here that my cabin had the form of the capital letter L, the door being within the angle and opening into the short part of the letter. A couch was to the left, the bed-place to the right; my writing-desk and the chronometer's table faced the door. But any one opening it, unless he stepped right inside, had no view of what I call the long (or vertical) part of the letter. It contained some lockers surmounted by a bookcase; and a few clothes, a thick jacket or two, caps, oilskin coat, and such like, hung on hooks. There was at the bottom of that part a door opening into my bathroom, which could be entered also directly from the saloon. But that way was never used.

The mysterious arrival had discovered the advantage of this particular shape. Entering my room, lighted strongly by a bulkhead lamp swung on gimbals above my writing-desk, I did not see him anywhere till he stepped out quietly from behind the coats hung in the recessed part.

"I heard somebody moving about, and went in there at once," he whispered.

I, too, spoke under my breath.

"Nobody is likely to come in here without knocking and getting permission."

He nodded. His face was thin and the sunburn faded, as though he had been ill. And no wonder. He had been, I heard presently, kept under arrest in his cabin for nearly seven weeks. But there was nothing sickly in his eyes or in his expression. He was not a bit like me, really; yet, as we stood leaning over my bed-place, whispering side by side, with our dark heads together and our backs to the door, anybody bold enough to open it stealthily would have been treated to the uncanny sight of a double captain busy talking in whispers with his other self.

"But all this doesn't tell me how you came to hang on to our side-ladder," I inquired, in the hardly audible murmurs we used, after he had told me something more of the proceedings on board the *Sephora* once the bad weather was over.

"When we sighted Java Head I had had time to think all those matters out several times over. I had six weeks of doing nothing else, and with only an hour or so every evening for a tramp on the quarter-deck."

He whispered, his arms folded on the side of my bed-place, staring through the open port. And I could imagine perfectly the manner of this thinking out—a stubborn if not a steadfast operation; something of which I should have been perfectly incapable.

"I reckoned it would be dark before we closed with the land," he continued, so low that I had to strain my hearing, near as we were to each other, shoulder touching shoulder almost. "So I asked to speak to the old man. He always seemed very sick when he came to see me—as if he could not look me in the face. You know, that foresail saved the ship. She was too deep to have run long under bare poles. And it was I that managed to set it for him. Anyway, he came. When I had him in my cabin—he stood by the door looking at me as if I had the halter round my neck already—I asked him right away to leave my cabin door unlocked at night while the ship was going through Sunda Straits. There would be the Java coast within two or three miles, off Angier Point. I wanted nothing more. I've had a prize for swimming my second year in the Conway."

"I can believe it," I breathed out.

"God only knows why they locked me in every night. To see some of their faces you'd have thought they were afraid I'd go about at night strangling people. Am I a murdering brute? Do I look it? By Jove! if I had been he wouldn't have trusted himself like that into my room. You'll say I might have chucked him aside and bolted out, there and then—it was dark already. Well, no. And for the same reason I wouldn't think of trying to smash the door. There would have been a rush to stop me at the noise, and I did not mean to get into a confounded scrimmage. Somebody else might have got killed—for I would not have broken out only to get chucked back, and I did not want any more of that work. He refused, looking more sick than ever. He was afraid of the men, and also of that old second mate of his who had been sailing with him for years—a grey-headed old humbug; and his steward, too, had been with him devil knows how long —seventeen years or more—a dogmatic sort of loafer who hated me like poison, just because I was the chief mate. No chief mate ever made more than one voyage in the *Sephora*, you know. Those two old chaps ran the ship. Devil only knows what the skipper wasn't afraid of (all his nerve went to pieces altogether in that hellish spell of bad weather we had)—of what the law would do to him—of his wife, perhaps. Oh, yes! she's on board. Though I don't think she would have meddled. She would have been only too glad to have me out of the ship in any way. The 'brand of Cain' business, don't you see. That's all right. I was ready enough to go off wandering on the face of the earth—and that was price enough to pay for an Abel of that sort. Anyhow, he wouldn't listen to me. 'This thing must take its course. I represent the law here.' He was shaking like a leaf. 'So you won't?' 'No!' 'Then I hope you will be able to sleep on that,' I said, and turned my back on him. 'I wonder that *you* can,' cries he, and locks the door.

"Well, after that, I couldn't. Not very well. That was three weeks ago. We have had a slow passage through the Java Sea; drifted about Carimata for ten days. When we anchored here they thought, I suppose, it was all right. The nearest land (and that's five miles) is the ship's destination; the consul would soon set about catching me; and there would have been no object in bolting to these islets there. I don't suppose there's a drop of water on them. I don't know how it was, but to-night that steward, after bringing me my supper, went out to let me eat it, and left the door unlocked. And I ate it—all there was, too. After I had finished I strolled out on the quarter-deck. I don't know that I meant to do anything. A breath of fresh air was all I wanted, I believe. Then a sudden temptation came over me. I kicked off my slippers and was in the water before I had made up my mind fairly. Somebody heard the splash and they raised an awful hullabaloo. 'He's gone! Lower the boats! He's committed suicide! No, he's swimming.' Certainly I was swimming. It's not so easy for a swimmer like me to commit suicide by drowning. I landed on the nearest islet before the boat left the ship's side. I heard them pulling about in the dark, hailing, and so on, but after a bit they gave up. Everything quieted down and the anchorage became as still as death. I sat down on a stone and began to think. I felt certain they would start searching for me at daylight. There was no place to hide on those stony things—and if there had been, what would have been the good? But now I was clear of that ship, I was not going back. So after a while I took off all my clothes, tied them up in a bundle with a stone inside, and dropped them in the deep water on the outer side of that islet. That was suicide enough for me. Let them think what they liked, but I didn't mean to drown myself. I meant to swim till I sank—but that's not the same thing. I struck out for another of these little islands, and it was from that one that I first saw your riding-light. Something to swim for. I went on easily, and on the way I came upon a flat rock a foot or two above water. In the daytime, I dare say, you might make it out with a glass from your poop. I scrambled up on it and rested myself for a bit. Then I made another start. That last spell must have been over a mile."

His whisper was getting fainter and fainter, and all the time he stared straight out through the port-hole, in which there was not even a star to be seen. I had not interrupted him. There was something that made comment impossible in his narrative, or perhaps in himself; a sort of feeling, a quality, which I can't find a name for. And when he ceased, all I found was a futile whisper: "So you swam for our light?"

"Yes—straight for it. It was something to swim for. I couldn't see any stars low down because the coast was in the way, and I couldn't see the land, either. The water was like glass. One might have been swimming in a confounded thousand-feet deep cistern with no place for scrambling out anywhere; but what I didn't like was the notion of swimming round and round like a crazed bullock before I gave out and as I didn't mean to go back . . . No. Do you see me being hauled back, stark naked, off one of these little islands by the scruff of the neck and fighting like a wild beast? Somebody would have got killed for certain, and I did not want any of that. So I went on. Then your ladder—"

"Why didn't you hail the ship?" I asked, a little louder.

He touched my shoulder lightly. Lazy footsteps came right over our heads and stopped. The second mate had crossed from the other side of the poop and might have been hanging over the rail, for all we knew.

"He couldn't hear us talking—could he?" My double breathed into my very ear, anxiously.

His anxiety was an answer, a sufficient answer, to the question I had put to him. An answer containing all the difficulty of that situation. I closed the porthole quietly, to make sure. A louder word might have been overheard.

"Who's that?" he whispered then.

"My second mate. But I don't know much more of the fellow than you do."

And I told him a little about myself. I had been appointed to take charge while I least expected anything of the sort, not quite a fortnight ago. I didn't know either the ship or the people. Hadn't had the time in port to look about me or size anybody up. And as to the crew, all they knew was that I was appointed to take the ship home. For the rest, I was almost as much of a stranger on board as himself, I said. And at the moment I felt it most acutely. I felt that it would take very little to make me a suspect person in the eyes of the ship's company.

He had turned about meantime; and we, the two strangers in the ship, faced each other in identical attitudes.

"Your ladder—" he murmured, after a silence. "Who'd have thought of finding a ladder hanging over at night in a ship anchored out here! I felt just then a very unpleasant faintness. After the life I've been leading for nine weeks, anybody would have got out of condition. I wasn't capable of swimming round as far as your rudder-chains. And, lo and behold! there was a ladder to get hold of. After I gripped it I said to myself, 'What's the good?' When I saw a man's head looking over I thought I would swim away presently and leave him shouting—in whatever language it was. I didn't mind being looked at. I—I liked it. And then you speaking to me so quietly—as if you had expected me—made me hold on a little longer. It had been a confounded lonely time—I don't mean while swimming. I was glad to talk a little to somebody that didn't belong to the *Sephora*. As to asking for the captain, that was a mere impulse. It could have been no use, with all the ship knowing about me and the other people pretty certain to be round here in the morning. I don't know—I wanted to be seen, to talk with somebody, before I went on. I don't know what I would have said. . . . 'Fine night isn't it?' or something of the sort."

"Do you think they will be round here presently?" I asked with some incredulity.

"Quite likely," he said, faintly.

He looked extremely haggard all of a sudden. His head rolled on his shoulders.

"H'm. We shall see then. Meantime get into that bed," I whispered. "Want help? There."

It was a rather high bed-place with a set of drawers underneath. This amazing swimmer really needed the lift I gave him by seizing his leg. He tumbled in, rolled over on his back, and flung one arm across his eyes. And then, with his face nearly hidden, he must have looked exactly as I used to look in that bed. I gazed upon my other self for a while before drawing across carefully the two green serge curtains which ran on a brass rod. I thought for a moment of pinning them together for greater safety, but I sat down on the couch, and once there I felt unwilling to rise and hunt for a pin. I would do it in a moment. I was extremely tired, in a peculiarly intimate way, by the strain of stealthiness, by the effort of whispering and the general secrecy of this excitement. It was three o'clock by now and I had been on my feet since nine, but I was not sleepy; I could not have gone to sleep. I sat there, fagged out, looking at the curtains, trying to clear my mind of the confused sensation of being in two places at once, and greatly bothered by an exasperating knocking in my head. It was a relief to discover suddenly that it was not in my head at all, but on the outside of the door. Before I could collect myself the words "Come in" were out of my mouth, and the steward entered with a tray, bringing in my morning coffee. I had slept, after all, and I was so frightened that I shouted, "This way! I am here, steward," as though he had been miles away. He put down the tray on the table next the couch and only then said, very quietly, "I can see you are here, sir." I felt him give me a keen look, but I dared not meet his eyes just then. He must have wondered why I had drawn the curtains of my bed before going to sleep on the couch. He went out, hooking the door open as usual.

I heard the crew washing decks above me. I knew I would have been told at once if there had been any wind. Calm, I thought, and I was doubly vexed. Indeed, I felt dual more than ever. The steward reappeared suddenly in the doorway. I jumped up from the couch so quickly that he gave a start.

"What do you want here?"

"Close your port, sir—they are washing decks."

"It is closed," I said, reddening.

"Very well, sir." But he did not move from the doorway and returned my stare in an extraordinary, equivocal manner for a time. Then his eyes wavered, all his expression changed, and in a voice unusually gentle, almost coaxingly:

"May I come in to take the empty cup away, sir?"

"Of course!" I turned my back on him while he popped in and out. Then I unhooked and closed the door and even pushed the bolt. This sort of thing could not go on very long. The cabin was as hot as an oven, too. I took a peep at my double, and discovered that he had not moved, his arm was still over his eyes; but his chest heaved; his hair was wet; his chin glistened with perspiration. I reached over him and opened the port.

"I must show myself on deck," I reflected.

Of course, theoretically, I could do what I liked, with no one to say nay to me within the whole circle of the horizon; but to lock my cabin door and take the key away I did not dare. Directly I put my head out of the companion I saw the group of my two officers, the second mate barefooted, the chief mate in long india-rubber boots, near the break of the poop, and the steward half-way down the poop-ladder talking to them eagerly. He happened to catch sight of me and dived, the second ran down on the main-deck shouting some order or other, and the chief mate came to meet me, touching his cap.

There was a sort of curiosity in his eye that I did not like. I don't know whether the steward had told them that I was "queer" only, or downright drunk, but I know the man meant to have a good look at me. I watched him coming with a smile which, as he got into point-blank range, took effect and froze his very whiskers. I did not give him time to open his lips.

"Square the yards by lifts and braces before the hands go to breakfast."

It was the first particular order I had given on board that ship; and I stayed on deck to see it executed, too. I had felt the need of asserting myself without loss of time. That sneering young cub got taken down a peg or two on that occasion, and I also seized the opportunity of having a good look at the face of every foremast man as they filed past me to go to the after braces. At breakfast time, eating nothing myself, I presided with such frigid dignity that the two mates were only too glad to escape from the cabin as soon as decency permitted; and all the time the dual working of my mind distracted me almost to the point of insanity. I was constantly watching myself, my secret self, as dependent on my actions as my own personality, sleeping in that bed, behind that door which faced me as I sat at the head of the table. It was very much like being mad, only it was worse because one was aware of it.

I had to shake him for a solid minute, but when at last he opened his eyes it was in the full possession of his senses, with an inquiring look.

"All's well so far," I whispered. "Now you must vanish into the bath-room."

He did so, as noiseless as a ghost, and then I rang for the steward, and facing him boldly, directed him to tidy up my stateroom while I was having my bath—" and be quick about it." As my tone admitted of no excuses, he said, "Yes, sir," and ran off to fetch his dust-pan and brushes. I took a bath and did most of my dressing, splashing, and whistling softly for the steward's edification, while the secret sharer of my life stood drawn up bolt upright in that little space, his face looking very sunken in day-light, his eyelids lowered under the stern, dark line of his eyebrows drawn together by a slight frown.

When I left him there to go back to my room the steward was finishing dusting. I sent for the mate and engaged him in some insignificant conver-sation. It was, as it were, trifling with the terrific character of his whiskers; but my object was to give him an opportunity for a good look at my cabin. And then I could at last shut, with a clear conscience, the door of my state-room and get my double back into the recessed part. There was nothing else for it. He had to sit still on a small folding stool, half smothered by the heavy coats hanging there. We listened to the steward going into the bath room out of the saloon, filling the water-bottles there, scrubbing the bath, setting things to rights, whisk, bang, clatter—out again into the sa-loon—turn the key—click. Such was my scheme for keeping my second self invisible. Nothing better could be contrived under the circumstances. And there we sat; I at my writing-desk ready to appear busy with some papers, he behind me out of sight of the door. It would not have been prudent to talk in day-time; and I could not have stood the excitement of that queer sense of whispering to myself. Now and then, glancing over my shoulder, I saw him far back there, sitting rigidly on the low stool, his bare feet close together, his arms folded, his head hanging on his breast—and perfectly still. Anybody would have taken him for me.

I was fascinated by it myself. Every moment I had to glance over my shoulder. I was looking at him when a voice outside the door said:

"Beg pardon, sir."

"Well!" . . . I kept my eyes on him, and so when the voice outside the door announced, "There's a ship's boat coming our way, sir," I saw him give a start—the first movement he had made for hours. But he did not raise his bowed head.

"All right. Get the ladder over."

I hesitated. Should I whisper something to him? But what? His immobility seemed to have been never disturbed. What could I tell him he did not know already? . . . Finally I went on deck.

II

The skipper of the *Sephora* had a thin red whisker all round his face, and the sort of complexion that goes with hair of that colour; also the particular, rather smeary shade of blue in the eyes. He was not exactly a showy figure; his shoulders were high, his stature but middling—one leg slightly more bandy than the other. He shook hands, looking vaguely around. A spiritless tenacity was his main characteristic, I judged. I behaved with a politeness which seemed to disconcert him. Perhaps he was shy. He mumbled to me as if he were ashamed of what he was saying; gave his name (it was something like Archbold—but at this distance of years I hardly am sure), his ship's name, and a few other particulars of that sort, in the manner of a criminal making a reluctant and doleful confession. He had had terrible weather on the passage out—terrible—terrible—wife aboard, too.

By this time we were seated in the cabin and the steward brought in a tray with a bottle and glasses. "Thanks! No." Never took liquor. Would have some water, though. He drank two tumblerfuls. Terrible thirsty work. Ever since daylight had been exploring the islands round his ship.

"What was that for—fun?" I asked, with an appearance of polite interest.

"No!" He sighed. "Painful duty."

As he persisted in his mumbling and I wanted my double to hear every word, I hit upon the notion of informing him that I regretted to say I was hard of hearing.

"Such a young man, too!" he nodded, keeping his smeary blue, unintelligent eyes fastened upon me. What was the cause of it—some disease? he inquired, without the least sympathy and as if he thought that, if so, I'd got no more than I deserved.

"Yes; disease," I admitted in a cheerful tone which seemed to shock him. But my point was gained, because he had to raise his voice to give me his tale. It is not worth while to record that version. It was just over two months since all this had happened, and he had thought so much about it that he seemed completely muddled as to its bearings, but still immensely impressed.

"What would you think of such a thing happening on board your own ship? I've had the *Sephora* for these fifteen years. I am a well-known shipmaster."

He was densely distressed—and perhaps I should have sympathised with him if I had been able to detach my mental vision from the unsuspected sharer of my cabin as though he were my second self. There he was on the other side of the bulkhead, four or five feet from us, no more, as we sat in the saloon. I looked politely at Captain Archbold (if that was his name), but it was the other I saw, in a grey sleeping suit, seated on a low stool, his bare feet close together, his arms folded, and every word said between us falling into the ears of his dark head bowed on his chest.

"I have been at sea now, man and boy, for seven-and-thirty years, and I've never heard of such a thing happening in an English ship. And that it should be my ship. Wife on board, too."

I was hardly listening to him.

"Don't you think," I said, "that the heavy sea which, you told me, came aboard just then might have killed the man? I have seen the sheer weight of a sea kill a man very neatly, by simply breaking his neck."

"Good God!" he uttered, impressively, fixing his smeary blue eyes on me. "The sea! No man killed by the sea every looked like that." He seemed positively scandalised at my suggestion. And as I gazed at him, certainly not prepared for anything original on his part, he advanced his head close to mine and thrust his tongue out at me so suddenly that I couldn't help starting back.

After scoring over my calmness in this graphic way he nodded wisely. If I had seen the sight, he assured me, I would never forget it as long as I lived. The weather was too bad to give the corpse a proper sea burial. So next day at dawn they took it up on the poop, covering its face with a bit of bunting; he read a short prayer, and then, just as it was, in its oilskins and long boots, they launched it amongst those mountainous seas that seemed ready every moment to swallow up the ship herself and the terrified lives on board of her.

"That reefed foresail saved you," I threw in.

"Under God—it did," he exclaimed fervently. "It was by a special mercy, I firmly believe, that it stood some of those hurricane squalls."

"It was the setting of that sail which—" I began.

"God's own hand in it," he interrupted me. "Nothing less could have done it. I don't mind telling you that I hardly dared give the order. It seemed impossible that we could touch anything without losing it, and then our last hope would have been gone."

The terror of that gale was on him yet. I let him go on for a bit, then said, casually—as if returning to a minor subject:

"You were very anxious to give up your mate to the shore people, I believe?"

He was. To the law. His obscure tenacity on that point had in it something incomprehensible and a little awful; something, as it were, mystical, quite apart from his anxiety that he should not be suspected of "countenancing any doings of that sort." Seven-and-thirty virtuous years at sea, of which over twenty of immaculate command, and the last fifteen in the *Sephora*, seemed to have laid him under some pitiless obligation.

"And you know," he went on, groping shamefacedly amongst his feelings, "I did not engage that young fellow. His people had some interest with my owners. I was in a way forced to take him on. He looked very smart, very gentlemanly, and all that. But do you know—I never liked him, somehow. I am a plain man. You see, he wasn't exactly the sort for the chief mate of a ship like the *Sephora*."

I had become so connected in thoughts and impressions with the secret sharer of my cabin that I felt as if I, personally, were being given to understand that I, too, was not the sort that would have done for the chief mate of a ship like the *Sephora*. I had no doubt of it in my mind.

"Not at all the style of man. You understand," he insisted, superfluously, looking hard at me.

I smiled urbanely. He seemed at a loss for a while.

"I suppose I must report a suicide."

"Beg pardon?"

"Sui-cide! That's what I'll have to write to my owners directly I get in."

"Unless you manage to recover him before to-morrow," I assented, dispassionately. . . . "I mean, alive."

He mumbled something which I really did not catch, and I turned my ear to him in a puzzled manner. He fairly bawled:

"The land—I say, the mainland is at least seven miles off my anchorage."

"About that."

My lack of excitement, of curiosity, of surprise, of any sort of pronounced interest, began to arouse his distrust. But except for the felicitous pretence of deafness I had not tried to pretend anything. I had felt utterly incapable of playing the part of ignorance properly, and therefore was afraid to try. It is also certain that he had brought some ready-made suspicions with him, and that he viewed my politeness as a strange and unnatural phenomenon. And yet how else could I have received him? Not heartily! That was impossible for psychological reasons, which I need not state here. My only object was to keep off his inquiries. Surlily? Yes, but surliness might have provoked a point-blank question. From its novelty to him and from its nature, punctilious courtesy was the manner best calculated to restrain the man. But there was the danger of his breaking through my defence bluntly. I could not, I think, have met him by a direct lie, also for psychological (not moral) reasons. If he had only known how afraid I was of his putting my feeling of identity with the other to the test! But, strangely enough—(I thought of it only afterwards)—I believe that he was not a little disconcerted by the reverse side of that weird situation, by something in me that reminded him of the man he was seeking—suggested a mysterious similitude to the young fellow he had distrusted and disliked from the first.

However that might have been, the silence was not very prolonged. He took another oblique step.

"I reckon I had no more than a two-mile pull to your ship. Not a bit more."

"And quite enough, too, in this awful heat," I said.

Another pause full of mistrust followed. Necessity, they say, is mother of invention, but fear, too, is not barren of ingenious suggestions. And I was afraid he would ask me point-blank for news of my other self.

"Nice little saloon, isn't it?" I remarked, as if noticing for the first time the way his eyes roamed from one closed door to the other. "And very well fitted out, too. Here, for instance," I continued, reaching over the back of my seat negligently and flinging the door open, "is my bath-room."

He made an eager movement, but hardly gave it a glance. I got up, shut the door of the bath-room, and invited him to have a look round, as if I were very proud of my accommodation. He had to rise and be shown round, but he went through the business without any raptures whatever.

"And now we'll have a look at my stateroom," I declared, in a voice as loud as I dared to make it, crossing the cabin to the starboard side with purposely heavy steps.

He followed me in and gazed around. My intelligent double had vanished. I played my part.

"Very convenient—isn't it?"

"Very nice. Very comf . . ." He didn't finish and went out brusquely as if to escape from some unrighteous wiles of mine. But it was not to be. I had been too frightened not to feel vengeful; I felt I had him on the run, and I meant to keep him on the run. My polite insistence must have had something menacing in it, because he gave in suddenly. And I did not let him off a single item; mate's room, pantry, storerooms, the very sail-locker which was also under the poop—he had to look into them all. When at last I showed him out on the quarter-deck he drew a long, spiritless sigh, and mumbled dismally that he must really be going back to his ship now. I desired my mate, who had joined us, to see to the captain's boat.

The man of whiskers gave a blast on the whistle which he used to wear hanging round his neck, and yelled, "*Sephora's* away!" My double down there in my cabin must have heard, and certainly could not feel more relieved than I. Four fellows came running out from somewhere forward and went over the side, while my own men, appearing on deck too, lined the rail. I escorted my visitor to the gangway ceremoniously, and nearly overdid it. He was a tenacious beast. On the very ladder he lingered, and in that unique, guiltily conscientious manner of sticking to the point:

"I say . . . you . . . you don't think that—"

I covered his voice loudly:

"Certainly not. . . . I am delighted. Good-bye."

I had an idea of what he meant to say, and just saved myself by the privilege of defective hearing. He was too shaken generally to insist, but my mate, close witness of that parting, looked mystified and his face took on a thoughtful cast. As I did not want to appear as if I wished to avoid all communication with my officers, he had the opportunity to address me.

"Seems a very nice man. His boat's crew told our chaps a very extraordinary story, if what I am told by the steward is true. I suppose you had it from the captain, sir?"

"Yes. I had a story from the captain."

"A very horrible affair—isn't it, sir?"

"It is."

"Beats all these tales we hear about murders in Yankee ships."

"I don't think it beats them. I don't think it resembles them in the least."

"Bless my soul—you don't say so! But of course I've no acquaintance whatever with American ships, not I, so I couldn't go against your knowledge. It's horrible enough for me. . . . But the queerest part is that those fellows seemed to have some idea the man was hidden aboard here. They had really. Did you ever hear of such a thing?"

"Preposterous—isn't it?"

We were walking to and fro athwart the quarter-deck. No one of the crew forward could be seen (the day was Sunday), and the mate pursued:

"There was some little dispute about it. Our chaps took offence. 'As if we would harbour a thing like that,' they said. 'Wouldn't you like to look for him in our coal-hold?' Quite a tiff. But they made it up in the end. I suppose he did drown himself. Don't you, sir?"

"I don't suppose anything."

"You have no doubt in the matter, sir?"

"None whatever."

I left him suddenly. I felt I was producing a bad impression, but with my double down there it was most trying to be on deck. And it was almost as trying to be below. Altogether a nerve-trying situation. But on the whole I felt less torn in two when I was with him. There was no one in the whole ship whom I dared take into my confidence. Since the hands had got to know his story, it would have been impossible to pass him off for any one else, and an accidental discovery was to be dreaded now more than ever. . . .

The stewart being engaged in laying the table for dinner, we could talk only with our eyes when I first went down. Later in the afternoon we had a cautious try at whispering. The Sunday quietness of the ship was against us; the stillness of air and water around her was against us; the elements, the men were against us—everything was against us in our secret partnership; time itself—for this could not go on forever. The very trust in Providence was, I suppose, denied to his guilt. Shall I confess that this thought cast me down very much? And as to the chapter of accidents which counts for so much in the book of success, I could only hope that it was closed. For what favourable accident could be expected?

"Did you hear everything?" were my first words as soon as we took up our position side by side, leaning over my bed-place.

He had. And the proof of it was his earnest whisper. "The man told you he hardly dared to give the order."

I understood the reference to be to that saving foresail.

"Yes. He was afraid of it being lost in the setting."

"I assure you he never gave the order. He may think he did, but he never gave it. He stood there with me on the break of the poop after the maintopsail blew away, and whimpered about our last hope—positively whimpered about it and nothing else—and the night coming on! To hear one's skipper go on like that in such weather was enough to drive any fellow out of his mind. It worked me up into a sort of desperation. I just took it into my own hands and went away from him, boiling, and— But what's the use telling you? *You* know! . . . Do you think that if I had not been pretty fierce with them I should have got the men to do anything? Not it! The bo's'n perhaps? Perhaps! It wasn't a heavy sea—it was a sea gone mad! I suppose the end of the world will be something like that; and a man may have the heart to see it coming once and be done with it—but to have to face it day after day—I don't blame anybody. I was precious little better than the rest. Only—I was an officer of that old coal-wagon, anyhow—"

"I quite understand," I conveyed that sincere assurance into his ear. He was out of breath with whispering; I could hear him pant slightly. It was all very simple. The same strung-up force which had given twenty-four men a chance, at least, for their lives, had, in a sort of recoil, crushed an unworthy mutinous existence.

But I had no leisure to weigh the merits of the matter—footsteps in the saloon, a heavy knock. "There's enough wind to get under way with, sir." Here was the call of a new claim upon my thoughts and even upon my feelings.

"Turn the hands up," I cried through the door. "I'll be on deck directly."

I was going out to make the acquaintance of my ship. Before I left the cabin our eyes met—the eyes of the only two strangers on board. I pointed to the recessed part where the little camp-stool awaited him and laid my finger on my lips. He made a gesture—somewhat vague—a little mysterious, accompanied by a faint smile, as if of regret.

This is not the place to enlarge upon the sensations of a man who feels for the first time a ship move under his feet to his own independent word. In my case they were not unalloyed. I was not wholly alone with my command; for there was that stranger in my cabin. Or rather, I was not completely and wholly with her. Part of me was absent. That mental feeling of being in two places at once affected me physically as if the mood of secrecy had penetrated my very soul. Before an hour had elapsed since the ship had begun to move, having occasion to ask the mate (he stood by my side) to take a compass bearing of the Pagoda, I caught myself reaching up to his ear in whispers. I say I caught myself, but enough had escaped to startle the man. I can't describe it otherwise than by saying that he shied. A grave, preoccupied manner, as though he were in possession of some perplexing intelligence, did not leave him henceforth. A little later I moved away from the rail to look at the compass with such a stealthy gait that the helmsman noticed it—and I could not help noticing the unusual roundness of his eyes. These are trifling instances, though it's to no commander's advantage to be suspected of ludicrous eccentricities. But I was also more seriously affected. There are to a seaman certain words, gestures, that should in given conditions come as naturally, as instinctively as the winking of a menaced eye. A certain order should spring on to his lips without thinking; a certain sign should get itself made, so to speak, without reflection. But all unconscious alertness had abandoned me. I had to make an effort of will to recall myself back (from the cabin) to the conditions of the moment. I felt that I was appearing an irresolute commander to those people who were watching me more or less critically.

And, besides, there were the scares. On the second day out, for instance, coming off the deck in the afternoon (I had straw slippers on my bare feet) I stopped at the open pantry door and spoke to the steward. He was doing something there with his back to me. At the sound of my voice he nearly jumped out of his skin, as the saying is, and incidentally broke a cup.

"What on earth's the matter with you?" I asked, astonished.

He was extremely confused. "Beg your pardon, sir. I made sure you were in your cabin."

"You see I wasn't."

"No, sir. I could have sworn I had heard you moving in there not a moment ago. It's most extraordinary . . . very sorry, sir."

I passed on with an inward shudder. I was so identified with my secret double that I did not even mention the fact in those scanty, fearful whispers we exchanged. I suppose he had made some slight noise of some kind or other. It would have been miraculous if he hadn't at one time or another. And yet, haggard as he appeared, he looked always perfectly self-controlled, more than calm—almost invulnerable. On my suggestion he remained almost entirely in the bath-room, which, upon the whole, was the safest place. There could be really no shadow of an excuse for any one ever wanting to go in there, once the steward had done with it. It was a very tiny place. Sometimes he reclined on the floor, his legs bent, his head sustained on one elbow. At others I would find him on the camp-stool, sitting in his grey sleeping-suit and with his cropped dark hair like a patient, unmoved convict. At night I would smuggle him into my bed-place, and we would whisper together, with the regular footfalls of the officer of the watch passing and repassing over our heads. It was an infinitely miserable time. It was lucky that some tins of fine preserves were stowed in a locker in my stateroom; hard bread I could always get hold of; and so he lived on stewed chicken, pâté de foie gras, asparagus, cooked oysters, sardines—on all sorts of abominable sham delicacies out of tins. My early morning coffee he always drank; and it was all I dared do for him in that respect.

Every day there was the horrible manoeuvring to go through so that my room and then the bath-room should be done in the usual way. I came to hate the sight of the steward, to abhor the voice of that harmless man. I felt that it was he who would bring on the disaster of discovery. It hung like a sword over our heads.

The fourth day out, I think (we were then working down the east side of the Gulf of Siam, tack for tack, in light winds and smooth water)—the fourth day, I say, of this miserable juggling with the unavoidable, as we sat at our evening meal, that man, whose slightest movement I dreaded, after putting down the dishes ran up on deck busily. This could not be dangerous. Presently he came down again; and then it appeared that he had remembered a coat of mine which I had thrown over a rail to dry after having been wetted in a shower which had passed over the ship in the afternoon. Sitting stolidly at the head of the table I became terrified at the sight of the garment on his arm. Of course he made for my door. There was no time to lose.

"Steward," I thundered. My nerves were so shaken that I could not govern my voice and conceal my agitation. This was the sort of thing that made my terrifically whiskered mate tap his forehead with his forefinger. I had detected him using that gesture while talking on deck with a confidential air to the carpenter. It was too far to hear a word, but I had no doubt that this pantomime could only refer to the strange new captain.

"Yes, sir," the pale-faced steward turned resignedly to me. It was this maddening course of being shouted at, checked without rhyme or reason, arbitrarily chased out of my cabin, suddenly called into it, sent flying out of his pantry on incomprehensible errands, that accounted for the growing wretchedness of his expression.

"Where are you going with that coat?"

"To your room, sir."

"Is there another shower coming?"

"I'm sure I don't know, sir. Shall I go up again and see, sir?"

"No! never mind."

My object was attained, as of course my other self in there would have heard everything that passed. During this interlude my two officers never raised their eyes off their respective plates; but the lip of that confounded cub, the second mate, quivered visibly.

I expected the steward to hook my coat on and come out at once. He was very slow about it; but I dominated my nervousness sufficiently not to shout after him. Suddenly I became aware (it could be heard plainly enough) that the fellow for some reason or other was opening the door of the bathroom. It was the end. The place was literally not big enough to swing a cat in. My voice died in my throat and I went stony all over. I expected to hear a yell of surprise and terror, and made a movement, but had not the strength to get on my legs. Everything remained still. Had my second self taken the poor wretch by the throat? I don't know what I could have done next moment if I had not seen the steward come out of my room, close the door, and then stand quietly by the sideboard.

"Saved," I thought. "But, no! Lost! Gone! He was gone!"

I laid my knife and fork down and leaned back in my chair. My head swam. After a while, when sufficiently recovered to speak in a steady voice, I instructed my mate to put the ship round at eight o'clock himself.

"I won't come on deck," I went on. "I think I'll turn in, and unless the wind shifts I don't want to be disturbed before midnight. I feel a bit seedy."

"You did look middling bad a little while ago," the chief mate remarked without showing any great concern.

They both went out, and I stared at the steward clearing the table. There was nothing to be read on that wretched man's face. But why did he avoid my eyes I asked myself. Then I thought I should like to hear the sound of his voice.

"Steward!"

"Sir!" Startled as usual.

"Where did you hang up that coat?"

"In the bath-room, sir." The usual anxious tone. "It's not quite dry yet, sir."

For some time longer I sat in the cuddy. Had my double vanished as he had come? But of his coming there was an explanation, whereas his disappearance would be inexplicable. . . . I went slowly in my dark room, shut the door, lighted the lamp, and for a time dared not turn round. When at last I did I saw him standing bolt upright in the narrow recessed part. It would not be true to say I had a shock, but an irresistible doubt of his bodily existence flitted through my mind. Can it be, I asked myself, that he is not visible to other eyes than mine? It was like being haunted. Motionless, with a grave face, he raised his hands slightly at me in a gesture which meant clearly, "Heavens! what a narrow escape!" Narrow indeed. I think I had come creeping quietly as near insanity as any man who has not actually gone over the border. That gesture restrained me, so to speak.

The mate with the terrific whiskers was not putting the ship on the other tack. In the moment of profound silence which follows upon the hands going to their stations I heard on the poop his raised voice: "Hard alee!" and the distant shout of the order repeated on the maindeck. The sails, in that light breeze, made but a faint fluttering noise. It ceased. The ship was coming round slowly; I held my breath in the renewed stillness of expectation; one wouldn't have thought that there was a single living soul on her decks. A sudden brisk shout, "Mainsail haul!" broke the spell, and in the noisy cries and rush overhead of the men running away with the mainbrace we two, down in my cabin, came together in our usual position by the bed-place.

He did not wait for my question. "I heard him fumbling here and just managed to squat myself down in the bath," he whispered to me. "The fellow only opened the door and put his arm in to hang the coat up. All the same—"

"I never thought of that," I whispered back, even more appalled than before at the closeness of the shave, and marvelling at that something unyielding in his character which was carrying him through so finely. There was no agitation in his whisper. Whoever was being driven distracted, it was not he. He was sane. And the proof of his sanity was continued when he took up the whispering again.

"It would never do for me to come to life again."

It was something that a ghost might have said. But what he was alluding to was his old captain's reluctant admission of the theory of suicide. It would obviously serve his turn—if I had understood at all the view which seemed to govern the unalterable purpose of his action.

"You must maroon me as soon as ever you can get amongst these islands off the Cambodje shore," he went on.

"Maroon you! We are not living in a boy's adventure tale," I protested. His scornful whispering took me up.

"We aren't indeed! There's nothing of a boy's tale in this. But there's nothing else for it. I want no more. You don't suppose I am afraid of what can be done to me? Prison or gallows or whatever they may please. But you don't see me coming back to explain such things to an old fellow in a wig and twelve respectable tradesmen, do you? What can they know whether I am guilty or not—or of *what* I am guilty, either? That's my affair. What does the Bible say? 'Driven off the face of the earth.' Very well. I am off the face of the earth now. As I came at night so I shall go."

"Impossible!" I murmured. "You can't."

"Can't? . . . Not naked like a soul on the Day of Judgment. I shall freeze on to this sleeping-suit. The Last Day is not yet—and . . . you have understood thoroughly. Didn't you?"

I felt suddenly ashamed of myself. I may say truly that I understood—and my hesitation in letting that man swim away from my ship's side had been a mere sham sentiment, a sort of cowardice.

"It can't be done now till next night," I breathed out. "The ship is on the off-shore tack and the wind may fail us."

"As long as I know that you understand," he whispered. "But of course you do. It's a great satisfaction to have got somebody to understand. You seem to have been there on purpose." And in the same whisper, as if we two whenever we talked had to say things to each other which were not fit for the world to hear, he added, "It's very wonderful."

We remained side by side talking in our secret way—but sometimes silent or just exchanging a whispered word or two at long intervals. And as usual he stared through the port. A breath of wind came now and again into our faces. The ship might have been moored in dock, so gently and on an even keel she slipped through the water, that did not murmur even at our passage, shadowy and silent like a phantom sea.

At midnight I went on deck, and to my mate's great surprise put the ship round on the other tack. His terrible whiskers flitted round me in silent criticism. I certainly should not have done it if it had been only a question of getting out of that sleepy gulf as quickly as possible. I believe he told the second mate, who relieved him, that it was a great want of judgment. The other only yawned. That intolerable cub shuffled about so sleepily and lolled against the rails in such a slack, improper fashion that I came down on him sharply.

"Aren't you properly awake yet?"

"Yes, sir! I am awake."

"Well, then, be good enough to hold yourself as if you were. And keep a look-out. If there's any current we'll be closing with some islands before daylight."

The east side of the gulf is fringed with islands, some solitary, others in groups. On the blue background of the high coast they seem to float on silvery patches of calm water, arid and grey, or dark green and rounded like clumps of evergreen bushes, with the larger ones, a mile or two long, showing the outlines of ridges, ribs of grey rock under the dank mantle of matted leafage. Unknown to trade, to travel, almost to geography, the manner of life they harbour is an unsolved secret. There must be villages —settlements of fishermen at least—on the largest of them, and some communication with the world is probably kept up by native craft. But all that forenoon, as we headed for them, fanned along by the faintest of breezes, I saw no sign of man or canoe in the field of the telescope I kept on pointing at the scattered group.

At noon I gave no orders for a change of course, and the mate's whiskers became much concerned and seemed to be offering themselves unduly to my notice. At last I said:

"I am going to stand right in. Quite in—as far as I can take her."

The stare of extreme surprise imparted an air of ferocity also to his eyes, and he looked truly terrific for a moment.

"We're not doing well in the middle of the gulf," I continued, casually. "I am going to look for the land breezes to-night."

"Bless my soul! Do you mean, sir, in the dark amongst the lot of all them islands and reefs and shoals?"

"Well—if there are any regular land breezes at all on this coast one must get close inshore to find them, mustn't one?"

"Bless my soul!" he exclaimed again under his breath. All that afternoon he wore a dreamy, contemplative appearance which in him was a mark of perplexity. After dinner I went into my stateroom as if I meant to take some rest. There we two bent our dark heads over a half-unrolled chart lying on my bed.

"There," I said. "It's got to be Koh-ring. I've been looking at it ever since sunrise. It has got two hills and a low point. It must be inhabited. And on the coast opposite there is what looks like the mouth of a biggish river—with some town, no doubt, not far up. It's the best chance for you that I can see."

"Anything. Koh-ring let it be."

He looked thoughtfully at the chart as if surveying chances and distances from a lofty height—and following with his eyes his own figure wandering on the blank land of Cochin-China, and then passing off that piece of paper clean out of sight into uncharted regions. And it was as if the ship had two captains to plan her course for her. I had been so worried and restless running up and down that I had not had the patience to dress that day. I had remained in my sleeping-suit, with straw slippers and a soft floppy hat. The closeness of the heat in the gulf had been most oppressive, and the crew were used to see me wandering in that airy attire.

"She will clear the south point as she heads now," I whispered into his ear. "Goodness only knows when, though, but certainly after dark. I'll edge her in to half a mile, as far as I may be able to judge in the dark—"

"Be careful," he murmured, warningly—and I realised suddenly that all my future, the only future for which I was fit, would perhaps go irretrievably to pieces in any mishap to my first command.

I could not stop a moment longer in the room. I motioned him to get out of sight and made my way on the poop. That unplayful cub had the watch. I walked up and down for a while thinking things out, then beckoned him over.

"Send a couple of hands to open the two quarter-deck ports," I said, mildly.

He actually had the impudence, or else so forgot himself in his wonder at such an incomprehensible order, as to repeat:

"Open the quarter-deck ports! What for, sir?"

"The only reason you need concern yourself about is because I tell you to do so. Have them open wide and fastened properly."

He reddened and went off, but I believe made some jeering remark to the carpenter as to the sensible practice of ventilating a ship's quarter-deck. I know he popped into the mate's cabin to impart the fact to him because the whiskers came on deck, as it were by chance, and stole glances at me from below—for signs of lunacy or drunkenness, I suppose.

A little before supper, feeling more restless than ever, I rejoined, for a moment, my second self. And to find him sitting so quietly was surprising, like something against nature, inhuman.

I developed my plan in a hurried whisper.

"I shall stand in as close as I dare and then put her round. I will presently find means to smuggle you out of here into the sail-locker, which communicates with the lobby. But there is an opening, a sort of square for hauling the sails out, which gives straight on the quarter-deck and which is never closed in fine weather, so as to give air to the sails. When the ship's way is deadened in stays and all the hands are aft at the main-braces you will have a clear road to slip out and get overboard through the open quarter-deck port. I've had them both fastened up. Use a rope's end to lower yourself into the water so as to avoid a splash—you know. It could be heard and cause some beastly complication."

He kept silent for a while, then whispered, "I understand."

"I won't be there to see you go," I began with an effort. "The rest . . . I only hope I have understood, too."

"You have. From first to last"—and for the first time there seemed to be a faltering, something strained in his whisper. He caught hold of my arm, but the ringing of the supper bell made me start. He didn't, though; he only released his grip.

After supper I didn't come below again till well past eight o'clock. The faint, steady breeze was loaded with dew; and the wet, darkened sails held all there was of propelling power in it. The night, clear and starry, sparkled darkly, and the opaque, lightless patches shifting slowly against the low stars were the drifting islets. On the port bow there was a big one more distant and shadowily imposing by the great space of sky it eclipsed.

On opening the door I had a back view of my very own self looking at a chart. He had come out of the recess and was standing near the table.

"Quite dark enough," I whispered.

He stepped back and leaned against my bed with a level, quiet glance. I sat on the couch. We had nothing to say to each other. Over our heads the officer of the watch moved here and there. Then I heard him move quickly. I knew what that meant. He was making for the companion; and presently his voice was outside my door.

"We are drawing in pretty fast, sir. Land looks rather close."

"Very well," I answered. "I am coming on deck directly."

I waited till he was gone out of the cuddy, then rose. My double moved too. The time had come to exchange our last whispers, for neither of us was ever to hear each other's natural voice.

"Look here!" I opened a drawer and took out three sovereigns. "Take this anyhow. I've got six and I'd give you the lot, only I must keep a little money to buy some fruit and vegetables for the crew from native boats as we go through Sunda Straits."

He shook his head.

"Take it," I urged him, whispering desperately. "No one can tell what—"

He smiled and slapped meaningly the only pocket of the sleeping-jacket. It was not safe, certainly. But I produced a large old silk handkerchief of mine, and tying the three pieces of gold in a corner, pressed it on him. He was touched, I suppose, because he took it at last, and tied it quickly round his waist under the jacket, on his bare skin.

Our eyes met; several seconds elapsed, till, our glances still mingled, I extended my hand and turned the lamp out. Then I passed through the cuddy, leaving the door of my room wide open. . . . "Steward!"

He was still lingering in the pantry in the greatness of his zeal, giving a rub-up to a plated cruet stand the last thing before going to bed. Being careful not to wake up the mate, whose room was opposite, I spoke in an undertone.

He looked round anxiously. "Sir!"

"Can you get me a little hot water from the galley?"

"I am afraid, sir, the galley fire's been out for some time now."

"Go and see."

He flew up the stairs.

"Now," I whispered, loudly, into the saloon—too loudly, perhaps, but I was afraid I couldn't make a sound. He was by my side in an instant—the double captain slipped past the stairs—through a tiny dark passage . . . a sliding door. We were in the sail-locker, scrambling on our knees over the sails. A sudden thought struck me. I saw myself wandering barefooted, bareheaded, the sun beating on my dark poll. I snatched off my floppy hat and tried hurriedly in the dark to ram it on my other self. He dodged and fended off silently. I wonder what he thought had come to me before he understood and suddenly desisted. Our hands met gropingly, lingered united in a steady, motionless clasp for a second. . . . No word was breathed by either of us when they separated.

I was standing quietly by the pantry door when the steward returned.

"Sorry, sir. Kettle barely warm. Shall I light the spirit-lamp?"

"Never mind."

I came out on deck slowly. It was now a matter of conscience to shave the land as close as possible—for now he must go overboard whenever the ship was put in stays. Must! There could be no going back for him. After a moment I walked over to leeward and my heart flew into my mouth at the nearness of the land on the bow. Under any other circumstances I would not have held on a minute longer. The second mate had followed me anxiously.

I looked on till I felt I could command my voice.

"She may weather," I said then in a quiet tone.

"Are you going to try that, sir?" he stammered out incredulously.

I took no notice of him and raised my tone just enough to be heard by the helmsman.

"Keep her good full."

"Good full, sir."

The wind fanned my cheek, the sails slept, the world was silent. The strain of watching the dark loom of the land grow bigger and denser was too much for me. I had shut my eyes—because the ship must go closer. She must! The stillness was intolerable. Were we standing still?

When I opened my eyes the second view started my heart with a thump. The black southern hill of Koh-ring seemed to hang right over the ship like a towering fragment of the everlasting night. On that enormous mass of blackness there was not a gleam to be seen, not a sound to be heard. It was gliding irresistibly towards us and yet seemed already within reach of the hand. I saw the vague figures of the watch grouped in the waist, gazing in awed silence.

"Are you going on, sir?" inquired an unsteady voice at my elbow.

I ignored it. I had to go on.

"Keep her full. Don't check her way. That won't do now," I said, warningly.

"I can't see the sails very well," the helmsman answered me, in strange, quavering tones.

Was she close enough? Already she was, I won't say in the shadow of the land, but in the very blackness of it, already swallowed up as it were, gone too close to be recalled, gone from me altogether.

"Give the mate a call," I said to the young man who stood at my elbow as still as death. "And turn all hands up."

My tone had a borrowed loudness reverberated from the height of the land. Several voices cried out together: "We are all on deck, sir."

Then stillness again, with the great shadow gliding closer, towering higher, without light, without a sound. Such a hush had fallen on the ship that she might have been a bark of the dead floating in slowly under the very gate of Erebus.

"My God! Where are we?"

It was the mate moaning at my elbow. He was thunderstruck, and as it were deprived of the moral support of his whiskers. He clapped his hands and absolutely cried out, "Lost!"

"Be quiet," I said, sternly.

He lowered his tone, but I saw the shadowy gesture of his despair. "What are we doing here?"

"Looking for the land wind."

He made as if to tear his hair, and addressed me recklessly.

"She will never get out. You have done it, sir. I knew it'd end in something like this. She will never weather, and you are too close now to stay. She'll drift ashore before she's round. O my God!"

I caught his arm as he was raising it to batter his poor devoted head, and shook it violently.

"She's ashore already," he wailed, trying to tear himself away.

"Is she? . . . Keep good full there!"

"Good full, sir," cried the helmsman in a frightened, thin, childlike voice.

I hadn't let go the mate's arm and went on shaking it. "Ready about, do you hear? You go forward"—shake—"and stop there"—shake—"and hold your noise"—shake—"and see these head-sheets properly overhauled"—shake, shake—shake.

And all the time I dared not look towards the land lest my heart should fail me. I released my grip at last and he ran forward as if fleeing for dear life.

I wondered what my double there in the sail-locker thought of this commotion. He was able to hear everything—and perhaps he was able to understand why, on my conscience, it had to be thus close—no less. My first order "Hard alee!" re-echoed ominously under the towering shadow of Koh-ring as if I had shouted in a mountain gorge. And then I watched the land intently. In that smooth water and light wind it was impossible to feel the ship coming-to. No! I could not feel her. And my second self was making now ready to slip out and lower himself overboard. Perhaps he was gone already . . . ?

The great black mass brooding over our very mastheads began to pivot away from the ship's side silently. And now I forgot the secret stranger ready to depart, and remembered only that I was a total stranger to the ship. I did not know her. Would she do it? How was she to be handled?

I swung the mainyard and waited helplessly. She was perhaps stopped, and her very fate hung in the balance, with the black mass of Koh-ring like the gate of the everlasting night towering over her taffrail. What would she do now? Had she way on her yet? I stepped to the side swiftly, and on the shadowy water I could see nothing except a faint phosphorescent flash revealing the glassy smoothness of the sleeping surface. It was impossible to tell—and I had not learned yet the feel of my ship. Was she moving? What I needed was something easily seen, a piece of paper, which I could throw overboard and watch. I had nothing on me. To run down for it I didn't dare. There was no time. All at once my strained, yearning stare distinguished a white object floating within a yard of the ship's side. White on the black water. A phosphorescent flash passed under it. What was that thing? . . . I recognised my own floppy hat. It must have fallen off his head . . . and he didn't bother. Now I had what I wanted—the saving mark for my eyes. But I hardly thought of my other self, now gone from the ship, to be hidden for ever from all friendly faces, to be a fugitive and a vagabond on the earth, with no brand of the curse on his sane forehead to stay a slaying hand . . . too proud to explain.

And I watched the hat—the expression of my sudden pity for his mere flesh. It had been meant to save his homeless head from the dangers of the sun. And now—behold—it was saving the ship, by serving me for a mark to help out the ignorance of my strangeness. Ha! It was drifting forward, warning me just in time that the ship had gathered sternway.

"Shift the helm," I said in a low voice to the seaman standing still like a statue.

The man's eyes glistened wildly in the binnacle light as he jumped round to the other side and spun round the wheel.

I walked to the break of the poop. On the over-shadowed deck all hands stood by the forebraces waiting for my order. The stars ahead seemed to be gliding from right to left. And all was so still in the world that I heard the quiet remark "She's round," passed in a tone of intense relief between two seamen.

"Let go and haul."

The foreyards ran round with a great noise, amidst cheery cries. And now the frightful whiskers made themselves heard giving various orders. Already the ship was drawing ahead. And I was alone with her. Nothing! no one in the world should stand now between us, throwing a shadow on the way of silent knowledge and mute affection, the perfect communion of a seaman with his first command.

Walking to the taffrail, I was in time to make out, on the very edge of a darkness thrown by a towering black mass like the very gateway of Erebus —yes, I was in time to catch an evanescent glimpse of my white hat left behind to mark the spot where the secret sharer of my cabin and of my thoughts, as though he were my second self, had lowered himself into the water to take his punishment: a free man, a proud swimmer striking out for a new destiny.

7

FRANZ KAFKA
The Metamorphosis

"As Gregor Samsa awoke one morning from uneasy dreams he found himself transformed in his bed into a gigantic insect." So begins Kafka's wildly impossible tale. People do not simply turn into insects in real life, nor do they in "realistic" fiction, a category into which *The Metamorphosis* seems to fit, except for Gregor's horrid transformation. Nevertheless, Kafka presents his invention with such force that we accept it from the start. Precisely drawn character, sophisticated use of point of view, and imagery so chillingly real as to communicate a sense of myopic horror—all conspire to convince us that what happens in the story is truth of an extraordinary kind. The single impossibility of the story initiates a painstakingly logical series of causes and effects. *The Metamorphosis* differs significantly in this respect from fantasy literature like science fiction, and from allegory, where one impossibility is generally expected to be followed by others.

Probably the most important effect of Gregor's presence as an insect is that it intensifies the sheer drama of the story. *The Metamorphosis* is remarkable in the way it maintains a consistently high degree of interest through revelation of complex, clearly presented characters within confined physical settings. The giant insect's presence rivets our attention and draws us subtly into the story's action. At the same time, Kafka plays cunningly on our conditioned fear of strange insects in order to repel our empathy. Most of us would be horrified to have an ugly beetle—even a small one—suddenly crawl across our skin, or worse yet bite us, or still worse fly into our mouth and be swallowed. The nature of this fright is important. It expresses a reaction not so much to real danger as to symbolic threat, the threat to bodily integrity and symbolically to human identity posed by something radically inhuman.

Kafka's story has a strong ring of personal truth, as well as great ambiguity, apparently because he wrote with nearly direct reference to the ambiguous psychological pressures of his own life. The close similarity of the names "Samsa" and "Kafka" has often been noticed, and certainly Gregor's fate is an expression of many fantasies which haunted Kafka with nightmare intensity. As a German-speaking Jew in turn-of-the-century Prague, as a seriously ill man, as a family pariah, and above all as an artist set apart from others by a piercing vision of life's horrors, Kafka knew the feeling of being trapped within nightmarish suffering and loneliness. His diaries reveal that the idea of being turned into an insect was prompted in part by the association between "Kafka" and *"Kafer,"* the German word for bug or beetle. In both German and English, also, the word "vermin" (German *Ungeziefer*) can mean a spineless, worthless person, and Kafka often felt just that way before his aggressive, successful, and demanding father. In real life Kafka often wished to take his father's place, and he suffered fantasies of guilt for doing so. The fictional transformation is logical: in the story Gregor does take his father's place, but then as an insect he suffers his father's revenge.

The wish to punish and the masochistic wish to be punished are central not only in *The Metamorphosis* but in Kafka's artistic process as well. One reason for the story's exceptional tone of personal truth and immediacy is that Kafka's creativity and his suffering were inseparable.

Confronted by the nonhuman form of Gregor, the members of his family begin an ironic process of becoming something less than human themselves. His father, for example, becomes stiff, vain, and vengeful, and his uncomfortable messenger's uniform is an ironic counterpart of Gregor's insect shell. Despite the family's attempts to preserve order by tolerating Gregor and retrenching their finances, irrationality overtakes them. Their increasingly zany behavior draws attention to the latent humor in the story. Kafka's humor is much like that of farce, a kind of comedy typically based on repressed desires, in which things become laughably complicated and desperate. The members of Gregor's family become strangely laughable in the way they lose touch with their own humanity, just as they literally lose the freedom of their own apartment to the three bearded lodgers. The lodgers, correspondingly, are laughable in their own deadpan, eerily inhuman way, and they provide a further reflection on the theme of irrationality. Their self-possessed bearing suggests that they might bring a measure of rationality to the Samsa household, but they prove to be as eccentric and intolerant as anyone.

To some, Gregor's plight as an insect may seem so alien and odd that it simply does not speak to the reality of their own world. Yet, the human meaning of the story is enormously compelling. Almost everyone, at some time, experiences life as a confrontation with boundless absurdity. Anyone who has suddenly found himself without a living, or seriously ill, or in an unfriendly country where everyone else speaks a foreign language, or the lone outsider in a cliquish group, has had the occasion to feel some of the anguish that befalls Gregor. Still, these are peripheral human situations, and the meaning of *The Metamorphosis* cuts even closer to the core of human experience. Kafka uncomfortably reminds us all of the insect within us; but, joyfully, he also allows us to recognize the universality of our fear, and he provides a devastating portrait of the world which denies us that recognition.

The Metamorphosis

I

As Gregor Samsa awoke one morning from uneasy dreams he found himself transformed in his bed into a gigantic insect. He was lying on his hard, as it were armor-plated, back and when he lifted his head a little he could see his dome-like brown belly divided into stiff arched segments on top of which the bed quilt could hardly keep in position and was about to slide off completely. His numerous legs, which were pitifully thin compared to the rest of his bulk, waved helplessly before his eyes.

What has happened to me? he thought. It was no dream. His room, a regular human bedroom, only rather too small, lay quiet between the four familiar walls. Above the table on which a collection of cloth samples was unpacked and spread out—Samsa was a commercial traveler—hung the picture which he had recently cut out of an illustrated magazine and put into a pretty gilt frame. It showed a lady, with a fur cap on and a fur stole, sitting upright and holding out to the spectator a huge fur muff into which the whole of her forearm had vanished!

Gregor's eyes turned next to the window, and the overcast sky—one could hear rain drops beating on the window gutter—made him quite melancholy. What about sleeping a little longer and forgetting all this nonsense, he thought, but it could not be done, for he was accustomed to sleep on his right side and in his present condition he could not turn himself

Reprinted by permission of Schocken Books Inc. from THE PENAL COLONY by Franz Kafka. Copyright © 1948 by Schocken Books Inc.

over. However violently he forced himself towards his right side he always rolled on to his back again. He tried it at least a hundred times, shutting his eyes to keep from seeing his struggling legs, and only desisted when he began to feel in his side a faint dull ache he had never experienced before.

Oh God, he thought, what an exhausting job I've picked on! Traveling about day in, day out. It's much more irritating work than doing the actual business in the office, and on top of that there's the trouble of constant traveling, of worrying about train connections, the bed and irregular meals, casual acquaintances that are always new and never become intimate friends. The devil take it all! He felt a slight itching up on his belly; slowly pushed himself on his back nearer to the top of the bed so that he could lift his head more easily; identified the itching place which was surrounded by many small white spots the nature of which he could not understand and made to touch it with a leg, but drew the leg back immediately, for the contact made a cold shiver run through him.

He slid down again into his former position. This getting up early, he thought, makes one quite stupid. A man needs his sleep. Other commercials live like harem women. For instance, when I come back to the hotel of a morning to write up the orders I've got, these others are only sitting down to breakfast. Let me just try that with my chief; I'd be sacked on the spot. Anyhow, that might be quite a good thing for me, who can tell? If I didn't have to hold my hand because of my parents I'd have given notice long ago, I'd have gone to the chief and told him exactly what I think of him. That would knock him endways from his desk! It's a queer way of doing, too, this sitting on high at a desk and talking down to employees, especially when they have to come quite near because the chief is hard of hearing. Well, there's still hope; once I've saved enough money to pay back my parents' debts to him—that should take another five or six years—I'll do it without fail. I'll cut myself completely loose then. For the moment, though, I'd better get up, since my train goes at five.

He looked at the alarm clock ticking on the chest. Heavenly Father! he thought. It was half-past six o'clock and the hands were quietly moving on, it was even past the half-hour, it was getting on toward a quarter to seven. Had the alarm clock not gone off? From the bed one could see that it had been properly set for four o'clock; of course it must have gone off. Yes, but was it possible to sleep quietly through that ear-splitting noise? Well, he had not slept quietly, yet apparently all the more soundly for that. But what was he to do now? The next train went at seven o'clock; to catch that he would need to hurry like mad and his samples weren't even packed up, and he himself wasn't feeling particularly fresh and active. And even if he did catch the train he wouldn't avoid a row with the chief, since the firm's porter would have been waiting for the five o'clock train and would have long since reported his failure to turn up. The porter was a creature of the chief's, spineless and stupid. Well, supposing he were to say he was sick? But that would be most unpleasant and would look suspicious, since during his five years' employment he had not been ill once. The chief himself would be sure to come with the sick-insurance doctor, would reproach his parents with their son's laziness and would cut all excuses short by referring to the insurance doctor, who of course regarded all mankind as perfectly healthy malingerers. And would he be so far wrong on this occasion? Gregor really felt quite well, apart from a drowsiness that was utterly superfluous after such a long sleep, and he was even unusually hungry.

As all this was running through his mind at top speed without his being able to decide to leave his bed—the alarm clock had just struck a quarter to seven—there came a cautious tap at the door behind the head of his bed. "Gregor," said a voice—it was his mother's—"it's a quarter to seven. Hadn't you a train to catch?" That gentle voice! Gregor had a shock as he heard his own voice answering hers, unmistakably his own voice, it was true, but with a persistent horrible twittering squeak behind it like an undertone, that left the words in their clear shape only for the first moment and then rose up reverberating round them to destroy their sense, so that one could not be sure one had heard them rightly. Gregor wanted to answer at length and explain everything, but in the circumstances he confined himself to saying: "Yes, yes, thank you, Mother, I'm getting up now." The wooden door between them must have kept the change in his voice from being noticeable outside, for his mother contented herself with this statement and shuffled away. Yet this brief exchange of words had made the other members of the family aware that Gregor was still in the house, as they had not expected, and at one of the side doors his father was already knocking, gently, yet with his fist. "Gregor, Gregor," he called, "what's the matter with you?" And after a little while he called again in a deeper voice: "Gregor! Gregor!" At the other side door his sister was saying in a low, plaintive tone: "Gregor? Aren't you well? Are you needing anything?" He answered them both at once: "I'm just ready," and did his best to make his voice sound as normal as possible by enunciating the words very clearly and leaving long pauses between them. So his father went back to his breakfast, but his sister whispered: "Gregor, open the door, do." However, he was not thinking of opening the door, and felt thankful for the prudent habit he had acquired in traveling of locking all doors during the night, even at home.

His immediate intention was to get up quietly without being disturbed, to put on his clothes and above all eat his breakfast, and only then to consider what else was to be done, since in bed, he was well aware, his meditations would come to no sensible conclusion. He remembered that often enough in bed he had felt small aches and pains, probably caused by awkward postures, which had proved purely imaginary once he got up, and he looked foward eagerly to seeing this morning's delusions gradually fall away. That the change in his voice was nothing but the precursor of a severe chill, a standing ailment of commercial travelers, he had not the least possible doubt.

To get rid of the quilt was quite easy; he had only to inflate himself a little and it fell off by itself. But the next move was difficult, especially because he was so uncommonly broad. He would have needed arms and hands to hoist himself up; instead he had only the numerous little legs which never stopped waving in all directions and which he could not control in the least. When he tried to bend one of them it was the first to stretch itself straight; and did he succeed at last in making it do what he wanted, all the other legs meanwhile waved the more wildly in a high degree of unpleasant agitation. "But what's the use of lying idle in bed," said Gregor to himself.

He thought that he might get out of bed with the lower part of his body first, but this lower part, which he had not yet seen and of which he could form no clear conception, proved too difficult to move; it shifted so slowly; and when finally, almost wild with annoyance, he gathered his forces together and thrust out recklessly, he had miscalculated the direction and bumped heavily against the lower end of the bed, and the stinging pain he felt informed him that precisely this lower part of his body was at the moment probably the most sensitive.

So he tried to get the top part of himself out first, and cautiously moved his head towards the edge of the bed. That proved easy enough, and despite its breadth and mass bulk of his body at last slowly followed the movement of his head. Still, when he finally got his head free over the edge of the bed he felt too scared to go on advancing, for after all if he let himself fall in this way it would take a miracle to keep his head from being injured. And at all costs he must not lose consciousness now, precisely now; he would rather stay in bed.

But when after a repetition of the same efforts he lay in his former position again, sighing, and watched his little legs struggling against each other more wildly than ever, if that were possible, and saw no way of bringing any order into this arbitrary confusion, he told himself again that it was impossible to stay in bed and that the most sensible course was to risk everything for the smallest hope of getting away from it. At the same time he did not forget meanwhile to remind himself that cool reflection, the coolest possible, was much better than desperate resolves. In such moments he focused his eyes as sharply as possible on the window, but, unfortunately, the prospect of the morning fog, which muffled even the other side of the narrow street, brought him little encouragement and comfort. "Seven o'clock already," he said to himself when the alarm clock chimed again, "seven o'clock already and still such a thick fog." And for a little while he lay quiet, breathing lightly, as if perhaps expecting such complete repose to restore all things to their real and normal condition.

But then he said to himself: "Before it strikes a quarter past seven I must be quite out of this bed, without fail. Anyhow, by that time someone will have come from the office to ask for me, since it opens before seven." And he set himself to rocking his whole body at once in a regular rhythm, with the idea of swinging it out of the bed. If he tipped himself out in that way he could keep his head from injury by lifting it at an acute angle when he fell. His back seemed to be hard and was not likely to suffer from a fall on the carpet. His biggest worry was the loud crash he would not be able to help making, which would probably cause anxiety, if not terror, behind all the doors. Still, he must take the risk.

When he was already half out of the bed—the new method was more a game than an effort, for he needed only to hitch himself across by rocking to and fro—it struck him how simple it would be if he could get help. Two strong people—he thought of his father and the servant girl—would be amply sufficient; they would only have to thrust their arms under his convex back, lever him out of the bed, bend down with their burden and then be patient enough to let him turn himself right over on to the floor, where it was to be hoped his legs would then find their proper function. Well, ignoring the fact that the doors were all locked, ought he really to call for help? In spite of his misery he could not suppress a smile at the very idea of it.

He had got so far that he could barely keep his equilibrium when he rocked himself strongly, and he would have to nerve himself very soon for the final decision since in five minutes' time it would be a quarter past seven—when the front door bell rang. "That's someone from the office," he said to himself, and grew almost rigid, while his little legs only jigged about all the faster. For a moment everything stayed quiet. "They're not going to open the door," said Gregor to himself, catching at some kind of irrational hope. But then of course the servant girl went as usual to the door with her heavy tread and opened it. Gregor needed only to hear the first good morning of the visitor to know immediately who it was—the chief clerk himself. What a fate, to be condemned to work for a firm where the smallest omission at once gave rise to the gravest suspicion! Were all employees in a body nothing but scoundrels, was there not among them one single loyal devoted man who, had he wasted only an hour or so of the firm's time in a morning, was so tormented by conscience as to be driven out of his mind and actually incapable of leaving his bed? Wouldn't it really have been sufficient to send an apprentice to inquire—if any inquiry were necessary at all—did the chief clerk himself have to come and thus indicate to the entire family, an innocent family, that this suspicious circumstance could be investigated by no one less versed in affairs than himself? And more through the agitation caused by these reflections than through any act of will Gregor swung himself out of bed with all his strength. There was a loud thump, but it was not really a crash. His fall was broken to some extent by the carpet, his back, too, was less stiff than he thought, and so there was merely a dull thud, not so very startling. Only he had not lifted his head carefully enough and had hit it; he turned it and rubbed it on the carpet in pain and irritation.

"That was something falling down in there," said the chief clerk in the next room to the left. Gregor tried to suppose to himself that something like what had happened to him today might some day happen to the chief clerk; one really could not deny that it was possible. But as if in brusque reply to this supposition the chief clerk took a couple of firm steps in the next-door room and his patent leather boots creaked. From the right-hand room his sister was whispering to inform him of the situation: "Gregor, the chief clerk's here." "I know," muttered Gregor to himself; but he didn't dare to make his voice loud enough for his sister to hear it.

"Gregor," said his father now from the left-hand room, "the chief clerk has come and wants to know why you didn't catch the early train. We don't know what to say to him. Besides, he wants to talk to you in person. So open the door, please. He will be good enough to excuse the untidiness of your room." "Good morning, Mr. Samsa," the chief clerk was calling amiably meanwhile. "He's not well," said his mother to the visitor, while his father was still speaking through the door "he's not well, sir, believe me. What else would make him miss a train! The boy thinks about nothing but his work. It makes me almost cross the way he never goes out in the evenings; he's been here the last eight days and has stayed at home every single evening. He just sits there quietly at the table reading a newspaper or looking through railway timetables. The only amusement he gets is doing fretwork. For instance, he spent two or three evenings cutting out a little picture frame; you would be surprised to see how pretty it is; it's hanging in his room; you'll see it in a minute when Gregor opens the door. I must say I'm glad you've come, sir; we should never have got him to unlock the door by ourselves; he's so obstinate; and I'm sure he's unwell, though he wouldn't have it to be so this morning." "I'm just coming," said Gregor slowly and carefully, not moving an inch for fear of losing one word of the conversation. "I can't think of any other explanation, madam," said the chief clerk, "I hope it's nothing serious. Although on the other hand I must say that we men of business—fortunately or unfortunately— very often simply have to ignore any slight indisposition, since business must be attended to." "Well, can the chief clerk come in now?" asked Gregor's father impatiently, again knocking on the door. "No," said Gregor. In the left-hand room a painful silence followed this refusal, in the right-hand room his sister began to sob.

Why didn't his sister join the others? She was probably newly out of bed and hadn't even begun to put on her clothes yet. Well, why was she crying? Because he wouldn't get up and let the chief clerk in, because he was in danger of losing his job, and because the chief would begin dunning his parents again for the old debts? Surely these were things one didn't need to worry about for the present. Gregor was still at home and not in the least thinking of deserting the family. At the moment, true, he was lying on the carpet and no one who knew the condition he was in could seriously expect him to admit the chief clerk. But for such a small discourtesy, which could plausibly be explained away somehow later on, Gregor could hardly be dismissed on the spot. And it seemed to Gregor that it would be much more sensible to leave him in peace for the present than to trouble him with tears and entreaties. Still, of course, their uncertainty bewildered them all and excused their behavior.

"Mr. Samsa," the chief clerk called now in a louder voice, "what's the matter with you? Here you are, barricading yourself in your room, giving only 'yes' and 'no' for answers, causing your parents a lot of unnecessary trouble and neglecting—I mention this only in passing—neglecting your business duties in an incredible fashion. I am speaking here in the name of your parents and of your chief, and I beg you quite seriously to give me an immediate and precise explanation. You amaze me, you amaze me. I thought you were a quiet, dependable person, and now all at once you seem bent on making a disgraceful exhibition of yourself. The chief did hint to me early this morning a possible explanation for your disappearance—with reference to the cash payments that were entrusted to you recently—but I almost pledged my solemn word of honor that this could not be so. But now that I see how incredibly obstinate you are, I no longer have the slightest desire to take your part at all. And your position in the firm is not so unassailable. I came with the intention of telling you all this in private, but since you are wasting my time so needlessly I don't see why your parents shouldn't hear it too. For some time past your work has been most unsatisfactory; this is not the season of the year for a business boom, of course, we admit that, but a season of the year for doing no business at all, that does not exist, Mr. Samsa, must not exist."

"But, sir," cried Gregor, beside himself and in his agitation forgetting everything else, "I'm just going to open the door this very minute. A slight illness, an attack of giddiness, has kept me from getting up. I'm still lying in bed. But I feel all right again. I'm getting out of bed now. Just give me a moment or two longer! I'm not quite so well as I thought. But I'm all right, really. How a thing like that can suddenly strike one down! Only last night I was quite well, my parents can tell you, or rather I did have a slight presentiment. I must have showed some sign of it. Why didn't I report it at the office! But one always thinks that an indisposition can be got over without staying in the house. Oh sir, do spare my parents! All that you're reproaching me with now has no foundation; no one has ever said a word to me about it. Perhaps you haven't looked at the last orders I sent in. Anyhow, I can still catch the eight o'clock train, I'm much the better for my few hours' rest. Don't let me detain you here, sir; I'll be attending to business very soon, and do be good enough to tell the chief so and to make my excuses to him!"

And while all this was tumbling out pell-mell and Gregor hardly knew what he was saying, he had reached the chest quite easily, perhaps because of the practice he had had in bed, and was now trying to lever himself upright by means of it. He meant actually to open the door, actually to show himself and speak to the chief clerk; he was eager to find out what the others, after all their insistence, would say at the sight of him. If they were horrified then the responsibility was no longer his and he could stay quiet. But if they took it calmly, then he had no reason either to be upset, and could really get to the station for the eight o'clock train if he hurried. At first he slipped down a few times from the polished surface of the chest, but at length with a last heave he stood upright; he paid no more attention to the pains in the lower part of his body, however they smarted. Then he let himself fall against the back of a near-by chair, and clung with his little legs to the edges of it. That brought him into control of himself again and he stopped speaking, for now he could listen to what the chief clerk was saying.

"Did you understand a word of it?" the chief clerk was asking; "surely he can't be trying to make fools of us?" "Oh dear," cried his mother, in tears, "perhaps he's terribly ill and we're tormenting him. Grete! Grete!" she called out then. "Yes Mother?" called his sister from the other side. They were calling to each other across Gregor's room. "You must go this minute for the doctor. Gregor is ill. Go for the doctor, quick. Did you hear how he was speaking?" "That was no human voice," said the chief clerk in a voice noticeably low beside the shrillness of the mother's. "Anna! Anna!" his father was calling through the hall to the kitchen, clapping his hands, "get a locksmith at once!" And the two girls were already running through the hall with a swish of skirts—how could his sister have got dressed so quickly?—and were tearing the front door open. There was no sound of its closing again; they had evidently left it open, as one does in houses where some great misfortune has happened.

But Gregor was now much calmer. The words he uttered were no longer understandable, apparently, although they seemed clear enough to him, even clearer than before, perhaps because his ear had grown accustomed to the sound of them. Yet at any rate people now believed that something was wrong with him, and were ready to help him. The positive certainty with which these first measures had been taken comforted him. He felt himself drawn once more into the human circle and hoped for great and remarkable results from both the doctor and the locksmith, without really distinguishing precisely between them. To make his voice as clear as possible for the decisive conversation that was now imminent he coughed a little, as quietly as he could, of course, since this noise too might not sound like a human cough for all he was able to judge. In the next room meanwhile there was complete silence. Perhaps his parents were sitting at the table with the chief clerk, whispering, perhaps they were all leaning against the door and listening.

Slowly Gregor pushed the chair towards the door, then let go of it, caught hold of the door for support—the soles at the end of his little legs were somewhat sticky—and rested against it for a moment after his efforts. Then he set himself to turning the key in the lock with his mouth. It seemed, unhappily, that he hadn't really any teeth—what could he grip the key with?—but on the other hand his jaws were certainly very strong; with their help he did manage to set the key in motion, heedless of the fact that he was undoubtedly damaging them somewhere, since a brown fluid issued from his mouth, flowed over the key and dripped on the floor. "Just listen to that," said the chief clerk next door; "he's turning the key." That was a great encouragement to Gregor; but they should all have shouted encouragement to him, his father and mother too: "Go on, Gregor," they should have called out, "keep going, hold on to that key!" And in the belief that they were all following his efforts intently, he clenched his jaws recklessly on the key with all the force at his command. As the turning of the key progressed he circled round the lock, holding on now only with his mouth, pushing on the key, as required, or pulling it down again with all the weight of his body. The louder click of the finally yielding lock literally quickened Gregor. With a deep breath of relief he said to himself: "So I didn't need the locksmith," and laid his head on the handle to open the door wide.

Since he had to pull the door towards him, he was still invisible when it was really wide open. He had to edge himself slowly round the near half of the double door, and to do it very carefully if he was not to fall plump upon his back just on the threshold. He was still carrying out this difficult manoeuvre, with no time to observe anything else, when he heard the chief clerk utter a loud "Oh!"—it sounded like a gust of wind—and now he could see the man, standing as he was nearest to the door, clapping one hand before his open mouth and slowly backing away as if driven by some invisible steady pressure. His mother—in spite of the chief clerk's being there her hair was still undone and sticking up in all directions—first clasped her hands and looked at his father, then took two steps towards Gregor and fell on the floor among her outspread skirts, her face quite hidden on her breast. His father knotted his fist with a fierce expression on his face as if he meant to knock Gregor back into his room, then looked uncertainly round the living room, covered his eyes with his hands and wept till his great chest heaved.

Gregor did not go now into the living room, but leaned against the inside of the firmly shut wing of the door, so that only half his body was visible and his head above it bending sideways to look at the others. The light had meanwhile strengthened; on the other side of the street one could see clearly a section of the endlessly long, dark gray building opposite—it was a hospital—abruptly punctuated by its row of regular windows; the rain was still falling, but only in large singly discernible and literally singly splashing drops. The breakfast dishes were set out on the table lavishly, for breakfast was the most important meal of the day to Gregor's father, who lingered it out for hours over various newspapers. Right opposite Gregor on the wall hung a photograph of himself on military service, as a lieutenant, hand on sword, a carefree smile on his face, inviting one to respect his uniform and military bearing. The door leading to the hall was open, and one could see that the front door stood open too, showing the landing beyond and the beginning of the stairs going down.

"Well," said Gregor, knowing perfectly that he was the only one who had retained any composure, "I'll put my clothes on at once, pack up my samples and start off. Will you only let me go? You see, sir, I'm not obstinate, and I'm willing to work; traveling is a hard life, but I couldn't live without it. Where are you going, sir? To the office? Yes? Will you give a true account of all this? One can be temporarily incapacitated, but that's just the moment for remembering former services and bearing in mind that later on, when the incapacity has been got over, one will certainly work with all the more industry and concentration. I'm loyally bound to serve the chief, you know that very well. Besides, I have to provide for my parents and my sister. I'm in great difficulties, but I'll get out of them again. Don't make things any worse for me than they are. Stand up for me in the firm. Travelers are not popular there, I know. People think they earn sacks of money and just have a good time. A prejudice there's no particular reason for revising. But you, sir, have a more comprehensive view of affairs than the rest of the staff, yes, let me tell you in confidence, a more comprehensive view than the chief himself, who, being the owner, lets his judgment easily be swayed against one of his employees. And you know very well that the traveler, who is never seen in the office almost the whole year round, can so easily fall a victim to gossip and ill luck and unfounded complaints, which he mostly knows nothing about, except when he comes back exhausted from his rounds, and only then suffers in person from their evil consequences, which he can no longer trace back to the original causes. Sir, sir, don't go away without a word to me to show that you think me in the right at least to some extent!"

But at Gregor's very first words the chief clerk had already backed away and only stared at him with parted lips over one twitching shoulder. And while Gregor was speaking he did not stand still one moment but stole away towards the door, without taking his eyes off Gregor, yet only an inch at a time, as if obeying some secret injunction to leave the room. He was already at the hall, and the suddenness with which he took his last step out of the living room would have made one believe he had burned the sole of his foot. Once in the hall he stretched his right arm before him towards the staircase, as if some supernatural power were waiting there to deliver him.

Gregor perceived that the chief clerk must on no account be allowed to go away in this frame of mind if his position in the firm were not to be endangered to the utmost. His parents did not understand this so well; they had convinced themselves in the course of years that Gregor was settled for life in this firm, and besides they were so occupied with their immediate troubles that all foresight had forsaken them. Yet Gregor had this foresight. The chief clerk must be detained, soothed, persuaded and finally won over; the whole future of Gregor and his family depended on it! If only

his sister had been there! She was intelligent; she had begun to cry while
Gregor was still lying quietly on his back. And no doubt the chief clerk, so
partial to ladies, would have been guided by her; she would have shut the
door of the flat and in the hall talked him out of his horror. But she was
not there, and Gregor would have to handle the situation himself. And
without remembering that he was still unaware what powers of movement
he possessed, without even remembering that his words in all possibility,
indeed in all likelihood, would again be unintelligible, he let go the wing
of the door, pushed himself through the opening, started to walk towards
the chief clerk, who was already ridiculously clinging with both hands to
the railing on the landing; but immediately, as he was feeling for a support, he fell down with a little cry upon all his numerous legs. Hardly was
he down when he experienced for the first time this morning a sense of
physical comfort; his legs had firm ground under them; they were completely obedient, as he noted with joy; they even strove to carry him forward in whatever direction he chose; and he was inclined to believe that a
final relief from all his sufferings was at hand. But in the same moment as
he found himself on the floor, rocking with suppressed eagerness to move,
not far from his mother, indeed just in front of her, she, who had seemed
so completely crushed, sprang all at once to her feet, her arms and fingers
outspread, cried: "Help, for God's sake, help!" bent her head down as if to
see Gregor better, yet on the contrary kept backing senselessly away; had
quite forgotten that the laden table stood behind her; sat upon it hastily, as
if in absence of mind, when she bumped into it; and seemed altogether
unaware that the big coffee pot beside her was upset and pouring coffee in a
flood over the carpet.

"Mother, Mother," said Gregor in a low voice, and looked up at her.
The chief clerk, for the moment, had quite slipped from his mind; instead,
he could not resist snapping his jaws together at the sight of the streaming
coffee. That made his mother scream again, she fled from the table and fell
into the arms of his father, who hastened to catch her. But Gregor had now
no time to spare for his parents; the chief clerk was already on the stairs;
with his chin on the banisters he was taking one last backward look. Gregor
made a spring, to be as sure as possible of overtaking him; the chief clerk
must have divined his intention, for he leaped down several steps and vanished; he was still yelling "Ugh!" and it echoed through the whole staircase.

Unfortunately, the flight of the chief clerk seemed completely to upset
Gregor's father, who had remained relatively calm until now, for instead of
running after the man himself, or at least not hindering Gregor in his pursuit, he seized in his right hand the walking stick which the chief clerk had
left behind on a chair, together with a hat and greatcoat, snatched in his
left hand a large newspaper from the table and began stamping his feet and
flourishing the stick and the newspaper to drive Gregor back into his room.
No entreaty of Gregor's availed, indeed no entreaty was even understood,

however humbly he bent his head his father only stamped on the floor the more loudly. Behind his father his mother had torn open a window, despite the cold weather, and was leaning far out of it with her face in her hands. A strong draught set in from the street to the staircase, the window curtains blew in, the newspapers on the table fluttered, stray pages whisked over the floor. Pitilessly Gregor's father drove him back, hissing and crying "Shoo!" like a savage. But Gregor was quite unpracticed in walking backwards, it really was a slow business. If he only had a chance to turn round he could get back to his room at once, but he was afraid of exasperating his father by the slowness of such a rotation and at any moment the stick in his father's hand might hit him a fatal blow on the back or on the head. In the end, however, nothing else was left for him to do since to his horror he observed that in moving backwards he could not even control the direction he took; and so, keeping an anxious eye on his father all the time over his shoulder, he began to turn round as quickly as he could, which was in reality very slowly. Perhaps his father noted his good intentions, for he did not interfere except every now and then to help him in the manoeuvre from a distance with the point of the stick. If only he would have stopped making that unbearable hissing noise! It made Gregor quite lose his head. He had turned almost completely round when the hissing noise so distracted him that he even turned a little the wrong way again. But when at last his head was fortunately right in front of the doorway, it appeared that his body was too broad simply to get through the opening. His father, of course, in his present mood was far from thinking of such a thing as opening the other half of the door, to let Gregor have enough space. He had merely the fixed idea of driving Gregor back into his room as quickly as possible. He would never have suffered Gregor to make the circumstantial preparations for standing up on end and perhaps slipping his way through the door. Maybe he was now making more noise than ever to urge Gregor forward, as if no obstacle impeded him: to Gregor, anyhow, the noise in his rear sounded no longer like the voice of one single father; this was really no joke, and Gregor thrust himself—come what might—into the doorway. One side of his body rose up, he was tilted at an angle in the doorway, his flank was quite bruised, horrid blotches stained the white door, soon he was stuck fast and, left to himself, could not have moved at all, his legs on one side fluttered trembling in the air, those on the other were crushed painfully to the floor—when from behind his father gave him a strong push which was literally a deliverance and he flew far into the room, bleeding freely. The door was slammed behind him with the stick, and then at last there was silence.

II

Not until it was twilight did Gregor awake out of a deep sleep, more like a swoon than a sleep. He would certainly have waked up of his own accord not much later, for he felt himself sufficiently rested and well-slept, but it

seemed to him as if a fleeting step and a cautious shutting of the door leading into the hall had aroused him. The electric lights in the street cast a
pale sheen here and there on the ceiling and the upper surfaces of the furniture, but down below, where he lay, it was dark. Slowly, awkwardly
trying out his feelers, which he now first learned to appreciate, he pushed
his way to the door to see what had been happening there. His left side felt
like one single long, unpleasantly tense scar, and he had actually to limp on
his two rows of legs. One little leg, moreover, had been severely damaged
in the course of that morning's events—it was almost a miracle that only
one had been damaged—and trailed uselessly behind him.

He had reached the door before he discovered what had really drawn
him to it: the smell of food. For there stood a basin filled with fresh milk
in which floated little sops of white bread. He could almost have laughed
with joy, since he was not still hungrier than in the morning, and he
dipped his head almost over the eyes straight into the milk. But soon in
disappointment he withdrew it again; not only did he find it difficult to
feed because of his tender left side—and he could only feed with the palpi-
tating collaboration of his whole body—he did not like the milk either,
although milk had been his favorite drink and that was certainly why his
sister had set it there for him, indeed it was almost with repulsion that he
turned away from the basin and crawled back to the middle of the room.

He could see through the crack of the door that the gas was turned on in
the living room, but while usually at this time his father made a habit of
reading the afternoon newspaper in a loud voice to his mother and occasionally to his sister as well, not a sound was now to be heard. Well, perhaps his father had recently given up this habit of reading aloud, which his
sister had mentioned so often in conversation and in her letters. But there
was the same silence all around, although the flat was certainly not empty
of occupants. "What a quiet life our family has been leading," said Gregor
to himself, and as he sat there motionless staring into the darkness he felt
great pride in the fact that he had been able to provide such a life for his
parents and sister in such a fine flat. But what if all the quiet, the comfort,
the contentment were now to end in horror? To keep himself from being
lost in such thoughts Gregor took refuge in movement and crawled up and
down the room.

Once during the long evening one of the side doors was opened a little
and quickly shut again, later the other side door too; someone had apparently wanted to come in and then thought better of it. Gregor now stationed himself immediately before the living room door, determined to
persuade any hesitating visitor to come in or at least to discover who it
might be; but the door was not opened again and he waited in vain. In the
early morning, when the doors were locked, they had all wanted to come
in, now that he had opened one door and the other had apparently been
opened during the day, no one came in and even the keys were on the other
side of the doors.

It was late at night before the gas went out in the living room, and Gregor could easily tell that his parents and his sister had all stayed awake until then, for he could clearly hear the three of them stealing away on tiptoe. No one was likely to visit him, not until the morning, that was certain; so he had plenty of time to meditate at his leisure on how he was to arrange his life afresh. But the lofty, empty room in which he had to lie flat on the floor filled him with an apprehension he could not account for, since it had been his very own room for the past five years—and with a half-unconscious action, not without a slight feeling of shame, he scuttled under the sofa, where he felt comfortable at once, although his back was a little cramped and he could not lift his head up, and his only regret was that his body was too broad to get the whole of it under the sofa.

He stayed there all night, spending the time partly in a light slumber, from which his hunger kept waking him up with a start, and partly in worrying and sketching vague hopes, which all led to the same conclusion, that he must lie low for the present and, by exercising patience and the utmost consideration, help the family to bear the inconvenience he was bound to cause them in his present condition.

Very early in the morning, it was still almost night, Gregor had the chance to test the strength of his new resolutions, for his sister, nearly fully dressed, opened the door from the hall and peered in. She did not see him at once, yet when she caught sight of him under the sofa—well, he had to be somewhere, he couldn't have flown away, could he?—she was so startled that without being able to help it she slammed the door shut again. But as if regretting her behavior she opened the door again immediately and came in on tiptoe, as if she were visiting an invalid or even a stranger. Gregor had pushed his head forward to the very edge of the sofa and watched her. Would she notice that he had left the milk standing, and not for lack of hunger, and would she bring in some other kind of food more to his taste? If she did not do it of her own accord, he would rather starve than draw her attention to the fact, although he felt a wild impulse to dart out from under the sofa, throw himself at her feet and beg her for something to eat. But his sister at once noticed, with surprise, that the basin was still full, except for a little milk that had been spilt all around it, she lifted it immediately, not with her bare hands, true, but with a cloth and carried it away. Gregor was wildly curious to know what she would bring instead, and made various speculations about it. Yet what she actually did next, in the goodness of her heart, he could never have guessed at. To find out what he liked she brought him a whole selection of food, all set out on an old newspaper. There were old, half-decayed vegetables, bones from last night's supper covered with a white sauce that had thickened; some raisins and almonds; a piece of cheese that Gregor would have called uneatable two days ago; a dry roll of bread, a buttered roll, and a roll both buttered and salted. Beides all that, she set down again the same basin, into which she had poured some water, and which was apparently to be reserved for his exclusive use. And with fine tact, knowing that Gregor would not eat in her presence, she withdrew quickly and even turned the key, to let him understand that he could take his ease as much as he liked. Gregor's legs all whizzed towards the food. His wounds must have healed completely, moreover, for he felt no disability, which amazed him and made him reflect how more than a month ago he had cut one finger a little with a knife and had still suffered pain from the wound only the day before yesterday. Am I less sensitive now? he thought, and sucked greedily at the cheese, which above all the other edibles attracted him at once and strongly. One after another and with tears of satisfaction in his eyes he quickly devoured the cheese, the vegetables and the sauce; the fresh food, on the other hand, had no charms for him, he could not even stand the smell of it and actually dragged away to some little distance the things he could eat. He had long finished his meal and was only lying lazily on the same spot when his sister turned the key slowly as a sign for him to retreat. That roused him at once, although he was nearly asleep, and he hurried under the sofa again. But it took considerable self-control for him to stay under the sofa, even for the short time his sister was in the room, since the large meal had swollen his body somewhat and he was so cramped he could hardly breathe. Slight attacks of breathlessness afflicted him and his eyes were starting a little out of his head as he watched his unsuspecting sister sweeping together with a broom not only the remains of what he had eaten, but even the things he had not touched, as if these were now of no use to anyone, and hastily shoveling it all into a bucket, which she covered with a wooden lid and carried away. Hardly had she turned her back when Gregor came from underneath the sofa and stretched and puffed himself out.

In this manner Gregor was fed, once in the early morning while his parents and the servant girl were still asleep, and a second time after they had all had their midday dinner, for then his parents took a short nap and the servant girl could be sent out on some errand or other by his sister. Not that they would have wanted him to starve, of course, but perhaps they could not have borne to know more about his feeding than from hearsay, perhaps too his sister wanted to spare them such little anxieties wherever possible, since they had quite enough to bear as it was.

Under what pretext the doctor and the locksmith had been got rid of on that first morning Gregor could not discover, for since what he said was not understood by the others it never struck any of them, not even his sister, that he could understand what they said, and so whenever his sister came into his room he had to content himself with hearing her utter only a sigh now and then and an occasional appeal to the saints. Later on, when she had got a little used to the situation—of course she could never get completely used to it—she sometimes threw out a remark which was kindly meant or could be so interpreted. "Well, he liked his dinner today," she would say when Gregor had made a good clearance of his food; and when he had not eaten, which gradually happened more and more often, she would say almost sadly: "Everything's been left standing again."

But although Gregor could get no news directly, he overheard a lot from the neighboring rooms, and as soon as voices were audible, he would run to the door of the room concerned and press his whole body against it. In the first few days especially there was no conversation that did not refer to him somehow, even if only indirectly. For two whole days there were family consultations at every mealtime about what should be done; but also between meals the same subject was discussed, for there were always at least two members of the family at home, since no one wanted to be alone in the flat and to leave it quite empty was unthinkable. And on the very first of these days the household cook—it was not quite clear what and how much she knew of the situaton—went down on her knees to his mother and begged leave to go, and when she departed, a quarter of an hour later, gave thanks for her dismissal with tears in her eyes as if for the greatest benefit that could have been conferred on her, and without any prompting swore a solemn oath that she would never say a single word to anyone about what had happened.

Now Gregor's sister had to cook too, helping her mother; true, the cooking did not amount to much, for they ate scarcely anything. Gregor was always hearing one of the family vainly urging another to eat and getting no answer but: "Thanks, I've had all I want," or something similar. Perhaps they drank nothing either. Time and again his sister kept asking his father if he wouldn't like some beer and offered kindly to go and fetch it herself, and when he made no answer suggested that she could ask the concierge to fetch it, so that he need feel no sense of obligation, but then a round "No" came from his father and no more was said about it.

In the course of that very first day Gregor's father explained the family's financial position and prospects to both his mother and his sister. Now and then he rose from the table to get some voucher or memorandum out of the small safe he had rescued from the collapse of his business five years earlier. One could hear him opening the complicated lock and rustling papers out and shutting it again. This statement made by his father was the first cheerful information Gregor had heard since his imprisonment. He had been of the opinion that nothing at all was left over from his father's business, at least his father had never said anything to the contrary, and of course he had not asked him directly. At that time Gregor's sole desire was to do his utmost to help the family to forget as soon as possible the catastrophe which had overwhelmed the business and thrown them all into a state of complete despair. And so he had set to work with unusual ardor and almost overnight had become a commercial traveler instead of a little clerk, with of course much greater chances of earning money, and his success was immediately translated into good round coin which he could lay on the table for his amazed and happy family. These had been fine times, and they had

never recurred, at least not with the same sense of glory, although later on
Gregor had earned so much money that he was able to meet the expenses of
the whole household and did so. They had simply got used to it, both the
family and Gregor; the money was gratefully accepted and gladly given, but
there was no special uprush of warm feeling. With his sister alone had he
remained intimate, and it was a secret plan of his that she, who loved
music, unlike himself, and could play movingly on the violin, should be
sent next year to study at the Conservatorium, despite the great expense that
would entail, which must be made up in some other way. During his brief
visits home the Conservatorium was often mentioned in the talks he had
with his sister, but always merely as a beautiful dream which could never
come true, and his parents discouraged even these innocent references to it;
yet Gregor had made up his mind firmly about it and meant to announce
the fact with due solemnity on Christmas Day.

Such were the thoughts, completely futile in his present condition, that
went through his head as he stood clinging upright to the door and listening. Sometimes out of sheer weariness he had to give up listening and let
his head fall negligently against the door, but he always had to pull himself
together again at once, for even the slight sound his head made was audible
next door and brought all conversation to a stop. "What can he be doing
now?" his father would say after a while, obviously turning towards the
door, and only then would the interrupted conversation gradually be set
going again.

Gregor was now informed as amply as he could wish—for his father
tended to repeat himself in his explanations, partly because it was a long
time since he had handled such matters and partly because his mother could
not always grasp things at once—that a certain amount of investments, a
very small amount it was true, had survived the wreck of their fortunes and
had even increased a little because the dividends had not been touched
meanwhile. And besides that, the money Gregor brought home every month
—he had kept only a few dollars for himself—had never been quite used
up and now amounted to a small capital sum. Behind the door Gregor
nodded his head eagerly, rejoiced at this evidence of unexpected thrift and
foresight. True, he could really have paid off some more of his father's
debts to the chief with his extra money, and so brought much nearer the
day on which he could quit his job, but doubtless it was better the way his
father had arranged it.

Yet this capital was by no means sufficient to let the family live on the
interest of it; for one year, perhaps, or at the most two, they could live on
the principal, that was all. It was simply a sum that ought not to be touched
and should be kept for a rainy day; money for living expenses would have
to be earned. Now his father was still hale enough but an old man, and he had
done no work for the past five years and could not be expected to do much;
during these five years, the first years of leisure in his laborious though
unsuccessful life, he had grown rather fat and become sluggish. And Greg-

or's old mother, how was she to earn a living with her asthma, which troubled her even when she walked through the flat and kept her lying on a sofa every other day panting for breath beside an open window? And was his sister to earn her bread, she who was still a child of seventeen and whose life hitherto had been so pleasant, consisting as it did in dressing herself nicely, sleeping long, helping in the housekeeping, going out to a few modest entertainments and above all playing the violin? At first whenever the need for earning money was mentioned Gregor let go his hold on the door and threw himself down on the cool leather sofa beside it, he felt so hot with shame and grief.

Often he just lay there the long nights through without sleeping at all, scrabbling for hours on the leather. Or he nerved himself to the great effort of pushing an armchair to the window, then crawled up over the window sill and, braced against the chair, leaned against the window panes, obviously in some recollection of the sense of freedom that looking out of a window always used to give him. For in reality day by day things that were even a little way off were growing dimmer to his sight; the hospital across the street, which he used to execrate for being all too often before his eyes, was now quite beyond his range of vision, and if he had not known that he lived in Charlotte Street, a quiet street but still a city street, he might have believed that his window gave on a desert waste where gray sky and gray land blended indistinguishably into each other. His quick-witted sister only needed to observe twice that the armchair stood by the window; after that whenever she had tidied the room she always pushed the chair back to the same place at the window and even left the inner casements open.

If he could have spoken to her and thanked her for all she had to do for him, he could have borne her ministrations better; as it was, they oppressed him. She certainly tried to make as light as possible of whatever was disagreeable in her task, and as time went on she succeeded, of course, more and more, but time brought more enlightenment to Gregor too. The very way she came in distressed him. Hardly was she in the room when she rushed to the window, without even taking time to shut the door, careful as she was usually to shield the sight of Gregor's room from the others, and as if she were almost suffocating tore the casements open with hasty fingers, standing then in the open draught for a while even in the bitterest cold and drawing deep breaths. This noisy scurry of hers upset Gregor twice a day; he would crouch trembling under the sofa all the time, knowing quite well that she would certainly have spared him such a disturbance had she found it at all possible to stay in his presence without opening the window.

On one occasion, about a month after Gregor's metamorphosis, when there was surely no reason for her to be still startled at his appearance, she came a little earlier than usual and found him gazing out of the window, quite motionless, and thus well placed to look like a bogey. Gregor would not have been surprised had she not come in at all, for she could not immediately open the window while he was there, but not only did she retreat, she jumped back as if in alarm and banged the door shut; a stranger might well have thought that he had been lying in wait for her there meaning to bite her. Of course he hid himself under the sofa at once, but he had to wait until midday before she came again, and she seemed more ill at ease than usual. This made him realize how repulsive the sight of him still was to her, and that it was bound to go on being repulsive, and what an effort it must cost her not to run away even from the sight of the small portion of his body that stuck out from under the sofa. In order to spare her that, therefore, one day he carried a sheet on his back to the sofa—it cost him four hours' labor—and arranged in there in such a way as to hide him completely, so that even if she were to bend down she could not see him. Had she considered the sheet unnecessary, she would certainly have stripped it off the sofa again, for it was clear enough that this curtaining and confining of himself was not likely to conduce Gregor's comfort, but she left it where it was, and Gregor even fancied that he caught a thankful glance from her eye when he lifted the sheet carefully a very little with his head to see how she was taking the new arrangement.

For the first fortnight his parents could not bring themselves to the point of entering his room, and he often heard them expressing their appreciation of his sister's activities, whereas formerly they had frequently scolded her for being as they thought a somewhat useless daughter. But now, both of them often waited outside the door, his father and his mother, while his sister tidied his room, and as soon as she came out she had to tell them exactly how things were in the room, what Gregor had eaten, how he had conducted himself this time and whether there was not perhaps some slight improvement in his condition. His mother, moreover, began relatively soon to want to visit him, but his father and sister dissuaded her at first with arguments which Gregor listened to very attentively and altogether approved. Later, however, she had to be held back by main force, and when she cried out: "Do let me in to Gregor, he is my unfortunate son! Can't you understand that I must go to him?" Gregor thought that it might be well to have her come in, not every day, of course, but perhaps once a week; she understood things, after all, much better than his sister, who was only a child despite the efforts she was making and had perhaps taken on so difficult a task merely out of childish thoughtlessness.

Gregor's desire to see his mother was soon fulfilled. During the daytime he did not want to show himself at the window, out of consideration for his parents, but he could not crawl very far around the few square yards of floor space he had, nor could he bear lying quietly at rest all during the night, while he was fast losing any interest he had ever taken in food, so that for mere recreation he had formed the habit of crawling crisscross over the walls and ceiling. He especially enjoyed hanging suspended from the ceiling; it was much better than lying on the floor; one could breathe more freely; one's body swung and rocked lightly; and in the almost blissful absorption induced by this suspension it could happen to his own surprise that he let go and fell plump on the floor. Yet he now had his body much better under control than formerly, and even such a big fall did him no harm. His sister at once remarked the new distraction Gregor had found for himself—he left traces behind him of the sticky stuff on his soles wherever he crawled—and she got the idea in her head of giving him as wide a field as possible to crawl in and of removing the pieces of furniture that hindered him, above all the chest of drawers and the writing desk. But that was more than she could manage all by herself; she did not dare ask her father to help her; and as for the servant girl, a young creature of sixteen who had had the courage to stay on after the cook's departure, she could not be asked to help, for she had begged as an especial favor that she might keep the kitchen door locked and open it only on a definite summons; so there was nothing left but to apply to her mother at an hour when her father was out. And the old lady did come, with exclamations of joyful eagerness, which, however, died away at the door of Gregor's room. Gregor's sister, of course, went in first, to see that everything was in order before letting his mother enter. In great haste Gregor pulled the sheet lower and rucked it more in folds so that it really looked as if it had been thrown accidentally over the sofa. And this time he did not peer out from under it; he renounced the pleasure of seeing his mother on this occasion and was only glad that she had come at all. "Come in, he's out of sight," said his sister, obviously leading her mother in by the hand. Gregor could now hear the two women struggling to shift the heavy old chest from its place, and his sister claiming the greater part of the labor for herself, without listening to the admonitions of her mother who feared she might overstrain herself. It took a long time. After at least a quarter of an hour's tugging his mother objected that the chest had better be left where it was, for in the first place it was too heavy and could never be got out before his father came home, and standing in the middle of the room like that it would only hamper Gregor's movements, while in the second place it was not at all certain that removing the furniture would be doing a service to Gregor. She was inclined to think to the contrary; the sight of the naked walls made her own heart heavy, and why shouldn't Gregor have the same feeling, considering that he had been used to his furniture for so long and might feel forlorn without it. "And doesn't it look," she concluded in a low voice—in fact she had been almost whispering all the time as if to avoid letting Gregor, whose exact whereabouts she did not know, hear even the tones of her voice, for she was convinced that he could not understand her words—"doesn't it look as if we were showing him, by taking away his furniture, that we have given up hope of his ever getting better and are just leaving him coldly to himself? I think it would be best to keep his room exactly as it has always been, so that when he comes back to us he will find everything unchanged and be able all the more easily to forget what has happened in between."

On hearing these words from his mother Gregor realized that the lack of

all direct human speech for the past two months together with the monot-
ony of family life must have confused his mind, otherwise he could not
account for the fact that he had quite earnestly looked forward to having
his room emptied of furnishing. Did he really want his warm room, so
comfortably fitted with old family furniture, to be turned into a naked den
in which he would certainly be able to crawl unhampered in all directions
but at the price of shedding simultaneously all recollection of his human
background? He had indeed been so near the brink of forgetfulness that
only the voice of his mother, which he had not heard for so long, had
drawn him back from it. Nothing should be taken out of his room; everything must stay as it was; he could not dispense with the good influence of
the furniture on his state of mind; and even if the furniture did hamper
him in his senseless crawling round and round, that was no drawback but a
great advantage.

Unfortunately his sister was of the contrary opinion; she had grown
accustomed, and not without reason, to consider herself an expert in Greg-
or's affairs as against her parents, and so her mother's advice was now
enough to make her determined on the removal not only of the chest and
the writing desk, which had been her first intention, but of all the furniture
except the indispensable sofa. This determination was not, of course,
merely the outcome of childish recalcitrance and of the self-confidence she
had recently developed so unexpectedly and at such cost; she had in fact
perceived that Gregor needed a lot of space to crawl about in, while on the
other hand he never used the furniture at all, so far as could be seen.
Another factor might have been also the enthusiastic temperament of an
adolescent girl, which seeks to indulge itself on every opportunity and
which now tempted Grete to exaggerate the horror of her brother's circumstances in order that she might do all the more for him. In a room where
Gregor lorded it all alone over empty walls no one save herself was likely
ever to set foot.

And so she was not to be moved from her resolve by her mother who
seemed moreover to be ill at ease in Gregor's room and therefore unsure of
herself, was soon reduced to silence and helped her daughter as best she
could to push the chest outside. Now, Gregor could do without the chest, if
need be, but the writing desk he must retain. As soon as the two women
had got the chest out of his room, groaning as they pushed it, Gregor stuck
his head out from under the sofa to see how he might intervene as kindly
and cautiously as possible. But as bad luck would have it, his mother was
the first to return, leaving Grete clasping the chest in the room next door
where she was trying to shift it all by herself, without of course moving it
from the spot. His mother however was not accustomed to the sight of him,
it might sicken her and so in alarm Gregor backed quickly to the other end
of the sofa, yet could not prevent the sheet from swaying a little in front.
That was enough to put her on the alert. She paused, stood still for a
moment and then went back to Grete.

Although Gregor kept reassuring himself that nothing out of the way was happening, but only a few bits of furniture were being changed round, he soon had to admit that all this trotting to and fro of the two women, their little ejaculations and the scraping of furniture along the floor affected him like a vast disturbance coming from all sides at once, and however much he tucked in his head and legs and cowered to the very floor he was bound to confess that he would not be able to stand it for long. They were clearing his room out; taking away everything he loved; the chest in which he kept his fret saw and other tools was already dragged off; they were now loosening the writing desk which had almost sunk into the floor, the desk at which he had done all his homework when he was at the commercial academy, at the grammer school before that, and, yes, even at the primary school—he had no more time to waste in weighing the good intentions of the two women, whose existence he had by now almost forgotten, for they were so exhausted that they were laboring in silence and nothing could be heard but the heavy scuffling of their feet.

And so he rushed out—the women were just leaning against the writing desk in the next room to give themselves a breather—and four times changed his direction, since he really did not know what to rescue first, then on the wall opposite, which was already otherwise cleared, he was struck by the picture of the lady muffled in so much fur and quickly crawled up to it and pressed himself to the glass, which was a good surface to hold on to and comforted his hot belly. This picture at least, which was entirely hidden beneath him, was going to be removed by nobody. He turned his head towards the door of the living room so as to observe the women when they came back.

They had not allowed themselves much of a rest and were already coming; Grete had twined her arm round her mother and was almost supporting her. "Well, what shall we take now?" said Grete, looking round. Her eyes met Gregor's from the wall. She kept her composure, presumably because of her mother, bent her head down to her mother, to keep her from looking up, and said, although in a fluttering, unpremeditated voice: "Come, hadn't we better go back to the living room for a moment?" Her intentions were clear enough to Gregor, she wanted to bestow her mother in safety and then chase him down from the wall. Well, just let her try it! He clung to his picture and would not give it up. He would rather fly in Grete's face.

But Grete's words had succeeded in disquieting her mother, who took a step to one side, caught sight of the huge brown mass on the flowered wallpaper, and before she was really conscious that what she saw was Gregor screamed in a loud, hoarse voice: "Oh God, oh God!" fell with outspread arms over the sofa as if giving up and did not move. "Gregor!" cried his sister, shaking her fist and glaring at him. This was the first time she had directly addressed him since his metamorphosis. She ran into the next room for some aromatic essence with which to rouse her mother from her fainting fit. Gregor wanted to help too—there was still time to rescue the picture—but he was stuck fast to the glass and had to tear himself loose; he then ran after his sister into the next room as if he could advise her, as he used to do; but then had to stand helplessly behind her; she meanwhile searched among various small bottles and when she turned round started in alarm at the sight of him; one bottle fell on the floor and broke; a splinter of glass cut Gregor's face and some kind of corrosive medicine splashed him; without pausing a moment longer Grete gathered up all the bottles she could carry and ran to her mother with them; she banged the door shut with her foot. Gregor was now cut off from his mother, who was perhaps nearly dying because of him; he dared not open the door for fear of frightening away his sister, who had to stay with her mother; there was nothing he could do but wait; and harassed by self-reproach and worry he began now to crawl to and fro, over everything, walls, furniture and ceiling, and finally in his despair, when the whole room seemed to be reeling round him, fell down on to the middle of the big table.

A little while elapsed, Gregor was still lying there feebly and all around was quiet, perhaps that was a good omen. Then the doorbell rang. The servant girl was of course locked in her kitchen, and Grete would have to open the door. It was his father. "What's been happening?" were his first words; Grete's face must have told him everything. Grete answered in a muffled voice, apparently hiding her head on his breast: "Mother has been fainting, but she's better now. Gregor's broken loose." "Just what I expected," said his father, "just what I've been telling you, but you women would never listen." It was clear to Gregor that his father had taken the worst interpretation of Grete's all too brief statement and was assuming that Gregor had been guilty of some violent act. Therefore Gregor must now try to propitiate his father, since he had neither time nor means for an explanation. And so he fled to the door of his own room and crouched against it to let his father see as soon as he came in from the hall that his son had the good intention of getting back into his room immediately and that it was not necessary to drive him there, but that if only the door were opened he would disappear at once.

Yet his father was not in the mood to perceive such fine distinctions. "Ah!" he cried as soon as he appeared, in a tone which sounded at once angry and exultant. Gregor drew his head back from the door and lifted it to look at his father. Truly, this was not the father he had imagined to himself; admittedly he had been too absorbed of late in his new recreation of crawling over the ceiling to take the same interest as before in what was happening elsewhere in the flat, and he ought really to be prepared for some changes. And yet, and yet, could that be his father? The man who used to lie wearily sunk in bed whenever Gregor set out on a business journey; who welcomed him back of an evening lying in a long chair in a dressing gown; who could not really rise to his feet but only lifted his arms in greeting, and on the rare occasions when he did go out with his family, on one to two Sundays a year and on high holidays, walked between Gregor and his mother, who were slow walkers anyhow, even more slowly than they did, muffled in his old greatcoat, shuffling laboriously forward with the help of his crook-handled stick which he set down most cautiously at every step and, whenever he wanted to say anything, nearly always came to a full stop and gathered his escort around him? Now he was standing there in fine shape; dressed in a smart blue uniform with gold buttons, such as bank messengers wear; his strong double chin bulged over the stiff high collar of his jacket; from under his bushy eyebrows his black eyes darted fresh and penetrating glances; his onetime tangled white hair had been combed flat on either side of a shining and carefully exact parting. He pitched his cap, which bore a gold monogram, probably the badge of some bank, in a wide sweep across the whole room on to a sofa and with the tail-ends of his jacket thrown back, his hands in his trouser pockets, advanced with a grim visage towards Gregor. Likely enough he did not himself know what he meant to do; at any rate he lifted his feet uncommonly high, and Gregor was dumbfounded at the enormous size of his shoe soles. But Gregor could not risk standing up to him, aware as he had been from the very first day of his new life that his father believed only the severest measures suitable for dealing with him. And so he ran before his father, stopping when he stopped and scuttling forward again when his father made any kind of move. In this way they circled the room several times without anything decisive happening; indeed the whole operation did not even look like a pursuit because it was carried out so slowly. And so Gregor did not leave the floor, for he feared that his father might take as a piece of peculiar wickedness any excursion of his over the walls or the ceiling. All the same, he could not stay this course much longer, for while his father took one step he had to carry out a whole series of movements. He was already beginning to feel breathless, just as in his former life his lungs had not been very dependable. As he was staggering along, trying to concentrate his energy on running, hardly keeping his eyes open; in his dazed state never even thinking of any other escape than simply going forward; and having almost forgotten that the walls were free to him, which in this room were well provided with finely carved pieces of furniture full of knobs and crevices—suddenly something lightly flung landed close behind him and rolled before him. It was an apple; a second apple followed immediately; Gregor came to a stop in alarm; there was no point in running on, for his father was determined to bombard him. He had filled his pockets with fruit from the dish on the sideboard and was now shying apple after apple, without taking particularly good aim for the moment. The small red apples rolled about the floor as if magnetized and cannoned into each other. An apple thrown without much force grazed Gregor's back and glanced off harmlessly. But another following immediately landed right on his back and sank in; Gregor wanted to drag himself forward, as if this startling, incredible pain could be left behind him; but he felt as if nailed to the spot and flattened himself out in a complete derangement of all his senses. With his last conscious look he saw the door of his room being torn open and his mother rushing out ahead of his screaming sister, in her underbodice, for her daughter had loosened her clothing to let her breathe more freely and recover from her swoon, he saw his mother rushing towards his father, leaving one after another behind her on the floor her loosened petticoats, stumbling over her petticoats straight to his father and embracing him, in complete union with him—but here Gregor's sight began to fail—with her hands clasped round his father's neck as she begged for her son's life.

III

The serious injury done to Gregor, which disabled him for more than a month—the apple went on sticking in his body as a visible reminder, since no one ventured to remove it—seemed to have made even his father recollect that Gregor was a member of the family, despite his present unfortunate and repulsive shape, and ought not to be treated as an enemy, that, on the contrary, family duty required the suppression of disgust and the exercise of patience, nothing but patience.

And although his injury had impaired, probably for ever, his power of movement, and for the time being it took him long, long minutes to creep across his room like an old invalid—there was no question now of crawling up the wall—yet in his own opinion he was sufficiently compensated for this worsening of his condition by the fact that towards evening the living-room door, which he used to watch intently for an hour or two beforehand, was always thrown open, so that lying in the darkness of his room, invisible to the family, he could see them all at the lamp-lit table and listen to their talk, by general consent as it were, very different from his earlier eavesdropping.

True, their intercourse lacked the lively character of former times, which he had always called to mind with a certain wistfulness in the small hotel bedrooms where he had been wont to throw himself down, tired out, on damp bedding. They were now mostly very silent. Soon after supper his father would fall asleep in his armchair; his mother and sister would admonish each other to be silent; his mother, bending low over the lamp, stitched at fine sewing for an underwear firm; his sister, who had taken a job as a salesgirl, was learning shorthand and French in the evenings on the chance of bettering herself. Sometimes his father woke up, and as if quite unaware that he had been sleeping said to his mother: "What a lot of sewing you're doing today!" and at once fell asleep again, while the two women exchanged a tired smile.

With a kind of mulishness his father persisted in keeping his uniform on even in the house; his dressing gown hung uselessly on its peg and he slept fully dressed where he sat, as if he were ready for service at any moment and even here only at the beck and call of his superior. As a result, his uniform, which was not brand-new to start with, began to look dirty, despite all the loving care of the mother and sister to keep it clean, and Gregor often spent whole evenings gazing at the many greasy spots on the garment, gleaming with gold buttons always in a high state of polish, in which the old man sat sleeping in extreme discomfort and yet quite peacefully.

As soon as the clock struck ten his mother tried to rouse his father with gentle words and to persuade him after that to get into bed, for sitting there he could not have a proper sleep and that was what he needed most, since he had to go to duty at six. But with the mulishness that had obsessed him since he became a bank messenger he always insisted on staying longer at the table, although he regularly fell asleep again and in the end only with the greatest trouble could be got out of his armchair and into his bed. However insistently Gregor's mother and sister kept urging him with gentle reminders, he would go on slowly shaking his head for a quarter of an hour, keeping his eyes shut, and refuse to get to his feet. The mother plucked at his sleeve, whispering endearments in his ear, the sister left her lessons to come to her mother's help, but Gregor's father was not to be caught. He would only sink down deeper in his chair. Not until the two women hoisted him up by the armpits did he open his eyes and look at them both, one after the other, usually with the remark: "This is a life. This is the peace and quiet of my old age." And leaning on the two of them he would heave himself up, with difficulty, as if he were a great burden to himself, suffer them to lead him as far as the door and then wave them off and go on alone, while the mother abandoned her needlework and the sister her pen in order to run after him and help him farther.

Who could find time, in this overworked and tired-out family, to bother about Gregor more than was absolutely needful? The household was reduced more and more; the servant girl was turned off; a gigantic bony charwoman with white hair flying round her head came in morning and evening to do the rough work; everything else was done by Gregor's mother, as well as great piles of sewing. Even various family ornaments, which his mother and sister used to wear with pride at parties and celebrations, had to be sold, as Gregor discovered of an evening from hearing them all discuss the prices obtained. But what they lamented most was the fact that they could not leave the flat which was much too big for their present circumstances, because they could not think of any way to shift Gregor. Yet Gregor saw well enough that consideration for him was not the main difficulty preventing the removal, for they could have easily shifted him in some suitable box with a few air holes in it; what really kept them from moving into another flat was rather their own complete hopelessness and the belief that they had been singled out for a misfortune such as had never happened to any of their relations or acquaintances. They fulfilled to the uttermost all that the world demands of poor people, the father fetched breakfast for the small clerks in the bank, the mother devoted her energy to making underwear for strangers, the sister trotted to and fro behind the counter at the behest of customers, but more than this they had not the strength to do. And the wound in Gregor's back began to nag at him afresh when his mother and sister, after getting his father into bed, came back again, left their work lying, drew close to each other and sat cheek by cheek; when his mother, pointing towards his room, said: "Shut that door now, Grete," and he was left again in darkness, while next door the women mingled their tears or perhaps sat dry-eyed staring at the table.

Gregor hardly slept at all by night or by day. He was often haunted by the idea that next time the door opened he would take the family's affairs in hand again just as he used to do; once more, after this long interval, there appeared in his thoughts the figures of the chief and the chief clerk, the commercial travelers and the apprentices, the porter who was so dull-witted, two or three friends in other firms, a chambermaid in one of the rural hotels, a sweet and fleeting memory, a cashier in a milliner's shop, whom he had wooed earnestly but too slowly—they all appeared, together with strangers or people he had quite forgotten, but instead of helping him and his family they were one and all unapproachable and he was glad when they vanished. At other times he would not be in the mood to bother about his family, he was only filled with rage at the way they were neglecting him, and although he had no clear idea of what he might care to eat he would make plans for getting into the larder to take the food that was after all his due, even if he were not hungry. His sister no longer took thought to bring him what might especially please him, but in the morning and at noon before she went to business hurriedly pushed into his room with her foot any food that was available, and in the evening cleared it out again with one sweep of the broom, heedless of whether it had been merely tasted, or—as most frequently happened—left untouched. The cleaning of his room, which she now did always in the evenings, could not have been more hastily done. Streaks of dirt stretched along the walls, here and there lay balls of dust and filth. At first Gregor used to station himself in some particularly filthy corner when his sister arrived, in order to reproach her with it, so to speak. But he could have sat there for weeks without getting her to make any improvements; she could see the dirt as well as he did, but she had simply made up her mind to leave it alone. And yet, with a touchiness that was new to her, which seemed anyhow to have infected the whole family, she jealously guarded her claim to be the sole caretaker of Gregor's room. His mother once subjected his room to a thorough cleaning, which was achieved only by means of several buckets of water—all this dampness of course upset Gregor too and he lay widespread, sulky and motionless on the sofa—but she was well punished for it. Hardly had his sister noticed the changed aspect of his room that evening than she rushed in high dudgeon into the living room and, despite the imploringly raised hands of her mother, burst into a storm of weeping, while her parents—her father had of course been startled out of his chair—looked on at first in helpless amazement; then they too began to go into action; the father reproached the mother on his right for not having left the cleaning of Gregor's room to his sister; shrieked at the sister on his left that never again was she to be allowed to clean Gregor's room; while the mother tried to pull the father into his bedroom, since he was beyond himself with agitation; the sister, shaken with sobs, then beat upon the table with her small fists; and Gregor hissed loudly with rage because not one of them thought of shutting the door to spare him such a spectacle and so much noise.

Still, even if the sister, exhausted by her daily work, had grown tired of looking after Gregor as she did formerly, there was no need for his mother's intervention or for Gregor's being neglected at all. The charwoman was there. This old widow, whose strong bony frame had enabled her to survive the worst a long life could offer, by no means recoiled from Gregor. Without being in the least curious she had once by chance opened the door of his room and at the sight of Gregor, who, taken by surprise, began to rush to and fro although no one was chasing him, merely stood there with her arms folded. From that time she never failed to open his door a little for a moment, morning and evening, to have a look at him. At first she even used to call him to her, with words which apparently she took to be friendly, such as "Come along, then, you old dung beetle!" or "Look at the old dung beetle, then!" To such allocutions Gregor made no answer, but stayed motionless where he was, as if the door had never been opened. Instead of being allowed to disturb him so senselessly whenever the whim took her, she should rather have been ordered to clean out his room daily, that charwoman! Once, early in the morning—heavy rain was lashing on the windowpanes, perhaps a sign that spring was on the way—Gregor was so exasperated when she began addressing him again that he ran at her, as if to attack her, although slowly and feebly enough. But the charwoman instead of showing fright merely lifted high a chair that happened to be beside the door, and as she stood there with her mouth wide open it was clear that she meant to shut it only when she brought the chair down on Gregor's back. "So you're not coming any nearer?" she asked, as Gregor turned away again, and quietly put the chair back into the corner.

Gregor was now eating hardly anything. Only when he happened to pass the food laid out for him did he take a bit of something in his mouth as a pastime, kept it there for an hour at a time and usually spat it out again. At first he thought it was chagrin over the state of his room that prevented him from eating, yet he soon got used to the various changes in his room. It had become a habit in the family to push into his room things there was no room for elsewhere, and there were plenty of these now, since one of the rooms had been let to three lodgers. These serious gentlemen—all three of them with full beards, as Gregor once observed through a crack in the door

—had a passion for order, not only in their own room but, since they were now members of the household, in all its arrangements, especially in the kitchen. Superfluous, not to say dirty, objects they could not bear. Besides, they had brought with them most of the furnishings they needed. For this reason many things could be dispensed with that it was no use trying to sell but that should not be thrown away either. All of them found their way into Gregor's room. The ash can likewise and the kitchen garbage can. Anything that was not needed for the moment was simply flung into Gregor's room by the charwoman, who did everything in a hurry; fortunately Gregor usually saw only the object, whatever it was, and the hand that held it. Perhaps she intended to take the things away again as time and opportunity offered, or to collect them until she could throw them all out in a heap, but in fact they just lay wherever she happened to throw them, except when Gregor pushed his way through the junk heap and shifted it somewhat, at first out of necessity, because he had not room enough to crawl, but later with increasing enjoyment, although after such excursions, being sad and weary to death, he would lie motionless for hours. And since the lodgers often ate their supper at home in the common living room, the living-room door stayed shut many an evening, yet Gregor reconciled himself quite easily to the shutting of the door, for often enough on evenings when it was opened he had disregarded it entirely and lain in the darkest corner of his room, quite unnoticed by the family. But on one occasion the charwoman left the door open a little and it stayed ajar even when the lodgers came in for supper and the lamp was lit. They set themselves at the top end of the table where formerly Gregor and his father and mother had eaten their meals, unfolded their napkins and took knife and fork in hand. At once his mother appeared in the other doorway with a dish of meat and close behind her his sister with a dish of potatoes piled high. The food steamed with a thick vapor. The lodgers bent over the food set before them as if to scrutinize it before eating, in fact the man in the middle, who seemed to pass for an authority with the other two, cut a piece of meat as it lay on the dish, obviously to discover if it were tender or should be sent back to the kitchen. He showed satisfaction, and Gregor's mother and sister, who had been watching anxiously, breathed freely and began to smile.

The family itself took its meals in the kitchen. None the less, Gregor's father came into the living room before going into the kitchen and with one prolonged bow, cap in hand, made a round of the table. The lodgers all stood up and murmured something in their beards. When they were alone again they ate their food in almost complete silence. It seemed remarkable to Gregor that among the various noises coming from the table he could always distinguish the sound of their masticating teeth, as if this were a sign to Gregor that one needed teeth in order to eat, and that with toothless jaws even of the finest make one could do nothing. "I'm hungry enough," said Gregor sadly to himself, "but not for that kind of food. How these lodgers are stuffing themselves, and here am I dying of starvation!"

On that very evening—during the whole of his time there Gregor could not remember ever having heard the violin—the sound of violin-playing came from the kitchen. The lodgers had already finished their supper, the one in the middle had brought out a newspaper and given the other two a page apiece, and now they were leaning back at ease reading and smoking. When the violin began to play they pricked up their ears, got to their feet, and went on tiptoe to the hall door where they stood huddled together. Their movements must have been heard in the kitchen, for Gregor's father called out: "Is the violin-playing disturbing you, gentlemen? It can be stopped at once." "On the contrary," said the middle lodger, "could not Fräulein Samsa come and play in this room, beside us, where it is much more convenient and comfortable?" "Oh certainly," cried Gregor's father, as if he were the violin-player. The lodgers came back into the living room and waited. Presently Gregor's father arrived with the music stand, his mother carrying the music and his sister with the violin. His sister quietly made everything ready to start playing; his parents, who had never let rooms before and so had an exaggerated idea of the courtesy due to lodgers, did not venture to sit down on their own chairs; his father leaned against the door, the right hand thrust between two buttons of his livery coat, which was formally buttoned up; but his mother was offered a chair by one of the lodgers and, since she left the chair just where he had happened to put it, sat down in a corner to one side.

Gregor's sister began to play; the father and mother, from either side, intently watched the movements of her hands. Gregor, atttracted by the playing, ventured to move forward a little until his head was actually inside the living room. He felt hardly any surprise at his growing lack of consideration for the others; there had been a time when he prided himself on being considerate. And yet just on this occasion he had more reason than ever to hide himself, since owing to the amount of dust which lay thick in his room and rose into the air at the slightest movement, he too was covered with dust; fluff and hair and remnants of food trailed with him, caught on his back and along his sides; his indifference to everything was much too great for him to turn on his back and scrape himself clean on the carpet, as once he had done several times a day. And in spite of his condition, no shame deterred him from advancing a little over the spotless floor of the living room.

To be sure, no one was aware of him. The family was entirely absorbed in the violin-playing; the lodgers, however, who first of all had stationed themselves, hands in pockets, much too close behind the music stand so that they could all have read the music, which must have bothered his sister, had soon retreated to the window, half-whispering with downbent heads, and stayed there while his father turned an anxious eye on them. Indeed, they were making it more than obvious that they had been disappointed in their expectation of hearing good or enjoyable violin-playing, that they had had more than enough of the performance and only out of courtesy suffered a continued disturbance of their peace. From the way they all kept blowing the smoke of their cigars high in the air through nose and mouth one could divine their irritation. And yet Gregor's sister was playing so beautifully. Her face leaned sideways, intently and sadly her eyes followed the notes of music. Gregor crawled a little farther forward and lowered his head to the ground so that it might be possible for his eyes to meet hers. Was he an animal, that music had such an effect upon him? He felt as if the way were opening before him to the unknown nourishment he craved. He was determined to push forward till he reached his sister, to pull at her skirt and so let her know that she was to come into his room with her violin, for no one here appreciated her playing as he would appreciate it. He would never let her out of his room, at least, not so long as he lived; his frightful appearance would become, for the first time, useful to him; he would watch all the doors of his room at once and spit at intruders; but his sister should need no constraint, she should stay with him of her own free will; she should sit beside him on the sofa, bend down her ear to him and hear him confide that he had had the firm intention of sending her to the Conservatorium, and that, but for his mishap, last Christmas—surely Christmas was long past?—he would have announced it to everybody without allowing a single objection. After this confession his sister would be so touched that she would burst into tears, and Gregor would then raise himself to her shoulder and kiss her on the neck, which, now that she went to business, she kept free of any ribbon or collar.

"Mr. Samsa!" cried the middle lodger, to Gregor's father, and pointed, without wasting any more words, at Gregor, now working himself slowly forwards. The violin fell silent, the middle lodger first smiled to his friends with a shake of the head and then looked at Gregor again. Instead of driving Gregor out, his father seemed to think it more needful to begin by soothing down the lodgers, although they were not at all agitated and apparently found Gregor more entertaining than the violin-playing. He hurried towards them and, spreading out his arms, tried to urge them back into their own room and at the same time to block their view of Gregor. They now began to be really a little angry, one could not tell whether because of the old man's behavior or because it had just dawned on them that all unwittingly they had such a neighbor as Gregor next door. They demanded explanations of his father, they waved their arms like him, tugged uneasily at their beards, and only with reluctance backed towards their room. Meanwhile Gregor's sister, who stood there as if lost when her playing was so abruptly broken off, came to life again, pulled herself together all at once after standing for a while holding violin and bow in nervelessly hanging hands and staring at her music, pushed her violin into the lap of her mother, who was still sitting in her chair fighting asthmatically for breath, and ran into the lodgers' room to which they were now being shepherded by her father rather more quickly than before. One could see the pillows and blankets on the beds flying under her accustomed fingers and being laid in order. Before the lodgers had actually reached their room she had finished making the beds and slipped out.

The old man seemed once more to be so possessed by his mulish self-assertiveness that he was forgetting all the respect he should show to his lodgers. He kept driving them on and driving them on until in the very door of the bedroom the middle lodger stamped his foot loudly on the floor and so brought him to a halt. "I beg to announce," said the lodger, lifting one hand and looking also at Gregor's mother and sister, "that because of the disgusting conditions prevailing in this household and family"—here he spat on the floor with emphatic brevity—"I give you notice on the spot. Naturally I won't pay you a penny for the days I have lived here, on the contrary I shall consider bringing an action for damages against you, based on claims—believe me—that will be easily susceptible of proof." He ceased and stared straight in front of him, as if he expected something. In fact his two friends at once rushed into the breach with these words: "And we too give notice on the spot." On that he seized the door-handle and shut the door with a slam.

Gregor's father, groping with his hands, staggered forward and fell into his chair; it looked as if he were stretching himself there for his ordinary evening nap, but the marked jerkings of his head, which was as if uncontrollable, showed that he was far from asleep. Gregor had simply stayed quietly all the time on the spot where the lodgers had espied him. Disappointment at the failure of his plan, perhaps also the weakness arising from extreme hunger, made it impossible for him to move. He feared, with a fair degree of certainty, that at any moment the general tension would discharge itself in a combined attack upon him, and he lay waiting. He did not react even to the noise made by the violin as it fell off his mother's lap from under her trembling fingers and gave out a resonant note.

"My dear parents," said his sister, slapping her hand on the table by way of introduction, "things can't go on like this. Perhaps you don't realize that, but I do. I won't utter my brother's name in the presence of this creature, and so all I say is: we must try to get rid of it. We've tried to look after it and to put up with it as far as is humanly possible, and I don't think anyone could reproach us in the slightest."

"She is more than right," said Gregor's father to himself. His mother, who was still choking for lack of breath, began to cough hollowly into her hand with a wild look in her eyes.

His sister rushed over to her and held her forehead. His father's thoughts seemed to have lost their vagueness at Grete's words, he sat more upright, fingering his service cap that lay among the plates still lying on the table from the lodgers' supper, and from time to time looked at the still form of Gregor.

"We must try to get rid of it," his sister now said explicitly to her father, since her mother was coughing too much to hear a word, "it will be the death of both of you, I can see that coming. When one has to work as hard as we do, all of us, one can't stand this continual torment at home on top of it. At least I can't stand it any longer." And she burst into such a passion of sobbing that her tears dropped on her mother's face, where she wiped them off mechanically.

"My dear," said the old man sympathetically, and with evident understanding, "but what can we do?"

Gregor's sister merely shrugged her shoulders to indicate the feeling of helplessness that had now overmastered her during her weeping fit, in contrast to her former confidence.

"If he could understand us," said her father, half questioningly; Grete, still sobbing, vehemently waved a hand to show how unthinkable that was.

"If he could understand us," repeated the old man, shutting his eyes to consider his daughter's conviction that understanding was impossible, "then perhaps we might come to some agreement with him. But as it is—"

"He must go," cried Gregor's sister, "that's the only solution, Father. You must try to get rid of the idea that this is Gregor. The fact that we've believed it for so long is the root of all our trouble. But how can it be Gregor? If this were Gregor, he would have realized long ago that human beings can't live with such a creature, and he'd have gone away on his own accord. Then we wouldn't have any brother, but we'd be able to go on living and keep his memory in honor. As it is, this creature persecutes us, drives away our lodgers, obviously wants the whole apartment to himself and would have us all sleep in the gutter. Just look, Father," she shrieked all at once, "he's at it again!" And in an access of panic that was quite incomprehensible to Gregor she even quitted her mother, literally thrusting the chair from her as if she would rather sacrifice her mother than stay so near to Gregor, and rushed behind her father, who also rose up, being simply upset by her agitation, and half-spread his arms out as if to protect her.

Yet Gregor had not the slightest intention of frightening anyone, far less his sister. He had only begun to turn round in order to crawl back to his room, but it was certainly a startling operation to watch, since because of his disabled condition he could not execute the difficult turning movements except by lifting his head and then bracing it against the floor over and over again. He paused and looked round. His good intentions seemed to have been recognized; the alarm had only been momentary. Now they were all watching him in melancholy silence. His mother lay in her chair, her legs stiffly outstretched and pressed together, her eyes almost closing for sheer weariness; his father and his sister were sitting beside each other, his sister's arm around the old man's neck.

Perhaps I can go on turning round now, thought Gregor, and began his labors again. He could not stop himself from panting with the effort, and had to pause now and then to take breath. Nor did anyone harass him, he was left entirely to himself. When he had completed the turn-round he began at once to crawl straight back. He was amazed at the distance separating him from his room and could not understand how in his weak state he had managed to accomplish the same journey so recently, almost without remarking it. Intent on crawling as fast as possible, he barely noticed that not a single word, not an ejaculation from his family, interfered with his progress. Only when he was already in the doorway did he turn his head round, not completely, for his neck muscles were getting stiff, but enough to see that nothing had changed behind him except that his sister had risen to her feet. His last glance fell on his mother, who was not quite overcome by sleep.

Hardly was he well inside his room when the door was hastily pushed shut, bolted and locked. The sudden noise in his rear startled him so much that his little legs gave beneath him. It was his sister who had shown such haste. She had been standing ready waiting and had made a light spring forward, Gregor had not even heard her coming, and she cried "At last!" to her parents as she turned the key in the lock.

"And what now?" said Gregor to himself, looking round in the darkness. Soon he made the discovery that he was now unable to stir a limb. This did not surprise him, rather it seemed unnatural that he should ever actually have been able to move on these feeble little legs. Otherwise he felt relatively comfortable. True, his whole body was aching, but it seemed that the pain was gradually growing less and would finally pass away. The rotting apple in his back and the inflamed area around it, all covered with soft dust, already hardly troubled him. He thought of his family with tenderness and love. The decision that he must disappear was one that he held to even more strongly than his sister, if that were possible. In this state of vacant and peaceful meditation he remained until the tower clock struck three in the morning. The first broadening of light in the world outside the window entered his consciousness once more. Then his head sank to the floor of its own accord and from his nostrils came the last faint flicker of his breath.

When the charwoman arrived early in the morning—what between her strength and her impatience she slammed all the doors so loudly, never mind how often she had been begged not to do so, that no one in the whole apartment could enjoy any quiet sleep after her arrival—she noticed nothing unusual as she took her customary peep into Gregor's room. She thought he was lying motionless on purpose, pretending to be in the sulks; she credited him with every kind of intelligence. Since she happened to have the long-handled broom in her hand she tried to tickle him up with it from the doorway. When that too produced no reaction she felt provoked and poked at him a little harder, and only when she had pushed him along the floor without meeting any resistance was her attention aroused. It did not take her long to establish the truth of the matter, and her eyes widened,

she let out a whistle, yet did not waste much time over it but tore open the
door of the Samsas' bedroom and yelled into the darkness at the top of her
voice: "Just look at this, it's dead; it's lying here dead and done for!"

Mr. and Mrs. Samsa started up in their double bed and before they realized the nature of the charwoman's announcement had some difficulty in
overcoming the shock of it. But then they got out of bed quickly, one on
either side, Mr. Samsa throwing a blanket over his shoulders, Mrs. Samsa
in nothing but her nightgown; in this array they entered Gregor's room.
Meanwhile the door of the living room opened, too, where Grete had been
sleeping since the advent of the lodgers; she was completely dressed as if
she had not been to bed, which seemed to be confirmed also by the paleness
of her face. "Dead?" said Mrs. Samsa, looking questioningly at the charwoman, although she could have investigated for herself, and the fact was
obvious enough without investigation. "I should say so," said the charwoman, proving her words by pushing Gregor's corpse a long way to one
side with her broomstick. Mrs. Samsa made a movement as if to stop her,
but checked it. "Well," said Mr. Samsa, "now thanks be to God." He
crossed himself, and the three women followed his example. Grete, whose
eyes never left the corpse, said: "Just see how thin he was. It's such a long
time since he's eaten anything. The food came out again just as it went in."
Indeed, Gregor's body was completely flat and dry, as could only now be
seen when it was no longer supported by the legs and nothing prevented
one from looking closely at it.

"Come in beside us, Grete, for a little while," said Mrs. Samsa with a
tremulous smile, and Grete, not without looking back at the corpse, followed her parents into their bedroom. The charwoman shut the door and
opened the window wide. Although it was so early in the morning a certain
softness was perceptible in the fresh air. After all, it was already the end of
March.

The three lodgers emerged from their room and were surprised to see no
breakfast; they had been forgotten. "Where's our breakfast?" said the
middle lodger peevishly to the charwoman. But she put her finger to her
lips and hastily, without a word, indicated by gestures that they should go
into Gregor's room. They did so and stood, their hands in the pockets of
their somewhat shabby coats, around Gregor's corpse in the room where it
was now fully light.

At that the door of the Samsas' bedroom opened and Mr. Samsa
appeared in his uniform, his wife on one arm, his daughter on the other.
They all looked a little as if they had been crying; from time to time Grete
hid her face on her father's arm.

"Leave my house at once!" said Mr. Samsa, and pointed to the door
without disengaging himself from the women. "What do you mean by
that?" said the middle lodger, taken somewhat aback, with a feeble smile.
The two others put their hands behind them and kept rubbing them
together, as if in gleeful expectation of a fine set-to in which they were

bound to come off the winners. "I mean just what I say," answered Mr. Samsa, and advanced in a straight line with his two companions towards the lodger. He stood his ground at first quietly, looking at the floor as if his thoughts were taking a new pattern in his head. "Then let us go, by all means," he said, and looked up at Mr. Samsa as if in a sudden access of humility he were expecting some renewed sanction for this decision. Mr. Samsa merely nodded briefly once or twice with meaning eyes. Upon that the lodger really did go with long strides into the hall, his two friends had been listening and had quite stopped rubbing their hands for some moments and now went scuttling after him as if afraid that Mr. Samsa might get into the hall before them and cut them off from their leader. In the hall they all three took their hats from the rack, their sticks from the umbrella stand, bowed in silence and quitted the apartment. With a suspiciousness which proved quite unfounded Mr. Samsa and the two women followed them out to the landing; leaning over the banister they watched the three figures slowly but surely going down the long stairs, vanishing from sight at a certain turn of the staircase on every floor and coming into view again after a moment or so; the more they dwindled, the more the Samsa family's interest in them dwindled, and when a butcher's boy met them and passed them on the stairs coming up proudly with a tray on his head, Mr. Samsa and the two women soon left the landing and as if a burden had been lifted from them went back into their apartment.

They decided to spend this day in resting and going for a stroll; they had not only deserved such a respite from work, but absolutely needed it. And so they sat down at the table and wrote three notes of excuse, Mr. Samsa to his board of management, Mrs. Samsa to her employer and Grete to the head of her firm. While they were writing, the charwoman came in to say that she was going now, since her morning's work was finished. At first they only nodded without looking up, but as she kept hovering there they eyed her irritably. "Well?" said Mr. Samsa. The charwoman stood grinning in the doorway as if she had good news to impart to the family but meant not to say a word unless properly questioned. The small ostrich feather standing upright on her hat, which had annoyed Mr. Samsa ever since she was engaged, was waving gaily in all directions. "Well, what is it then?" asked Mrs. Samsa, who obtained more respect from the charwoman than the others. "Oh," said the charwoman, giggling so amiably that she could not at once continue, "just this, you don't need to bother about how to get rid of the thing next door. It's been seen to already." Mrs. Samsa and Grete bent over their letters again, as if preoccupied; Mr. Samsa, who perceived that she was eager to begin describing it all in detail, stopped her with a decisive hand. But since she was not allowed to tell her story, she remembered the great hurry she was in, being obviously deeply huffed: "Bye, everybody," she said, whirling off violently, and departed with a frightful slamming of doors.

"She'll be given notice tonight," said Mr. Samsa, but neither from his wife nor his daughter did he get any answer, for the charwoman seemed to have shattered again the composure they had barely achieved. They rose, went to the window and stayed there, clasping each other tight. Mr. Samsa turned in his chair to look at them and quietly observed them for a little. Then he called out: "Come along, now, do. Let bygones be bygones. And you might have some consideration for me." The two of them complied at once, hastened to him, caressed him and quickly finished their letters.

Then they all three left the apartment together, which was more than they had done for months, and went by tram into the open country outside the town. The tram, in which they were the only passengers, was filled with warm sunshine. Leaning comfortably back in their seats they canvassed their prospects for the future, and it appeared on closer inspection that these were not at all bad, for the jobs they had got, which so far they had never really discussed with each other, were all three admirable and likely to lead to better things later on. The greatest immediate improvement in their condition would of course arise from moving to another house; they wanted to take a smaller and cheaper but also better situated and more easily run apartment than the one they had, which Gregor had selected. While they were thus conversing, it struck both Mr. and Mrs. Samsa, almost at the same moment, as they became aware of their daughter's increasing vivacity, that in spite of all the sorrow of recent times, which had made her cheeks pale, she had bloomed into a pretty girl with a good figure. They grew quieter and half unconsciously exchanged glances of complete agreement, having come to the conclusion that it would soon be time to find a good husband for her. And it was like a confirmation of their new dreams and excellent intentions that at the end of the journey their daughter sprang to her feet first and stretched her young body.

8

D. H. LAWRENCE
The Fox

From the outset, Lawrence intimates that the two women's attempts to make a livelihood at Bailey Farm are strangely blighted. He quite clearly intends that their attempts to embrace pastoral "nature"—with its idyllic landscape, rhythmic life, and supposedly fertile animals—are an unconscious and misguided means of compensating for the fulfillment they deny themselves by their retreat from men. It must be remembered that, to Lawrence, rejection of passionate heterosexual love led to grave personal and social ills. His disapproval of Banford and March can often be felt in the mocking tone of his narrative, as well as in the faintly condescending, ironic neatness of having the women prefer pastoral nature over the sexual complications of human nature.

March must suffer by far the greater self-repression in clinging to farm life. Banford, perhaps because of her father's influence, seems to fit more naturally into a maleless environment. Both women harbor deep feelings toward the possibility of masculine intrusion. Banford is "physically afraid," but March is ambivalent. March fears involvement with a man, but she also desires involvement, and her dream-

like aloofness reflects the self-destructive contradiction within her. Her characteristic way of puckering her lips, an expression associated with her dream of the fox, seems to be both a gesture of distrust and a gesture of sexual beckoning. Her obsessive fascination with the fox is consistent with her ambiguous nature. The fox is a fitting symbol of the intruding male, and he is also a symbol of March's ambiguous impulses toward fulfillment and denial.

The masculine intruder, it turns out, is young, charming, innocent-seeming Henry Grenfel, just back from the war on the Continent. Like many young men returning from war, he has about him the deliberateness and newly gained maturity of one who has recently been through trying experiences. His name fittingly links him with forces of nature, associating him symbolically with such mythological figures as the Medieval English "Green Knight" whose vitality becomes a social menace. After their initial fright the women are disarmed by Henry's demeanor of wholesome innocence. "He was such a boy," Banford thinks. In fact, Henry Grenfel does possess a fascinating innocence, primarily because he is guided by almost pure instinct, and his lack of self-awareness blinds him to the other side of his nature. Although his destructiveness is disguised by innocence, it begins to have effect almost as soon as he enters the story. The women are embarrassed because there is little food to serve their guest—a small enough problem, circumstantially, but through the course of the story food and eating become symbols that comment significantly on the inability of the women to confront Henry in what is from the start a subtle battle of wills. March readily identifies Henry with the fox, and the youth now becomes the visible focus of her conflicting desires.

Henry's motives in courting March are as complex as they are sinister. Note what he says immediately prior to his first mention of marrying her. More important than his greedy impulse to "use" March is understanding why he has an ingrained instinct to nourish the power of his own being by possessing some sustaining reality larger than himself. The farm itself is that kind of reality to him, and unlike the women, Henry is sustained magnificently by nature in this literal form. When he is out in the woods —especially at night, with his gun —his spirit soars, and his will, as Lawrence describes in a masterful key passage, enters into a cunning and fatal contest with that of his prey. Yet, nature, in its maternal way, contains and surpasses him and draws him onward into dimensions of being which he cannot fully possess within himself. March, like nature, has maternal qualities for Henry, yet this threatens him. At the last, complete possession of March still eludes him, and the enigmatic depths of her womanhood continue to draw him onwards in a mutually destructive battle of wills.

The passion of Lawrence's writing owes much to the austere and religious fervor of his philosophy. At the core of his vision was what he regarded as the profound spirituality of the human body. He championed exuberant sex, vitality, and the body's "blood consciousness" as the only genuine sources of morality. "That which is good, and moral, is that which brings us into a stronger, deeper flow of life and life-energy: evil is that which impairs the life-flow." He despised everything in modern life that seemed to destroy life-energy—sexual prudery, the restrictedness of conventional family life, urban blight, and the menace of machines and machine warfare.

Based upon such a tumultuous philosophy, Lawrence's fiction is predictably uneven in quality, and some critics have charged that his characterization is often weak, his symbolism heavy-handed. But even when his craftsmanship seems uncertain, his fiction is often made extraordinary by his literary "voice" —the projection of a characteristic spirit in his writing. One is made constantly aware of the energy and presence of the man himself, animating his words, propelling the story onwards with a numb, breathless, rushing force.

The Fox

The two girls were usually known by
their surnames, Banford and March. They had taken the farm together,
intending to work it all by themselves: that is, they were going to rear
chickens, make a living by poultry, and add to this by keeping a cow, and
raising one or two young beasts. Unfortunately, things did not turn out
well.

Banford was a small, thin, delicate thing with spectacles. She, however,
was the principal investor, for March had little or no money. Banford's
father, who was a tradesman in Islington, gave his daughter the start, for
her health's sake, and because he loved her, and because it did not look as
if she would marry. March was more robust. She had learned carpentry
and joinery at the evening classes in Islington. She would be the man
about the place. They had, moreover, Banford's old grandfather living with
them at the start. He had been a farmer. But unfortunately the old man
died after he had been at Bailey Farm for a year. Then the two girls were
left alone.

They were neither of them young: that is, they were near thirty. But they
certainly were not old. They set out quite gallantly with their enterprise.
They had numbers of chickens, black Leghorns and white Leghorns, Plym-
ouths and Wyandottes; also some ducks; also two heifers in the fields. One
heifer, unfortunately, refused absolutely to stay in the Bailey Farm closes.

No matter how March made up the fences, the heifer was out, wild in the woods, or trespassing on the neighbouring pasture, and March and Banford were away, flying after her, with more haste than success. So this heifer they sold in despair. Then, just before the other beast was expecting her first calf, the old man died, and the girls, afraid of the coming event, sold her in a panic, and limited their attentions to fowls and ducks.

In spite of a little chagrin, it was a relief to have no more cattle on hand. Life was not made merely to be slaved away. Both girls agreed in this. The fowls were quite enough trouble. March had set up her carpenter's bench at the end of the open shed. Here she worked, making coops and doors and other appurtenances. The fowls were housed in the bigger building, which had served as barn and cow-shed in old days. They had a beautiful home, and should have been perfectly content. Indeed, they looked well enough. But the girls were disgusted at their tendency to strange illnesses, at their exacting way of life, and at their refusal, obstinate refusal to lay eggs.

March did most of the outdoor work. When she was out and about, in her puttees and breeches, her belted coat and her loose cap, she looked almost like some graceful, loose-balanced young man, for her shoulders were straight, and her movements easy and confident, even tinged with a little indifference or irony. But her face was not a man's face, ever. The wisps of her crisp dark hair blew about her as she stopped, her eyes were big and wide and dark, when she looked up again, strange, startled, shy and sardonic at once. Her mouth, too, was almost pinched as if in pain and irony. There was something odd and unexplained about her. She would stand balanced on one hip, looking at the fowls pattering about in the obnoxious fine mud of the sloping yard, and calling to her favourite white hen, which came in answer to her name. But there was an almost satirical flicker in March's big, dark eyes, as she looked at her three-toed flock pottering about under her gaze, and the same slight dangerous satire in her voice as she spoke to the favoured Patty, who pecked at March's boot by way of friendly demonstration.

Fowls did not flourish at Bailey Farm, in spite of all that March did for them. When she provided hot food for them in the morning, according to rule, she noticed that it made them heavy and dozy for hours. She expected to see them lean against the pillars of the shed in their languid processes of digestion. And she knew quite well that they ought to be busily scratching and foraging about, if they were to come to any good. She she decided to give them their hot food at night, and let them sleep on it. Which she did. But it made no difference.

War conditions, again, were very unfavourable to poultry-keeping. Food was scarce and bad. And when the Daylight Saving Bill was passed, the fowls obstinately refused to go to bed as usual, about nine o'clock in the summer-time. That was late enough, indeed, for there was no peace till they were shut up and asleep. Now they cheerfully walked around, without so much as glancing at the barn, until ten o'clock or later. Both Banford and March disbelieved in living for work alone. They wanted to read or take a cycle-ride in the evening, or perhaps March wished to paint curvilinear swans on porcelain, with green background, or else make a marvelous fire-screen by processes of elaborate cabinet work. For she was a creature of odd whims and unsatisfied tendencies. But from all these things she was prevented by the stupid fowls.

One evil there was greater than any other. Bailey Farm was a little homestead, with ancient wooden barn and low-gabled farm-house, lying just one field removed from the edge of the wood. Since the war the fox was a demon. He carried off the hens under the very noses of March and Banford. Banford would start and stare through her big spectacles with all her eyes, as another squawk and flutter took place at her heels. Too late! Another white Leghorn gone. It was disheartening.

They did what they could to remedy it. When it became permitted to shoot foxes, they stood sentinel with their guns, the two of them, at the favoured hours. But it was no good. The fox was too quick for them. So another year passed, and another, and they were living on their losses, as Banford said. They let their farm-house one summer, and retired to live in a railway-carriage that was deposited as a sort of out-house in a corner of the field. This amused them, and helped their finances. None the less, things looked dark.

Although they were usually the best of friends, because Banford, though nervous and delicate, was a warm, generous soul, and March, though so odd and absent in herself, had a strange magnanimity, yet, in the long solitude, they were apt to become a little irritable with one another, tired of one another. March had four-fifths of the work to do, and though she did not mind, there seemed no relief, and it made her eyes flash curiously sometimes. Then Banford, feeling more nerve-worn than ever, would become despondent, and March would speak sharply to her. They seemed to be losing ground, somehow, losing hope as the months went by. There alone in the fields by the wood, with the wide country stretching hollow and dim to the round hills of the White Horse, in the far distance, they seemed to have to live too much off themselves. There was nothing to keep them up—and no hope.

The fox really exasperated them both. As soon as they had let the fowls out, in the early summer mornings, they had to take their guns and keep guard: and then again as soon as evening began to mellow, they must go once more. And he was so sly. He slid along in the deep grass; he was difficult as a serpent to see. And he seemed to circumvent the girls deliberately. Once or twice March had caught sight of the white tip of his brush, or the ruddy shadow of him in the deep grass, and she had let fire at him. But he made no account of this.

One evening March was standing with her back to the sunset, her gun under her arm, her hair pushed under her cap. She was half watching, half musing. It was her constant state. Her eyes were keen and observant, but her inner mind took no notice of what she saw. She was always lapsing into this odd, rapt state, her mouth rather screwed up. It was a question whether she was there, actually consciously present, or not.

The trees on the wood-edge were a darkish, brownish green in the full light—for it was the end of August. Beyond, the naked, copper-like shafts and limbs of the pine trees shone in the air. Nearer the rough grass, with its long, brownish stalks all agleam, was full of light. The fowls were round about—the ducks were still swimming on the pond under the pine trees. March looked at it all, saw it all, and did not see it. She heard Banford speaking to the fowls in the distance—and she did not hear. What was she thinking about? Heaven knows. Her consciousness was, as it were, held back.

She lowered her eyes, and suddenly saw the fox. He was looking up at her. His chin was pressed down, and his eyes were looking up. They met her eyes. And he knew her. She was spellbound—she knew he knew her. So he looked into her eyes, and her soul failed her. He knew her, he was not daunted.

She struggled, confusedly she came to herself, and saw him making off, with slow leaps over some fallen boughs, slow, impudent jumps. Then he glanced over his shoulder, and ran smoothly away. She saw his brush held smooth like a feather, she saw his white buttocks twinkle. And he was gone, softly, soft as the wind.

She put her gun to her shoulder, but even then pursed her mouth, knowing it was nonsense to pretend to fire. So she began to walk slowly after him, in the direction he had gone, slowly, pertinaciously. She expected to find him. In her heart she was determined to find him. What she would do when she saw him again she did not consider. But she was determined to find him. So she walked abstractedly about on the edge of the wood, with wide, vivid dark eyes, and a faint flush in her cheeks. She did not think. In strange mindlessness she walked hither and thither.

At last she became aware that Banford was calling her. She made an effort of attention, turned, and gave some sort of screaming call in answer. Then again she was striding off towards the homestead. The red sun was setting, the fowls were retiring towards their roost. She watched them, white creatures, black creatures, gathering to the barn. She watched them spellbound, without seeing them. But her automatic intelligence told her when it was time to shut the door.

She went indoors to supper, which Banford had set on the table. Banford chatted easily. March seemed to listen, in her distant, manly way. She answered a brief word now and then. But all the time she was as if spellbound. And as soon as supper was over, she rose again to go out, without saying why.

She took her gun again and went to look for the fox. For he had lifted

his eyes upon her, and his knowing look seemed to have entered her brain.
She did not so much think of him: she was possessed by him. She saw his
dark, shrewd, unabashed eye looking into her knowing her. She felt him
invisibly master her spirit. She knew the way he lowered his chin as he
looked up, she knew his muzzle, the golden brown, and the greyish white.
And again she saw him glance over his shoulder at her, half inviting, half
contemptuous and cunning. So she went, with her great startled eyes glowing, her gun under her arm, along the wood edge. Meanwhile the night
fell, and a great moon rose above the pine trees. And again Banford was
calling.

So she went indoors. She was silent and busy. She examined her gun,
and cleaned it, musing abstractedly by the lamplight. Then she went out
again, under the great moon, to see if everything was right. When she saw
the dark crests of the pine trees against the blood-red sky, again her heart
beat to the fox, the fox. She wanted to follow him, with her gun.

It was some days before she mentioned the affair to Banford. Then suddenly one evening she said:

"The fox was right at my feet on Saturday night."

"Where?" said Banford, her eyes opening behind her spectacles.

"When I stood just above the pond."

"Did you fire?" cried Banford.

"No, I didn't."

"Why not?"

"Why, I was too much surprised, I suppose."

It was the same old, slow, laconic way of speech March always had. Banford stared at her friend for a few moments.

"You saw him?" she cried.

"Oh yes! He was looking up at me, cool as anything."

"I tell you," cried Banford—"the cheek! They're not afraid of us,
Nellie."

"Oh no," said March.

"Pity you didn't get a shot at him," said Banford.

"Isn't it a pity! I've been looking for him ever since. But I don't suppose
he'll come so near again."

"I don't suppose he will," said Banford.

And she proceeded to forget about it, except that she was more indignant
than ever at the impudence of the beggar. March also was not conscious
that she thought of the fox. But whenever she fell into her half-musing,
when she was half rapt and half intelligently aware of what passed under
her vision, then it was the fox which somehow dominated her unconscious-
ness, possessed the blank half of her musing. And so it was for weeks, and
months. No matter whether she had been climbing the trees for the apples,
or beating down the last of the damsons, or whether she had been digging
out the ditch from the duck-pound, or clearing out the barn, when she had
finished, or when she straightened herself, and pushed the wisps of hair

away again from her forehead, and pursed up her mouth again in an odd, screwed fashion, much too old for her years, there was sure to come over her mind the old spell of the fox, as it came when he was looking at her. It was as if she could smell him at these times. And it always recurred, at unexpected moments, just as she was going to sleep at night, or just as she was pouring the water into the tea-pot to make tea—it was the fox, it came over her like a spell.

So the months passed. She still looked for him unconsciously when she went towards the wood. He had become a settled effect in her spirit, a state permanently established, not continuous, but always recurring. She did not know what she felt or thought: only the state came over her, as when he looked at her.

The months passed, the dark evenings came, heavy, dark November, when March went about in high boots, ankle deep in mud, when the night began to fall at four o'clock, and the day never properly dawned. Both girls dreaded these times. They dreaded the almost continuous darkness that enveloped them on their desolate little farm near the wood. Banford was physically afraid. She was afraid of tramps, afraid lest someone should come prowling around. March was not so much afraid as uncomfortable, and disturbed. She felt discomfort and gloom in all her physique.

Usually the two girls had tea in the sitting-room. March lighted a fire at dusk, and put on the wood she had chopped and sawed during the day. Then the long evening was in front, dark, sodden, black outside, lonely and rather oppressive inside, a little dismal. March was content not to talk, but Banford could not keep still. Merely listening to the wind in the pines outside, or the drip of water, was too much for her.

One evening the girls had washed up the tea-cups in the kitchen, and March had put on her house-shoes, and taken up a roll of crochet-work, which she worked at slowly from time to time. So she lapsed into silence. Banford stared at the red fire, which, being of wood, needed constant attention. She was afraid to begin to read too early, because her eyes would not bear any strain. So she sat staring at the fire, listening to the distant sounds, sound of cattle lowing, of a dull, heavy moist wind, of the rattle of the evening train on the little railway not far off. She was almost fascinated by the red glow of the fire.

Suddenly both girls started, and lifted their heads. They heard a footstep —distinctly a footstep. Banford recoiled in fear. March stood listening. Then rapidly she approached the door that led into the kitchen. At the same time they heard the footsteps approach the back door. They waited a second. The back door opened softly. Banford gave a loud cry. A man's voice said softly:

"Hello!"

March recoiled, and took a gun from a corner.

"What do you want?" she cried, in a sharp voice.

Again the soft, softly-vibrating man's voice said:

"Hello! What's wrong?"

"I shall shoot!" cried March. "What do you want?"

"Why, what's wrong? What's wrong?" came the soft, wondering, rather scared voice: and a young soldier, with his heavy kit on his back, advanced into the dim light.

"Why," he said, "who lives here then?"

"We live here," said March. "What do you want?"

"Oh!" came the long, melodious, wonder-note from the young soldier. "Doesn't William Grenfel live here then?"

"No—you know he doesn't."

"Do I? Do I? I don't, you see. He *did* live here, because he was my grandfather, and I lived here myself five years ago. What's become of him then?"

The young man—or youth, for he would not be more than twenty—now advanced and stood in the inner doorway. March, already under the influence of his strange, soft, modulated voice, stared at him spellbound. He had a ruddy, roundish face, with fairish hair, rather long, flattened to his forehead with sweat. His eyes were blue, and very bright and sharp. On his cheeks, on the fresh ruddy skin were fine, fair hairs, like a down, but sharper. It gave him a slightly glistening look. Having his heavy sack on his shoulders, he stooped, thrusting his head forward. His hat was loose in one hand. He stared brightly, very keenly from girl to girl, particularly at March, who stood pale, with great dilated eyes, in her belted coat and puttees, her hair knotted in a big crisp knot behind. She still had the gun in her hand. Behind her, Banford, clinging to the sofa-arm, was shrinking away, with half-averted head.

"I thought my grandfather still lived here? I wonder if he's dead."

"We've been here for three years," said Banford, who was beginning to recover her wits, seeing something boyish in the round head with its rather long, sweaty hair.

"Three years! You don't say so! And you don't know who was here before you?"

"I know it was an old man, who lived by himself."

"Ay! Yes, that's him! And what became of him then?"

"He died. I know he died."

"Ay! He's dead then!"

The youth stared at them without changing colour or expression. If he had any expression, besides a slight baffled look of wonder, it was one of sharp curiosity concerning the two girls; sharp, impersonal curiosity, the curiosity of that round young head.

But to March he was the fox. Whether it was the thrusting forward of his head, or the glisten of fine whitish hairs on the ruddy cheek bones, or the bright, keen eyes, that can never be said: but the boy was to her the fox, and she could not see him otherwise.

"How is it you didn't know if your grandfather was alive or dead?" asked Banford, recovering her natural sharpness.

"Ay, that's it," replied the softly-breathing youth. "You see, I joined up in Canada, and I hadn't heard for three or four years. I ran away to Canada."

"And now have you just come from France?"

"Well—from Salonika really."

There was a pause, nobody knowing quite what to say.

"So you've nowhere to go now?" said Banford rather lamely.

"Oh, I know some people in the village. Anyhow, I can go to the 'Swan.' "

"You came on the train, I suppose. Would you like to sit down a bit?"

"Well—I don't mind."

He gave an odd little groan as he swung off his kit. Banford looked at March.

"Put the gun down," she said. "We'll make a cup of tea."

"Ay," said the youth. "We've seen enough of rifles."

He sat down rather tired on the sofa, leaning forward.

March recovered her presence of mind, and went into the kitchen. There she heard the soft young voice musing:

"Well, to think I should come back and find it like this!" He did not seem sad, not at all—only rather interestingly surprised.

"And what a difference in the place, eh?" he continued, looking round the room.

"You see a difference, do you?" said Banford.

"Yes—don't I!"

His eyes were unnaturally clear and bright, though it was the brightness of abundant health.

March was busy in the kitchen preparing another meal. It was about seven o'clock. All the time, while she was active, she was attending to the youth in the sitting-room, not so much listening to what he said as feeling the soft run of his voice. She primmed up her mouth tighter and tighter, puckering it as if it were sewed, in her effort to keep her will uppermost. Yet her large eyes dilated and glowed in spite of her; she lost herself. Rapidly and carelessly she prepared the meal, cutting large chunks of bread and margarine—for there was no butter. She racked her brain to think of something else to put on the tray—she had only bread, margarine, and jam, and the larder was bare. Unable to conjure anything up, she went into the sitting-room with her tray.

She did not want to be noticed. Above all, she did not want him to look at her. But when she came in, and was busy setting the table just behind him, he pulled himself up from his sprawling, and turned and looked over his shoulder. She became pale and wan.

The youth watched her as she bent over the table, looked at her slim, well-shapen legs, at the belted coat dropping around her thighs, at the knot of dark hair, and his curiosity, vivid and widely alert, was again arrested by her.

The lamp was shaded with a dark-green shade, so that the light was thrown downwards and the upper half of the room was dim. His face moved bright under the light, but March loomed shadowy in the distance.

She turned round, but kept her eyes sideways, dropping and lifting her dark lashes. Her mouth unpuckered as she said to Banford:

"Will you pour out?"

Then she went into the kitchen again.

"Have your tea where you are, will you?" said Banford to the youth—"unless you'd rather come to the table."

"Well," said he, "I'm nice and comfortable here, aren't I? I will have it here, if you don't mind."

"There's nothing but bread and jam," she said. And she put his plate on a stool by him. She was very happy now, waiting on him. For she loved company. And now she was no more afraid of him than if he were her own younger brother. He was such a boy.

"Nellie," she called. "I've poured you a cup out."

March appeared in the doorway, took her cup, and sat down in a corner, as far from the light as possible. She was very sensitive in her knees. Having no skirts to cover them, and being forced to sit with them boldly exposed, she suffered. She shrank and shrank, trying not to be seen. And the youth, sprawling low on the couch, glanced up at her, with long, steady, penetrating looks, till she was almost ready to disappear. Yet she held her cup balanced, she drank her tea, screwed up her mouth and held her head averted. Her desire to be invisible was so strong that it quite baffled the youth. He felt he could not see her distinctly. She seemed like a shadow within the shadow. And ever his eyes came back to her, searching, unremitting, with unconscious fixed attention.

Meanwhile he was talking softly and smoothly to Banford, who loved nothing so much as gossip, and who was full of perky interest, like a bird. Also he ate largely and quickly and voraciously, so that March had to cut more chunks of bread and margarine, for the roughness of which Banford apologised.

"Oh, well," said March, suddenly speaking, "if there's no butter to put on it, it's no good trying to make dainty pieces."

Again the youth watched her, and he laughed, with a sudden, quick laugh, showing his teeth and wrinkling his nose.

"It isn't, is it," he answered in his soft, near voice.

It appeared he was Cornish by birth and upbringing. When he was twelve years old he had come to Bailey Farm with his grandfather, with whom he had never agreed very well. So he had run away to Canada, and worked far away in the West. Now he was here—and that was the end of it.

He was very curious about the girls, to find out exactly what they were doing. His questions were those of a farm youth; acute, practical, a little mocking. He was very much amused by their attitude to their losses; for they were amusing on the score of heifers and fowls.

"Oh, well," broke in March, "we don't believe in living for nothing but work."

"Don't you?" he answered. And again the quick young laugh came over his face. He kept his eyes steadily on the obscure woman in the corner.

"But what will you do when you've used up all your capital?" he said.

"Oh, I don't know," answered March laconically. "Hire ourselves out for land-workers, I suppose."

"Yes, but there won't be any demand for women landworkers now the war's over," said the youth.

"Oh, we'll see. We shall hold on a bit longer yet," said March, with a plangent, half-sad, half-ironical indifference.

"There wants a man about the place," said the youth softly.

Banford burst out laughing.

"Take care what you say," she interrupted. "We consider ourselves quite efficient."

"Oh," came March's slow plangent voice, "it isn't a case of efficiency, I'm afraid. If you're going to do farming you must be at it from morning till night, and you might as well be a beast yourself."

"Yes, that's it," said the youth. "You aren't willing to put yourselves into it."

"We aren't," said March, "and we know it."

"We want some of our time for ourselves," said Banford.

The youth threw himself back on the sofa, his face tight with laughter, and laughed silently but thoroughly. The calm scorn of the girls tickled him tremendously.

"Yes," he said, "but why did you begin then?"

"Oh," said March, "we had a better opinion of the nature of fowls then than we have now."

"Of Nature altogether, I'm afraid," said Banford. "Don't talk to me about Nature."

Again the face of the youth tightened with delighted laughter.

"You haven't a very high opinion of fowls and cattle, have you?" he said.

"Oh no—quite a low one," said March.

He laughed out.

"Neither fowls nor heifers," said Banford, "nor goats nor the weather."

The youth broke into a sharp yap of laughter, delighted. The girls began to laugh too, March turning aside her face and wrinkling her mouth in amusement.

"Oh, well," said Banford, "we don't mind, do we, Nellie?"

"No," said March, "we don't mind."

The youth was very pleased. He had eaten and drunk his fill. Banford began to question him. His name was Henry Grenfel—no, he was not called Harry, always Henry. He continued to answer with courteous simplicity, grave and charming. March, who was not included, cast long, slow glances at him from her recess, as he sat there on the sofa, his hands clasping his knees, his face under the lamp bright and alert, turned to Banford. She became almost peaceful at last. He was identified with the fox—and he was here in full presence. She need not go after him any more. There in the shadow of her corner she gave herself up to a warm, relaxed peace, almost like sleep, accepting the spell that was on her. But she wished to remain hidden. She was only fully at peace whilst he forgot her, talking to Banford. Hidden in the shadow of the corner, she need not any more be divided in herself, trying to keep up two planes of consciousness. She could at last lapse into the odour of the fox.

For the youth, sitting before the fire in his uniform, sent a faint but distinct odour into the room, indefinable, but something like a wild creature. March no longer tried to reserve herself from it. She was still and soft in her corner like a passive creature in its cave.

At last the talk dwindled. The youth relaxed his clasp of his knees, pulled himself together a little, and looked round. Again he became aware of the silent, half-invisible woman in the corner.

"Well," he said unwillingly, "I suppose I'd better be going, or they'll be in bed at the 'Swan.' "

"I'm afraid they're in bed, anyhow," said Banford. "They've all got this influenza."

"Have they!" he exclaimed. And he pondered. "Well," he continued, "I shall find a place somewhere."

"I'd say you could stay here, only——" Banford began.

He turned and watched her, holding his head forward.

"What?" he asked.

"Oh, well," she said, "propriety, I suppose." She was rather confused.

"It wouldn't be improper, would it?" he said, gently surprised.

"Not as far as we're concerned," said Banford.

"And not as far as *I'm* concerned," he said, with grave naiveté. "After all, it's my own home, in a way."

Banford smiled at this.

"It's what the village will have to say," she said.

There was a moment's blank pause.

"What do you say, Nellie?" asked Banford.

"I don't mind," said March, in her distinct tone. "The village doesn't matter to me, anyhow."

"No," said the youth, quick and soft. "Why should it? I mean, what should they say?"

"Oh, well," came March's plangent, laconic voice, "they'll easily find something to say. But it makes no difference what they say. We can look after ourselves."

"Of course you can," said the youth.

"Well then, stop if you like," said Banford. "The spare room is quite ready."

His face shone with pleasure.

"If you're quite sure it isn't troubling you too much," he said, with that soft courtesy which distinguished him.

"Oh, it's no trouble," they both said.

He looked, smiling with delight, from one to another.

"It's awfully nice not to have to turn out again, isn't it?" he said gratefully.

"I suppose it is," said Banford.

March disappeared to attend to the room. Banford was as pleased and thoughtful as if she had her own younger brother home from France. It gave her just the same kind of gratification to attend on him, to get out the bath for him, and everything. Her natural warmth and kindliness had now an outlet. And the youth luxuriated in her sisterly attention. But it puzzled him slightly to know that March was silently working for him too. She was so curiously silent and obliterated. It seemed to him he had not really seen her. He felt he should not know her if he met her in the road.

That night March dreamed vividly. She dreamed she heard a singing outside which she could not understand, a singing that roamed round the house, in the fields, and in the darkness. It moved her so that she felt she must weep. She went out, and suddenly she knew it was the fox singing. He was very yellow and bright, like corn. She went nearer to him, but he ran away and ceased singing. He seemed near, and she wanted to touch him. She stretched out her hand, but suddenly he bit her wrist, and at the same instant, as she drew back, the fox, turning round to bound away, whisked his brush across her face, and it seemed his brush was on fire, for it seared and burned her mouth with a great pain. She awoke with the pain of it, and lay trembling as if she were really seared.

In the morning, however, she only remembered it as a distant memory. She arose and was busy preparing the house and attending to the fowls. Banford flew into the village on her bicycle to try and buy food. She was a hospitable soul. But alas, in the year 1918 there was not much good to buy. The youth came downstairs in his shirt-sleeves. He was young and fresh, but he walked with his head thrust forward, so that his shoulders seemed raised and rounded, as if he had a slight curvature of the spine. It must have been only a manner of bearing himself, for he was young and vigorous. He washing himself and went outside, whilst the women were preparing breakfast.

He saw everything, and examined everything. His curiosity was quick and insatiable. He compared the state of things with that which he remembered before, and cast over in his mind the effect of the changes. He watched the fowls and the ducks, to see their condition; he noticed the flight of wood-pigeons overhead: they were very numerous; he saw the few apples high up, which March had not been able to reach; he remarked that they had borrowed a draw-pump, presumably to empty the big soft-water cistern which was on the north side of the house.

"It's a funny, dilapidated old place," he said to the girls, as he sat at breakfast.

His eyes were wise and childish, with thinking about things. He did not say much, but ate largely. March kept her face averted. She, too, in the early morning could not be aware of him, though something about the glint of his khaki reminded her of the brilliance of her dream-fox.

During the day the girls went about their business. In the morning he attended to the guns, shot a rabbit and a wild duck that was flying high towards the wood. That was a great addition to the empty larder. The girls felt that already he had earned his keep. He said nothing about leaving, however. In the afternoon he went to the village. He came back at tea-time. He had the same alert, forward-reaching look on his roundish face. He hung his hat on a peg with a little swinging gesture. He was thinking about something.

"Well," he said to the girls, as he sat at table. "What am I going to do?"

"How do you mean—what are you going to do?" said Banford.

"Where am I going to find a place in the village to stay?" he said.

"I don't know," said Banford. "Where do you think of staying?"

"Well"—he hesitated—"at the 'Swan' they've got this 'flu, and at the 'Plough and Harrow' they've got the soldiers who are collecting the hay for the army: besides, in the private houses, there's ten men and a corporal altogether billeted in the village, they tell me. I'm not sure where I could get a bed."

He left the matter to them. He was rather calm about it. March sat with her elbows on the table, her two hands supporting her chin, looking at him unconsciously. Suddenly he lifted his clouded blue eyes, and unthinking looked straight into March's eyes. He was startled as well as she. He, too, recoiled a little. March felt the same sly, taunting, knowing spark leap out of her eyes, as he turned his head aside, and fall into her soul, as had fallen from the dark eyes of the fox. She pursed her mouth as if in pain, as if asleep too.

"Well, I don't know," Banford was saying. She seemed reluctant, as if she were afraid of being imposed upon. She looked at March. But, with her weak, troubled sight, she only saw the usual semi-abstraction on her friend's face. "Why don't you speak, Nellie?" she said.

But March was wide-eyed and silent, and the youth, as if fascinated, was watching her without moving his eyes.

"Go on—answer something," said Banford. And March turned her head slightly aside, as if coming to consciousness, or trying to come to consciousness.

"What do you expect me to say?" she asked automatically.

"Say what you think," said Banford.

"It's all the same to me," said March.

And again there was silence. A pointed light seemed to be on the boy's eyes, penetrating like a needle.

"So it is to me," said Banford. "You can stop on here if you like."

A smile like a cunning little flame came over his face, suddenly and involuntarily. He dropped his head quickly to hide it, and remained with his head dropped, his face hidden.

"You can stop on here if you like. You can please yourself, Henry," Banford concluded.

Still he did not reply, but remained with his head dropped. Then he lifted his face. It was bright with a curious light, as if exultant, and his eyes were strangely clear as he watched March. She turned her face aside, her mouth suffering as if wounded, and her consciousness dim.

Banford became a little puzzled. She watched the steady, pellucid gaze of the youth's eyes as he looked at March, with the invisible smile gleaming on his face. She did not know how he was smiling, for no feature moved. It seemed only in the gleam, almost the glitter of the fine hairs on his cheeks. Then he looked with quite a changed look at Banford.

"I'm sure," he said in his soft, courteous voice, "you're awfully good. You're too good. You don't want to be bothered with me, I'm sure."

"Cut a bit of bread, Nellie," said Banford uneasily, adding: "It's no bother, if you like to stay. It's like having my own brother here for a few days. He's a boy like you are."

"That's awfully kind of you," the lad repeated. "I should like to stay ever so much, if you're sure I'm not a trouble to you."

"No, of course you're no trouble. I like you, it's a pleasure to have somebody in the house besides ourselves," said warm-hearted Banford.

"But Miss March?" he said in his soft voice, looking at her.

"Oh, it's quite all right as far as I'm concerned," said March vaguely.

His face beamed, and he almost rubbed his hands with pleasure.

"Well then," he said, "I should love it, if you'd let me pay my board and help with the work."

"You've no need to talk about board," said Banford.

One or two days went by, and the youth stayed on at the farm. Banford was quite charmed by him. He was so soft and courteous in speech, not wanting to say much himself, preferring to hear what she had to say, and to laugh in his quick, half-mocking way. He helped readily with the work— but not too much. He loved to be out alone with the gun in his hands, to watch, to see. For his sharp-eyed, impersonal curiosity was insatiable, and he was most free when he was quite alone, half-hidden, watching.

Particularly he watched March. She was a strange character to him. Her figure, like a graceful young man's piqued him. Her dark eyes made some-thing rise in his soul, with a curious elate excitement, when he looked into them, an excitement he was afraid to let be seen, it was so keen and secret. And then her odd, shrewd speech made him laugh outright. He felt he must go further, he was inevitably impelled. But he put away the thought of her and went off towards the wood's edge with the gun.

The dusk was falling as he came home, and with the dusk, a fine, late November rain. He saw the fire-light leaping in the window of the sitting-room, a leaping light in the little cluster of the dark buildings. And he thought to himself it would be a good thing to have this place for his own. And then the thought entered him shrewdly: Why not marry March? He stood still in the middle of the field, for some moments, the dead rabbit hanging still in his hand, arrested by this thought. His mind waited in amazement—it seemed to calculate—and then he smiled curiously to him-self in acquiescence. Why not? Why not indeed? It was a good idea. What if it was rather ridiculous? What did it matter? What if she was older than he? It didn't matter. When he thought of her dark, startled, vulnerable eyes he smiled subtly to himself. He was older than she, really. He was master of her.

He scarcely admitted his intention even to himself. He kept it as a secret even from himself. It was all too uncertain as yet. He would have to see how things went. Yes, he would have to see how things went. If he wasn't careful, she would just simply mock at the idea. He knew, sly and subtle as he was, that if he went to her plainly and said: "Miss March, I love you and want you to marry me," her inevitable answer would be: "Get out. I don't want any of that tomfoolery." This was her attitude to men and their 'tomfoolery'. If he was not careful, she would turn round on him with her savage, sardonic ridicule, and dismiss him from the farm and from her own mind for ever. He would have to go gently. He would have to catch her as you catch a deer or a woodcock when you go out shooting. It's no good walking into the forest and saying to the deer: "Please fall to my gun." No, it is a slow, subtle battle. When you really go out to get a deer, you gather yourself together, you coil yourself inside yourself, and you advance secretly, before dawn, into the mountains. It is not so much what you do, when you go out hunting, as how you feel. You have to be subtle and cun-ning and absolutely fatally ready. It becomes like a fate. Your own fate overtakes and determines the fate of the deer you are hunting. First of all, even before you come in sight of your quarry, there is a strangle battle, like mesmerism. Your own soul, as a hunter, has gone out to fasten on the soul of the deer, even before you see any deer. And the soul of the deer fights to escape. Even before the deer has any wind of you, it is so. It is a subtle, profound battle of wills which takes place in the invisible. And it is a battle never finished till your bullet goes home. When you are *really* worked up to the true pitch, and you come at last into range, you don't then aim as you do when you are firing at a bottle. It is your own *will* which carries the bullet into the heart of your quarry. The bullet's flight home is a sheer projection of your own fate into the fate of the deer. It happens like a supreme wish, a supreme act of volition, not as a dodge of cleverness.

He was a huntsman in spirit, not a farmer, and not a soldier stuck in a regiment. And it was as a young hunter that he wanted to bring down March as his quarry, to make her his wife. So he gathered himself subtly together, seemed to withdraw into a kind of invisibility. He was not quite sure how he would go on. And March was suspicious as a hare. So he remained in appearance just the nice, odd stranger-youth, staying for a fortnight on the place.

He had been sawing logs for the fire in the afternoon. Darkness came very early. It was still a cold, raw mist. It was getting almost too dark to see. A pile of short sawed logs lay beside the trestle. March came to carry them indoors, or into the shed, as he was busy sawing the last log. He was working in his shirt-sleeves, and did not notice her approach; she came unwillingly, as if shy. He saw her stooping to the bright-ended logs, and he stopped sawing. A fire like lightning flew down his legs in the nerves.

"March?" he said in his quiet, young voice.

She looked up from the logs she was piling.

"Yes!" she said.

He looked down on her in the dusk. He could see her not too distinctly.

"I wanted to ask you something," he said.

"Did you? What was it?" she said. Already the fright was in her voice. But she was too much mistress of herself.

"Why"—his voice seemed to draw out soft and subtle, it penetrated her nerves—"why, what do you think it is?"

She stood up, placed her hands on her hips, and stood looking at him transfixed, without answering. Again he burned with a sudden power.

"Well," he said, and his voice was so soft it seemed rather like a subtle touch, like the merest touch of a cat's paw, a feeling rather than a sound. "Well—I wanted to ask you to marry me."

March felt rather than heard him. She was trying in vain to turn aside her face. A great relaxation seemed to have come over her. She stood silent, her head slightly on one side. He seemed to be bending towards her, invisibly smiling. It seemed to her fine sparks came out of him.

Then very suddenly she said:

"Don't try any of your tomfoolery on me."

A quiver went over his nerves. He had missed. He waited a moment to collect himself again. Then he said, putting all the strange softness into his voice, as if he were imperceptibly stroking her:

"Why, it's not tomfoolery. It's not tomfoolery. I mean it. I mean it. What makes you disbelieve me?"

He sounded hurt. And his voice had such a curious power over her;

making her feel loose and relaxed. She struggled somewhere for her own power. She felt for a moment that she was lost—lost—lost. The word seemed to rock in her as if she were dying. Suddenly again she spoke.

"You don't know what you are talking about," she said, in a brief and transient stroke of scorn. "What nonsense! I'm old enough to be your mother."

"Yes, I do know what I'm talking about. Yes, I do," he persisted softly, as if he were producing his voice in her blood. "I know quite well what I'm talking about. You're not old enough to be my mother. That isn't true. And what does it matter even if it was? You can marry me whatever age we are. What is age to me? And what is age to you! Age is nothing."

A swoon went over her as he concluded. He spoke rapidly—in the rapid Cornish fashion—and his voice seemed to sound in her somewhere where she was helpless against it. "Age is nothing!" The soft, heavy insistence of it made her sway dimly out there in the darkness. She could not answer.

A great exultance leaped like fire over his limbs. He felt he had won.

"I want to marry you, you see. Why shouldn't I?" he proceeded, soft and rapid. He waited for her to answer. In the dusk he saw her almost phosphorescent. Her eyelids were dropped, her face half-averted and unconscious. She seemed to be in his power. But he waited, watchful. He dared not yet touch her.

"Say then," he said, "say then you'll marry me. Say—say!" He was softly insistent.

"What?" she asked, faint, from a distance, like one in pain. His voice was now unthinkably near and soft. He drew very near to her.

"Say yes."

"Oh, I can't," she wailed helplessly, half-articulate, as if semi-conscious, and as if in pain, like one who dies. "How can I?"

"You can," he said softly, laying his hand gently on her shoulder as she stood with her head averted and dropped, dazed. "You can. Yes, you can. What makes you say you can't? You can. You can." And with awful softness he bent forward and just touched her neck with his mouth and his chin.

"Don't!" she cried, with a faint mad cry like hysteria, starting away and facing round on him. "What do you mean?" But she had no breath to speak with. It was as if she was killed.

"I mean what I say," he persisted softly and cruelly. "I want you to marry me. I want you to marry me. You know that, now, don't you? You know that, now? Don't you? Don't you?"

"What?" she said.

"Know," he replied.

"Yes," she said. "I know you say so."

"And you know I mean it, don't you?"

"I know you say so."

"You believe me?" he said.

She was silent for some time. Then she pursed her lips.

"I don't know what I believe," she said.

"Are you out there?" came Banford's voice, calling from the house.

"Yes, we're bringing in the logs," he answered.

"I thought you'd gone lost," said Banford disconsolately. "Hurry up, do, and come let's have tea. The kettle's boiling."

He stooped at once to take an armful of little logs and carry them into the kitchen, where they were piled in a corner. March also helped, filling her arms and carrying the logs on her breast as if they were some heavy child. The night had fallen cold.

When the logs were all in, the two cleaned their boots noisily on the scraper outside, then rubbed them on the mat. March shut the door and took off her old felt hat—her farm-girl hat. Her thick, crisp, black hair was loose, her face was pale and strained. She pushed back her hair vaguely and washed her hands. Banford came hurrying into the dimly-lighted kitchen, to take from the oven the scones she was keeping hot.

"Whatever have you been doing all this time?" she asked fretfully. "I thought you were never coming in. And it's ages since you stopped sawing. What were you doing out there?"

"Well," said Henry, "We had to stop that hole in the barn to keep the rats out."

"Why, I could see you standing there in the shed. I could see your shirt-sleeves," challenged Banford.

"Yes, I was just putting the saw away."

They went in to tea. March was quite mute. Her face was pale and strained and vague. The youth, who always had the same ruddy, self-contained look on his face, as though he were keeping himself to himself, had come to tea in his shirt-sleeves as if he were at home. He bent over his plate as he ate his food.

"Aren't you cold?" said Banford spitefully. "In your shirt-sleeves."

He looked up at her, with his chin near his plate, and his eyes very clear, pellucid, and unwavering as he watched her.

"No, I'm not cold," he said with his usual soft courtesy. "It's much warmer in here than it is outside, you see."

"I hope it is," said Banford, feeling nettled by him. He had a strange suave assurance and a wide-eyed bright look that got on her nerves this evening.

"But perhaps," he said softly and courteously, "you don't like me coming to tea without my coat. I forgot that."

"Oh, I don't mind," said Banford: although she *did*.

"I'll go and get it, shall I?" he said.

March's dark eyes turned slowly down to him.

"No, don't you bother," she said in her queer, twanging tone. "If you feel all right as you are, stop as you are." She spoke with a crude authority.

"Yes," said he, "I *feel* all right, if I'm not rude."

"It's usually considered rude," said Banford. "But we don't mind."

"Go along, 'considered rude,'" ejaculated March. "Who considers it rude?"

"Why, you do, Nellie, in anybody else," said Banford, bridling a little behind her spectacles, and feeling her food stick in her throat.

But March had again gone vague and unheeding, chewing her food as if she did not know she was eating at all. And the youth looked from one to another, with bright, watching eyes.

Banford was offended. For all his suave courtesy and soft voice, the youth seemed to her impudent. She did not like to look at him. She did not like to meet his clear, watchful eyes, she did not like to see the strange glow in his face, his cheeks with their delicate fine hair, and his ruddy skin that was quite dull and yet which seemed to burn with a curious heat of life. It made her feel a little ill to look at him: the quality of his physical presence was too penetrating, too hot.

After tea the evening was very quiet. The youth rarely went into the village. As a rule, he read: he was a great reader, in his own hours. That is, when he did begin, he read absorbedly. But he was not very eager to begin. Often he walked about the fields and along the hedges alone in the dark at night, prowling with a queer instinct for the night, and listening to the wild sounds.

To-night, however, he took a Captain Mayne Reid book from Banford's shelf and sat down with his knees wide apart and immersed himself in his story. His brownish fair hair was long, and lay on his head like a thick cap, combed sideways. He was still in his shirt-sleeves, and bending forward under the lamp-light, with his knees stuck wide apart and the book in his hand and his whole figure absorbed in the rather strenuous business of reading, he gave Banford's sitting-room the look of a lumber-camp. She resented this. For on her sitting-room floor she had a red Turkey rug and dark stain round, the fire-place had fashionable green tiles, the piano stood open with the latest dance music: she played quite well: and on the walls were March's hand-painted swans and water-lilies. Moreover, with the logs nicely, tremulously burning in the grate, the thick curtains drawn, the doors all shut, and the pine trees hissing and shuddering in the wind outside, it was cosy, it was refined and nice. She resented the big, raw, long-legged youth sticking his khaki knees out and sitting there with his soldier's shirt-cuffs buttoned on his thick red wrists. From time to time he turned a page, and from time to time he gave a sharp look at the fire, settling the logs. Then he immersed himself again in the intense and isolated business of reading.

March, on the far side of the table, was spasmodically crochetting. Her mouth was pursed in an odd way, as when she had dreamed the fox's brush burned it, her beautiful, crisp black hair strayed in wisps. But her whole figure was absorbed in its bearing, as if she herself was miles away. In a sort of semi-dream she seemed to be hearing the fox singing round the house in the wind, singing wildly and sweetly and like a madness. With red but well-shaped hands she slowly crochetted the white cotton, very slowly, awkwardly.

Banford was also trying to read, sitting in her low chair. But between those two she felt fidgetty. She kept moving and looking round and listening to the wind, and glancing secretly from one to the other of her companions. March, seated on a straight chair, with her knees in their close breeches crossed, and slowly, laboriously crochetting, was also a trial.

"Oh dear!" said Banford. "My eyes are bad to-night." And she pressed her fingers on her eyes.

The youth looked up at her with his clear, bright look, but did not speak.

"Are they, Jill?" said March absently.

The youth began to read again, and Banford perforce returned to her book. But she could not keep still. After a while she looked up at March, and a queer, almost malignant little smile was on her thin face.

"A penny for them, Nell," she said suddenly.

March looked round with big, startled black eyes, and went pale as if with terror. She had been listening to the fox singing so tenderly, so tenderly, as he wandered round the house.

"What?" she said vaguely.

"A penny for them," said Banford sarcastically. "Or twopence, if they're as deep as all that."

The youth was watching with bright, clear eyes from beneath the lamp.

"Why," came March's vague voice, "what do you want to waste your money for?"

"I thought it would be well spent," said Banford.

"I wasn't thinking of anything except the way the wind was blowing," said March.

"Oh dear," replied Banford, "I could have had as original thoughts as that myself. I'm afraid I *have* wasted my money this time."

"Well, you needn't pay," said March.

The youth suddenly laughed. Both women looked at him: March rather surprised-looking, as if she had hardly known he was there.

"Why, do you ever pay up on these occasions?" he asked.

"Oh yes," said Banford. "We always do. I've sometimes had to pass a shilling a week to Nellie, in the winter-time. It costs much less in summer."

"What, paying for each other's thoughts?" he laughed.

"Yes, when we've absolutely come to the end of everything else."

He laughed quickly, wrinkling his nose sharply like a puppy and laughing with quick pleasure, his eyes shining.

"It's the first time I ever heard of that," he said.

"I guess you'd hear of it often enough if you stayed a winter on Bailey Farm," said Banford lamentably.

"Do you get so tired, then?" he asked.

"So bored," said Banford.

"Oh!" he said gravely. "But why should you be bored?"

"Who wouldn't be bored?" said Banford.

"I'm sorry to hear that," he said gravely.

"You must be, if you were hoping to have a lively time here," said Banford.

He looked at her long and gravely.

"Well," he said, with his odd, young seriousness, "it's quite lively enough for me."

"I'm glad to hear it," said Banford.

And she returned to her book. In her thin, frail hair were already many threads of grey, though she was not yet thirty. The boy did not look down, but turned his eyes to March, who was sitting with pursed mouth laboriously crochetting, her eyes wide and absent. She had a warm, pale, fine skin and a delicate nose. Her pursed mouth looked shrewish. But the shrewish look was contradicted by the curious lifted arch of her dark brows, and the wideness of her eyes; a look of startled wonder and vagueness. She was listening again for the fox, who seemed to have wandered farther off into the night.

From under the edge of the lamp-light the boy sat with his face looking up, watching her silently, his eyes round and very clear and intent. Banford, biting her fingers irritably, was glancing at him under her hair. He sat there perfectly still, his ruddy face tilted up from the low level under the light, on the edge of the dimness, and watching with perfect abstract intentness. March suddenly lifted her great, dark eyes from her crochetting and saw him. She started, giving a little exclamation.

"There he is!" she cried involuntarily, as if terribly startled.

Banford looked around in amazement, sitting up straight.

"Whatever has got you, Nellie?" she cried.

But March, her face flushed a delicate rose colour, was looking away to the door.

"Nothing! Nothing!" she said crossly. "Can't one speak?"

"Yes, if you speak sensibly," said Banford. "Whatever did you mean?"

"I don't know what I meant," cried March testily.

"Oh, Nellie, I hope you aren't going jumpy and nervy. I feel I can't stand another *thing!* Whoever did you mean? Did you mean Henry?" cried poor, frightened Banford.

"Yes. I suppose so," said March laconically. She would never confess to the fox.

"Oh dear, my nerves are all gone for to-night," wailed Banford.

At nine o'clock March brought in a tray with bread and cheese and tea

—Henry had confessed that he liked a cup of tea. Banford drank a glass of milk and ate a little bread. And soon she said:

"I'm going to bed, Nellie. I'm all nerves to-night. Are you coming?"

"Yes, I'm coming the minute I've taken the tray away," said March.

"Don't be long then," said Banford fretfully. "Good-night, Henry. You'll see the fire is safe, if you come up last, won't you?"

"Yes, Miss Banford, I'll see it's safe," he replied in his reassuring way.

March was lighting the candle to go to the kitchen. Banford took her candle and went upstairs. When March came back to the fire, she said to him:

"I suppose we can trust you to put out the fire and everything?" She stood there with her hand on her hip, and one knee loose, her head averted shyly, as if she could not look at him. He had his face lifted, watching her.

"Come and sit down a minute," he said softly.

"No, I'll be going. Jill will be waiting, and she'll get upset, if I don't come."

"What made you jump like that this evening?" he asked.

"When did I jump?" she retorted, looking at him.

"Why, just now you did," he said. "When you cried out."

"Oh!" she said. "Then!—Why, I thought you were the fox!" And her face screwed into a queer smile, half-ironic.

"The fox! Why the fox?" he asked softly.

"Why, one evening last summer when I was out with the gun I saw the fox in the grass nearly at my feet, looking straight up at me. I don't know —I suppose he made an impression on me." She turned aside her head again and let one foot stray loose, self-consciously.

"And did you shoot him?" asked the boy.

"No, he gave me such a start, staring straight at me as he did, and then stopping to look back at me over his shoulder with a laugh on his face."

"A laugh on his face!" repeated Henry, also laughing. "He frightened you, did he?"

"No, he didn't frighten me. He made an impression on me, that's all."

"And you thought I was the fox, did you?" he laughed with the same queer, quick little laugh, like a puppy wrinkling his nose.

"Yes, I did, for the moment," she said. "Perhaps he'd been in my mind without my knowing."

"Perhaps you think I've come to steal your chickens or something," he said, with the same young laugh.

But she only looked at him with a wide, dark, vacant eye.

"It's the first time," he said, "that I've ever been taken for a fox. Won't you sit down for a minute?" His voice was very soft and cajoling.

"No," she said. "Jill will be waiting." But still she did not go, but stood with one foot loose and her face turned aside, just outside the circle of light.

"But won't you answer my question?" he said, lowering his voice still more.

"I don't know what question you mean."

"Yes, you do. Of course you do. I mean the question of you marrying me."

"No, I shan't answer that question," she said flatly.

"Won't you?" The queer, young laugh came on his nose again. "Is it because I'm like the fox? Is that why?" And still he laughed.

She turned and looked at him with a long, slow look.

"I wouldn't let that put you against me," he said. "Let me turn the lamp low, and come and sit down a minute."

He put his red hand under the glow of the lamp and suddenly made the light very dim. March stood there in the dimness quite shadowy, but unmoving. He rose silently to his feet, on his long legs. And now his voice was extraordinarily soft and suggestive, hardly audible.

"You'll stay a moment," he said. "Just a moment." And he put his hand on her shoulder. She turned her face from him. "I'm sure you don't really think I'm like the fox," he said, with the same softness and with a suggestion of laughter in his tone, a subtle mockery. "Do you now?" And he drew her gently towards him and kissed her neck, softly. She winced and trembled and hung away. But his strong, young arm held her, and he kissed her softly again, still on the neck, for her face was averted.

"Won't you answer my question? Won't you now?" came his soft, lingering voice. He was trying to draw her near to kiss her face. And he kissed her cheek softly, near the ear.

At that moment Banford's voice was heard calling fretfully, crossly from upstairs.

"There's Jill!" cried March, starting and drawing erect.

And as she did so, quick as lightning he kissed her on the mouth, with a quick, brushing kiss. It seemed to burn through her every fibre. She gave a queer little cry.

"You will, won't you? You will?" he insisted softly.

"Nellie! *Nellie!* Whatever are you so long for?" came Banford's faint cry fom the outer darkness.

But he held her fast, and was murmuring with that intolerable softness and insistency:

"You will, won't you? Say yes! Say yes!"

March, who felt as if the fire had gone through her and scathed her, and as if she could do no more, murmured:

"Yes! Yes! Anything you like! Anything you like! Only let me go! Only let me go! Jill's calling."

"You know you've promised," he said insidiously.

"Yes! Yes! I do!" Her voice suddenly rose into a shrill cry. "All right, Jill, I'm coming."

Startled, he let her go, and she went straight upstairs.

In the morning at breakfast, after he had looked round the place and attended to the stock and thought to himself that one could live easily enough here, he said to Banford:

"Do you know what, Miss Banford?"

"Well, what?" said the good-natured, nervy Banford.

He looked at March, who was spreading jam on her bread.

"Shall I tell?" he said to her.

She looked up at him, and a deep pink colour flushed over her face.

"Yes, if you mean Jill," she said. "I hope you won't go talking all over the village, that's all." And she swallowed her dry bread with difficulty.

"Whatever's coming?" said Banford, looking up with wide, tired, slightly reddened eyes. She was a thin, frail little thing, and her hair, which was delicate and thin, was bobbed, so it hung softly by her worn face in its faded brown and grey.

"Why, what do you think?" he said, smiling like one who has a secret.

"How do I know!" said Banford.

"Can't you guess?" he said, making bright eyes and smiling, pleased with himself.

"I'm sure I can't. What's more, I'm not going to try."

"Nellie and I are going to be married."

Banford put down her knife out of her thin, delicate fingers, as if she would never take it up to eat any more. She stared with blank, reddened eyes.

"You what?" she exclaimed.

"We're going to get married. Aren't we, Nellie?" and he turned to March.

"You say so, anyway," said March, laconically. But again she flushed with an agonised flush. She, too, could swallow no more.

Banford looked at her like a bird that has been shot: a poor, little sick bird. She gazed at her with all her wounded soul in her face, at the deep-flushed March.

"Never!" she exclaimed, helpless.

"It's quite right," said the bright and gloating youth.

Banford turned aside her face, as if the sight of the food on the table made her sick. She sat like this for some moments, as if she were sick. Then, with one hand on the edge of the table, she rose to her feet.

"I'll *never* believe it, Nellie," she cried. "It's absolutely impossible!"

Her plaintive, fretful voice had a thread of hot anger and despair.

"Why? Why shouldn't you believe it?" asked the youth, with all his soft, velvety impertinence in his voice.

Banford looked at him from her wide, vague eyes, as if he were some creature in a museum.

"Oh," she said languidly, "because she can never be such a fool. She can't lose her self-respect to such an extent." Her voice was cold and plain-tive, drifting.

"In what way will she lose her self-respect?" asked the boy.

Banford looked at him with vague fixity from behind her spectacles.

"If she hasn't lost it already," she said.

He became very red, vermilion, under the slow, vague stare from behind the spectacles.

"I don't see it at all," he said.

"Probably you don't. I shouldn't expect you would," said Banford, with that straying mild tone of remoteness which made her words even more insulting.

He sat stiff in his chair, staring with hot, blue eyes from his scarlet face. An ugly look had come on his brow.

"My word, she doesn't know what she's letting herself in for," said Ban-ford, in her plaintive, drifting, insulting voice.

"What has it got to do with you, anyway?" said the youth, in a temper.

"More than it has to do with you, probably," she replied, plaintive and venomous.

"Oh, has it! I don't see that at all," he jerked out.

"No, you wouldn't," she answered, drifting.

"Anyhow," said March, pushing back her hair and rising uncouthly. "It's no good arguing about it." And she seized the bread and tea-pot and strode away to the kitchen.

Banford let her fingers stray across her brow and along her hair, like one bemused. Then she turned and went away upstairs.

Henry sat stiff and sulky in his chair, with his face and his eyes on fire. March came and went, clearing the table. But Henry sat on, stiff with temper. He took no notice of her. She had regained her composure and her soft, even, creamy complexion. But her mouth was pursed up. She glanced at him each time as she came to take things from the table, glanced from her large, curious eyes, more in curiosity than anything. Such a long, red-faced, sulky boy! That was all he was. He seemed as remote from her as if his red face were a red chimney-pot on a cottage across the fields, and she looked at him just as objectively, as remotely.

At length he got up and stalked out into the fields with the gun. He came in only at dinner-time, with the devil still in his face, but his manners quite polite. Nobody said anything particular; they sat each one at the sharp corner of a triangle, in obstinate remoteness. In the afternoon he went out again at once with the gun. He came in at nightfall with a rabbit and a pigeon. He stayed in all the evening, but hardly opened his mouth. He was in the devil of a temper, feeling he had been insulted.

Banford's eyes were red, she had evidently been crying. But the manner was more remote and supercilious than ever; the way she turned her head if he spoke at all, as if he were some tramp or inferior intruder of that sort, made his blue eyes go almost black with rage. His face looked sulkier. But he never forgot his polite intonation, if he opened his mouth to speak.

March seemed to flourish in this atmosphere. She seemed to sit between the two antagonists with a little wicked smile on her face, enjoying herself. There was even a sort of complacency in the way she laboriously crochetted this evening.

When he was in bed, the youth could hear the two women talking and arguing in their room. He sat up in bed and strained his ears to hear what they said. But he could hear nothing, it was too far off. Yet he could hear the soft, plaintive drip of Banford's voice, and March's deeper note.

The night was quiet, frosty. Big stars were snapping outside, beyond the ridge-tops of the pine trees. He listened and listened. In the distance he heard a fox yelping: and the dogs from the farms barking in answer. But it was not that he wanted to hear. It was what the two women were saying.

He got stealthily out of bed and stood by his door. He could hear no more than before. Very, very carefully he began to lift the door latch. After quite a time he had his door open. Then he stepped stealthily out into the passage. The old oak planks were cold under his feet, and they creaked preposterously. He crept very, very gently up the one step, and along by the wall, till he stood outside their door. And there he held his breath and listened. Banford's voice:

"No, I simply couldn't stand it. I should be dead in a month. Which is just what he would be aiming at, of course. That would just be his game, to see me in the churchyard. No, Nellie, if you were to do such a thing as to marry him, you could never stop here. I couldn't, I couldn't live in the same house with him. Oh!—h! I feel quite sick with the smell of his clothes. And his red face simply turns me over. I can't eat my food when he's at the table. What a fool I was ever to let him stop. One ought *never* to try to do a kind action. It always flies back in your face like a boomerang."

"Well, he's only got two more days," said March.

"Yes, thank heaven. And when he's gone he'll never come in this house again. I feel so bad while he's here. And I know, I know he's only counting what he can get out of you. I *know* that's all it is. He's just a good-for-nothing, who doesn't want to work, and who thinks he'll live on us. But he won't live on me. If you're such a fool, then it's your own lookout. Mrs. Burgess knew him all the time he was here. And the old man could never get him to do any steady work. He was off with the gun on every occasion, just as he is now. Nothing but the gun! Oh, I do hate it. You don't know what you're doing, Nellie, you don't. If you marry him he'll just make a fool of you. He'll go off and leave you stranded. I know he will, if he can't get Bailey Farm out of us—and he's not going to, while I live. While I live he's never going to set foot here. I know what it would be. He'd soon think he was master of both of us, as he thinks he's master of you already."

"But he isn't," said Nellie.

"He thinks he is, anyway. And that's what he wants: to come and be master here. Yes, imagine it! That's what we've got the place together for, is it, to be bossed and bullied by a hateful, red-faced boy, a beastly labourer. Oh, we *did* make a mistake when we let him stop. We ought never to have lowered ourselves. And I've had such a fight with all the people here, not to be pulled down to their level. No, he's not coming here. And then you see—if he can't have the place, he'll run off to Canada or somewhere again, as if he'd never known you. And here you'll be, absolutely ruined and made a fool of. I know I shall never have any peace of mind again."

"We'll tell him he can't come here. We'll tell him that," said March.

"Oh, don't you bother; I'm going to tell him that, and other things as well, before he goes. He's not going to have all his own way while I've got the strength left to speak. Oh, Nellie, he'll despise you, he'll despise you, like the awful little beast he is, if you give way to him. I'd no more trust him than I'd trust a cat not to steal. He's deep, he's deep, and he's bossy, and he's selfish through and through, as cold as ice. All he wants is to make use of you. And when you're no more use to him, then I pity you."

"I don't think he's as bad as all that," said March.

"No, because he's been playing up to you. But you'll find out, if you see much of him. Oh, Nellie, I can't bear to think of it."

"Well, it won't hurt you, Jill, darling."

"Won't it! Won't it! I shall never know a moment's peace again while I live, nor a moment's happiness. No, Nellie—" and Banford began to weep bitterly.

The boy outside could hear the stifled sound of the woman's sobbing, and could hear March's soft, deep, tender voice comforting, with wonderful gentleness and tenderness, the weeping woman.

His eyes were so round and wide that he seemed to see the whole night, and his ears were almost jumping off his head. He was frozen stiff. He crept back to bed, but felt as if the top of his head were coming off. He could not sleep. He could not keep still. He rose, quietly dressed himself, and crept out onto the landing once more. The women were silent. He went softly downstairs and out to the kitchen.

Then he put on his boots and his overcoat and took the gun. He did not think to go away from the farm. No, he only took the gun. As softly as possible he unfastened the door and went out into the frosty December night. The air was still, the stars bright, the pine trees seemed to bristle audibly in the sky. He went stealthily away down a fence-side, looking for something to shoot. At the same time he remembered that he ought not to shoot and frighten the women.

So he prowled round the edge of the gorse cover, and through the grove of tall old hollies, to the woodside. There he skirted the fence, peering through the darkness with dilated eyes that seemed to be able to grow black and full of sight in the dark, like a cat's. An owl was slowly and mournfully whooing round a great oak tree. He stepped stealthily with his gun, listening, listening, watching.

As he stood under the oaks of the wood-edge he heard the dogs from the neighbouring cottage up the hill yelling suddenly and startlingly, and the wakened dogs from the farms around barking answer. And suddenly it seemed to him England was little and tight, he felt the landscape was constricted even in the dark, and that there were too many dogs in the night, making a noise like a fence of sound, like the network of English hedges netting the view. He felt the fox didn't have a chance. For it must be the fox that had started all this hullabaloo.

Why not watch for him, anyhow! He would, no doubt, be coming sniffing round. The lad walked downhill to where the farmstead with its few pine trees crouched blackly. In the angle of the long shed, in the black dark, he crouched down. He knew the fox would be coming. It seemed to him it would be the last of the foxes in this loudly-barking, thick-voiced England, tight with innumerable little houses.

He sat a long time with his eyes fixed unchanging upon the open gateway, where a little light seemed to fall from the stars or from the horizon, who knows. He was sitting on a log in a dark corner with the gun across his knees. The pine trees snapped. Once a chicken fell off its perch in the barn with a loud crawk and cackle and commotion that startled him, and he stood up, watching with all his eyes, thinking it might be a rat. But he *felt* it was nothing. So he sat down again with the gun on his knees and his hands tucked in to keep them warm, and his eyes fixed unblinking on the pale reach of the open gateway. He felt he could smell the hot, sickly, rich smell of live chickens on the cold air.

And then—a shadow. A sliding shadow in the gateway. He gathered all his vision into a concentrated spark, and saw the shadow of the fox, the fox creeping on his belly through the gate. There he went, on his belly like a snake. The boy smiled to himself and brought the gun to his shoulder. He knew quite well what would happen. He knew the fox would go to where the fowl door was boarded up and sniff there. He knew he would lie there for a minute, sniffing the fowls within. And then he would start again prowling under the edge of the old barn, waiting to get in.

The fowl door was at the top of a slight incline. Soft, soft as a shadow the fox slid up this incline, and crouched with his nose to the boards. And at the same moment there was the awful crash of a gun reverberating between the old buildings, as if all the night had gone smash. But the boy watched keenly. He saw even the white belly of the fox as the beast beat his paws in death. So he went forward.

There was a commotion everywhere. The fowls were scuffling and crawking, the ducks were quark-quarking, the pony had stamped wildly to his feet. But the fox was on his side, struggling in his last tremors. The boy bent over him and smelt his foxy smell.

There was a sound of a window opening upstairs, then March's voice calling:

"Who is it?"

"It's me," said Henry; "I've shot the fox."

"Oh, goodness! You nearly frightened us to death."

"Did I? I'm awfully sorry."

"Whatever made you get up?"

"I heard him about."

"And have you shot him?"

"Yes, he's here," and the boy stood in the yard holding up the warm, dead brute. "You can't see, can you? Wait a minute." And he took his flash-light from his pocket and flashed it on to the dead animal. He was holding it by the brush. March saw, in the middle of the darkness, just the reddish fleece and the white belly and the white underneath of the pointed chin, and the queer, dangling paws. She did not know what to say.

"He's a beauty," he said. "He will make you a lovely fur."

"You don't catch me wearing a fox fur," she replied.

"Oh!" he said. And he switched off the light.

"Well, I should think you'll come in and go to bed again now," she said.

"Probably I shall. What time is it?"

"What time is it, Jill?" called March's voice. It was a quarter to one.

That night March had another dream. She dreamed that Banford was dead, and that she, March, was sobbing her heart out. Then she had to put Banford into her coffin. And the coffin was the rough wood-box in which the bits of chopped wood were kept in the kitchen, by the fire. This was the coffin, and there was no other, and March was in agony and dazed bewilderment, looking for something to line the box with, something to make it soft with, something to cover up the poor, dead darling. Because she couldn't lay her in there just in her white, thin night-dress, in the horrible wood-box. So she hunted and hunted, and picked up thing after thing, and threw it aside in the agony of dream-frustration. And in her dream-despair all she could find that would do was a fox-skin. She knew that it wasn't right, that this was not what she should have. But it was all she could find. And so she folded the brush of the fox, and laid her darling Jill's head on this, and she brought round the skin of the fox and laid it on the top of the body, so that it seemed to make a whole ruddy, fiery coverlet, and she cried and cried, and woke to find the tears streaming down her face.

The first thing that both she and Banford did in the morning was to go out to see the fox. Henry had hung it up by the heels in the shed, with its poor brush falling backwards. It was a lovely dog-fox in its prime, with a handsome, thick, winter coat: a lovely golden-red colour, with grey as it passed to the belly, and belly all white, and a great full brush with a delicate black and grey and pure white tip.

"Poor brute!" said Banford. "If it wasn't such a thieving wretch, you'd feel sorry for it."

March said nothing, but stood with her foot trailing aside, one hip out; her face was pale and her eyes big and black, watching the dead animal that was suspended upside down. White and soft as snow his belly: white and soft as snow. She passed her hand softly down it. And his wonderful black-glinted brush was full and frictional, wonderful. She passed her hand down this also, and quivered. Time after time she took the full fur of that thick tail between her fingers, and passed her hand slowly downwards. Wonderful, sharp, thick, splendour of a tail. And he was dead! She pursed her lips, and her eyes went black and vacant. Then she took the head in her hand.

Henry was sauntering up, so Banford walked rather pointedly away. March stood there bemused, with the head of the fox in her hand. She was wondering, wondering, wondering over his long, fine muzzle. For some reason it reminded her of a spoon or a spatula. She felt she could not understand it. The beast was a strange beast to her, incomprehensible, out of her range. Wonderful silver whiskers he had, like ice-threads. And pricked ears with hair inside. But that long, long, slender spoon of a nose! —and the marvellous white teeth beneath! It was to thrust forward and bite with, deep, deep, deep into the living prey, to bite and bite the blood.

"He's a beauty, isn't he?" said Henry, standing by.

"Oh yes, he's a fine big fox. I wonder how many chickens he's responsible for," she replied.

"A good many. Do you think he's the same one you saw in the summer?"

"I should think very likely he is," she replied.

He watched her, but he could make nothing of her. Partly she was so shy and virgin, and partly she was so grim, matter-of-fact, shrewish. What she said seemed to him so different from the look of her big, queer, dark eyes.

"Are you going to skin him?" she asked.

"Yes, when I've had breakfast, and got a board to peg him on."

"My word, what a strong smell he's got! Pooo! It'll take some washing off one's hands. I don't know why I was so silly as to handle him." And she looked at her right hand, that had passed down his belly and along his tail, and had even got a tiny streak of blood from one dark place in his fur.

"Have you seen the chickens when they smell him, how frightened they are?" he said.

"Yes, aren't they!"

"You must mind you don't get some of his fleas."

"Oh, fleas!" she replied, nonchalant.

Later in the day she saw the fox's skin nailed flat on a board, as if crucified. It gave her an uneasy feeling.

The boy was angry. He went about with his mouth shut, as if he had swallowed part of his chin. But in behaviour he was polite and affable. He did not say anything about his intention. And he left March alone.

That evening they sat in the dining-room. Banford wouldn't have him in her sitting-room any more. There was a very big log on the fire. And every-body was busy. Banford had letters to write, March was sewing a dress, and he was mending some little contrivance.

Banford stopped her letter-writing from time to time to look round and rest her eyes. The boy had his head down, his face hidden over his job.

"Let's see," said Banford. "What train do you go by, Henry?"

He looked up straight at her.

"The morning train. In the morning," he said.

"What, the eight-ten or the eleven-twenty?"

"The eleven-twenty, I suppose," he said.

"That is the day after to-morrow?" said Banford.

"Yes, the day after to-morrow."

"Mm!" murmured Banford, and she returned to her writing. But as she was licking her envelope, she asked:

"And what plans have you made for the future, if I may ask?"

"Plans?" he said, his face very bright and angry.

"I mean about you and Nellie, if you are going on with this business. When do you expect the wedding to come off?" She spoke in a jeering tone.

"Oh, the wedding!" he replied. "I don't know."

"Don't you know anything?" said Banford. "Are you going to clear out on Friday and leave things no more settled than they are?"

"Well, why shouldn't I? We can always write letters."

"Yes, of course you can. But I wanted to know because of this place. If Nellie is going to get married all of a sudden, I shall have to be looking round for a new partner."

"Couldn't she stay on here if she were married?" he said. He knew quite well what was coming.

"Oh," said Banford, "this is no place for a married couple. There's not enough work to keep a man going, for one thing. And there's no money to be made. It's quite useless your thinking of staying on here if you marry. Absolutely!"

"Yes, but I wasn't thinking of staying on here," he said.

"Well, that's what I want to know. And what about Nellie, then? How long is she going to be here with me, in that case?"

The two antagonists looked at one another.

"That I can't say," he answered.

"Oh, go along," she cried petulantly. "You must have some idea what you are going to do, if you ask a woman to marry you. Unless it's all a hoax."

"Why should it be a hoax? I am going back to Canada."

"And taking her with you?"

"Yes, certainly."

"You hear that, Nellie?" said Banford.

March, who had had her head bent over her sewing, now looked up with a sharp, pink blush on her face, and a queer, sardonic laugh in her eyes and on her twisted mouth.

"That's the first time I've heard that I was going to Canada," she said.

"Well, you have to hear it for the first time, haven't you?" said the boy.

"Yes, I suppose I have," she said nonchalantly. And she went back to her sewing.

"You're quite ready, are you, to go to Canada? Are you, Nellie?" asked Banford.

March looked up again. She let her shoulders go slack, and let her hand that held the needle lie loose in her lap.

"It depends on *how* I'm going," she said. "I don't think I want to go jammed up in the steerage, as a soldier's wife. I'm afraid I'm not used to that way."

The boy watched her with bright eyes.

"Would you rather stay over here while I go first?" he asked.

"I would, if that's the only alternative," she replied.

"That's much the wisest. Don't make it any fixed engagement," said Banford. "Leave yourself free to go or not after he's got back and found you a place, Nellie. Anything else is madness, madness."

"Don't you think," said the youth, "we ought to get married before I go —and then go together, or separate, according to how it happens?"

"I think it's a terrible idea," cried Banford.

But the boy was watching March.

"What do you think?" he asked her.

She let her eyes stray vaguely into space.

"Well, I don't know," she said. "I shall have to think about it."

"Why?" he asked pertinently.

"Why?" She repeated his question in a mocking way and looked at him laughing, though her face was pink again. "I should think there's plenty of reasons why."

He watched her in silence. She seemed to have escaped him. She had got into league with Banford against him. There was again the queer, sardonic look about her; she would mock stoically at everything he said or which life offered.

"Of course," he said, "I don't want to press you to do anything you don't wish to do."

"I should think not, indeed," cried Banford indignantly.

At bed-time Banford said plaintively to March:

"You take my hot bottle up for me, Nellie, will you?"

"Yes, I'll do it," said March, with the kind of willing unwillingness she so often showed towards her beloved but uncertain Jill.

The two women went upstairs. After a time March called from the top of the stairs: "Good-night, Henry. I shan't be coming down. You'll see to the lamp and the fire, won't you?"

The next day Henry went about with the cloud on his brow and his young cub's face shut up tight. He was cogitating all the time. He had wanted March to marry him and go back to Canada with him. And he had been sure she would do it. Why he wanted her he didn't know. But he did want her. He had set his mind on her. And he was convulsed with a youth's fury at being thwarted. To be thwarted, to be thwarted! It made him so furious inside that he did not know what to do with himself. But he kept himself in hand. Because even now things might turn out differently. She might come over to him. Of course she might. It was her business to do so.

Things drew to a tension again toward evening. He and Banford had avoided each other all day. In fact, Banford went in to the little town by the 11.20 train. It was market day. She arrived back on the 4.25. Just as the night was falling Henry saw her little figure in a dark-blue coat and a dark-blue tam-o'-shanter hat crossing the first meadow from the station. He stood under one of the wild pear trees, with the old dead leaves round his feet. And he watched the little blue figure advancing persistently over the rough winter-ragged meadow. She had her arms full of parcels, and advanced slowly, frail thing she was, but with that devilish little certainty which he so detested in her. He stood invisible under the pear tree, watching her every step. And if looks could have affected her, she would have felt a log of iron on each of her ankles as she made her way forward. "You're a nasty little thing, you are," he was saying softly, across the distance. "You're a nasty little thing. I hope you'll be paid back for all the harm you've done me for nothing. I hope you will—you nasty little thing. I hope you'll have to pay for it. You will, if wishes are anything. You nasty little creature that you are."

She was toiling slowly up the slope. But if she had been slipping back at every step towards the Bottomless Pit, he would not have gone to help her with her parcels. Aha, there went March, striding with her long, land stride in her breeches and her short tunic! Striding downhill at a great pace, and even running a few steps now and then, in her great solicitude and desire to come to the rescue of the little Banford. The boy watched her with rage in his heart. See her leap a ditch, and run, run as if a house was on fire, just to get to that creeping, dark little object down there! So, the Banford just stood still and waited. And March strode up and took *all* the parcels except a bunch of yellow chrysanthemums. These the Banford still carried—yellow chrysanthemums!

"Yes, you look well, don't you?" he said softly into the dusk air. "You look well, pottering up there with a bunch of flowers, you do. I'd make you eat them for your tea if you hug them so tight. And I'd give them you for breakfast again, I would. I'd give you flowers. Nothing but flowers."

He watched the progress of the two women. He could hear their voices: March always outspoken and rather scolding in her tenderness, Banford murmuring rather vaguely. They were evidently good friends. He could not hear what they said till they came to the fence of the home meadow, which they must climb. Then he saw March manfully climbing over the bars with all her packages in her arms, and on the still air he heard Banford's fretful:

"Why don't you let me help you with the parcels?" She had a queer, plaintive hitch in her voice. Then came March's robust and reckless:

"Oh, I can manage. Don't you bother about me. You've all you can do to get yourself over."

"Yes, that's all very well," said Banford fretfully. "You say, *Don't you bother about me*, and then all the while you feel injured because nobody thinks of you."

"When do I feel injured?" said March.

"Always. You always feel injured. Now you're feeling injured because I won't have that boy to come and live on the farm."

"I'm not feeling injured at all," said March.

"I know you are. When he's gone you'll sulk over it. I know you will."

"Shall I?" said March. "We'll see."

"Yes, we *shall* see, unfortunately. I can't think how you can make yourself so cheap. I can't *imagine* how you can lower yourself like it."

"I haven't lowered myself," said March.

"I don't know what you call it, then. Letting a boy like that come so cheeky and impudent and make a mug of you. I don't know what you think of yourself. How much respect do you think he's going to have for you afterwards? My word, I wouldn't be in your shoes, if you married him."

"Of course you wouldn't. My boots are a good bit too big for you, and not half dainty enough," said March, with rather a misfire sarcasm.

"I thought you had too much pride, really I did. A woman's got to hold herself high, especially with a youth like that. Why, he's impudent. Even the way he forced himself on us at the start."

"We asked him to stay," said March.

"Not till he'd almost forced us to. And then he's so cocky and self-assured. My word, he puts my back up. I simply can't imagine how you can let him treat you so cheaply."

"I don't let him treat me cheaply," said March. "Don't you worry yourself, nobody's going to treat me cheaply. And even you aren't, either." She had a tender defiance and a certain fire in her voice.

"Yes, it's sure to come back to me," said Banford bitterly. "That's always the end of it. I believe you only do it to spite me."

They went now in silence up the steep, grassy slope and over the brow, through the gorse bushes. On the other side of the hedge the boy followed in the dusk, at some little distance. Now and then, through the huge ancient hedge of hawthorn, risen into trees, he saw the two dark figures creeping up the hill. As he came to the top of the slope he saw the homestead dark in the twilight, with a huge old pear tree leaning from the near gable, and a little yellow light twinkling in the small side windows of the kitchen. He heard the clink of the latch and saw the kitchen door open into light as the two women went indoors. So they were at home.

And so!—this was what they thought of him. It was rather in his nature to be a listener, so he was not at all surprised whatever he heard. The things people said about him always missed him personally. He was only rather surprised at the women's way with one another. And he disliked the Banford with an acid dislike. And he felt drawn to the March again. He felt again irresistibly drawn to her. He felt there was a secret bond, a secret thread between him and her, something very exclusive, which shut out everybody else and made him and her possess each other in secret.

He hoped again that she would have him. He hoped with his blood suddenly firing up that she would agree to marry him quite quickly: at Christmas, very likely. Christmas was not far off. He wanted, whatever else happened, to snatch her into a hasty marriage and a consummation with him. Then for the future, they could arrange later. But he hoped it would happen as he wanted it. He hoped that to-night she would stay a little while with him, after Banford had gone upstairs. He hoped he could touch her soft, creamy cheek, her strange, frightened face. He hoped he could look into her dilated, frightened dark eyes, quite near. He hoped he might even put his hand on her bosom and feel her soft breasts under her tunic. His heart beat deep and powerful as he thought of that. He wanted very much to do so. He wanted to make sure of her soft woman's breasts under her tunic. She always kept the brown linen coat buttoned so close up to her throat. It seemed to him like some perilous secret, that her soft woman's breasts must be buttoned up in that uniform. It seemed to him, moreover, that they were so much softer, tenderer, more lovely and lovable, shut up in that tunic, than were the Banford's breasts, under her soft blouses and chiffon dresses. The Banford would have little iron breasts, he said to himself. For all her frailty and fretfulness and delicacy, she would have tiny iron breasts. But March, under her crude, fast, workman's tunic, would have soft, white breasts, white and unseen. So he told himself, and his blood burned.

When he went in to tea, he had a surprise. He appeared at the inner door, his face very ruddy and vivid and his blue eyes shining, dropping his head forward as he came in, in his usual way, and hesitating in the doorway to watch the inside of the room, keenly and cautiously, before he entered. He was wearing a long-sleeved waistcoat. His face seemed extraordinarily like a piece of the out-of-doors come indoors: as holly-berries do. In his second of pause in the doorway he took in the two women sitting at table, at opposite ends, saw them sharply. And to his amazement March was dressed in a dress of dull, green silk crape. His mouth came open in surprise. If she had suddenly grown a moustache he could not have been more surprised.

"Why," he said, "do you wear a dress, then?"

She looked up, flushing a deep rose colour, and twisting her mouth with a smile, said:

"Of course I do. What else do you expect me to wear but a dress?"

"A land girl's uniform, of course," said he.

"Oh," she cried, nonchalant, "that's only for this dirty, mucky work about here."

"Isn't it your proper dress, then?" he said.

"No, not indoors it isn't," she said. But she was blushing all the time as she poured out his tea. He sat down in his chair at table, unable to take his eyes off her. Her dress was a perfectly simple slip of bluey-green crape, with a line of gold stitching round the top and round the sleeves, which came to the elbow. It was cut just plain and round at the top, and showed her white, soft throat. Her arms he knew, strong and firm muscled, for he had often seen her with her sleeves rolled up. But he looked her up and down, up and down.

Banford, at the other end of the table, said not a word, but piggled with the sardine on her plate. He had forgotten her existence. He just simply stared at March while he ate his bread and margarine in huge mouthfuls, forgetting even his tea.

"Well, I never knew anything make such a difference!" he murmured, across his mouthfuls.

"Oh, goodness!" cried March, blushing still more. "I might be a pink monkey!"

And she rose quickly to her feet and took the tea-pot to the fire, to the kettle. And as she crouched on the hearth with her green slip about her, the boy stared more wide-eyed than ever. Through the crape her woman's form seemed soft and womanly. And when she stood up and walked he saw her legs move soft within her modernly short skirt. She had on black silk stockings, and small patent shoes with little gold buckles.

No, she was another being. She was something quite different. Seeing her always in the hard-cloth breeches, wide on the hips, buttoned on the knee, strong as armour, and in the brown puttees and thick boots, it had never occurred to him that she had a woman's legs and feet. Now it came upon him. She had a woman's soft, skirted legs, and she was accessible. He blushed to the roots of his hair, shoved his nose in his tea-cup and drank his tea with a little noise that made Banford simply squirm: and strangely, suddenly he felt a man, no longer a youth. He felt a man, with all a man's grave weight of responsibility. A curious quietness and gravity came over his soul. He felt a man, quiet, with a little of the heaviness of male destiny upon him.

She was soft and accessible in her dress. The thought went home in him like an everlasting responsibility.

"Oh, for goodness' sake, say something, somebody," cried Banford fretfully. "It might be a funeral." The boy looked at her, and she could not bear his face.

"A funeral!" said March, with a twisted smile. "Why, that breaks my dream."

Suddenly she had thought of Banford in the wood-box for a coffin.

"What, have you been dreaming of a wedding?" said Banford sarcastically.

"Must have been," said March.

"Whose wedding?" asked the boy.

"I can't remember," said March.

She was shy and rather awkward that evening, in spite of the fact that, wearing a dress, her bearing was much more subdued than in her uniform. She felt unpeeled and rather exposed. She felt almost improper.

They talked desultorily about Henry's departure next morning, and made the trivial arrangement. But of the matter on their minds, none of them spoke. They were rather quiet and friendly this evening; Banford had practically nothing to say. But inside herself she seemed still, perhaps kindly.

At nine o'clock March brought in the tray with the everlasting tea and a little cold meat which Banford had managed to procure. It was the last supper, so Banford did not want to be disagreeable. She felt a bit sorry for the boy, and felt she must be as nice as she could.

He wanted her to go to bed. She was usually the first. But she sat on in her chair under the lamp, glancing at her book now and then, and staring into the fire. A deep silence had come into the room. It was broken by March asking, in a rather small tone:

"What time is it, Jill?"

"Five past ten," said Banford, looking at her wrist.

And then not a sound. The boy had looked up from the book he was holding between his knees. His rather wide, cat-shaped face had its obstinate look, his eyes were watchful.

"What about bed?" said March at last.

"I'm ready when you are," said Banford.

"Oh, very well," said March. "I'll fill your bottle."

She was as good as her word. When the hot-water bottle was ready, she lit a candle and went upstairs with it. Banford remained in her chair, listening acutely. March came downstairs again.

"There you are, then," she said. "Are you going up?"

"Yes, in a minute," said Banford. But the minute passed, and she sat on in her chair under the lamp.

Henry, whose eyes were shining like a cat's as he watched from under his brows, and whose face seemed wider, more chubbed and cat-like with unalterable obstinacy, now rose to his feet to try his throw.

"I think I'll go and look if I can see the she-fox," he said. "She may be creeping round. Won't you come as well for a minute, Nellie, and see if we see anything?"

"Me!" cried March, looking up with her startled, wondering face.

"Yes. Come on," he said. It was wonderful how soft and warm and coaxing his voice could be, how near. The very sound of it made Banford's blood boil. "Come on for a minute," he said, looking down into her uplifted, unsure face.

And she rose to her feet as if drawn up by his young, ruddy face that was looking down on her.

"I should think you're never going out at this time of night, Nellie!" cried Banford.

"Yes, just for a minute," said the boy, looking round on her, and speaking with an odd, sharp yelp in his voice.

March looked from one to the other, as if confused, vague. Banford rose to her feet for battle.

"Why, it's ridiculous. It's bitter cold. You'll catch your death in that thin frock. And in those slippers. You're not going to do any such thing."

There was a moment's pause. Banford turtled up like a little fighting cock, facing March and the boy.

"Oh, I don't think you need worry yourself," he replied. "A moment under the stars won't do anybody any damage. I'll get the rug off the sofa in the dining-room. You're coming, Nellie."

His voice had so much anger and contempt and fury in it as he spoke to Banford: and so much tenderness and proud authority as he spoke to March, that the latter answered:

"Yes, I'm coming."

And she turned with him to the door.

Banford, standing there in the middle of the room, suddenly burst into a long wail and a spasm of sobs. She covered her face with her poor, thin hands, and her thin shoulders shook in an agony of weeping. March looked back from the door.

"Jill!" she cried in a frantic tone, like someone just coming awake. And she seemed to start towards her darling.

But the boy had March's arm in his grip, and she could not move. She did not know why she could not move. It was as in a dream when the heart strains and the body cannot stir.

"Never mind," said the boy softly. "Let her cry. Let her cry. She will have to cry sooner or later. And the tears will relieve her feelings. They will do her good."

So he drew March slowly through the doorway. But her last look was back to the poor little figure which stood in the middle of the room with covered face and thin shoulders shaken with bitter weeping.

In the dining-room he picked up the rug and said:

"Wrap yourself up in this."

She obeyed—and they reached the kitchen door, he holding her soft and firm by the arm, though she did not know it. When she saw the night outside she started back.

"I must go back to Jill," she said. "I *must!* Oh yes, I must."

Her tone sounded final. The boy let go of her and she turned indoors. But he seized her again and arrested her.

"Wait a minute," he said. "Wait a minute. Even if you go, you're not going yet."

"Leave go! Leave go!" she cried. "My place is at Jill's side. Poor little thing, she's sobbing her heart out."

"Yes," said the boy bitterly. "And your heart too, and mine as well."

"Your heart?" said March. He still gripped her and detained her.

"Isn't it as good as her heart?" he said. "Or do you think it's not?"

"Your heart?" she said again, incredulous.

"Yes, mine! Mine! Do you think I haven't *got* a heart?" And with his hot grasp he took her hand and pressed it under his left breast. "There's my heart," he said, "if you don't believe in it."

It was wonder which made her attend. And then she felt the deep, heavy, powerful stroke of his heart, terrible, like something from beyond. It was like something from beyond, something awful from outside, signalling to her. And the signal paralysed her. It beat upon her very soul, and made her helpless. She forgot Jill. She could not think of Jill any more. She could not think of her. That terrible signalling from outside!

The boy put his arm round her waist.

"Come with me," he said gently. "Come and let us say what we've got to say."

And he drew her outside, closed the door. And she went with him darkly down the garden path. That he should have a beating heart! And that he should have his arm round her, outside the blanket! She was too confused to think who he was or what he was.

He took her to a dark corner of the shed, where there was a tool-box with a lid, long and low.

"We'll sit here a minute," he said.

And obediently she sat down by his side.

"Give me your hand," he said.

She gave him both her hands, and he held them between his own. He was young, and it made him tremble.

"You'll marry me. You'll marry me before I go back, won't you?" he pleaded.

"Why, aren't we both a pair of fools?" she said.

He had put her in the corner, so that she should not look out and see the lighted window of the house across the dark garden. He tried to keep her all there inside the shed with him.

"In what way a pair of fools?" he said. "If you go back to Canada with me, I've got a job and a good wage waiting for me, and it's a nice place, near the mountains. Why shouldn't you marry me? Why shouldn't we marry? I should like to have you there with me. I should like to feel I'd got somebody there, at the back of me, all my life."

"You'd easily find somebody else who'd suit you better," she said.

"Yes, I might easily find another girl. I know I could. But not one I really wanted. I've never met one I really wanted for good. You see, I'm thinking of all my life. If I marry, I want to feel it's for all my life. Other girls: well, they're just girls, nice enough to go a walk with now and then. Nice enough for a bit of play. But when I think of my life, then I should be very sorry to have to marry one of them, I should indeed."

"You mean they wouldn't make you a good wife."

"Yes, I mean that. But I don't mean they wouldn't do their duty by me. I mean—I don't know what I mean. Only when I think of my life, and of you, then the two things go together."

"And what if they didn't?" she said, with her odd, sardonic touch.

"Well, I think they would."

They sat for some time silent. He held her hands in his, but he did not make love to her. Since he had realised that she was a woman, and vulnerable, accessible, a certain heaviness had possessed his soul. He did not want to make love to her. He shrank from any such performance, almost with fear. She was a woman, and vulnerable, accessible to him finally, and he held back from that which was ahead, almost with dread. It was a kind of darkness he knew he would enter finally, but of which he did not want as yet even to think. She was the woman, and he was responsible for the strange vulnerability he had suddenly realised in her.

"No," she said at last, "I'm a fool. I know I'm a fool."

"What for?" he asked.

"To go on with this business."

"Do you mean me?" he asked.

"No, I mean myself. I'm making a fool of myself, and a big one."

"Why, because you don't want to marry me, really?"

"Oh, I don't know whether I'm against it, as a matter of fact. That's just it. I don't know."

He looked at her in the darkness, puzzled. He did not in the least know what she meant.

"And don't you know whether you like to sit here with me this minute or not?" he asked.

"No, I don't really. I don't know whether I wish I was somewhere else, or whether I like being here. I don't know, really."

"Do you wish you were with Miss Banford? Do you wish you'd gone to bed with her?" he asked, as a challenge.

She waited a long time before she answered.

"No," she said at last. "I don't wish that."

"And do you think you would spend all your life with her—when your hair goes white, and you are old?" he said.

"No," she said, without much hesitation. "I don't see Jill and me two old women together."

"And don't you think, when I'm an old man and you're an old woman, we might be together still, as we are now?" he said.

"Well, not as we are now," she replied. "But I could imagine—no, I can't. I can't imagine you an old man. Besides, it's dreadful!"

"What, to be an old man?"

"Yes, of course."

"Not when the time comes," he said. "But it hasn't come. Only it will. And when it does, I should like to think you'd be there as well."

"Sort of old age pensions," she said dryly.

Her kind of witless humour always startled him. He never knew what she meant. Probably she didn't quite know herself.

"No," he said, hurt.

"I don't know why you harp on old age," she said. "I'm not ninety."

"Did anybody ever say you were?" he asked, offended.

They were silent for some time, pulling different ways in the silence.

"I don't want you to make fun of me," he said.

"Don't you?" she replied, enigmatic.

"No, because just this minute I'm serious. And when I'm serious, I believe in not making fun of it."

"You mean nobody else must make fun of you," she replied.

"Yes, I mean that. And I mean I don't believe in making fun of it myself. When it comes over me so that I'm serious, then—there it is, I don't want it to be laughed at."

She was silent for some time. Then she said, in a vague, almost pained voice:

"No, I'm not laughing at you."

A hot wave rose in his heart.

"You believe me, do you?" he asked.

"Yes, I believe you," she replied, with a twang of her old, tired nonchalance, as if she gave in because she was tired. But he didn't care. His heart was hot and clamorous.

"So you agree to marry me before I go?—perhaps at Christmas?"

"Yes, I agree."

"There!" he exclaimed. "That's settled it."

And he sat silent, unconscious, with all the blood burning in all his veins, like fire in all the branches and twigs of him. He only pressed her two hands to his chest, without knowing. When the curious passion began to die down, he seemed to come awake to the world.

"We'll go in, shall we?" he said: as if he realised it was cold.

She rose without answering.

"Kiss me before we go, now you've said it," he said.

And he kissed her gently on the mouth, with a young, frightened kiss. It made her feel so young, too, and frightened, and wondering: and tired, tired, as if she were going to sleep.

They went indoors. And in the sitting-room, there, crouched by the fire like a queer little witch, was Banford. She looked round with reddened eyes as they entered, but did not rise. He thought she looked frightening, unnatural crouching there and looking round at them. Evil he thought her look was, and he crossed his fingers.

Banford saw the ruddy, elate face on the youth: he seemed strangely tall and bright and looming. And March had a delicate look on her face; she wanted to hide her face, to screen it, to let it not be seen.

"You've come at last," said Banford uglily.

"Yes, we've come," said he.

"You've been long enough for anything," she said.

"Yes, we have. We've settled it. We shall marry as soon as possible," he replied.

"Oh, you've settled it, have you! Well, I hope you won't live to repent it," said Banford.

"I hope so too," he replied.

"Are you going to bed *now*, Nellie?" said Banford.

"Yes, I'm going now."

"Then for goodness' sake come along."

March looked at the boy. He was glancing with his very bright eyes at her and at Banford. March looked at him wistfully. She wished she could stay with him. She wished she had married him already, and it was all over. For oh, she felt suddenly so safe with him. She felt so strangely safe and peaceful in his presence. If only she could sleep in his shelter, and not with Jill. She felt afraid of Jill. In her dim, tender state, it was agony to have to go with Jill and sleep with her. She wanted the boy to save her. She looked again at him.

And he, watching with bright eyes, divined something of what she felt. It puzzled and distressed him that she must go with Jill.

"I shan't forget what you've promised," he said, looking clear into her eyes, right into her eyes, so that he seemed to occupy all herself with his queer, bright look.

She smiled at him faintly, gently. She felt safe again—safe with him.

But in spite of all the boy's precautions, he had a setback. The morning he was leaving the farm he got March to accompany him to the market-town, about six miles away, where they went to the registrar and had their names stuck up as two people who were going to marry. He was to come at Christmas, and the wedding was to take place then. He hoped in the spring to be able to take March back to Canada with him, now the war was really over. Though he was so young, he had saved some money.

"You never have to be without *some* money at the back of you, if you can help it," he said.

So she saw him off in the train that was going West: his camp was on Salisbury Plain. And with big, dark eyes she watched him go, and it seemed as if everything real in life was retreating as the train retreated with his queer, chubby, ruddy face, that seemed so broad across the cheeks, and which never seemed to change its expression, save when a cloud of sulky anger hung on the brow, or the bright eyes fixed themselves in their stare. This was what happened now. He leaned there out of the carriage window as the train drew off, saying good-bye and staring back at her, but his face quite unchanged. There was no emotion on his face. Only his eyes tightened and became fixed and intent in their watching like a cat's when suddenly she sees something and stares. So the boy's eyes stared fixedly as the train drew away, and she was left feeling intensely forlorn. Failing his physical presence, she seemed to have nothing of him. And she had nothing of anything. Only his face was fixed in her mind: the full, ruddy unchanging cheeks, and the straight snout of a nose and the two eyes staring above. All she could remember was how he suddenly wrinkled his nose when he laughed, as a puppy does when he is playfully growling. But him, himself, and what he was—she knew nothing, she had nothing of him when he left her.

On the ninth day after he had left her he received this letter.

"Dear Henry,

"I have been over it all again in my mind, this business of me and you, and it seems to me impossible. When you aren't there I see what a fool I am. When you are there you seem to blind me to things as they actually are. You make me see things all unreal, and I don't know what. Then when I am alone again with Jill I seem to come to my own senses and realise what a fool I am making of myself, and how I am treating you unfairly. Because it must be unfair to you for me to go on with this affair when I can't feel in my heart that I really love you. I know people talk a lot of stuff and nonsense about love, and I don't want to do that. I want to keep to plain facts and act in a sensible way. And that seems to me what I'm not doing. I don't see on what grounds I am going to marry you. I know I am not head over heels in love with you, as I have fancied myself to be with fellows when I was a young fool of a girl. You are an absolute stranger to me, and it seems to me you will always be one. So on what grounds am I going to marry you? When I think of Jill, she is ten times more real to me. I know her and I'm awfully fond of her, and I hate myself for a beast if I ever hurt her little finger. We have a life together. And even if it can't last for ever, it is a life while it does last. And it might last as long as either of us lives. Who knows how long we've got to live? She is a delicate little thing, perhaps nobody but me knows how delicate. And as for me, I feel I might fall down the well any day. What I don't seem to see at all is you. When I think of what I've been and what I've done with you, I'm afraid I am a few screws loose. I should be sorry to think that softening of the brain is setting in so soon, but that is what it seems like. You are such an absolute stranger, and so different from what I'm used to, and we don't seem to have a thing in common. As for love, the very word seems impossible. I know what love means even in Jill's case, and I know that in this affair with you it's an absolute impossibility. And then going to Canada. I'm sure I must have been clean off my chump when I promised such a thing. It makes me feel fairly frightened of myself. I feel I might do something really silly that I wasn't responsible for—and end my days in a lunatic asylum. You may think that's all I'm fit for after the way I've gone on, but it isn't a very nice thought for me. Thank goodness Jill is here, and her being here makes me feel sane again, else I don't know what I might do; I might have an accident with the gun one evening. I love Jill, and she makes me feel safe and sane, with her loving anger against me for being such a fool. Well, what I want to say is, won't you let us cry the whole thing off? I can't marry you, and really, I won't do such a thing if it seems to me wrong. It is all a great mistake. I've made a complete fool of myself, and all I can do is to apologise to you and ask you please to forget it, and please to take no further notice of me. Your fox-skin is nearly ready, and seems all right. I will post it to you if you will let me know if this address is still right, and if you will accept my apology for the awful and lunatic way I have behaved with you, and then let the matter rest.

"Jill sends her kindest regards. Her mother and father are staying with us over Christmas.

> "Yours very sincerely,
>
> "ELLEN MARCH"

The boy read this letter in camp as he was cleaning his kit. He set his teeth, and for a moment went almost pale, yellow round the eyes with fury. He said nothing and saw nothing and felt nothing but a livid rage that was quite unreasoning. Balked! Balked again! Balked! He wanted the woman, he had fixed like doom upon having her. He felt that was his doom, his destiny, and his reward to have this woman. She was his heaven and hell on earth, and he would have none elsewhere. Sightless with rage and thwarted madness he got through the morning. Save that in his mind he was lurking and scheming towards an issue, he would have committed some insane act. Deep in himself he felt like roaring and howling and gnashing his teeth and breaking things. But he was too intelligent. He knew society was on top of him, and he must scheme. So with his teeth bitten together, and his nose curiously slightly lifted, like some creature that is vicious, and his eyes fixed and staring, he went through the morning's affairs drunk with anger and suppression. In his mind was one thing—Banford. He took no heed of all March's outpouring: none. One thorn rankled, stuck in his mind. Banford. In his mind, in his soul, in his whole being, one thorn rankling to insanity. And he would have to get it out. He would have to get the thorn of Banford out of his life, if he died for it.

With this one fixed idea in his mind, he went to ask for twenty-four hours' leave of absence. He knew it was not due to him. His consciousness was supernaturally keen. He knew where he must go—he must go to the captain. But how could he get at the captain? In that great camp of wooden huts and tents he had no idea where his captain was.

But he went to the officers' canteen. There was his captain standing talking with three other officers. Henry stood in the doorway at attention.

"May I speak to Captain Berryman?" The captain was Cornish like himself.

"What do you want?" called the captain.

"May I speak to you, Captain?"

"What do you want?" replied the captain, not stirring from among his group of fellow officers.

Henry watched his superior for a minute without speaking.

"You won't refuse me, sir, will you?" he asked gravely.

"It depends what it is."

"Can I have twenty-four hours' leave?"

"No, you've no business to ask."

"I know I haven't. But I must ask you."

"You've had your answer."

"Don't send me away, Captain."

There was something strange about the boy as he stood there so everlasting in the doorway. The Cornish captain felt the strangeness at once, and eyed him shrewdly.

"Why, what's afoot?" he said, curious.

"I'm in trouble about something. I must go to Blewbury," said the boy.

"Blewbury, eh? After the girls?"

"Yes, it is a woman, Captain." And the boy, as he stood there with his head reaching forward a little, went suddenly terribly pale, or yellow, and his lips seemed to give off pain. The captain saw and paled a little also. He turned aside.

"Go on, then," he said. "But for God's sake don't cause any trouble of any sort."

"I won't, Captain, thank you."

He was gone. The captain, upset, took a gin and bitters. Henry managed to hire a bicycle. It was twelve o'clock when he left the camp. He had sixty miles of wet and muddy crossroads to ride. But he was in the saddle and down the road without a thought of food.

At the farm, March was busy with a work she had had some time in hand. A bunch of Scotch fir trees stood at the end of the open shed, on a little bank where ran the fence between two of the gorse-shaggy meadows. The farthest of these trees was dead—it had died in the summer, and stood with all its needles brown and sere in the air. It was not a very big tree. And it was absolutely dead. So March determined to have it, although they were not allowed to cut any of the timber. But it would make such splendid firing, in these days of scarce fuel.

She had been giving a few stealthy chops at the trunk for a week or more, every now and then hacking away for five minutes, low down, near the ground, so no one should notice. She had not tried the saw, it was such hard work, alone. Now the tree stood with a great yawning gap in his base, perched, as it were, on one sinew, and ready to fall. But he did not fall.

It was late in the damp December afternoon, with cold mists creeping out of the woods and up the hollows, and darkness waiting to sink in from above. There was a bit of yellowness where the sun was fading away beyond the low woods of the distance. March took her axe and went to the tree. The small thud-thud of her blows resounded rather ineffectual about the wintry homestead. Banford came out wearing her thick coat, but with no hat on her head, so that her thin, bobbed hair blew on the uneasy wind that sounded in the pines and in the wood.

"What I'm afraid of," said Banford, "is that it will fall on the shed and we sh'll have another job repairing that."

"Oh, I don't think so," said March, straightening herself and wiping her arm over her hot brow. She was flushed red, her eyes were very wide open and queer, her upper lip lifted away from her two white front teeth with a curious, almost rabbit look.

A little stout man in a black overcoat and a bowler hat came pottering across the yard. He had a pink face and a white beard and smallish, pale-blue eyes. He was not very old, but nervy, and he walked with little short steps.

"What do you think, father?" said Banford. "Don't you think it might hit the shed in falling?"

"Shed, no!" said the old man. "Can't hit the shed. Might as well say the fence."

"The fence doesn't matter," said March, in her high voice.

"Wrong as usual, am I!" said Banford, wiping her straying hair from her eyes.

The tree stood as it were on one spelch of itself, leaning, and creaking in the wind. It grew on the bank of a little dry ditch between the two meadows. On the top of the bank straggled one fence, running to the bushes up-hill. Several trees clustered there in the corner of the field near the shed and near the gate which led into the yard. Towards this gate, horizontal across the weary meadows, came the grassy, rutted approach from the high road. There trailed another rickety fence, long split poles joining the short, thick, wide-apart uprights. The three people stood at the back of the tree, in the corner of the shed meadow, just above the yard gate. The house, with its two gables and its porch, stood tidy in a little grassed garden across the yard. A little, stout, rosy-faced woman in a little red woollen shoulder shawl had come and taken her stand in the porch.

"Isn't it down yet?" she cried, in a high little voice.

"Just thinking about it," called her husband. His tone towards the two girls was always rather mocking and satirical. March did not want to go on with her hitting while he was there. As for him, he wouldn't lift a stick from the ground if he could help it, complaining, like his daughter, of rheumatics in his shoulder. So the three stood there a moment silent in the cold afternoon, in the bottom corner near the yard.

They heard the far-off taps of a gate, and craned to look. Away across, on the green horizontal approach, a figure was just swinging on to a bicycle again, and lurching up and down over the grass, approaching.

"Why, it's one of our boys—it's Jack," said the old man.

"Can't be," said Banford.

March craned her head to look. She alone recognised the khaki figure. She flushed, but said nothing.

"No, it isn't Jack, I don't think," said the old man, staring with little round blue eyes under his white lashes.

In another moment the bicycle lurched into sight, and the rider dropped off at the gate. It was Henry, his face wet and red and spotted with mud. He was altogether a muddy sight.

"Oh!" cried Banford, as if afraid. "Why, it's Henry!"

"What!" muttered the old man. He had a thick, rapid, muttering way of speaking, and was slightly deaf. "What? What? Who is it? Who is it, do you say? That young fellow? That young fellow of Nellie's? Oh! Oh!" And the satiric smile came on his pink face and white eyelashes.

Henry, pushing the wet hair off his steaming brow, had caught sight of them and heard what the old man said. His hot, young face seemed to flame in the cold light.

"Oh, are you all there!" he said, giving his sudden, puppy's little laugh. He was so hot and dazed with cycling he hardly knew where he was. He leaned the bicycle against the fence and climbed over into the corner on to the bank, without going into the yard.

"Well, I must say, we weren't expecting *you*," said Banford laconically.

"No, I suppose not," said he, looking at March.

She stood aside, slack, with one knee dropped and the axe resting its head loosely on the ground. Her eyes were wide and vacant, and her upper lip lifted from her teeth in that helpless, fascinated rabbit look. The moment she saw his glowing, red face it was all over with her. She was as helpless as if she had been bound. The moment she saw the way his head seemed to reach forward.

"Well, who is it? Who is it, anyway?" asked the smiling, satiric old man in his muttering voice.

"Why, Mr. Grenfel, whom you've heard us tell about, father," said Banford coldly.

"Heard you tell about, I should think so. Heard of nothing else practically," muttered the elderly man, with his queer little jeering smile on his face. "How do you do," he added, suddenly reaching out his hand to Henry.

The boy shook hands just as startled. Then the two men fell apart.

"Cycled over from Salisbury Plain, have you?" asked the old man.

"Yes."

"Hm! Longish ride. How long d'it take you, eh? Some time, eh? Several hours, I suppose."

"About four."

"Eh? Four! Yes, I should have thought so. When are you going back, then?"

"I've got till to-morrow evening."

"Till to-morrow evening, eh? Yes. Hm! Girls weren't expecting you, were they?"

And the old man turned his pale-blue, round little eyes under their white lashes mockingly towards the girls. Henry also looked round. He had become a little awkward. He looked at March, who was still staring away into the distance as if to see where the cattle were. Her hand was on the pommel of the axe, whose head rested loosely on the ground.

"What were you doing there?" he asked in his soft, courteous voice. "Cutting a tree down?"

March seemed not to hear, as if in a trance.

"Yes," said Banford. "We've been at it for over a week."

"Oh! And have you done it all by yourselves then?"

"Nellie's done it all, I've done nothing," said Banford.

"Really! You must have worked quite hard," he said, addressing himself in a curious gentle tone direct to March. She did not answer, but remained half averted staring away towards the woods above as if in a trance.

"*Nellie!*" cried Banford sharply. "Can't you answer?"

"What—me?" cried March, starting round and looking from one to the other. "Did anyone speak to me?"

"Dreaming!" muttered the old man, turning aside to smile. "Must be in love, eh, dreaming in the day-time!"

"Did you say anything to me?" said March, looking at the boy as from a strange distance, her eyes wide and doubtful, her face delicately flushed.

"I said you must have worked hard at the tree," he replied courteously.

"Oh, that! Bit by bit. I thought it would have come down by now."

"I'm thankful it hasn't come down in the night, to frighten us to death," said Banford.

"Let me just finish it for you, shall I?" said the boy.

March slanted the axe-shaft in his direction.

"Would you like to?" she said.

"Yes, if you wish it," he said.

"Oh, I'm thankful when the thing's down, that's all," she replied, non-chalant.

"Which way is it going to fall?" said Banford. "Will it hit the shed?"

"No it won't hit the shed," he said. "I should think it will fall there— quite clear. Though it might give a twist and catch the fence."

"Catch the fence!" cried the old man. "What, catch the fence! When it's leaning at that angle? Why, it's farther off than the shed. It won't catch the fence."

"No," said Henry, "I don't suppose it will. It has plenty of room to fall quite clear, and I suppose it will fall clear."

"Won't tumble backwards on top of *us*, will it?" asked the old man, sarcastic.

"No, it won't do that," said Henry, taking off his short overcoat and his tunic. "Ducks! Ducks! Go back!"

A line of four brown-speckled ducks led by a brown-and-green drake were stemming away downhill from the upper meadow, coming like boats running on a ruffled sea, cockling their way top speed downwards towards the fence and towards the little group of people, and cackling as excitedly as if they brought news of the Spanish Armada.

"Silly things! Silly things!" cried Banford, going forward to turn them off. But they came eagerly towards her, opening their yellow-green beaks and quacking as if they were so excited to say something.

"There's no food. There's nothing here. You must wait a bit," said Banford to them. "Go away. Go away. Go round to the yard."

They didn't go, so she climbed the fence to swerve them round under the gate and into the yard. So off they waggled in an excited string once more, wagging their rumps like the stems of little gondolas, ducking under the bar of the gate. Banford stood on the top of the bank, just over the fence, looking down on the other three.

Henry looked up at her, and met her queer, round pupilled, weak eyes staring behind her spectacles. He was perfectly still. He looked away, up at the weak, leaning tree. And as he looked into the sky, like a huntsman who is watching a flying bird, he thought to himself: "If the tree falls in just such a way, and spins just so much as it falls, then the branch there will strike her exactly as she stands on top of that bank."

He looked at her again. She was wiping the hair from her brow again, with that perpetual gesture. In his heart he had decided her death. A terrible still force seemed in him, and a power that was just his. If he turned even a hair's breadth in the wrong direction, he would lose the power.

"Mind yourself, Miss Banford," he said. And his heart held perfectly still, in the terrible pure will that she should not move.

"Who, me, mind myself?" she cried, her father's jeering tone in her voice. "Why, do you think you might hit me with the axe?"

"No, it's just possible the tree might, though," he answered soberly. But the tone of his voice seemed to her to imply that he was only being falsely solicitous, and trying to make her move because it was his will to move her.

"Absolutely impossible," she said.

He heard her. But he held himself icy still, lest he should lose his power.

'No, it's just possible. You'd better come down this way."

"Oh, all right. Let us see some crack Canadian tree-felling," she retorted.

"Ready, then," he said, taking the axe, looking round to see he was clear.

There was a moment of pure, motionless suspense, when the world seemed to stand still. Then suddenly his form seemed to flash up enormously tall and fearful, he gave two swift, flashing blows, in immediate succession, the tree was severed, turning slowly, spinning strangely in the air and coming down like a sudden darkness on the earth. No one saw what was happening except himself. No one heard the strange little cry which the Banford gave as the dark end of the bough swooped down, down on her. No one saw her crouch a little and receive the blow on the back of the neck. No one saw her flung outwards and laid, a little twitching heap at the foot of the fence. No one except the boy. And he watched with intense bright eyes, as he would watch a wild goose he had shot. Was it winged or dead? Dead!

Immediately he gave a loud cry. Immediately March gave a wild shriek that went far, far down the afternoon. And the father started a strange bellowing sound.

The boy leapt the fence and ran to the fringe. The back of the neck and head was a mass of blood, of horror. He turned it over. The body was quivering with little convulsions. But she was dead really. He knew it, that it was so. He knew it in his soul and his blood. The inner necessity of his life was fulfilling itself, it was he who was to live. The thorn was drawn out of his bowels. So he put her down gently. She was dead.

He stood up. March was standing there petrified and absolutely motionless. Her face was dead white, her eyes big black pools. The old man was scrambling horribly over the fence.

"I'm afraid it's killed her," said the boy.

The old man was making curious, blubbering noises as he huddled over the fence. "What!" cried March, starting electric.

"Yes, I'm afraid," repeated the boy.

March was coming forward. The boy was over the fence before she reached it.

"What do you say, killed her?" she asked in a sharp voice.

"I'm afraid so," he answered softly.

She went still whiter, fearful. The two stood facing one another. Her black eyes gazed on him with the last look of resistance. And then in a last agonised failure she began to grizzle, to cry in a shivery little fashion of a child that doesn't want to cry, but which is beaten from within, and gives that little first shudder of sobbing which is not yet weeping, dry and fearful.

He had won. She stood there absolutely helpless, shuddering her dry sobs and her mouth trembling rapidly. And then, as in a child, with a little crash came the tears and the blind agony of sightless weeping. She sank down on the grass, and sat there with her hands on her breast and her face lifted in sightless, convulsed weeping. He stood above her, looking down on her, mute, pale, and everlasting seeming. He never moved, but looked down on her. And among all the torture of the scene, the torture of his own heart and bowels, he was glad, he had won.

After a long time he stooped to her and took her hands.

"Don't cry," he said softly. "Don't cry."

She looked up at him with tears running from her eyes, a senseless look of helplessness and submission. So she gazed on him as if sightless, yet looking up to him. She would never leave him again. He had won her. And he knew it and was glad, because he wanted her for his life. His life must have her. And now he had won her. It was what his life must have.

But if he had won her he had not yet got her. They were married at Christmas as he had planned, and he got again ten days' leave. They went to Cornwall, to his own village, on the sea. He realised that it was awful for her to be at the farm any more.

But though she belonged to him, though she lived in his shadow, as if she could not be away from him, she was not happy. She did not want to leave him: and yet she did not feel free with him. Everything round her seemed to watch her, seemed to press on her. He had won her, he had her with him, she was his wife. And she—she belonged to him, she knew it. But she was not glad. And he was still foiled. He realised that though he was married to her and possessed her in every possible way, apparently, and though she *wanted* him to possess her, she wanted it, she wanted nothing else, now, still he did not quite succeed.

Something was missing. Instead of her soul swaying with new life, it seemed to droop, to bleed as if it were wounded. She would sit for a long time with her hand in his, looking away at the sea. And in her dark, vacant eyes was a sort of wound, and her face looked a little peaked. If he spoke to her, she would turn to him with a faint new smile, the strange, quivering little smile of a woman who has died in the old way of love, and can't quite rise to the new way. She still felt she ought to *do* something, to strain herself in some direction. And there was nothing to do, and no direction in which to strain herself. And she could not quite accept the submergence which his new love put upon her. If she was in love, she ought to *exert* herself, in some way, loving. She felt the weary need of our day to *exert* herself in love. But she knew that in fact she must no more exert herself in love. He would not have the love which exerted itself towards him. It made his brow go black. No, he wouldn't let her exert her love towards him. No, she had to be passive, to acquiesce, and to be submerged under the surface of love. She had to be like the seaweeds she saw as she peered down from the boat, swaying forever delicately under water, with all their delicate fibrils put tenderly out upon the flood, sensitive, utterly sensitive and receptive within the shadowy sea, and never, never rising and looking forth above water while they lived. Never. Never looking forth from the water until they died, only then washing, corpses, upon the surface. But while they lived, always submerged, always beneath the wave. Beneath the wave they might have powerful roots, stronger than iron; they might be tenacious and dangerous in their soft waving within the flood. Beneath the water they might be stronger, more indestructible than resistant oak trees are on land. But it was always under-water, always under-water. And she, being a woman, must be like that.

And she had been so used to the very opposite. She had had to take all the thought for love and for life, and all the responsibility. Day after day she had been responsible for the coming day, for the coming year: for her dear Jill's health and happiness and well-being. Verily, in her own small way, she had felt herself responsible for the well-being of the world. And this had been her great stimulant, this grand feeling that, in her own small sphere, she was responsible for the well-being of the world.

And she had failed. She knew that, even in her small way, she had failed. She had failed to satisfy her own feeling of responsibility. It was so difficult. It seemed so grand and easy at first. And the more you tried, the more difficult it became. It had seemed so easy to make one beloved creature happy. And the more you tried, the worse the failure. It was terrible. She had been all her life reaching, reaching, and what she reached for seemed so near, until she had stretched to her utmost limit. And then it was always beyond her.

Always beyond her, vaguely, unrealisably beyond her, and she was left with nothingness at last. The life she reached for, the happiness she reached for, the well-being she reached for all slipped back, became unreal, the farther she stretched her hand. She wanted some goal, some finality—and there was none. Always this ghastly reaching, reaching, striving for something that might be just beyond. Even to make Jill happy. She was glad Jill was dead. For she had realised that she could never make her happy. Jill would always be fretting herself thinner and thinner, weaker and weaker. Her pains grew worse instead of less. It would be so for ever. She was glad she was dead.

And if Jill had married a man it would have been just the same. The woman striving, striving to make the man happy, striving within her own limits for the well-being of her world. And always achieving failure. Little, foolish successes in money or in ambition. But at the very point where she most wanted success, in the anguished effort to make some one beloved human being happy and perfect, there the failure was almost catastrophic. You wanted to make your beloved happy, and his happiness seemed always achievable. If only you did just this, that and the other. And you did this, that, and the other, in all good faith, and every time the failure became a little more ghastly. You could love yourself to ribbons and strive and strain yourself to the bone, and things would go from bad to worse, bad to worse, as far as happiness went. The awful mistake of happiness.

Poor March, in her good-will and her responsibility, she had strained herself till it seemed to her that the whole of life and everything was only a horrible abyss of nothingness. The more you reach after the fatal flower of happiness, which trembles so blue and lovely in a crevice just beyond your grasp, the more fearfully you become aware of the ghastly and awful gulf of the precipice below you, into which you will inevitably plunge, as into the bottomless pit, if you reach any farther. You pluck flower after flower —it is never *the* flower. The flower itself—its calyx is a horrible gulf, it is the bottomless pit.

That is the whole history of the search for happiness, whether it be your own or somebody else's that you want to win. It ends, and it always ends, in the ghastly sense of the bottomless nothingness into which you will inevitably fall if you strain any farther.

And women?—what goal can any woman conceive, except happiness? Just happiness for herself and the whole world. That, and nothing else. And so, she assumes the responsibility and sets off towards her goal. She can see it there, at the foot of the rainbow. Or she can see it a little way beyond, in the blue distance. Not far, not far.

But the end of the rainbow is a bottomless gulf down which you can fall forever without arriving, and the blue distance is a void pit which can swallow you and all your efforts into its emptiness, and still be no emptier. You and all your efforts. So, the illusion of attainable happiness!

Poor March, she had set off so wonderfully towards the blue goal. And the farther and farther she had gone, the more fearful had become the realisation of emptiness. An agony, an insanity at last.

She was glad it was over. She was glad to sit on the shore and look westwards over the sea, and know the great strain had ended. She would never strain for love and happiness any more. And Jill was safely dead. Poor Jill, poor Jill. It must be sweet to be dead.

For her own part, death was not her destiny. She would have to leave her destiny to the boy. But then, the boy. He wanted more than that. He wanted her to give herself without defences, to sink and become submerged in him. And she—she wanted to sit still, like a woman on the last milestone, and watch. She wanted to see, to know, to understand. She wanted to be alone: with him at her side.

And he! He did not want her to watch any more, to see any more, to understand any more. He wanted to veil her woman's spirit, as Orientals veil the woman's face. He wanted her to commit herself to him, and to put her independent spirit to sleep. He wanted to take away from her all her effort, all that seemed her very *raison d'être*. He wanted to make her submit, yield, blindly pass away out of all her strenuous consciousness. He wanted to take away her consciousness, and make her just his woman. Just his woman.

And she was so tired, so tired, like a child that wants to go to sleep, but which fights against sleep as if sleep were death. She seemed to stretch her eyes wider in the obstinate effort and tension of keeping awake. She *would* keep awake. She *would* know. She *would* consider and judge and decide. She *would* have the reins of her own life between her own hands. She *would* be an independent woman to the last. But she was so tired, so tired of everything. And sleep seemed near. And there was such rest in the boy.

Yet there, sitting in a niche of the high, wild cliffs of West Cornwall, looking over the westward sea, she stretched her eyes wider and wider. Away to the West, Canada, America. She *would* know and she *would* see what was ahead. And the boy, sitting beside her, staring down at the gulls, had a cloud between his brows and the strain of discontent in his eyes. He wanted her asleep, at peace in him. He wanted her at peace, asleep in him. And *there* she was, dying with the strain of her own wakefulness. Yet she would not sleep: no, never. Sometimes he thought bitterly that he ought to have left her. He ought never to have killed Banford. He should have left Banford and March to kill one another.

But that was only impatience: and he knew it. He was waiting, waiting to go West. He was aching almost in torment to leave England, to go West, to take March away. To leave this shore! He believed that as they crossed the seas, as they left this England which he so hated, because in some way it seemed to have stung him with poison, she would go to sleep. She would close her eyes at last and give in to him.

And then he would have her, and he would have his own life at last. He chafed, feeling he hadn't got his own life. He would never have it till she yielded and slept in him. Then he would have all his own life as a young man and a male, and she would have all her own life as a woman and a female. There would be no more of this awful straining. She would not be a man any more, an independent woman with a man's responsibility. Nay, even the responsibility for her own soul she would have to commit to him. He knew it was so, and obstinately held out against her, waiting for the surrender.

"You'll feel better when once we get over the seas to Canada over there," he said to her as they sat among the rocks on the cliff.

She looked away to the sea's horizon, as if it were not real. Then she looked round at him, with the strained, strange look of a child that is struggling against sleep.

"Shall I?" she said.

"Yes," he answered quietly.

And her eyelids dropped with the slow motion, sleep weighing them unconscious. But she pulled them open again to say:

"Yes, I may. I can't tell. I can't tell what it will be like over there."

"If only we could go soon!" he said, with pain in his voice.

9

KATHERINE ANNE PORTER
Pale Horse, Pale Rider

Although *Pale Horse, Pale Rider* is not predominantly a historical short novel, it cannot be fully appreciated without reference to what has been one of the most influential historical events of the twentieth century—World War I. The first mechanized war ever, World War I introduced the machine gun, the tank, and poison gas to the battlefield, and the protractedness of trench warfare inflicted a qualitatively new kind of suffering on troops. Many literary works, T. S. Eliot's poem *The Wasteland* and Ernest Hemingway's novel *The Sun Also Rises* notable among them, have portrayed this period as a historical watershed which initiated an age of bitterness, disillusionment, and spiritual bankruptcy.

The effects of the war can be felt throughout *Pale Horse, Pale Rider*. To Miranda the war is no more than a hoax, futile and deadly. In a virtue-ridden Western town (implicitly, Denver) where blind patriotism has been made a religion, her indifference puts her on a collision course with the community. Periodically she comes into conflict with patriotic types. The men who come to sell her Savings Bonds, the women who ply hospitalized soldiers with candy, and the Bond salesman at the theater—"a neat little melon buttoned into his trousers"—all appal her with dreariness. Her relationship with Adam Barclay is also poisoned by the war. He is certain to be sent overseas within days. As an officer in the Corps of Engineers he expects to take part in demolition raids, whose members, he jokes, have a life expectancy of exactly nine minutes after their job is done. Adam shares Miranda's perception of the war's hypocrisies. Yet because he loves his country, and perhaps because of his dashing uniform and the idea of glory in a land far from Texas, he submits good-naturedly to his role as a sacrificial lamb. This, too, saddens Miranda.

Even before the beginning of the story, her revulsion against the war is intensified by the illness taking hold within her. During sleep, her body communicates the onset of crisis through the dream of the pale rider. The influenza epidemic sweeps through the city like a medieval plague, so that the city ironically begins to resemble a battlefield, a landscape of death. The parallel drawn between war and epidemic, two apocalyptic horsemen, is meaningful. *Pale Horse, Pale Rider* is not just a story about Miranda, Adam, and World War I, but a reflection on man's fallen and mortal condition. War and pestilence are ancient, symbolic bringers of death; to a certain extent, they represent all that is deathly in human existence, especially the failure of human will to choose life over death.

The question of will, of the potential transcendence of human spirit, is central in this short novel. Can the human will to live—more specifically, can Miranda's will to live—triumph over life's onslaught of dreariness, hostility, failure, and sickness? The implied answer is obscure, but it does not seem optimistic. Throughout the story Miranda is portrayed as a rather delicate person with a frail but tenacious hold on life. She lives in a world devitalized by weak people. Towney, Chuck, the old vaudeville performer, the soldier and the old women in the hospital—all are somehow mis-shapen or beaten down by life, and they in turn seem to drain the spirit from Miranda's life. The title folksong about the pale rider claims that death has taken everyone but the singer. And so it seems: death-in-life has claimed nearly everyone. The saving exception is Adam, who is vital and strong, but he is ultimately betrayed into death.

At her nearest point to death, Miranda experiences a kind of heavenly vision. Unconscious, she realizes a vividly imaged state of peace and joy. Whether her vision expresses a will to live or a longing for the otherworldliness of death is hard to say. But her return to life is clearly unwilling, and even during the interval between the news of the war's end and the news of Adam's death, a time when she might have taken hope, "she folded her painful body together and wept silently, shamelessly, in pity for herself and her lost rapture."

Pale Horse, Pale Rider

In sleep she knew she was in her bed, but not the bed she had lain down in a few hours since, and the room was not the same but it was a room she had known somewhere. Her heart was a stone lying upon her breast outside of her; her pulses lagged and paused, and she knew that something strange was going to happen, even as the early morning winds were cool through the lattice, the streaks of light were dark blue and the whole house was snoring in its sleep.

Now I must get up and go while they are all quiet. Where are my things? Things have a will of their own in this place and hide where they like. Daylight will strike a sudden blow on the roof startling them all up to their feet; faces will beam asking, Where are you going, What are you doing, What are you thinking, How do you feel, Why do you say such things, What do you mean? No more sleep. Where are my boots and what horse shall I ride? Fiddler or Graylie or Miss Lucy with the long nose and the wicked eye? How I have loved this house in the morning before we are all awake and tangled together like badly cast fishing lines. Too many people have been born here, and have wept too much here, and have laughed too much, and have been too angry and outrageous with each other here. Too many have died in this bed already, there are far too many ancestral bones propped up on the mantelpieces, there have been too damned many antimacassars in this house, she said loudly, and oh, what accumulation of storied dust never allowed to settle in peace for one moment.

And the stranger? Where is that lank greenish stranger I remember hanging about the place, welcomed by my grandfather, my great-aunt, my five times removed cousin, my decrepit hound and my silver kitten? Why did they take to him, I wonder? And where are they now? Yet I saw him pass the window in the evening. What else besides them did I have in the world? Nothing. Nothing is mine, I have only nothing but it is enough, it is beautiful and it is all mine. Do I even walk about in my own skin or is it something I have borrowed to spare my modesty? Now what horse shall I borrow for this journey I do not mean to take, Graylie or Miss Lucy or Fiddler who can jump ditches in the dark and knows how to get the bit between his teeth? Early morning is best for me because trees are trees in one stroke, stones are stones set in shades known to be grass, there are no false shapes or surmises, the road is still asleep with the crust of dew unbroken. I'll take Graylie because he is not afraid of bridges.

Come now, Graylie, she said, taking his bridle, we must outrun Death and the Devil. You are no good for it, she told the other horses standing saddled before the stable gate, among them the horse of the stranger, gray also, with tarnished nose and ears. The stranger swung into his saddle beside her, leaned far towards her and regarded her without meaning, the blank still stare of mindless malice that makes no threats and can bide its time. She drew Graylie around sharply, urged him to run. He leaped the low rose hedge and the narrow ditch beyond, and the dust of the lane flew heavily under his beating hoofs. The stranger rode beside her, easily, lightly, his reins loose in his half-closed hand, straight and elegant in dark shabby garments that flapped upon his bones; his pale face smiled in an evil trance, he did not glance at her. Ah, I have seen this fellow before, I know this man if I could place him. He is no stranger to me.

She pulled Graylie up, rose in her stirrups and shouted, I'm not going with you this time—ride on! Without pausing or turning his head the stranger rode on. Graylie's ribs heaved under her, her own ribs rose and fell, Oh, why am I so tired, I must wake up. "But let me get a fine yawn first," she said, opening her eyes and stretching, "a slap of cold water in my face, for I've been talking in my sleep again, I heard myself but what was I saying?"

Slowly, unwillingly, Miranda drew herself up inch by inch out of the pit of sleep, waited in a daze for life to begin again. A single word struck in her mind, a gong of warning, reminding her for the daylong what she forgot happily in sleep, and only in sleep. The war, said the gong, and she shook her head. Dangling her feet idly with their slippers hanging, she was reminded of the way all sorts of persons sat upon her desk at the newspaper office. Every day she found someone there, sitting upon her desk instead of the chair provided, dangling his legs, eyes roving, full of his important affairs, waiting to pounce about something or other. "*Why* won't they sit in the chair? Should I put a sign on it, saying, 'For God's sake, sit here'?"

Far from putting up a sign, she did not even frown at her visitors.

Usually she did not notice them at all until their determination to be seen was greater than her determination not to see them. Saturday, she thought, lying comfortably in her tub of hot water, will be payday, as always. Or I hope always. Her thoughts roved hazily in a continual effort to bring together and unite firmly the disturbing oppositions in her day-to-day existence, where survival, she could see clearly, had become a series of feats of sleight of hand. I owe—let me see, I wish I had a pencil and paper—well, suppose I *did* pay five dollars now on a Liberty Bond, I couldn't possibly keep it up. Or maybe. Eighteen dollars a week. So much for rent, so much for food, and I mean to have a few things besides. About five dollars' worth. Will leave me twenty-seven cents. I suppose I can make it. I suppose I should be worried. I am worried. Very well, now I am worried and what next? Twenty-seven cents. That's not so bad. Pure profit, really. Imagine if they should suddenly raise me to twenty I should then have two dollars and twenty-seven cents left over. But they aren't going to raise me to twenty. They are in fact going to throw me out if I don't buy a Liberty Bond. I hardly believe that. I'll ask Bill. (Bill was the city editor.) I wonder if a threat like that isn't a kind of blackmail. I don't believe even a Lusk Committeeman can get away with that.

Yesterday there had been two pairs of legs dangling, on either side of her typewriter, both pairs stuffed thickly into funnels of dark expensive-looking material. She noticed at a distance that one of them was oldish and one was youngish, and they both of them had a stale air of borrowed importance which apparently they had got from the same source. They were both much too well nourished and the younger one wore a square little mustache. Being what they were, no matter what their business was it would be something unpleasant. Miranda had nodded at them, pulled out her chair and without removing her cap or gloves had reached into a pile of letters and sheets from the copydesk as if she had not a moment to spare. They did not move, or take off their hats. At last she had said "Good morning" to them, and asked if they were, perhaps, waiting for her?

The two men slid off the desk, leaving some of her papers rumpled, and the oldish man had inquired why she had not bought a Liberty Bond. Miranda had looked at him then, and got a poor impression. He was a pursy-faced man, gross-mouthed, with little lightless eyes, and Miranda wondered why nearly all of those selected to do the war work at home were of his sort. He might be anything at all, she thought; advance agent for a road show, promoter of a wildcat oil company, a former saloon keeper announcing the opening of a new cabaret, an automobile salesman—any follower of any one of the crafty, haphazard callings. But he was now all Patriot, working for the government. "Look here," he asked her, "do you know there's a war, or don't you?"

Did he expect an answer to that? Be quiet, Miranda told herself, this was bound to happen. Sooner or later it happens. Keep your head. The man wagged his finger at her. "Do you?" he persisted, as if he were prompting an obstinate child.

"Oh, the war," Miranda had echoed on a rising note and she almost smiled at him. It was habitual, automatic, to give that solemn, mystically uplifted grin when you spoke the words or heard them spoken. *"C'est la guerre,"* whether you could pronounce it or not, was even better, and always, always, you shrugged.

"Yeah," said the younger man in a nasty way, "the war." Miranda, startled by the tone, met his eye; his stare was really stony, really viciously cold, the kind of thing you might expect to meet behind a pistol on a deserted corner. This expression gave temporary meaning to a set of features otherwise nondescript, the face of those men who have no business of their own. "We're having a war, and some people are buying Liberty Bonds and others just don't seem to get around to it," he said. "That's what we mean."

Miranda frowned with nervousness, the sharp beginnings of fear. "Are you selling them?" she asked, taking the cover off her typewriter and putting it back again.

"No, we're not selling them," said the older man. "We're just asking you why you haven't bought one." The voice was persuasive and ominous.

Miranda began to explain that she had no money, and did not know where to find any, when the older man interrupted: "That's no excuse, no excuse at all, and you know it, with the Huns overrunning martyred Belgium."

"With our American boys fighting and dying in Belleau Wood," said the younger man, "anybody can raise fifty dollars to help beat the Boche."

Miranda said hastily, "I have eighteen dollars a week and not another cent in the world. I simply cannot buy anything."

"You can pay for it five dollars a week," said the older man (they had stood there cawing back and forth over her head), "like a lot of other people in this office, and a lot of other offices besides are doing."

Miranda, desperately silent, had thought, "Suppose I were not a coward, but said what I really thought? Suppose I said to hell with this filthy war? Suppose I asked that little thug, What's the matter with you, why aren't you rotting in Belleau Wood? I wish you were. . . ."

She began to arrange her letters and notes, her fingers refusing to pick up things properly. The older man went on making his little set speech. It was hard, of course. Everybody was suffering, naturally. Everybody had to do his share. But as to that, a Liberty Bond was the safest investment you could make. It was just like having the money in the bank. Of course. The government was back of it and where better could you invest?

"I agree with you about that," said Miranda, "but I haven't any money to invest."

And of course, the man had gone on, it wasn't so much her fifty dollars that was going to make any difference. It was just a pledge of good faith on her part. A pledge of good faith that she was a loyal American doing her duty. And the thing was safe as a church. Why, if he had a million dollars he'd be glad to put every last cent of it in these Bonds. . . . "You can't lose by it," he said, almost benevolently, "and you can lose a lot if you don't. Think it over. You're the only one in this whole newspaper office that hasn't come in. And every firm in this city has come in one hundred per cent. Over at the *Daily Clarion* nobody had to be asked twice."

"They pay better over there," said Miranda. "But next week, if I can. Not now, next week."

"See that you do," said the younger man. "This ain't any laughing matter."

They lolled away, past the Society Editor's desk, past Bill the City Editor's desk, past the long copydesk where old man Gibbons sat all night shouting at intervals, "Jarge! Jarge!" and the copyboy would come flying. "Never say *people* when you mean *persons*," old man Gibbons had instructed Miranda, "and never say *practically*, say *virtually*, and don't for God's sake ever so long as I am at this desk use the barbarism *inasmuch* under any circumstances whatsoever. Now you're educated, you may go." At the head of the stairs her inquisitors had stopped in their fussy pride and vainglory, lighting cigars and wedging their hats more firmly over their eyes.

Miranda turned over in the soothing water, and wished she might fall asleep there, to wake up only when it was time to sleep again. She had a burning slow headache, and noticed it now, remembering she had waked up with it and it had in fact begun the evening before. While she dressed she tried to trace the insidious career of her headache, and it seemed reasonable to suppose it had started with the war. "It's been a headache, all right, but not quite like this." After the Committeemen had left, yesterday, she had gone to the cloakroom and had found Mary Townsend, the Society Editor, quietly hysterical about something. She was perched on the edge of the shabby wicker couch with ridges down the center, knitting on something rose-colored. Now and then she would put down her knitting, seize her head with both hands and rock, saying "My *God*," in a surprised, inquiring voice. Her column was called Ye Towne Gossyp, so of course everybody called her Towney. Miranda and Towney had a great deal in common, and liked each other. They had both been real reporters once, and had been sent together to "cover" a scandalous elopement in which no marriage had taken place, after all, and the recaptured girl, her face swollen, had sat with her mother who was moaning steadily under a mound of blankets. They had both wept painfully and implored the young reporters to suppress the worst of the story. They had suppressed it, and the rival newspaper printed it all the next day. Miranda and Towney had then taken their punishment together, and had been degraded publicly to routine female jobs, one to the theaters, the other to society. They had this in common, that neither of them could see what else they could possibly have done, and they knew they were considered fools by the rest of the staff—nice girls, but fools. At sight of Miranda, Towney had broken out in a rage, "I can't do it, I'll never be able to raise the money, I told them, I can't, I can't, but they wouldn't listen."

Miranda said, "I knew I wasn't the only person in this office who couldn't raise five dollars. I told them I couldn't, too, and I can't."

"My *God*," said Towney, in the same voice, "they told me I'd lose my job—"

"I'm going to ask Bill," Miranda said; "I don't believe Bill would do that."

"It's not up to Bill," said Towney. "He'd have to if they got after him. Do you suppose they could put us in jail?"

"I don't know," said Miranda. "If they do, we won't be lonesome." She sat down beside Towney and held her own head. "What kind of soldier are you knitting that for? It's a sprightly color, it ought to cheer him up."

"Like hell," said Towney, her needles going again. "I'm making this for myself. That's that."

"Well," said Miranda, "we won't be lonesome and we'll catch up on our sleep." She washed her face and put on fresh makeup. Taking clean gray gloves out of her pocket she went out to join a group of young women fresh from the country club dances, the morning bridge, the charity bazaar, the Red Cross workrooms, who were wallowing in good works. They gave tea dances and raised money, and with the money they bought quantities of sweets, fruit, cigarettes, and magazines for the men in the cantonment hospitals. With this loot they were now setting out, a gay procession of high-powered cars and brightly tinted faces to cheer the brave boys who already, you might very well say, had fallen in defense of their country. It must be frightfully hard on them, the dears, to be floored like this when they're all crazy to get overseas and into the trenches as quickly as possible. Yes, and some of them are the cutest things you ever saw, I didn't know there were so many good-looking men in this country, good heavens, I said, where do they come from? Well, my dear, you may ask yourself that question, who knows where they did come from? You're quite right, the way I feel about it is this, we must do everything we can to make them contented, but I draw the line at talking to them. I told the chaperons at those dances for enlisted men, I'll dance with them, every dumbbell who asks me, but I will NOT talk to them, I said, even if there is a war. So I danced hundreds of miles without opening my mouth except to say, Please keep your knees to yourself. I'm glad we gave those dances up. Yes, and the men stopped coming, anyway. But listen, I've heard that a great many of the enlisted men come from very good families; I'm not good at catching names, and those I did catch I'd never heard before, so I don't know . . . but it seems to me if they were from good families, you'd know it, wouldn't you? I mean, if a man is well bred he doesn't step on your feet, does he? At least not that. I used to have a pair of sandals ruined at every one of those dances. Well, I think any kind of social life is in very poor taste just now, I think we should all put on our Red Cross headdresses and wear them for the duration of the war—

Miranda, carrying her basket and her flowers, moved in among the young women, who scattered out and rushed upon the ward uttering girlish laughter meant to be refreshingly gay, but there was a grim determined clang in it calculated to freeze the blood. Miserably embarrassed at the idiocy of her errand, she walked rapidly between the long rows of high beds, set foot to foot with a narrow aisle between. The men, a selected presentable lot, sheets drawn up to their chins, not seriously ill, were bored and restless, most of them willing to be amused at anything. They were for the most part picturesquely bandaged as to arm or head, and those who were not visibly wounded invariably replied "Rheumatism" if some tactless girl, who had been solemnly warned never to ask this question, still forgot and asked a man what his illness was. The good-natured, eager ones, laughing and calling out from their hard narrow beds, were soon surrounded. Miranda, with her wilting bouquet and her basket of sweets and cigarettes, looking about, caught the unfriendly bitter eye of a young fellow lying on his back, his right leg in a cast and pulley. She stopped at the foot of his bed and continued to look at him, and he looked back with an unchanged, hostile face. Not having any, thank you and be damned to the whole business, his eyes said plainly to her, and will you be so good as to take your trash off my bed? For Miranda had set it down, leaning over to place it where he might be able to reach it if he would. Having set it down, she was incapable of taking it up again, but hurried away, her face burning, down the long aisle and out into the cool October sunshine, where the dreary raw barracks swarmed and worked with an aimless life of scurrying, dun-colored insects; and going around to a window near where he lay, she looked in, spying upon her soldier. He was lying with his eyes closed, his eyebrows in a sad bitter frown. She could not place him at all, she could not imagine where he came from nor what sort of being he might have been "in life," she said to herself. His face was young and the features sharp and plain, the hands were not laborer's hands but not well-cared-for hands either. They were good useful properly shaped hands, lying there on the coverlet. It occurred to her that it would be her luck to find him, instead of a jolly hungry puppy glad of a bite to eat and a little chatter. It is like turning a corner absorbed in your painful thoughts and meeting your state of mind embodied, face to face, she said. "My own feelings about this whole thing, made flesh. Never again will I come here, this is no sort of thing to be doing. This is disgusting," she told herself plainly. "Of course I would pick him out," she thought, getting into the back seat of the car she came in, "serves me right, I know better."

Another girl came out looking very tired and climbed in beside her.

After a short silence, the girl said in a puzzled way, "I don't know what good it does, really. Some of them wouldn't take anything at all. I don't like this, do you?"

"I hate it," said Miranda.

"I suppose it's all right, though," said the girl cautiously.

"Perhaps," said Miranda, turning cautious also.

That was for yesterday. At this point Miranda decided there was no good in thinking of yesterday, except for the hour after midnight she had spent dancing with Adam. He was in her mind so much, she hardly knew when she was thinking about him directly. His image was simply always present in more or less degree, he was sometimes nearer the surface of her thoughts, the pleasantest, the only really pleasant thought she had. She examined her face in the mirror between the windows and decided that her uneasiness was not all imagination. For three days at least she had felt odd and her expression was unfamiliar. She would have to raise that fifty dollars somehow, she supposed, or who knows what can happen? She was hardened to stories of personal disaster, of outrageous and extraordinarily bitter penalties that had grown monstrously out of incidents very little more important than her failure—her refusal—to buy a Bond. No, she did not find herself a pleasing sight, flushed and shiny, and even her hair felt as if it had decided to grow in the other direction. I must do something about this, I can't let Adam see me like this, she told herself, knowing that even now at that moment he was listening for the turn of her doorknob, and he would be in the hallway, or on the porch when she came out, as if by sheerest coincidence. The noon sunlight cast cold slanting shadows in the room where, she said, I suppose I live, and this day is beginning badly, but they all do now, for one reason or another. In a drowse, she sprayed perfume on her hair, put on her moleskin cap and jacket, now in their second winter, but still good, still nice to wear, again being glad she had paid a frightening price for them. She had enjoyed them all this time, and in no case would she have had the money now. Maybe she could manage for that Bond. She could not find the lock without leaning to search for it, then stood undecided a moment possessed by the notion that she had forgotten something she would miss seriously later on.

Adam was in the hallway, a step outside his own door; he swung about as if quite startled to see her, and said, "Hello. I don't have to go back to camp today after all—isn't that luck?"

Miranda smiled at him gaily because she was always delighted at the sight of him. He was wearing his new uniform, and he was all olive and tan and tawny, hay colored and sand colored from hair to boots. She half noticed again that he always began by smiling at her; that his smile faded gradually; that his eyes became fixed and thoughtful as if he were reading in a poor light.

They walked out together into the fine fall day, scuffling bright ragged leaves under their feet, turning their faces up to a generous sky really blue and spotless. At the first corner they waited for a funeral to pass, the mourners seated straight and firm as if proud in their sorrow.

"I imagine I'm late," said Miranda, "as usual. What time is it?"

"Nearly half past one," he said, slipping back his sleeve with an exaggerated thrust of his arm upward. The young soldiers were still self-conscious about their wristwatches. Such of them as Miranda knew were boys from southern and southwestern towns, far off the Atlantic seaboard, and they had always believed that only sissies wore wristwatches. "I'll slap you on the wristwatch," one vaudeville comedian would simper to another, and it was always a good joke, never stale.

"I think it's a most sensible way to carry a watch," said Miranda. "You needn't blush."

"I'm nearly used to it," said Adam, who was from Texas. "We've been told time and again how all the he-manly regular army men wear them. It's the horrors of war," he said; "are we downhearted? I'll say we are."

It was the kind of patter going the rounds. "You look it," said Miranda.

He was tall and heavily muscled in the shoulders, narrow in the waist and flanks, and he was infinitely buttoned, strapped, harnessed into a uniform as tough and unyielding in cut as a straitjacket, though the cloth was fine and supple. He had his uniforms made by the best tailor he could find, he confided to Miranda one day when she told him how squish he was looking in his new soldier suit. "Hard enough to make anything of the outfit, anyhow," he told her. "It's the least I can do for my beloved country, not to go around looking like a tramp." He was twenty-four years old and a Second Lieutenant in an Engineers Corps, on leave because his outfit expected to be sent over shortly. "Came in to make my will," he told Miranda, "and get a supply of toothbrushes and razor blades. By what gorgeous luck do you suppose," he asked her, "I happened to pick on your rooming house? How did I know you were there?"

Strolling, keeping step, his stout polished well-made boots setting themselves down firmly beside her thin-soled black suede, they put off as long as they could the end of their moment together, and kept up as well as they could their small talk that flew back and forth over little grooves worn in the thin upper surface of the brain, things you could say and hear clink reassuringly at once without disturbing the radiance which played and darted about the simple and lovely miracle of being two persons named Adam and Miranda, twenty-four years old each, alive and on the earth at the same moment: "Are you in the mood for dancing, Miranda?" and "I'm always in the mood for dancing, Adam!" but there were things in the way, the day that ended with dancing was a long way to go.

He really did look, Miranda thought, like a fine healthy apple this morning. One time or another in their talking, he had boasted that he had never had a pain in his life that he could remember. Instead of being horrified at this monster, she approved his monstrous uniqueness. As for herself, she had had too many pains to mention, so she did not mention them. After working for three years on a morning newspaper she had an illusion of maturity and experience; but it was fatigue merely, she decided, from keeping what she had been brought up to believe were unnatural hours, eating casually at dirty little restaurants, drinking bad coffee all night, and smoking too much. When she said something of her way of living to Adam, he studied her face a few seconds as if he had never seen it before, and said in a forthright way, "Why, it hasn't hurt you a bit, I think you're beautiful," and left her dangling there, wondering if he had thought she wished to be praised. She did wish to be praised, but not at that moment. Adam kept unwholesome hours too, or had in the ten days they had known each other, staying awake until one o'clock to take her out for supper; he smoked also continually, though if she did not stop him he was apt to explain to her exactly what smoking did to the lungs. "But," he said, "does it matter so much if you're going to war, anyway?"

"No," said Miranda, "and it matters even less if you're staying at home knitting socks. Give me a cigarette, will you?" They paused at another corner, under a half-foliaged maple, and hardly glanced at a funeral procession approaching. His eyes were pale tan with orange flecks in them, and his hair was the color of a haystack when you turn the weathered top back to the clear straw beneath. He fished out his cigarette case and snapped his silver lighter at her, snapped it several times in his own face, and they moved on, smoking.

"I can see you knitting socks," he said. "That would be just your speed. You know perfectly well you can't knit."

"I do worse," she said, soberly; "I write pieces advising other young women to knit and roll bandages and do without sugar and help win the war."

"Oh, well," said Adam, with the easy masculine morals in such questions, "that's merely your job, that doesn't count."

"'I wonder," said Miranda. "How did you manage to get an extension of leave?"

"They just gave it," said Adam, "for no reason. The men are dying like flies out there, anyway. This funny new disease. Simply knocks you into a cocked hat."

"It seems to be a plague," said Miranda, "something out of the Middle Ages. Did you ever see so many funerals, ever?"

"Never did. Well, let's be strong-minded and not have any of it. I've got four days more straight from the blue and not a blade of grass must grow under our feet. What about tonight?"

"Same thing," she told him, "but make it about half past one. I've got a special job beside my usual run of the mill."

"What a job you've got," said Adam, "nothing to do but run from one dizzy amusement to another and then write a piece about it."

"Yes, it's too dizzy for words," said Miranda. They stood while a funeral passed, and this time they watched it in silence. Miranda pulled her cap to an angle and winked in the sunlight, her head swimming slowly "like goldfish," she told Adam, "my head swims. I'm only half awake, I must have some coffee."

They lounged on their elbows over the counter of a drugstore. "No more cream for the stay-at-homes," she said, "and only one lump of sugar. I'll have two or none; that's the kind of martyr I'm being. I mean to live on boiled cabbage and wear shoddy from now on and get in good shape for the next round. No war is going to sneak up on me again."

"Oh, there won't be any more wars, don't you read the newspapers?" asked Adam. "We're going to mop 'em up this time, and they're going to stay mopped, and this is going to be all."

"So they told me," said Miranda, tasting her bitter luke-warm brew and making a rueful face. Their smiles approved of each other, they felt they had got the right tone, they were taking the war properly. Above all, thought Miranda, no tooth-gnashing, no hair-tearing, it's noisy and unbecoming and it doesn't get you anywhere.

"Swill," said Adam rudely, pushing back his cup. "Is that all you're having for breakfast?"

"It's more than I want," said Miranda.

"I had buckwheat cakes, with sausage and maple syrup, and two bananas, and two cups of coffee, at eight o'clock, and right now, again, I feel like a famished orphan left in the ashcan. I'm all set," said Adam, "for broiled steak and fried potatoes and—"

"Don't go on with it," said Miranda, "it sounds delirious to me. Do all that after I'm gone." She slipped from the high seat, leaned against it slightly, glanced at her face in her round mirror, rubbed rouge on her lips and decided that she was past praying for.

"There's something terribly wrong," she told Adam. "I feel too rotten. It can't just be the weather, and the war."

"The weather is perfect," said Adam, "and the war is simply too good to be true. But since when? You were all right yesterday."

"I don't know," she said slowly, her voice sounding small and thin. They stopped as always at the open door before the flight of littered steps leading up to the newspaper loft. Miranda listened for a moment to the rattle of typewriters above, the steady rumble of presses below. "I wish we were going to spend the whole afternoon on a park bench," she said; "or drive to the mountains."

"I do too," he said; "let's do that tomorrow."

"Yes, tomorrow, unless something else happens. I'd like to run away," she told him; "let's both."

"Me?" said Adam. "Where I'm going there's no running to speak of. You mostly crawl about on your stomach here and there among the debris. You know, barbed wire and such stuff. It's going to be the kind of thing that happens once in a lifetime." He reflected a moment, and went on, "I don't know a darned thing about it, really, but they make it sound awfully messy. I've heard so much about it I feel as if I had been there and back. It's going to be an anticlimax," he said, "like seeing the pictures of a place so often you can't see it at all when you actually get there. Seems to me I've been in the army all my life."

Six months, he meant. Eternity. He looked so clear and fresh, and he had never had a pain in his life. She had seen them when they had been there and back and they never looked like this again. "Already the returned hero," she said, "and don't I wish you were."

"When I learned the use of the bayonet in my first training camp," said Adam, "I gouged the vitals out of more sandbags and sacks of hay than I could keep track of. They kept bawling at us, 'Get him, get that Boche, stick him before he sticks you'—and we'd go for those sandbags like wild-fire, and honestly, sometimes I felt a perfect fool for getting so worked up when I saw the sand trickling out. I used to wake up in the night sometimes feeling silly about it."

"I can imagine," said Miranda. "It's perfect nonsense." They lingered, unwilling to say good-by. After a little pause, Adam, as if keeping up the conversation, asked, "Do you know what the average life expectation of a sapping party is after it hits the job?"

"Something speedy, I suppose."

"Just nine minutes," said Adam; "I read that in your own newspaper not a week ago."

"Make it ten and I'll come along," said Miranda.

"Not another second," said Adam, "exactly nine minutes, take it or leave it."

"Stop bragging," said Miranda. "Who figured that out?"

"A noncombatant," said Adam, "a fellow with rickets."

This seemed very comic, they laughed and leaned towards each other and Miranda heard herself being a little shrill. She wiped the tears from her eyes. "My, it's a funny war," she said; "isn't it? I laugh every time I think about it."

Adam took her hand in both of his and pulled a little at the tips of her gloves and sniffed them. "What nice perfume you have," he said, "and such a lot of it, too. I like a lot of perfume on gloves and hair," he said, sniffing again.

"I've got probably too much," she said. "I can't smell or see or hear today. I must have a fearful cold."

"Don't catch cold," said Adam; "my leave is nearly up and it will be the last, the very last." She moved her fingers in her gloves as he pulled at the fingers and turned her hands as if they were something new and curious and of great value, and she turned shy and quiet. She liked him, she liked him, and there was more than this but it was no good even imagining, because he was not for her nor for any woman, being beyond experience already, committed without any knowledge or act of his own to death. She took back her hands. "Good-by," she said finally, "until tonight."

She ran upstairs and looked back from the top. He was still watching her, and raised his hand without smiling. Miranda hardly ever saw anyone look back after he had said good-by. She could not help turning sometimes for one glimpse more of the person she had been talking with, as if that would save too rude and too sudden a snapping of even the lightest bond. But people hurried away, their faces already changed, fixed, in their straining towards their next stopping place, already absorbed in planning their next act or encounter. Adam was waiting as if he expected her to turn, and under his brows fixed in a strained frown, his eyes were very black.

At her desk she sat without taking off jacket or cap, slitting envelopes and pretending to read the letters. Only Chuck Rouncivale, the sports reporter, and Ye Towne Gossyp were sitting on her desk today, and them she liked having there. She sat on theirs when she pleased. Towney and Chuck were talking and they went on with it.

"They say," said Towney, "that it is really caused by germs brought by a German ship to Boston, a camouflaged ship, naturally, it didn't come in under its own colors. Isn't that ridiculous?"

"Maybe it was a submarine," said Chuck, "sneaking in from the bottom of the sea in the dead of night. Now that sounds better."

"Yes, it does," said Towney; "they always slip up somewhere in these details . . . and they think the germs were sprayed over the city—it started in Boston, you know—and somebody reported seeing a strange, thick, greasy-looking cloud float up out of Boston Harbor and spread slowly all over that end of town. I think it was an old woman who saw it."

"Should have been," said Chuck.

"I read it in a New York newspaper," said Towney; "so it's bound to be true."

Chuck and Miranda laughed so loudly at this that Bill stood up and glared at them. "Towney still reads the newspapers," explained Chuck.

"Well, what's funny about that?" asked Bill, sitting down again and frowning into the clutter before him.

"It was a noncombatant saw that cloud," said Miranda.

"Naturally," said Towney.

"Member of the Lusk Committee, maybe," said Miranda.

"The Angel of Mons," said Chuck, "or a dollar-a-year man."

Miranda wished to stop hearing and talking, she wished to think for just five minutes of her own about Adam, really to think about him, but there was no time. She had seen him first ten days ago, and since then they had been crossing streets together, darting between trucks and limousines and pushcarts and farm wagons; he had waited for her in doorways and in little restaurants that smelled of stale frying fat; they had eaten and danced to the urgent whine and bray of jazz orchestras, they had sat in dull theaters because Miranda was there to write a piece about a play. Once they had gone to the mountains and, leaving the car, had climbed a stony trail, and had come out on a ledge upon a flat stone, where they sat and watched the lights change on a valley landscape that was, no doubt, Miranda said, quite aprocryphal—"We need not believe it, but it is fine poetry," she told him; they had leaned their shoulders together there, and had sat quite still, watching. On two Sundays they had gone to the geological museum, and had pored in shared fascination over bits of meteors, rock formations, fossilized tusks and trees, Indian arrows, grottoes from the silver and gold lodes. "Think of those old miners washing out their fortunes in little pans beside the streams," said Adam, "and inside the earth there was this—" and he had told her he liked better those things that took long to make; he loved airplanes too, all sorts of machinery, things carved out of wood or stone. He knew nothing much about them, but he recognized them when he saw them. He had confessed that he simply could not get through a book, any kind of book except textbooks on engineering; reading bored him to crumbs; he regretted now he hadn't brought his roadster, but he hadn't thought he would need a car; he loved driving, he wouldn't expect her to believe how many hundreds of miles he could get over in a day . . . he had showed her snapshots of himself at the wheel of his roadster; of himself sailing a boat, looking very free and windblown, all angles, hauling on the ropes; he would have joined the air force but his mother had hysterics every time he mentioned it. She didn't seem to realize that dogfighting in the air was a good deal safer than sapping parties on the ground at night. But he hadn't argued, because of course she did not realize about sapping parties. And here he was, stuck, on a plateau a mile high with no water for a boat and his car at home, otherwise they could really have had a good time. Miranda knew he was trying to tell what kind of person he was when he had his machinery with him. She felt she knew pretty well what kind of person he was, and would have liked to tell him that if he thought he had left himself at home in a boat or an automobile, he was much mistaken. The telephones were ringing, Bill was shouting at somebody who kept saying, "Well, but listen, well, but listen—" but nobody was going to listen, of course, nobody. Old man Gibbons bellowed in despair, "Jarge, Jarge—"

"Just the same," Towney was saying in her most complacent patriotic voice, "Hut Service is a fine idea, and we should all volunteer even if they don't want us." Towney does well at this, thought Miranda, look at her; remembering the rose-colored sweater and the tight rebellious face in the cloakroom. Towney was now all open-faced glory and goodness, willing to sacrifice herself for her country. "After all," said Towney, "I *can* sing and dance well enough for the Little Theater, and I could write their letters for them, and at a pinch I might drive an ambulance. I have driven a Ford for years."

Miranda joined in: "Well, I can sing and dance too, but who's going to do the bed-makng and the scrubbing up? Those huts are hard to keep, and it would be a dirty job and we'd be perfectly miserable; and as I've got a hard dirty job and am perfectly miserable, I'm going to stay at home."

"I think the women should keep out of it," said Chuck Rouncivale. "They just add skirts to the horrors of war." Chuck had bad lungs and fretted a good deal about missing the show. "I could have been there and back with a leg off by now; it would have served the old man right. Then he'd either have to buy his own hooch or sober up."

Miranda had seen Chuck on payday giving the old man money for hooch. He was a good-humored ingratiating old scoundrel, too, that was the worst of him. He slapped his son on the back and beamed upon him with the bleared eye of paternal affection while he took his last nickel.

"It was Florence Nightingale ruined wars," Chuck went on. "What's the idea of petting soldiers and binding up their wounds and soothing their fevered brows? That's not war. Let 'em perish where they fall. That's what they're there for."

"You can talk," said Towney, with a slantwise glint at him.

"Whats the idea?" asked Chuck, flushing and hunching his shoulders. "You know I've got this lung, or maybe half of it anyway by now."

"You're much too sensitive," said Towney. "I didn't mean a thing."

Bill had been raging about, chewing his half-smoked cigar, his hair standing up in a brush, his eyes soft and lambent but wild, like a stag's. He would never, thought Miranda, be more than fourteen years old if he lived for a century, which he would not at the rate he was going. He behaved exactly like city editors in the moving pictures, even to the chewed cigar. Had he formed his style on the films, or had scenario writers seized once for all on the type Bill in its inarguable purity? Bill was shouting to Chuck: *"And if he comes back here take him up the alley and saw his head off by hand!"*

Chuck said, "He'll be back, don't worry." Bill said mildly, already off on another track, "Well, saw him off." Towney went to her own desk, but Chuck sat waiting amiably to be taken to the new vaudeville show. Miranda, with two tickets, always invited one of the reporters to go with her on Monday. Chuck was lavishly hardboiled and professional in his sports writing, but he had told Miranda that he didn't give a damn about sports, really; the job kept him out in the open, and paid him enough to buy the old man's hooch. He preferred shows and didn't see why women always had the job.

"Who does Bill want sawed today?" asked Miranda.

"That hoofer you panned in this morning's," said Chuck. "He was up here bright and early asking for the guy that writes up the show business. He said he was going to take the goof who wrote that piece up the alley and bop him in the nose. He said . . ."

"I hope he's gone," said Miranda; "I do hope he had to catch a train."

Chuck stood up and arranged his maroon-colored turtlenecked sweater, glanced down at the peasoup tweed plus fours and the hobnailed tan boots which he hoped would help to disguise the fact that he had a bad lung and didn't care for sports, and said, "He's long gone by now, don't worry. Let's get going; you're late as usual."

Miranda, facing about, almost stepped on the toes of a little drab man in a derby hat. He might have been a pretty fellow once, but now his mouth drooped where he had lost his side teeth, and his sad red-rimmed eyes had given up coquetry. A thin brown wave of hair was combed out with brilliantine and curled against the rim of the derby. He didn't move his feet, but stood planted with a kind of inert resistance, and asked Miranda: "are you the so-called dramatic critic on this hick newspaper?"

"I'm afraid I am," said Miranda.

"Well," said the little man, "I'm just asking for one minute of your valuable time." His underlip shot out, he began with shaking hands to fish about in his waistcoat pocket. "I just hate to let you get away with it, that's all." He riffled through a collection of shabby newspaper clippings. "Just give these the once-over, will you? And then let me ask you if you think I'm gonna stand for being knocked by a tanktown critic," he said, in a toneless voice; "look here, here's Buffalo, Chicago, Saint Looey, Philadelphia, Frisco, besides New York. Here's the best publications in the business, *Variety*, the *Billboard*, they all broke down and admitted that Danny Dickerson knows his stuff. So you don't think so, hey? That's all I wanta ask you."

"No, I don't," said Miranda, as bluntly as she could, "and I can't stop to talk about it."

The little man leaned nearer, his voice shook as if he had been nervous for a long time. "Look here, what was there you didn't like about me? Tell me that."

Miranda said, "You shouldn't pay any attention at all. What does it matter what I think?"

"I don't care what you think, it ain't that," said the little man, "but these things get round and booking agencies back East don't know how it is out here. We get panned in the sticks and they think it's the same as getting panned in Chicago, see? They don't know the difference. They don't know that the more high class an act is the more the hick critics pan it. But I've been called the best in the business by the best in the business and I wanta know what you think is wrong with me."

Chuck said, "Come on, Miranda, curtain's going up." Miranda handed the little man his clippings, they were mostly ten years old, and tried to edge past him. He stepped before her again and said without much conviction. "If you was a man I'd knock your block off." Chuck got up at that and lounged over, taking his hands out of his pockets, and said, "Now you've done your song and dance you'd better get out. Get the hell out now before I throw you downstairs."

The little man pulled at the top of his tie, a small blue tie with red polka dots, slightly frayed at the knot. He pulled it straight and repeated as if he had rehearsed it, "Come out in the alley." The tears filled his thickened red lids. Chuck said, "Ah, shut up," and followed Miranda, who was running towards the stairs. He overtook her on the sidewalk. "I left him sniveling and shuffling his publicity trying to find the joker," said Chuck, "the poor old heel."

Miranda said, "There's too much of everything in this world just now. I'd like to sit down here on the curb, Chuck, and die, and never again see— I wish I could lose my memory and forget my own name. . . . I wish—"

Chuck said, "Toughen up, Miranda. This is no time to cave in. Forget that fellow. For every hundred people in show business, there are ninety-nine like him. But you don't manage right, anyway. You bring it on yourself. All you have to do is play up the headliners, and you needn't even mention the also-rans. Try to keep in mind that Rypinsky has got show business cornered in this town; please Rypinsky and you'll please the advertising department, please them and you'll get a raise. Hand-in-glove, my poor dumb child, will you ever learn?"

"I seem to keep learning all the wrong things," said Miranda hopelessly.

"You do that for a fact," Chuck told her cheerfully. "You are as good at it as I ever saw. Now do you feel better?"

"This is a rotten show you've invited me to," said Chuck. "Now what are you going to do about it? If I were writing it up, I'd—"

"Do write it up," said Miranda. "You write it up this time. I'm getting ready to leave, anyway, but don't tell anybody yet."

"You mean it? All my life," said Chuck, "I've yearned to be a so-called dramatic critic on a hick newspaper, and this is positvely my first chance."

"Better take it," Miranda told him. "It may be your last." She thought, This is the beginning of the end of something. Something terrible is going to happen to me. I shan't need bread and butter where I'm going. I'll will it to Chuck, he has a venerable father to buy hooch for. I hope they let him have it. Oh, Adam, I hope I see you once more before I go under with whatever is the matter with me. "I wish the war were over," she said to Chuck, as if they had been talking about that. "I wish it were over and I wish it had never begun."

Chuck had got out his pad and pencil and was already writing his review. What she had said seemed safe enough but how would he take it? "I don't care how it started or when it ends," said Chuck, scribbling away. "I'm not going to be there."

All the rejected men talked like that, thought Miranda. War was the only thing they wanted, now they couldn't have it. Maybe they had wanted badly to go, some of them. All of them had a sidelong eye for the women they talked with about it, a guarded resentment which said, "Don't pin a white feather on me, you bloodthirsty female. I've offered my meat to the crows and they won't have it." The worst thing about war for the stay-at-homes is there isn't anyone to talk to any more. The Lusk Committee will get you if you don't watch out. Bread will win the war. Work will win, sugar will win, peach pits will win the war. Nonsense. *Not* nonsense, I tell you, there's some kind of valuable high explosive to be got out of peach pits. So all the happy housewives hurry during the canning season to lay their baskets of peach pits on the altar of their country. It keeps them busy and makes them feel useful, and all these women running wild with the men away are dangerous, if they aren't given something to keep their little minds out of mischief. So rows of young girls, the intact cradles of the future, with their pure serious faces framed becomingly in Red Cross wimples, roll cockeyed bandages that will never reach a base hospital, and knit sweaters that will never warm a manly chest, their minds dwelling lovingly on all the blood and mud and the next dance at the Acanthus Club for the officers of the flying corps. Keeping still and quiet will win the war.

"I'm simply not going to be there," said Chuck, absorbed in his review. No, Adam will be there, thought Miranda. She slipped down in the chair and leaned her head against the dusty plush, closed her eyes and faced for one instant that was a lifetime the certain, the overwhelming and awful knowledge that there was nothing at all ahead for Adam and for her. Nothing. She opened her eyes and held her hands together palms up, gazing at them and trying to understand oblivion.

"Now look at this," said Chuck, for the lights had come on and the audience was rustling and talking again. "I've got it all done, even before the headliner comes on. It's old Stella Mayhew, and she's always good, she's been good for forty years, and she's going to sing 'O the blues ain't nothin' but the easy-going heart disease.' That's all you need to know about her. Now just glance over this. Would you be willing to sign it?"

Miranda took the pages and stared at them conscientiously, turning them over, she hoped, at the right moment, and gave them back. "Yes, Chuck, yes, I'd sign that. But I won't. We must tell Bill you wrote it, because it's your start, maybe."

"You don't half appreciate it," said Chuck. "You read it too fast. Here, listen to this—" and he began to mutter excitedly. While he was reading she watched his face. It was a pleasant face with some kind of spark of life in it, and a good severity in the modeling of the brow above the nose. For the first time since she had known him she wondered what Chuck was thinking about. He looked preoccupied and unhappy, he wasn't so frivolous as he sounded. The people were crowding into the aisle, bringing out their cigarette cases ready to strike a match the instant they reached the lobby; women with waved hair clutched at their wraps, men stretched their chins to ease them of their stiff collars, and Chuck said, "We might as well go now." Miranda, buttoning her jacket, stepped into the moving crowd, thinking, What did I ever know about them? There must be a great many of them here who think as I do, and we dare not say a word to each other of our desperation, we are speechless animals letting ourselves be destroyed, and why? Does anybody here believe the things we say to each other?

Stretched in unease on the ridge of the wicker couch in the cloakroom, Miranda waited for time to pass and leave Adam with her. Time seemed to proceed with more than usual eccentricity, leaving twilight gaps in her mind for thirty minutes which seemed like a second, and then hard flashes of light that shone clearly on her watch proving that three minutes is an intolerable stretch of waiting, as if she were hanging by her thumbs. At last it was reasonable to imagine Adam stepping out of the house in the early darkness into the blue mist that might soon be rain, he would be on the way, and there was nothing to think about him, after all. There was only the wish to see him and the fear, the present threat, of not seeing him again; for every step they took towards each other seemed perilous, drawing them apart instead of together, as a swimmer in spite of his most determined strokes is yet drawn slowly backward by the tide. "I don't want to love," she would think in spite of herself, "not Adam, there is no time and we are not ready for it and yet this is all we have—"

And there he was on the sidewalk, with his foot on the first step, and Miranda almost ran down to meet him. Adam, holding her hands, asked, "Do you feel well now? Are you hungry? Are you tired? Will you feel like dancing after the show?"

"Yes to everything," said Miranda, "yes, yes. . . ." Her head was like a feather, and she steadied herself on his arm. The mist was still mist that might be rain later, and though the air was sharp and clean in her mouth, it did not, she decided, make breathing any easier. "I hope the show is good, or at least funny," she told him, "but I promise nothing."

It was a long, dreary play, but Adam and Miranda sat very quietly together waiting patiently for it to be over. Adam carefully and seriously pulled off her glove and held her hand as if he were accustomed to holding her hand in theaters. Once they turned and their eyes met, but only once, and the two pairs of eyes were equally steady and noncommittal. A deep tremor set up in Miranda, and she set about resisting herself methodically as if she were closing windows and doors and fastening down curtains against a rising storm. Adam sat watching the monotonous play with a strange shining excitement, his face quite fixed and still.

When the curtain rose for the third act, the third act did not take place at once. There was instead disclosed a backdrop almost covered with an American flag improperly and disrespectfully exposed, nailed at each upper corner, gathered in the middle and nailed again, sagging dustily. Before it posed a local dollar-a-year man, now doing his bit as a Liberty Bond salesman. He was an ordinary man past middle life, with a neat little melon buttoned into his trousers and waistcoat, an opinionated tight mouth, a face and figure in which nothing could be read save the inept sensual record of fifty years. But for once in his life he was an important fellow in an impressive situation, and he reveled, rolling his words in an actorish tone.

"Looks like a penguin," said Adam. They moved, smiled at each other, Miranda reclaimed her hand, Adam folded his together and they prepared to wear their way again through the same old moldy speech with the same old dusty blackdrop. Miranda tried not to listen, but she heard. These vile Huns—glorious Belleau Wood—our keyword is Sacrifice—Martyred Belgium—give till it hurts—our noble boys Over There—Big Berthas—the death of civilization—the Boche—"My head aches," whispered Miranda. "Oh, why won't he hush?"

"He won't," whispered Adam. "I'll get you some aspirin."

"In Flanders Field the poppies grow, Between the crosses row on row" —"He's getting into the home stretch," whispered Adam—atrocities, innocent babes hoisted on Boche bayonets—your child and my child—if our children are spared these things, then let us say with all reverence that these dead have not died in vain—the war, the *war*, the WAR to end WAR, war for Democracy, for humanity, a safe world forever and ever—and to prove our faith in Democracy to each other, and to the world, let everybody get together and buy Liberty Bonds and do without sugar and wool socks—was that it? Miranda asked herself, Say that over, I didn't catch the last line. Did you mention Adam? If you didn't I'm not interested. What about Adam, you little pig? And what are we going to sing this time, "Tipperary" or "There's a Long, Long Trail"? Oh, please do let the show go on and get over with. I must write a piece about it before I can go dancing with Adam and we have no time. Coal, oil, iron, gold, international finance, why don't you tell us about them, you little liar?

The audience rose and sang, "There's a Long, Long Trail A-winding," their opened mouths black and faces pallid in the reflected footlights; some of the faces grimaced and wept and had shining streaks like snail's tracks on them. Adam and Miranda joined in at the tops of their voices, grinning shamefacedly at each other once or twice.

In the street, they lit their cigarettes and walked slowly as always. "Just another nasty old man who would like to see the young one killed," said Miranda in a low voice; "the tomcats try to eat the little tom-kittens, you know. They don't fool you really, do they, Adam?"

The young people were talking like that about the business by then. They felt they were seeing pretty clearly through that game. She went on, "I hate these pot-bellied baldheads, too fat, too old, too cowardly, to go to war themselves, they know they're safe; it's you they are sending instead—"

Adam turned eyes of genuine surprise upon her. "Oh, *that* one," he said. "Now what could the poor sap do if they did take him? It's not his fault," he explained, "he can't do anything but talk." His pride in his youth, his forbearance and tolerance and contempt for that unlucky being breathed out of his very pores as he strolled, straight and relaxed in his strength. "What *could* you expect of him, Miranda?"

She spoke his name often, and he spoke hers rarely. The little shock of pleasure the sound of her name in his mouth gave her stopped her answer. For a moment she hesitated, and began at another point of attack. "Adam," she said, "the worst of war is the fear and suspicion and the awful expression in all the eyes you meet . . . as if they had pulled down the shutters over their minds and their hearts and were peering out at you, ready to leap if you make one gesture or say one word they do not understand instantly. It frightens me; I live in fear too, and no one should have to live in fear. It's the skulking about, and the lying. It's what war does to the mind and the heart, Adam, and you can't separate these two—what it does to them is worse than what it can do to the body."

Adam said soberly, after a moment, "Oh, yes, but suppose one comes back whole? The mind and the heart sometimes get another chance, but if anything happens to the poor old human frame, why, it's just out of luck, that's all."

"Oh, yes," mimicked Miranda. "It's just out of luck, that's all."

"If I didn't go," said Adam, in a matter-of-fact voice, "I couldn't look myself in the face."

So that's all settled. With her fingers flattened on his arm, Miranda was silent, thinking about Adam. No, there was no resentment or revolt in him. Pure, she thought, all the way through, flawless, complete, as the sacrificial lamb must be. The sacrificial lamb strode along casually, accommodating his long pace to hers, keeping her on the inside of the walk in the good American style, helping her across street corners as if she were a cripple —"I hope we don't come to a mud puddle, he'll carry me over it"—giving off whiffs of tobacco smoke, a manly smell of scentless soap, freshly cleaned leather and freshly washed skin, breathing through his nose and carrying his chest easily. He threw back his head and smiled into the sky which still misted, promising rain. "Oh, boy," he said, "what a night. Can't you hurry that review of yours so we can get started?"

He waited for her before a cup of coffee in the restaurant next to the pressroom, nicknamed The Greasy Spoon. When she came down at last, freshly washed and combed and powdered, she saw Adam first, sitting near the dingy big window, face turned to the street, but looking down. It was an extraordinary face, smooth and fine and golden in the shabby light, but now set in a blind melancholy, a look of painted suspense and disillusion. For just one split second she got a glimpse of Adam when he would have been older, the face of the man he would not live to be. He saw her then, rose, and the bright glow was there.

Adam pulled their chairs together at their table; they drank hot tea and listened to the orchestra jazzing "Pack Up Your Troubles."

"'In an old kit bag, and smoil, smoil, smoil,'" shouted half a dozen boys under the draft age, gathered around a table near the orchestra. They yelled incoherently, laughed in great hysterical bursts of something that appeared to be merriment, and passed around under the tablecloth flat bottles containing a clear liquid—for in this western city founded and built by roaring drunken miners, no one was allowed to take his alcohol openly—splashed it into their tumblers of ginger ale, and went on singing, "It's a Long Way to Tipperary." When the tune changed to "Madelon," Adam said, "Let's dance." It was a tawdry little place, crowded and hot and full of smoke, but there was nothing better. The music was gay; and life is completely crazy anyway, thought Miranda, so what does it matter? This is what we have, Adam and I, this is all we're going to get, this is the way it is with us. She wanted to say, "Adam, come out of your dream and listen to me. I have pains in my chest and my head and my heart and they're real. I am in pain all over, and you are in such danger as I can't bear to think about, and why can we not save each other?" When her hand tightened on his shoulder his arm tightened about her waist instantly, and stayed there, holding firmly. They said nothing but smiled continually at each other, odd changing smiles as though they had found a new language. Miranda, her face near Adam's shoulder, noticed a dark young pair sitting at a corner table, each with an arm around the waist of the other, their heads together, they eyes staring at the same thing, whatever it was, that hovered in space before them. Her right hand lay on the table, his hand over it, and her face was a blur with weeping. Now and then he raised her hand and kissed it, and set it down and held it, and her eyes would fill again. They were not shameless, they had merely forgotten where they were, or they had no other place to go, perhaps. They said not a word, and the small pantomime repeated itself, like a melancholy short film running monotonously over and over again. Miranda envied them. She envied that girl. At least she can weep if that helps, and he does not even have to ask, What is the matter? Tell me. They had cups of coffee before them, and after a long while—Miranda and Adam had danced and sat down again twice—when the coffee was quite cold, they drank it suddenly, then embraced as before, without a word and scarcely a glance at each other. Something was done and settled between them, at least; it was enviable, enviable, that they could sit quietly together and have the same expression on their faces while they looked into the hell they shared, no matter what kind of hell, it was theirs, they were together.

At the table nearest Adam and Miranda a young woman was leaning on her elbow, telling her young man a story. "And I don't like him because he's too fresh. He kept on asking me to take a drink and I kept telling him, I don't drink and he said, Now look here, I want a drink the worst way and I think it's mean of you not to drink with me. I can't sit up here and drink by myself, he said. I told him, You're not by yourself in the first place; I like that, I said, and if you want a drink go ahead and have it, I told him, why drag *me* in? So he called the waiter and ordered ginger ale and two glasses and I drank straight ginger ale like I always do but he poured a shot of hooch in his. He was awfully proud of that hooch, said he made it himself out of potatoes. Nice homemade likker, warm from the pipe, he told me, three drops of this and your ginger ale will taste like Mumm's Extry. But I said, No, and I mean no, can't you get that through your bean? He took another drink and said, Ah, come on, honey, don't be so stubborn, this'll make your shimmy shake. So I just got tired of the argument, and I said, I don't need to drink, to shake my shimmy, I can strut my stuff on tea, I said. Well, why don't you then, he wanted to know, and I just told him—"

She knew she had been asleep for a long time when all at once without even a warning footstep or creak of the door hinge, Adam was in the room turning on the light, and she knew it was he, though at first she was blinded and turned her head away. He came over at once and sat on the side of the bed and began to talk as if he were going on with something they had been talking about before. He crumpled a square of paper and tossed it in the fireplace.

"You didn't get my note," he said. "I left it under the door. I was called back suddenly to camp for a lot of inoculations. They kept me longer than I expected, I was late. I called the office and they told me you were not coming in today. I called Miss Hobbe here and she said you were in bed and couldn't come to the telephone. Did she give you my message?"

"No," said Miranda drowsily, "but I think I have been asleep all day. Oh, I do remember. There was a doctor here. Bill sent him. I was at the telephone once, for Bill told me he would send an ambulance and have me taken to the hospital. The doctor tapped my chest and left a prescription and said he would be back, but he hasn't come."

"Where is it, the prescription?" asked Adam.

"I don't know. He left it, though, I saw him."

Adam moved about searching the tables and the mantelpiece. "Here it is," he said. "I'll be back in a few minutes. I must look for an all-night drugstore. It's after one o'clock. Good-by."

Good-by, good-by. Miranda watched the door where he had disappeared for quite a while, then closed her eyes, and thought, When I am not here I cannot remember anything about this room where I have lived for nearly a year, except that the curtains are too thin and there was never any way of shutting out the morning light. Miss Hobbe had promised heavier curtains, but they had never appeared. When Miranda in her dressing gown had been at the telephone that morning, Miss Hobbe had passed through, carrying a tray. She was a little red-haired nervously friendly creature, and her manner said all too plainly that the place was not paying and she was on the ragged edge.

"My dear *child*," she said sharply, with a glance at Miranda's attire, "what is the matter?"

Miranda, with the receiver to her ear, said, "Influenza, I think."

"*Horrors,*" said Miss Hobbe, in a whisper, and the tray wavered in her hands. "Go back to bed at once . . . go at *once!*"

"I must talk to Bill first," Miranda had told her, and Miss Hobbe had hurried on and had not returned. Bill had shouted directions at her, promising everything, doctor, nurse, ambulance, hospital, her check every week as usual, everything, but she was to get back to bed and stay there. She dropped into bed, thinking that Bill was the only person she had ever seen who actually tore his own hair when he was excited enough . . . I suppose I should ask to be sent home, she thought, it's a respectable old custom to inflict your death on the family if you can manage it. No, I'll stay here, this is my business, but not in this room, I hope. . . . I wish I were in the cold mountains in the snow, that's what I should like best; and all about her rose the measured ranges of the Rockies wearing their perpetual snow, their majestic blue laurels of cloud, chilling her to the bone with their sharp breath. Oh, no, I must have warmth—and her memory turned and roved after another place she had known first and loved best, that now she could see only in drifting fragments of palm and cedar, dark shadows and a sky that warmed without dazzling, as this strange sky had dazzled without warming her; there was the long slow wavering of gray moss in the drowsy oak shade, the spacious hovering of buzzards overhead, the smell of crushed water herbs along a bank, and without warning a broad tranquil river into which flowed all the rivers she had known. The walls shelved away in one deliberate silent movement on either side, and a tall sailing ship was moored near by, with a gangplank weathered to blackness touching the foot of her bed. Back of the ship was jungle, and even as it appeared before her, she knew it was all she had ever read or had been told or felt or thought about jungles; a writhing terribly alive and secret place of death, creeping with tangles of spotted serpents, rainbow-colored birds with malign eyes, leopards with human wise faces and extravagantly crested lions; screaming long-armed monkeys tumbling among broad fleshy leaves that glowed with sulphur-colored light and exuded the ichor of death, and rotting trunks of unfamiliar trees sprawled in crawling slime. Without surprise, watching from her pillow, she saw herself run swiftly down this gangplank to the slanting deck, and standing there, she leaned on the rail and waved gaily to her in bed, and the slender ship spread its wings and sailed away into the jungle. The air trembled with the shattering scream and the hoarse bellow of voices all crying together, rolling and colliding above her like ragged stormclouds, and the words became two words only rising and falling and clamoring about her head. Danger, danger, danger, the voices said, and War, war, war. There was her door half open, Adam standing with his hand on the knob, and Miss Hobbe with her face all out of shape with terror was crying shrilly, "I tell you, they must come for her *now,* or I'll put her on the sidewalk. . . . I tell you, this is a plague, a plague, my God, and I've got a houseful of people to think about!"

Adam said, "I know that. They'll come for her tomorrow morning."

"Tomorrow morning, my God, they'd better come now!"

"They can't get an ambulance," said Adam, "and there aren't any beds.

And we can't find a doctor or a nurse. They're all busy. That's all there is to it. You stay out of the room, and I'll look after her."

"Yes, you'll look after her, I can see that," said Miss Hobbe, in a particularly unpleasant tone.

"Yes, that's what I said," answered Adam, drily, "and you keep out."

He closed the door carefully. He was carrying an assortment of misshapen packages, and his face was astonishingly impassive.

"Did you hear that?" he asked, leaning over and speaking very quietly.

"Most of it," said Miranda, "it's nice prospect, isn't it?"

"I've got your medicine," said Adam, "and you're to begin with it this minute. She can't put you out."

"So it's really as bad as that," said Miranda.

"It's as bad as anything can be," said Adam, "all the theaters and nearly all the shops and restaurants are closed, and the streets have been full of funerals all day and ambulances all night—"

"But not one for me," said Miranda, feeling hilarious and lightheaded. She sat up and beat her pillow into shape and reached for her robe. "I'm glad you're here, I've been having a nightmare. Give me a cigarette, will you, and light one for yourself and open all the windows and sit near one of them. You're running a risk," she told him, "don't you know that? Why do you do it?"

"Never mind," said Adam, "take your medicine," and offered her two large cherry-colored pills. She swallowed them promptly and instantly vomited them up. *"Do* excuse me," she said, beginning to laugh. "I'm so sorry." Adam without a word and with a very concerned expression washed her face with a wet towel, gave her some cracked ice from one of the packages, and firmly offered her two more pills. "That's what they always did at home," she explained to him, "and it worked." Crushed with humiliation, she put her hands over her face and laughed again, painfully.

"There are two more kinds yet," said Adam, pulling her hands from her face and lifting her chin. "You've hardly begun. And I've got other things, like orange juice and ice cream—they told me to feed you ice cream—and coffee in a thermos bottle, and a thermometer. You have to work through the whole lot so you'd better take it easy."

"This time last night we were dancing," said Miranda, and drank something from a spoon. Her eyes followed him about the room, as he did things for her with an absentminded face, like a man alone; now and again he would come back, and slipping his hand under her head, would hold a cup or a tumbler to her mouth, and she drank, and followed him with her eyes again, without a clear notion of what was happening.

"Adam," she said, "I've just thought of something. Maybe they forgot St. Luke's Hospital. Call the sisters there and ask them not to be so selfish with their silly old rooms. Tell them I only want a very small dark ugly one for three days, or less. Do try them, Adam."

He believed, apparently, that she was still more or less in her right mind, for she heard him at the telephone explaining in his deliberate voice. He was back again almost at once, saying, "This seems to be my day for getting mixed up with peevish old maids. The sister said that even if they had a room you couldn't have it without doctor's orders. But they didn't have one, anyway. She was pretty sour about it."

"Well," said Miranda in a thick voice, "I think that's abominably rude and mean, don't you?" She sat up with a wide gesture of both arms, and began to retch again, violently.

"Hold it, as you were," called Adam, fetching the basin. He held her head, washed her face and hands with ice water, put her head straight on the pillow, and went over and looked out of the window. "Well," he said at last, sitting beside her again, "they haven't got a room. They haven't got a bed. They haven't even got a baby crib, the way she talked. So I think that's straight enough, and we may as well dig in."

"Isn't the ambulance coming?"

"Tomorrow, maybe."

He took off his tunic and hung it on the back of a chair. Kneeling before the fireplace, he began carefully to set kindling sticks in the shape of an Indian tepee, with a little paper in the center for them to lean upon. He lighted this and placed other sticks upon them, and larger bits of wood. When they were going nicely he added still heavier wood, and coal a few lumps at a time, until there was a good blaze, and a fire that would not need rekindling. He rose and dusted his hands together, the fire illuminated him from the back and his hair shone.

"Adam," said Miranda, "I think you're very beautiful." He laughed out at this, and shook his head at her. "What a hell of a word," he said, "for me." "It was the first that occurred to me," she said, drawing up on her elbow to catch the warmth of the blaze. "That's a good job, that fire."

He sat on the bed again, dragging up a chair and putting his feet on the rungs. They smiled at each other for the first time since he had come in that night. "How do you feel now?" he asked.

"Better, much better," she told him. "Let's talk. Let's tell each other what we meant to do."

"You tell me first," said Adam. "I want to know about you."

"You'd get the notion I had a very sad life," she said, "and perhaps it was, but I'd be glad enough to have it now. If I could have it back, it would be easy to be happy about almost anything at all. That's not true, but that's the way I feel now." After a pause, she said, "There's nothing to tell, after all, if it ends now, for all this time I was getting ready for something that was going to happen later, when the time came. So now it's nothing much."

"But it must have been worth having until now, wasn't it?" he asked seriously as if it were something important to know.

"Not if this is all," she repeated obstinately.

"Weren't you ever—happy?" asked Adam, and he was plainly afraid of the word; he was shy of it as he was of the word *love,* he seemed never to have spoken it before, and was uncertain of its sound or meaning.

"I don't know," she said, "I just lived and never thought about it. I remember things I liked, though, and things I hoped for."

"I was going to be an electrical engineer," said Adam. He stopped short. "And I shall finish up when I get back," he added, after a moment.

"Don't you love being alive?" asked Miranda. "Don't you love weather and the colors at different times of the day, and all the sounds and noises like children screaming in the next lot, and automobile horns and little bands playing in the street and the smell of food cooking?"

"I love to swim, too," said Adam.

"So do I," said Miranda; "we never did swim together."

"Do you remember any prayers?" she asked him suddenly. "Did you ever learn anything at Sunday School?"

"Not much," confessed Adam without contrition. "Well, the Lord's Prayer."

"Yes, and there's Hail Mary," she said, "and the really useful one beginning, I confess to Almighty God and to blessed Mary ever virgin and to the holy Apostles Peter and Paul—"

"Catholic," he commented.

"Prayers just the same, you big Methodist. I'll bet you *are* a Methodist."

"No, Presbyterian."

"Well, what others do you remember?"

"Now I lay me down to sleep—" said Adam.

"Yes, that one, and Blessed Jesus meek and mild—you see that my religious education wasn't neglected either. I even know a prayer beginning O Apollo. Want to hear it?"

"No," said Adam, "you're making fun."

"I'm not," said Miranda, "I'm trying to keep from going to sleep. I'm afraid to go to sleep, I may not wake up. Don't let me got to sleep, Adam. Do you know Matthew, Mark, Luke and John? Bless the bed I lie upon?"

"If I should die before I wake, I pray the Lord my soul to take. Is that it?" asked Adam. "It doesn't sound right, somehow."

"Light me a cigarette, please, and move over and sit near the window. We keep forgetting about fresh air. You must have it." He lighted the cigarette and held it to her lips. She took it between her fingers and dropped it under the edge of her pillow. He found it and crushed it out in the saucer under the water tumbler. Her head swam in darkness for an instant, cleared, and she sat up in panic, throwing off the covers and breaking into a sweat. Adam leaped up with an alarmed face, and almost at once was holding a cup of hot coffee to her mouth.

"You must have some too," she told him, quiet again, and they sat huddled together on the edge of the bed, drinking coffee in silence.

Adam said, "You must lie down again. You're awake now."

"Let's sing," said Miranda. "I know an old spiritual, I can remember some of the words." She spoke in a natural voice. "I'm fine now." She began in a hoarse whisper, " 'Pale horse, pale rider, done taken my lover away. . . .' Do you know that song?"

"Yes," said Adam, "I heard Negroes in Texas sing it, in an oil field."

"I heard them sing it in a cotton field," she said; "it's a good song."

They sang that line together. "But I can't remember what comes next," said Adam.

" 'Pale horse, pale rider,' " said Miranda. "(We really need a good banjo) 'done taken my lover away—' " Her voice cleared and she said, "But we ought to get on with it. What's the next line?"

"There's a lot more to it than that," said Adam, "about forty verses, the rider done taken away mammy, pappy, brother, sister, the whole family besides the lover—"

"But not the singer, not yet," said Miranda. "Death always leaves one singer to mourn. 'Death,' " she sang, " 'oh, leave one singer to mourn—' "

" 'Pale horse, pale rider,' " chanted Adam, coming in on the beat, " 'done taken my lover away!' (I think we're good, I think we ought to get up and act—)"

"Go in Hut Service," said Miranda, "entertain the poor defenseless heroes Over There."

"We'll play banjos," said Adam; "I always wanted to play the banjo."

Miranda sighed, and lay back on the pillow and thought, I must give up, I can't hold out any longer. There was only that pain, only that room, and only Adam. There were no longer any multiple planes of living, no tough filaments of memory and hope pulling taut backwards and forwards holding her upright between them. There was only this one moment and it was a dream of time, and Adam's face, very near hers, eyes still and intent, was a shadow, and there was to be nothing more. . . .

"Adam," she said out of the heavy soft darkness that drew her down, down, "I love you, and I was hoping you would say that to me, too."

He lay down beside her with his arm under her shoulder, and pressed his smooth face against hers, his mouth moved towards her mouth and stopped. "Can you hear what I am saying? . . . What do you think I have been trying to tell you all this time?"

She turned towards him, the cloud cleared and she saw his face for an instant. He pulled the covers about her and held her, and said, "Go to sleep, darling, darling, if you will go to sleep now for one hour I will wake you up and bring you hot coffee and tomorrow we will find somebody to help. I love you, go to sleep—"

Almost with no warning at all, she floated into the darkness, holding his hand, in sleep that was not sleep but clear evening light in a small green wood, an angry dangerous wood full of inhuman concealed voices singing sharply like the whine of arrows and she saw Adam transfixed by a flight of these singing arrows that struck him in the heart and passed shrilly cutting their path through the leaves. Adam fell straight back before her eyes, and rose again unwounded and alive; another flight of arrows loosed from the invisible bow struck him again and he fell, and yet he was there before her untouched in a perpetual death and resurrection. She threw herself before him, angrily and selfishly she interposed between him and the track of the arrow, crying, No, no, like a child cheated in a game, it's my turn now, why must you always be the one to die? and the arrows struck her cleanly through the heart and through his body and he lay dead, and she still lived, and the wood whistled and sang and shouted, every branch and leaf and blade of grass had its own terrible accusing voice. She ran then, and Adam caught her in the middle of the room, running, and said, "Darling, I must have been asleep too. What happened, you screamed terribly?"

After he had helped her to settle again, she sat with her knees drawn up under her chin, resting her head on her folded arms and began carefully searching for her words because it was important to explain clearly. "It was a very odd sort of dream, I don't know why it could have frightened me. There was something about an old-fashioned valentine. There were two hearts carved on a tree, pierced by the same arrow—you know, Adam—"

"Yes, I know, honey," he said in the gentlest sort of way, and sat kissing her on the cheek and forehead with a kind of accustomedness, as if he had been kissing her for years, "one of those lace paper things."

"Yes, and yet they were alive, and were us, you understand—this doesn't seem to be quite the way it was, but it was something like that. It was in a wood—"

"Yes," said Adam. He got up and put on his tunic and gathered up the thermos bottle. "I'm going back to that little stand and get us some ice cream and hot coffee," he told her, "and I'll be back in five minutes, and you keep quiet. Good-by for five minutes," he said, holding her chin in the palm of his hand and trying to catch her eye, "and you be very quiet."

"Good-by," she said. "I'm awake again." But she was not, and the two alert young internes from the County hospital who had arrived, after frantic urgings from the noisy city editor of the Blue Mountain *News,* to carry her away in a police ambulance, decided that they had better go down and get the stretcher. Their voices roused her, she sat up, got out of bed at once and stood glancing about brightly. "Why, you're all right," said the darker and stouter of the two young men, both extremely fit and competent-looking in their white clothes, each with a flower in his buttonhole. "I'll just carry you." He unfolded a white blanket and wrapped it around her. She gathered up the folds and asked, "But where is Adam?" taking hold of the doctor's arm. He laid a hand on her drenched forehead, shook his head, and gave her a shrewd look. "Adam?"

"Yes," Miranda told him, lowering her voice confidentially, "he was here and now he is gone."

"Oh, he'll be back," the interne told her easily, "he's just gone round the block to get cigarettes. Don't worry about Adam. He's the least of your troubles."

"Will he know where to find me?" she asked, still holding back.

"We'll leave him a note," said the interne. "Come now, it's time we got out of here."

He lifted and swung her up to his shoulder. "I feel very badly," she told him; "I don't know why."

"I'll bet you do," said he, stepping out carefully, the other doctor going before them, and feeling for the first step of the stairs. "Put your arms around my neck," he instructed her. "It won't do you any harm and it's a great help to me."

"What's your name?" Miranda asked as the other doctor opened the front door and they stepped out into the frosty sweet air.

"Hildesheim," he said, in the tone of one humoring a child.

"Well, Dr. Hildesheim, aren't we in a pretty mess?"

"We certainly are," said Dr. Hildesheim.

The second young interne, still quite fresh and dapper in his white coat, though his carnation was withering at the edges, was leaning over listening to her breathing through a stethoscope, whistling thinly, "There's a Long, Long Trail—" From time to time he tapped her ribs smartly with two fingers, whistling. Miranda observed him for a few moments until she fixed his bright busy hazel eye not four inches from hers. "I'm not unconscious," she explained, "I know what I want to say." Then to her horror she heard herself babbling nonsense, knowing it was nonsense though she could not hear what she was saying. The flicker of attention in the eye near her vanished, the second interne went on tapping and listening, hissing softly under his breath.

"I wish you'd stop whistling," she said clearly. The sound stopped. "It's a beastly tune," she added. Anything, anything at all to keep her small hold on the life of human beings, a clear line of communication, no matter what, between her and the receding world. "Please let me see Dr. Hildesheim," she said, "I have something important to say to him. I must say it now." The second interne vanished. He did not walk away, he fled into the air without a sound, and Dr. Hildesheim's face appeared in his stead.

"Dr. Hildesheim, I want to ask you about Adam."

"That young man? He's been here, and left you a note, and has gone again," said Dr. Hildesheim, "and he'll be back tomorrow and the day after." His tone was altogether too merry and flippant.

"I don't believe you," said Miranda bitterly, closing her lips and eyes and hoping she might not weep.

"Miss Tanner," called the doctor, "have you got that note?"

Miss Tanner appeared beside her, handed her an unsealed envelope, took it back, unfolded the note and gave it to her.

"I can't see it," said Miranda, after a pained search of the page full of hasty scratches in black ink.

"Here, I'll read it," said Miss Tanner. "It says, 'They came and took you while I was away and now they will not let me see you. Maybe tomorrow they will, with my love, Adam,' " read Miss Tanner in a firm dry voice, pronouncing the words distinctly. "Now, do you see?" she asked soothingly.

Miranda, hearing the words one by one, forgot them one by one. "Oh, read it again, what does it say?" she called out over the silence that pressed upon her, reaching towards the dancing words that just escaped as she almost touched them. "That will do," said Dr. Hildesheim, calmly authoritarian. "Where is that bed?"

"There is no bed yet," said Miss Tanner, as if she said, We are short of oranges. Dr. Hildesheim said, "Well, we'll manage something," and Miss Tanner drew the narrow trestle with bright crossed metal supports and small rubbery wheels into a deep jut of the corridor, out of the way of the swift white figures darting about, whirling and skimming like water flies all in silence. The white walls rose sheer as cliffs, a dozen frosted moons followed each other in perfect self-possession down a white lane and dropped mutely one by one into a snowy abyss.

What is this whiteness and silence but the absence of pain? Miranda lay lifting the nap of her white blanket softly between eased fingers, watching a dance of tall deliberate shadows moving behind a wide screen of sheets spread upon a frame. It was there, near her, on her side of the wall where she could see it clearly and enjoy it, and it was so beautiful she had no curiosity as to its meaning. Two dark figures nodded, bent, curtsied to each other, retreated and bowed again, lifted long arms and spread great hands against the white shadow of the screen; then with a single round movement, the sheets were folded back, disclosing two speechless men in white, standing, and another speechless man in white, lying on the bare springs of a white iron bed. The man on the springs was swathed smoothly from head to foot in white, with folded bands across the face, and a large stiff bow like merry rabbit ears dangled at the crown of his head.

The two living men lifted a mattress standing hunched against the wall, spread it tenderly and exactly over the dead man. Wordless and white they vanished down the corridor, pushing the wheeled bed before them. It had been an entrancing and leisurely spectacle, but now it was over. A pallid white fog rose in their wake insinuatingly and floated before Miranda's eyes, a fog in which was concealed all terror and all weariness, all the wrung faces and twisted backs and broken feet of abused, outraged living things, all the shapes of their confused pain and their estranged hearts; the fog might part at any moment and loose the horde of human torments. She put up her hands and said, Not yet, not yet, but it was too late. The fog parted and two executioners, white clad, moved towards her pushing between them with marvelously deft and practiced hands the misshapen figure of an old man in filthy rags whose scanty beard waggled under his opened mouth as he bowed his back and braced his feet to resist and delay the fate they had prepared for him. In a high weeping voice he was trying to explain to them that the crime of which he was accused did not merit the punishment he was about to receive; and except for this whining cry there was silence as they advanced. The soiled cracked bowls of the old man's hands were held before him beseechingly as a beggar's as he said, "Before God I am not guilty," but they held his arms and drew him onward, passed, and were gone.

The road to death is a long march beset with all evils, and the heart fails little by little at each new terror, the bones rebel at each step, the mind sets up its own bitter resistance and to what end? The barriers sink one by one, and no covering of the eyes shuts out the landscape of disaster, nor the sight of crimes committed there. Across the field came Dr. Hildesheim, his face a skull beneath his German helmet, carrying a naked infant writhing on the point of his bayonet, and a huge stone pot marked Poison in Gothic letters. He stopped before the well that Miranda remembered in a pasture on her father's farm, a well once dry but now bubbling with living water, and into its pure depths he threw the child and the poison, and the violated water sank back soundlessly into the earth. Miranda, screaming, ran with her arms above her head; her voice echoed and came back to her like a wolf's howl, Hildesheim is a Boche, a spy, a Hun, kill him, kill him before he kills you. . . . She woke howling, she heard the foul words accusing Hildesheim tumbling from her mouth; opened her eyes and knew she was in a bed in a small white room, with Dr. Hildesheim sitting beside her, two firm fingers on her pulse. His hair was brushed sleekly and his buttonhole flower was fresh. Stars gleamed through the window, and Dr. Hildesheim seemed to be gazing at them with no particular expression, his stethoscope dangling around his neck. Miss Tanner stood at the foot of the bed writing something on a chart.

"Hello," said Dr. Hildesheim, "at least you take it out in shouting. You don't try to get out of bed and go running around." Miranda held her eyes open with a terrible effort, saw his rather heavy, patient face clearly even as her mind tottered and slithered again, broke from its foundation and spun like a cast wheel in a ditch. "I didn't mean it, I never believed it, Dr. Hildesheim, you mustn't remember it—" and was gone again, not being able to wait for an answer.

The wrong she had done followed her and haunted her dream: this wrong took vague shapes of horror she could not recognize or name, though her heart cringed at sight of them. Her mind, split in two, acknowledged and denied what she saw in the one instant, for across an abyss of complaining darkness her reasoning coherent self watched the strange frenzy of the other coldly, reluctant to admit the truth of its visions, its tenacious remorses and despairs.

"I know those are your hands," she told Miss Tanner. "I know it, but to me they are white tarantulas, don't touch me."

"Shut your eyes," said Miss Tanner.

"Oh, no," said Miranda, "for then I see worse things," but her eyes closed in spite of her will, and the midnight of her internal torment closed about her.

Oblivion, thought Miranda, her mind feeling among her memories of words she had been taught to describe the unseen, the unknowable, is a whirlpool of gray water turning upon itself for all eternity . . . eternity is perhaps more than the distance to the farthest star. She lay on a narrow ledge over a pit that she knew to be bottomless, though she could not comprehend it; the ledge was her childhood dream of danger, and she strained back against a reassuring wall of granite at her shoulders, staring into the pit, thinking, There it is, there it is at last, it is very simple; and soft carefully shaped words like oblivion and eternity are curtains hung before nothing at all. I shall not know when it happens, I shall not feel or remember, why can't I consent now, I am lost, there is no hope for me. Look, she told herself, there it is, that is death and there is nothing to fear. But she could not consent, still shrinking stiffly against the granite wall that was her childhood dream of safety, breathing slowly for fear of squandering breath, saying desperately, Look, don't be afraid, it is nothing, it is only eternity.

Granite walls, whirlpools, stars, are things. None of them is death, nor the image of it. Death is death, said Miranda, and for the dead it has no attributes. Silenced, she sank easily through deeps under deeps of darkness until she lay like a stone at the farthest bottom of life, knowing herself to be blind, deaf, speechless, no longer aware of the members of her own body, entirely withdrawn from all human concerns, yet alive with a peculiar lucidity and coherence; all notions of the mind, the reasonable inquiries of doubt, all ties of blood and the desires of the heart, dissolved and fell away from her, and there remained of her only a minute fiercely burning particle of being that knew itself alone, that relied upon nothing beyond itself for its strength; not susceptible to any appeal or inducement, being itself composed entirely of one single motive, the stubborn will to live. This fiery motionless particle set itself unaided to resist destruction, to survive and to be in its own madness of being, motiveless and planless beyond that one essential end. Trust me, the hard unwinking angry point of light said. Trust me. I stay.

At once it grew, flattened, thinned to a fine radiance, spread like a great fan and curved out into a rainbow through which Miranda, enchanted, altogether believing, looked upon a deep clear landscape of sea and sand, of soft meadow and sky, freshly washed and glistening with transparencies of blue. Why, of course, of course, said Miranda, without surprise but with serene rapture as if some promise made to her had been kept long after she had ceased to hope for it. She rose from her narrow ledge and ran lightly through the tall portals of the great bow that arched in its splendor over the burning blue of the sea and the cool green of the meadow on either hand.

The small waves rolled in and over unhurriedly, lapped upon the sand in silence and retreated; the grasses flurried before a breeze that made no sound. Moving towards her leisurely as clouds through the shimmering air came a great company of human beings, and Miranda saw in an amazement of joy that they were all the living she had known. Their faces were transfigured, each in its own beauty, beyond what she remembered of them, their eyes were clear and untroubled as good weather, and they cast no shadows. They were pure identities and she knew them every one without calling their names or remembering what relation she bore to them. They surrounded her smoothly on silent feet, then turned their entranced faces again towards the sea, and she moved among them easily as a wave among waves. The drifting circle widened, separated, and each figure was alone but not solitary; Miranda, alone too, questioning nothing, desiring nothing, in the quietude of her ecstasy, stayed where she was, eyes fixed on the overwhelming deep sky where it was always morning.

Lying at ease, arms under her head, in the prodigal warmth which flowed evenly from sea and sky and meadow, within touch but not touching the serenely smiling familiar beings about her, Miranda felt without warning a vague tremor of apprehension, some small flick of distrust in her joy; a thin frost touched the edges of this confident tranquillity; something, somebody, was missing, she had lost something, she had left something valuable in another country, oh, what could it be? There are no trees, no trees here, she said in fright, I have left something unfinished. A thought struggled at the back of her mind, came clearly as a voice in her ear. Where are the dead? We have forgotten the dead, oh, the dead, where are they? At once as if a curtain had fallen, the bright landscape faded, she was alone in a strange stony place of bitter cold, picking her way along a steep path of slippery snow, calling out, Oh, I must go back! But in what direction? Pain returned, a terrible compelling pain running through her veins like heavy fire, the stench of corruption filled her nostrils, the sweetish sickening smell of rotting flesh and pus; she opened her eyes and saw pale light through a coarse white cloth over her face, knew that the smell of death was in her own body and struggled to lift her hand. The cloth was drawn away; she saw Miss Tanner filling a hypodermic needle in her methodical expert way, and heard Dr. Hildesheim saying, "I think that will do the trick. Try another." Miss Tanner plucked firmly at Miranda's arm near the shoulder, and the unbelievable current of agony ran burning through her veins again. She struggled to cry out, saying, Let me go, let me go; but heard only incoherent sounds of animal suffering. She saw doctor and nurse glance at each other with the glance of initiates at a mystery, nodding in silence, their eyes alive with knowledgeable pride. They looked briefly at their handiwork and hurried away.

Bells screamed all off key, wrangling together as they collided in midair, horns and whistles mingled shrilly with cries of human distress; sulphur-colored light exploded through the black windowpane and flashed away in darkness. Miranda waking from a dreamless sleep asked without expecting an answer, "What is happening?" for there was a bustle of voices and footsteps in the corridor, and a sharpness in the air; the far clamor went on, a furious exasperated shrieking like a mob in revolt.

The light came on, and Miss Tanner said in a furry voice, "Hear that? They're celebrating. It's the Armistice. The war is over, my dear." Her hands trembled. She rattled a spoon in a cup, stopped to listen, held the cup out to Miranda. From the ward for old bedridden women down the hall floated a ragged chorus of cracked voices singing, "My country, 'tis of thee . . ."

Sweet land . . . oh, terrible land of this bitter world where the sound of rejoicing was a clamor of pain, where ragged tuneless old women, sitting up waiting for their evening bowl of cocoa, were singing, "Sweet land of Liberty—"

"Oh, say, can you see?" their hopeless voices were asking next, the hammer strokes of metal tongues drowning them out. "The war is over," said Miss Tanner, her underlip held firmly, her eyes blurred. Miranda said, "Please open the window, please, I smell death in here."

Now if real daylight such as I remember having seen in this world would only come again, but it is always twilight or just before morning, a promise of day that is never kept. What has become of the sun? That was the longest and loneliest night and yet it will not end and let the day come. Shall I ever see light again?

Sitting in a long chair, near a window, it was in itself a melancholy wonder to see the colorless sunlight slanting on the snow, under a sky drained of its blue. "Can this be my face?" Miranda asked her mirror. "Are these my own hands?" she asked Miss Tanner, holding them up to show the yellow tint like melted wax glimmering between the closed fingers. The body is a curious monster, no place to live in, how could anyone feel at home there? Is it possible I can ever accustom myself to this place? she asked herself. The human faces around her seemed dulled and tired, with no radiance of skin and eyes as Miranda remembered radiance; the once white walls of her room were now a soiled gray. Breathing slowly, falling asleep and waking again, feeling the splash of water on her flesh, taking food, talking in bare phrases with Dr. Hildesheim and Miss Tanner, Miranda looked about her with the covertly hostile eyes of an alien who does not like the country in which he finds himself, does not understand the language nor wish to learn it, does not mean to live there and yet is helpless, unable to leave it at his will.

"It is morning," Miss Tanner would say, with a sigh, for she had grown old and weary once for all in the past month, "morning again, my dear," showing Miranda the same monotonous landscape of dulled evergreens and leaden snow. She would rustle about in her starched skirts, her face bravely powdered, her spirit unbreakable as good steel, saying, "Look, my dear, what a heavenly morning, like a crystal," for she had an affection for the salvaged creature before her, the silent ungrateful human being whom she, Cornelia Tanner, a nurse who knew her business, had snatched back from death with her own hands. "Nursing is nine-tenths, just the same," Miss Tanner would tell the other nurses; "keep that in mind." Even the sunshine was Miss Tanner's own prescription for the further recovery of Miranda, this patient the doctors had given up for lost, and who yet sat here, visible proof of Miss Tanner's theory. She said, "Look at the sunshine, now," as she might be saying, "I ordered this for you, my dear, so sit up and take it."

"It's beautiful," Miranda would answer, even turning her head to look, thanking Miss Tanner for her goodness, most of all her goodness about the weather, "beautiful, I always loved it." And I might love it again if I saw it, she thought, but truth was, she could not see it. There was no light, there might never be light again, compared as it must always be with the light she had seen beside the blue sea that lay so tranquilly along the shore of her paradise. That was a child's dream of the heavenly meadow, the vision of repose that comes to a tired body in sleep, she thought, but I have seen it when I did not know it was a dream. Closing her eyes she would rest for a moment remembering that bliss which had repaid all the pain of the journey to reach it; opening them again she saw with a new anguish the dull world to which she was condemned, where the light seemed filmed over with cobwebs, all the bright surfaces corroded, the sharp planes melted and formless, all objects and beings meaningless, ah, dead and withered things that believed themselves alive!

At night, after the long effort of lying in her chair, in her extremity of grief for what she had so briefly won, she folded her painful body together and wept silently, shamelessly, in pity for herself and her lost rapture. There was no escape. Dr. Hildesheim, Miss Tanner, the nurses in the diet kitchen, the chemist, the surgeon, the precise machine of the hospital, the whole humane conviction and custom of society, conspired to pull her inseparable rack of bones and wasted flesh to its feet, to put in order her disordered mind, and to set her once more safely on the road that would lead her again to death.

Chuck Rouncivale and Mary Townsend came to see her, bringing her a bundle of letters they had guarded for her. They brought a basket of delicate small hothouse flowers, lilies of the valley with sweet peas and feathery fern, and above these blooms their faces were merry and haggard.

Mary said, "You *have* had a tussle, haven't you?" and Chuck said, "Well, you made it back, didn't you?" Then after an uneasy pause, they told her that everybody was waiting to see her again at her desk. "They've put me back on sports already, Miranda," said Chuck. For ten minutes Miranda smiled and told them how gay and what a pleasant surprise it was to find herself alive. For it will not do to betray the conspiracy and tamper with the courage of the living; there is nothing better than to be alive, everyone has agreed on that; it is past argument, and who attempts to deny it is justly outlawed. "I'll be back in no time at all," she said; "this is almost over."

Her letters lay in a heap in her lap and beside her chair. Now and then she turned one over to read the inscription, recognizing this handwriting or that, examined the blotted stamps and the postmarks, and let them drop again. For two or three days they lay upon the table beside her, and she continued to shrink from them. "They will all be telling me again how good it is to be alive, they will say again they love me, they are glad I am living too, and what can I answer to that?" and her hardened, indifferent heart shuddered in despair at itself, because before it had been tender and capable of love.

Dr. Hildesheim said, "What, all these letters not opened yet?" and Miss Tanner said, "Read your letters, my dear, I'll open them for you." Standing beside the bed, she slit them cleanly with a paper knife. Miranda, cornered, picked and chose until she found a thin one in an unfamiliar handwriting. "Oh, no, now," said Miss Tanner, "take them as they come. Here, I'll hand them to you." She sat down, prepared to be helpful to the end.

What a victory, what triumph, what happiness to be alive, sang the letters in a chorus. The names were signed with flourishes like the circles in air of bugle notes, and they were the names of those she had loved best; some of those she had known well and pleasantly; and a few who meant nothing to her, then or now. The thin letter in the unfamiliar handwriting was from a strange man at the camp where Adam had been, telling her that Adam had died of influenza in the camp hospital. Adam had asked him, in case anything happened, to be sure to let her know.

If anything happened. To be sure to let her know. If anything happened. "Your friend, Adam Barclay," wrote the strange man. It had happened— she looked at the date—more than a month ago.

"I've been here a long time, haven't I?" she asked Miss Tanner, who was folding letters and putting them back in their proper envelopes.

"Oh, quite a while," said Miss Tanner, "but you'll be ready to go soon now. But you must be careful of yourself and not overdo, and you should come back now and then and let us look at you, because sometimes the after-effects are very—"

Miranda, sitting up before the mirror, wrote carefully: "One lipstick, medium, one ounce flask Bois d'Hiver perfume, one pair of gray suede gauntlets without straps, two pair gray sheer stockings without clocks—"

Towney, reading after her, said, "Everything without something so that it will be almost impossible to get?"

"Try it, though," said Miranda, "they're nicer without. One walking stick of silvery wood with a silver knob."

"That's going to be expensive," warned Towney. "Walking is hardly worth it."

"You're right," said Miranda, and wrote in the margin, "a nice one to match my other things. Ask Chuck to look for this, Mary. Good-looking and not too heavy." Lazarus, come forth. Not unless you bring me my top hat and stick. Stay where you are then, you snob. Not at all, I'm coming forth. "A jar of cold cream," wrote Miranda, "a box of apricot powder— and, Mary, I don't need eye shadow, do I?" She glanced at her face in the mirror and away again. "Still, no one need pity this corpse if we look properly to the art of the thing."

Mary Townsend said, "You won't recognize yourself in a week."

"Do you suppose, Mary," asked Miranda, "I could have my old room back again?"

"That should be easy," said Mary. "We stored away all your things there with Miss Hobbe." Miranda wondered again at the time and trouble the living took to be helpful to the dead. But not quite dead now, she reassured herself, one foot in either world now; soon I shall cross back and be at home again. The light will seem real and I shall be glad when I hear that someone I know has escaped from death. I shall visit the escaped ones and help them dress and tell them how lucky they are, and how lucky I am still to have them. Mary will be back soon with my gloves and my walking stick, I must go now, I must begin saying good-by to Miss Tanner and Dr. Hildesheim. Adam, she said, now you need not die again, but still I wish you were here; I wish you had come back, what do you think I came back for, Adam, to be deceived like this?

At once he was there beside her, invisible but urgently present, a ghost but more alive than she was, the last intolerable cheat of her heart; for knowing it was false she still clung to the lie, the unpardonable lie of her bitter desire. She said, "I love you," and stood up trembling, trying by the mere act of her will to bring him to sight before her. If I could call you up from the grave I would, she said, if I could see your ghost I would say, I believe. . . . "I believe," she said aloud. "Oh, let me see you once more." The room was silent, empty, the shade was gone from it, struck away by the sudden violence of her rising and speaking aloud. She came to herself as if out of sleep. Oh, no, that is not the way, I must never do that, she warned herself. Miss Tanner said, "Your taxicab is waiting, my dear," and there was Mary. Ready to go.

No more war, no more plague, only the dazed silence that follows the ceasing of the heavy guns; noiseless houses with the shades drawn, empty streets, the dead cold light of tomorrow. Now there would be time for everything.

10

RICHARD WRIGHT
The Man Who Lived Underground

The Man Who Lived Underground has many of the characteristics of allegory. As in an allegory, nearly every scene is a vehicle for conveying symbolic meaning, and the meanings generated by various scenes fit together in a carefully structured way so as to contribute to moral insight. In particular, Fred Daniels' escape underground and his successive experiences there have moral implications. Wright was inspired partly by Dostoevsky's *Notes from Underground* in using the underground as a symbol of repression, suffering, and insight into cultural truth. Instead of using the underground purely as a metaphor, as Dostoevsky does, Wright transforms the literal underground of a city sewer system into a symbolic world. Free for a time from the immediate threat of white repression, Fred Daniels stumbles onto truths which, as a black man, he has repressed within himself most of his life. The scenes he encounters have the kind of imagistic clarity and sequential structure characteristic of allegorical symbolism. By the end of his stay underground, he is obsessed with the realization that urban blacks are complicit in their own destruction

under the yoke of white wealth and power.

Because Wright's primary purpose is to reveal moral and psychological truth through symbolic events, his techniques often depart from those of strictly realistic fiction. He uses improbability and contrivance, somewhat as Conrad does in *The Secret Sharer,* to pack his story with more meaning than he might by simply portraying life as it usually is. Fred Daniels' extraordinary luck in gaining access to various buildings from his sewer hideout is of course improbable. Even more improbably, he witnesses the interrogation of the night watchman by the same three policemen who had extracted his own false confession of murder. But improbability opens the way to meaning: in this case, the reappearance of the policemen develops the theme of innocence and guilt. The same three policemen torture two equally innocent black men. In the second case it is Fred Daniels who is actually guilty, but his is only a symbolic, underground guilt—unconscious, absurd, and unrelated to the conventional above-ground morality of greed and necessity. This is the black man's plight: to be essentially innocent, but to suffer endlessly from a guilt "which one could not forget or shake off, but which had been forgotten by the conscious mind, creating in one's life a state of eternal anxiety."

The Man Who Lived Underground is a psychological study as well as a moral one, and much of its powerful appeal stems from the acting out of unconscious desires common to all people. Fred Daniels' escape through underground tunnels reawakens childhood passions for "escapes" into caves, tunnels, and the like. His almost magical ease of movement can be compared to such magical powers of mobility as flying in myths and dreams. There is also strong appeal to the human impulse for exploration, for going where no one else has been and seeing things as they have not been seen before.

In history and mythology two kinds of imaginative places have especially motivated man's zest for exploration: the ultimately good place, the Eldorado or Shangri-la, and the ultimately bad place, the symbolic hell where the adventurer may discover fascinating truths by seeing the very worst of worlds. Dante's mythological hell is of this type. Wright succeeds in evoking the imaginative power of both kinds of places. The sewer is a terrifying place. It is dark, rat-infested, and lonely. The scenes Fred Daniels sees there chill his soul with the awful truth of black subjection. At the same time, he is quite safe underground, and his steadily growing capability there gives him access to food and treasure. In its own way the underground becomes a kind of perverse Eden, and he finds in it a knowledge of good and evil.

The Man
Who Lived
Underground

I've got to hide, he told himself. His chest heaved as he waited, crouching in a dark corner of the vestibule. He was tired of running and dodging. Either he had to find a place to hide, or he had to surrender. A police car swished by through the rain, its siren rising sharply. They're looking for me all over . . . He crept to the door and squinted through the fogged plate glass. He stiffened as the siren rose and died in the distance. Yes, he had to hide, but where? He gritted his teeth. Then a sudden movement in the street caught his attention. A throng of tiny columns of water snaked into the air from the perforations of a manhole cover. The columns stopped abruptly, as though the perforations had become clogged; a gray spout of sewer water jutted up from underground and lifted the circular metal cover, juggled it for a moment, then let it fall with a clang.

He hatched a tentative plan: he would wait until the siren sounded far off, then he would go out. He smoked and waited, tense. At last the siren gave him his signal; it wailed, dying, going away from him. He stepped to the sidewalk, then paused and looked curiously at the open manhole, half expecting the cover to leap up again. He went to the center of the street and stooped and peered into the hole, but could see nothing. Water rustled in the black depths.

He started with terror; the siren sounded so near that he had the idea that he had been dreaming and had awakened to find the car upon him. He dropped instinctively to his knees and his hands grasped the rim of the manhole. The siren seemed to hoot directly above him and with a wild gasp of exertion he snatched the cover far enough off to admit his body. He swung his legs over the opening and lowered himself into watery darkness. He hung for an eternal moment to the rim by his finger tips, then he felt rough metal prongs and at once he knew that sewer workmen used these ridges to lower themselves into manholes. Fist over fist, he let his body sink until he could feel no more prongs. He swayed in dank space; the siren seemed to howl at the very rim of the manhole. He dropped and was washed violently into an ocean of warm, leaping water. His head was battered against a wall and he wondered if this were death. Frenziedly his fingers clawed and sank into a crevice. He steadied himself and measured the strength of the current with his own muscular tension. He stood slowly in water that dashed past his knees with fearful velocity.

He heard a prolonged scream of brakes and the siren broke off. Oh, God! They had found him! Looming above his head in the rain a white face hovered over the hole. "How did this damn thing get off?" he heard a policeman ask. He saw the steel cover move slowly until the hole looked like a quarter moon turned black. "Give me a hand here," someone called. The cover clanged into place, muffling the sights and sounds of the upper world. Knee-deep in the pulsing current, he breathed with aching chest, filling his lungs with the hot stench of yeasty rot.

From the perforations of the manhole cover, delicate lances of hazy violet sifted down and wove a mottled pattern upon the surface of the streaking current. His lips parted as a car swept past along the wet pavement overhead, its heavy rumble soon dying out, like the hum of a plane speeding through a dense cloud. He had never thought that cars could sound like that; everything seemed strange and unreal under here. He stood in darkness for a long time, knee-deep in rustling water, musing.

The odor of rot had become so general that he no longer smelled it. He got his cigarettes, but discovered that his matches were wet. He searched and found a dry folder in the pocket of his shirt and managed to strike one; it flared weirdly in the wet gloom, glowing greenishly, turning red, orange, then yellow. He lit a crumpled cigarette; then, by the flickering light of the match, he looked for support so that he would not have to keep his muscles flexed against the pouring water. His pupils narrowed and he saw to either side of him two steaming walls that rose and curved inward some six feet above his head to form a dripping, mouse-colored dome. The bottom of the sewer was a sloping V-trough. To the left, the sewer vanished in ashen fog. To the right was a steep down-curve into which water plunged.

He saw now that had he not regained his feet in time, he would have been swept to death, or had he entered any other manhole he would have probably drowned. Above the rush of the current he heard sharper juttings of water; tiny streams were spewing into the sewer from smaller conduits. The match died; he struck another and saw a mass of debris sweep past him and clog the throat of the down-curve. At once the water began rising rapidly. Could he climb out before he drowned? A long hiss sounded and the debris was sucked from sight; the current lowered. He understood now what had made the water toss the manhole cover; the down-curve had become temporarily obstructed and the perforations had been clogged.

He was in danger; he might slide into a down-curve; he might wander with a lighted match into a pocket of gas and blow himself up; or he might contract some horrible disease . . . Though he wanted to leave, an irrational impulse held him rooted. To the left, the convex ceiling swooped to a height of less than five feet. With cigarette slanting from pursed lips, he waded with taut muscles, his feet sloshing over the slimy bottom, his shoes sinking into spongy slop, the slate-colored water cracking in creamy foam against his knees. Pressing his flat left palm against the lowered ceiling, he struck another match and saw a metal pole nestling in a niche of the wall. Yes, some sewer workman had left it. He reached for it, then jerked his head away as a whisper of scurrying life whisked past and was still. He held the match close and saw a huge rat, wet with slime, blinking beady eyes and baring tiny fangs. The light blinded the rat and the frizzled head moved aimlessly. He grabbed the pole and let it fly against the rat's soft body; there was shrill piping and the grizzly body splashed into the dun-colored water and was snatched out of sight, spinning in the scuttling stream.

He swallowed and pushed on, following the curve of the misty cavern, sounding the water with the pole. By the faint light of another manhole cover he saw, amid loose wet brick, a hole with walls of damp earth leading into blackness. Gingerly he poked the pole into it; it was hollow and went beyond the length of the pole. He shoved the pole before him, hoisted himself upward, got to his hands and knees, and crawled. After a few yards he paused, struck to wonderment by the silence; it seemed that he had traveled a million miles away from the world. As he inched forward again he could sense the bottom of the dirt tunnel becoming dry and lowering slightly. Slowly he rose and to his astonishment he stood erect. He could not hear the rustling of the water now and he felt confoundingly alone, yet lured by the darkness and silence.

He crept a long way, then stopped, curious, afraid. He put his right foot forward and it dangled in space; he drew back in fear. He thrust the pole outward and it swung in emptiness. He trembled, imagining the earth crumbling and burying him alive. He scratched a match and saw that the dirt floor sheered away steeply and widened into a sort of cave some five feet below him. An old sewer, he muttered. He cocked his head, hearing a feathery cadence which he could not identify. The match ceased to burn.

Using the pole as a kind of ladder, he slid down and stood in darkness. The air was a little fresher and he could still hear vague noises. Where was he? He felt suddenly that someone was standing near him and he turned sharply, but there was only darkness. He poked cautiously and felt a brick wall; he followed it and the strange sounds grew louder. He ought to get out of here. This was crazy. He could not remain here for any length of time; there was no food and no place to sleep. But the faint sounds tantalized him; they were strange but familiar. Was it a motor? A baby crying? Music? A siren? He groped on, and the sounds came so clearly that he could feel the pitch and timbre of human voices. Yes, singing! That was it! He listened with open mouth. It was a church service. Enchanted, he groped toward the waves of melody.

> Jesus, take me to your home above
> And fold me in the bosom of Thy love . . . . . .

The singing was on the other side of a brick wall. Excited, he wanted to watch the service without being seen. Whose church was it? He knew most of the churches in this area above ground, but the singing sounded too strange and detached for him to guess. He looked to the left, to the right, down to the black dirt, then upward and was startled to see a bright sliver of light slicing the darkness like the blade of a razor. He struck one of his two remaining matches and saw rusty pipes running along an old concrete ceiling. Photographically he located the exact position of the pipes in his mind. The match flame sank and he sprang upward; his hands clutched a pipe. He swung his legs and tossed his body onto the bed of pipes and they creaked, swaying up and down; he thought that the tier was about to crash, but nothing happened. He edged to the crevice and saw a segment of black men and women, dressed in white robes, singing, holding tattered songbooks in their black palms. His first impulse was to laugh, but he checked himself.

What was he doing? He was crushed with a sense of guilt. Would God strike him dead for that? The singing swept on and he shook his head, disagreeing in spite of himself. They oughtn't do that, he thought. But he could think of no reason *why* they should not do it. Just singing with the air of the sewer blowing in on them . . . He felt that he was gazing upon something abysmally obscene, yet he could not bring himself to leave.

After a long time he grew numb and dropped to the dirt. Pain throbbed in his legs and a deeper pain, induced by the sight of those black people groveling and begging for something they could never get, churned in him. A vague conviction made him feel that those people should stand unrepentant and yield no quarter in singing and praying, yet *he* had run away from the police, had pleaded with them to believe in *his* innocence. He shook his head, bewildered.

How long had he been down here? He did not know. This was a new kind of living for him; the intensity of feelings he had experienced when looking at the church people sing made him certain that he had been down here a long time, but his mind told him that the time must have been short.

In this darkness the only notion he had of time was when a match flared and measured time by its fleeting light. He groped back through the hole toward the sewer and the waves of song subsided and finally he could not hear them at all. He came to where the earth hole ended and he heard the noise of the current and time lived again for him, measuring the moments by the wash of water.

The rain must have slackened, for the flow of water had lessened and came only to his ankles. Ought he to go up into the streets and take his chances on hiding somewhere else? But they would surely catch him. The mere thought of dodging and running again from the police made him tense. No, he would stay and plot how to elude them. But what could he do down here? He walked forward into the sewer and came to another manhole cover; he stood beneath it, debating. Fine pencils of gold spilled suddenly from the little circles in the manhole cover and trembled on the surface of the current. Yes, street lamps . . . It must be night . . .

He went forward for about a quarter of an hour, wading aimlessly, poking the pole carefully before him. Then he stopped, his eyes fixed and intent. What's that? A strangely familiar image attracted and repelled him. Lit by the yellow stems from another manhole cover was a tiny nude body of a baby snagged by debris and half-submerged is water. Thinking that the baby was alive, he moved impulsively to save it, but his roused feelings told him that it was dead, cold, nothing, the same nothingness he had felt while watching the men and women singing in the church. Water blossomed about the tiny legs, the tiny arms, the tiny head, and rushed onward. The eyes were closed, as though in sleep; the fists were clenched, as though in protest; and the mouth gaped black in a soundless cry.

He straightened and drew in his breath, feeling that he had been staring for all eternity at the ripples of veined water skimming impersonally over the shriveled limbs. He felt as condemned as when the policemen had accused him. Involuntarily he lifted his hand to brush the vision away, but his arm fell listlessly to his side. Then he acted; he closed his eyes and reached forward slowly with the soggy shoe of his right foot and shoved the dead baby from where it had been lodged. He kept his eyes closed, seeing the little body twisting in the current as it floated from sight. He opened his eyes, shivered, placed his knuckles in the sockets, hearing the water speed in the somber shadows.

He tramped on, sensing at times a sudden quickening in the current as he passed some conduit whose waters were swelling the stream that slid by his feet. A few minutes later he was standing under another manhole cover, listening to the faint rumble of noises above ground. Streetcars and trucks, he mused. He looked down and saw a stagnant pool of gray-green sludge; at intervals a balloon pocket rose from the scum, glistening a bluish-purple, and burst. Then another. He turned, shook his head, and tramped back to the dirt cave by the church, his lips quivering.

Back in the cave, he sat and leaned his back against a dirt wall. His body was trembling slightly. Finally his senses quieted and he slept. When he awakened he felt stiff and cold. He had to leave this foul place, but leaving meant facing those policemen who had wrongly accused him. No, he could not go back aboveground. He remembered the beating they had given him and how he had signed his name to a confession, a confession which he had not even read. He had been too tired when they had shouted at him, demanding that he sign his name; he had signed it to end his pain.

He stood and groped about in the darkness. The church singing had stopped. How long had he slept? He did not know. But he felt refreshed and hungry. He doubled his fist nervously, realizing that he could not make a decision. As he walked about he stumbled over an old rusty iron pipe. He picked it up and felt a jagged edge. Yes, there was a brick wall and he could dig into it. What would he find? Smiling, he groped to the brick wall, sat, and began digging idly into damp cement. I can't make any noise, he cautioned himself. As time passed he grew thirsty, but there was no water. He had to kill time or go aboveground. The cement came out of the wall easily; he extracted four bricks and felt a soft draft blowing into his face. He stopped, afraid. What was beyond? He waited a long time and nothing happened; then he began digging again, soundlessly, slowly; he enlarged the hole and crawled through into a dark room and collided with another wall. He felt his way to the right; the wall ended and his fingers toyed in space, like the antennae of an insect.

He fumbled on and his feet struck something hollow, like wood. What's this? He felt with his fingers. Steps . . . He stopped and pulled off his shoes and mounted the stairs and saw a yellow chink of light shining and heard a low voice speaking. He placed his eye to a keyhole and saw the nude waxen figure of a man stretched out upon a white table. The voice, low-pitched and vibrant, mumbled indistinguishable words, neither rising nor falling. He craned his neck and squinted to see the man who was talking, but he could not locate him. Above the naked figure was suspended a huge glass container filled with a blood-red liquid from which a white rubber tube dangled. He crouched closer to the door and saw the tip end of a black object lined with pink satin. A coffin, he breathed. This is an undertaker's establishment . . . A fine-spun lace of ice covered his body and he shuddered. A throaty chuckle sounded in the depths of the yellow room.

He turned to leave. Three steps down it occurred to him that a light switch should be nearby; he felt along the wall, found an electric button, pressed it, and a blinding glare smote his pupils so hard that he was sightless, defenseless. His pupils contracted and he wrinkled his nostrils at a peculiar odor. At once he knew that he had been dimly aware of this odor in the darkness, but the light had brought it sharply to his attention. Some kind of stuff they use to embalm, he thought. He went down the steps and saw piles of lumber, coffins, and a long workbench. In one corner was a tool chest. Yes, he could use tools, could tunnel through walls with them. He lifted the lid of the chest and saw nails, a hammer, a crowbar, a screwdriver, a light bulb, a long length of electric wire. Good! He would lug these back to his cave.

He was about to hoist the chest to his shoulders when he discovered a door behind the furnace. Where did it lead? He tried to open it and found it securely bolted. Using the crowbar so as to make no sound, he pried the door open; it swung on creaking hinges, outward. Fresh air came to his face and he caught the faint roar of faraway sound. Easy now, he told himself. He widened the door and a lump of coal rattled toward him. A coalbin . . . Evidently the door led into another basement. The roaring noise was louder now, but he could not identify it. Where was he? He groped slowly over the coal pile, then ranged in darkness over a gritty floor. The roaring noise seemed to come from above him, then below. His fingers followed a wall until he touched a wooden ridge. A door, he breathed.

The noise died to a low pitch; he felt his skin prickle. It seemed that he was playing a game with an unseen person whose intelligence outstripped his. He put his ear to the flat surface of the door. Yes, voices . . . Was this a prize fight stadium? The sound of the voices came near and sharp, but he could not tell if they were joyous or despairing. He twisted the knob until he heard a soft click and felt the springy weight of the door swinging toward him. He was afraid to open it, yet captured by curiosity and wonder. He jerked the door wide and saw on the far side of the basement a furnace glowing red. Ten feet away was still another door, half ajar. He crossed and peered through the door into an empty, high-ceilinged corridor that terminated in a dark complex of shadow. The belling voices rolled about him and his eagerness mounted. He stepped into the corridor and the voices swelled louder. He crept on and came to a narrow stairway leading circularly upward; there was no question but what he was going to ascend those stairs.

Mounting the spiraled staircase, he heard the voices roll in a steady wave, then leap to crescendo, only to die away, but always remaining audible. Ahead of him glowed red letters: E—X—I—T. At the top of the steps he paused in front of a black curtain that fluttered uncertainly. He parted the folds and looked into a convex depth that gleamed with clusters of shimmering lights. Sprawling below him was a stretch of human faces, tilted upward, chanting, whistling, screaming, laughing. Dangling before the faces, high upon a screen of silver, were jerking shadows. A movie, he said with slow laughter breaking from his lips.

He stood in a box in the reserved section of a movie house and the impulse he had had to tell the people in the church to stop their singing seized him. These people were laughing at their lives, he thought with amazement. They were shouting and yelling at the animated shadows of themselves. His compassion fired his imagination and he stepped out of the box, walked out upon thin air, walked on down to the audience; and, hovering in the air just above them, he stretched out his hand to touch them . . .

His tension snapped and he found himself back in the box, looking down into the sea of faces. No; it could not be done; he could not awaken them. He sighed. Yes, these people were children, sleeping in their living, awake in their dying.

He turned away, parted the black curtain, and looked out. He saw no one. He started down the white stone steps and when he reached the bottom he saw a man in trim blue uniform coming toward him. So used had he become to being underground that he thought that he could walk past the man, as thought he were a ghost. But the man stopped. And he stopped.

"Looking for the men's room sir?" the man asked, and, without waiting for an answer, he turned and pointed. "This way, sir. The first door to your right."

He watched the man turn and walk up the steps and go out of sight. Then he laughed. What a funny fellow! He went back to the basement and stood in the red darkness, watching the glowing embers in the furnace. He went to the sink and turned the faucet and the water flowed in a smooth silent stream that looked like a spout of blood. He brushed the mad image from his mind and began to wash his hands leisurely, looking about for the usual bar of soap. He found one and rubbed it in his palms until a rich lather bloomed in his cupped fingers, like a scarlet sponge. He scrubbed and rinsed his hands meticulously, then hunted for a towel; there was none. He shut off the water, pulled off his shirt, dried his hands on it; when he put it on again he was grateful for the cool dampness that came to his skin.

Yes, he was thirsty; he turned on the faucet again, bowled his fingers and when the water bubbled over the brim of his cupped palms, he drank in long, slow swallows. His bladder grew tight; he shut off the water, faced the wall, bent his head, and watched a red stream strike the floor. He nostrils wrinkled against acrid wisps of vapor; though he had tramped in the waters of the sewer, he stepped back from the wall so that his shoes, wet with sewer slime, would not touch his urine.

He heard footsteps and crawled quickly into the coalbin. Lumps rattled noisily. The footsteps came into the basement and stopped. Who was it? Had someone heard him and come down to investigate? He waited, crouching, sweating. For a long time there was silence, then he heard the clang of metal and a brighter glow lit the room. Somebody's tending the furnace, he thought. Footsteps came closer and he stiffened. Looming before him was a white face lined with coal dust, the face of an old man with watery blue eyes. Highlights spotted his gaunt cheekbones, and he held a huge shovel. There was a screechy scrape of metal against stone, and the old man lifted a shovelful of coal and went from sight.

The room dimmed momentarily, then a yellow glare came as coal flared at the furnace door. Six times the old man came to the bin and went to the furnace with shovels of coal, but not once did he lift his eyes. Finally he dropped the shovel, mopped his face with a dirty handkerchief, and sighed: "Wheeew!" He turned slowly and trudged out of the basement, his footsteps dying away.

He stood, and lumps of coal clattered down the pile. He stepped from the bin and was startled to see the shadowy outline of an electric bulb hanging above his head. Why had not the old man turned it on? Oh, yes . . . He understood. The old man had worked here for so long that he had no need for light; he had learned a way of seeing in his dark world, like those sightless worms that inch along underground by a sense of touch.

His eyes fell upon a lunch pail and he was afraid to hope that it was full. He picked it up; it was heavy. He opened it. *Sandwiches!* He looked guiltily around; he was alone. He searched farther and found a folder of matches and a half-empty tin of tobacco; he put them eagerly into his pocket and clicked off the light. With the lunch pail under his arm, he went through the door, groped over the pile of coal, and stood again in the lighted basement of the undertaking establishment. I've got to get those tools, he told himself. And turn off that light. He tiptoed back up the steps and switched off the light; the invisible voice still droned on behind the door. He crept down and, seeing with his fingers, opened the lunch pail and tore off a piece of paper bag and brought out the tin and spilled grains of tobacco into the makeshift concave. He rolled it and wet it with spittle, then inserted one end into his mouth and lit it: he sucked smoke that bit his lungs. The nicotine reached his brain, went out along his arms to his finger tips, down to his stomach, and over the tired nerves of his body.

He carted the tools to the hole he had made in the wall. Would the noise of the falling chest betray him? But he would have to take a chance; he had to have those tools. He lifted the chest and shoved it; it hit the dirt on the other side of the wall with a loud clatter. He waited, listening; nothing happened. Head first, he slithered through and stood in the cave. He grinned, filled with a cunning idea. Yes, he would now go back into the basement of the undertaking establishment and crouch behind the coal pile and dig another hole. Sure! Fumbling, he opened the tool chest and extracted a crowbar, a screwdriver, and a hammer; he fastened them securely about his person.

With another lumpish cigarette in his flexed lips, he crawled back through the hole and over the coal pile and sat, facing the brick wall. He jabbed with the crowbar and the cement sheered away; quicker than he thought, a brick came loose. He worked an hour; the other bricks did not come easily. He sighed, weak from effort. I ought to rest a little, he thought. I'm hungry. He felt his way back to the cave and stumbled along the wall till he came to the tool chest. He sat upon it, opened the lunch pail, and took out two thick sandwiches. He smelled them. Pork chops . . . His mouth watered. He closed his eyes and devoured a sandwich, savoring the smooth rye bread and juicy meat. He ate rapidly, gulping down lumpy mouthfuls that made him long for water. He ate the other sandwich and found an apple and gobbled that up too, sucking the core till the last trace of flavor was drained from it. Then, like a dog, he ground the meat bones with his teeth, enjoying the salty, tangy marrow. He finished and stretched out full length on the ground and went to sleep. . . .

. . . His body was washed by cold water that gradually turned warm and he was buoyed upon a stream and swept out to sea where waves rolled gently and suddenly he found himself walking upon the water how strange and delightful to walk upon the water and he came upon a nude woman holding a nude baby in her arms and the woman was sinking into the water holding the baby above her head and screaming *help* and he ran over the water to the woman and he reached her just before she went down and he took the baby from her hands and stood watching the breaking bubbles where the woman sank and he called *lady* and still no answer yes dive down there and rescue that woman but he could not take this baby with him and he stooped and laid the baby tenderly upon the surface of the water expecting it to sink but it floated and he leaped into the water and held his breath and strained his eyes to see through the gloomy volume of water but there was no woman and he opened his mouth and called *lady* and the water bubbled and his chest ached and his arms were tired but he could not see the woman and he called again *lady lady* and his feet touched sand at the bottom of the sea and his chest felt as though it would burst and he bent his knees and propelled himself upward and water rushed past him and his head bobbed out and he breathed deeply and looked around where was the baby the baby was gone and he rushed over by the water looking for the baby calling *where is it* and the empty sky and sea threw back his voice *where is it* and he began to doubt that he could stand upon the water and then he was sinking and as he struggled the water rushed him downward spinning dizzily and he opened his mouth to call for help and water surged into his lungs and he choked . . .

He groaned and leaped erect in the dark, his eyes wide. The images of terror that thronged his brain would not let him sleep. He rose, made sure that the tools were hitched to his belt, and groped his way to the coal pile and found the rectangular gap from which he had taken the bricks. He took out the crowbar and hacked. Then dread paralyzed him. How long had he slept? Was it day or night now? He had to be careful. Someone might hear him if it were day. He hewed softly for hours at the cement, working silently. Faintly quivering in the air above him was the dim sound of yelling voices. Crazy people, he muttered. They're still there in that movie . . .

Having rested, he found the digging much easier. He soon had a dozen bricks out. His spirits rose. He took out another brick and his fingers fluttered in space. Good! What lay ahead of him? Another basement? He made the hole larger, climbed through, walked over an uneven floor and felt a metal surface. He lighted a match and saw that he was standing behind a furnace in a basement; before him, on the far side of the room, was a door. He crossed and opened it; it was full of odds and ends. Daylight spilled from a window above his head.

Then he was aware of a soft, continuous tapping. What was it? A clock? No, it was louder than a clock and more irregular. He placed an old empty box beneath the window, stood upon it, and looked into an areaway. He eased the window up and crawled through; the sound of the tapping came clearly now. He glanced about; he was alone. Then he looked upward at a series of window ledges. The tapping identified itself. That's a typewriter, he said to himself. It seemed to be coming from just above. He grasped the ridges of a rain pipe and lifted himself upward; through a half-inch opening of window he saw a doorknob about three feet away. No, it was not a doorknob; it was a small circular disk made of stainless steel with many fine markings upon it. He held his breath: an eerie white hand, seemingly detached from its arm, touched the metal knob and whirled it, first to the left, then to right. It's a safe! . . . Suddenly he could see the dial no more; a huge metal door swung slowly toward him and he was looking into a safe filled with green wads of paper money, rows of coins wrapped in brown paper, and glass jars and boxes of various sizes. His heart quickened. Good Lord! The white hand went in and out of the safe, taking wads of bills and cylinders of coins. The hand vanished and he heard the muffled click of the big door as it closed. Only the steel dial was visible now. The typewriter still tapped in his ears, but he could not see it. He blinked, wondering if what he had seen was real. There was more money in that safe than he had seen in all his life.

As he clung to the rain pipe, a daring idea came to him and he pulled the screwdriver from his belt. If the white hand twirled that dial again, he would be able to see how far to the left and right it spun and he would have the combination! His blood tingled. I can scratch the numbers right here, he thought. Holding the pipe with one hand, he made the sharp edge of the screwdriver bite into the brick wall. Yes, he could do it. Now, he was set. Now, he had a reason for staying here in the underground. He waited for a long time, but the white hand did not return. Goddamn! Had he been more alert, he would have counted the twirls and he would have had the combination. He got down and stood in the areaway, sunk in reflection.

How could he get into that room? He climbed back into the basement and saw wooden steps leading upward. Was that the room where the safe stood? Fearing that the dial was now being twirled, he clambered through the window, hoisted himself up the rain pipe, and peered; he saw only the naked gleam of the steel dial. He got down and doubled his fists. Well, he would explore the basement. He returned to the basement room and mounted the steps to the door and squinted through the keyhole; all was dark, but the tapping was still somewhere near, still faint and directionless. He pushed the door in; along one wall of a room was a table piled with radios and electrical equipment. A radio shop, he muttered.

Well, he could rig up a radio in his cave. He found a sack, slid the radio into it, and slung it across his back. Closing the door, he went down the steps and stood again in the basement, disappointed. He had not solved the problem of the steel dial and he was irked. He set the radio on the floor and again hoisted himself through the window and up the rain pipe and squinted; the metal door was swinging shut. Goddamn! He's worked the combination again. If I had been patient, I'd have had it! How could he get into that room? He *had* to get into it. He could jimmy the window, but it would be much better if he could get in without any traces. To the right of him, he calculated, should be the basement of the building that held the safe; therefore, if he dug a hole right *here* he ought to reach his goal.

He began a quiet scraping; it was hard work, for the bricks were not damp. He eventually got one out and lowered it softly to the floor. He had to be careful; perhaps people were beyond this wall. He extracted a second layer of brick and found still another. He gritted his teeth, ready to quit. I'll dig one more, he resolved. When the next brick came out he felt air blowing into his face. He waited to be challenged, but nothing happened.

He enlarged the hole and pulled himself through and stood in quiet darkness. He scratched a match to flame and saw steps; he mounted and peered through a keyhole: Darkness . . . He strained to hear the typewriter, but there was only silence. Maybe the office had closed? He twisted the knob and swung the door in; a frigid blast made him shiver. In the shadows before him were halves and quarters of hogs and lambs and steers hanging from metal hooks on the low ceiling, red meat encased in folds of cold white fat. Fronting him was frost-coated glass from behind which came indistinguishable sounds. The odor of fresh raw meat sickened him and he backed away. A meat market, he whispered.

He ducked his head, suddenly blinded by light. He narrowed his eyes; the red-white rows of meat were drenched in yellow glare. A man wearing a crimson-spotted jacket came in and took down a bloody meat clever. He eased the door to, holding it ajar just enough to watch the man, hoping that the darkness in which he stood would keep him from being seen. The man took down a hunk of steer and placed it upon a bloody wooden block and bent forward and whacked with the cleaver. The man's face was hard, square, grim; a jet of mustache smudged his upper lip and a glistening cowlick of hair fell over his left eye. Each time he lifted the cleaver and brought it down upon the meat, he let out a short, deep-chested grunt. After he had cut the meat, he wiped blood off the wooden block with a sticky wad of gunny sack and hung the cleaver upon a hook. His face was proud as he placed the chunk of meat in the crook of his elbow and left.

The door slammed and the light went off; once more he stood in shadow. His tension ebbed. From behind the frosted glass he heard the man's voice: "Forty-eight cents a pound, ma'am." He shuddered, feeling that there was something he had to do. But what? He stared fixedly at the cleaver, then he sneezed and was terrified for fear that the man had heard him. But the door did not open. He took down the cleaver and examined the sharp edge smeared with cold blood. Behind the ice-coated glass a cash register rang with a vibrating, musical tinkle.

Absent-mindedly holding the meat cleaver, he rubbed the glass with his thumb and cleared a spot that enabled him to see into the front of the store. The shop was empty, save for the man who was now putting on his hat and coat. Beyond the front window a wan sun shone in the streets; people passed and now and then a fragment of laughter or the whir of a speeding auto came to him. He peered closer and saw on the right counter of the shop a mosquito netting covering pears, grapes, lemons, oranges, bananas, peaches, and plums. His stomach contracted.

The man clicked out the light and he gritted his teeth, muttering, Don't lock the icebox door . . . The man went through the door of the shop and locked it from the outside. Thank God! Now, he would eat some more! He waited, trembling. The sun died and its rays lingered on in the sky, turning the streets to dusk. He opened the door and stepped inside the shop. In reverse letters across the front window was: NICK'S FRUITS AND MEATS. He laughed, picked up a soft ripe yellow pear and bit into it; juice squirted; his mouth ached as his saliva glands reacted to the acid of the fruit. He ate three pears, gobbled six bananas, and made away with several oranges, taking a bite out of their tops and holding them to his lips and squeezing them as he hungrily sucked the juice.

He found a faucet, turned it on, laid the cleaver aside, pursed his lips under the stream until his stomach felt about to burst. He straightened and belched, feeling satisfied for the first time since he had been underground. He sat upon the floor, rolled and lit a cigarette, his bloodshot eyes squinting against the film of drifting smoke. He watched a patch of sky turn red, then purple; night fell and he lit another cigarette, brooding. Some part of him was trying to remember the world he had left, and another part of him did not want to remember it. Sprawling before him in his mind was his wife, Mrs. Wooten for whom he worked, the three policemen who had picked him up . . . He possessed them now more completely than he had ever possessed them when he had lived aboveground. How this had come about he could not say, but he had no desire to go back to them. He laughed, crushed the cigarette, and stood up.

He went to the front door and gazed out. Emotionally he hovered between the world aboveground and the world underground. He longed to go out, but sober judgment urged him to remain here. Then impulsively he pried the lock loose with one swift twist of the crowbar; the door swung outward. Through the twilight he saw a white man and a white woman coming toward him. He held himself tense, waiting for them to pass; but they came directly to the door and confronted him.

"I want to buy a pound of grapes," the woman said.

Terrified, he stepped back into the store. The white man stood to one side and the woman entered.

"Give me a pound of dark ones," the woman said.

The white man came slowly forward, blinking his eyes.

"Where's Nick?" the man asked.

"Were you just closing?" the woman asked.

"Yes, ma'am," he mumbled. For a second he did not breathe, then he mumbled again: "Yes, ma'am."

"I'm sorry," the woman said.

The street lamps came on, lighting the store somewhat. Ought he run? But that would raise an alarm. He moved slowly, dreamily, to a counter and lifted up a bunch of grapes and showed them to the woman.

"Fine," the woman said. "But isn't that more than a pound?"

He did not answer. The man was staring at him intently.

"Put them in a bag for me," the woman said, fumbling with her purse.

"Yes, ma'am."

He saw a pile of paper bags under a narrow ledge; he opened one and put the grapes in.

"Thanks," the woman said, taking the bag and placing a dime in his dark palm.

"Where's Nick?" the man asked again. "At supper?"

"Sir? Yes, sir," he breathed.

They left the store and he stood trembling in the doorway. When they were out of sight, he burst out laughing and crying. A trolley car rolled noisily past and he controlled himself quickly. He flung the dime to the pavement with a gesture of contempt and stepped into the warm night air. A few shy stars trembled above him. The look of things was beautiful, yet he felt a lurking threat. He went to an unattended newsstand and looked at a stack of papers. He saw a headline: HUNT NEGRO FOR MURDER.

He felt that someone had slipped up on him from behind and was stripping off his clothes; he looked about wildly, went quickly back into the store, picked up the meat cleaver where he had left it near the sink, then made his way through the icebox to the basement. He stood for a long time, breathing heavily. They know I didn't do anything, he muttered. But how could he prove it? He had signed a confession. Though innocent, he felt guilty, condemned. He struck a match and held it near the steel blade, fascinated and repelled by the dried blotches of blood. Then his fingers gripped the handle of the cleaver with all the strength of his body, he wanted to fling the cleaver from him, but he could not. The match flame wavered and fled; he struggled through the hole and put the cleaver in the sack with the radio. He was determined to keep it, for what purpose he did not know.

He was about to leave when he remembered the safe. Where was it? He wanted to give up, but felt that he ought to make one more try. Opposite the last hole he had dug, he tunneled again, plying the crowbar. Once he was so exhausted that he lay on the concrete floor and panted. Finally he made another hole. He wriggled through and his nostrils filled with the fresh smell of coal. He struck a match; yes, the usual steps led upward. He tiptoed to a door and eased it open. A fair-haired white girl stood in front of a steel cabinet, her blue eyes wide upon him. She turned chalky and gave a high-pitched scream. He bounded down the steps and raced to his hole and clambered through, replacing the bricks with nervous haste. He paused, hearing loud voices.

"What's the matter, Alice?"

"A man . . ."

"What man? Where?"

"A man was at that door . . ."

"Oh, nonsense!"

"He was looking at me through the door!"

"Aw, you're dreaming."

"I *did* see a man!"

The girl was crying now.

"There's nobody here."

Another man's voice sounded.

"What is it, Bob?"

"Alice says she saw a man in here, in that door!"

"Let's take a look."

He waited, poised for flight. Footsteps descended the stairs.

"There's nobody down here."

"The window's locked."

"And there's no door."

"You ought to fire that dame."

"Oh, I don't know. Women are that way."

"She's too hysterical."

The men laughed. Footsteps sounded again on the stairs. A door slammed. He sighed, relieved that he had escaped. But he had not done what he had set out to do; his glimpse of the room had been too brief to determine if the safe was there. He had to know. Boldly he groped through the hole once more; he reached the steps and pulled off his shoes and tiptoed up and peered through the keyhole. His head accidentally touched the door and it swung silently in a fraction of an inch; he saw the girl bent over the cabinet, her back to him. Beyond her was the safe. He crept back down the steps, thinking exultingly: I found it!

Now he had to get the combination. Even if the window in the areaway was locked and bolted, he could gain entrance when the office closed. He scoured through the hole he had dug and stood again in the basement where he had left the radio and the cleaver. Again he crawled out of the window and lifted himself up the rain pipe and peered. The steel dial showed lonely and bright, reflecting the yellow glow of an unseen light. Resigned to a long wait, he sat and leaned against a wall. From far off came the faint sounds of life aboveground; once he looked with a baffled expression at the dark sky. Frequently he rose and climbed the pipe to see the white hand spin the dial, but nothing happened. He bit his lip with impatience. It was not the money that was luring him, but the mere fact that he could get it with impunity. Was the hand now twirling the dial? He rose and looked, but the white hand was not in sight.

Perhaps it would be better to watch continuously? Yes; he clung to the pipe and watched the dial until his eyes thickened with tears. Exhausted, he stood again in the areaway. He heard a door being shut and he clawed up the pipe and looked. He jerked tense as a vague figure passed in front of him. He stared unblinkingly, hugging the pipe with one hand and holding the screwdriver with the other, ready to etch the combination upon the wall. His ears caught: *Dong* . . . *Dong* . . . *Dong* . . . *Dong* . . . *Dong* . . . *Dong* . . . *Dong* . . . Seven o'clock, he whispered. Maybe they were closing now? What kind of a store would be open as late as this? he wondered. Did anyone live in the rear? Was there a night watchman? Perhaps the safe was *already* locked for the night! Goddamn! While he had been eating in that shop, they had locked up everything . . . Then, just as he was about to give up, the white hand touched the dial and turned it once to the right and stopped at six. With quivering fingers, he etched 1—R—6 upon the brick wall with the tip of the screwdriver. The hand twirled the dial twice to the left and stopped at two, and he engraved 2—L—2 upon the wall. The dial was spun four times to the right and stopped at six again; he wrote 4—R—6. The dial rotated three times to the left and was centered straight up and down; he wrote 3—L—0. The door swung open and again he saw the piles of green money and the rows of wrapped coins. I got it, he said grimly.

Then he was stone still, astonished. There were two hands now. A right hand lifted a wad of green bills and deftly slipped it up the sleeve of a left arm. The hands trembled; again the right hand slipped a packet of bills up the left sleeve. He's stealing, he said to himself. He grew indignant, as if the money belonged to him. Though *he* had planned to steal the money, he despised and pitied the man. He felt that his stealing the money and the man's stealing were two entirely different things. He wanted to steal the money merely for the sensation involved in getting it, and he had no intention whatever of spending a penny of it; but he knew that the man who was now stealing it was going to spend it, perhaps for pleasure. The huge steel door closed with a soft click.

Though angry, he was somewhat satisfied. The office would close soon. I'll clean the place out, he mused. He imagined the entire office staff cringing with fear; the police would question everyone for a crime they had not committed, just as they had questioned him. And they would have no idea of how the money had been stolen until they discovered the holes, he had tunneled in the walls of the basements. He lowered himself and laughed mischievously, with the abandoned glee of an adolescent.

He flattened himself against the wall as the window above him closed with rasping sound. He looked; somebody was bolting the window securely with a metal screen. That won't help you, he snickered to himself. He clung to the rain pipe until the yellow light in the office went out. He went back into the basement, picked up the sack containing the radio and cleaver, and crawled through the two holes he had dug and groped his way into the basement of the building that held the safe. He moved in slow motion, breathing softly. Be careful now, he told himself. There might be a night watchman . . . In his memory was the combination written in bold white characters as upon a blackboard. Eel-like he squeezed through the last hole and crept up the steps and put his hand on the knob and pushed the door in about three inches. Then his courage ebbed; his imagination wove dangers for him.

Perhaps the night watchman was waiting in there, ready to shoot. He dangled his cap on a forefinger and poked it past the jamb of the door. If anyone fired, they would hit his cap; but nothing happened. He widened the door, holding the crowbar high above his head, ready to beat off an assailant. He stood like that for five minutes; the rumble of a streetcar brought him to himself. He entered the room. Moonlight floated in from a wide window. He confronted the safe, then checked himself. Better take a look around first . . . He stepped about and found a closed door. Was the night watchman in there? He opened it and saw a washbowl, a faucet, and a commode. To the left was still another door that opened into a huge dark room that seemed empty; on the far side of that room he made out the shadow of still another door. Nobody's here, he told himself.

He turned back to the safe and fingered the dial; it spun with ease. He laughed and twirled it just for fun. Get to work, he told himself. He turned the dial to the figures he saw on the blackboard of his memory; it was so easy that he felt that the safe had not been locked at all. The heavy door eased loose and he caught hold of the handle and pulled hard, but the door swung open with a slow momentum of its own. Breathless, he gaped at wads of green bills, rows of wrapped coins, curious glass jars full of white pellets, and many oblong green metal boxes. He glanced guiltily over his shoulder; it seemed impossible that someone should not call to him to stop.

They'll be surprised in the morning, he thought. He opened the top of the sack and lifted a wad of compactly tied bills; the money was crisp and new. He admired the smooth, clean-cut edges. The fellows in Washington sure know how to make this stuff, he mused. He rubbed the money with his fingers, as though expecting it to reveal hidden qualities. He lifted the wad to his nose and smelled the fresh odor of ink. Just like any other paper, he mumbled. He dropped the wad into the sack and picked up another. Holding the bag, he thought and laughed.

There was in him no sense of possessiveness; he was intrigued with the form and color of the money, with the manifold reactions which he knew that men aboveground held toward it. The sack was one-third full when it occurred to him to examine the denominations of the bills; without realizing it, he had put many wads of one-dollar bills into the sack, Aw, nuts, he said in disgust. Take the big ones . . . He dumped the one-dollar bills onto the floor and swept all the hundred-dollar bills he could find into the sack, then he raked in rolls of coins with crooked fingers.

He walked to a desk upon which sat a typewriter, the same machine which the blond girl had used. He was fascinated by it; never in his life had he used one of them. It was a queer instrument of business, something beyond the rim of his life. Whenever he had been in an office where a girl was typing, he had almost always spoken in whispers. Remembering vaguely what he had seen others do, he inserted a sheet of paper into the machine; it went in lopsided and he did not know how to straighten it. Spelling in a soft diffident voice, he pecked out his name on the keys: *fred-daniels*. He looked at it and laughed. He would learn to type correctly one of these days.

Yes, he would take the typewriter too. He lifted the machine and placed it atop the bulk of money in the sack. He did not feel that he was stealing, for the cleaver, the radio, the money, and the typewriter were all on the same level of value, all meant the same thing to him. They were the serious toys of the men who lived in the dead world of sunshine and rain he had left, the world that had condemned him, branded him guilty.

But what kind of a place is this? He wondered. What was in that dark room to his rear? He felt for his matches and found that he had only one left. He leaned the sack against the safe and groped forward into the room, encountering smooth, metallic objects that felt like machines. Baffled, he touched a wall and tried vainly to locate an electric switch. Well, he *had* to strike his last match. He knelt and struck it, cupping the flame near the floor with his palms. The place seemed to be a factory, with benches and tables. There were bulbs with green shades spaced about the tables; he turned on a light and twisted it low so that the glare was limited. There were stools at the benches and he concluded that men worked here at some trade. He wandered and found a few half-used folders of matches. If only he could find more cigarettes! But there were none.

But what kind of a place was this? On a bench he saw a pad of paper captioned: PEER'S—MANUFACTURING JEWELERS. His lips formed an "O," then he snapped off the light and ran back to the safe and lifted one of the glass jars and stared at the tiny white pellets. Gingerly he picked up one and found that it was wrapped in tissue paper. He peeled the paper and saw a glittering stone that looked like glass, glinting white and blue sparks. Diamonds, he breathed.

Roughly he tore the paper from the pellets and soon his palm quivered with precious fire. Trembling, he took all four glass jars from the safe and put them into the sack. He grabbed one of the metal boxes, shook it, and heard a tinny rattle. He pried off the lid with the screwdriver. Rings! Hundreds of them . . . Were they worth anything? He scooped up a hand-ful and jets of fire shot fitfully from the stones. These are diamonds too, he said. He pried open another box. Watches! A chorus of soft, metallic ticking filled his ears. For a moment he could not move, then he dumped all the boxes into the sack.

He shut the safe door, then stood looking around, anxious not to over-look anything. Oh! He had seen a door in the room where the machines were. What was in there? More valuables? He re-entered the room, crossed the floor, and stood undecided before the door. He finally caught hold of the knob and pushed the door in; the room beyond was dark. He advanced cautiously inside and ran his fingers along the wall for the usual switch, then he was stark still. *Something had moved in the room!* What was it? Ought he to creep out, taking the rings and diamonds and money? Why risk what he already had? He waited and the ensuing silence gave him con-fidence to explore further. Dare he strike a match? Would not a match flame make him a good target? He tensed again as he heard a faint sigh; he was now convinced that there was something alive near him, something that lived and breathed. On tiptoe he felt slowly along the wall, hoping that he would not collide with anything. Luck was with him; he found the light switch.

No; don't turn the light on . . . Then suddenly he realized that he did not know in what direction the door was. Goddamn! He had to turn the light on or strike a match. He fingered the switch for a long time, then thought of an idea. He knelt upon the floor, reached his arm up to the switch and flicked the button, hoping that if anyone shot, the bullet would go above his head. The moment the light came on he narrowed his eyes to see quickly. He sucked in his breath and his body gave a violent twitch and was still. In front of him, so close that it made him want to bound up and scream, was a human face.

He was afraid to move lest he touch the man. If the man had opened his eyes at that moment, there was no telling what he might have done. The man—long and rawboned—was stretched out on his back upon a little cot, sleeping in his clothes, his head cushioned by a dirty pillow; his face, clouded by a dark stubble of beard, looked straight up to the ceiling. The man sighed, and he grew tense to defend himself; the man mumbled and turned his face away from the light. I've got to turn off that light, he thought. Just as he was about to rise, he saw a gun and cartridge belt on the floor at the man's side. Yes, he would take the gun and cartridge belt, not to use them, but just to keep them, as one stakes a memento from a country fair. He picked them up and was about to click off the light when his eyes fell upon a photograph perched upon a chair near the man's head; it was the picture of a woman, smiling, shown against a background of open fields; at the woman's side were two young children, a boy and a girl. He smiled indulgently; he could send a bullet into that man's brain and time would be over for him . . .

He clicked off the light and crept silently back into the room where the safe stood; he fastened the cartridge belt about him and adjusted the hol-ster at his right hip. He strutted about the room on tiptoe, lolling his head nonchalantly, then paused abruptly, pulled the gun and pointed it with grim face toward an imaginary foe. "Boom!" he whispered fiercely. Then he bent forward with silent laughter. That's just like they do it in the movies, he said.

He contemplated his loot for a long time, then got a towel from the washroom and tied the sack securely. When he looked up he was momentarily frightened by his shadow looming on the wall before him. He lifted the sack, dragged it down the basement steps, lugged it across the basement, gasping for breath. After he had struggled through the hole, he clumsily replaced the bricks, then tussled with the sack until he got it to the cave. He stood in the dark, wet with sweat, brooding about the diamonds, the rings, the watches, the money; he remembered the singing in the church, the people yelling in the movie, the dead baby, the nude man stretched out upon the white table . . . He saw these items hovering before his eyes and felt that some dim meaning linked them together, that some magical relationship made them kin. He stared with vacant eyes, convinced that all of these images, with their tongueless reality, were striving to tell him something . . .

Later, seeing with his fingers, he untied the sack and set each item neatly upon the dirt floor. Exploring, he took the bulb, the socket, and the wire out of the tool chest; he was elated to find a double socket at one end of the wire. He crammed the stuff into his pockets and hoisted himself upon the rusty pipes and squinted into the church; it was dim and empty. Somewhere in this wall were live electric wires; but where? He lowered himself, groped and tapped the wall with the butt of the screwdriver, listening vainly for hollow sounds. I'll just take a chance and dig, he said.

For an hour he tried to dislodge a brick, and when he struck a match, he found that he had dug a depth of only an inch! No use in digging here, he sighed. By the flickering light of a match, he looked upward, then lowered his eyes, only to glance up again, startled. Directly above his head, beyond the pipes, was a wealth of electric wiring. I'll be damned, he snickered.

He got an old dull knife from the chest and, seeing again with his fingers, separated the two strands of wire and cut away the insulation. Twice he received a slight shock. He scraped the wiring clean and managed to join the two twin ends, then screwed in the bulb. The sudden illumination blinded him and he shut his lids to kill the pain in his eyeballs. I've got that much done, he thought jubilantly.

He placed the bulb on the dirt floor and the light cast a blatant glare on the bleak clay walls. Next he plugged one end of the wire that dangled from the radio into the light socket and bent down and switched on the button; almost at once there was the harsh sound of static, but no words or music. Why won't it work? he wondered. Had he damaged the mechanism in any way? Maybe it needed grounding? Yes . . . He rummaged in the tool chest and found another length of wire, fastened it to the ground of the radio, and then tied the opposite end to a pipe. Rising and growing distinct, a slow strain of music entranced him with its measured sound. He sat upon the chest, deliriously happy.

Later he searched again in the chest and found a half-gallon can of glue; he opened it and smelled a sharp odor. Then he recalled that he had not even looked at the money. He took a wad of green bills and weighed it in his palm, then broke the seal and held one of the bills up to the light and studied it closely. *The United States of America will pay to the bearer on demand one hundred dollars,* he read in slow speech; then: *This note is legal tender for all debts, public and private. . . .* He broke into a musing laugh, feeling that he was reading of the doings of people who lived on some far-off planet. He turned the bill over and saw on the other side of it a delicately beautiful building gleaming with paint and set amidst green grass. He had no desire whatever to count the money; it was what it stood for—the various currents of life swirling aboveground—that captivated him. Next he opened the rolls of coins and let them slide from their paper wrappings to the ground; the bright, new gleaming pennies and nickels and dimes piled high at his feet, a glowing mound of shimmering copper and silver. He sifted them through his fingers, listening to their tinkle as they struck the conical heap.

Oh, yes! He had forgotten. He would now write his name on the type-writer. He inserted a piece of paper and poised his fingers to write. But what was his name? He stared, trying to remember. He stood and glared about the dirt cave, his name on the tip of his lips. But it would not come to him. Why was he here? Yes, he had been running away from the police. But why? His mind was blank. He bit his lips and sat again, feeling a vague terror. But why worry? He laughed, then pecked slowly: *itwasa-longhotday.* He was determined to type the sentence without making any mistakes. How did one make capital letters? He experimented and luckily discovered how to lock the machine for capital letters and then shift it back to lower case. Next he discovered how to make spaces, then he wrote neatly and correctly: *It was a long hot day.* Just why he selected that sentence he did not know; it was merely the ritual of performing the thing that ap-pealed to him. He took the sheet out of the machine and looked around with stiff neck and hard eyes and spoke to an imaginary person:

"Yes, I'll have the contracts ready tomorrow."

He laughed. That's just the way they talk, he said. He grew weary of the game and pushed the machine aside. His eyes fell upon the can of glue, and a mischievous idea bloomed in him, filling him with nervous eager-ness. He leaped up and opened the can of glue, then broke the seals on all the wads of money. I'm going to have some wallpaper, he said with a lux-urious, physical laugh that made him bend at the knees. He took the towel with which he had tied the sack and balled it into a swab and dipped it into the can of glue and dabbed glue onto the wall; then he pasted one green bill by the side of another. He stepped back and cocked his head. Jesus! That's funny . . . He slapped his thighs and guffawed. He had triumphed over the world aboveground! He was free! If only people could see this! He wanted to run from this cave and yell his discovery to the world.

He swabbed all the dirt walls of the cave and pasted them with green bills; when he had finished the walls blazed with a yellow-green fire. Yes, this room would be his hide-out; between him and the world that had branded him guilty would stand this mocking symbol. He had not stolen the money; he had simply picked it up, just as a man would pick up fire-wood in a forest. And that was how the world aboveground now seemed to him, a wild forest filled with death.

The walls of money finally palled on him and he looked about for new interests to feed his emotions. The cleaver! He drove a nail into the wall and hung the bloody cleaver upon it. Still another idea welled up. He pried open the metal boxes and lined them side by side on the dirt floor. He grinned at the gold and fire. From one box he lifted up a fistful of ticking gold watches and dangled them by their gleaming chains. He stared with an idle smile, then began to wind them up; he did not attempt to set them at any given hour, for there was no time for him now. He took a fistful of nails and drove them into the papered walls and hung the watches upon them, letting them swing down by their glittering chains, trembling and ticking busily against the backdrop of green with the lemon sheen of the electric light shining upon the metal watch casings, converting the golden disks into blobs of liquid yellow. Hardly had he hung up the last watch than the idea extended itself; he took more nails from the chest and drove them into the green paper and took the boxes of rings and went from nail to nail and hung up the golden bands. The blue and white sparks from the stones filled the cave with brittle laughter, as though enjoying his hilarious secret. People certainly can do some funny things, he said to himself.

He sat upon the tool chest, alternately laughing and shaking his head soberly. Hours later he became conscious of the gun sagging at his hip and he pulled it from the holster. He had seen men fire guns in movies, but somehow his life had never led him into contact with firearms. A desire to feel the sensation others felt in firing came over him. But someone might hear . . . Well, what if they did? They would not know where the shot had come from. Not in their wildest notions would they think that it had come from under the streets! He tightened his finger on the trigger; there was a deafening report and it seemed that the entire underground had caved in upon his eardrums; and in the same instant there flashed an orange-blue spurt of flame that died quickly but lingered on as a vivid after-image. He smelled the acrid stench of burnt powder filling his lungs and he dropped the gun abruptly.

The intensity of his feelings died and he hung the gun and cartridge belt upon the wall. Next he lifted the jars of diamonds and turned them bottom upward, dumping the white pellets upon the ground. One by one he picked them up and peeled the tissue paper from them and piled them in a neat heap. He wiped his sweaty hands on his trousers, lit a cigarette, and commenced playing another game. He imagined that he was a rich man who lived aboveground in the obscene sunshine and he was strolling through a park of a summer morning, smiling, nodding to his neighbors, sucking an after-breakfast cigar. Many times he crossed the floor of the cave, avoiding the diamonds with his feet, yet subtly gauging his footsteps so that his shoes, wet with sewer slime, would strike the diamonds at some undetermined moment. After twenty minutes of sauntering, his right foot smashed into the heap and diamonds lay scattered in all directions, glinting with a million tiny chuckles of icy laughter. Oh, shucks, he mumbled in mock regret, intrigued by the damage he had wrought. He continued walking, ignoring the brittle fire. He felt he had a glorious victory locked in his heart.

He stooped and flung the diamonds more evenly over the floor and they showered rich sparks, collaborating with him. He went over the floor and trampled the stones just deep enough for them to be faintly visible, as though they were set delicately in the prongs of a thousand rings. A ghostly light bathed the cave. He sat on the chest and frowned. Maybe *any*thing's right, he mumbled. Yes, if the world as men had made it was right, then anything else was right, any act a man took to satisfy himself, murder, theft, torture.

He straightened with a start. What was happening to him? He was drawn to these crazy thoughts, yet they made him feel vaguely guilty. He would stretch out upon the ground, then get up; he would want to crawl again through the holes he had dug, but would restrain himself; he would think of going again up into the streets, but fear would hold him still. He stood in the middle of the cave, surrounded by green walls and a laughing floor, trembling. He was going to do something, but what? Yes, he was afraid of himself, afraid of doing some nameless thing.

To control himself, he turned on the radio. A melancholy piece of music rose. Brooding over the diamonds on the floor was like looking up into a sky full of restless stars; then the illusion turned into its opposite: he was high up in the air looking down at the twinkling lights of a sprawling city. The music ended and a man recited news events. In the same attitude in which he had contemplated the city, so now, as he heard the cultivated tone, he looked upon land and sea as men fought, as cities were razed, as planes scattered death upon open towns, as long lines of trenches wavered and broke. He heard the names of generals and the names of mountains and the names of countries and the names and numbers of divisions that were in action on different battle fronts. He saw black smoke billowing from the stacks of warships as they neared each other over wastes of water and he heard their huge guns thunder as red-hot shells screamed across the surface of night seas. He saw hundreds of planes wheeling and droning in the sky and heard the clatter of machine guns as they fought each other and he saw planes falling in plumes of smoke and blaze of fire. He saw steel tanks rumbling across fields of ripe wheat to meet other tanks and there was a loud clang of steel as numberless tanks collided. He saw troops with fixed bayonets and men groaned as steel ripped into their bodies and they went down to die . . . The voice of the radio faded and he was staring at the diamonds on the floor at his feet.

He shut off the radio, fighting an irrational compulsion to act. He walked aimlessly about the cave, touching the walls with his finger tips. Suddenly he stood still. *What was the matter with him?* Yes, he knew . . . It was these walls; these crazy walls were filling him with a wild urge to climb out into the dark sunshine aboveground. Quickly he doused the light to banish the shouting walls, then sat again upon the tool chest. Yes, he was trapped. His muscles were flexed taut and sweat ran down his face. He knew now that he could not stay here and he could not go out. He lit a cigarette with shaking fingers; the match flame revealed the green-papered walls with militant distinctness; the purple on the gun barrel glinted like a threat; the meat cleaver brooded with its eloquent splotches of blood; the mound of silver and copper smoldered angrily; the diamonds winked at him from the floor; and the gold watches ticked and trembled, crowning time the king of consciousness, defining the limits of living . . . The match blaze died and he bolted from where he stood and collided brutally with the nails upon the walls. The spell was broken. He shuddered, feeling that, in spite of his fear, sooner or later he would go up into the dead sunshine and somehow say something to somebody about all this.

He sat again upon the tool chest. Fatigue weighed upon his forehead and eyes. Minutes passed and he relaxed. He dozed, but his imagination was alert. He saw himself rising, wading again in the sweeping water of the sewer; he came to a manhole and climbed out and was amazed to discover that he had hoisted himself into a room with armed policemen who were watching him intently. He jumped awake in the dark; he had not moved. He sighed, closed his eyes, and slept again; this time his imagination designed a scheme of protection for him. His dreaming made him feel that he was standing in a room watching over his own nude body lying stiff and cold upon a white table. At the far end of the room he saw a crowd of people huddled in a corner, afraid of his body. Though lying dead upon the table, he was standing in some mysterious way at his side, warding off the people guarding his body, and laughing to himself as he observed the situation. They're scared of me, he thought.

He awakened with a start, leaped to his feet, and stood in the center of the black cave. It was a full minute before he moved again. He hovered between sleeping and waking, unprotected, a prey of wild fears. He could neither see nor hear. One part of him was asleep; his blood coursed slowly and his flesh was numb. On the other hand he was roused to a strange, high pitch of tension. He lifted his fingers to his face, as though about to weep. Gradually his hands lowered and he struck a match, looking about, expecting to see a door through which he could walk to safety: but there was no door, only the green walls and the moving floor. The match flame died and it was dark again.

Five minutes later he was still standing when the thought came to him that he had been asleep. Yes . . . But he was not yet fully awake; he was still queerly blind and deaf. How long had he slept? Where was he? Then suddenly he recalled the green-papered walls of the cave and in the same instant he heard loud singing coming from the church beyond the wall. Yes, they woke me up, he muttered. He hoisted himself and lay atop the bed of pipes and brought his face to the narrow slit. Men and women stood here and there between pews. A song ended and a young black girl tossed back her head and closed her eyes and broke plaintively into another hymn:

> Glad, glad, glad, oh, so glad
> I got Jesus in my soul . . .

Those few words were all she sang, but what her words did not say, her emotions said as she repeated the lines, varying the mood and tempo, making her tone express meanings which her conscious mind did not know. Another woman melted her voice with the girl's, and then an old man's voice merged with that of the two women. Soon the entire congregation was singing:

> Glad, glad, glad, oh, so glad
> I got Jesus in my soul . . .

They're wrong, he whispered in the lyric darkness. He felt that their search for a happiness they could never find made them feel that they had committed some dreadful offense which they could not remember or understand. He was now in possession of the feeling that had gripped him when he had first come into the underground. It came to him in a series of questions: Why was this sense of guilt so seemingly innate, so easy to come by, to think, to feel, so verily physical? It seemed that when one felt this guilt one was retracing in one's feelings a faint pattern designed long before; it seemed that one was always trying to remember a gigantic shock that had left a haunting impression upon one's body which one could not forget or shake off, but which had been forgotten by the conscious mind, creating in one's life a state of eternal anxiety.

He had to tear himself away from this; he got down from the pipes. His nerves were so taut that he seemed to feel his brain pushing through his skull. He felt that he had to do something, but he could not figure out what it was. Yet he knew that if he stood here until he made up his mind, he would never move. He crawled through the hole he had made in the brick wall and the exertion afforded him respite from tension. When he entered the basement of the radio store, he stopped in fear, hearing loud voices.

"Come on, boy! Tell us what you did with the radio!"

"Mister, I didn't steal the radio! I swear!"

He heard a dull thumping sound and he imagined a boy being struck violently.

"Please, mister!"

"Did you take it to a pawn shop?"

"No, sir! I didn't steal the radio! I got a radio at home," the boy's voice pleaded hysterically. "Go to my home and look!"

There came to his ears the sound of another blow. It was so funny that he had to clap his hand over his mouth to keep from laughing out loud. They're beating some poor boy, he whispered to himself, shaking his head. He felt a sort of distant pity for the boy and wondered if he ought to bring back the radio and leave it in the basement. No. Perhaps it was a good thing that they were beating the boy; perhaps the beating would bring to the boy's attention, for the first time in his life, the secret of his existence, the guilt that he could never get rid of.

Smiling, he scampered over a coal pile and stood again in the basement of the building where he had stolen the money and jewelry. He lifted himself into the areaway, climbed the rain pipe, and squinted through a two-inch opening of window. The guilty familiarity of what he saw made his muscles tighten. Framed before him in a bright tableau of daylight was the night watchman sitting upon the edge of a chair, stripped to the waist, his head sagging forward, his eyes red and puffy. The watchman's face and shoulders were stippled with red and black welts. Back of the watchman stood the safe, the steel door wide open showing the empty vault. Yes, they think he did it, he mused.

Footsteps sounded in the room and a man in a blue suit passed in front of him, then another, then still another. Policemen, he breathed. Yes, they were trying to make the watchman confess, just as they had once made him confess to a crime he had not done. He stared into the room, trying to recall something. Oh . . . Those were the same policemen who had beaten him, had made him sign that paper when he had been too tired and sick to care. Now, they were doing the same thing to the watchman. His heart pounded as he saw one of the policemen shake a finger into the watchman's face.

"Why don't you admit it's an inside job, Thompson?" the policeman said.

"I've told you all I know," the watchman mumbled through swollen lips.

"But nobody was here but you!" the policeman shouted.

"I was sleeping," the watchman said. "It was wrong, but I was sleeping all that night!"

"Stop telling us that lie!"

"It's the truth!"

"When did you get the combination?"

"I don't know how to open the safe," the watchman said.

He clung to the rain pipe, tense; he wanted to laugh, but he controlled himself. He felt a great sense of power; yes, he could go back to the cave, rip the money off the walls, pick up the diamonds and rings, and bring them here and write a note, telling them where to look for their foolish toys. No . . . What good would that do? It was not worth the effort. The watchman was guilty; although he was not guilty of the crime of which he had been accused, he was guilty, had always been guilty. The only thing that worried him was that the man who had been really stealing was not being accused. But he consoled himself: they'll catch him sometime during his life.

He saw one of the policemen slap the watchman across the mouth.

"Come clean, you bastard!"

"I've told you all I know," the watchman mumbled like a child.

One of the police went to the rear of the watchman's chair and jerked it from under him; the watchman pitched forward upon his face.

"Get up!" a policeman said.

Trembling, the watchman pulled himself up and sat limply again in the chair.

"Now, are you going to talk?"

"I've told you all I know," the watchman gasped.

"Where did you hide the stuff?"

"I didn't take it!"

"Thompson, your brains are in your feet," one of the policemen said. "We're going to string you up and get them back into your skull."

He watched the policemen clamp handcuffs on the watchman's wrists and ankles; then they lifted the watchman and swung him upside-down and hoisted his feet to the edge of a door. The watchman hung, head down, his eyes bulging. They're crazy, he whispered to himself as he clung to the ridges of the pipe.

"You going to talk?" a policeman shouted into the watchman's ear.

He heard the watchman groan.

"We'll let you hang there till you talk, see?"

He saw the watchman close his eyes.

"Let's take 'im down. He passed out," a policeman said.

He grinned as he watched them take the body down and dump it carelessly upon the floor. The policeman took off the handcuffs.

"Let 'im come to. Let's get a smoke," a policeman said.

The three policemen left the scope of his vision. A door slammed. He had an impulse to yell to the watchman that he could escape through the hole in the basement and live with him in the cave. But he wouldn't understand, he told himself. After a moment he saw the watchman rise and stand swaying from weakness. He stumbled across the room to a desk, opened a drawer, and took out a gun. He's going to kill himself, he thought, intent, eager, detached, yearning to see the end of the man's actions. As the watchman stared vaguely about he lifted the gun to his temple; he stood like that for some minutes, biting his lips until a line of blood etched its way down a corner of his chin. No, he oughtn't do that, he said to himself in a mood of pity.

"Don't!" he half whispered and half yelled.

The watchman looked wildly about; he had heard him. But it did not help; there was a loud report and the watchman's head jerked violently and he fell like a log and lay prone, the gun clattering over the floor.

The three policemen came running into the room with drawn guns. One of the policemen knelt and rolled the watchman's body over and stared at a ragged, scarlet hole in the temple.

"Our hunch was right," the kneeling policeman said. "He was guilty, all right."

"Well, this ends the case," another policeman said.

"He knew he was licked," the third one said with grim satisfaction.

He eased down the rain pipe, crawled back through the holes he had made, and went back into his cave. A fever burned in his bones. He had to act, yet he was afraid. His eyes stared in the darkness as though propped open by invisible hands, as though they had become lidless. His muscles were rigid and he stood for what seemed to him a thousand years.

When he moved again his actions were informed with precision, his muscular system reinforced from a reservoir of energy. He crawled through the hole of earth, dropped into the gray sewer current, and sloshed ahead. When his right foot went forward at a street intersection, he fell backward and shot down into water. In a spasm of terror his right hand grabbed the concrete ledge of a down-curve and he felt the streaking water tugging violently at his body. The current reached his neck and for a moment he was still. He knew that if he moved clumsily he would be sucked under. He held onto the ledge with both hands and slowly pulled himself up. He sighed, standing once more in the sweeping water, thankful that he had missed death.

He waded on through sludge, moving with care, until he came to a web of light sifting down from a manhole cover. He saw steel hooks running up the side of the sewer wall; he caught hold and lifted himself and put his shoulder to the cover and moved it an inch. A crash of sound came to him as he looked into a hot glare of sunshine through which blurred shapes moved. Fear scalded him and he dropped back into the pallid current and stood paralyzed in the shadows. A heavy car rumbled past overhead, jarring the pavement, warning him to stay in his world of dark light, knocking the cover back into place with an imperious clang.

He did not know how much fear he felt, for fear claimed him completely; yet it was not a fear of the police or of people, but a cold dread at the thought of the actions he knew he would perform if he went out into that cruel sunshine. His mind said no; his body said yes; and his mind could not understand his feelings. A low whine broke from him and he was in the act of uncoiling. He climbed upward and heard the faint honking of auto horns. Like a frantic cat clutching a rag, he clung to the steel prongs and heaved his shoulder against the cover and pushed it off halfway. For a split second his eyes were drowned in the terror of yellow light and he was in a deeper darkness than he had ever known in the underground.

Partly out of the hole, he blinked, regaining enough sight to make out meaningful forms. An odd thing was happening: No one was rushing forward to challenge him. He had imagined the moment of his emergence as a desperate tussle with men who wanted to cart him off to be killed; instead, life froze about him as the traffic stopped. He pushed the cover aside, stood, swaying in the world so fragile that he expected it to collapse and drop him into some deep void. But nobody seemed to pay him heed. The cars were now swerving to shun him and the gaping hole.

"Why in hell don't you put up a red light, dummy?" a raucous voice yelled.

He understood; they thought that he was a sewer workman. He walked toward the sidewalk, weaving unsteadily through the moving traffic.

"Look where you're going, nigger!"

"That's right! Stay there and get killed!"

"You blind, you bastard?"

"Go home and sleep your drunk off!"

A policeman stood at the curb, looking in the opposite direction. When he passed the policeman, he feared that he would be grabbed, but nothing happened. Where was he? Was this real? He wanted to look about to get his bearings, but felt that something awful would happen to him if he did. He wandered into a spacious doorway of a store that sold men's clothing and saw his reflection in a long mirror: his cheekbones protruded from a hairy black face; his greasy cap was perched askew upon his head and his eyes were red and glassy. His shirt and trousers were caked with mud and hung loosely. His hands were gummed with a black stickiness. He threw back his head and laughed so loudly that passers-by stopped and stared.

He ambled on down the sidewalk, not having the merest notion of where he was going. Yet, sleeping within him, was the drive to go somewhere and say something to somebody. Half an hour later his ears caught the sound of spirited singing.

> The Lamb, the Lamb, the Lamb
> I hear thy voice a-calling
> The Lamb, the Lamb, the Lamb
> I feel thy grace a-falling

A church! he exclaimed. He broke into a run and came to brick steps leading downward to a subbasement. This is it! The church into which he had peered. Yes, he was going in and tell them. What? He did not know; but, once face to face with them, he would think of what to say. Must be

Sunday, he mused. He ran down the steps and jerked the door open; the church was crowded and a deluge of song swept over him.

> The Lamb, the Lamb, the Lamb
> Tell me again your story
> The Lamb, the Lamb, the Lamb
> Flood my soul with your glory

He stared at the singing faces with a trembling smile.

"Say!" he shouted.

Many turned to look at him, but the song rolled on. His arm was jerked violently.

"I'm sorry, Brother, but you can't do that in here," a man said.

"But, mister!"

"You can't act rowdy in God's house," the man said.

"He's filthy," another man said.

"But I want to tell 'em," he said loudly.

"He stinks," someone muttered.

The song had stopped, but at once another one began.

> Oh, wondrous sight upon the cross
> Vision sweet and divine
> Oh, wondrous sight upon the cross
> Full of such love sublime

He attempted to twist away, but other hands grabbed him and rushed him into the doorway.

"Let me alone!" he screamed, struggling.

"Get out!"

"He's drunk," somebody said. "He ought to be ashamed!"

"He acts crazy!"

He felt that he was failing and he grew frantic.

"But, mister, let me tell—"

"Get away from this door, or I'll call the police!"

He stared, his trembling smile fading in a sense of wonderment.

"The police," he repeated vacantly.

"Now, get!"

He was pushed toward the brick steps and the door banged shut. The waves of song came.

> Oh, wondrous sight, wondrous sight
> Lift my heavy heart above
> Oh, wondrous sight, wondrous sight
> Fill my weary soul with love

He was smiling again now. Yes, the police . . . That was it! Why had he not thought of it before? The idea had been deep down in him, and only now did it assume supreme importance. He looked up and saw a street sign: COURT STREET—HARTSDALE AVENUE. He turned and walked northward, his mind filled with the image of the police station. Yes, that was where they had beaten him, accused him, and had made him sign a confession of his guilt. He would go there and clear up everything, make a statement. What statement? He did not know. He was the statement, and since it was all so clear to him, surely he would be able to make it clear to others.

He came to the corner of Hartsdale Avenue and turned westward. Yeah, there's the station . . . A policeman came down the steps and walked past him without a glance. He mounted the stone steps and went through the door, paused; he was in a hallway where several policemen were standing, talking, smoking. One turned to him.

"What do you want, boy?"

He looked at the policeman and laughed.

"What in hell are you laughing about?" the policeman asked.

He stopped laughing and stared. His whole being was full of what he wanted to say to them, but he could not say it.

"Are you looking for the Desk Sergeant?"

"Yes, sir," he said quickly; then: "Oh, no, sir."

"Well, make up your mind, now."

Four policemen grouped themselves around him.

"I'm looking for the men," he said.

"What men?"

Peculiarly, at that moment he could not remember the names of the policemen; he recalled their beating him, the confession he had signed, and how he had run away from them. He saw the cave next to the church, the money on the walls, the guns, the rings, the cleaver, the watches, and the diamonds on the floor.

"They brought me here," he began.

"When?"

His mind flew back over the blur of the time lived in the underground blackness. He had no idea of how much time had elapsed, but the intensity of what had happened to him told him that it could not have transpired in a short space of time, yet his mind told him that time must have been brief.

"It was a long time ago." He spoke like a child relating a dimly remembered dream. "It was a long time," he repeated, following the promptings of his emotions. "They beat me . . . I was scared . . . I ran away."

A policeman raised a finger to his temple and made a derisive circle.

"Nuts," the policeman said.

"Do you know what place this is, boy?"

"Yes, sir. The police station," he answered sturdily, almost proudly.

"Well, who do you want to see?"

"The men," he said again, feeling that surely they knew the men. "You know the men," he said in a hurt tone.

"What's your name?"

He opened his lips to answer and no words came. He had forgotten. But what did it matter is he had? It was not important.

"Where do you live?"

Where did he live? It had been so long ago since he had lived up here in this strange world that he felt it was foolish even to try to remember. Then for a moment the old mood that had dominated him in the underground surged back. He leaned forward and spoke eagerly.

"They said I killed the woman."

"What woman?" a policeman asked.

"And I signed a paper that said I was guilty," he went on, ignoring theirs questions. "Then I ran off . . ."

"Did you run off from an institution?"

"No, sir," he said, blinking and shaking his head. "I came from under the ground. I pushed off the manhole cover and climbed out . . ."

"All right, now," a policeman said, placing an arm about his shoulder. "We'll send you to the psycho and you'll be taken care of."

"Maybe he's a Fifth Columnist!" a policeman shouted.

There was laughter and, despite his anxiety, he joined in. But the laughter lasted so long that it irked him.

"I got to find those men," he protested mildly.

"Say, boy, what have you been drinking?"

"Water," he said. "I got some water in a basement."

"Were the men you ran away from dressed in white, boy?"

"No, sir," he said brightly. "They were men like you."

An elderly policeman caught hold of his arm.

"Try and think hard. Where did they pick you up?"

He knitted his brows in an effort to remember, but he was blank inside. The policeman stood before him demanding logical answers and he could no longer think with his mind; he thought with his feelings and no words came.

"I was guilty," he said. "Oh, no, sir. I wasn't then, I mean, mister!"

"Aw, talk sense. Now, where did they pick you up?"

He felt challenged and his mind began reconstructing events in reverse; his feelings ranged back over the long hours and he saw the cave, the sewer, the bloody room where it was said that a woman had been killed.

"Oh, yes, sir," he said, smiling. "I was coming from Mrs. Wooten's."

"Who is she?"

"I work for her."

"Where does she live?"

"Next door to Mrs. Peabody, the woman who was killed."

The policemen were very quiet now, looking at him intently.

"What do you know about Mrs. Peabody's death, boy?"

"Nothing, sir. But they said I killed her. But it doesn't make any difference. I'm guilty!"

"What are you talking about, boy?"

His smile faded and he was possessed with memories of the underground; he saw the cave next to the church and his lips moved to speak. But how could he say it? The distance between what he felt and what these men meant was vast. Something told him, as he stood there looking into their faces, that he would never be able to tell them, that they would never believe him even if he told them.

"All the people I saw was guilty," he began slowly.

"Aw, nuts," a policeman muttered.

"Say," another policeman said, "that Peabody woman was killed over on Winewood. That's Number Ten's beat."

"Where's Number Ten?" a policeman asked.

"Upstairs in the swing room," someone answered.

"Take this boy up, Sam," a policeman ordered.

"O.K. Come along, boy."

An elderly policeman caught hold of his arm and led him up a flight of wooden stairs, down a long hall, and to a door.

"Squad Ten!" the policeman called through the door.

"What?" a gruff voice answered.

"Someone to see you!"

"About what?"

The old policeman pushed the door in and then shoved him into the room.

He stared, his lips open, his heart barely beating. Before him were the three policemen who had picked him up and had beaten him to extract the confession. They were seated about a small table, playing cards. The air was blue with smoke and sunshine poured through a high window, lighting up fantastic smoke shapes. He saw one of the policemen look up; the policeman's face was tired and a cigarette dropped limply from one corner of his mouth and both of his fat, puffy eyes were squinting and his hands gripped his cards.

"Lawson!" the man exclaimed.

The moment the man's name sounded he remembered the names of all of them: Lawson, Murphy, and Johnson. How simple it was. He waited, smiling, wondering how they would react when they knew that he had come back.

"Looking for me?" the man who been called Lawson mumbled, sorting his cards. "For what?"

So far only Murphy, the red-headed one, had recognized him.

"Don't you-all remember me?" he blurted, running to the table.

All three of the policemen were looking at him now. Lawson, who seemed the leader, jumped to his feet.

"Where in hell have you been?"

"Do you know 'im, Lawson?" the old policeman asked.

"Huh?" Lawson frowned. "Oh, yes, I'll handle 'im." The old policeman left the room and Lawson crossed to the door and turned the key in the lock. "Come here, boy," he ordered in a cold tone.

He did not move; he looked from face to face. Yes, he would tell them about his cave.

"He looks batty to me," Johnson said, the one who had not spoken before.

"Why in hell did you come back here?" Lawson said.

"I—I just didn't want to run away no more," he said. "I'm all right, now." He paused; the men's attitude puzzled him.

"You've been hiding, huh?" Lawson asked in a tone that denoted that he had not heard his previous words. "You told us you were sick, and when we left you in the room, you jumped out of the window and ran away."

Panic filled him. Yes, they were indifferent to what he would say! They were waiting for him to speak and they would laugh at him. He had to rescue himself from this bog; he had to force the reality of himself upon them.

"Mister, I took a sackful of money and pasted it on the walls . . ." he began.

"I'll be damned," Lawson said.

"Listen," said Murphy, "let me tell you something for your own good. We don't want you, see? You're free, free as air. Now go home and forget it. It was all a mistake. We caught the guy who did the Peabody job. He wasn't colored at all. He was an Eyetalian."

"Shut up!" Lawson yelled. "Have you no sense!"

"But I want to tell 'im," Murphy said.

"We can't let this crazy fool go," Lawson exploded. "He acts nuts, but this may be a stunt . . ."

"I was down in the basement," he began in a childlike tone as though repeating a lesson learned by heart; "and I went into a movie . . ." His voice failed. He was getting ahead of his story. First, he ought to tell them about the singing in the church, but what words could he use? He looked at them appealingly. "I went into a shop and took a sackful of money and diamonds and watches and rings . . . I didn't steal 'em; I'll give 'em all back. I just took 'em to play with . . ." He paused, stunned by their disbelieving eyes.

Lawson lit a cigarette and looked at him coldly.

"What did you do with the money?" he asked in a quiet, waiting voice.

"I pasted the hundred-dollar bills on the walls."

"What walls?" Lawson asked.

"The walls of the dirt room," he said, smiling, "the room next to the church. I hung up the rings and the watches and I stamped the diamonds into the dirt . . ." He saw that they were not understanding what he was saying. He grew frantic to make them believe, his voice tumbled on eagerly. "I saw a dead baby and a dead man . . ."

"Aw, you're nuts," Lawson snarled, shoving him into a chair.

"But, mister . . ."

"Johnson, where's the paper he signed?" Lawson asked.

"What paper?"

"The confession, fool!"

Johnson pulled out his billfold and extracted a crumpled piece of paper.

"Yes, sir, mister," he said, stretching forth his hand. "That's the paper I signed . . ."

Lawson slapped him and he would have toppled had his chair not struck a wall behind him. Lawson scratched a match and held the paper over the flame; the confession burned down to Lawson's fingertips.

He stared, thunderstruck; the sun of the underground was fleeing and the terrible darkness of the day stood before him. They did not believe him, but he *had* to make them believe him!

"But, mister . . ."

"It's going to be all right, boy," Lawson said with a quiet, soothing laugh. "I've burned your confession, see? You didn't sign anything." Lawson came close to him with the black ashed cupped in his palm. "You don't remember a thing about this, do you?"

"Don't you-all be scared of me," he pleaded, sensing their uneasiness. "I'll sign another paper, if you want me to. I'll show you the cave."

"What's your game, boy?" Lawson asked suddenly.

"What are you trying to find out?" Johnson asked.

"Who sent you here?" Murphy demanded.

"Nobody sent me, mister," he said. "I just want to show you the room."

"Aw, he's plumb bats," Murphy said. "Let's ship 'im to the psycho."

"No," Lawson said. "He's playing a game and I wish to God I knew what it was."

There flashed through his mind a definite way to make them believe him; he rose from the chair with nervous excitement.

"Mister, I saw the night watchman blow his brains out because you accused him of stealing," he told them. "But he didn't steal the money and diamonds. I took 'em."

Tigerishly Lawson grabbed his collar and lifted him bodily.

"*Who told you about that?*"

"Don't get excited, Lawson," Johnson said. "He read about it in the papers."

Lawson flung him away.

"He couldn't have," Lawson said, pulling papers from his pocket. "I haven't turned in the reports yet."

"Then how *did* he find out?" Murphy asked.

"Let's get out of here," Lawson said with quick resolution. "Listen, boy, we're going to take you to a nice, quiet place, see?"

"Yes, sir," he said. "And I'll show you the underground."

"Goddamn," Lawson muttered, fastening the gun at his hip. He narrowed his eyes at Johnson and Murphy. "Listen," he spoke just above a whisper, "say nothing about this, you hear?"

"O.K.," Johnson said.

"Sure," Murphy said.

Lawson unlocked the door and Johnson and Murphy led him down the stairs. The hallway was crowded with policemen.

"What have you got there, Lawson?"

"What did he do, Lawson?"

"He's psycho, ain't he, Lawson?"

Lawson did not answer; Johnson and Murphy led him to the car parked at the curb, pushed him into the back seat. Lawson got behind the steering wheel and the car rolled forward.

"What's up, Lawson?" Murphy asked.

"Listen," Lawson began slowly, "we tell the papers that he spilled about the Peabody job, then he escapes. The Wop is caught and we tell the papers that we steered them wrong to trap the real guy, see? Now this dope shows up and acts nuts. If we let him go, he'll squeal that we framed him, see?"

"I'm all right, mister," he said, feeling Murphy's and Johnson's arms locked rigidly into his. "I'm guilty . . . I'll show you everything in the underground. I laughed and laughed . . ."

"Shut that fool up!" Lawson ordered.

Johnson tapped him across the head with a blackjack and he fell back against the seat cushion, dazed.

"Yes, sir," he mumbled. "I'm all right."

The car sped along Hartsdale Avenue, then swung onto Pine Street and rolled to State Street, then turned south. It slowed to a stop, turned in the middle of a block, and headed north again.

"You're going around in circles, Lawson," Murphy said.

Lawson did not answer; he was hunched over the steering wheel. Finally he pulled the car to a stop at the curb.

"Say, boy, tell us the truth," Lawson asked quietly. "Where did you hide?"

"I didn't hide, mister."

The three policemen were staring at him now; he felt that for the first time they were willing to understand him.

"Then what happened?"

"Mister, when I looked through all of those holes and saw how people were living, I loved 'em. . . ."

"Cut out that crazy talk!" Lawson snapped. "Who sent you back here?"

"Nobody, mister."

"Maybe he's talking straight," Johnson ventured.

"All right," Lawson said. "Nobody hid you. Now, tell us *where* you hid."

"I went underground . . ."

"What goddamn underground do you keep talking about?"

"I just went . . ." He paused and looked into the street, then pointed to a manhole cover. "I went down in there and stayed."

"In the *sewer?*"

"Yes, sir."

The policemen burst into a sudden laugh and ended quickly. Lawson swung the car around and drove to Woodside Avenue; he brought the car to a stop in front of a tall apartment building.

"What're we going to do, Lawson?" Murphy asked.

"I'm taking him up to my place," Lawson said. "We've got to wait until night. There's nothing we can do now."

They took him out of the car and led him into a vestibule.

"Take the steps," Lawson muttered.

They led him up four flights of stairs and into the living room of a small apartment. Johnson and Murphy let go of his arms and he stood uncertainly in the middle of the room.

"Now, listen, boy," Lawson began, "forget those wild lies you've been telling us. Where did you hide?"

"I just went underground, like I told you."

The room rocked with laughter. Lawson went to a cabinet and got a bottle of whisky; he placed glasses for Johnson and Murphy. The three of them drank.

He felt that he could not explain himself to them. He tried to muster all the sprawling images that floated in him; the images stood out sharply in his mind, but he could not make them have the meaning for others that they had for him. He felt so helpless that he began to cry.

"He's nuts, all right," Johnson said. "All nuts cry like that."

Murphy crossed the room and slapped him.

"Stop that raving!"

A sense of excitement flooded him; he ran to Murphy and grabbed his arm.

"Let me show you the cave," he said. "Come on, and you'll see!"

Before he knew it a sharp blow had clipped him on the chin; darkness covered his eyes. He dimly felt himself being lifted and laid out on the sofa. He heard low voices and struggled to rise, but hard hands held him down. His brain was clearing now. He pulled to a sitting posture and stared with glazed eyes. It had grown dark. How long had he been out?

"Say, boy," Lawson said soothingly, "will you show us the underground?"

His eyes shone and his heart swelled with gratitude. Lawson believed him! He rose, glad; he grabbed Lawson's arm, making the policeman spill whisky from the glass to his shirt.

"Take it easy, goddammit," Lawson said.

"Yes, sir."

"O.K. We'll take you down. But you'd better be telling us the truth, you hear?"

He clapped his hands in wild joy.

"I'll show you everything!"

He had triumphed at last! He would now do what he had felt was compelling him all along. At last he would be free of his burden.

"Take 'im down," Lawson ordered.

They led him down to the vestibule; when he reached the sidewalk he saw that it was night and a fine rain was falling.

"It's just like when I went down," he told them.

"What?" Lawson asked.

"The rain," he said, sweeping his arm in a wide arc. "It was raining when I went down. The rain made the water rise and lift the cover off."

"Cut it out," Lawson snapped.

They did not believe him now, but they would. A mood of high selflessness throbbed in him. He could barely contain his rising spirits. They would see what he had seen; they would feel what he had felt. He would lead them through all the holes he had dug and . . . He wanted to make a hymn, prance about in physical ecstasy, throw his arms about the policemen in fellowship.

"Get into the car," Lawson ordered.

He climbed in and Johnson and Murphy sat at either side of him; Lawson slid behind the steering wheel and started the motor.

"Now, tell us where to go," Lawson said.

"It's right around the corner from where the lady was killed," he said.

The car rolled slowly and he closed his eyes, remembering the song he had heard in the church, the song that had wrought him to such a high pitch of terror and pity. He sang softly, lolling his head:

> Glad, glad, glad, oh, so glad
> I got Jesus in my soul . . .

"Mister," he said, stopping his song, "you ought to see how funny the rings look on the wall." He giggled. "I fired a pistol, too. Just once, to see how it felt."

"What do you suppose he's suffering from?" Johnson asked.

"Delusions of grandeur, maybe," Murphy said.

"Maybe it's because he lives in a white man's world," Lawson said.

"Say, boy, what did you eat down there?" Murphy asked, prodding Johnson anticipatorily with his elbow.

"Pears, oranges, bananas, and pork chops," he said.

The car filled with laughter.

"You didn't eat any watermelon?" Lawson asked, smiling.

"No, sir," he answered calmly. "I didn't see any."

The three policemen roared harder and louder.

"Boy, you're sure some case," Murphy said, shaking his head in wonder. The car pulled to a curb.

"All right, boy," Lawson said. "Tell us where to go."

He peered through the rain and saw where he had gone down. The streets, save for a few dim lamps glowing softly through the rain, were dark and empty.

"Right there, mister," he said, pointing.

"Come on; let's take a look," Lawson said.

"Well, suppose he did hide down there," Johnson said, "what is that supposed to prove?"

"I don't believe he hid down there," Murphy said.

"It won't hurt to look," Lawson said. "Leave things to me."

Lawson got out of the car and looked up and down the street.

He was eager to show them the cave now. If he could show them what he had seen, then they would feel what he had felt and they in turn would show it to others and those others would feel as they had felt, and soon everybody would be governed by the same impulse of pity.

"Take 'im out," Lawson ordered.

Johnson and Murphy opened the door and pushed him out; he stood trembling in the rain, smiling. Again Lawson looked up and down the street; no one was in sight. The rain came down hard, slanting like black wires across the windswept air.

"All right," Lawson said. "Show us."

He walked to the center of the street, stopped and inserted a finger in one of the tiny holes of the cover and tugged, but he was too weak to budge it.

"Did you really go down in there, boy?" Lawson asked; there was a doubt in his voice.

"Yes, sir. Just a minute. I'll show you."

"Help 'im get that damn thing off," Lawson said.

Johnson stepped forward and lifted the cover; it clanged against the wet pavement. The hole gaped round and black.

"I went down in there," he announced with pride.

Lawson gazed at him for a long time without speaking, then he reached his right hand to his holster and drew his gun.

"Mister, I got a gun just like that down there," he said, laughing and looking into Lawson's face. "I fired it once then hung it on the wall. I'll show you."

"Show us how you went down," Lawson said quietly.

"I'll go down first, mister, and then you-all can come after me, hear?" He spoke like a little boy playing a game.

"Sure, sure," Lawson said soothingly. "Go ahead. We'll come."

He looked brightly at the policemen; he was bursting with happiness. He bent down and placed his hands on the rim of the hole and sat on the edge, his feet dangling into watery darkness. He heard the familiar drone of the gray current. He lowered his body and hung for a moment by his fingers, then he went downward on the steel prongs, hand over hand, until he reached the last rung. He dropped and his feet hit the water and he felt the stiff current trying to suck him away. He balanced himself quickly and looked back upward at the policemen.

"Come on, you-all!" he yelled, casting his voice above the rustling at his feet.

The vague forms that towered above him in the rain did not move. He laughed, feeling that they doubted him. But, once they saw the things he had done, they would never doubt again.

"Come on! The cave isn't far!" he yelled. "But be careful when your feet hit the water, because the current's pretty rough down here!"

Lawson still held the gun. Murphy and Johnson looked at Lawson quizzically.

"What are we going to do, Lawson?" Murphy asked.

"We are not going to follow that crazy nigger down into that sewer, are we?" Johnson asked.

"Come on, you-all!" he begged in a shout.

He saw Lawson raise the gun and point it directly at him. Lawson's face twitched, as though he were hesitating.

Then there was a thunderous report and a streak of fire ripped through his chest. He was hurled into the water, flat on his back. He looked in amazement at the blurred white faces looming above him. They shot me, he said to himself. The water flowed past him, blossoming in foam about his arms, his legs, and his head. His jaw sagged and his mouth gaped soundless. A vast pain gripped his head and gradually squeezed out consciousness. As from a great distance he heard hollow voices.

"What did you shoot him for, Lawson?"

"I had to."

"Why?"

"You've got to shoot his kind. They'd wreck things."

As though in a deep dream, he heard a metallic clank; they had replaced the manhole cover, shutting out forever the sound of wind and rain. From overhead came the muffled roar of a powerful motor and the swish of a speeding car. He felt the strong tide pushing him slowly into the middle of the sewer, turning him about. For a split second there hovered before his eyes the glittering cave, the shouting walls, and the laughing floor . . . Then his mouth was full of thick, bitter water. The current spun him around. He sighed and closed his eyes, a whirling object rushing alone in the darkness, veering, tossing, lost in the heart of the earth.

11

CARSON McCULLERS
The Ballad of the Sad Café

The coming of the hunchback Cousin Lymon causes Miss Amelia to sublimate her aggressiveness, awakening in her an almost super-human capacity for good. Before his arrival, the forbidding side of her personality predominated. She had been masculine, vindictive, and greedy, and her inner bene-ficence had found expression in little other than her extraordinary doctoring practice. With the arrival of Lymon and the birth of the café, her capacity for kindness transforms the entire town as if by magic. Suggestions of magic, in fact, surround Miss Amelia, and she is deliberately made to seem like some good-evil witch from a fairy tale, with powers both to heal and to de-stroy. Amelia's café soon becomes a magic place, a sacred place, although no one in town would be likely to describe it in such words. In a town where the value of life is constantly threatened by boredom, purposeless-ness, and collective stupidity, the café provides an atmosphere of dig-nity and warmth in which human self-respect is renewed.

Miss Amelia's love for Cousin Lymon, like the story's two other strange loves, defies any wholly sat-isfactory explanation. However, it is apparent that her powerful attrac-tion to her father has much to do with her behavior toward Lymon.

The café is a direct outgrowth of Amelia's love for Lymon. Rumors claim that she runs it in order to distract him in the late hours, when terrifying thoughts haunt him. It is Lymon's presence there, as well as Amelia's, that makes the café such an important place. There is always an undercurrent of excitement when he is present at the nightly gather-ings. Despite the hushed and proper atmosphere of the place, there is the feeling that anything might happen. Lymon is a figure of tantalizing mys-tery. No one knows how old he is, where he comes from, or what, if any, is his precise blood relationship to Amelia. His dwarfish stature and his hunchback add to the impression that he is something out of the or-dinary, not quite human. Like many of the dwarfish creatures in myths and fairy tales, he is associated with hidden treasure, subterranean magic, and ambiguous good and evil. He has a way of insinuating himself into forbidden places and taking possession of secret things. Much as he has made himself at home in the fabled second story of Amelia's store—and even gained possession of her cabinet of treasured curios— he also worms his way into the secrets of all the café's patrons, so that in the end he possesses the power of their collective aspirations, fears, and antagonisms. In short, Lymon becomes an embodiment of folk-energy, of the commonly shared and unconscious forces which, for example, bring the silent group of men into Miss Amelia's store on the night the café is created.

The emphasis on Lymon's power to create antagonism sets the stage for his role in the confrontation between Miss Amelia and Marvin Macy. Somewhat like the potential violence in Miss Amelia and Lymon, Marvin has been hidden away (specifically, in the Atlanta Penitentiary) during the years of the café. Marvin's imprisonment creates a vague threat of gathering evil which Miss Amelia and the townspeople never entirely forget, and this threat gives an added tang of sweetness to the café's four happy years. His return precipitates the emergence of destructive instincts on the part of all three main characters. Lymon's immediate infatuation with Marvin stems from their mutual recognition of criminal instinct. And probably from even before their first exchange of glances, Lymon is drawn to Marvin by their mutual desire for revenge on Miss Amelia. In Marvin's case, the desire for revenge is understandable. But Lymon's revenge seems explicable only through the inverse logic of love provided by the narrator—a rationale in which there is chilling truth: "The beloved fears and hates the lover, and with the best of reasons. For the lover is forever trying to strip bare his beloved. The lover craves any possible relation with the beloved, even if this experience can cause him only pain."

Carson McCullers calls her story a "ballad." The best-known ballad form is the folk song composed of short stanzas alternating with a refrain verse. Such ballads often deal with colorful outlaws or other legendary figures; they stress the outlandish and the grotesque, and their endings are typically bittersweet. Most of these characteristics are obviously present in *The Ballad of the Sad Café*. Although most ballads are predominantly sad, or at least muted in tone, their effect is more pleasing than saddening partly because they tend to celebrate the character of those about whom—and by whom and for whom—they are sung. Gifted with a certain pride, talent, and resignation, the ballad singer can sing sweetly even of life's most abject miseries, and whoever is taken by the song and sings it again celebrates misery and the miserable, the former singer and the song, and himself. The spirit of celebration is important throughout *The Ballad of the Sad Café,* and McCullers' awareness of this is apparent in the epilogue, "Twelve Mortal Men," which deals directly with the idea of the orally transmitted folk song as the common man's deliverance from the misery of human bondage. The haunting song of the chain gang, like McCullers' telling of the story itself, is celebration in the most meaningful sense: a discovery of shared joy and hope in the depths of suffering.

The successful joining of celebration and sadness in *The Ballad of the Sad Café* is partly the result of the story's simultaneous imitation and parody of the folk ballad. The author gives the whole story a playful air by taking the ballad's positive characteristics, such as color, exuberance, and improbability, and exaggerating them enough so that they come across with a ring of mellow laughter. So, also, the very process of rumor and folk energy which gives such folk tales their birth is related with a mixed tone of mockery and awe. Suffering itself becomes slyly melodramatic, as in the list of awful things Lymon and Marvin do to Miss Amelia's property before leaving town. What gives all these devices such subtlety is above all the author's careful distancing of her own voice from that of the narrator—presumably some lady neighbor of Miss Amelia's who is by turns sophisticated and naïve, generous and rather petty. The author is constantly there, however, just behind the narrator, informing the reader through minute signs about what is silly, improbable, or in poor taste. When, for example, we are told that Miss Amelia kept her two kidney stones "in a velvet box" in her cabinet, and that "in the second year of Cousin Lymon's stay with her she had them set as ornaments in a watch chain which she gave to him," it becomes apparent that Carson McCullers is making fun of the sublime grotesquerie with which folk tales abound. At the same time, the business about the kidney stones is a genuinely imaginative *tour de force,* and a meaningful bit of symbolism.

The Ballad
of the Sad Café

The town itself is dreary; not much is
there except the cotton mill, the two-room houses where the workers live, a
few peach trees, a church with two colored windows, and a miserable main
street only a hundred yards long. On Saturdays the tenants from the near-by
farms come in for a day of talk and trade. Otherwise the town is lonesome,
sad, and like a place that is far off and estranged from all other places in
the world. The nearest train stop is Society City, and the Greyhound and
White Bus Lines use the Forks Falls Road which is three miles away. The
winters here are short and raw, the summers white with glare and fiery hot.

If you walk along the main street on an August afternoon there is nothing whatsoever to do. The largest building, in the very center of the town,
is boarded up completely and leans so far to the right that it seems bound
to collapse at any minute. The house is very old. There is about it a curious,
cracked look that is very puzzling until you suddenly realize that at one
time, and long ago, the right side of the front porch had been painted, and
part of the wall—but the painting was left unfinished and one portion of
the house is darker and dingier than the other. The building looks completely deserted. Nevertheless, on the second floor there is one window
which is not boarded; sometimes in the late afternoon when the heat is at
its worst a hand will slowly open the shutter and a face will look down on
the town. It is a face like the terrible dim faces known in dreams—sexless

and white, with two gray crossed eyes which are turned inward so sharply that they seem to be exchanging with each other one long and secret gaze of grief. The face lingers at the window for an hour or so, then the shutters are closed once more, and as likely as not there will not be another soul to be seen along the main street. These August afternoons—when your shift is finished there is absolutely nothing to do; you might as well walk down to the Forks Falls Road and listen to the chain gang.

However, here in this very town there was once a café. And this old boarded-up house was unlike any other place for many miles around. There were tables with cloths and paper napkins, colored streamers from the electric fans, great gatherings on Saturday nights. The owner of the place was Miss Amelia Evans. But the person most responsible for the success and gaiety of the place was a hunchback called Cousin Lymon. One other person had a part in the story of this café—he was the former husband of Miss Amelia, a terrible character who returned to the town after a long term in the penitentiary, caused ruin, and then went on his way again. The café has long since been closed, but it is still remembered.

The place was not always a café. Miss Amelia inherited the building from her father, and it was a store that carried mostly feed, guano, and staples such as meal and snuff. Miss Amelia was rich. In addition to the store she operated a still three miles back in the swamp, and ran out the best liquor in the county. She was a dark, tall woman with bones and muscles like a man. Her hair was cut short and brushed back from the forehead, and there was about her sunburned face a tense, haggard quality. She might have been a handsome woman if, even then, she was not slightly cross-eyed. There were those who would have courted her, but Miss Amelia cared nothing for the love of men and was a solitary person. Her marriage had been unlike any other marriage ever contracted in this county—it was a strange and dangerous marriage, lasting only for ten days, that left the whole town wondering and shocked. Except for this queer marriage, Miss Amelia had lived her life alone. Often she spent whole nights back in her shed in the swamp, dressed in overalls and gum boots, silently guarding the low fire of the still.

With all things which could be made by the hands Miss Amelia prospered. She sold chitterlings and sausage in the town near-by. On fine autumn days, she ground sorghum, and the syrup from her vats was dark golden and delicately flavored. She built the brick privy behind her store in only two weeks and was skilled in carpentering. It was only with people that Miss Amelia was not at ease. People, unless they are nilly-willy or very sick, cannot be taken into the hands and changed overnight to something more worthwhile and profitable. So that the only use that Miss Amelia had for other people was to make money out of them. And in this she succeeded. Mortgages on crops and property, a sawmill, money in the bank—she was the richest woman for miles around. She would have been rich as a

congressman if it were not for her one great failing, and that was her passion for lawsuits and the courts. She would involve herself in long and
bitter litigation over just a trifle. It was said that if Miss Amelia so much as
stumbled over a rock in the road she would glance around instinctively as
though looking for something to sue about it. Aside from these lawsuits
she lived a steady life and every day was very much like the day that had
gone before. With the exception of her ten-day marriage, nothing happened
to change this until the spring of the year that Miss Amelia was thirty years
old.

It was toward midnight on a soft quiet evening in April. The sky was
the color of a blue swamp iris, the moon clear and bright. The crops that
spring promised well and in the past weeks the mill had run a night shift.
Down by the creek the square brick factory was yellow with light, and there
was the faint, steady hum of the looms. It was such a night when it is good
to hear from faraway, across the dark fields, the slow song of a Negro on
his way to make love. Or when it is pleasant to sit quietly and pick a
guitar, or simply to rest alone and think of nothing at all. The street that
evening was deserted, but Miss Amelia's store was lighted and on the porch
outside there were five people. One of these was Stumpy MacPhail, a foreman with a red face and dainty, purplish hands. On the top step were two
boys in overalls, the Rainey twins—both of them lanky and slow, with
white hair and sleepy green eyes. The other man was Henry Macy, a shy
and timid person with gentle manners and nervous ways, who sat on the
edge of the bottom step. Miss Amelia herself stood leaning against the side
of the open door, her feet crossed in their big swamp boots, patiently unty-
ing knots in a rope she had come across. They had not talked for a long
time.

One of the twins, who had been looking down the empty road, was the
first to speak. 'I see something coming,' he said.

'A calf got loose,' said his brother.

The approaching figure was still too distant to be clearly seen. The moon
made dim, twisted shadows of the blossoming peach trees along the side of
the road. In the air the odor of blossoms and sweet spring grass mingled
with the warm, sour smell of the near-by lagoon.

'No. It's somebody's youngun,' said Stumpy MacPhail.

Miss Amelia watched the road in silence. She had put down her rope
and was fingering the straps of her overalls with her brown bony hand. She
scowled, and a dark lock of hair fell down on her forehead. While they
were waiting there, a dog from one of the houses down the road began a
wild, hoarse howl that continued until a voice called out and hushed him.
It was not until the figure was quite close, within the range of the yellow
light from the porch, that they saw clearly what had come.

The man was a stranger, and it is rare that a stranger enters the town on
foot at that hour. Besides, the man was a hunchback. He was scarcely more
than four feet tall and he wore a ragged, dusty coat that reached only to his

knees. His crooked little legs seemed too thin to carry the weight of his great warped chest and the hump that sat on his shoulders. He had a very large head, with deep-set blue eyes and a sharp little mouth. His face was both soft and sassy—at the moment his pale skin was yellowed by dust and there were lavendar shadows beneath his eyes. He carried a lopsided old suitcase which was tied with a rope.

'Evening,' said the hunchback, and he was out of breath.

Miss Amelia and the men on the porch neither answered his greeting nor spoke. They only looked at him.

'I am hunting for Miss Amelia Evans.'

Miss Amelia pushed back her hair from her forehead and raised her chin. 'How come?'

'Because I am kin to her,' the hunchback said.

The twins and Stumpy MacPhail looked up at Miss Amelia.

'That's me,' she said. 'How do you mean, "kin"?'

'Because——' the hunchback began. He looked uneasy, almost as though he was about to cry. He rested the suitcase on the bottom step, but did not take his hand from the handle. 'My mother was Fanny Jesup and she come from Cheehaw. She left Cheehaw some thirty years ago when she married her first husband. I remember hearing her tell how she had a half-sister named Martha. And back in Cheehaw today they tell me that was your mother.'

Miss Amelia listened with her head turned slightly aside. She ate her Sunday dinners by herself; her place was never crowded with a flock of relatives, and she claimed kin with no one. She had had a great-aunt who owned the livery stable in Cheehaw, but that aunt was now dead. Aside from her there was only one double first cousin who lived in a town twenty miles away, but this cousin and Miss Amelia did not get on so well, and when they chanced to pass each other they spat on the side of the road. Other people had tried very hard, from time to time, to work out some kind of far-fetched connection with Miss Amelia, but with absolutely no success.

The hunchback went into a long rigmarole, mentioning names and places that were unknown to the listeners on the porch and seemed to have nothing to do with the subject. 'So Fanny and Martha Jesup were half-sisters. And I am the son of Fanny's third husband. So that would make you and I ——' He bent down and began to unfasten his suitcase. His hands were like dirty sparrow claws and they were trembling. The bag was full of all manner of junk—ragged clothes and odd rubbish that looked like parts out of a sewing machine, or something just as worthless. The hunchback scrambled among these belongings and brought out an old photograph. 'This is a picture of my mother and her half-sister.'

Miss Amelia did not speak. She was moving her jaw slowly from side to side, and you could tell from her face what she was thinking about. Stumpy MacPhail took the photograph and held it out toward the light. It was a picture of two pale, withered up little children of about two and three years of age. The faces were tiny white blurs, and it might have been an old picture in anyone's album.

Stumpy MacPhail handed it back with no comment. 'Where you come from?' he asked.

The hunchback's voice was uncertain. 'I was traveling.'

Still Miss Amelia did not speak. She just stood leaning against the side of the door, and looked down at the hunchback. Henry Macy winked nervously and rubbed his hands together. Then quietly he left the bottom step and disappeared. He is a good soul, and the hunchback's situation had touched his heart. Therefore he did not want to wait and watch Miss Amelia chase this newcomer off her property and run him out of town. The hunchback stood with his bag open on the bottom step; he sniffed his nose, and his mouth quivered. Perhaps he began to feel his dismal predicament. Maybe he realized what a miserable thing it was to be a stranger in the town with a suitcase full of junk, and claiming kin with Miss Amelia. At any rate he sat down on the steps and suddenly began to cry.

It was not a common thing to have an unknown hunchback walk to the store at midnight and then sit down and cry. Miss Amelia rubbed back her hair from her forehead and the men looked at each other uncomfortably. All around the town was very quiet.

At last one of the twins said: 'I'll be damned if he ain't a regular Morris Finestein.'

Everyone nodded and agreed, for that is an expression having a certain special meaning. But the hunchback cried louder because he could not know what they were talking about. Morris Finestein was a person who had lived in the town years before. He was only a quick, skipping little Jew who cried if you called him Christ-killer, and ate light bread and canned salmon every day. A calamity had come over him and he had moved away to Society City. But since then if a man were prissy in any way, or if a man ever wept, he was known as a Morris Finestein.

'Well, he is afflicted,' said Stumpy MacPhail. 'There is some cause.'

Miss Amelia crossed the porch with two slow, gangling strides. She went down the steps and stood looking thoughtfully at the stranger. Gingerly, with one long brown forefinger, she touched the hump on his back. The hunchback still wept, but he was quieter now. The night was silent and the moon still shone with a soft, clear light—it was getting colder. Then Miss Amelia did a rare thing; she pulled out a bottle from her hip pocket and after polishing off the top with the palm of her hand she handed it to the hunchback to drink. Miss Amelia could seldom be persuaded to sell her liquor on credit, and for her to give so much as a drop away free was almost unknown.

'Drink,' she said. 'It will liven your gizzard.'

The hunchback stopped crying, neatly licked the tears from around his mouth, and did as he was told. When he was finished, Miss Amelia took a slow swallow, warmed and washed her mouth with it, and spat. Then she also drank. The twins and the foreman had their own bottle they had paid for.

'It is smooth liquor,' Stumpy MacPhail said. 'Miss Amelia, I have never known you to fail.'

The whisky they drank that evening (two big bottles of it) is important. Otherwise, it would be hard to account for what followed. Perhaps without it there would never have been a café. For the liquor of Miss Amelia has a special quality of its own. It is clean and sharp on the tongue, but once down a man it glows inside him for a long time afterward. And that is not all. It is known that if a message is written with lemon juice on a clean sheet of paper there will be no sign of it. But if the paper is held for a moment to the fire then the letters turn brown and the meaning becomes clear. Imagine that the whisky is the fire and that the image is that which is known only in the soul of a man—then the worth of Miss Amelia's liquor can be understood. Things that have gone unnoticed, thoughts that have been harbored far back in the dark mind, are suddenly recognized and comprehended. A spinner who has thought only of the loom, the dinner pail, the bed, and then the loom again—this spinner might drink some on a Sunday and come across a marsh lily. And is his palm he might hold this flower, examining the golden dainty cup, and in him suddenly might come a sweetness keen as pain. A weaver might look up suddenly and see for the first time the cold, weird radiance of midnight January sky, and a deep fright at his own smallness stop his heart. Such things as these, then, happen when a man has drunk Miss Amelia's liquor. He may suffer, or he may be spent with joy—but the experience has shown the truth; he has warmed his soul and seen the message hidden there.

They drank until it was past midnight, and the moon was clouded over so that the night was cold and dark. The hunchback still sat on the bottom steps, bent over miserably with his forehead resting on his knee. Miss Amelia stood with her hands in her pockets, one foot resting on the second step of the stairs. She had been silent for a long time. Her face had the expression often seen in slightly cross-eyed persons who are thinking deeply, a look that appears to be both very wise and very crazy. At last she said: 'I don't know your name.'

'I'm Lymon Willis,' said the hunchback.

'Well, come on in,' she said. 'Some supper was left in the stove and you can eat.'

Only a few times in her life had Miss Amelia invited anyone to eat with her, unless she were planning to trick them in some way, or make money out of them. So the men on the porch felt there was something wrong. Later, they said among themselves that she must have been drinking back in the swamp the better part of the afternoon. At any rate she left the porch, and Stumpy MacPhail and the twins went on off home. She bolted the front door and looked all around to see that her goods were in order. Then she went to the kitchen, which was at the back of the store. The hunchback followed her, dragging his suitcase, sniffling and wiping his nose on the sleeve of his dirty coat.

'Sit down,' said Miss Amelia. 'I'll just warm up what's here.'

It was a good meal they had together on that night. Miss Amelia was rich and she did not grudge herself food. There was fried chicken (the breast of which the hunchback took on his own plate), mashed rootabeggars, collard greens, and hot, pale golden, sweet potatoes. Miss Amelia ate slowly and with the relish of a farm hand. She sat with both elbows on the table, bent over the plate, her knees spread wide apart and her feet braced on the rungs of the chair. As for the hunchback, he gulped down his supper as though he had not smelled food in months. During the meal one tear crept down his dingy cheek—but it was just a little leftover tear and meant nothing at all. The lamp on the table was well-trimmed, burning blue at the edges of the wick, and casting a cheerful light in the kitchen. When Miss Amelia had eaten her supper she wiped her plate carefully with a slice of light bread, and then poured her own clear, sweet syrup over the bread. The hunchback did likewise—except that he was more finicky and asked for a new plate. Having finished, Miss Amelia tilted back her chair, tightened her fist, and felt the hard, supple muscles of her right arm beneath the clean, blue cloth of her shirtsleeves—an unconscious habit with her, at the close of a meal. Then she took the lamp from the table and jerked her head toward the staircase as an invitation for the hunchback to follow after her.

Above the store there were the three rooms where Miss Amelia had lived during all her life—two bedrooms with a large parlor in between. Few people had even seen these rooms, but it was generally known that they were well-furnished and extremely clean. And now Miss Amelia was taking up with her a dirty little hunch-backed stranger, come from God knows where. Miss Amelia walked slowly, two steps at a time, holding the lamp high. The hunchback hovered so close behind her that the swinging light made on the staircase wall one great, twisted shadow of the two of them. Soon the premises above the store were dark as the rest of the town.

The next morning was serene, with a sunrise of warm purple mixed with rose. In the fields around the town the furrows were newly plowed, and very early the tenants were at work setting out the young, deep green tobacco plants. The wild crows flew down close to the fields, making swift blue shadows on the earth. In town the people set out early with their dinner pails, and the windows of the mill were blinding gold in the sun. The air was fresh and the peach trees light as March clouds with their blossoms.

Miss Amelia came down at about dawn, as usual. She washed her head at the pump and very shortly set about her business. Later in the morning she saddled her mule and went to see about her property, planted with cotton, up near the Forks Falls Road. By noon, of course, everybody had heard about the hunchback who had come to the store in the middle of the night. But no one as yet had seen him. The day soon grew hot and the sky was a rich, midday blue. Still no one had laid an eye on this strange guest. A few people remembered that Miss Amelia's mother had had a half-sister—but there was some difference of opinion as to whether she had died or had run off with a tobacco stringer. As for the hunchback's claim, everyone thought it was a trumped-up business. And the town, knowing Miss Amelia, decided that surely she had put him out of the house after feeding him. But toward evening, when the sky had whitened, and the shift was done, a woman claimed to have seen a crooked face at the window of one of the rooms up over the store. Miss Amelia herself said nothing. She clerked in the store for a while, argued for an hour with a farmer over a plow shaft, mended some chicken wire, locked up near sundown, and went to her rooms. The town was left puzzled and talkative.

The next day Miss Amelia did not open the store, but stayed locked up inside her premises and saw no one. Now this was the day that the rumor started—the rumor so terrible that the town and all the country about were stunned by it. The rumor was started by a weaver called Merlie Ryan. He is a man of not much account—sallow, shambling, and with no teeth in his head. He has the three-day malaria, which means that every third day the fever comes on him. So on two days he is dull and cross, but on the third day he livens up and sometimes has an idea or two, most of which are foolish. It was while Merlie Ryan was in his fever that he turned suddenly and said:

'I know what Miss Amelia done. She murdered that man for something in that suitcase.'

He said this in a calm voice, as a statement of fact. And within an hour the news had swept through the town. It was a fierce and sickly tale the town built up that day. In it were all the things which cause the heart to shiver—a hunchback, a midnight burial in the swamp, the dragging of Miss Amelia through the streets of the town on the way to prison, the squabbles over what would happen to her property—all told in hushed voices and repeated with some fresh and weird detail. It rained and women forgot to bring in the washing from the lines. One or two mortals, who were in debt to Miss Amelia, even put on Sunday clothes as though it were a holiday. People clustered together on the main street, talking and watching the store.

It would be untrue to say that all the town took part in this evil festival. There were a few sensible men who reasoned that Miss Amelia, being rich, would not go out of her way to murder a vagabond for a few trifles of junk. In the town there were even three good people, and they did not want this crime, not even for the sake of the interest and the great commotion it would entail; it gave them no pleasure to think of Miss Amelia holding to the bars of the penitentiary and being electrocuted in Atlanta. These good people judged Miss Amelia in a different way from what the others judged her. When a person is as contrary in every single respect as she was and when the sins of a person have amounted to such a point that they can hardly be remembered all at once—then this person plainly requires a special judgment. They remembered that Miss Amelia had been born dark and somewhat queer of face, raised motherless by her father who was a solitary man, that early in youth she had grown to be six feet two inches tall which in itself is not natural for a woman, and that her ways and habits of life were too peculiar ever to reason about. Above all, they remembered her puzzling marriage, which was the most unreasonable scandal ever to happen in this town.

So these good people felt toward her something near to pity. And when she was out on her wild business, such as rushing in a house to drag forth a sewing machine in payment for a debt, or getting herself worked up over some matter concerning the law—they had toward her a feeling which was a mixture of exasperation, a ridiculous little inside tickle, and a deep, unnamable sadness. But enough of the good people, for there were only three of them; the rest of the town was making a holiday of this fancied crime the whole of the afternoon.

Miss Amelia herself, for some strange reason, seemed unaware of all this. She spent most of her day upstairs. When down in the store, she prowled around peacefully, her hands deep in the pockets of her overalls and head bent so low that her chin was tucked inside the collar of her shirt. There was no bloodstain on her anywhere. Often she stopped and just stood somberly looking down at the cracks on the floor, twisting a lock of her short-cropped hair, and whispering something to herself. But most of the day was spent upstairs.

Dark came on. The rain that afternoon had chilled the air, so that the evening was bleak and gloomy as in wintertime. There were no stars in the sky, and a light, icy drizzle had set in. The lamps in the houses made mournful, wavering flickers when watched from the street. A wind had come up, not from the swamp side of the town but from the cold black pinewoods to the north.

The clocks in the town struck eight. Still nothing had happened. The bleak night, after the gruesome talk of the day, put a fear in some people, and they stayed home close to the fire. Others were gathered in groups together. Some eight or ten men had convened on the porch of Miss Amelia's store. They were silent and were indeed just waiting about. They themselves did not know what they were waiting for, but it was this: in times of tension, when some great action is impending, men gather and wait in this way. And after a time there will come a moment when all together they will act in unison, not from thought or from the will of any one man, but as though their instincts had merged together so that the decision belongs to no single one of them, but to the group as a whole. At such a time, no individual hesitates. And whether the matter will be settled peaceably, or whether the joint action will result in ransacking, violence, and crime, depends on destiny. So the men waited soberly on the porch of Miss Amelia's store, not one of them realizing what they would do, but knowing inwardly that they must wait, and that the time had almost come.

Now the door to the store was open. Inside it was bright and natural-looking. To the left was the counter where slabs of white meat, rock candy, and tobacco were kept. Behind this were shelves of salted white meat and meal. The right side of the store was mostly filled with farm implements and such. At the back of the store, to the left, was the door leading up the stairs, and it was open. And at the far right of the store there was another door which led to a litttle room that Miss Amelia called her office. This door was also open. And at eight o'clock that evening Miss Amelia could be seen there sitting before her rolltop desk, figuring with a fountain pen and some pieces of paper.

The office was cheerfully lighted, and Miss Amelia did not seem to notice the delegation on the porch. Everything around her was in great order, as usual. This office was a room well-known, in a dreadful way, throughout the country. It was there Miss Amelia transacted all business. On the desk was a carefully covered typewriter which she knew how to run, but used only for the most important documents. In the drawers were literally thousands of papers, all filed according to the alphabet. This office was also the place where Miss Amelia received sick people, for she enjoyed doctoring and did a great deal of it. Two whole shelves were crowded with bottles and various paraphernalia. Against the wall was a bench where the patients sat. She could sew up a wound with a burnt needle so that it would not turn green. For burns she had a cool, sweet syrup. For unlocated sickness there were any number of different medicines which she had brewed herself from unknown recipes. They wrenched loose the bowels very well, but they could not be given to small children, as they caused bad convulsions; for them she had an entirely separate draught, gentler and sweet-flavored. Yes, all in all, she was considered a good doctor. Her hands, though very large and bony, had a light touch about them. She possessed great imagination and used hundreds of different cures. In the face of the most dangerous and extraordinary treatment she did not hesitate, and no disease was so terrible but what she would undertake to cure it. In this there was one exception. If a patient came with a female complaint she could do nothing. Indeed at the mere mention of the words her face would slowly darken with shame, and she would stand there craning her neck against the collar of her shirt, or rubbing her swamp boots together, for all the world like a great, shamed, dumb-tongued child. But in other matters people trusted her. She charged no fee whatsoever and always had a raft of patients.

On this evening, Miss Amelia wrote with her fountain pen a good deal. But even so she could not be forever unaware of the group waiting out there on the dark porch, and watching her. From time to time she looked up and regarded them steadily. But she did not holler out to them .o demand why they were loafing around her property like a sorry bunch of gabbies. Her face was proud and stern, as it always was when she sat at the desk of her office. After a time their peering in like that seemed to annoy her. She wiped her cheek with a red handkerchief, got up, and closed the office door.

Now to the group on the porch this gesture acted as a signal. The time had come. They had stood for a long while with the night raw and gloomy in the street behind them. They had waited long and just at that moment the instinct to act came on them. All at once, as though moved by one will, they walked into the store. At that moment the eight men looked very much alike—all wearing blue overalls, most of them with whitish hair, all pale of face, and all with a set, dreaming look in the eye. What they would have done next no one knows. But at that instant there was a noise at the head of the staircase. The men looked up and then stood dumb with shock. It was the hunchback, whom they had already murdered in their minds. Also, the creature was not at all as had been pictured to them—not a pitiful and dirty little chatterer, alone and beggared in this world. Indeed, he was like nothing any man among them had ever beheld until that time. The room was still as death.

The hunchback came down slowly with the proudness of one who owns every plank of the floor beneath his feet. In the past days he had greatly changed. For one thing he was clean beyond words. He still wore his little coat, but it was brushed off and neatly mended. Beneath this was a fresh red and black checkered shirt belonging to Miss Amelia. He did not wear trousers such as ordinary men are meant to wear, but a pair of tight-fitting little knee-length breeches. On his skinny legs he wore black stockings, and his shoes were of a special kind, being queerly shaped, laced up over the ankles, and newly cleaned and polished with wax. Around his neck, so that his large, pale ears were almost completely covered, he wore a shawl of lime-green wool, the fringes of which almost touched the floor.

The hunchback walked down the store with his stiff strut and then stood in the center of the group that had come inside. They cleared a space about him and stood looking with hands loose at their sides and eyes wide open. The hunchback himself got his bearings in an odd manner. He regarded each person steadily at his own eye-level, which was about belt line for an ordinary man. Then with shrewd deliberation he examined each man's lower regions—from the waist to the sole of the shoe. When he had satisfied himself he closed his eyes for a moment and shook his head, as though in his opinion what he had seen did not amount to much. Then with assurance, only to confirm himself, he tilted back his head and took in the halo of faces around him with one long, circling stare. There was a half-filled sack of guano on the left side of the store, and when he had found his bearings in this way, the hunchback sat down upon it. Cozily settled, with his little legs crossed, he took from his coat pocket a certain object.

Now it took some moments for the men in the store to regain their ease. Merlie Ryan, he of the three-day fever who had started the rumor that day, was the first to speak. He looked at the object which the hunchback was fondling, and said in a hushed voice:

'What is it you have there?'

Each man knew well what it was the hunchback was handling. For it was the snuffbox which had belonged to Miss Amelia's father. The snuffbox was of blue enamel with a dainty embellishment of wrought gold on the lid. The group knew it well and marveled. They glanced warily at the closed office door, and heard the low sound of Miss Amelia whistling to herself.

'Yes, what is it, Peanut?'

The hunchback looked up quickly and sharpened his mouth to speak. 'Why, this is a lay-low to catch meddlers.'

The hunchback reached in the box with his scrambly little fingers and ate something, but he offered no one around him a taste. It was not even proper snuff which he was taking, but a mixture of sugar and cocoa. This he took, though, as snuff, pocketing a little wad of it beneath his lower lip and licking down neatly into this with a flick of his tongue which made a frequent grimace come over his face.

'The very teeth in my head have always tasted sour to me,' he said 'in explanation. 'That is the reason why I take this kind of sweet snuff.'

The group still clustered around, feeling somewhat gawky and bewildered. This sensation never quite wore off, but it was soon tempered by another feeling—an air of intimacy in the room and a vague festivity. Now the names of the men of the group there on that evening were as follows: Hasty Malone, Robert Calvert Hale, Merlie Ryan, Reverend T. M. Willin, Rosser Cline, Rip Wellborn, Henry Ford Crimp, and Horace Wells. Except for Reverend Willin, they are all alike in many ways as has been said—all having taken pleasure from something or other, all having wept and suffered in some way, most of them tractable unless exasperated. Each of them worked in the mill, and lived with others in a two- or three-room house for which the rent was ten dollars or twelve dollars a month. All had been paid that afternoon, for it was Saturday. So, for the present, think of them as a whole.

The hunchback, however, was already sorting them out in his mind. Once comfortably settled he began to chat with everyone, asking questions such as if a man was married, how old he was, how much his wages came to in an average week, et cetera—picking his way along to inquiries which were downright intimate. Soon the group was joined by others in the town, Henry Macy, idlers who had sensed something extraordinary, women come to fetch their men who lingered on, and even one loose, towhead child who tiptoed into the store, stole a box of animal crackers, and made off very quietly. So the premises of Miss Amelia were soon crowded, and she herself had not yet opened her office door.

There is a type of person who has a quality about him that sets him apart from other and more ordinary human beings. Such a person has an instinct which is usually found only in small children, an instinct to establish immediate and vital contact between himself and all things in the world. Certainly the hunchback was of this type. He had only been in the store half an hour before an immediate contact had been established between him and each other individual. It was as though he had lived in the town for years, was a well-known character, and had been sitting and talking there on that guano sack for countless evenings. This, together with the fact that it was Saturday night, could account for the air of freedom and illicit gladness in the store. There was a tension, also, partly because of the oddity of the situation and because Miss Amelia was still closed off in her office and had not yet made her appearance.

She came out that evening at ten o'clock. And those who were expecting some drama at her entrance were disappointed. She opened the door and walked in with her slow, gangling swagger. There was a streak of ink on on side of her nose, and she had knotted the red handkerchief about her neck. She seemed to notice nothing unusual. Her gray, crossed eyes glanced over to the place where the hunchback was sitting, and for a moment lingered there. The rest of the crowd in her store she regarded with only a peaceable surprise.

'Does anyone want waiting on?' she asked quietly.

There were a number of customers, because it was Saturday night, and they all wanted liquor. Now Miss Amelia had dug up an aged barrel only three days past and had siphoned it into bottles back by the still. This night she took the money from the customers and counted it beneath the bright light. Such was the ordinary procedure. But after this what happened was not ordinary. Always before, it was necessary to go around to the dark back yard, and there she would hand out your bottle through the kitchen door. There was no feeling of joy in the transaction. After getting his liquor the customer walked off into the night. Or, if his wife would not have it in the home, he was allowed to come back around to the front porch of the store and guzzle there or in the street. Now, both the porch and the street before it were the property of Miss Amelia, and no mistake about it—but she did not regard them as her premises; the premises began at the front door and took in the entire inside of the building. There she had never allowed liquor to be opened or drunk by anyone but herself. Now for the first time she broke this rule. She went to the kitchen, with the hunchback close at her heels, and she brought back the bottles into the warm, bright store. More than that she furnished some glasses and opened two boxes of crackers so that they were there hospitably in a platter on the counter and anyone who wished could take one free.

She spoke to no one but the hunchback, and she only asked him in a somewhat harsh and husky voice: 'Cousin Lymon, will you have yours straight, or warmed in a pan with water on the stove?'

'If you please, Amelia,' the hunchback said. (And since what time had anyone presumed to address Miss Amelia by her bare name, without a title of respect?—Certainly not her bridegroom and her husband of ten days. In fact, not since the death of her father, who for some reason had always called her Little, had anyone dared to address her in such a familiar way.) 'If you please, I'll have it warmed.'

Now, this was the beginning of the café. It was as simple as that. Recall that the night was gloomy as in wintertime, and to have sat around the property outside would have made a sorry celebration. But inside there was company and a genial warmth. Someone had rattled up the stove in the rear, and those who bought bottles shared their liquor with friends. Several women were there and they had twists of licorice, a Nehi, or even a swallow of the whisky. The hunchback was still a novelty and his presence amused everyone. The bench in the office was brought in, together with several extra chairs. Other people leaned against the counter or made themselves comfortable on barrels and sacks. Nor did the opening of liquor on the premises cause any rambunctiousness, indecent giggles, or misbehavior whatsoever. On the contrary the company was polite even to the point of a certain timidity. For people in this town were then unused to gathering together for the sake of pleasure. They met to work in the mill. Or on Sunday there would be an all-day camp meeting—and though that is a pleasure, the intention of the whole affair is to sharpen your view of Hell and put into you a keen fear of the Lord Almighty. But the spirit of a café is altogether different. Even the richest, greediest old rascal will behave himself, insulting no one in a proper café. And poor people look about them gratefully and pinch up the salt in a dainty and modest manner. For the atmosphere of a proper café implies these qualities: fellowship, the satisfactions of the belly, and a certain gaiety and grace of behavior. This had never been told to the gathering in Miss Amelia's store that night. But they knew it of themselves, although never, of course, until that time had there been a café in the town.

Now, the cause of all this, Miss Amelia, stood most of the evening in the doorway leading to the kitchen. Outwardly she did not seem changed at all. But there were many who noticed her face. She watched all that went on, but most of the time her eyes were fastened lonesomely on the hunchback. He strutted about the store, eating from his snuffbox, and being at once sour and agreeable. Where Miss Amelia stood, the light from the chinks of the stove cast a glow, so that her brown, long face was somewhat brightened. She seemed to be looking inward. There was in her expression pain, perplexity, and uncertain joy. Her lips were not so firmly set as usual, and she swallowed often. Her skin had paled and her large empty hands were sweating. Her look that night, then, was the lonesome look of the lover.

This opening of the café came to an end at midnight. Everyone said good-bye to everyone else in a friendly fashion. Miss Amelia shut the front door of her premises, but forgot to bolt it. Soon everything—the main street with its three stores, the mill, the houses—all the town, in fact—was dark and silent. And so ended three days and nights in which had come an arrival of a stranger, an unholy holiday, and the start of the café.

Now time must pass. For the next four years are much alike. There are great changes, but these changes are brought about bit by bit, in simple steps which in themselves do not appear to be important. The hunchback continued to live with Miss Amelia. The café expanded in a gradual way. Miss Amelia began to sell her liquor by the drink, and some tables were brought into the store. There were customers every evening, and on Saturday a great crowd. Miss Amelia began to serve fried catfish suppers at fifteen cents a plate. The hunchback cajoled her into buying a fine mechanical piano. Within two years the place was a store no longer, but had been converted into a proper café, open every evening from six until twelve o'clock.

Each night the hunchback came down the stairs with the air of one who has a grand opinion of himself. He always smelled slightly of turnip greens, as Miss Amelia rubbed him night and morning with pot liquor to give him strength. She spoiled him to a point beyond reason, but nothing seemed to strengthen him; food only made his hump and his head grow larger while the rest of him remained weakly and deformed. Miss Amelia was the same in appearance. During the week she still wore swamp boots and overalls, but on Sunday she put on a dark red dress that hung on her in a most peculiar fashion. Her manners, however, and her way of life were greatly changed. She still loved a fierce lawsuit, but she was not so quick to cheat her fellow man and to exact cruel payments. Because the hunchback was so extremely sociable, she even went about a little—to revivals, to funerals, and so forth. Her doctoring was as successful as ever, her liquor even finer than before, if that were possible. The café itself proved profitable and was the only place of pleasure for many miles around.

So for the moment regard these years from random and disjointed views. See the hunchback marching in Miss Amelia's footsteps when on a red winter morning they set out for the pinewoods to hunt. See them working on her properties—with Cousin Lymon standing by and doing absolutely nothing, but quick to point out any laziness among the hands. On autumn afternoons they sat on the back steps chopping sugar cane. The glaring summer days they spent back in the swamp where the water cypress is a deep black green, where beneath the tangled swamp trees there is a drowsy gloom. When the path leads through a bog or a stretch of blackened water see Miss Amelia bend down to let Cousin Lymon scramble on her back—and see her wading forward with the hunchback settled on her shoulders, clinging to her ears or to her broad forehead. Occasionally Miss Amelia cranked up the Ford which she had bought and treated Cousin Lymon to a picture-show in Cheehaw, or to some distant fair or cockfight; the hunchback took a passionate delight in spectacles. Of course, they were in their café every morning, they would often sit for hours together by the fireplace in the parlor upstairs. For the hunchback was sickly at night and dreaded to lie looking into the dark. He had a deep fear of death. And Miss Amelia would not leave him by himself to suffer with this fright. It may even be reasoned that the growth of the café came about mainly on this account; it was a thing that brought him company and pleasure and that helped him through the night. *So compose from such flashes an image of these years as a whole.* And for a moment let it rest.

Now some explanation is due for all this behavior. The time has come to speak about love. For Miss Amelia loved Cousin Lymon. So much was clear to everyone. They lived in the same house together and were never seen apart. Therefore, according to Mrs. MacPhail, a warty-nosed old busybody who is continually moving her sticks of furniture from one part of the front room to another; according to her and to certain others, these two were living in sin. If they were related, they were only a cross between first and second cousins, and even that could in no way be proved. Now, of course, Miss Amelia was a powerful blunderbuss of a person, more than six feet tall—and Cousin Lymon a weakly little hunchback reaching only to her waist. But so much the better for Mrs. Stumpy MacPhail and her cronies, for they and their kind glory in conjunctions which are ill-matched and pitiful. So let them be. The good people thought that if those two had found some satisfaction of the flesh between themselves, then it was a matter concerning them and God alone. All sensible people agreed in their opinion about this conjecture—and their answer was a plain, flat no. What sort of thing, then, was this love?

First of all, love is a joint experience between two persons—but the fact that it is a joint experience does not mean that it is a similar experience to the two people involved. There are the lover and the beloved, but these two come from different countries. Often the beloved is only a stimulus for all the stored-up love which has lain quiet within the lover for a long time hitherto. And somehow every lover knows this. *He feels in his soul that his love is a solitary thing.* He comes to know a new, strange loneliness and it is this knowledge which makes him suffer. So there is only one thing for the lover to do. He must house his love within himself as best he can; *he must create for himself a whole new-inward world—a world intense and strange, complete in himself.* Let it be added here that his lover about whom we speak need not necessarily be a young man saving for a wedding ring—this lover can be man, woman, child, or indeed any human creature on this earth.

Now, the beloved can also be of any description. The most outlandish people can be the stimulus for love. A man may be a doddering great-grandfather and still love only a strange girl he saw in the streets of Chee-haw one afternoon two decades past. The preacher may love a fallen woman. The beloved may be treacherous, greasy-headed, and given to evil habits. Yes, and the lover may see this as clearly as anyone else—but that does not affect the evolution of his love one whit. A most mediocre person can be the object of a love which is wild, extravagant, and beautiful as the poison lilies of the swamp. A good man may be the stimulus for a love both violent and debased, *or a jabbering madman may bring about in the soul of someone a tender and simple idyll. Therefore, the value and quality of any love is determined solely by the lover himself.*

It is for this reason that most of us would rather love than be loved. Almost everyone wants to be the lover. And the curt truth is that, in a deep secret way, the state of being beloved is intolerable to many. The beloved fears and hates the lover, and with the best of reasons. For the lover is for-ever trying to strip bare his beloved. The lover craves any possible relation with the beloved, even if this experience can cause him only pain.

It has been mentioned before that Miss Amelia was once married. And this curious episode might as well be accounted for at this point. Remember that it all happened long ago, and that it was Miss Amelia's only personal contact, before the hunchback came to her, with this phenomenon—love.

The town then was the same as it is now, except there were two stores instead of three and the peach trees along the street were more crooked and smaller than they are now. Miss Amelia was nineteen years old at the time, and her father had been dead many months. There was in the town at that time a loom-fixer named Marvin Macy. He was the brother of Henry Macy, although to know them you would never guess that those two could be kin. For Marvin Macy was the handsomest man in this region—being six feet one inch tall, hard-muscled, and with slow gray eyes and curly hair. He was well off, made good wages, and had a gold watch which opened in the back to a picture of a waterfall. From the outward and worldly point of view Marvin Macy was a fortunate fellow; he needed to bow and scrape to no one and always got just what he wanted. But from a more serious and thoughtful viewpoint Marvin Macy was not a person to be envied, for he was an evil character. His reputation was as bad, if not worse, than that of any young man in the county. For years, when he was a boy, he had carried about with him the dried and salted ear of a man he had killed in a razor fight. He had chopped off the tails of squirrels in the pinewoods just to please his fancy, and in his left hip pocket he carried forbidden marijuana weed to tempt those who were discouraged and drawn toward death. Yet in spite of his well-known reputation he was the beloved of many females in this region—and there were at the time several young girls who were clean-haired and soft-eyed, with tender sweet little buttocks and charming ways. These gentle young girls he degraded and shamed. Then finally, at the age of twenty-two, this Marvin Macy chose Miss Amelia. That solitary, gangling, queer-eyed girl was the one he longed for. Nor did he want her because of her money, but solely out of love.

And love changed Marvin Macy. Before the time when he loved Miss Amelia it could be questioned if such a person had within him a heart and soul. Yet there is some explanation for the ugliness of his character, for Marvin Macy had had a hard beginning in this world. He was one of six unwanted children whose parents could hardly be called parents at all; these parents were wild younguns who liked to fish and roam around the swamp. Their own children, and there was a new one almost every year, were only a nuisance to them. At night when they came home from the mill they would look at the children as though they did not know wherever they had come from. If the children cried they were beaten, and the first thing they learned in this world was to seek the darkest corner of the room and try to hide themselves as best they could. They were as thin as little white-haired ghosts, and they did not speak, not even to each other. Finally, they were abandoned by their parents altogether and left to the mercies of the town. It was a hard winter, with the mill closed down almost three months, and much misery everywhere. But this is not a town to let white orphans perish in the road before your eyes. So here is what came about: the eldest child, who was eight years old, walked into Cheehaw and disappeared—perhaps he took a freight train somewhere and went out into the world, nobody knows. Three other children were boarded out amongst the town, being sent around from one kitchen to another, and as they were delicate they died before Easter time. The last two children were Marvin Macy and Henry Macy, and they were taken into a home. There was a good woman in the town named Mrs. Mary Hale, and she took Marvin Macy and Henry Macy and loved them as her own. They were raised in her household and treated well.

But the hearts of small children are delicate organs. A cruel beginning in this world can twist them into curious shapes. The heart of a hurt child can shrink so that forever afterward it is hard and pitted as the seed of a peach. Or again, the heart of such a child may fester and swell until it is a misery to carry within the body, easily chafed and hurt by the most ordinary things. This last is what happened to Henry Macy, who is so opposite to his brother, is the kindest and gentlest man in town. He lends his wages to those who are unfortunate, and in the old days he used to care for the children whose parents were at the café on Saturday night. But he is a shy man, and he has the look of one who has a swollen heart and suffers. Marvin

Macy, however, grew to be bold and fearless and cruel. His heart turned tough as the horns of Satan, and until the time when he loved Miss Amelia he brought to his brother and the good woman who raised him nothing but shame and trouble.

But love reversed the character of Marvin Macy. For two years he loved Miss Amelia, but he did not declare himself. He would stand near the door of her premises, his cap in his hand, his eyes meek and longing and misty gray. He reformed himself completely. He was good to his brother and foster mother, and he saved his wages and learned thrift. Moreover, he reached out toward God. No longer did he lie around on the floor of the front porch all day Sunday, singing and playing his guitar; he attended church services and was present at all religious meetings. He learned good manners: he trained himself to rise and give his chair to a lady, and he quit swearing and fighting and using holy names in vain. So for two years he passed through this transformation and improved his character in every way. Then at the end of the two years he went one evening to Miss Amelia, carrying a bunch of swamp flowers, a sack of chitterlings, and a silver ring —that night Marvin Macy declared himself.

And Miss Amelia married him. Later everyone wondered why. Some said it was because she wanted to get herself some wedding presents. Others believed it came about through the nagging of Miss Amelia's great-aunt in Cheehaw, who was a terrible old woman. Anyway, she strode with great steps down the aisle of the church wearing her dead mother's bridal gown, which was of yellow satin and at least twelve inches too short for her. It was a winter afternoon and the clear sun shone through the ruby windows of the church and put a curious glow on the pair before the altar. As the marriage lines were read Miss Amelia kept making an odd gesture —she would rub the palm of her right hand down the side of her satin wedding gown. She was reaching for the pocket of her overalls, and being unable to find it her face became impatient, bored, and exasperated. At last when the lines were spoken and the marriage prayer was done Miss Amelia hurried out of the church, not taking the arm of her husband, but walking at least two paces ahead of him.

The church is no distance from the store so the bride and groom walked home. It is said that on the way Miss Amelia began to talk about some deal she had worked up with a farmer over a load of kindling wood. In fact, she treated her groom in exactly the same manner she would have used with some customer who had come into the store to buy a pint from her. But so far all had gone decently enough; the town was gratified, as people had seen what this love had done to Marvin Macy and hoped that it might also reform his bride. At least, they counted on the marriage to tone down Miss Amelia's temper, to put a bit of bride-fat on her, and to change her at last into a calculable woman.

They were wrong. The young boys who watched through the window on that night said that this is what actually happened: The bride and groom ate a grand supper prepared by Jeff, the old Negro who cooked for Miss Amelia. The bride took second servings of everything, but the groom picked with his food. Then the bride went about her ordinary business— reading the newspaper, finishing an inventory of the stock in the store, and so forth. The groom hung about in the doorway with a loose, foolish, blissful face and was not noticed. At eleven o'clock the bride took a lamp and went upstairs. The groom followed close behind her. So far all had gone decently enough, but what followed after was unholy.

Within half an hour Miss Amelia had stomped down the stairs in breeches and a khaki jacket. Her face had darkened so that it looked quite black. She slammed the kitchen door and gave it an ugly kick. Then she controlled herself. She poked up the fire, sat down, and put her feet up on the kitchen stove. She read the Farmer's Almanac, drank coffee, and had a smoke with her father's pipe. Her face was hard, stern, and had now whitened to its natural color. Sometimes she paused to jot down some information from the Almanac on a piece of paper. Toward dawn she went into her office and uncovered her typewriter, which she had recently bought and was only just learning how to run. That was the way in which she spent the whole of her wedding night. At daylight she went out to her yard as though nothing whatsoever had occurred and did some carpentering on a rabbit hutch which she had begun the week before and intended to sell somewhere.

A groom is in a sorry fix when he is unable to bring his well-beloved bride to bed with him, and the whole town knows it. Marvin Macy came down that day still in his wedding finery, and with a sick face. God knows how he had spent the night. He moped about the yard, watching Miss Amelia, but keeping some distance away from her. Then toward noon an idea came to him and he went off in the direction of Society City. He returned with presents—an opal ring, a pink enamel doreen of the sort which was then in fashion, a silver bracelet with two hearts on it, and a box of candy which had cost two dollars and a half. Miss Amelia looked over these fine gifts and opened the box of candy, for she was hungry. The rest of the presents she judged shrewdly for a moment to sum up their value— then she put them in the counter out for sale. The night was spent in much the same manner as the preceding one—except that Miss Amelia brought her feather mattress to make a pallet by the kitchen stove, and she slept fairly well.

Things went on like this for three days. Miss Amelia went about her business as usual, and took great interest in some rumor that a bridge was to be built some ten miles down the road. Marvin Macy still followed her about around the premises, and it was plain from his face how he suffered. Then on the fourth day he did an extremely simple-minded thing: he went to Cheehaw and came back with a lawyer. Then in Miss Amelia's office he signed over to her the whole of his worldly goods, which was ten acres of timberland which he had bought with the money he had saved. She studied the paper sternly to make sure there was no possibility of a trick and filed it soberly in the drawer of her desk. That afternoon Marvin Macy took a quart bottle of whisky and went with it alone out in the swamp while the sun was still shining. Toward evening he came in drunk, went up to Miss Amelia with wet wide eyes, and put his hand on her shoulder. He was trying to tell her something, but before he could open his mouth she had swung once with her fist and hit his face so hard that he was thrown back against the wall and one of his front teeth was broken.

The rest of this affair can only be mentioned in bare outline. After this first blow Miss Amelia hit him whenever he came within arm's reach of her, and whenever he was drunk. At last she turned him off the premises altogether, and he was forced to suffer publicly. During the day he hung around just outside the boundary line of Miss Amelia's property and sometimes with a drawn crazy look he would fetch his rifle and sit there cleaning it, peering at Miss Amelia steadily. If she was afraid she did not show it, but her face was sterner than ever, and often she spat on the ground. His last foolish effort was to climb in the window of her store one night and to sit there in the dark, for no purpose whatsoever, until she came down the stairs next morning. For this Miss Amelia set off immediately to the courthouse in Cheehaw with some notion that she could get him locked in the penitentiary for trespassing. Marvin Macy left the town that day, and no one saw him go, or knew just where he went. On leaving he put a long curious letter, partly written in pencil and partly with ink, beneath Miss Amelia's door. It was a wild love letter—but in it were also included threats, and he swore that in his life he would get even with her. His marriage had lasted for ten days. And the town felt the special satisfaction that people feel when someone has been thoroughly done in by some scandalous and terrible means.

Miss Amelia was left with everything that Marvin Macy had ever owned —his timberwood, his gilt watch, every one of his possessions. But she seemed to attach little value to them and that spring she cut up his Klansman's robe to cover her tobacco plants. So all that he had ever done was to make her richer and to bring her love. But, strange to say, she never spoke of him but with a terrible and spiteful bitterness. She never once referred to him by name but always mentioned him scornfully as 'that loom-fixer I was married to.'

And later, when horrifying rumors concerning Marvin Macy reached the town, Miss Amelia was very pleased. For the true character of Marvin Macy finally revealed itself, once he had freed himself of his love. He became a criminal whose picture and name were in all the papers in the state. He robbed three filling stations and held up the A & P store of Society City with a sawed-off gun. He was suspected of the murder of Slit-

Eye Sam who was a noted highjacker. All these crimes were connected with the name of Marvin Macy, so that his evil became famous through many countries. Then finally the law captured him, drunk, on the floor of a tourist cabin, his guitar by his side, and fifty-seven dollars in his right shoe. He was tried, sentenced, and sent off to the penitentiary near Atlanta. Miss Amelia was deeply gratified.

Well, all this happened a long time ago, and it is the story of Miss Amelia's marriage. The town laughed a long time over this grotesque affair. But though the outward facts of this love are indeed sad and ridiculous, it must be remembered that the real story was that which took place in the soul of the lover himself. So who but God can be the final judge of this or any other love? On the very first night of the café there were several who suddenly thought of this broken bridegroom, locked in the gloomy penitentiary, many miles away. And in the years that followed, Marvin Macy was not altogether forgotten in the town. His name was never mentioned in the presence of Miss Amelia or the hunchback. But the memory of his passion and his crimes, and the thought of him trapped in his cell in the penitentiary was like a troubling undertone beneath the happy love of Miss Amelia and the gaiety of the café. So do not forget this Marvin Macy, as he is to act a terrible part in the story which is yet to come.

During the four years in which the store became a café the rooms upstairs were not changed. This part of the premises remained exactly as it had been all of Miss Amelia's life, as it was in the time of her father, and most likely his father before him. The three rooms, it is already known, were immaculately clean. The smallest object had its exact place, and everything was wiped and dusted by Jeff, the servant of Miss Amelia, each morning. The front room belonged to Cousin Lymon—it was the room where Marvin Macy had stayed during the few nights he was allowed on the premises, and before that it was the bedroom of Miss Amelia's father. The room was furnished with a large chifforobe, a bureau covered with a stiff white linen cloth crocheted at the edges, and a marble-topped table. The bed was immense, an old fourposter made of carved dark rosewood. On it were two feather mattresses, bolsters, and a number of handmade comforts. The bed was so high that beneath it were two wooden steps—no occupant had ever used these steps before, but Cousin Lymon drew them out each night and walked up in state. Beside the steps, but pushed modestly out of view, there was a china chamber-pot painted with pink roses. No rug covered the dark, polished floor and the curtains were of some white stuff, also crocheted at the edges.

On the other side of the parlor was Miss Amelia's bedroom, and it was smaller and very simple. The bed was narrow and made of pine. There was a bureau for her breeches, shirts, and Sunday dress, and she had hammered two nails in the closet wall on which to hang her swamp boots. There were no curtains, rugs, or ornaments of any kind.

The large middle room, the parlor, was elaborate. The rosewood sofa, upholstered in threadbare green silk, was before the fireplace. Marble-topped tables, two Singer sewing machines, a big vase of pampas grass—everything was rich and grand. The most important piece of furniture in the parlor was a big, glassed-doored cabinet in which was kept a number of treasures and curios. Miss Amelia had added two objects to this collection —one was a large acorn from a water oak, the other little velvet box holding two small, grayish stones. Sometimes when she had nothing much to do, Miss Amelia would take out this velvet box and stand by the window with the stones in the palm of her hand, looking down at them with a mixture of fascination, dubious respect, and fear. They were the kidney stones of Miss Amelia herself, and had been taken from her by the doctor in Cheehaw some years ago. It had been a terrible experience, from the first minute to the last, and all she had got out of it were those two little stones; she was bound to set great store by them, or else admit to a mighty sorry bargain. So she kept them and in the second year of Cousin Lymon's stay with her she had them set as ornaments in a watch chain which she gave to him. The other object she had added to the collection, the large acorn, was precious to her—but when she looked at it her face was always saddened and perplexed.

'Amelia, what does it signify?' Cousin Lymon asked her.

'Why, it's just an acorn,' she answered. 'Just an acorn I picked up on the afternoon Big Papa died.'

'How do you mean?' Cousin Lymon insisted.

'I mean it's just an acorn I spied on the ground that day. I picked it up and put in my pocket. But I don't know why.'

'What a peculiar reason to keep it,' Cousin Lymon said.

The talks of Miss Amelia and Cousin Lymon in the rooms upstairs, usually in the first few hours of the morning when the hunchback could not sleep, were many. As a rule, Miss Amelia was a silent woman, not letting her tongue run wild on any subject that happened to pop into her head. There were certain topics of conversation, however, in which she took pleasure. All these subjects had one point in common—they were interminable. She liked to contemplate problems which could be worked over for decades and still remain insoluble. Cousin Lymon, on the other hand, enjoyed talking on any subject whatsoever, as he was a great chatterer. Their approach to any conversation was altogether different. Miss Amelia always kept to the broad, rambling generalities of the matter, going on endlessly in a low, thoughtful voice and getting nowhere—while Cousin Lymon would interrupt her suddenly to pick up, magpie fashion, some detail which, even if unimportant, was at least concrete and bearing on some practical facet close at hand. Some of the favorite subjects of Miss Amelia were: the stars, the reason why Negroes are black, the best treatment for cancer, and so forth. Her father was also an interminable subject which was dear to her

'Why, Law,' she would say to Lymon. 'Those days I slept. I'd go to bed just as the lamp was turned on and sleep—why, I'd sleep like I was drowned in warm axle grease. Then come daybreak Big Papa would walk in and put his hand down on my shoulder. "Get stirring, Little," he would say. Then later he would holler up the stairs from the kitchen when the stove was hot. "Fried grits," he would holler. "White meat and gravy. Ham and eggs." And I'd run down the stairs and dress by the hot stove while he was out washing at the pump. Then off we'd go to the still or maybe—'

'The grits we had this morning was poor,' Cousin Lymon said. 'Fried too quick so that the inside never heated.'

'And when Big Papa would run off the liquor in those days—' The conversation would go on endlessly, with Miss Amelia's long legs stretched out before the hearth; for winter or summer there was always a fire in the grate, as Lymon was cold-natured. He sat in a low chair across from her, his feet not quite touching the floor and his torso usually well-wrapped in a blanket or the green wool shawl. Miss Amelia never mentioned her father to anyone else except Cousin Lymon.

That was one of the ways in which she showed her love for him. He had her confidence in the most delicate and vital matters. He alone knew where she kept the chart that showed where certain barrels of whisky were buried on a piece of property near by. He alone had access to her bank-book and the key to the cabinet of curios. He took money from the cash register, whole handfuls of it, and appreciated the loud jingle it made inside his pockets. He owned almost everything on the premises, for when he was cross Miss Amelia would prowl about and find him some present—so that now there was hardly anything left close at hand to give him. The only part of her life that she did not want Cousin Lymon to share with her was the memory of her ten-day marriage. Marvin Macy was the one subject that was never, at any time, discussed between the two of them.

So let the slow years pass and come to a Saturday evening six years after the time when Cousin Lymon came first to the town. It was August and the sky had burned above the town like a sheet of flame all day. Now the green twilight was near and there was a feeling of repose. The street was coated an inch deep with dry golden dust and the little children ran about half-naked, sneezed often, sweated, and were fretful. The mill had closed down at noon. People in the houses along the main street sat resting on their steps and the women had palmetto fans. At Miss Amelia's there was a sign at the front of the premises saying CAFÉ. The back porch was cool with latticed shadows and there Cousin Lymon sat turning the ice-cream freezer—often he unpacked the salt and ice and removed the dasher to lick a bit and see how the work was coming on. Jeff cooked in the kitchen. Early that morning Miss Amelia had put a notice on the wall of the front porch reading: Chicken Dinner—Twenty Cents Tonite. The café was already open and

Miss Amelia had just finished a period of work in her office. All the eight tables were occupied and from the mechanical piano came a jingling tune.

In a corner near the door and sitting at a table with a child, was Henry Macy. He was drinking a glass of liquor, which was unusual for him, as liquor went easily to his head and made him cry or sing. His face was very pale and his left eye worked constantly in a nervous tic, as it was apt to do when he was agitated. He had come into the café sidewise and silent, and when he was greeted he did not speak. The child next to him belonged to Horace Wells, and he had been left at Miss Amelia's that morning to be doctored.

Miss Amelia came out from her office in good spirits. She attended to a few details in the kitchen and entered the café with the pope's nose of a hen between her fingers, as that was her favorite piece. She looked about the room, saw that in general all was well, and went over to the corner table by Henry Macy. She turned the chair around and sat straddling the back, as she only wanted to pass the time of day and was not yet ready for her supper. There was a bottle of Kroup Kure in the hip pocket of her overalls —a medicine made from whisky, rock candy, and a secret ingredient. Miss Amelia uncorked the bottle and put it to the mouth of the child. Then she turned to Henry Macy and, seeing the nervous winking of his left eye, she asked:

'What ails you?'

Henry Macy seemed on the point of saying something difficult, but, after a long look into the eyes of Miss Amelia, he swallowed and did not speak.

So Miss Amelia returned to her patient. Only the child's head showed above the table top. His face was very red, with the eyelids half-closed and the mouth partly open. He had a large, hard, swollen boil on his thigh, and had been brought to Miss Amelia so that it could be opened. But Miss Amelia used a special method with children; she did not like to see them hurt, struggling, and terrified. So she had kept the child around the premises all day, giving him licorice and frequent doses of the Kroup Kure, and toward evening she tied a napkin around his neck and let him eat his fill of the dinner. Now as he sat at the table his head wobbled slowly from side to side and sometimes as he breathed there came from him a little worn-out grunt.

There was a stir in the café and Miss Amelia looked around quickly. Cousin Lymon had come in. The hunchback strutted into the café as he did every night, and when he reached the exact center of the room he stopped short and looked shrewdly around him, summing up the people and making a quick pattern of the emotional material at hand that night. The hunchback was a great mischief-maker. He enjoyed any kind of to-do, and without saying a word he could set the people at each other in a way that was miraculous. It was due to him that the Rainey twins had quarreled over a jackknife two years past, and had not spoken one word to each other since. He was present at the big fight between Rip Wellborn and Robert Calvert Hale, and every other fight for that matter since he had come into the town. He nosed around everywhere, knew the intimate business of everybody, and trespassed every waking hour. Yet, queerly enough, in spite of this it was the hunchback who was most responsible for the great popularity of the café. Things were never so gay as when he was around. When he walked into the room there was always a quick feeling of tension, because with this busybody about there was never any telling what might descend on you, or what might suddenly be brought to happen in the room. People are never so free with themselves and so recklessly glad as when there is some possibility of commotion or calamity ahead. So when the hunchback marched into the café everyone looked around at him and there was a quick outburst of talking and a drawing of corks.

Lymon waved his hand to Stumpy MacPhail who was sitting with Merlie Ryan and Henry Ford Crimp. 'I walked to Rotten Lake today to fish,' he said. 'And on the way I stepped over what appeared at first to be a big fallen tree. But then as I stepped over I felt something stir and I taken this second look and there I was straddling this here alligator long as from the front door to the kitchen and thicker than a hog.'

The hunchback chattered on. Everyone looked at him from time to time, and some kept track of his chattering and others did not. There were times when every word he said was nothing but lying and bragging. Nothing he said tonight was true. He had lain in bed with a summer quinsy all day long, and had only got up in the late afternoon in order to turn the ice-cream freezer. Everybody knew this, yet he stood there in the middle of the café and held forth with such lies and boasting that it was enough to shrivel the ears.

Miss Amelia watched him with her hands in her pockets and her head turned to one side. There was a softness about her gray, queer eyes and she was smiling gently to herself. Occasionally she glanced from the hunchback to the other people in the café—and then her look was proud, and there was in it the hint of a threat, as though daring anyone to try to hold him to account for all his foolery. Jeff was bringing in the suppers, already served on the plates, and the new electric fans in the café made a pleasant stir of coolness in the air.

'The little youngun is asleep,' said Henry Macy finally.

Miss Amelia looked down at the patient beside her, and composed her face for the matter in hand. The child's chin was resting on the table edge and a trickle of spit or Kroup Kure had bubbled from the corner of his mouth. His eyes were quite closed, and a little family of gnats had clustered peacefully in the corners. Miss Amelia put her hand on his head and shook it roughly, but the patient did not awake. So Miss Amelia lifted the child from the table, being careful not to touch the sore part of his leg, and went into the office. Henry Macy followed after her and they closed the office door.

Cousin Lymon was bored that evening. There was not much going on, and in spite of the heat the customers in the café were good-humored. Henry Ford Crimp and Horace Wells sat at the middle table with their arms around each other, sniggering over some long joke—but when he approached them he could make nothing of it as he had missed the beginning of the story. The moonlight brightened the dusty road, and the dwarfed peach trees were black and motionless; there was no breeze. The drowsy buzz of swamp mosquitoes was like an echo of the silent night. The town seemed dark, except far down the road to the right there was the flicker of a lamp. Somewhere in the darkness a woman sang in a high wild voice and the tune had no start and no finish and was made up of only three notes which went on and on and on. The hunchback stood leaning against the banister of the porch, looking down the empty road as though hoping that someone would come along.

There were footsteps behind him, then a voice: 'Cousin Lymon, your dinner is set out upon the table.'

'My appetite is poor tonight,' said the hunchback, who had been eating sweet snuff all the day. 'There is a sourness in my mouth.'

'Just a pick,' said Miss Amelia. 'The breast, the liver, and the heart.'

Together they went back into the bright café, and sat down with Henry Macy. Their table was the largest one in the café, and on it there was a bouquet of swamp lilies in a Coca Cola bottle. Miss Amelia had finished with her patient and was satisfied with herself. From behind the closed office door there had come only a few sleepy whimpers, and before the patient could wake up and become terrified it was all over. The child was now slung across the shoulder of his father, sleeping deeply, his little arms dangling loose along his father's back, and his puffed-up face very red—they were leaving the café to go home.

Henry Macy was still silent. He ate carefully, making no noise when he swallowed, and was not a third as greedy as Cousin Lymon who had claimed to have no appetite and was now putting down helping after helping of the dinner. Occasionally Henry Macy looked across at Miss Amelia and again held his peace.

It was a typical Saturday night. An old couple who had come in from the country hesitated for a moment at the doorway, holding each other's hand, and finally decided to come inside. They had lived together so long, this old country couple, that they looked as similar as twins. They were brown, shriveled, and like two little walking peanuts. They left early, and by midnight most of the other customers were gone. Rosser Cline and Merlie Ryan still played checkers, and Stumpy MacPhail sat with a liquor bottle on his table (his wife would not allow it in the home) and carried on peaceable conversations with himself. Henry Macy had not yet gone away, and this was unusual, as he almost always went to bed soon after nightfall. Miss Amelia yawned sleepily, but Lymon was restless and she did not suggest that they close up for the night.

Finally, at one o'clock, Henry Macy looked up at the corner of the ceiling and said quietly to Miss Amelia: 'I got a letter today.'

Miss Amelia was not one to be impressed by this, because all sorts of business letters and catalogues came addressed to her.

'I got a letter from my brother,' said Macy.

The hunchback, who had been goose-stepping about the café with his hands clasped behind his head, stopped suddenly. He was quick to sense any change in the atmosphere of a gathering. He glanced at each face in the room and waited.

Miss Amelia scowled and hardened her right fist. 'You are welcome to it,' she said.

'He is on parole. He is out of the penitentiary.'

The face of Miss Amelia was very dark, and she shivered although the night was warm. Stumpy MacPhail and Merlie Ryan pushed aside their checker game. The café was very quiet.

'Who?' asked Cousin Lymon. His large, pale ears seemed to grow on his head and stiffen. 'What?'

Miss Amelia slapped her hands palm down on the table. 'Because Marvin Macy is a——' But her voice hoarsened and after a few moments she only said: 'He belongs to be in that penitentiary the balance of his life.'

'What did he do?' asked Cousin Lymon.

There was a long pause, as no one knew exactly how to answer this. 'He robbed three filling stations,' said Stumpy MacPhail. But his words did not sound complete and there was a feeling of sins left unmentioned.

The hunchback was impatient. He could not bear to be left out of anything, even a great misery. The name Marvin Macy was unknown to him, but it tantalized him as did any mention of subjects which others knew about and of which he was ignorant—such as any reference to the old sawmill that had been torn down before he came, or a chance word about poor Morris Finestein, or the recollection of any event that had occurred before his time. Aside from this inborn curiosity, the hunchback took a great interest in robbers and crimes of all varieties. As he strutted around the table he was muttering the words 'released on parole' and 'penitentiary' to himself. But although he questioned insistently, he was unable to find anything, as nobody would dare to talk about Marvin Macy before Miss Amelia in the café.

'The letter did not say very much,' said Henry Macy. 'He did not say where he was going.'

'Humph!' said Amelia, and her face was still hardened and very dark. 'He will never set his split hoof on my premises.'

She pushed back her chair from the table, and made ready to close the café. Thinking about Marvin Macy may have set her to brooding, for she hauled the cash register back to the kitchen and put it in a private place. Henry Macy went off down the dark road. But Henry Ford Crimp and

Merlie Ryan lingered for a time on the front porch. Later Merlie Ryan was to make certain claims, to swear that on that night he had a vision of what was to come. But the town paid no attention, for that was just the sort of thing that Merlie Ryan would claim. Miss Amelia and Cousin Lymon talked for a time in the parlor. And when at last the hunchback thought that he could sleep she arranged the mosquito netting over his bed and waited until he had finished with his prayers. Then she put on her long nightgown, smoked two pipes, and only after a long time went to sleep.

That autumn was a happy time. The crops around the countryside were good, and over at the Forks Falls market the price of tobacco held firm that year. After the long hot summer the first cool days had a clean bright sweetness. Goldenrod grew along the dusty roads, and the sugar cane was ripe and purple. The bus came each day from Cheehaw to carry off a few of the younger children to the consolidated school to get an education. Boys hunted foxes in the pinewoods, winter quilts were aired out on the wash lines, and sweet potatoes bedded in the ground with straw against the colder months to come. In the evening, delicate shreds of smoke rose from the chimneys, and the moon was round and orange in the autumn sky. There was no stillness like the quiet of the first cold nights in the fall. Some-times, late in the night when there was no wind, there could be heard in the town the thin wild whistle of the train that goes through Society City on its way far off to the North.

For Miss Amelia Evans this was a time of greaty activity. She was at work from dawn until sundown. She made a new and bigger condenser for her still, and in one week ran off enough liquor to souse the whole county. Her old mule was dizzy from grinding so much sorghum, and she scalded her Mason jars and put away pear preserves. She was looking forward greatly to the first frost, because she had traded for three tremendous hogs, and intended to make much barbecue, chitterlings, and sausage.

During these weeks there was a quality about Miss Amelia that many people noticed. She laughed often, with a deep ringing laugh, and her whistling had a sassy, tuneful trickery. She was forever trying out her strength, lifting up heavy objects, or poking her tough biceps with her fin-ger. One day she sat down to her typewriter and wrote a story—a story in which there were foreigners, trap doors, and millions of dollars. Cousin Lymon was with her always, traipsing along behind her coat-tails, and when she watched him her face had a bright, soft look, and when she spoke his name there lingered in her voice the undertone of love.

The first cold spell came at last. When Miss Amelia awoke one morning there were frost flowers on the windowpanes, and rime had silvered the patches of grass in the yard. Miss Amelia built a roaring fire in the kitchen stove, then went out of doors to judge the day. The air was cold and sharp, the sky pale green and cloudless. Very shortly people began to come in from the country to find out what Miss Amelia thought of the weather; she decided to kill the biggest hog, and word got round the countryside. The hog was slaughtered and a low oak fire started in the barbecue pit. There was the warm smell of pig blood and smoke in the back yard, the stamp of footsteps, the ring of voices in the winter air. Miss Amelia walked around giving orders and soon most of the work was done.

She had some particular business to do in Cheehaw that day, so after making sure that all was going well, she cranked up her car and got ready to leave. She asked Cousin Lymon to come with her, in fact, she asked him seven times, but he was loath to leave the commotion and wanted to remain. This seemed to trouble Miss Amelia, as she always liked to have him near to her, and was prone to be terribly homesick when she had to go any distance away. But after asking him seven times, she did not urge him any further. Before leaving she found a stick and drew a heavy line all around the barbecue pit, about two feet back from the edge, and told him not to trespass beyond that boundary. She left after dinner and intended to be back before dark.

Now, it is not so rare to have a truck or an automobile pass along the road and through the town on the way from Cheehaw to somewhere else. Every year the tax collector comes to argue with rich people such as Miss Amelia. And if somebody in the town, such as Merlie Ryan, takes a notion that he can connive to get a car on credit, or to pay down three dollars and have a fine electric icebox such as they advertise in the store windows of Cheehaw, then a city man will come out asking meddlesome questions, finding out all his troubles, and ruining his chances of buying anything on the installment plan. Sometimes, especially since they are working on the Forks Falls highway, the cars hauling the chain gang come through the town. And frequently people in automobiles get lost and stop to inquire how they can find the right road again. So, late that afternoon it was nothing unusual to have a truck pass the mill and stop in the middle of the road near the café of Miss Amelia. A man jumped down from the back of the truck, and the truck went on its way.

The man stood in the middle of the road and looked about him. He was a tall man, with brown curly hair, and slow-moving, deep-blue eyes. His lips were red and he smiled the lazy, half-mouthed smile of the braggart. The man wore a red shirt, and a wide belt of tooled leather; he carried a tin suitcase and a guitar. The first person in the town to see this newcomer was Cousin Lymon, who had heard the shifting gears and come around to investigate. The hunchback stuck his head around the corner of the porch, but did not step out altogether into full view. He and the man stared at each other, and it was not the look of two strangers meeting for the first time and swiftly summing up each other. It was a peculiar stare they exchanged between them, like the look of two criminals who recognize each other. Then the man in the red shirt shrugged his left shoulder and turned away. The face of the hunchback was very pale as he watched the man go down the road, and after a few moments he began to follow along carefully, keeping many paces away.

It was immediately known throughout the town that Marvin Macy had come back again. First, he went to the mill, propped his elbows lazily on a window sill and looked inside. He liked to watch others hard at work, as do all born loafers. The mill was thrown into a sort of numb confusion. The dyers left the hot vats, the spinners and weavers forgot about their machines, and even Stumpy MacPhail, who was foreman, did not know exactly what to do. Marvin Macy still smiled his wet half-mouthed smiles, and when he saw his brother, his bragging expression did not change. After looking over the mill Marvin Macy went down the road to the house where he had been raised, and left his suitcase and guitar on the front porch. Then he walked around the millpond, looked over the church, the three stores, and the rest of the town. The hunchback trudged along quietly at some distance behind him, his hands in his pockets, and his little face still very pale.

It had grown late. The red winter sun was setting, and to the west the sky was deep gold and crimson. Ragged chimney swifts flew to their nests; lamps were lighted. Now and then there was the smell of smoke, and the warm rich odor of the barbecue slowly cooking in the pit behind the café. After making the rounds of the town Marvin Macy stopped before Miss Amelia's premises and read the sign above the porch. Then, not hesitating to trespass, he walked through the side yard. The mill whistle blew a thin, lonesome blast, and the day's shift was done. Soon there were others in Miss Amelia's back yard beside Marvin Macy—Henry Ford Crimp, Merlie Ryan, Stumpy MacPhail, and any number of children and people who stood around the edges of the property and looked on. Very little was said. Marvin Macy stood by himself on one side of the pit, and the rest of the people clustered together on the other side. Cousin Lymon stood somewhat apart from everyone, and he did not take his eyes from the face of Marvin Macy.

'Did you have a good time in the penitentiary?' asked Merlie Ryan, with a silly giggle.

Marvin Macy did not answer. He took from his hip pocket a large knife, opened it slowly, and honed the blade on the seat of his pants. Merlie Ryan grew suddenly very quiet and went to stand directly behind the broad back of Stumpy MacPhail.

Miss Amelia did not come home until almost dark. They heard the rattle of her automobile while she was still a long distance away, then the slam of the door and a bumping noise as though she were hauling something up the front steps of her premises. The sun had already set, and in the air there was the blue smoky glow of early winter evenings. Miss Amelia came down the back steps slowly, and the group in her yard waited very quietly. Few people in this world could stand up to Miss Amelia, and against Marvin Macy she had this special and bitter hate. Everyone waited to see her burst into a terrible holler, snatch up some dangerous object, and chase him altogether out of town. At first she did not see Marvin Macy, and her face had the relieved and dreamy expression that was natural to her when she reached home after having gone some distance away.

Miss Amelia must have seen Marvin Macy and Cousin Lymon at the same instant. She looked from one to the other, but it was not the wastrel from the penitentiary on whom she finally fixed her gaze of sick amazement. She, and everyone else, was looking at Cousin Lymon, and he was a sight to see.

The hunchback stood at the end of the pit, his pale face lighted by the soft glow from the smoldering oak fire. Cousin Lymon had a very peculiar accomplishment, which he used whenever he wished to ingratiate himself with someone. He would stand very still, and with just a little concentration, he could wiggle his large pale ears with marvelous quickness and ease. This trick he always used when he wanted to get something special out of Miss Amelia, and to her it was irresistible. Now as he stood there the hunchback's ears were wiggling furiously on his head, but it was not Miss Amelia at whom he was looking this time. The hunchback was smiling at Marvin Macy with an entreaty that was near to desperation. At first Marvin Macy paid no attention to him, and when he did finally glance at the hunchback it was without any appreciation whatsoever.

'What ails this Brokeback?' he asked with a rough jerk of his thumb.

No one answered. And Cousin Lymon, seeing that his accomplishment was getting him nowhere, added new efforts of persuasion. He fluttered his eyelids, so that they were like pale, trapped moths in his sockets. He scraped his feet around on the ground, waved his hands about, and finally began doing a little trotlike dance. In the last gloomy light of the winter afternoon he resembled the child of a swamp-haunt.

Marvin Macy, alone of all the people in the yard, was unimpressed.

'Is the runt throwing a fit?' he asked, and when no one answered he stepped forward and gave Cousin Lymon a cuff on the side of the head. The hunchback staggered, then fell back on the ground. He sat where he had fallen, still looking up at Marvin Macy, and with great effort his ears managed one last forlorn little flap.

Now everyone turned to Miss Amelia to see what she would do. In all these years no one had so much as touched a hair of Cousin Lymon's head, although many had had the itch to do so. If anyone even spoke crossly to the hunchback, Miss Amelia would cut off this rash mortal's credit and find ways of making things go hard for him a long time afterward. So now if Miss Amelia had split open Marvin Macy's head with the ax on the back porch no one would have been surprised. But she did nothing of the kind.

'There were times when Miss Amelia seemed to go into a sort of trance. And the cause of these trances was usually known and understood. For Miss Amelia was a fine doctor, and did not grind up swamp roots and other untried ingredients and give them to the first patient who came along; whenever she invented a new medicine she always tried it out first on herself. She would swallow an enormous dose and spend the following day walking thoughtfully back and forth from the café to the brick privy. Often, when there was a sudden keen gripe, she would stand quite still, her queer eyes staring down at the ground and her fists clenched; she was trying to decide which organ was being worked upon, and what misery the new medicine might be most likely to cure. And now as she watched the hunchback and Marvin Macy, her face wore this same expression, tense with reckoning some inward pain, although she had taken no new medicine that day.

'That will learn you, Brokeback,' said Marvin Macy.

Henry Macy pushed back his limp whitish hair from his forehead and coughed nervously. Stumpy MacPhail and Merlie Ryan shuffled their feet, and the children and black people on the outskirts of the property made not a sound. Marvin Macy folded the knife he had been honing, and after looking about him fearlessly he swaggered out of the yard. The embers in the pit were turning to gray feathery ashes and it was now quite dark.

That was the way Marvin Macy came back from the penitentiary. Not a living soul in all the town was glad to see him. Even Mrs. Mary Hale, who was a good woman and had raised him with love and care—at the first sight of him even this old foster mother dropped the skillet she was holding and burst into tears. But nothing could faze that Marvin Macy. He sat on the back steps of the Hale house, lazily picking his guitar, and when the supper was ready, he pushed the children of the household out of the way and served himself a big meal, although there had been barely enough hoecakes and white meat to go round. After eating he settled himself in the best and warmest sleeping place in the front room and was untroubled by dreams.

Miss Amelia did not open the café that night. She locked the doors and all the windows very carefully, nothing was seen of her and Cousin Lymon, and a lamp burned in her room all the night long.

Marvin Macy brought with him bad fortune, right from the first, as could be expected. The next day the weather turned suddenly, and it became hot. Even in the early morning there was a sticky sultriness in the atmosphere, the wind carried the rotten smell of the swamp, and delicate shrill mosquitoes webbed the green millpond. It was unseasonable, worse than August, and much damage was done. For nearly everyone in the county who owned a hog had copied Miss Amelia and slaughtered the day before. And what sausage could keep in such weather as this? After a few days there was everywhere the smell of slowly spoiling meat, and an atmosphere of dreary waste. Worse yet, a family reunion near the Forks Falls highway ate pork roast and died, every one of them. It was plain that their hog had been infected—and who could tell whether the rest of the meat was safe or not? People were torn between the longing for the good taste of pork, and the fear of death. It was a time of waste and confusion.

The cause of all this, Marvin Macy, had no shame in him. He was seen everywhere. During work hours he loafed about the mill, looking in at the windows, and on Sundays he dressed in his red shirt and paraded up and down the road with his guitar. He was still handsome—with his brown hair, his red lips, and his broad strong shoulders; but the evil in him was now too famous for his good looks to get him anywhere. And this evil was not measured only by the actual sins he had committed. True, he had robbed those filling stations. And before that he had ruined the tenderest girls in the county, and laughed about it. Any number of wicked things could be listed against him, but quite apart from these crimes there was about him a secret meanness that clung to him almost like a smell. Another thing—he never sweated, not even in August, and that surely is a sign worth pondering over.

Now it seemed to the town that he was more dangerous than he had ever been before, as in the penitentiary in Atlanta he must have learned the method of laying charms. Otherwise how could his effect on Cousin Lymon be explained? For since first setting eyes on Marvin Macy the hunchback was possessed by an unnatural spirit. Every minute he wanted to be following along behind this jailbird, and he was full of silly schemes to attract attention to himself. Still Marvin Macy either treated him hatefully or failed to notice him at all. Sometimes the hunchback would give up, perch himself on the banister of the front porch much as a sick bird huddles on a telephone wire, and grieve publicly.

'But why?' Miss Amelia would ask, staring at him with her crossed, gray eyes, and her fists closed tight.

'Oh, Marvin Macy,' groaned the hunchback, and the sound of the name was enough to upset the rhythm of his sobs so that he hiccuped. 'He has been to Atlanta.'

Miss Amelia would shake her head and her face was dark and hardened. To begin with she had no patience with any traveling; those who had made the trip to Atlanta or traveled fifty miles from home to see the ocean— those restless people she despised. 'Going to Atlanta does no credit to him.'

'He has been to the penitentiary,' said the hunchback, miserable with longing.

How are you going to argue against such envies as these? In her perplexity Miss Amelia did not herself sound any too sure of what she was saying. 'Been to the penitentiary, Cousin Lymon? Why, a trip like that is no travel to brag about.'

During these weeks Miss Amelia was closely watched by everyone. She went about absent-mindedly, her face remote as though she had lapsed into one of her gripe trances. For some reason, after the day of Marvin Macy's arrival, she put aside her overalls and wore always the red dress she had before this time reserved for Sundays, funerals, and sessions of the court. Then as the weeks passed she began to take some steps to clear up the situation. But her efforts were hard to understand. If it hurt her to see Cousin Lymon follow Marvin Macy about the town, why did she not make the issues clear once and for all, and tell the hunchback that if he had dealings with Marvin Macy she would turn him off the premises? That would have been simple, and Cousin Lymon would have had to submit to her, or else face the sorry business of finding himself loose in the world. But Miss Amelia seemed to have lost her will; for the first time in her life she hesitated as to just what course to pursue. And, like most people in such a position of uncertainty, she did the worst thing possible—she began following several courses at once, all of them contrary to each other.

The café was opened every night as usual, and, strangely enough, when Marvin Macy came swaggering through the door, with the hunchback at his heels, she did not turn him out. She even gave him free drinks and smiled at him in a wild, crooked way. At the same time she set a terrible trap for him out in the swamp that surely would have killed him if he had got caught. She let Cousin Lymon invite him to Sunday dinner, and then tried to trip him up as he went down the steps. She began a great campaign of pleasure for Cousin Lymon—making exhausting trips to various spectacles being held in distant places, driving the automobile thirty miles to a Chautauqua, taking him to Forks Falls to watch a parade. All in all it was a distracting time for Miss Amelia. In the opinion of most people she was well on her way in the climb up fools' hill, and everyone waited to see how it would all turn out.

The weather turned cold again, the winter was upon the town, and night came before the last shift in the mill was done. Children kept on all their garments when they slept, and women raised the backs of their skirts to toast themselves dreamily at the fire. After it rained, the mud in the road made hard frozen ruts, there were faint flickers of lamplight from the windows of the houses, the peach trees were scrawny and bare. In the dark, silent nights of winter-time the café was the warm center point of the town, the lights shining so brightly that they could be seen a quarter of a mile away. The great iron stove at the back of the room roared, crackled, and turned red. Miss Amelia had made red curtains for the windows, and from a salesman who passed through the town she bought a great bunch of paper roses that looked very real.

But it was not only the warmth, the decorations, and the brightness, that made the café what it was. There is a deeper reason why the café was so precious to this town. And this deeper reason has to do with a certain pride that had not hitherto been known in these parts. To understand this new pride the cheapness of human life must be kept in mind. There were always plenty of people clustered around a mill—but it was seldom that every family had enough meal, garments, and fat back to go the rounds. Life could become one long dim scramble just to get the things needed to keep alive. And the confusing point is this: All useful things have a price, and are bought only with money, as that is the way the world is run. You know without having to reason about it the price of a bale of cotton, or a quart of molasses. But no value has been put on human life; it is given to us free and taken without being paid for. What is it worth? If you look around, at times the value may seem to be little or nothing at all. Often after you have sweated and tried and things are not better for you, there comes a feeling deep down in the soul that you are not worth much.

But the pride that the café brought to this town had an effect on almost everyone, even the children. For in order to come to the café you did not have to buy the dinner, or a portion of liquor. There were cold bottled drinks for a nickel. And if you could not even afford that, Miss Amelia had a drink called Cherry Juice which sold for a penny a glass, and was pink-colored and very sweet. Almost everyone, with the exception of Reverend T. M. Willin, came to the café at least once during the week. Children love to sleep in houses other than their own, and to eat at a neighbor's table; on such occasions they behave themselves decently and are proud. The people in the town were likewise proud when sitting at the tables in the café. They washed before coming to Miss Amelia's, and scraped their feet very politely on the threshold as they entered the café. There, for a few hours at least, the deep bitter knowing that you are not worth much in this world could be laid low.

The café was a special benefit to bachelors, unfortunate people, and consumptives. And here it may be mentioned that there was some reason to suspect that Cousin Lymon was consumptive. The brightness of his gray eyes, his insistence, his talkativeness, and his cough—these were all signs. Besides, there is generally supposed to be some connection between a hunched spine and consumption. But whenever this subject had been mentioned to Miss Amelia she had become furious; she denied these symptoms with bitter vehemence, but on the sly she treatd Cousin Lymon with hot chest platters, Kroup Kure, and such. Now this winter the hunchback's cough was worse, and sometimes even on cold days he would break out in a heavy sweat. But this did not prevent him from following along after Marvin Macy.

Early every morning he left the premises and went to the back door of Mrs. Hale's house, and waited and waited—as Marvin Macy was a lazy sleeper. He would stand there and call out softly. His voice was just like the voices of children who squat patiently over those tiny little holes in the ground where doodlebugs are thought to live, poking the hold with a broom straw, and calling plaintively: 'Doodlebug, Doodlebug—fly away home. Mrs. Doodlebug, Mrs. Doodlebug. Come out, come out. Your house is on fire and all your children are burning up.' In just such a voice—at once sad, luring, and resigned—would the hunchback call Marvin Macy's name each morning. Then when Marvin Macy came out for the day, he would trail him about the town, and sometimes they would be gone for hours together out in the swamp.

And Miss Amelia continued to do the worst thing possible: that is, to try to follow several courses at once. When Cousin Lymon left the house she did not call him back, but only stood in the middle of the road and watched lonesomely until he was out of sight. Nearly every day Marvin Macy turned up with Cousin Lymon at dinnertime, and ate at her table. Miss Amelia opened the pear preserves, and the table was well-set with ham or chicken, great bowls of hominy grits, and winter peas. It is true that on one occasion Miss Amelia tried to poison Marvin Macy—but there was a mistake, the plates were confused, and it was she herself who got the poisoned dish. This she quickly realized by the slight bitterness of the food, and that day she ate no dinner. She sat tilted back in her chair, feeling her muscle, and looking at Marvin Macy.

Every night Marvin Macy came to the café and settled himself at the best and largest table, the one in the center of the room. Cousin Lymon brought him liquor, for which he did not pay a cent. Marvin Macy brushed the hunchback aside as if he were a swamp mosquito, and not only did he show no gratitude for these favors, but if the hunchback got in his way he would cuff him with the back of his hand, or say: 'Out of my way, Brokeback— I'll snatch you baldheaded.' When this happened Miss Amelia would come out from behind her counter and approach Marvin Macy very slowly, her fists clenched, her peculiar red dress hanging awkwardly around her bony knees. Marvin Macy would also clench his fists and they would walk slowly and meaningfully around each other. But, although everyone watched breathlessly, nothing ever came of it. The time for the fight was not yet ready.

There is one particular reason why this winter is remembered and still talked about. A great thing happened. People woke up on the second of January and found the whole world about them altogether changed. Little ignorant children looked out of the windows, and they were so puzzled that they began to cry. Old people harked back and could remember nothing in these parts to equal the phenomenon. For in the night it had snowed. In the dark hours after midnight the dim flakes started falling softly on the town. By dawn the ground was covered, and the strange snow banked the ruby windows of the church, and whitened the roofs of the houses. The snow gave the town a drawn, bleak look. The two-room houses near the mill were dirty, crooked, and seemed about to collapse, and somehow everything was dark and shrunken. But the snow itself—there was a beauty about it few people around here had ever known before. The snow was not white, as Northerners had pictured it to be; in the snow there were soft colors of blue and silver, the sky was a gentle shining gray. And the dreamy quietness of falling snow—when had the town been so silent?

People reacted the the snowfall in various ways. Miss Amelia, on looking out of her window, thoughtfully wiggled the toes of her bare foot,
gathered close to her neck the collar of her nightgown. She stood there for
some time, then commenced to draw the shutters and lock every window on
the premises. She closed the place completely, lighted the lamps, and sat
solemnly over her bowl of grits. The reason for this was not that Miss
Amelia feared the snowfall. It was simply that she was unable to form an
immediate opinion of this new event, and unless she knew exactly and definitely what she thought of a matter (which was nearly always the case)
she preferred to ignore it. Snow had never fallen in this county in her lifetime, and she had never thought about it one way or the other. But if she
admitted this snowfall she would have to come to some decision, and in
those days there was enough distraction in her life as it was already. So she
poked about the gloomy, lamp-lighted house and pretended that nothing
had happened. Cousin Lymon, on the contrary, chased around in the wildest excitement, and when Miss Amelia turned her back to dish him some
breakfast he slipped out of the door.

Marvin Macy laid claim to the snowfall. He said that he knew snow, had
seen it in Atlanta, and from the way he walked about the town that day it
was as though he owned every flake. He sneered at the little children who
crept timidly out of the houses and scooped up handfuls of snow to taste.
Reverend Willin hurried down the road with a furious face, as he was
thinking deeply and trying to weave the snow into his Sunday sermon.
Most people were humble and glad about his marvel; they spoke hushed
voices and said 'thank you' and 'please' more than was necessary. A few
weak characters, of course, were demoralized and got drunk—but they
were not numerous. To everyone this was an occasion and many counted
their money and planned to go to the café that night.

Cousin Lymon followed Marvin Macy about all day, seconding his claim
to the snow. He marveled that snow did not fall as does rain, and stared up
at the dreamy, gently falling flakes until he stumbled from dizziness. And
the pride he took on himself, basking in the glory of Marvin Macy—it was
such that many people could not resist calling out to him: ' "Oho," said the
fly on the chariot wheel. "What a dust we do raise." '

Miss Amelia did not intend to serve dinner. But when, at six o'clock,
there was the sound of footsteps on the porch she opened the front door
cautiously. It was Henry Ford Crimp, and though there was no food, she
let him sit at a table and served him a drink. Others came. The evening was
blue, bitter, and though the snow fell no longer there was a wind from the
pine trees that swept up delicate flurries from the ground. Cousin Lymon
did not come until after dark, with him Marvin Macy, and he carried his
tin suitcase and his guitar.

'So you mean to travel?' said Miss Amelia quickly.

Marvin Macy warmed himself at the stove. Then he settled down at his table and carefully sharpened a little stick. He picked his teeth, frequently taking the stick out of his mouth to look at the end and wipe it on the sleeve of his coat. He did not bother to answer.

The hunchback looked at Miss Amelia, who was behind the counter. His face was not in the least beseeching; he seemed quite sure of himself. He folded his hands behind his back and perked up his ears confidently. His cheeks were red, his eyes shining, and his clothes were soggy wet. 'Marvin Macy is going to visit a spell with us,' he said.

Miss Amelia made no protest. She only came out from behind the counter and hovered over the stove, as though the news had made her suddenly cold. She did not warm her backside modestly, lifting her skirt only an inch or so, as do most women when in public. There was not a grain of modesty about Miss Amelia, and she frequently seemed to forget altogether that there were men in the room. Now as she stood warming herself, her red dress was pulled up quite high in the back so that a piece of her strong, hairy thigh could be seen by anyone who cared to look at it. Her head was turned to one side, and she had begun talking with herself, nodding and wrinkling her forehead, and there was the tone of accusation and reproach in her voice although the words were not plain. Meanwhile, the hunchback and Marvin Macy had gone upstairs—up to the parlor with the pampas grass and the two sewing machines, to the private rooms where Miss Amelia had lived the whole of her life. Down in the café you could hear them bumping around, unpacking Marvin Macy, and getting him settled.

That is the way Marvin Macy crowded into Miss Amelia's home. At first Cousin Lymon, who had given Marvin Macy his own room, slept on the sofa in the parlor. But the snowfall had a bad effect on him; he caught a cold that turned into a winter quinsy, so Miss Amelia gave up her bed to him. The sofa in the parlor was much too short for her, her feet lapped over the edges, and often she rolled off onto the floor. Perhaps it was this lack of sleep the clouded her wits; everything she tried to do against Marvin Macy rebounded on herself. She got caught in her own tricks, and found herself in many pitiful positions. But still she did not put Marvin Macy off the premises, as she was afraid that she would be left alone. Once you have lived with another, it is a great torture to have to live alone. The silence of a firelit room where suddenly the clock stops ticking, the nervous shadows in an empty house—it is better to take in your mortal enemy than face the terror of living alone.

The snow did not last. The sun came out and within two days the town was just as it had always been before. Miss Amelia did not open her house until every flake had melted. Then she had a big house cleaning and aired everything out in the sun. But before that, the very first thing she did on going out again into her yard, was to tie a rope to the largest branch of the chinaberry tree. At the end of the rope she tied a crocus sack tightly stuffed with sand. This was the punching bag she made for herself and from that day on she would box with it out in her yard every morning. Already she was a fine fighter—a little heavy on her feet, but knowing all manner of mean holds and squeezes to make up for this.

Miss Amelia, as has been mentioned, measured six feet two inches in height. Marvin Macy was one inch shorter. In weight they were about even —both of them weighing close to a hundred and sixty pounds. Marvin Macy had the advantage in slyness of movement, and in toughness of chest. In fact from the outward point of view the odds were altogether in his favor. Yet almost everybody in the town was betting on Miss Amelia; scarcely a person would put up money on Marvin Macy. The town remembered the great fight between Miss Amelia and a Fork Falls lawyer who had tried to cheat her. He had been a huge strapping fellow, but he was left three-quarters dead when she had finished with him. And it was not only her talent as a boxer that had impressed everyone—she could demoralize her enemy by making terrifying faces and fierce noises, so that even the spectators were sometimes cowed. She was brave, she practiced faithfully with her punching bag, and in this case she was clearly in the right. So people had confidence in her, and they waited. Of course there was no set date for this fight. There were just the signs that were too plain to be overlooked.

During these times the hunchback strutted around with a pleased little pinched-up face. In many delicate and clever ways he stirred up trouble between them. He was constantly plucking at Marvin Macy's trouser leg to draw attention to himself. Sometimes he followed in Miss Amelia's footsteps—but these days it was only in order to imitate her awkward long-legged walk; he crossed his eyes and aped her gestures in a way that made her appear to be a freak. There was something so terrible about this that even the silliest customers of the café, such as Merlie Ryan, did not laugh. Only Marvin Macy drew up the left corner of his mouth and chuckled. Miss Amelia, when this happened, would be divided between two emotions. She would look at the hunchback with a lost, dismal reproach—then turn toward Marvin Macy with her teeth clamped.

'Bust a gut!' she would say bitterly.

And Marvin Macy, most likely, would pick up the guitar from the floor beside his chair. His voice was wet and slimy, as he always had too much spit in his mouth. And the tunes he sang glided slowly from his throat like eels. His strong fingers picked the strings with dainty skill, and everything he sang both lured and exasperated. This was usually more than Miss Amelia could stand.

'Bust a gut!' she would repeat, in a shout.

But always Marvin Macy had the answer ready for her. He would cover the strings to silence the quivering leftover tones, and reply with slow, sure insolence.

'Everything you holler at me bounces back on yourself. Yah! Yah!'

Miss Amelia would have to stand there helpless, as no one has ever invented a way out of this trap. She could not shout out abuse that would bounce back on herself. He had the best of her, there was nothing she could do.

So things went on like this. What happened between the three of them during the nights in the rooms upstairs nobody knows. But the café became more and more crowded every night. A new table had to be brought in. Even the Hermit, the crazy man named Rainer Smith, who took to the swamps years ago, heard something of the situation and came one night to look in at the window and brood over the gathering in the bright café. And the climax each evening was the time when Miss Amelia and Marvin Macy doubled their fists, squared up, and glared at each other. Usually this did not happen after any especial argument, but it seemed to come about mysteriously, by means of some instinct on the part of both of them. At these times the café would become so quiet that you could hear the bouquet of paper roses rustling in the draft. And each night they held this fighting stance a little longer than the night before.

The fight took place on Ground Hog Day, which is the second of February. The weather was favorable, being neither rainy nor sunny, and with a neutral temperature. There were several signs that this was the appointed day, and by ten o'clock the news spread all over the county. Early in the morning Miss Amelia went out and cut down her punching bag. Marvin Macy sat on the back step with a tin can of hog fat between his knees and carefully greased his arms and his legs. A hawk with a bloody breast flew over the town and circled twice around the property of Miss Amelia. The tables in the café were moved out to the back porch, so that the whole big room was cleared for the fight. There was every sign. Both Miss Amelia and Marvin Macy ate four helpings of half-raw roast for dinner, and then lay down in the afternoon to store up strength. Marvin Macy rested in the big room upstairs, while Miss Amelia stretched herself out on the bench in her office. It was plain from her white stiff face what a torment it was for her to be lying still and doing nothing, but she lay there quiet as a corpse with her eyes closed and her hands crossed on her chest.

Cousin Lymon had a restless day, and his little face was drawn and tightened with excitement. He put himself up a lunch, and set out to find the ground hog—within an hour he returned, the lunch eaten, and said that the ground hog had seen his shadow and there was to be bad weather ahead. Then, as Miss Amelia and Marvin Macy were both resting to gather strength, and he was left to himself, it occurred to him that he might as well paint the front porch. The house had not been painted for years—in fact, God knows if it had ever been painted at all. Cousin Lymon scrambled around, and soon he had painted half the floor of the porch a gay bright green. It was a loblolly job, and he smeared himself all over. Typically enough he did not even finish the floor, but changed over to the walls, painting as high as he could reach and then standing on a crate to get up a foot higher. When the paint ran out, the right side of the floor was bright green and there was a jagged portion of wall that had been painted. Cousin Lymon left it at that.

There was something childish about his satisfaction with his painting. And in this respect a curious fact should be mentioned. No one in the town, not even Miss Amelia, had any idea how old the hunchback was. Some maintained that when he came to town he was about twelve years old, still a child—others were certain that he was well past forty. His eyes were blue and steady as a child's but there were lavender crêpy shadows beneath these blue eyes that hinted of age. It was impossible to guess his age by his hunched queer body. And even his teeth gave no clue—they were all still in his head (two were broken from cracking a pecan), but he had stained them with so much sweet snuff that it was impossible to decide whether they were old teeth or young teeth. When questioned directly about his age the hunchback professed to know absolutely nothing—he had no idea how long he had been on the earth, whether for ten years or a hundred! So his age remained a puzzle.

Cousin Lymon finished his painting at five-thirty o'clock in the afternoon. The day had turned colder and there was a wet taste in the air. The wind came up from the pinewoods, rattling windows, blowing an old newspaper down the road until at last it caught upon a thorn tree. People began to come in from the country; packed automobiles that bristled with the poked-out heads of children, wagons drawn by old mules who seemed to smile in a weary, sour way and plodded along with their tired eyes half-closed. Three young boys came from Society City. All three of them wore yellow rayon shirts and caps put on backward—they were as much alike as triplets, and could always be seen at cock fights and camp meetings. At six o'clock the mill whistle sounded the end of the day's shift and the crowd was complete. Naturally, among the newcomers there were some riffraff, unknown characters, and so forth—but even so the gathering was quiet. A hush was on the town and the faces of people were strange in the fading light. Darkness hovered softly; for a moment the sky was a pale clear yellow against which the gables of the church stood out in dark and bare outline, then the sky died slowly and the darkness gathered into night.

Seven is a popular number, and especially it was a favorite with Miss Amelia. Seven swallows of water for hiccups, seven runs around the mill-pond for cricks in the neck, seven doses of Amelia Miracle Mover as a worm cure—her treatment nearly always hinged on this number. It is a number of mingled possibilities, and all who love mystery and charms set store by it. So the fight was to take place at seven o'clock. This was known to everyone, not by announcement or words, but understood in the un-questioning way that rain is understood, or an evil odor from the swamp. So before seven o'clock everyone gathered gravely around the property of Miss Amelia. The cleverest got into the café itself and stood lining the walls of the room. Others crowded onto the front porch, or took a stand in the yard.

Miss Amelia and Marvin Macy had not yet shown themselves. Miss Amelia, after resting all afternoon on the office bench, had gone upstairs. On the other hand Cousin Lymon was at your elbow every minute, threading his way through the crowd, snapping his fingers nervously, and batting his eyes. At one minute to seven o'clock he squirmed his way into the café and climbed up on the counter. All was very quiet.

It must have been aranged in some manner beforehand. For just at the stroke of seven Miss Amelia showed herself at the head of the stairs. At the same instant Marvin Macy appeared in front of the café and the crowd made way for him silently. They walked toward each other with no haste, their fists already gripped, and their eyes like the eyes of dreamers. Miss Amelia had changed her red dress for her old overalls, and they were rolled up to the knees. She was barefooted and she had an iron strength-band around her right wrist. Marvin Macy had also rolled his trouser legs —he was naked to the waist and heavily greased; he wore the heavy shoes that had been issued him when he left the penitentiary. Stumpy MacPhail stepped forward from the crowd and slapped their hip pockets with the palm of his right hand to make sure there would be no sudden knives. Then they were alone in the cleared center of the bright café.

There was no signal, but they both struck out simultaneously. Both blows landed on the chin, so that the heads of Miss Amelia and Marvin Macy bobbed back and they were left a little groggy. For a few seconds after the first blows they merely shuffled their feet around on the bare floor, experimenting with various positions, and making mock fists. Then, like wildcats, they were suddenly on each other. There was the sound of knocks, panting, and thumpings on the floor. They were so fast that it was hard to take in what was going on—but once Miss Amelia was hurled backward so that she staggered and almost fell, and another time Marvin Macy caught a knock on the shoulder that spun him around like a top. So the fight went on in this wild violent way with no sign of weakening on either side.

During a struggle like this, when the enemies are as quick and strong as these two, it is worth-while to turn from the confusion of the fight itself and observe the spectators. The people had flattened back as close as possible against the walls. Stumpy MacPhail was in a corner, crouched over and with his fists tight in sympathy, making strange noises. Poor Merlie Ryan had his mouth so wide open that a fly buzzed into it, and was swallowed before Merlie realized what had happened. And Cousin Lymon—he was worth watching. The hunchback still stood on the counter, so that he was raised up above everyone else in the café. He had his hands on his hips, his big head thrust forward, and his little legs bent so that the knees jutted outward. The excitement had made him break out in a rash, and his pale mouth shivered.

Perhaps it was half an hour before the course of the fight shifted. Hundreds of blows had been exchanged, and there was still a deadlock. Then suddenly Marvin Macy managed to catch hold of Miss Amelia's left arm and pinion it behind her back. She struggled and got a grasp around his waist; the real fight was now begun. Wrestling is the natural way of fighting in this county—as boxing is too quick and requires much thinking and concentration. And now that Miss Amelia and Marvin were locked in a hold together the crowd came out of its daze and pressed in closer. For a while the fighters grappled muscle to muscle, their hipbones braced against each other. Backward and forward, from side to side, they swayed in this way. Marvin Macy still had not sweated, but Miss Amelia's overalls were drenched and so much sweat had trickled down her legs that she left wet footprints on the floor. Now the test had come, and in these moments of terrible effort, it was Miss Amelia who was the stronger. Marvin Macy was greased and slippery, tricky to grasp, but she was stronger. Gradually she bent him over backward, and inch by inch she forced him to the floor. It was a terrible thing to watch and their deep hoarse breaths were the only sound in the café. At last she had him down, and straddled; her strong big hands were on his throat.

But at that instant, just as the fight was won, a cry sounded in the café that caused a shrill bright shiver to run down the spine. And what took place has been a mystery ever since. The whole town was there to testify what happened, but there were those who doubted their own eyesight. For the counter on which Cousin Lymon stood was at least twelve feet from the fighters in the center of the café. Yet at the instant Miss Amelia grasped the throat of Marvin Macy the hunchback sprang forward and sailed through the air as though he had grown hawk wings. He landed on the broad strong back of Miss Amelia and clutched at her neck with his clawed little fingers.

The rest is confusion. Miss Amelia was beaten before the crowd could come to their senses. Because of the hunchback the fight was won by Marvin Macy, and at the end Miss Amelia lay sprawled on the floor, her arms flung outward and motionless. Marvin Macy stood over her, his face somewhat popeyed, but smiling his old half-mouthed smile. And the hunchback, he had suddenly disappeared. Perhaps he was frightened about what he had done, or maybe he was so delighted that he wanted to glory with himself alone—at any rate he slipped out of the café and crawled under the back steps. Someone poured water on Miss Amelia, and after a time she got up slowly and dragged herself into her office. Through the open door the crowd could see her sitting at her desk, her head in the crook of her arm, and she was sobbing with the last of her grating, winded breath. Once she gathered her right fist together and knocked it three times on the top of her office desk, then her hand opened feebly and lay palm upward and still. Stumpy MacPhail stepped forward and closed the door.

The crowd was quiet, and one by one the people left the café. Mules were waked up and untied, automobiles cranked, and the three boys from Society City roamed off down the road on foot. This was not a fight to hash over and talk about afterward; people went home and pulled the covers up over their heads. The town was dark, except for the premises of Miss Amelia, but every room was lighted there the whole night long.

Marvin Macy and the hunchback must have left the town an hour or so before daylight. And before they went away this is what they did:

They unlocked the private cabinet of curios and took everything in it.

They broke the mechanical piano.

They carved terrible words on the café tables.

They found the watch that opened in the back to show a picture of a waterfall and took that also.

They poured a gallon of sorghum syrup all over the kitchen floor and smashed the jars of preserves.

They went out in the swamp and completely wrecked the still, ruining the big new condenser and the cooler, and setting fire to the shack itself.

They fixed a dish of Miss Amelia's favorite food, grits with sausage, seasoned it with enough poison to kill off the county, and placed this dish temptingly on the café counter.

They did everything ruinous they could think of without actually breaking into the office where Miss Amelia stayed the night. Then they went off together, the two of them.

That was how Miss Amelia was left alone in the town. The people would have helped her if they had known how, as people in this town will as often as not be kindly if they have a chance. Several housewives nosed around with brooms and offered to clear up the wreck. But Miss Amelia only looked at them with lost crossed eyes and shook her head. Stumpy Mac-Phail came in on the third day to buy a plug of Queenie tobacco, and Miss Amelia said the price was one dollar. Everything in the café had suddenly risen in price to be worth one dollar. And what sort of a café is that? Also, she changed very queerly as a doctor. In all the years before she had been much more popular than the Cheehaw doctor. She had never monkeyed with a patient's soul, taking away from him such real necessities as liquor, tobacco, and so forth. Once in a great while she might carefully warn a patient never to eat fried watermelon or some such dish it had never occurred to a person to want in the first place. Now all this wise doctoring was over. She told one-half of her patients that they were going to die outright, and to the remaining half she recommended cures so far-fetched and agonizing that no one in his right mind would consider them for a moment.

Miss Amelia let her hair grow ragged, and it was turning gray. Her face lengthened, and the great muscles of her body shrank until she was thin as old maids are thin when they go crazy. And those gray eyes—slowly day by day they were more crossed, and it was as though they sought each other out to exchange a little glance of grief and lonely recognition. She was not pleasant to listen to; her tongue had sharpened terribly.

When anyone mentioned the hunchback she would say only this: 'Ho! if I could lay hand to him I would rip out his gizzard and throw it to the cat!' But it was not so much the words that were terrible, but the voice in which they were said. Her voice had lost its old vigor; there was none of the ring of vengeance it used to have when she would mention 'that loom-fixer I was married to,' or some other enemy. Her voice was broken, soft, and sad as the wheezy whine of the church pump-organ.

For three years she sat out on the front steps every night, alone and silent, looking down the road and waiting. But the hunchback never returned. There were rumors that Marvin Macy used him to climb into windows and steal, and other rumors that Marvin Macy had sold him into a side show. But both these reports were traced back to Merlie Ryan. Nothing true was ever heard of him. It was in the fourth year that Miss Amelia hired a Cheehaw carpenter and had him board up the premises, and there in those closed rooms she has remained ever since.

Yes, the town is dreary. On August afternoons the road is empty, white with dust, and the sky above is bright as glass. Nothing moves—there are no children's voices, only the hum of the mill. The peach trees seem to grow more crooked every summer, and the leaves are dull gray and of a sickly delicacy. The house of Miss Amelia leans so much to the right that it is now only a question of time when it will collapse completely, and people are careful not to walk around the yard. There is no good liquor to be bought in the town; the nearest still is eight miles away, and the liquor is such that those who drink it grow warts on their livers the size of goobers, and dream themselves into a dangerous inward world. There is absolutely nothing to do in the town. Walk around the millpond, stand kicking at a rotten stump, figure out what you can do with the old wagon wheel by the side of the road near the church. The soul rots with boredom. You might as well go down to the Forks Falls highway and listen to the chain gang.

The Twelve Mortal Men

The Forks Falls highway is three miles from the town, and it is here the chain gang has been working. The road is of macadam, and the county decided to patch up the rough places and widen it at a certain dangerous place. The gang is made up of twelve men, all wearing black and white striped prison suits, and chained at the ankles. There is a guard, with a gun, his eyes drawn to red slits by the glare. The gang works all the day long, arriving huddled in the prison cart soon after daybreak, and being driven off again in the gray August twilight. All day there is the sound of the picks striking into the clay earth, hard sunlight, the smell of sweat. And every day there is music. One dark voice will start a phrase, half-sung, and like a question. And after a moment another voice will join in, soon the whole gang will be singing. The voices are dark in the golden glare, the music intricately blended, both somber and joyful. The music will swell until at last it seems that the sound does not come from the twelve men on the gang, but from the earth itself, or the wide sky. It is music that causes the heart to broaden and the listener to grow cold with ecstasy and fright. Then slowly the music will sink down until at last there remains one lonely voice, then a great hoarse breath, the sun, the sound of the picks in the silence.

And what kind of gang is this that can make such music? Just twelve mortal men, seven of them black and five of them white boys from this county. Just twelve mortal men who are together.

12

SAUL BELLOW
Seize the Day

There is considerable similarity among Saul Bellow's main characters, enough so that the "Bellow character" has joined the "Hemingway hero" and others as a distinct literary type. Among Bellow characters, Tommy Wilhelm shares much in common with the heroes of *Henderson the Rain King* and *Herzog*: he goofs and stumbles, he laughs at himself and cries, and he proceeds to complicate his life with mistake after mistake. His misfortunes are so compounded that, as depressing as they are to him, they become a major source of the story's color and interest. Like New York City, like Bellow's style itself, Wilhelm's suffering is strikingly multidimensional. Family, friends, job, all are sources of trouble. He is victimized by nearly every mental capacity, vice, and virtue he possesses. His sloth and self-pity hamstring his attempts to live prosperously, and his misplaced faith in his friend Tamkin and the talent agent Maurice Venice betray him. His considerable love for his sons, for his father, and for his would-be bride Olive cripple him with remorse. The working of time itself adds to his woes, for he suffers in the pres-

ent and he suffers for the past. Bellow skillfully laces Wilhelm's present experiences with flashbacks, and each reveals still further dimensions of misfortune, so that pain of both present and past springs with redoubled force on character and reader alike. Physically, too, Wilhelm endures pain. A remarkable effect of *Seize the Day* is its sense of physical reality. Wilhelm comes alive before us as a physical presence, so that we are made acutely aware of his huge body's revolt against intolerable circumstances: "Wilhelm made a great preliminary summary which involved the whole of his body. He drew and held a long breath, and his color changed and his eyes swam. 'New?' he said."

Moral and psychological ambiguity comprise another source of interest in the story. Even though key personalities are rendered in great detail, questions about who is right or wrong, who is blameworthy and why, are not easily answered. In a number of ways Wilhelm seems to be morally responsible for his own situation. Yet he has a redeeming largeness of soul, an openness of heart, a sweetness that defies cynicism and is perhaps one of the finest and most humanly engaging qualities in the story. The morality of his behavior is further complicated by his unconscious need for suffering and guilt. His personality is definitely not all of one piece, and unconscious forces drive him so powerfully that the scope of his will at times seems severely limited. Dr. Adler is the opposite of his son in nearly every respect, but the moral value of his actions is similarly difficult to judge. Wilhelm seems justified in his bitter protest that the old man at least owes him compassion because he is his father. But should Dr. Adler begin to finance his son and his son's greedy wife, there is every indication that the demands would be endless. Then there is Tamkin—the amazing Tamkin! A genuine *tour de force* of creation on Bellow's part, he is layer upon layer of philosopher, egoist, do-gooder, madman, poet, con man, psychologist. His improbable stories add circles within circles of absurdity to Wilhelm's sorry state of confusion. Whether or not he purposely swindles Wilhelm is one of the story's more interesting riddles.

Bellow is obviously an author who takes joy in using abundant and often eye-catching literary technique. He knows New York City intimately, and his imagery brings the story's setting alive in full sound and color. He does not relate imagery in a wholly realistic way, but somewhat impressionistically, so that we perceive things more or less as Wilhelm would. "The traffic seemed to come down Broadway out of the sky, where the hot spokes of sun rolled from the south. Hot, stony odors arose from the subway grating in the street." Bellow's style is marked by exceptional energy and virtuosity. With great agility his prose glides from one narrative mode to another—from dialogue to interior monologue, from monologue to third-person narrative. Often the terse rhythms, quick transitions, inverted sentence structures, and wry humor of his writing stress the distinctive qualities of Jewish speech.

An abundant, soulful sense of humor pervades Bellow's writing, and most of his main characters share in it. Even in the darkest moments one senses the twinkling authorial eye in the quick movement, mock heaviness, or giddy rhetorical loops of his prose. Through humor and piercing intellect—and through the immense joy of his spirit, which undoubtedly owes something to Hasidic tradition—he distances his work purposefully from the fiction of cheap pessimism and black humor. Admittedly, much pessimism clouds the ruminations of Wilhelm and Tamkin, and to some extent one must assume that Wilhelm's outcry against greed and inhumanity is Bellow's own. Nevertheless these views should not be taken incautiously as the author's. Although most of his own characters are made to fight desperately for self and salvation through love, Bellow is deeply suspicious of the literary pose which holds that the self is destroyed by modern life and that civilization has reached a dead end.

Seize
the Day

1

When it came to concealing his troubles, Tommy Wilhelm was not less capable than the next fellow. So at least he thought, and there was a certain amount of evidence to back him up. He had once been an actor—no, not quite, an extra—and he knew what acting should be. Also, he was smoking a cigar, and when a man is smoking a cigar, wearing a hat, he has an advantage; it is harder to find out how he feels. He came from the twenty-third floor down the lobby on the mezzanine to collect his mail before breakfast, and he believed—he hoped—that he looked passably well: doing all right. It was a matter of sheer hope, because there was not much that he could add to his present effort. On the fourteenth floor he looked for his father to enter the elevator; they often met at this hour, on the way to breakfast. If he worried about his appearance it was mainly for his old father's sake. But there was no stop on the fourteenth, and the elevator sank and sank. Then the smooth door opened and the great dark red uneven carpet that covered the lobby billowed toward Wilhelm's feet. In the foreground the lobby was dark, sleepy. French drapes like sails kept out the sun, but three high, narrow windows were open, and in the blue air Wilhelm saw a pigeon about to light on the great chain that supported the marquee of the movie house directly underneath the lobby. For one moment he heard the wings beating strongly.

Most of the guests at the Hotel Gloriana were past the age of retirement. Along Broadway in the Seventies, Eighties, and Nineties, a great part of New York's vast population of old men and women lives. Unless the weather is too cold or wet they fill the benches about the tiny railed parks and along the subway gratings from Verdi Square to Columbia University, they crowd the shops and cafeterias, the dime stores, the tea-rooms, the bakeries, the beauty parlors, the reading rooms and club rooms. Among these old people at the Gloriana, Wilhelm felt out of place. He was comparatively young, in his middle forties, large and blond, with big shoulders; his back was heavy and strong, if already a little stooped or thickened. After breakfast the old guests sat down on the green leather armchairs and sofas in the lobby and began to gossip and look into the papers; they had nothing to do but wait out the day. But Wilhelm was used to an active life and liked to go out energetically in the morning. And for several months, because he had no position, he had kept up his morale by rising early; he was shaved and in the lobby by eight o'clock. He bought the paper and some cigars and drank a Coca-Cola or two before he went in to breakfast with his father. After breakfast—out, out to attend to business. The getting out had in itself become the chief business. But he had realized that he could not keep this up much longer, and today he was afraid. He was aware that his routine was about to break up and he sensed that a huge trouble long presaged but till now formless was due. Before evening, he'd know.

Nevertheless he followed his daily course and crossed the lobby.

Rubin, the man at the newsstand, had poor eyes. They may not have been actually weak but they were poor in expression, with lacy lids that furled down at the corners. He dressed well. It didn't seem necessary—he was behind the counter most of the time—but he dressed very well. He had on a rich brown suit; the cuffs embarrassed the hairs on his small hands. He wore a Countess Mara painted necktie. As Wilhelm approached, Rubin did not see him; he was looking out dreamily at the Hotel Ansonia, which was visible from his corner, several blocks away. The Ansonia, the neighborhood's great landmark, was built by Stanford White. It looks like a baroque palace from Prague or Munich enlarged a hundred times, with towers, domes, huge swells and bubbles of metal gone green from exposure, iron fretwork and festoons. Black television antennae are densely planted on its round summits. Under the changes of weather it may look like marble or like sea water, black as slate in the fog, white as tufa in sunlight. This morning it looked like the image of itself reflected in deep water, white and cumulous above, with cavernous distortions underneath. Together, the two men gazed at it.

Then Rubin said, "Your dad is in to breakfast already, the old gentleman."

"Oh, yes? Ahead of me today?"

"That's a real knocked-out shirt you got on," said Rubin. "Where's it from, Saks?"

"No, it's a Jack Fagman—Chicago."

Even when his spirits were low, Wilhelm could still wrinkle his fore-head in a pleasing way. Some of the slow, silent movements of his face were very attractive. He went back a step, as if to stand away from himself and get a better look at his shirt. His glance was comic, a comment upon his untidiness. He liked to wear good clothes, but once he had put it on each article appeared to go its own way. Wilhelm, laughing, panted a little; his teeth were small; his cheeks when he laughed and puffed grew round, and he looked much younger than his years. In the old days when he was a college freshman and wore a raccoon coat and a beanie on his large blond head his father used to say that, big as he was, he could charm a bird out of a tree. Wilhelm had great charm still.

"I like this dove-gray color," he said in his sociable, good-natured way. "It isn't washable. You have to send it to the cleaner. It never smells as good as washed. But it's a nice shirt. It cost sixteen, eighteen bucks."

This shirt had not been bought by Wilhelm; it was a present from his boss—his former boss, with whom he had had a falling out. But there was no reason why he should tell Rubin the history of it. Although perhaps Rubin knew—Rubin was the kind of man who knew, and knew and knew. Wilhelm also knew many things about Rubin, for that matter, about Rubin's wife and Rubin's business, Rubin's health. None of these could be mentioned, and the great weight of the unspoken left them little to talk about.

"Well, y'lookin' pretty sharp today," Rubin said.

And Wilhelm said gladly, "Am I? Do you really think so?" He could not believe it. He saw his reflection in the glass cupboard full of cigar boxes, among the grand seals and paper damask and the gold-embossed portraits of famous men, García, Edward the Seventh, Cyrus the Great. You had to allow for the darkness and deformations of the glass, but he thought he didn't look too good. A wide wrinkle like a comprehensive bracket sign was written upon his forehead, the point between his brows, and there were patches of brown on his dark blond skin. He began to be half amused at the shadow of his own marveling, troubled, desirous eyes, and his nostrils and his lips. Fair-haired hippopotamus!—that was how he looked to himself. He saw a big round face, a wide, flourishing red mouth, stump teeth. And the hat, too; and the cigar, too. I should have done hard labor all my life, he reflected. Hard honest labor that tires you out and makes you sleep. I'd have worked off my energy and felt better. Instead, 1 had to distinguish myself—yet.

He had put forth plenty of effort, but that was not the same as working hard, was it? And if as a young man he had got off to a bad start it was due to this very same face. Early in the nineteen-thirties, because of his striking looks, he had been very briefly considered star material, and he had gone to Hollywood. There for seven years, stubbornly, he had tried to become a screen artist. Long before that time his ambition or delusion had ended, but through pride and perhaps also through laziness he had remained in California. At last he turned to other things, but those seven years of persistence and defeat had unfitted him somehow for trades and businesses, and then it was too late to go into one of the professions. He had been slow to mature, and he had lost ground, and so he hadn't been able to get rid of his energy and he was convinced that this energy itself had done him the greatest harm.

"I didn't see you at the gin game last night," said Rubin.

"I had to miss it. How did it go?"

For the last few weeks Wilhelm had played gin almost nightly, but yesterday he had felt that he couldn't afford to lose any more. He had never won. Not once. And while the losses were small they weren't gains, were they? They were losses. He was tired of losing, and tired also of the company, and so he had gone by himself to the movies.

"Oh," said Rubin, "it went okay. Carl made a chump of himself yelling at the guys. This time Doctor Tamkin didn't let him get away with it. He told him the psychological reason why."

"What was the reason?"

Rubin said, "I can't quote him. Who could? You know the way Tamkin talks. Don't ask me. Do you want the *Trib?* Aren't you going to look at the closing quotations?"

"It won't help much to look. I know what they were yesterday at three," said Wilhelm. "But I suppose I better had get the paper." It seemed necessary for him to lift one shoulder in order to put his hand into his jacket pocket. There, among little packets of pills and crushed cigarette butts and strings of cellophane, the red tapes of packages which he sometimes used as dental floss, he recalled that he had dropped some pennies.

"That doesn't sound so good," said Rubin. He meant to be conversationally playful, but his voice had no tone and his eyes, slack and lid-blinded, turned elsewhere. He didn't want to hear. It was all the same to him. Maybe he already knew, being the sort of man who knew and knew.

No, it wasn't good. Wilhelm had three orders of lard in the commodities market. He and Dr. Tamkin had bought this lard together four days ago at 12.96, and the price at once began to fall and was still falling. In the mail this morning there was sure to be a call for additional margin payment. One came every day.

The psychologist, Dr. Tamkin, had got him into this. Tamkin lived at the Gloriana and attended the card game. He had explained to Wilhelm that you could speculate in commodities at one of the uptown branches of a good Wall Street house without making the full deposit of margin legally required. It was up to the branch manager. If he knew you—and all the branch managers knew Tamkin—he would allow you to make short-term purchases. You needed only to open a small account.

"The whole secret of this type of speculation," Tamkin had told him, "is in the alertness. You have to act fast—buy it and sell it; sell it and buy in again. But quick! Get to the window and have them wire Chicago at just the right second. Strike and strike again! Then get out the same day. In no time at all you turn over fifteen, twenty thousand dollars' worth of soy beans, coffee, corn, hides, wheat, cotton." Obviously the doctor understood the market well. Otherwise he could not make it sound so simple. "People lose because they are greedy and can't get out when it starts to go up. They gamble, but I do it scientifically. This is not guesswork. You must take a few points and get out. Why, ye gods!" said Dr. Tamkin with his bulging eyes, his bald head, and his drooping lip. "Have you stopped to think how much dough people are making in the market?"

Wilhelm with a quick shift from gloomy attention to the panting laugh which entirely changed his face had said, "Ho, have I ever! What do you think? Who doesn't know it's way beyond nineteen-twenty-eight—twenty-nine and still on the rise? Who hasn't read the Fulbright investigation? There's money everywhere. Everyone is shoveling it in. Money is—is—"

"And can you rest—can you sit still while this is going on?" said Dr. Tamkin. "I confess to you I can't. I think about people, just because they have a few bucks to invest, making fortunes. They have no sense, they have no talent, they just have the extra dough and it makes them more dough. I get so worked up and tormented and restless, so restless! I haven't even been able to practice my profession. With all this money around you don't want to be a fool while everyone else is making. I know guys who make five, ten thousand a week just by fooling around. I know a guy at the Hotel Pierre. There's nothing to him, but he has a whole case of Mumm's champagne at lunch. I know another guy on Central Park South— But what's the use of talking. They make millions. They have smart lawyers who get them out of taxes by a thousand schemes."

"Whereas I got taken," said Wilhelm. "My wife refused to sign a joint return. One fairly good year and I got into the thirty-two-percent bracket and was stripped bare. What of all my bad years?"

"It's a businessmen's government," said Dr. Tamkin. "You can be sure that these men making five thousand a week—"

"I don't need that sort of money," Wilhelm had said. "But oh! if I could only work out a little steady income from this. Not much. I don't ask much. But how badly I need—! I'd be so grateful if you'd show me how to work it."

"Sure I will. I do it regularly. I'll bring you my receipts if you like. And do you want to know something? I approve of your attitude very much. You want to avoid catching the money fever. This type of activity is filled with hostile feeling and lust. You should see what it does to some of these fellows. They go on the market with murder in their hearts."

"What's that I once heard a guy say?" Wilhelm remarked. "A man is only as good as what he loves."

"That's it—just it," Tamkin said. "You don't have to go about it their way. There's also a calm and rational, a psychological approach."

Wilhelm's father, old Dr. Adler, lived in an entirely different world from his son, but he had warned him once against Dr. Tamkin. Rather casually—he was a very bland old man—he said, "Wilky, perhaps you listen too much to this Tamkin. He's interesting to talk to. I don't doubt it. I think he's pretty common but he's a persuasive man. However, I don't know how reliable he may be."

It made Wilhelm profoundly bitter that his father should speak to him with such detachment about his welfare. Dr. Adler liked to appear affable. Affable! His own son, his one and only son, could not speak his mind or ease his heart to him. I wouldn't turn to Tamkin, he thought, if I could turn to him. At least Tamkin sympathizes with me and tries to give me a hand, whereas Dad doesn't want to be disturbed.

Old Dr. Adler had retired from practice; he had a considerable fortune and could easily have helped his son. Recently Wilhelm had told him, "Father—it so happens that I'm in a bad way now. I hate to have to say it. You realize that I'd rather have good news to bring you. But it's true. And since it's true, Dad— What else am I supposed to say? It's true."

Another father might have appreciated how difficult this confession was —so much bad luck, weariness, weakness, and failure. Wilhelm had tried to copy the old man's tone and made himself sound gentlemanly, low-voiced, tasteful. He didn't allow his voice to tremble; he made no stupid gesture. But the doctor had no answer. He only nodded. You might have told him that Seattle was near Puget Sound, or that the Giants and Dodgers were playing a night game, so little was he moved from his expression of healthy, handsome, good-humored old age. He behaved toward his son as he had formerly done toward his patients, and it was a great grief to Wilhelm; it was almost too much to bear. Couldn't he see—couldn't he feel? Had he lost his family sense?

Greatly hurt, Wilhelm struggled however to be fair. Old people are bound to change, he said. They have hard things to think about. They must prepare for where they are going. They can't live by the old schedule any longer and all their perspectives change, and other people become alike, kin and acquaintances. Dad is no longer the same person, Wilhelm reflected. He was thirty-two when I was born, and now he's going on eighty. Furthermore, it's time I stopped feeling like a kid toward him, a small son.

The handome old doctor stood well above the other old people in the hotel. He was idolized by everyone. This was what people said: "That's old Professor Adler, who used to teach internal medicine. He was a diagnostician, one of the best in New York, and had a tremendous practice. Isn't he a wonderful-looking old guy? It's a pleasure to see such a fine old scientist, clean and immaculate. He stands straight and understands every single thing you say. He still has all his buttons. You can discuss any subject with him." The clerks, the elevator operators, the telephone girls and waitresses and chambermaids, and management flattered and pampered him. That was what he wanted. He had always been a vain man. To see how his father loved himself sometimes made Wilhelm madly indignant.

He folded over the *Tribune* with its heavy, black, crashing sensational print and read without recognizing any of the words, for his mind was still on his father's vanity. The doctor had created his own praise. People were primed and did not know it. And what did he need praise for? In a hotel where everyone was busy and contacts were so brief and had such small weight, how could it satisfy him? He could be in people's thoughts here and there for a moment; in and then out. He could never matter much to them. Wilhelm let out a long, hard breath and raised the brows of his round and somewhat circular eyes. He stared beyond the thick borders of the paper.

> . . . love that well which thou must leave ere long.

Involuntary memory brought him this line. At first he thought it referred to his father, but then he understood that it was for himself, rather. *He* should love that well. "This thou perceivest, which makes *thy* love more strong." Under Dr. Tamkin's influence Wilhelm had recently begun to remember the poems he used to read. Dr. Tamkin knew, or said he knew, the great English poets and once in a while he mentioned a poem of his own. It was a long time since anyone had spoken to Wilhelm about this sort of thing. He didn't like to think about his college days, but if there was one course that now made sense it was Literature I. The textbook was Lieder and Lovett's *British Poetry and Prose,* a black heavy book with thin pages. Did I read that? he asked himself. Yes, he had read it and there was one accomplishment at least he could recall with pleasure. He had read "Yet once more, O ye laurels." How pure this was to say! It was beautiful.

> Sunk though he be beneath the wat'ry floor . . .

Such things had always swayed him, and now the power of such words was far, far greater.

Wilhelm respected the truth, but he could lie and one of the things he lied often about was his education. He said he was an alumnus of Penn State; in fact he had left school before his sophomore year was finished. His sister Catherine had a B.S. degree. Wilhelm's late mother was a graduate of Bryn Mawr. He was the only member of the family who had no education. This was another sore point. His father was ashamed of him.

But he had heard the old man bragging to another old man, saying: "My son is a sales executive. He didn't have the patience to finish school. But he does all right for himself. His income is up in the five figures somewhere."

"What—thirty, forty thousand?" said his stooped old friend.

"Well, he needs at least that much for his style of life. Yes, he needs that."

Despite his troubles, Wilhelm almost laughed. Why, that boasting old hypocrite. He knew the sales executive was no more. For many weeks there had been no executive, no sales, no income. But how we love looking fine in the eyes of the world—how beautiful are the old when they are doing a snow job! It's Dad, thought Wilhelm, who is the salesman. He's selling me. *He* should have gone on the road.

But what of the truth? Ah, the truth was that there were problems, and of these problems his father wanted no part. His father was ashamed of him. The truth, Wilhelm thought, was very awkward. He pressed his lips together, and his tongue went soft; it pained him far at the back, in the cords and throat, and a knot of ill formed in his chest. Dad never was a pal to me when I was young, he reflected. He was at the office or the hospital, or lecturing. He expected me to look out for myself and never gave me much thought. Now he looks down on me. And maybe in some respects he's right.

No wonder Wilhelm delayed the moment when he would have to go into the dining room. He had moved to the end of Rubin's counter. He had opened the *Tribune;* the fresh pages drooped from his hands; the cigar was smoked out and the hat did not defend him. He was wrong to suppose that he was more capable than the next fellow when it came to concealing his troubles. They were clearly written out upon his face. He wasn't even aware of it.

There was the matter of the different names, which, in the hotel, came up frequently. "Are you Doctor Adler's son?" "Yes, but my name is Tommy Wilhelm." And the doctor would say, "My son and I use different monickers. I uphold tradition. He's for the new." The Tommy was Wilhelm's own invention. He adopted it when he went to Hollywood, and dropped the Adler. Hollywood was his own idea, too. He used to pretend that it had all been the doing of a certain talent scout named Maurice Venice. But the scout had never made him a definite offer of a studio connection. He had approached him, but the results of the screen tests had not been good. After the test Wilhelm took the initiative and pressed Maurice Venice until he got him to say, "Well, I suppose you might make it out there." On the strength of this Wilhelm had left college and had gone to California.

Someone had said, and Wilhelm agreed with the saying, that in Los Angeles all the loose objects in the country were collected, as if America had been tilted and everything that wasn't tightly screwed down had slid into Southern California. He himself had been one of these loose objects. Sometimes he told people, "I was too mature for college. I was a big boy, you see. Well, I thought, when do you start to become a man?" After he had driven a painted flivver and had worn a yellow slicker with slogans on it, and played illegal poker, and gone out on Coke dates, he had *had* college. He wanted to try something new and quarreled with his parents about his career. And then a letter came from Maurice Venice.

The story of the scout was long and intricate and there were several versions of it. The truth about it was never told. Wilhelm had lied first boastfully and then out of charity to himself. But his memory was good, he could still separate what he had invented from the actual happenings, and this morning he found it necessary as he stood by Rubin's showcase with his *Tribune* to recall the crazy course of the true events.

I didn't seem even to realize that there was a depression. How could I have been such a jerk as not to prepare for anything and just go on luck and inspiration? With round gray eyes expanded and his large shapely lips closed in severity toward himself he forced open all that had been hidden. Dad I couldn't affect one way or another. Mama was the one who tried to stop me, and we carried on and yelled and pleaded. The more I lied the louder I raised my voice, and charged—like a hippopotamus. Poor Mother! How I disappointed her. Rubin heard Wilhelm give a broken sign as he stood with the forgotten *Tribune* crushed under his arm.

When Wilhelm was aware that Rubin watched him, loitering and idle, apparently not knowing what to do with himself this morning, he turned to the Coca-Cola machine. He swallowed hard at the Coke bottle and coughed over it, but he ignored his coughing, for he was still thinking, his eyes upcast and his lips closed behind his hand. By a peculiar twist of habit he wore his coat collar turned up always, as though there were a wind. It never lay flat. But on his broad back, stooped with its own weight, its strength warped almost into deformity, the collar of his sports coat appeared anyway to be no wider than a ribbon.

He was listening to the sound of his own voice as he explained, twenty-five years ago in the living room on West End Avenue, "But Mother, if I don't pan out as an actor I can still go back to school."

But she was afraid he was going to destroy himself. She said, "Wilky, Dad could make it easy for you if you wanted to go into medicine." To remember this stifled him.

"I can't bear hospitals. Besides, I might make a mistake and hurt someone or even kill a patient. I couldn't stand that. Besides, I haven't got that sort of brains."

Then his mother made the mistake of mentioning her nephew Artie, Wilhelm's cousin, who was an honor student at Columbia in math and languages. That dark little gloomy Artie with his disgusting narrow face, and his moles and self-sniffing ways and his unclean table manners, the boring habit he had of conjugating verbs when you want for a walk with him. "Roumanian is an easy language. You just add a *tl* to everything." He was now a professor, this same Artie with whom Wilhelm had played near the soldiers' and sailors' monument on Riverside Drive. Not that to be a professor was in itself so great. How could anyone bear to know so many languages? And Artie also had to remain Artie, which was a bad deal. But perhaps success had changed him. Now that he had a place in the world perhaps he was better. Did Artie love his languages, and live for them, or was he also, in his heart, cynical? So many people nowadays were. No one seemed satisfied, and Wilhelm was especially horrified by the cynicism of successful people. Cynicism was bread and meat to everyone. And irony, too. Maybe it couldn't be helped. It was probably even necessary. Wilhelm, however, feared it intensely. Whenever at the end of the day he was unusually fatigued he attributed it to cynicism. Too much of the world's business done. Too much falsity. He had various words to express the effect this had on him. Chicken! Unclean! Congestion! he exclaimed in his heart. Rat race! Phony! Murder! Play the Game! Buggers!

At first the letter from the talent scout was nothing but a flattering sort of joke. Wilhelm's picture in the college paper when he was running for class treasurer was seen by Maurice Venice, who wrote to him about a screen test. Wilhelm at once took the train to New York. He found the scout to be huge and oxlike, so stout that his arms seemed caught from beneath in a grip of flesh and fat; it looked as though it must be positively painful. He had little hair. Yet he enjoyed a healthy complexion. His breath was noisy and his voice rather difficult and husky because of the fat in his throat. He had on a double-breasted suit of the type then known as the pillbox; it was chalk-striped, pink on blue; the trousers hugged his ankles.

They met and shook hands and sat down. Together these two big men dwarfed the tiny Broadway office and made the furnishings look like toys. Wilhelm had the color of a Golden Grimes apple when he was well, and then his thick blond hair had been vigorous and his wide shoulders unwarped; he was leaner in the jaws, his eyes fresher and wider; his legs were then still awkward but he was impressively handsome. And he was about to make his first great mistake. Like, he sometimes thought, I was going to pick up a weapon and strike myself a blow with it.

Looming over the desk in the small office darkened by overbuilt midtown—sheer walls, gray spaces, dry lagoons of tar and pebbles—Maurice Venice proceeded to establish his credentials. He said, "My letter was on the regular stationery, but maybe you want to check on me?"

"Who, *me?*" said Wilhelm. "Why?"

"There's guys who think I'm in a racket and make a charge for the test. I don't ask a cent. I'm no agent. There ain't no commission."

"I never even thought of it," said Wilhelm. Was there perhaps something fishy about this Maurice Venice? He protested too much.

In his husky, fat-weakened voice he finally challenged Wilhelm, "If you're not sure, you can call the distributor and find out who I am, Maurice Venice."

Wilhelm wondered at him. "Why shouldn't I be sure? Of course I am."

"Because I can see the way you size me up, and because this is a dinky office. Like you don't believe me. Go ahead. Call. I won't care if you're cautious. I mean it. There's quite a few people who doubt me at first. They can't really believe that fame and fortune are going to hit 'em."

"But I tell you I do believe you," Wilhelm had said, and bent inward to accommodate the pressure of his warm, panting laugh. It was purely nervous. His neck was ruddy and neatly shaved about the ears—he was fresh from the barbershop; his face anxiously glowed with his desire to make a pleasing impression. It was all wasted on Venice, who was just as concerned about the impression *he* was making.

"If you're surprised, I'll just show you what I mean," Venice had said. "It was about fifteen months ago right in this identical same office when I saw a beautiful thing in the paper. It wasn't even a photo but a drawing, a brassière ad, but I knew right away that this was star material. I called up the paper to ask who the girl was, they gave me the name of the advertising agency; I phoned the agency and they gave me the name of the artist; I got hold of the artist and he gave me the number of the model agency. Finally, finally I got her number and phoned her and said, 'This is Maurice Venice, scout for Kaskaskia Films.' So right away she says, 'Yah, so's your old lady.' Well, when I saw I wasn't getting nowhere with her I said to her, 'Well, miss. I don't blame you. You're a very beautiful thing and must have a dozen admirers after you all the time, boy friends who like to call and pull your leg and give a tease. But as I happen to be a very busy fellow and don't have the time to horse around or argue, I tell you what to do. Here's my number, and here's the number of the Kaskaskia Distributors, Inc. Ask them who am I, Maurice Venice. The scout.' She did it. A little while later she phoned me back, all apologies and excuses, but I didn't want to embarrass her and get off on the wrong foot with an artist. I know better than to do that. So I told her it was a natural precaution, never mind. I wanted to run a screen test right away. Because I seldom am wrong about talent. If I see it, it's there. Get that, please. And do you know who that little girl is today?"

"No," Wilhelm said eagerly. "Who is she?"

Venice said impressively, " 'Nita Christenberry."

Wilhelm sat utterly blank. This was failure. He didn't know the name, and Venice was waiting for his response and would be angry.

And in fact Venice had been offended. He said, "What's the matter with you! Don't you read a magazine? She's a starlet."

"I'm sorry," Wilhelm answered. "I'm at school and don't have time to keep up. If I don't know her, it doesn't mean a thing. She made a big hit, I'll bet."

"You can say that again. Here's a photo of her." He handed Wilhelm some pictures. She was a bathing beauty—short, the usual breasts, hips, and smooth thighs. Yes, quite good, as Wilhelm recalled. She stood on high heels and wore a Spanish comb and mantilla. In her hand was a fan.

He had said, "She looks awfully peppy."

"Isn't she a divine girl? And what personality! Not just another broad in the show business, believe me." He had a surprise for Wilhelm. "I have found happiness with her," he said.

"You have?" said Wilhelm, slow to understand.

"Yes, boy, we're engaged."

Wilhelm saw another photograph, taken on the beach. Venice was dressed in a terry-cloth beach outfit, and he and the girl, cheek to cheek, were looking into the camera. Below, in white ink, was written "Love at Malibu Colony."

"I'm sure you'll be very happy. I wish you—"

"I *know*," said Venice firmly, "I'm going to be happy. When I saw that drawing, the breath of fate breathed on me. I felt it over my entire body."

"Say, it strikes a bell suddenly," Wilhelm had said. "Aren't you related to Martial Venice the producer?

Venice was either a nephew of the producer or the son of a first cousin. Decidedly he had not made good. It was easy enough for Wilhelm to see this now. The office was so poor, and Venice bragged so nervously and identified himself so scrupulously—the poor guy. He was the obscure failure of an aggressive and powerful clan. As such he had the greatest sympathy from Wilhelm.

Venice had said, "Now I suppose you want to know where you come in. I seen your school paper, by accident. You take quite a remarkable picture."

"It can't be so much," said Wilhelm, more panting than laughing.

"You don't want to tell me my business," Venice said. "Leave it to me. I studied up on this."

"I never imagined— Well, what kind of roles do you think I'd fit?"

"All this time that we've been talking, I've been watching. Don't think I haven't. You remind me of someone. Let's see who it can be—one of the great old-timers. Is it Milton Sills? No, that's not the one. Conway Tearle, Jack Mulhall? George Bancroft? No, his face was ruggeder. One thing I can tell you, though, a George Raft type you're not—those tough, smooth, black little characters."

"No, I wouldn't seem to be."

"No, you're not that flyweight type, with the fists, from a nightclub, and the glamorous sideburns, doing the tango or the bolero. Not Edward G. Robinson, either—I'm thinking aloud. Or the Cagney fly-in-your-face role, a cabbie, with that mouth and those punches."

"I realize that."

"Not suave like William Powell, or a lyric juvenile like Buddy Rogers. I suppose you don't play the sax? No. But—"

"But what?"

"I have you placed as the type that loses the girl to the George Raft type or the William Powell type. You are steady, faithful, you get stood up. The older women would know better. The mothers are on your side. With what they been through, if it was up to them, they'd take you in a minute. You're very sympathetic, even the young girls feel that. You'd make a good provider. But they go more for the other types. It's as clear as anything."

This was not how Wilhelm saw himself. And as he surveyed the old ground he recognized now that he had been not only confused but hurt. Why, he thought, he cast me even then for a loser.

Wilhelm had said, with half a mind to be defiant, "Is that your opinion?"

It never occurred to Venice that a man might object to stardom in such a role. "Here is your chance," he said. "Now you're just in college. What are you studying?" He snapped his fingers. "Stuff." Wilhelm himself felt this way about it. "You may plug along fifty years before you get anywheres. This way, in one jump, the world knows who you are. You become a name like Roosevelt, Swanson. From east to west, out to China, into South America. This is no bunk. You become a lover to the whole world. The world wants it, needs it. One fellow smiles, a billion people also smile. One fellow cries, the other billion sob with him. Listen, bud—" Venice had pulled himself together to make an effort. On his imagination there was some great weight which he could not discharge. He wanted Wilhelm, too, to feel it. He twisted his large, clean, well-meaning, rather foolish features as though he were their unwilling captive, and said in his choked, fat-obstructed voice, "Listen, everywhere there are people trying hard, miserable, in trouble, downcast, tired, trying and trying. They need a break, right? A break through, a help, luck or sympathy."

"That certainly is the truth," said Wilhelm. He had seized the feeling and he waited for Venice to go on. But Venice had no more to say; he had concluded. He gave Wilhelm several pages of blue hectographed script, stapled together, and told him to prepare for the screen test. "Study your lines in front of a mirror," he said. "Let yourself go. The part should take ahold of you. Don't be afraid to make faces and be emotional. Shoot the works. Because when you start to act you're no more an ordinary person, and those things don't apply to you. You don't behave the same way as the average."

And so Wilhelm had never returned to Penn State. His roommate sent his things to New York for him, and the school authorities had to write to Dr. Adler to find out what had happened.

Still, for three months Wilhelm delayed his trip to California. He wanted to start out with the blessings of his family, but they were never given. He quarreled with his parents and his sister. And then, when he was best aware of the risks and knew a hundred reasons against going and had made himself sick with fear, he left home. This was typical of Wilhelm. After much thought and hesitation and debate he invariably took the course he had rejected innumerable times. Ten such decisions made up the history of his life. He had decided that it would be a bad mistake to go to Hollywood, and then he went. He had made up his mind not to marry his wife, but ran off and got married. He had resolved not to invest money with Tamkin, and then had given him a check.

But Wilhelm had been eager for life to start. College was merely another delay. Venice had approached him and said that the world had named Wilhelm to shine before it. He was to be freed from the anxious and narrow life of the average. Moreover, Venice had claimed that he never made a mistake. His instinct for talent was infallible, he said.

But when Venice saw the results of the screen test he did a quick about-face. In those days Wilhelm had had a speech difficulty. It was not a true stammer, it was a thickness of speech which the sound track exaggerated. The film showed that he had many peculiarities, otherwise unnoticeable. When he shrugged, his hands drew up within his sleeves. The vault of his chest was huge, but he really didn't look strong under the lights. Though he called himself a hippopotamus, he more nearly resembled a bear. His walk was bearlike, quick and rather soft, toes turned inward, as though his shoes were an impediment. About one thing Venice had been right. Wilhelm was photogenic, and his wavy blond hair (now graying) came out well, but after the test Venice refused to encourage him. He tried to get rid of him. He couldn't afford to take a chance on him, he had made too many mistakes already and lived in fear of his powerful relatives.

Wilhelm had told his parents, "Venice says I owe it to myself to go." How ashamed he was now of this lie! He had begged Venice not to give him up. He had said, "Can't you help me out? It would kill me to get back to school now."

Then when he reached the Coast he learned that a recommendation from Maurice Venice was the kiss of death. Venice needed help and charity more than he, Wilhelm, ever had. A few years later when Wilhelm was down on his luck and working as an orderly in a Los Angeles hospital, he saw Venice's picture in the papers. He was under indictment for pandering. Closely following the trial, Wilhelm found out that Venice had indeed been employed by Kaskaskia Films but that he had evidently made use of the connection to organize a ring of call girls. Then what did he want with me? Wilhelm had cried to himself. He was unwilling to believe anything very bad about Venice. Perhaps he was foolish and unlucky, a fall guy, a dupe, a sucker. You didn't give a man fifteen years in prison for that. Wilhelm often thought that he might write him a letter to say how sorry he was. He remembered the breath of fate and Venice's certainty that he would be happy. 'Nita Christenberry was sentenced to three years. Wilhelm recognized her although she had changed her name.

By that time Wilhelm too had taken his new name. In California he became Tommy Wilhelm. Dr. Adler would not accept the change. Today he still called his son Wilky, as he had done for more than forty years. Well, now, Wilhelm was thinking, the paper crowded in disarray under his arm, there's really very little that a man can change at will. He can't change his lungs, or nerves, or constitution or temperament. They're not under his control. When he's young and strong and impulsive and dissatisfied with the way things are he wants to rearrange them to assert his freedom. He can't overthrow the government or be differently born; he only has a little scope and maybe a foreboding, too, that essentially you can't change. Nevertheless, he makes a gesture and becomes Tommy Wilhelm. Wilhelm had always had a great longing to be Tommy. He had never, however, succeeded in feeling like Tommy, and in his soul had always remained Wilky. When he was drunk he reproached himself horribly as Wilky. "You fool, you clunk, you Wilky!" he called himself. He thought that it was a good thing perhaps that he had not become a success as Tommy since that would not have been a genuine success. Wilhelm would have feared that not he but Tommy had brought it off, cheating Wilky of his birthright. Yes, it had been a stupid thing to do, but it was his imperfect judgment at the age of twenty which should be blamed. He had cast off his father's name, and with it his father's opinion of him. It was, he knew it was, his bid for liberty, Adler being in his mind the title of the species, Tommy the freedom of the person. But Wilky was his inescapable self.

In middle age you no longer thought such thoughts about free choice. Then it came over you that from one grandfather you had inherited such and such a head of hair which looked like honey when it whitens or sugars in the jar; from another, broad thick shoulders; an oddity of speech from one uncle, and small teeth from another, and the gray eyes with darkness diffused even into the whites, and a wide-lipped mouth like a statue from Peru. Wandering races have such looks, the bones of one tribe, the skin of another. From his mother he had gotten sensitive feelings, a soft heart, a brooding nature, a tendency to be confused under pressure.

The changed name was a mistake, and he would admit it as freely as you liked. But this mistake couldn't be undone now, so why must his father continually remind him how he had sinned? It was too late. He would have to go back to the pathetic day when the sin was committed. And where was that day? Past and dead. Whose humiliating memories were these? His and not his father's. What had he to think back on that he could call good? Very, very little. You had to forgive. First, to forgive yourself, and then general forgiveness. Didn't he suffer from his mistakes far more than his father could?

"Oh, God," Wilhelm prayed. "Let me out of my trouble. Let me out of my thoughts, and let me do something better with myself. For all the time I have wasted I am very sorry. Let me out of the clutch and into a different life. For I am all balled up. Have mercy."

II

The mail.

The clerk who gave it to him did not care what sort of appearance he made this morning. He only glanced at him from under his brows, upward, as the letters changed hands. Why should the hotel people waste courtesies on him? They had his number. The clerk knew that he was handing him, along with the letters, a bill for his rent. Wilhelm assumed a look that removed him from all such things. But it was bad. To pay the bill he would have to withdraw money from his brokerage account, and the account was being watched because of the drop in lard. According to the *Tribune*'s figures lard was still twenty points below last year's level. There were government price supports. Wilhelm didn't know how these worked but he understood that the farmer was protected and that the SEC kept an eye on the market and therefore he believed that lard would rise again and he wasn't greatly worried as yet. But in the meantime his father might have offered to pick up his hotel tab. Why didn't he? What a selfish old man he was! He saw his son's hardships; he could so easily help him. How little it would mean to him, and how much to Wilhelm! Where was the old man's heart? Maybe, thought Wilhelm, I was sentimental in the past and exaggerated his kindliness—warm family life. It may never have been there.

Not long ago his father had said to him in his usual affable, pleasant way, "Well, Wilky, here we are under the same roof again, after all these years."

Wilhelm was glad for an instant. At last they would talk over old times. But he was also on guard against insinuations. Wasn't his father saying, "Why are you here in a hotel with me and not at home in Brooklyn with your wife and two boys? You're neither a widower nor a bachelor. You have brought me all your confusions. What do you expect me to do with them?"

So Wilhelm studied the remark for a bit, then said, "The roof is twenty-six stories up. But how many years has it been?"

"That's what I was asking you."

"Gosh, Dad, I'm not sure. Wasn't it the year Mother died? What year was that?"

He asked this question with an innocent frown on his Golden Grimes, dark blond face. *What year was it!* As though he didn't know the year, the month, the day, the very hour of his mother's death.

"Wasn't it nineteen-thirty-one?" said Dr. Adler.

"Oh, was it?" said Wilhelm. And in hiding the sadness and the overwhelming irony of the question he gave a nervous shiver and wagged his head and felt the ends of his collar rapidly.

"Do you know?" his father said. "You must realize, an old fellow's memory becomes unreliable. It was in winter, that I'm sure of. Nineteen-thirty-two?"

Yes, it was age. Don't make an issue of it, Wilhelm advised himself. If you were to ask the old doctor in what year he had interned, he'd tell you correctly. All the same, don't make an issue. Don't quarrel with your own father. Have pity on an old man's failings.

"I believe the year was closer to nineteen-thirty-four, Dad," he said.

But Dr. Adler was thinking, Why the devil can't he stand still when we're talking? He's either hoisting his pants up and down by the pockets or jittering with his feet. A regular mountain of tics, he's getting to be. Wilhelm had a habit of moving his feet back and forth as though, hurrying into a house, he had to clean his shoes first on the doormat.

Then Wilhem had said, "Yes, that was the beginning of the end, wasn't it, Father?"

Wilhelm often astonished Dr. Adler. Beginning of the end? What could he mean—what was he fishing for? Whose end? The end of family life? The old man was puzzled but he would not give Wilhelm an opening to introduce his complaints. He had learned that it was better not to take up Wilhelm's strange challenges. So he merely agreed pleasantly, for he was a master of social behavior, and said, "It was an awful misfortune for us all."

He thought, What business has he to complain to *me* of his mother's death?

Face to face they had stood, each declaring himself silently after his own way. It was: it was not, the beginning of the end—*some* end.

Unaware of anything odd in his doing it, for he did it all the time. Wilhelm had punched out the coal of his cigarette and dropped the butt in his pocket, where there were many more. And as he gazed at his father the little finger of his right hand began to twitch and tremble; of that he was unconscious, too.

And yet Wilhelm believed that when he put his mind to it he could have perfect and even distinguished manners, outdoing his father. Despite the slight thickness in his speech—it amounted almost to a stammer when he started the same phrase over several times in his effort to eliminate the thick sound—he could be fluent. Otherwise he would never have made a good salesman. He claimed also that he was a good listener. When he listened he made a tight mouth and rolled his eyes thoughtfully. He would soon tire and begin to utter short, loud, impatient breaths, and he would say, "Oh yes . . . yes . . . yes. I couldn't agree more." When he was forced to differ he would declare, "Well, I'm not sure. I don't really see it that way. I'm of two minds about it." He would never willingly hurt any man's feelings.

But in conversation with his father he was apt to lose control of himself. After any talk with Dr. Adler, Wilhelm generally felt dissatisfied, and his dissatisfaction reached its greatest intensity when they discussed family matters. Ostensibly he had been trying to help the old man to remember a date, but in reality he meant to tell him, "You were set free when Ma died. You wanted to forget her. You'd like to get rid of Catherine, too. Me, too. You're not kidding anyone"—Wilhelm striving to put this cross, and the old man not having it. In the end he was left struggling, while his father seemed unmoved.

And then once more Wilhelm had said to himself, "But man! you're not a kid. Even then you weren't a kid!" He looked down over the front of his big, indecently big, spoiled body. He was beginning to lose his shape, his gut was fat, and he looked like a hippopotamus. His younger son called him "a hummuspotamus"; that was little Paul. And here he was still struggling with his old dad, filled with ancient grievances. Instead of saying, "Good-by, youth! Oh, good-by those marvelous, foolish wasted days. What a big clunk I was—I *am*."

Wilhelm was still paying heavily for his mistakes. His wife Margaret would not give him a divorce, and he had to support her and the two children. She would regularly agree to divorce him, and then think things over again and set new and more difficult conditions. No court would have awarded her the amounts he paid. One of today's letters, as he had expected, was from her. For the first time he had sent her a postdated check, and she protested. She also enclosed bills for the boys' educational insurance policies, due next week. Wilhelm's mother-in-law had taken out these policies in Beverly Hills, and since her death two years ago he had to pay the premiums. Why couldn't she have minded her own business! They were his kids and he took care of them and always would. He had planned to set up a trust fund. But that was on his former expectations. Now he had to rethink the future, because of the money problem. Meanwhile, here were the bills to be paid. When he saw the two sums punched out so neatly on the cards he cursed the company and its IBM equipment. His heart and his head were congested with anger. Everyone was supposed to have money. It was nothing to the company. It published pictures of funerals in the magazines and frightened the suckers, and then punched out little holes, and the customers would lie awake to think out ways to raise the dough. They'd be ashamed not to have it. They couldn't let a great company down, either, and they got the scratch. In the old days a man was put in prison for debt, but there were subtler things now. They made it a shame not to have money and set everybody to work.

Well, and what else had Margaret sent him? He tore the envelope open with his thumb, swearing that he would send any other bills back to her. There was, luckily, nothing more. He put the holepunched cards in his pocket. Didn't Margaret know that he was nearly at the end of his rope? Of course. Her instinct told her that this was her opportunity, and she was giving him the works.

He went into the dining room, which was under Austro-Hungarian management at the Hotel Gloriana. It was run like a European establishment. The pastries were excellent, especially the strudel. He often had apple strudel and coffee in the afternoon.

As soon as he entered he saw his father's small head in the sunny bay at the farther end, and heard his precise voice. It was with an odd sort of perilous expression that Wilhelm crossed the dining room.

Dr. Adler liked to sit in a corner that looked across Broadway down to the Hudson and New Jersey. On the other side of the street was a supermodern cafeteria with gold and purple mosaic columns. On the second floor a private-eye school, a dental laboratory, a reducing parlor, a veteran's club, and a Hebrew school shared the space. The old man was sprinkling sugar on his strawberries. Small hoops of brilliance were cast by the water glasses on the white tablecloth, despite a faint murkiness in the sunshine. It was early summer, and the long window was turned inward; a moth was on the pane; the putty was broken and the white enamel on the frames was streaming with wrinkles.

"Ha, Wilky," said the old man to his tardy son. "You haven't met our neighbor Mr. Perls, have you? From the fifteenth floor."

"How d'do," Wilhelm said. He did not welcome this stranger; he began at once to find fault with him. Mr. Perls carried a heavy cane with a crutch tip. Dyed hair, a skinny forehead—these were not reasons for bias. Nor was it Mr. Perls's fault that Dr. Adler was using him, not wishing to have breakfast with his son alone. But a gruffer voice within Wilhelm spoke, asking, "Who is this damn frazzle-faced herring with his dyed hair and his fish teeth and this drippy mustache? Another one of Dad's German friends. Where does he collect all these guys? What is the stuff on his teeth? I never saw such pointed crowns. Are they stainless steel, or a kind of silver? How can a human face get into this condition. Uch!" Staring with his widely spaced gray eyes, Wilhelm sat, his broad back stooped under the sports jacket. He clasped his hands on the table with an implication of suppliance. Then he began to relent a little toward Mr. Perls, beginning at the teeth. Each of those crowns represented a tooth ground to the quick, and estimating a man's grief with his teeth as two per cent of the total, and adding to that his flight from Germany and the probable origin of his wincing wrinkles, not to be confused with the wrinkles of his smile, it came to a sizable load.

"Mr. Perls was a hosiery wholesaler," said Dr. Adler.

"Is this the son you told me was in the selling line?" said Mr. Perls.

Dr. Adler replied, "I have only this one son. One daughter. She was a medical technician before she got married—anesthetist. At one time she had an important position in Mount Sinai."

He couldn't mention his children without boasting. In Wilhelm's opinion, there was little to boast of. Catherine, like Wilhelm, was big and fair-haired. She had married a court reporter who had a pretty hard time of it. She had taken a professional name, too—Philippa. At forty she was still ambitious to become a painter. Wilhelm didn't venture to criticize her work. It didn't do much to him, he said, but then he was no critic. Anyway, he and his sister were generally on the outs and he didn't often see her paintings. She worked very hard, but there were fifty thousand people in New York with paints and brushes, each practically a law unto himself. It was the Tower of Babel in paint. *He* didn't want to go far into this. Things were chaotic all over.

Dr. Adler thought that Wilhelm looked particularly untidy this morning —unrested, too, his eyes red-rimmed from excessive smoking. He was breathing through his mouth and he was evidently much distracted and rolled his red-shot eyes barbarously. As usual, his coat collar was turned up as though he had had to go out in the rain. When he went to business he pulled himself together a little; otherwise he let himself go and looked like hell.

"What's the matter, Wilky, didn't you sleep last night?"

"Not very much."

"You take too many pills of every kind—first stimulants and then depressants, anodynes followed by analeptics, until the poor organism doesn't know what's happened. Then the luminal won't put people to sleep, and the Pervitin or Benzedrine won't wake them. God knows! These things get to be as serious as poisons, and yet everyone puts all their faith in them."

"No, Dad, it's not the pills. It's that I'm not used to New York any more. For a native, that's very peculiar, isn't it? It was never so noisy at night as now, and every little thing is a strain. Like the alternate parking. You have to run out at eight to move your car. And where can you put it? If you forget for a minute they tow you away. Then some fool puts advertising leaflets under your windshield wiper and you have heart failure a block away because you think you've got a ticket. When you do get stung with a ticket, you can't argue. You haven't got a chance in court and the city wants the revenue."

"But in your line you have to have a car, eh?" said Mr. Perls.

"Lord knows why any lunatic would want one in the city who didn't need it for his livelihood."

Wilhelm's old Pontiac was parked in the street. Formerly, when on an expense account, he had always put it up in a garage. Now he was afraid to move the car from Riverside Drive lest he lose his space, and he used it only on Saturdays when the Dodgers were playing in Ebbets Field and he took his boys to the game. Last Saturday, when the Dodgers were out of town, he had gone out to visit his mother's grave.

Dr. Adler had refused to go along. He couldn't bear his son's driving. Forgetfully, Wilhelm traveled for miles in second gear; he was seldom in the right lane and he neither gave signals nor watched for lights. The upholstery of his Pontiac was filthy with grease and ashes. One cigarette burned in the ashtray, another in his hand, a third on the floor with maps and other waste paper and Coca-Cola bottles. He dreamed at the wheel or argued and gestured, and therefore the old doctor would not ride with him.

Then Wilhelm had come back from the cemetery angry because the stone bench between his mother's and his grandmother's graves had been overturned and broken by vandals. "Those damn teen-age hoodlums get worse and worse," he said. "Why, they must have used a sledge-hammer to break the seat smack in half like that. If I could catch one of them!" He wanted the doctor to pay for a new seat, but his father was cool to the idea. He said he was going to have himself cremated.

Mr. Perls said, "I don't blame you if you get no sleep up where you are." His voice was tuned somewhat sharp, as though he were slightly deaf. "Don't you have Parigi the singing teacher there? God, they have some queer elements in this hotel. On which floor is that Estonian woman with all her cats and dogs? They should have made her leave long ago."

"They've moved her down to twelve," said Dr. Adler.

Wilhelm ordered a large Coca-Cola with his breakfast. Working in secret at the small envelopes in his pocket, he found two pills by touch. Much fingering had worn and weakened the paper. Under cover of a napkin he swallowed a Phenaphen sedative and a Unicap, but the doctor was sharp-eyed and said, "Wilky, what are you taking now?"

"Just my vitamin pills." He put his cigar butt in an ashtray on the table behind him, for his father did not like the odor. Then he drank his Coca-Cola.

"That's what you drink for breakfast, and not orange juice?" said Mr. Perls. He seemed to sense that he would not lose Dr. Adler's favor by taking an ironic tone with his son.

"The caffeine stimulates brain activity," said the old doctor. "It does all kinds of things to the respiratory center."

"It's just a habit of the road, that's all," Wilhelm said. "If you drive around long enough it turns your brains, your stomach, and everything else."

His father explained, "Wilky used to be with the Rojax Corporation. He was their northeastern sales representative for a good many years but recently ended the connection."

"Yes," said Wilhelm, "I was with them from the end of the war." He sipped the Coca-Cola and chewed the ice, glancing at one and the other with his attitude of large, shaky, patient dignity. The waitress set two boiled eggs before him.

"What kind of line does this Rojax company manufacture?" said Mr. Perls.

"Kiddies' furniture. Little chairs, rockers, tables, Jungle-Gyms, slides, swings, seesaws."

Wilhelm let his father do the explaining. Large and stiff-backed, he tried to sit patiently, but his feet were abnormally restless. All right! His father had to impress Mr. Perls? He would go along once more, and play his part. Fine! He would play along and help his father maintain his style. Style was the main consideration. That was just fine!

"I was with the Rojax Corporation for almost ten years," he said. "We parted ways because they wanted me to share my territory. They took a son-in-law into the business—a new fellow. It was his idea."

To himself, Wilhelm said, Now God alone can tell why I have to lay my whole life bare to this blasted herring here. I'm sure nobody else does it. Other people keep their business to themselves. Not me.

He continued, "But the rationalization was that it was too big a territory tor one man. I had a monopoly. That wasn't so. The real reason was that they had gotten to the place where they would have to make me an officer of the corporation. Vice presidency. I was in line for it, but instead this son-in-law got in, and—"

Dr. Adler thought Wilhelm was discussing his grievances much too openly and said, "My son's income was up in the five figures."

As soon as money was mentioned, Mr. Perls's voice grew eagerly sharper. "Yes? What, the thirty-two-per-cent bracket? Higher even, I guess?" He asked for a hint, and he named the figures not idly but with a sort of hugging relish. Uch! How they love money, thought Wilhelm. They adore money! Holy money! Beautiful money! It was getting so that people were feeble-minded about everything except money. While if you didn't have it you were a dummy, a dummy! You had to excuse yourself from the face of the earth. Chicken! that's what it was. The world's business. If only he could find a way out of it.

Such thinking brought on the usual congestion. It would grow into a fit of passion if he allowed it to continue. Therefore he stopped talking and began to eat.

Before he struck the egg with his spoon he dried the moisture with his napkin. Then he battered it (in his father's opinion) more than was necessary. A faint grime was left by his fingers on the white of the egg after he had picked away the shell. Dr. Adler saw it with silent repugnance. What a Wilky he had given to the world! Why, he didn't even wash his hands in the morning. He used an electric razor so that he didn't have to touch water. The doctor couldn't bear Wilky's dirty habits. Only once—and never again, he swore—had he visited his room. Wilhelm, in pajamas and stockings had sat on his bed, drinking gin from a coffee mug and rooting for the Dodgers on television. "That's two and two on you, Duke. Come on—hit it, now." He came down on the mattress—bam! The bed looked kicked to pieces. Then he drank the gin as though it were tea, and urged his team on with his fist. The smell of dirty clothes was outrageous. By the bedside lay a quart bottle and foolish magazines and mystery stories for the hours of insomnia. Wilhelm lived in worse filth than a savage. When the Doctor spoke to him about this he answered, "Well, I have no wife to look after my things." And who—*who!*—had done the leaving? Not Margaret. The Doctor was certain that she wanted him back.

Wilhelm drank his coffee with a trembling hand. In his full face his abused bloodshot gray eyes moved back and forth. Jerkily he set his cup back and put half the length of a cigarette into his mouth; he seemed to hold it with his teeth, as though it were a cigar.

"I can't let them get away with it," he said. "It's also a question of morale."

His father corrected him. "Don't you mean a moral question, Wilky?"

"I mean that, too. I have to do something to protect myself. I was promised executive standing." Correction before a stranger mortified him, and his dark blond face changed color, more pale, and then more dark. He went on talking to Perls but his eyes spied on his father. "I was the one who opened the territory for them. I could go back for one of their competitors and take away their customers. *My* customers. Morale enters into it because they've tried to take away my confidence."

"Would you offer a different line to the same people?" Mr. Perls wondered.

"Why not? I know what's wrong with the Rojax product."

"Nonsense," said his father. "Just nonsense and kid's talk, Wilky. You're only looking for trouble and embarrassment that way. What would you gain by such a silly feud? You have to think about making a living and meeting your obligations."

Hot and bitter, Wilhelm said with pride, while his feet moved angrily under the table, "I don't have to be told about my obligations. I've been meeting them for years. In more than twenty years I've never had a penny of help from anybody. I preferred to dig a ditch on the WPA but never asked anyone to meet my obligations for me."

"Wilky has had all kinds of experiences," said Dr. Adler.

The old doctor's face had a wholesome reddish and almost translucent color, like a ripe apricot. The wrinkles beside his ears were deep because the skin conformed so tightly to his bones. With all his might, he was a healthy and fine small old man. He wore a white vest of a light check pattern. His hearing-aid doodad was in the pocket. An unusual shirt of red and black stripes covered his chest. He bought his clothes in a college shop farther uptown. Wilhelm thought he had no business to get himself up like a jockey, out of respect for his profession.

"Well," said Mr. Perls. "I can understand how you feel. You want to fight it out. By a certain time of life, to have to start all over again can't be a pleasure, though a good man can always do it. But anyway you want to keep on with a business you know already, and not have to meet a whole lot of new contacts."

Wilhelm again thought, Why does it have to be me and my life that's discussed, and not him and his life? He would never allow it. But I am an idiot. I have no reserve. To me it can be done. I talk. I must ask for it. Everybody wants to have intimate conversations, but the smart fellows don't give out, only the fools. The smart fellows talk intimately about the fools, and examine them all over and give them advice. Why do I allow it? The hint about his age had hurt him. No, you can't admit it's as good as ever, he conceded. Things do give out.

"In the meanwhile," Dr. Adler said, "Wilky is taking it easy and considering various propositions. Isn't that so?"

"More or less," said Wilhelm. He suffered his father to increase Mr. Perls's respect for him. The WPA ditch had brought the family into contempt. He was a little tired. The spirit, the peculiar burden of his existence lay upon him like an accretion, a load, a hump. In any moment of quiet, when sheer fatigue prevented him from struggling, he was apt to feel this mysterious weight, this growth or collection of nameless things which it was the business of his life to carry about. That must be what a man was for. This large, odd, excited, fleshy, blond, abrupt personality named Wilhelm, or Tommy, was here, present, in the present—Dr. Tamkin had been putting into his mind many suggestions about the present moment, the here and now—this Wilky, or Tommy Wilhelm, forty-four years old, father of two sons, at present living in the Hotel Gloriana, was assigned to be the carrier of a load which was his own self, his characteristic self. There was no figure or estimate for the value of his load. But it is probably exaggerated by the subject, T. W. Who is a visionary sort of animal. Who has to believe that he can know why he exists. Though he has never seriously tried to find out why.

Mr. Perls said, "If he wants time to think things over and have a rest, why doesn't he run down to Florida for a while? Off season it's cheap and quite. Fairyland. The mangoes are just coming in. I got two acres down there. You'd think you were in India."

Mr. Perls utterly astonished Wilhelm when he spoke of fairyland with a foreign accent. Mangoes—India? What did he mean, India?

"Once upon a time," said Wilhelm, "I did some public-relations work for a big hotel down in Cuba. If I could get them a notice in Leonard Lyons or one of the other columns it might be good for another holiday there, gratis. I haven't had a vacation for a long time, and I could stand a rest after going so hard. You know that's true, Father." He meant that his father knew how deep the crisis was becoming; how badly he was strapped for money; and that he could not rest but would be crushed if he stumbled; and that his obligations would destroy him. He couldn't falter. He thought, The money! When I had it, I flowed money. They bled it away from me. I hemorrhaged money. But now it's almost all gone, and where am I supposed to turn for more?

He said, "As a matter of fact, Father, I am tired as hell."

But Mr. Perls began to smile and said, "I understand from Doctor Tamkin that you're going into some kind of investment with him, partners."

"You know, he's a very ingenious fellow," said Dr. Adler. "I really enjoy hearing him go on. I wonder if he really is a medical doctor."

"Isn't he?" said Perls. "Everybody thinks he is. He talks about his patients. Doesn't he write prescriptions?"

"I don't really know what he does," said Dr. Adler. "He's a cunning man."

"He's a psychologist, I understand," said Wilhelm.

"I don't know what sort of psychologist or psychiatrist he may be," said his father. "He's a little vague. It's growing into a major industry, and a very expensive one. Fellows have to hold down very big jobs in order to pay those fees. Anyway, this Tamkin is clever. He never said he practiced here, but I believe he was a doctor in California. They don't seem to have much legislation out there to cover these things, and I hear a thousand dollars will get you a degree from a Los Angeles correspondence school. He gives the impression of knowing something about chemistry, and things like hypnotism. I wouldn't trust him, though."

"And why wouldn't you?" Wilhelm demanded.

"Because he's probably a liar. Do you believe he invented all the things he claims?"

Mr. Perls was grinning.

"He was written up in *Fortune*," said Wilhelm. "Yes, in *Fortune* magazine. He showed me the article. I've seen his clippings."

"That doesn't make him legitimate," said Dr. Adler. "It might have been another Tamkin. Make no mistake, he's an operator. Perhaps even crazy."

"Crazy, you say?"

Mr. Perls put in, "He could be both sane and crazy. In these days nobody can tell for sure which is which."

"An electrical device for truck drivers to wear in their caps," said Dr. Adler, describing one of Tamkin's proposed inventions. "To wake them with a shock when they begin to be drowsy at the wheel. It's triggered by the change in blood-pressure when they start to doze."

"It doesn't sound like such an impossible thing to me," said Wilhelm.

Mr. Perls said, "To me he described an underwater suit so a man could walk on the bed of the Hudson in case of an atomic attack. He said he could walk to Albany in it."

"Ha, ha, ha, ha, ha!" cried Dr. Adler in his old man's voice. "Tamkin's Folly. You could go on a camping trip under Niagara Falls."

"This is just his kind of fantasy," said Wilhelm. "It doesn't mean a thing. Inventors are supposed to be like that. I get funny ideas myself. Everybody wants to make something. Any American does."

But his father ignored this and said to Perls, "What other inventions did he describe?"

While the frazzle-faced Mr. Perls and his father in the unseemly, monkey-striped shirt were laughing, Wilhelm could not restrain himself and joined in with his own panting laugh. But he was in despair. They were laughing at the man to whom he had given a power of attorney over his last seven hundred dollars to speculate for him in the commodities market. They had bought all that lard. It had to rise today. By ten o'clock, or half-past ten, trading would be active, and he would see.

III

Between white tablecloths and glassware and glancing silverware, through overfull light, the long figure of Mr. Perls went away into the darkness of the lobby. He thrust with his cane, and dragged a large built-up shoe which Wilhelm had not included in his estimate of troubles. Dr. Adler wanted to talk about him. "There's a poor man," he said, "with a bone condition which is gradually breaking him up."

"One of those progressive diseases?" said Wilhelm.

"Very bad. I've learned," the doctor told him, "to keep my sympathy for the real ailments. This Perls is more to be pitied than any man I know."

Wilhelm understood he was being put on notice and did not express his opinion. He ate and ate. He did not hurry but kept putting food on his plate until he had gone through the muffins and his father's strawberries, and then some pieces of bacon that were left; he had several cups of coffee, and when he was finished he sat gigantically in a state of arrest and didn't seem to know what he should do next.

For a while father and son were uncommonly still. Wilhelm's preparations to please Dr. Adler had failed completely, for the old man kept thinking. You'd never guess he had a clean upbringing, and, What a dirty devil this son of mine is. Why can't he try to sweeten his appearance a little? Why does he want to drag himself like this? And he makes himself look so idealistic.

Wilhelm sat, mountainous. He was not really so slovenly as his father found him to be. In some aspects he even had a certain delicacy. His mouth, though broad, had a fine outline, and his brow and his gradually incurved nose, dignity, and in his blond hair there was white but there were also shades of gold and chestnut. When he was with the Rojax Corporation Wilhelm had kept a small apartment in Roxbury, two rooms in a large house with a small porch and garden, and on mornings of leisure, in late spring weather like this, he used to sit expanded in a wicker chair with the sunlight pouring through the weave, and sunlight through the slug-eaten holes of the young hollyhocks and as deeply as the grass allowed into small flowers. This peace (he forgot that that time had had its troubles, too), this peace was gone. It must not have belonged to him, really, for to be here in New York with his old father was more genuinely like his life. He was well aware that he didn't stand a chance of getting sympathy from his father, who said he kept his for real ailments. Moreover, he advised himself repeatedly not to discuss his vexatious problems with him, for his father, with some justice, wanted to be left in peace. Wilhelm also knew that when he began to talk about these things he made himself feel worse, he became congested with them and worked himself into a clutch. Therefore he warned himself, Lay off, pal. It'll only be an aggravation. From a deeper source, however, came other promptings. If he didn't keep his troubles before him he risked losing them altogether, and he knew by experience that this was worse. And furthermore, he could not succeed in excusing his father on the ground of old age. No. No, he could not. I am his son, he thought. He is my father. He is as much father as I am son—old or not. Affirming this, though in complete silence, he sat, and sitting, he kept his father at the table with him.

"Wilky," said the old man, "have you gone down to the baths here yet?"

"No, Dad, not yet."

"Well, you know the Gloriana has one of the finest pools in New York. Eighty feet, blue tile. It's a beauty."

Wilhelm had seen it. On the way to the gin game you passed the stairway to the pool. He did not care for the odor of the wall-locked and chlorinated water

"You ought to investigate the Russian and Turkish baths, and the sunlamps and massage. I don't hold with sunlamps. But the massage does a world of good, and there's nothing better than hydrotherapy when you come right down to it. Simple water has a calming effect and would do you more good than all the barbiturates and alcohol in the world."

Wilhelm reflected that this advice was as far as his father's help and sympathy would extend.

"I thought," he said, "that the water cure was for lunatics."

The doctor received this as one of his son's jokes and said with a smile, "Well, it won't turn a sane man into a lunatic. It does a great deal for me. I couldn't live without my massages and steam."

"You're probably right. I ought to try it one of these days. Yesterday, late in the afternoon, my head was about to bust and I just had to have a little air, so I walked around the reservoir, and I sat down for a while in a playground. It rests me to watch the kids play potsy and skiprope."

The doctor said with approval, "Well, now, that's more like the idea."

"It's the end of the lilacs," said Wilhelm. "When they burn it's the beginning of summer. At least, in the city. Around the time of year when the candy stores take down the windows and start to sell sodas on the sidewalk. But even though I was raised here, Dad, I can't take city life any more, and I miss the country. There's too much push here for me. It works me up too much. I take things too hard. I wonder why you never retired to a quieter place."

The doctor opened his small hand on the table in a gesture so old and so typical that Wilhelm felt it like an actual touch upon the foundations of his life. "I am a city boy myself, you must remember," Dr. Adler explained. "But if you find the city so hard on you, you ought to get out."

"I'll do that," said Wilhelm, "as soon as I can make the right connection. Meanwhile—"

His father interrupted, "Meanwhile I suggest you cut down on drugs."

"You exaggerate that, Dad. I don't really— I give myself a little boost against—" He almost pronounced the word "misery" but he kept his resolution not to complain.

The doctor, however, fell into the error of pushing his advice too hard. It was all he had to give his son and he gave it once more. "Water and exercise," he said.

He wants a young, smart, successful son, thought Wilhelm, and he said, "Oh, Father, it's nice of you to give me this medical advice, but steam isn't going to cure what ails me."

The doctor measurably drew back, warned by the sudden weak strain of Wilhelm's voice and all that the droop of his face, the swell of his belly against the restraint of his belt intimated.

"Some new business?" he asked unwillingly.

Wilhelm made a great preliminary summary which involved the whole of his body. He drew and held a long breath, and his color changed and his eyes swam. "New?" he said.

"You make too much of your problems," said the doctor. "They ought not to be turned into a career. Concentrate on real troubles—fatal sickness, accidents." The old man's whole manner said, Wilky, don't start this on me. I have a right to be spared.

Wilhelm himself prayed for restraint; he knew this weakness of his and fought it. He knew, also, his father's character. And he began mildly, "As far as the fatal part of it goes, everyone on this side of the grave is the same distance from death. No, I guess my trouble is not exactly new. I've got to pay premiums on two policies for the boys. Margaret sent them to me. She unloads everything on me. Her mother left her an income. She won't even file a joint tax return. I get stuck. Etcetera. But you've heard the whole story before."

"I certainly have," said the old man. "And I've told you to stop giving her so much money."

Wilhelm worked his lips in silence before he could speak. The congestion was growing. "Oh, but my kids, Father. My kids. I love them. I don't want them to lack anything."

The doctor said with a half-deaf benevolence. "Well, naturally. And she, I'll bet, is the beneficiary of that policy."

"Let her be. I'd sooner die myself before I collected a cent of such money."

"Ah yes." The old man sighed. He did not like the mention of death. "Did I tell you that your sister Catherine—Philippa—is after me again."

"What for?"

"She wants to rent a gallery for an exhibition."

Stiffly fair-minded, Wilhelm said, "Well, of course that's up to you, Father."

The round-headed old man with his fine, feather-white, ferny hair said, "No, Wilky. There's not a thing on those canvases. I don't believe it; it's a case of the emperor's clothes. I may be old enough for my second childhood, but at least the first is well behind me. I was glad enough to buy crayons for her when she was four. But now she's a woman of forty and too old to be encouraged in her delusions. She's no painter."

"I wouldn't go so far as to call her a born artist," said Wilhelm, "but you can't blame her for trying something worth while."

"Let her husband pamper her."

Wilhelm had done his best to be just to his sister, and he had sincerely meant to spare his father, but the old man's tight, benevolent deafness had its usual effect on him. He said, "When it comes to women and money, I'm completely in the dark. What makes Margaret act like this?"

"She's showing you that you can't make it without her," said the doctor. "She aims to bring you back by financial force."

"But if she ruins me, Dad, how can she expect me to come back? No, I have a sense of honor. What you don't see is that she's trying to put an end to me."

His father stared. To him this was absurd. And Wilhelm thought, Once a guy starts to slip, he figures he might as well be a clunk. A real big clunk. He even takes pride in it. But there's nothing to be proud of—hey, boy? Nothing. I don't blame Dad for his attitude. And it's no cause for pride.

"I don't understand that. But if you feel like this why don't you settle with her once and for all?"

"What do you mean, Dad?" said Wilhelm, surprised. "I thought I told you. Do you think I'm not willing to settle? Four years ago when we broke up I gave her everything—goods, furniture, savings. I tried to show good will, but I didn't get anywhere. Why when I wanted Scissors, the dog, because the animal and I were so attached to each other—it was bad enough to leave the kids—she absolutely refused me. Not that she cared a damn about the animal. I don't think you've seen him. He's an Australian sheep dog. They usually have one blank or whitish eye which gives a misleading look, but they're the gentlest dogs and have unusual delicacy about eating or talking. Let me at least have the companionship of this animal. Never." Wilhelm was greatly moved. He wiped his face at all corners with his napkin. Dr. Adler felt that his son was indulging himself too much in his emotions.

"Whenever she can hit me, she hits, and she seems to live for that alone. And she demands more and more, and still more. Two years ago she wanted to go back to college and get another degree. It increased my burden but I thought it would be wiser in the end if she got a better job through it. But still she takes as much from me as before. Next thing she'll want to be a Doctor of Philosophy. She says the women in her family live long, and I'll have to pay and pay for the rest of my life."

The doctor said impatiently, "Well, these are details, not principles. Just details which you can leave out. The dog! You're mixing up all kinds of irrelevant things. Go to a good lawyer."

"But I've already told you, Dad. I got a lawyer, and she got one, too, and both of them talk and send me bills, and I eat my heart out. Oh, Dad, Dad, what a hole I'm in!" said Wilhelm in utter misery. "The lawyers—see?—draw up an agreement, and she says okay on Monday and wants more money on Tuesday. And it begins again."

"I always thought she was a strange kind of woman," said Dr. Adler. He felt that by disliking Margaret from the first and disapproving of the marriage he had done all that he could be expected to do.

"Strange, Father? I'll show you what she's like." Wilhelm took hold of his broad throat with brown-stained fingers and bitten nails and began to choke himself.

"What are you doing?" cried the old man.

"I'm showing you what she does to me."

"Stop that—stop it!" the old man said and tapped the table commandingly.

"Well, Dad, she hates me. I feel that she's strangling me. I can't catch my breath. She just has fixed herself on me to kill me. She can do it at long distance. One of these days I'll be struck down by suffocation or apoplexy because of her. I just can't catch my breath."

"Take your hands off your throat, you foolish man," said his father. "Stop this bunk. Don't expect me to believe in all kinds of voodoo."

"If that's what you want to call it, all right." His face flamed and paled and swelled and his breath was laborious.

"But I'm telling you that from the time I met her I've been a slave. The Emancipation Proclamation was only for colored people. A husband like me is a slave, with an iron collar. The churches go up to Albany and supervise the law. They won't have divorces. The court says, 'You want to be free. Then you have to work twice as hard—twice, at least! Work! you bum.' So then guys kill each other for the buck, and they may be free of a wife who hates them but they are sold to the company. The company knows a guy has got to have his salary, and takes full advantage of him. Don't talk to me about being free. A rich man may be free on an income of a million net. A poor man may be free because nobody cares what he does. But a fellow in my position has to sweat it out until he drops dead."

His father replied to this, "Wilky, it's entirely your own fault. You don't have to allow it."

Stopped in his eloquence, Wilhelm could not speak for a while. Dumb and incompetent, he struggled for breath and frowned with effort into his father's face.

"I don't understand your problems," said the old man. "I never had any like them."

By now Wilhelm had lost his head and he waved his hands and said over and over, "Oh, Dad, don't give me that stuff, don't give me that. Please don't give me that sort of thing."

"It's true," said his father. "I come from a different world. Your mother and I led an entirely different life."

"Oh, how can you compare Mother," Wilhelm said. "Mother was a help to you. Did she harm you ever?"

"There's no need to carry on like an opera, Wilky," said the doctor. "This is only your side of things."

"What? It's the truth," said Wilhelm.

The old man could not be persuaded and shook his round head and drew his vest down over the gilded shirt, and leaned back with a completeness of style that made this look, to anyone out of hearing, like an ordinary conversation between a middle-aged man and his respected father. Wilhelm towered and swayed, big and sloven, with gray eyes red-shot and his honey-colored hair twisted in flaming shapes upward. Injustice made him angry, made him beg. But he wanted an understanding with his father, and he tried to capitulate to him. He said, "You can't compare Mother and Margaret, and neither can you and I be compared, because you, Dad, were a success. And a success—is a success. I never made a success."

The doctor's old face lost all of its composure and became hard and angry. His small breast rose sharply under the red and black shirt and he said, "Yes. Because of hard work. I was not self-indulgent, not lazy. My old man sold dry goods in Williamsburg. We were nothing, do you understand? I knew I couldn't afford to waste my chances."

"I wouldn't admit for one minute that I was lazy," said Wilhelm. "If anything, I tried too hard. I admit I made many mistakes. Like I thought I shouldn't do things you had done already. Study chemistry. You had done it already. It was in the family."

His father continued, "I didn't run around with fifty women, either. I was not a Hollywood star. I didn't have time to go to Cuba for a vacation. I stayed at home and took care of my children."

Oh, thought Wilhelm, eyes turning upward. Why did I come here in the first place, to live near him? New York is like a gas. The colors are running. My head feels so tight, I don't know what I'm doing. He thinks I want to take away his money or that I envy him. He doesn't see what I want.

"Dad," Wilhelm said aloud, "you're being very unfair. It's true the movies was a false step. But I love my boys. I didn't abandon them. I left Margaret because I had to."

"Why did you have to?"

"Well—" said Wilhelm, struggling to condense his many reasons into a few plain words. "I had to—I had to."

With sudden and surprising bluntness his father said, "Did you have bed-trouble with her? Then you should have stuck it out. Sooner or later everyone has it. Normal people stay with it. It passes. But you wouldn't, so now you pay for your stupid romantic notions. Have I made my view clear?"

It was very clear. Wilhelm seemed to hear it repeated from various sides and inclined his head different ways, and listened and thought. Finally he said, "I guess that's the medical standpoint. You may be right. I just couldn't live with Margaret. I wanted to stick it out, but I was getting very sick. She was one way and I was another. She wouldn't be like me, so I tried to be like her, and I couldn't do it."

"Are you sure she didn't tell *you* to go?" the doctor said.

"I wish she had. I'd be in a better position now. No, it was me. I didn't want to leave, but I couldn't stay. Somebody had to take the initiative. I did. Now I'm the fall guy too."

Pushing aside in advance all the objections that his son would make, the doctor said, "Why did you lose your job with Rojax?"

"I didn't, I've told you."

"You're lying. You wouldn't have ended the connection. You need the money too badly. But you must have got into trouble." The small old man spoke concisely and with great strength. "Since you have to talk and can't let it alone, tell the truth. Was there a scandal—a woman?"

Wilhelm fiercely defended himself. "No, Dad, there wasn't any woman. I told you how it was."

"Maybe it was a man, then," the old man said wickedly.

Shocked, Wilhelm stared at him with burning pallor and dry lips. His skin looked a little yellow. "I don't think you know what you're talking about," he answered after a moment. "You shouldn't let your imagination run so free. Since you've been living here on Broadway you must think you understand life, up to date. You ought to know your own son a little better. Let's drop that, now."

"All right, Wilky, I'll withdraw it. But something must have happened in Roxbury nevertheless. You'll never go back. You're just talking wildly about representing a rival company. You won't. You've done something to spoil your reputation, I think. But you've got girl friends who are expecting you back, isn't that so?"

"I take a lady out now and then while on the road," said Wilhelm. "I'm not a monk."

"No one special? Are you sure you haven't gotten into complications?"

He had tried to unburden himself and instead, Wilhelm thought, he had to undergo an inquisition to prove himself worthy of a sympathetic word. Because his father believed that he did all kinds of gross things.

"There is a woman in Roxbury that I went with. We fell in love and wanted to marry, but she got tired of waiting for my divorce. Margaret figured that. On top of which the girl was a Catholic and I had to go with her to the priest and make an explanation."

Neither did this last confession touch Dr. Adler's sympathies or sway his calm old head or affect the color of his complexion.

"No, no, no, no; all wrong," he said.

Again Wilhelm cautioned himself. Remember his age. He is no longer the same person. He can't bear trouble. I'm so choked up and congested anyway I can't see straight. Will I ever get out of the woods, and recover my balance? You're never the same afterward. Trouble rusts out the system.

"You really *want* a divorce?" said the old man.

"For the price I pay I should be getting something."

"In that case," Dr. Adler said, "it seems to me no normal person would stand for such treatment from a woman."

"Ah, Father, Father!" said Wilhelm. "It's always the same thing with you. Look how you lead me on. You always start out to help me with my problems, and be sympathetic and so forth. It gets my hopes up and I begin to be grateful. But before we're through I'm a hundred times more depressed than before. Why is that? You have no sympathy. You want to shift all the blame on to me. Maybe you're wise to do it." Wilhelm was beginning to lose himself. "All you seem to think about is your death. Well, I'm sorry. But I'm going to die too. And I'm your son. It isn't my fault in the first place. There ought to be a right way to do this, and be fair to each other. But what I want to know is, why do you start up with me if you're not going to help me? What do you want to know about my problems for, Father? So you can lay the whole responsibility on me—so that you won't have to help me? D'you want me to comfort you for having such a son?" Wilhelm had a great knot of wrong tied tight within his chest, and tears approached his eyes but he didn't let them out. He looked shabby enough as it was. His voice was thick and hazy, and he was stammering and could not bring his awful feelings forth.

"You have some purpose of your own," said the doctor, "in acting so unreasonable. What do you want from me? What do you expect?"

"What do I expect?" said Wilhelm. He felt as though he were unable to recover something. Like a ball in the surf, washed beyond reach, his self-control was going out. "I expect *help!*" The words escaped him in a loud, wild, frantic cry and startled the old man, and two or three breakfasters within hearing glanced their way. Wilhelm's hair, the color of whitened honey, rose dense and tall with the expansion of his face, and he said, "When I suffer—you aren't even sorry. That's because you have no affection for me, and you don't want any part of me."

"Why must I like the way you behave? No, I don't like it," said Dr. Adler.

"All right. You want me to change myself. But suppose I could do it— what would I become? What could I? Let's suppose that all my life I have had the wrong ideas about myself and wasn't what I thought I was. And wasn't even careful to take a few precautions, as most people do—like a woodchuck has a few exits to his tunnel. But what shall I do now? More than half my life is over. More than half. And now you tell me I'm not even normal."

The old man too had lost his calm. "You cry about being helped," he said. "When you thought you had to go into the service I sent a check to Margaret every month. As a family man you could have had an exemption. But no! The war couldn't be fought without you and you had to get yourself drafted and be an office-boy in the Pacific theater. Any clerk could have done what you did. You could find nothing better to become than a GI."

Wilhelm was going to reply, and half raised his bearish figure from the chair, his fingers spread and whitened by their grip on the table, but the old man would not let him begin. He said, "I see other elderly people here with children who aren't much good, and they keep backing them and holding them up at a great sacrifice. But I'm not going to make that mistake. It doesn't enter your mind that when I die—a year, two years from now—you'll still be here. I do think of it."

He had intended to say that he had a right to be left in peace. Instead he gave Wilhelm the impression that he meant it was not fair for the better man of the two, and the more useful, the more admired, to leave the world first. Perhaps he meant that, too—a little; but he would not under other circumstances have come out with it so flatly.

"Father," said Wilhelm with an unusual openness of appeal. "Don't you think I know how you feel? I have pity. I want you to live on and on. If you outlive me, that's perfectly okay by me." As his father did not answer this avowal and turned away his glance, Wilhelm suddenly burst out, "No, but you hate me. And if I had money you wouldn't. By God, you have to admit it. The money makes the difference. Then we would be a fine father and son, if I was a credit to you—so you could boast and brag about me all over the hotel. But I'm not the right type of son. I'm too old. I'm too old and too unlucky."

His father said, "I can't give you any money. There would be no end to it if I started. You and your sister would take every last buck from me. I'm still alive, not dead. I am still here. Life isn't over yet. I am as much alive as you or anyone. And I want nobody on my back. Get off! And I give you the same advice, Wilky. Carry nobody on your back."

"Just keep your money," said Wilhelm miserably. "Keep it and enjoy it yourself. That's the ticket!"

IV

Ass! Idiot! Wild boar! Dumb mule! Slave! Lousy, wallowing hippopotamus! Wilhelm called himself as his bending legs carried him from the dining room. His pride! His inflamed feelings! His begging and feebleness! And trading insults with his old father—and spreading confusion over everything. Oh, how poor, contemptible, and ridiculous he was! When he remembered how he had said, with great reproof, "You ought to know your own son"—why, how corny and abominable it was.

He could not get out of the sharply brilliant dining room fast enough. He was horribly worked up; his neck and shoulders, his entire chest ached as though they had been tightly tied with ropes. He smelled the salt odor of tears in his nose.

But at the same time, since there were depths in Wilhelm not unsuspected by himself, he received a suggestion from some remote element in his thoughts that the business of life, the real business—to carry his peculiar burden, to feel shame and impotence, to taste these quelled tears—the only important business, the highest business was being done. Maybe the making of mistakes expressed the very purpose of his life and the essence of his being here. Maybe he was supposed to make them and suffer from them on this earth. And though he had raised himself above Mr. Perls and his father because they adored money, still they were called to act energetically and this was better than to yell and cry, pray and beg, poke and blunder and go by fits and starts and fall upon the thorns of life. And finally sink beneath that watery floor—would that be tough luck, or would it be good riddance?

But he raged once more against his father. Other people with money, while they're still alive, want to see it do some good. Granted, he shouldn't support me. But have I ever asked him to do that? Have I ever asked for dough at all, either for Margaret or for the kids or for myself? It isn't the money, but only the assistance; not even assistance, but just the feeling. But he may be trying to teach me that a grown man should be cured of such feeling. Feeling got me in dutch at Rojax. I had the *feeling* that I belonged to the firm, and my *feelings* were hurt when they put Gerber in over me. Dad thinks I'm too simple. But I'm not so simple as he thinks. What about his feelings? He doesn't forget death for one single second, and that's what makes him like this. And not only is death on his mind but through money he forces me to think about it, too. It gives him power over me. He forces me that way, he himself, and then he's sore. If he was poor, I could care for him and show it. The way I *could* care, too, if I only had a chance. He'd see how much love and respect I had in me. It would make him a different man, too. He'd put his hands on me and give me his blessing.

Someone in a gray straw hat with a wide cocoa-colored band spoke to Wilhelm in the lobby. The light was dusky, splotched with red underfoot; green, the leather furniture; yellow, the indirect lighting.

"Hey, Tommy. Say, there."

"Excuse me," said Wilhelm, trying to reach a house phone. But this was Dr. Tamkin, whom he was just about to call.

"You have a very obsessional look on your face," said Dr. Tamkin.

Wilhelm thought, Here he is, Here he is. If I could only figure this guy out.

"Oh," he said to Tamkin. "Have I got such a look? Well, whatever it is, you name it and I'm sure to have it."

The sight of Dr. Tamkin brought his quarrel with his father to a close. He found himself flowing into another channel.

"What are we doing?" he said. "What's going to happen to lard today?"

"Don't worry yourself about that. All we have to do is hold on to it and it's sure to go up. But what's made you so hot under the collar, Wilhelm?"

"Oh, one of those family situations." This was the moment to take a new look at Tamkin, and he viewed him closely but gained nothing by the new effort. It was conceivable that Tamkin was everything that he claimed to be, and all the gossip false. But was he a scientific man, or not? If he was not, this might be a case for the district attorney's office to investigate. Was he a liar? That was a delicate question. Even a liar might be trustworthy in some ways. Could he trust Tamkin—could he? He feverishly, fruitlessly sought an answer.

But the time for this question was past, and he had to trust him now. After a long struggle to come to a decision, he had given him the money. Practical judgment was in abeyance. He had worn himself out, and the decision was no decision. How had this happened? But how had his Hollywood career begun? It was not because of Maurice Venice, who turned out to be a pimp. It was because Wilhelm himself was ripe for the mistake. His marriage, too, had been like that. Through such decisions somehow his life had taken form. And so, from the moment when he tasted the peculiar flavor of fatality in Dr: Tamkin, he could no longer keep back the money.

Five days ago Tamkin had said, "Meet me tomorrow, and we'll go to the market." Wilhelm, therefore, had had to go. At eleven o'clock they had walked to the brokerage office. On the way, Tamkin broke the news to Wilhelm that though this was an equal partnership he couldn't put up his half of the money just yet; it was tied up for a week or so in one of his patents. Today he would be two hundred dollars short; next week, he'd make it up. But neither of them needed an income from the market, of course. This was only a sporting proposition anyhow, Tamkin said. Wilhelm had to answer, "Of course." It was too late to withdraw. What else could he do? Then came the formal part of the transaction, and it was frightening. The very shade of green of Tamkin's check looked wrong; it was a false, disheartening color. His handwriting was peculiar, even monstrous; the e's were like i's, the t's and l's the same, and the h's like wasps' bellies. He wrote like a fourth-grader. Scientists, however, dealt mostly in symbols they printed. This was Wilhelm's explanation.

Dr. Tamkin had given him his check for three hundred dollars. Wilhelm, in a blinded and convulsed aberration, pressed and pressed to try to kill the trembling of his hand as he wrote out his check for a thousand. He set his lips tight, crouched with his huge back over the table, and wrote with crumbling, terrified fingers, knowing that if Tamkin's check bounced his own would not be honored either. His sole cleverness was to set the date ahead by one day to give the green check time to clear.

Next he had signed a power of attorney, allowing Tamkin to speculate with his money, and this was an even more frightening document. Tamkin never said a word about it, but here they were and it had to be done.

After delivering his signatures, the only precaution Wilhelm took was to come back to the manager of the brokerage office and ask him privately, "Uh, about Doctor Tamkin. We were in here a few minutes ago, remember?"

That day had been a weeping, smoky one and Wilhelm had gotten away from Tamkin on the pretext of having to run to the post office. Tamkin had gone to lunch alone, and here was Wilhelm, back again, breathless, his hat dripping, needlessly asking the manager if he remembered.

"Yes, sir, I know," the manager had said. He was a cold, mild, lean German who dressed correctly and around his neck wore a pair of opera glasses with which he read the board. He was an extremely correct person except that he never shaved in the morning, not caring, probably, how he looked to the fumblers and the old people and the operators and the gamblers and the idlers of Broadway uptown. The market closed at three. Maybe, Wilhelm guessed, he had a thick beard and took a lady out to dinner later and wanted to look fresh-shaven.

"Just a question," said Wilhelm. "A few minutes ago I signed a power of attorney so Doctor Tamkin could invest for me. You gave me the blanks."

"Yes, sir, I remember."

"Now this is what I want to know," Wilhelm had said. "I'm no lawyer and I only gave the paper a glance. Does this give Doctor Tamkin power of attorney over any other assets of mine—money, or property?"

The rain had dribbled from Wilhelm's deformed, transparent raincoat; the buttons of his shirt, which always seemed tiny, were partly broken, in pearly quarters of the moon, and some of the dark, thick golden hairs that grew on his belly stood out. It was the manager's business to conceal his opinion of him; he was shrewd, gray, correct (although unshaven) and had little to say except on matters that came to his desk. He must have recognized in Wilhelm a man who reflected long and then made the decision he had rejected twenty separate times. Silvery, cool, level, long-profiled, experienced, indifferent, observant, with unshaven refinement, he scarcely looked at Wilhelm, who trembled with fearful awkwardness. The manager's face, low-colored, long-nostriled, acted as a unit of perception; his eyes merely did their reduced share. Here was a man, like Rubin, who knew and knew and knew. He, a foreigner, knew; Wilhelm, in the city of his birth, was ignorant.

The manager had said, "No, sir, it does not give him."

"Only over the funds I deposited with you?"

"Yes, that is right, sir."

"Thank you, that's what I wanted to find out," Wilhelm had said, grateful.

The answer comforted him. However, the question had no value. None at all. For Wilhelm had no other assets. He had given Tamkin his last money. There wasn't enough of it to cover his obligations anyway, and Wilhelm had reckoned that he might as well go bankrupt now as next month. "Either broke or rich," was how he had figured, and that formula had encouraged him to make the gamble. Well, not rich; he did not expect that, but perhaps Tamkin might really show him how to earn what he needed in the market. By now, however, he had forgotten his own reckoning and was aware only that he stood to lose his seven hundred dollars to the last cent.

Dr. Tamkin took the attitude that they were a pair of gentlemen experimenting with lard and grain futures. The money, a few hundred dollars, meant nothing much to either of them. He said to Wilhelm, "Watch. You'll get a big kick out of this and wonder why more people don't go into it. You think the Wall Street guys are so smart—geniuses? That's because most of us are psychologically afraid to think about the details. Tell me this. When you're on the road, and you don't understand what goes on under the hood of your car, you'll worry what'll happen if something goes wrong with the engine. Am I wrong?" No, he was right. "Well," said Dr. Tamkin with an expression of quiet triumph about his mouth, almost the suggestion of a jeer. "It's the same psychological principle, Wilhelm. They are rich because you don't understand what goes on. But it's no mystery, and by putting in a little money and applying certain principles of observation, you begin to grasp it. It can't be studied in the abstract. You have to take a specimen risk so that you feel the process, the money-flow, the whole complex. To know how it feels to be a seaweed you have to get in the water. In a very short time we'll take out a hundred-per-cent profit." Thus Wilhelm had had to pretend at the outset that his interest in the market was theoretical.

"Well," said Tamkin when he met him now in the lobby, "what's the problem, what is this family situation? Tell me." He put himself forward as the keen mental scientist. Whenever this happened Wilhelm didn't know what to reply. No matter what he said or did it seemed that Dr. Tamkin saw through him.

"I had some words with my dad."

Dr. Tamkin found nothing extraordinary in this. "It's the eternal same story," he said. "The elemental conflict of parent and child. It won't end, ever. Even with a fine old gentleman like your dad."

"I don't suppose it will. I've never been able to get anywhere with him. He objects to my feelings. He thinks they're sordid. I upset him and he gets mad at me. But maybe all old men are alike."

"Sons, too. Take it from one of them," said Dr. Tamkin. "All the same, you should be proud of such a fine old patriarch of a father. It should give you hope. The longer he lives, the longer your life-expectancy becomes."

Wilhelm answered, brooding, "I guess so. But I think I inherit more from my mother's side, and she died in her fifties."

"A problem arose between a young fellow I'm treating and his dad—I just had a consultation," said Dr. Tamkin as he removed his dark gray hat.

"So early in the morning?" said Wilhelm with suspicion.

"Over the telephone, of course."

What a creature Tamkin was when he took off his hat! The indirect light showed the many complexities of his bald skull, his gull's nose, his rather handsome eyebrows, his vain mustache, his deceiver's brown eyes. His figure was stocky, rigid, short in the neck, so that the large ball of the occiput touched his collar. His bones were peculiarly formed, as though twisted twice where the ordinary human bone was turned only once, and his shoulders rose in two pagoda-like points. At mid-body he was thick. He stood pigeon-toed, a sign perhaps that he was devious or had much to hide. The skin of his hands was aging, and his nails were moonless, concave, clawlike, and they appeared loose. His eyes were as brown as beaver fur and full of strange lines. The two large brown naked balls looked thoughtful—but were they? And honest—but was Dr. Tamkin honest? There was a hypnotic power in his eyes, but this was not always of the same strength, nor was Wilhelm convinced that it was completely natural. He felt that Tamkin tried to make his eyes deliberately conspicuous, with studied art, and that he brought forth his hypnotic effect by an exertion. Occasionally it failed or drooped, and when this happened the sense of his face passed downward to his heavy (possibly foolish?) red underlip.

Wilhelm wanted to talk about the lard holdings, but Dr. Tamkin said, "This father-and-son case of mine would be instructive to you. It's a different psychological type completely than your dad. This man's father thinks that he isn't his son."

"Why not?"

"Because he has found out something about the mother carrying on with a friend of the family for twenty-five years."

"Well, what do you know!" said Wilhelm. His silent thought was, Pure bull. Nothing but bull!

"You must note how interesting the woman is, too. She has two husbands. Whose are the kids? The fellow detected her and she gave a signed confession that two of the four children were not the father's."

"It's amazing," said Wilhelm, but he said it in a rather distant way. He was always hearing such stories from Dr. Tamkin. If you were to believe Tamkin, most of the world was like this. Everybody in the hotel had a mental disorder, a secret history, a concealed disease. The wife of Rubin at the newsstand was supposed to be kept by Carl, the yelling, loud-mouthed gin-rummy player. The wife of Frank in the barbershop had disappeared with a GI while he was waiting for her to disembark at the French Lines pier. Everyone was like the faces on a playing card, upside down either way. Every public figure had a character-neurosis. Maddest of all were the businessmen, the heartless, flaunting, boisterous business class who ruled this country with their hard manners and their bold lies and their absurd words that nobody could believe. They were crazier than anyone. They spread the plague. Wilhelm, thinking of the Rojax Corporation, was inclined to agree that many businessmen were insane. And he supposed that Tamkin, for all his peculiarities, spoke a kind of truth and did some people a sort of good. It confirmed Wilhelm's suspicions to hear that there was a plague, and he said, "I couldn't agree with you more. They trade on anything, they steal everything, they're cynical right to the bones."

"You have to realize," said Tamkin, speaking of his patient, or his client, "that the mother's confession isn't good. It's a confession of duress.

I try to tell the young fellow he shouldn't worry about a phony confession. But what does it help him if I am rational with him?"

"No?" said Wilhelm, intensely nervous. "I think we ought to go over to the market. It'll be opening pretty soon."

"Oh, come on," said Tamkin. "It isn't even nine o'clock, and there isn't much trading the first hour anyway. Things don't get hot in Chicago until half-past ten, and they're an hour behind us, don't forget. Anyway, I say lard will go up, and it will. Take my word. I've made a study of the guilt-aggression cycle which is behind it. I ought to know *something* about that. Straighten your collar."

"But meantime," said Wilhelm, "we have taken a licking this week. Are you sure your insight is at its best? Maybe when it isn't we should lay off and wait."

"Don't you realize," Dr. Tamkin told him, "you can't march in a straight line to the victory? You fluctuate toward it. From Euclid to Newton there was straight lines. The modern age analyzes the wavers. On my own accounts, I took a licking in hides and coffee. But I have confidence. I'm sure I'll outguess them." He gave Wilhelm a narrow smile, friendly, calming, shrewd, and wizard-like, patronizing, secret, potent. He saw his fears and smiled at them. "It's something," he remarked, "to see how the competition-factor will manifest itself in different individuals."

"So? Let's go over."

"But I haven't had my breakfast yet."

"I've had mine."

"Come, have a cup of coffee."

"I wouldn't want to meet my dad." Looking through the glass doors, Wilhelm saw that his father had left by the other exit. Wilhelm thought, He didn't want to run into me, either. He said to Dr. Tamkin, "Okay, I'll sit with you, but let's hurry it up because I'd like to get to the market while there's still a place to sit. Everybody and his uncle gets in ahead of you."

"I want to tell you about this boy and his dad. It's highly absorbing. The father was a nudist. Everybody went naked in the house. Maybe the woman found men *with* clothes attractive. Her husband didn't believe in cutting his hair, either. He practiced dentistry. In his office he wore riding pants and a pair of boots, and he wore a green eyeshade."

"Oh, come off it," said Wilhelm.

"This is a true case history."

Without warning, Wilhelm began to laugh. He himself had had no premonition of his change of humor. His face became warm and pleasant, and he forgot his father, his anxieties; he panted bearlike, happily, through his teeth. "This sounds like a horse-dentist. He wouldn't have to put on pants to treat a horse. Now what else are you going to tell me? Did the wife play the mandolin? Does the boy join the cavalry? Oh, Tamkin, you really are a killer-diller."

"Oh, you think I'm trying to amuse you," said Tamkin. "That's because you aren't familiar with my outlook. I deal in facts. Facts always are sensational. I'll say that a second time. Facts *always!* are sensational."

Wilhelm was reluctant to part with his good mood. The doctor had little sense of humor. He was looking at him earnestly.

"I'd bet you any amount of money," said Tamkin, "that the facts about you are sensational."

"Oh—ha, ha! You want them? You can sell them to a true confession magazine."

"People forget how sensational the things are that they do. They don't see it on themselves. It blends into the background of their daily life."

Wilhelm smiled. "Are you sure this boy tells you the truth?"

"Yes, because I've known the whole family for years."

"And you do psychological work with your own friends? I didn't know that was allowed."

"Well, I'm a radical in the profession. I have to do good wherever I can."

Wilhelm's face became ponderous again and pale. His whitened gold hair lay heavy on his head, and he clasped uneasy fingers on the table. Sensational, but oddly enough, dull, too. Now how do you figure that out? It blends with the background. Funny but unfunny. True but false. Casual but laborious, Tamkin was. Wilhelm was most suspicious of him when he took his driest tone.

"With me," said Dr. Tamkin, "I am at my most efficient when I don't need the fee. When I only love. Without a financial reward. I remove myself from the social influence. Especially money. The spiritual compensation is what I look for. Bringing people into the here-and-now. The real universe. That's the present moment. The past is no good to us. The future is full of anxiety. Only the present is real—the here-and-now. Seize the day."

"Well," said Wilhelm, his earnestness returning. "I know you are a very unusual man. I like what you say about here-and-now. Are all the people who come to see you personal friends and patients too? Like that tall handsome girl, the one who always wears those beautiful broomstick skirts and belts?"

"She was an epileptic, and a most bad and serious pathology, too. I'm curing her successfully. She hasn't had a seizure in six months, and she used to have one every week."

"And that young cameraman, the one who showed us those movies from the jungles of Brazil, isn't he related to her?"

"Her brother. He's under my care, too. He has some terrible tendencies, which are to be expected when you have an epileptic sibling. I came into their lives when they needed help desperately, and took hold of them. A certain man forty years older than she had her in his control and used to give her fits by suggestion whenever she tried to leave him. If you only knew one per cent of what goes on in the city of New York! You see, I understand what it is when the lonely person begins to feel like an animal. When the night comes and he feels like howling from his window like a wolf. I'm taking complete care of that young fellow and his sister. I have to steady him down or he'll go from Brazil to Australia the next day. The way I keep him in the here-and-now is by teaching him Greek."

This was a complete surprise! "What, do you know Greek?"

"A friend of mine taught me when I was in Cairo. I studied Aristotle with him to keep from being idle."

Wilhelm tried to take in these new claims and examine them. Howling from the window like a wolf when night comes sounded genuine to him. That was something really to think about. But the Greek! He realized that Tamkin was watching to see how he took it. More elements were continually being added. A few days ago Tamkin had hinted that he had once been in the underworld, one of the Detroit Purple Gang. He was once head of a mental clinic in Toledo. He had worked with a Polish inventor on an unsinkable ship. He was a technical consultant in the field of television. In the life of a man of genius, all of these things might happen. But had they happened to Tamkin? Was he a genius? He often said that he had attended some of the Egyptian royal family as a psychiatrist. "But everybody is alike, common or aristocrat," he told Wilhelm. "The aristocrat knows less about life."

An Egyptian princess whom he had treated in California, for horrible disorders he had described to Wilhelm, retained him to come back to the old country with her, and there he had had many of her friends and relatives under his care. They turned over a villa on the Nile to him. "For ethical reasons, I can't tell you many of the details about them," he said—but Wilhelm had already heard all these details, and strange and shocking they were, if true. *If* true—he could not be free from doubt. For instance, the general who had to wear ladies' silk stockings and stand otherwise naked before the mirror—and all the rest. Listening to the doctor when he was so strangely factual, Wilhelm had to translate his words into his own language, and he could not translate fast enough or find terms to fit what he heard.

"Those Egyptian big shots invested in the market, too, for the heck of it. What did they need extra money for? By association, I almost became a millionaire myself, and if I had played it smart there's no telling what might have happened. I could have been the ambassador." The American? The Egyptian ambassador? "A friend of mine tipped me off on the cotton. I made a heavy purchase of it. I didn't have that kind of money, but everybody there knew me. It never entered their minds that a person of their social circle didn't have dough. The sale was made on the phone. Then, while the cotton shipment was at sea, the price tripled. When the stuff suddenly became so valuable all hell broke loose on the world cotton market, they looked to see who was the owner of this big shipment. Me! They investigated my credit and found out I was a mere doctor, and they canceled. This was illegal. I sued them. But as I didn't have the money to fight them I sold the suit to a Wall Street lawyer for twenty thousand dollars. He fought it and was winning. They settled with him out of court for more than a million. But on the way back from Cairo, flying, there was a crash. All on board died. I have this guilt on my conscience, of being the murderer of that lawyer. Although he was a crook."

Wilhelm thought, I must be a real jerk to sit and listen to such impossible stories. I guess I am a sucker for people who talk about the deeper things of life, even the way he does.

"We scientific men speak of irrational guilt, Wilhelm," said Dr. Tamkin, as if Wilhelm were a pupil in his class. "But in such a situation, because of the money, I wished him harm. I realize it. This isn't the time to describe all the details, but the money made me guilty. Money and Murder both begin with M. Machinery. Mischief."

Wilhelm, his mind thinking for him at random, said, "What about Mercy? Milk-of-human-kindness?"

"One fact should be clear to you by now. Money-making is aggression. That's the whole thing. The functionalistic explanation is the only one. People come to the market to kill. They say, 'I'm going to make a killing.' It's not accidental. Only they haven't got the genuine courage to kill, and they erect a symbol of it. The money. They make a killing by a fantasy. Now, counting and number is always a sadistic activity. Like hitting. In the Bible, the Jews wouldn't allow you to count them. They knew it was sadistic."

"I don't understand what you mean," said Wilhelm. A strange uneasiness tore at him. The day was growing too warm and his head felt dim. "What makes them want to kill?"

"By and by, you'll get the drift," Dr. Tamkin assured him. His amazing eyes had some of the rich dryness of a brown fur. Innumerable crystalline hairs or spicules of light glittered in their bold surfaces. "You can't understand without first spending years on the study of the ultimates of human and animal behavior, the deep chemical, organismic, and spiritual secrets of life. I am a psychological poet."

"If you're this kind of poet," said Wilhelm, whose fingers in his pocket were feeling in the little envelopes for the Phenaphen capsules, "what are you doing on the market?"

"That's a good question. Maybe I am better at speculation because I don't care. Basically, I don't wish hard enough for money, and therefore I come with a cool head to it."

Wilhelm thought, Oh, sure! That's the answer, is it? I bet that if I took a strong attitude he'd back down on everything. He'd grovel in front of me. The way he looks at me on the sly, to see if I'm being taken in! He swallowed his Phenaphen pill with a long gulp of water. The rims of his eyes grew red as it went down. And then he felt calmer.

"Let me see if I can give you an answer that will satisfy you," said Dr. Tamkin. His flapjacks were set before him. He spread the butter on them, poured on brown maple syrup, quartered them, and began to eat with hard, active, muscular jaws which sometimes gave a creak at the hinges. He pressed the handle of his knife against his chest and said, "In here, the human bosom—mine, yours, everybody's—there isn't just one soul. There's a lot of souls. But there are two main ones, the real soul and a pretender soul. Now! Every man realizes that he has to love something or somebody. He feels that he must go outward. 'If thou canst not love, what art thou?' Are you with me?"

"Yes, Doc, I think so," said Wilhelm listening—a little skeptically but nonetheless hard.

" 'What art thou?' Nothing. That's the answer. Nothing. In the heart of hearts—Nothing! So of course you can't stand that and want to be Something, and you try. But instead of being this Something, the man puts it over on everybody instead. You can't be that strict to yourself. You love a *little*. Like you have a dog" (*Scissors!*) "or give some money to a charity drive. Now that isn't love, is it? What is it? Egotism, pure and simple. It's a way to love the pretender soul. Vanity. Only vanity, is what it is. And social control. The interest of the pretender soul is the same as the interest of the social life, the society mechanism. This is the main tragedy of human life. Oh, it is terrible! Terrible! You are not free. Your own betrayer is inside of you and sells you out. You have to obey him like a slave. He makes you work like a horse. And for what? For who?"

"Yes, for what?" The doctor's words caught Wilhelm's heart. "I couldn't agree more," he said. "When do we get free?"

"The purpose is to keep the whole thing going. The true soul is the one that pays the price. It suffers and gets sick, and it realizes that the pretender can't be loved. Because the pretender is a lie. The true soul loves the truth. And when the true soul feels like this, it wants to kill the pretender. The love has turned into hate. Then you become dangerous. A killer. You have to kill the deceiver."

"Does this happen to everybody?"

The doctor answered simply. "Yes, to everybody. Of course, for simplification purposes, I have spoken of the soul; it isn't a scientific term, but it helps you to understand it. Whenever the slayer slays, he wants to slay the soul in him which has gypped and deceived him. Who is his enemy? Him. And his lover? Also. Therefore, all suicide is murder, and all murder is suicide. It's the one and identical phenomenon. Biologically, the pretender soul takes away the energy of the true soul and makes it feeble, like a parasite. It happens unconsciously, unawaringly, in the depths of the organism. Ever take up parasitology?"

"No, it's my dad who's the doctor."

"You should read a book about it."

Wilhelm said, "But this means that the world is full of murderers. So it's not the world. It's a kind of hell."

"Sure," the doctor said. "At least a kind of purgatory. You walk on the bodies. They are all around. I can hear them cry *de profundis* and wring their hands. I hear them, poor human beasts. I can't help hearing. And my eyes are open to it. I have to cry, too. This is the human tragedy-comedy."

Wilhelm tried to capture his vision. And again the doctor looked untrustworthy to him, and he doubted him. "Well," he said, "there are also kind, ordinary, helpful people. They're—out in the country. All over. What kind of morbid stuff do you read, anyway?" The doctor's room was full of books.

"I read the best of literature, science and philosophy," Dr. Tamkin said. Wilhelm had observed that in his room even the TV aerial was set upon a pile of volumes. "Korzybski, Aristotle, Freud, W. H. Sheldon, and all the great poets. You answer me like a layman. You haven't applied your mind strictly to this."

"Very interesting," said Wilhelm. He was aware that he hadn't applied his mind strictly to anything. "You don't have to think I'm a dummy, though. I have ideas, too." A glance at the clock told him that the market would soon open. They could spare a few minutes yet. There were still more things he wanted to hear from Tamkin. He realized that Tamkin spoke faultily, but then scientific men were not always strictly literate. It was the description of the two souls that had awed him. In Tommy he saw the pretender. And even Wilky might not be himself. Might the name of his true soul be the one by which his old grandfather had called him—Velvel? The name of a soul, however, must be only that—soul. What did it look like? Does my soul look like me? Is there a soul that looks like Dad? like Tamkin? Where does the true soul get its strength? Why does it have to love truth? Wilhelm was tormented, but tried to be oblivious to his torment. Secretly, he prayed the doctor would give him some useful advice and transform his life. "Yes, I understand you," he said. "It isn't lost on me."

"I never said you weren't intelligent, but only you just haven't made a study of it all. As a matter of fact you're a profound personality with very profound creative capacities but also disturbances. I've been concerned with you, and for some time I've been treating you."

"Without my knowing it? I haven't felt you doing anything. What do you mean? I don't think I like being treated without my knowledge. I'm of two minds. What's the matter, don't you think I'm normal?" And he really was divided in mind. That the doctor cared about him pleased him. This was what he craved, that someone should care about him, wish him well. Kindness, mercy, he wanted. But—and here he retracted his heavy shoulders in his peculiar way, drawing his hands up into his sleeves; his feet moved uneasily under the table—but he was worried, too, and even somewhat indignant. For what right had Tamkin to meddle without being asked? What kind of privileged life did this man lead? He took other people's money and speculated with it. Everybody came under his care. No one could have secrets from him.

The doctor looked at him with his deadly brown, heavy, impenetrable eyes, his naked shining head, his red hanging underlip, and said, "You have lots of guilt in you."

Wilhelm helplessly admitted, as he felt the heat rise to his wide face, "Yes, I think so too. But personally," he added, "I don't feel like a murderer. I always try to lay off. It's the others who get me. You know—make me feel oppressed. And if you don't mind, and it's all the same to you, I would rather know it when you start to treat me. And now, Tamkin, for Christ's sake, they're putting out the lunch menus already. Will you sign the check, and let's go!"

Tamkin did as he asked, and they rose. They were passing the bookkeeper's desk when he took out a substantial bundle of onionskin papers and said, "These are receipts of the transactions. Duplicates. You'd better keep them as the account is in your name and you'll need them for income taxes. And here is a copy of a poem I wrote yesterday."

"I have to leave something at the desk for my father," Wilhelm said, and he put his hotel bill in an envelope with a note. *Dear Dad, Please carry me this month, Yours, W.* He watched the clerk with his sullen pug's profile and his stiff-necked look push the envelope into his father's box.

"May I ask you really why you and your dad had words?" said Dr. Tamkin, who had hung back, waiting.

"It was about my future," said Wilhelm. He hurried down the stairs with swift steps, like a tower in motion, his hands in his trousers pockets. He was ashamed to discuss the matter. "He says there's a reason why I can't go back to my old territory, and there is. I told everybody I was going to be an officer of the corporation. And I was supposed to. It was promised. But then they welshed because of the son-in-law. I bragged and made myself look big."

"If you was humble enough, you could go back. But it doesn't make much difference. We'll make you a good living on the market."

They came into the sunshine of upper Broadway, not clear but throbbing through the dust and fumes, a false air of gas visible at eye-level as it spurted from the bursting buses. From old habit, Wilhelm turned up the collar of his jacket.

"Just a technical question," Wilhelm said. "What happens if your losses are bigger than your deposit?"

"Don't worry. They have ultra-modern electronic bookkeeping machinery, and it won't let you get in debt. It puts you out automatically. But I want you to read this poem. You haven't read it yet."

Light as a locust, a helicopter bringing mail from Newark Airport to La Guardia sprang over the city in a long leap.

The paper Wilhelm unfolded had ruled borders in red ink. He read:

Mechanism vs Functionalism
Ism vs Hism

If thee thyself couldst only see
Thy greatness that is and yet to be,
Thou would feel joy-beauty-what ecstasy.
They are at thy feet, earth-moon-sea, the trinity.

Why-forth then dost thou tarry
And partake thee only of the crust
And skim the earth's surface narry
When all creations art thy just?

Seek ye then that which art not there
In thine own glory let thyself rest.
Witness. Thy power is not bare.
Thou art King. Thou art at thy best.

Look then right before thee.
Open thine eyes and see.
At the foot of Mt. Serenity
Is thy cradle to eternity.

Utterly confused, Wilhelm said to himself explosively, What kind of mishmash, claptrap is this! What does he want from me? Damn him to hell, he might as well hit me on the head, and lay me out, kill me. What does he give me this for? What's the purpose? Is it a deliberate test? Does he want to mix me up? He's already got me mixed up completely. I was never good at riddles. Kiss those seven hundred bucks good-by, and call it one more mistake in a long line of mistakes— Oh, Mama, what a line! He stood near the shining window of a fancy fruit store, holding Tamkin's paper, rather dazed, as though a charge of photographer's flash powder had gone up in his eyes.

But he's waiting for my reaction. I have to say something to him about his poem. It really is no joke. What will I tell him? Who is this King? The poem is written *to* someone. But who? I can't even bring myself to talk. I feel too choked and strangled. With all the books he reads, how come the guy is so illiterate? And why do people just naturally assume that you'll know what they're talking about? No. I don't know, and nobody knows. The planets don't, the stars don't, infinite space doesn't. It doesn't square with Planck's Constant or anything else. So what's the good of it? Where's the need of it? What does he mean here by Mount Serenity? Could it be a figure of speech for Mount Everest? As he says people are all committing suicide, maybe those guys who climbed Everest were only trying to kill themselves, and if we want peace we should stay at the foot of the mountain. In the here-and-now. But it's also here-and-now on the slope, and on the top, where they climbed to seize the day. Surface narry is something he can't mean, I don't believe. I'm about to start foaming at the mouth. "Thy cradle . . ." *Who* is resting in his cradle—in his glory? My thoughts are at an end. I feel the wall. No more. So ——k it all! The money and everything. Take it away! When I have the money they eat me alive, like those piranha fish in the movie about the Brazilian jungle. It was hideous when they ate up that Brahma bull in the river. He turned pale, just like clay, and in five minutes nothing was left except the skeleton still in one piece, floating away. When I haven't got it any more, at least they'll let me alone.

"Well, what do you think of this?" said Dr. Tamkin. He gave a special sort of wise smile, as though Wilhelm must now see what kind of man he was dealing with.

"Nice. Very nice. Have you been writing long?"

"I've been developing this line of thought for years and years. You follow it all the way?"

"I'm trying to figure out who this Thou is."

"Thou? Thou is you."

"Me! Why? This applies to *me?*"

"Why shouldn't it apply to you. You were in my mind when I composed it. Of course, the hero of the poem is sick humanity. If it would open its eyes it would be great."

"Yes, but how do I get into this?"

"The main idea of the poem is *con*struct or *de*struct. There is no ground in between. Mechanism is *de*struct. Money of course is *de*struct. When the last grave is dug, the gravedigger will have to be paid. If you could have confidence in nature you would not have to fear. It would keep you up. Creative is natue. Rapid. Lavish. Inspirational. It shapes leaves. It rolls the waters of the earth. Man is the chief of all this. All creations are his just inheritance. You don't know what you've got within you. A person either creates or he destroys. There is no neutrality . . ."

"I realized you were no beginner," said Wilhelm with propriety. "I have only one crticism to make. I think 'why-forth' is wrong. You should write 'Wherefore then dost thou . . .' " And he reflected, So? I took a gamble. It'll have to be a miracle, though, to save me. My money will be gone, then it won't be able to destruct me. He can't just take and lose it, though. He's in it, too. I think he's in a bad way himself. He must be. I'm sure because, come to think of it, he sweated blood when he signed that check. But what have I let myself in for? The waters of the earth are going to roll over me.

V

Patiently, in the window of the fruit store, a man with a scoop spread crushed ice between his rows of vegetables. There were also Persian melons, lilacs, tulips with radiant black at the middle. The many street noises came back after a little while from the caves of the sky. Crossing the tide of Broadway traffic, Wilhelm was saying to himself, The reason Tamkin lectures me is that somebody has lectured him, and the reason for the poem is that he wants to give me good advice. Everybody seems to know something. Even fellows like Tamkin. Many people know what to do, but how many can do it?

He believed that he must, that he could and would recover the good things, the happy things, the easy tranquil things of life. He had made mistakes, but he could overlook these. He had been a fool, but that could be forgiven. The time wasted—must be relinquished. What else could one do about it? Things were too complex, but they might be reduced to simplicity again. Recovery was possible. First he had to get out of the city. No, first he had to pull out his money. . . .

From the carnival of the street—pushcarts, accordion and fiddle, shoeshine, begging, the dust going round like a woman on stilts—they entered the narrow crowded theater of the brokerage office. From front to back it was filled with the Broadway crowd. But how was lard doing this morning? From the rear of the hall Wilhelm tried to read the tiny figures. The German manager was looking through his binoculars. Tamkin placed himself on Wilhelm's left and covered his conspicuous bald head. "The guy'll ask me about the margin," he muttered. They passed, however, unobserved. "Look, the lard has held its place," he said.

Tamkin's eyes must be very sharp to read the figures over so many heads and at this distance—another respect in which he was unusual.

The room was always crowded. Everyone talked. Only at the front could you hear the flutter of the wheels within the board. Teletyped news items crossed the illuminated screen above.

"Lard. Now what about rye?" said Tamkin, rising on his toes. Here he was a different man, active and impatient. He parted people who stood in his way. His face turned resolute, and on either side of his mouth odd bulges formed under his mustache. Already he was pointing out to Wilhelm the appearance of a new pattern on the board. "There's something up today," he said.

"Then why'd you take so long with breakfast?" said Wilhelm.

There were no reserved seats in the room, only customary ones. Tamkin always sat in the second row, on the commodities side of the aisle. Some of his acquaintances kept their hats on the chairs for him.

"Thanks. Thanks," said Tamkin, and he told Wilhelm, "I fixed it up yesterday."

"That was a smart thought," said Wilhelm. They sat down.

With folded hands, by the wall, sat an old Chinese businessman in a seersucker coat. Smooth and fat, he wore a white Vandyke. One day Wilhelm had seen him on Riverside Drive pushing two little girls along in a baby carriage—his grandchildren. Then there were two women in their fifties, supposed to be sisters, shrewd and able money-makers, according to

Tamkin. They had never a word to say to Wilhelm. But they would chat with Tamkin. Tamkin talked to everyone.

Wilhelm sat between Mr. Rowland, who was elderly, and Mr. Rappaport, who was very old. Yesterday Rowland had told him that in the year 1908, when he was a junior at Harvard, his mother had given him twenty shares of steel for his birthday, and then he had started to read the financial news and had never practiced law but instead followed the market for the rest of his life. Now he speculated only in soy beans, of which he had made a specialty. By his conservative method, said Tamkin, he cleared two hundred a week. Small potatoes, but then he was a bachelor, retired, and didn't need money.

"Without dependents," said Tamkin. "He doesn't have the problems that you and I do."

Did Tamkin have dependents? He had everything that it was possible for a man to have—science, Greek, chemistry, poetry, and now dependents too. That beautiful girl with epilepsy, perhaps. He often said that she was a pure, marvelous, spiritual child who had no knowledge of the world. He protected her, and, if he was not lying, adored her. And if you encouraged Tamkin by believing him, or even if you refrained from questioning him, his hints became more daring. Sometimes he said that he paid for her music lessons. Sometimes he seemed to have footed the bill for the brother's camera expedition to Brazil. And he spoke of paying for the support of the orphaned child of a dead sweetheart. These hints, made dully as asides, grew by repetition into sensational claims.

"For myself, I don't need much," said Tamkin. "But a man can't live for himself and I need the money for certain important things. What do you figure you have to have, to get by?"

"Not less than fifteen grand, after taxes. That's for my wife and the two boys."

"Isn't there anybody else?" said Tamkin with a shrewdness almost cruel. But his look grew more sympathetic as Wilhelm stumbled, not willing to recall another grief.

"Well—there was. But it wasn't a money matter."

"I should hope!" said Tamkin. "If love is love, it's free. Fifteen grand, though, isn't too much for a man of your intelligence to ask out of life. Fools, hard-hearted criminals, and murderers have millions to squander. They burn up the world—oil, coal, wood, metal, and soil, and suck even the air and the sky. They consume, and they give back no benefit. A man like you, humble for life, who wants to feel and live, has trouble—not wanting," said Tamkin in his parenthetical fashion, "to exchange an ounce of soul for a pound of social power—he'll never make it without help in a world like this. But don't you worry." Wilhelm grasped at this assurance. "Just you never mind. We'll go easily beyond your figure."

Dr. Tamkin gave Wilhelm comfort. He often said that he had made as much as a thousand a week in commodities. Wilhelm had examined the receipts, but until this moment it had never occurred to him that there must be debit slips too; he had been shown only the credits.

"But fifteen grand is not an ambitious figure," Tamkin was telling him. "For that you don't have to wear yourself out on the road, dealing with narrow-minded people. A lot of them don't like Jews, either, I suppose?"

"I can't afford to notice. I'm lucky when I have my occupation. Tamkin, do you mean you can save our money?"

"Oh, did I forget to mention what I did before closing yesterday? You see, I closed out one of the lard contracts and bought a hedge of December rye. The rye is up three points already and takes some of the sting out. But lard will go up, too."

"Where? God, yes, you're right," said Wilhelm, eager, and got to his feet to look. New hope freshened his heart. "Why didn't you tell me before?"

And Tamkin, smiling like a benevolent magician, said, "You must learn to have trust. The slump in lard can't last. And just take a look at eggs. Didn't I predict they couldn't go any lower? They're rising and rising. If we had taken eggs we'd be far ahead."

"Then why didn't we take them?"

"We were just about to. I had a buying order in at .24, but the tide turned at .26¼ and we barely missed. Never mind. Lard will go back to last year's levels."

Maybe. But when? Wilhelm could not allow his hopes to grow too strong. However, for a little while he could breathe more easily. Late-morning trading was getting active. The shining numbers whirred on the board which sounded like a huge cage of artificial birds. Lard fluctuated between two points, but rye slowly climbed.

He closed his strained, greatly earnest eyes briefly and nodded his Buddha's head, too large to suffer such uncertainties. For several moments of peace he was removed to his small yard in Roxbury.

He breathed in the sugar of the pure morning.

He heard the long phrases of the birds.

No enemy wanted his life.

Wilhelm thought, I will get out of here. I don't belong in New York any more. And he sighed like a sleeper.

Tamkin said, "Excuse me," and left his seat. He could not sit still in the room but passed back and forth between the stocks and commodities sections. He knew dozens of people and was continually engaging in discussions. Was he giving advice, gathering information, or giving it, or practicing—whatever mysterious profession he practiced? Hypnotism? Perhaps he could put people in a trance while he talked to them. What a rare, peculiar bird he was, with those pointed shoulders, that bare head, his loose nails, almost claws, and those brown, soft, deadly, heavy eyes.

He spoke of things that mattered, and as very few people did this he could take you by surprise, excite you, move you. Maybe he wished to do good, maybe give himself a lift to a higher level, maybe believe his own prophecies, maybe touch his own heart. Who could tell? He had picked up a lot of strange ideas; Wilhelm could only suspect, he could not say with certainty, that Tamkin hadn't made them his own.

Now Tamkin and he were equal partners, but Tamkin had put up only three hundred dollars. Suppose he did this not only once but five times; then an investment of fifteen hundred dollars gave him five thousand to speculate with. If he had power of attorney in every case, he could shift the money from one account to another. No, the German probably kept an eye on him. Nevertheless it was possible. Calculations like this made Wilhelm feel ill. Obviously Tamkin was a plunger. But how did he get by? He must be in his fifties. How did he support himself? Five years in Egypt; Hollywood before that; Michigan; Ohio; Chicago. A man of fifty has supported himself for at least thirty years. You could be sure that Tamkin had never worked in a factory or in an office. How did he make it? His taste in clothes was horrible, but he didn't buy cheap things. He wore corduroy or velvet shirts from Clyde's, painted neckties, striped socks. There was a slightly acid or pasty smell about his person; for a doctor, he didn't bathe much. Also, Dr. Tamkin had a good room at the Gloriana and had had it for about a year. But so was Wilhelm himself a guest, with an unpaid bill at present in his father's box. Did the beautiful girl with the skirts and belts pay him? Was he defrauding his so-called patients? So many questions impossible to answer could not be asked about an honest man. Nor perhaps about a sane man. Was Tamkin a lunatic, then? That sick Mr. Perls at breakfast had said that there was no easy way to tell the sane from the mad, and he was right about that in any big city and especially in New York— the end of the world, with its complexity and machinery, bricks and tubes, wires and stones, holes and heights. And was everybody crazy here? What sort of people did you see? Every other man spoke a language entirely his own, which he had figured out by private thinking; he had his own ideas and peculiar ways. If you wanted to talk about a glass of water, you had to start back with God creating the heavens and earth; the apple; Abraham; Moses and Jesus; Rome; the Middle Ages; gunpowder; the Revolution; back to Newton; up to Einstein; then war and Lenin and Hitler. After reviewing this and getting it all straight again you could proceed to talk about a glass of water. "I'm fainting, please get me a little water." You were lucky even then to make yourself understood. And this happened over and over and over with everyone you met. You had to translate and translate, explain and explain, back and forth, and it was the punishment of hell itself not to understand or be understood, not to know the crazy from the sane, the wise from the fools, the young from the old or the sick from the well. The fathers were no fathers and the sons no sons. You had to talk with yourself in the daytime and reason with yourself at night. Who else was there to talk to in a city like New York?

A queer look came over Wilhelm's face with its eyes turned up and his silent mouth with its high upper lip. He went several degrees further—when you are like this, dreaming that everybody is outcast, you realize that this must be one of the small matters. There is a larger body, and from this you cannot be separated. The glass of water fades out. You do not go from simple *a* and simple *b* to the great *x* and *y*, nor does it matter whether you agree about the glass but, far beneath such details, what Tamkin would call the real soul says plain and understandable things to everyone. There sons and fathers are themselves, and a glass of water is only an ornament; it makes a hoop of brightness on the cloth; it is an angel's mouth. There truth for everybody may be found, and confusion is only—only temporary, thought Wilhelm.

The idea of this larger body had been planted in him a few days ago beneath Times Square, when he had gone downtown to pick up tickets for the baseball game on Saturday (a double-header at the Polo Grounds). He was going through an underground corridor, a place he had always hated and hated more than ever now. On the walls between the advertisements were words in chalk: "Sin No More," and "Do Not Eat the Pig," he had particularly noticed. And in the dark tunnel, in the haste, heat, and darkness which disfigure and make freaks and fragments of nose and eyes and teeth, all of a sudden, unsought, a general love for all these imperfect and lurid-looking people burst out in Wilhelm's breast. He loved them. One and all, he passionately loved them. They were his brothers and his sisters. He was imperfect and disfigured himself, but what difference did that make if he was united with them by this blaze of love? And as he walked he began to say, "Oh my brothers—my brothers and my sisters," blessing them all as well as himself.

So what did it matter how many languages there were, or how hard it was to describe a glass of water? Or matter that a few minutes later he didn't feel anything like a brother toward the man who sold him the tickets?

On that very same afternoon he didn't hold so high an opinion of this same onrush of loving kindness. What did it come to? As they had the capacity and must use it once in a while, people were bound to have such involuntary feelings. It was only another one of those subway things. Like having a hard-on at random. But today, his day of reckoning, he consulted his memory again and thought, I must go back to that. That's the right clue and may do me the most good. Something very big. Truth, like.

The old fellow on the right, Mr. Rappaport, was nearly blind and kept asking Wilhelm, "What's the new figure on November wheat? Give me July soy beans too." When you told him he didn't say thank you. He said, "Okay," instead, or, "Check," and turned away until he needed you again. He was very old, older even than Dr. Adler, and if you believed Tamkin he had once been the Rockefeller of the chicken business and had retired with a large fortune.

Wilhelm had a queer feeling about the chicken industry, that it was sin-

Ister. On the road, he frequently passed chicken farms. Those big, rambling, wooden buildings out in the neglected fields; they were like prisons. The lights burned all night in them to cheat the poor hens into laying. Then the slaughter. Pile all the coops of the slaughtered on end, and in one week they'd go higher than Mount Everest or Mount Serenity. The blood filling the Gulf of Mexico. The chicken shit, acid, burning the earth.

How old—old this Mr. Rappaport was! Purple stains were buried in the flesh of his nose, and the cartilage of his ear was twisted like a cabbage heart. Beyond remedy by glasses, his eyes were smoky and faded.

"Read me that soy-bean figure now, boy," he said, and Wilhelm did. He thought perhaps the old man might give him a tip, or some useful advice or information about Tamkin. But no. He only wrote memoranda on a pad, and put the pad in his pocket. He let no one see what he had written. And Wilhelm thought this was the way a man who had grown rich by the murder of millions of animals, little chickens, would act. If there was a life to come he might have to answer for the killing of all those chickens. What if they all were waiting? But if there was a life to come, everybody would have to answer. But if there was a life to come, the chickens themselves would be all right.

Well! What stupid ideas he was having this morning. Phooey!

Finally old Rappaport did address a few remarks to Wilhelm. He asked him whether he had reserved his seat in the synagogue for Yom Kippur.

"No," said Wilhelm.

"Well, you better hurry up if you expect to say *Yiskor* for your parents. I never miss."

And Wilhelm thought, Yes, I suppose I should say a prayer for Mother once in a while. His mother had belonged to the Reform congregation. His father had no religion. At the cemetery Wilhelm had paid a man to say a prayer for her. He was among the tombs and he wanted to be tipped for the *El molai rachamin.* "Thou God of Mercy," Wilhelm thought that meant. *B'gan Aden*—"in Paradise." Singing, they drew it out. *B'gan Ay-den.* The broken bench beside the grave made him wish to do something. Wilhelm often prayed in his own manner. He did not go to the synagogue but he would occasionally perform certain devotions, according to his feelings. Now he reflected, In Dad's eyes I am the wrong kind of Jew. He doesn't like the way I act. Only he is the right kind of Jew. Whatever you are, it always turns out to be the wrong kind.

Mr. Rappaport grumbled and whiffed at his long cigar, and the board, like a swarm of electrical bees, whirred.

"Since you were in the chicken business, I thought you'd speculate in eggs, Mr. Rappaport." Wilhelm, with his warm, panting laugh, sought to charm the old man.

"Oh. Yeah. Loyalty, hey?" said old Rappaport. "I should stick to them. I spent a lot of time amongst chickens. I got to be an expert chicken-sexer When the chick hatches you have to tell the boys from the girls. It's not easy. You need long, long experience. What do you think, it's a joke? A whole industry depends on it. Yes, now and then I buy a contract eggs. What have you got today?"

Wilhelm said anxiously, "Lard. Rye."

"Buy? Sell?"

"Bought."

"Uh," said the old man. Wilhelm could not determine what he meant by this. But of course you couldn't expect him to make himself any clearer. It was not in the code to give information to anyone. Sick with desire, Wilhelm waited for Mr. Rappaport to make an exception in his case. Just this once! Because it was critical. Silently, by a sort of telepathic concentration, he begged the old man to speak the single word that would save him, give him the merest sign. "Oh, please—please help," he nearly said. If Rappaport would close one eye, or lay his head to one side, or raise his finger and point to a column in the paper or to a figure on his pad. A hint! A hint!

A long perfect ash formed on the end of the cigar, the white ghost of the leaf with all its veins and its fainter pungency. It was ignored, in its beauty, by the old man. For it was beautiful. Wilhelm he ignored as well.

Then Tamkin said to him, "Wilhelm, look at the jump our rye just took."

December rye climbed three points as they tensely watched; the tumblers raced and the machine's lights buzzed.

"A point and a half more, and we can cover the lard losses," said Tamkin. He showed him his calculations on the margin of the *Times*.

"I think you should put in the selling order now. Let's get out with a small loss."

"Get out now? Nothing doing."

"Why not? Why should we wait?"

"Because," said Tamkin with a smiling, almost openly scoffing look, "you've got to keep your nerve when the market starts to go places. Now's when you can make something."

"I'd get out while the getting's good."

"No, you shouldn't lose your head like this. It's obvious to me what the mechanism is, back in the Chicago market. There's a short supply of December rye. Look, it's just gone up another quarter. We should ride it."

"I'm losing my taste for the gamble," said Wilhelm. "You can't feel safe when it goes up so fast. It's liable to come down just as quick."

Dryly, as though he were dealing with a child, Tamkin told him in a tone of tiring patience, "Now listen, Tommy. I have it diagnosed right. If you wish I should sell I can give the sell order. But this is the difference between healthiness and pathology. One is objective, doesn't change his mind every minute, enjoys the risk element. But that's not the neurotic character. The neurotic character—"

"Damn it, Tamkin!" said Wilhelm roughly. "Cut that out. I don't like it. Leave my character out of consideration. Don't pull any more of that stuff on me. I tell you I don't like it."

Tamkin therefore went no further; he backed down. "I meant," he said, softer, "that as a salesman you are basically an artist type. The seller is in the visionary sphere of the business function. And then you're an actor, too."

"No matter what type I am—" An angry and yet weak sweetness rose into Wilhelm's throat. He coughed as though he had the flu. It was twenty years since he had appeared on the screen as an extra. He blew the bagpipes in a film called *Annie Laurie*. Annie had come to warn the young Laird; he would not believe her and called the bagpipers to drown her out. He made fun of her while she wrung her hands. Wilhelm, in a kilt, barelegged, blew and blew and blew and not a sound came out. Of course all the music was recorded. He fell sick with the flu after that and still suffered sometimes from chest weakness.

"Something stuck in your throat?" said Tamkin. "I think maybe you are too disturbed to think clearly. You should try some of my 'here-and-now' mental exercises. It stops you from thinking so much about the future and the past and cuts down confusion."

"Yes, yes, yes, yes," said Wilhelm, his eyes fixed on December rye.

"Nature only knows one thing, and that's the present. Present, present, eternal present, like a big, huge, giant wave—colossal, bright and beautiful, full of life and death, climbing into the sky, standing in the seas. You must go along with the actual, the Here-and-Now, the glory—"

. . . chest weakness, Wilhelm's recollection went on. Margaret nursed him. They had had two rooms of furniture, which was later seized. She sat on the bed and read to him. He made her read for days, and she read stories, poetry, everything in the house. He felt dizzy, stifled when he tried to smoke. They had him wear a flannel vest.

> Come then, Sorrow!
> Sweetest Sorrow!
> Like an own babe I nurse thee on my breast!

Why did he remember that? Why?

"You have to pick out something that's in the actual, immediate present moment," said Tamkin. "And say to yourself here-and-now, here-and-now, here-and-now. 'Where am I?' 'Here.' 'When is it?' 'Now.' Take an object or a person. Anybody. 'Here and now I see a person.' 'Here and now I see a man.' 'Here and now I see a man sitting on a chair.' Take me, for instance. Don't let your mind wander. 'Here and now I see a man in a brown suit. Here and now I see a corduroy shirt.' You have to narrow it down, one item at a time, and not let your imagination shoot ahead. Be in the present. Grasp the hour, the moment, the instant."

Is he trying to hypnotize or con me? Wilhelm wondered. To take my mind off selling? But even if I'm back at seven hundred bucks, then where am I?

As if in prayer, his lids coming down with raised veins, frayed out, on his significant eyes. Tamkin said, " 'Here and now I see a button. Here and now I see the thread that sews the button. Here and now I see the green thread.' " Inch by inch he contemplated himself in order to show Wilhelm how calm it would make him. But Wilhelm was hearing Margaret's voice as she read, somewhat unwillingly,

> Come then, Sorrow!
>
> I thought to leave thee,
> And deceive thee,
> But now of all the world I love thee best.

Then Mr Rappaport's old hand pressed his thigh, and he said, "What's my wheat? Those damn guys are blocking the way. I can't see."

VI

Rye was still ahead when they went out to lunch, and lard was holding its own.

They ate in the cafeteria with the gilded front. There was the same art inside as outside. The food looked sumptuous. Whole fishes were framed like pictures with carrots, and the salads were like terraced landscapes or like Mexican pyramids; slices of lemon and onion and radishes were like sun and moon and stars; the cream pies were about a foot thick and the cakes swollen as if sleepers had baked them in their dreams.

"What'll you have?" said Tamkin.

"Not much. I ate a big breakfast. I'll find a table. Bring me some yogurt and crackers and a cup of tea. I don't want to spend much time over lunch."

Tamkin said, "You've got to eat."

Finding an empty place at this hour was not easy. The old people idled and gossiped over their coffee. The elderly ladies were rouged and mascaraed and hennaed and used blue hair rinse and eye shadow and wore costume jewelry, and many of them were proud and stared at your with expressions that did not belong to their age. Were there no longer any respectable old ladies who knitted and cooked and looked after their grandchildren? Wilhelm's grandmother had dressed him in a sailor suit and danced him on her knee, blew on the porridge for him and said, "Admiral, you must eat." But what was the use of remembering this so late in the day?

He managed to find a table, and Dr. Tamkin came along with a tray piled with plates and cups. He had Yankee pot roast, purple cabbage, potatoes, a big slice of watermelon, and two cups of coffee. Wilhelm could not even swallow his yogurt. His chest pained him still.

At once Tamkin involved him in a lengthy discussion. Did he do it to stall Wilhelm and prevent him from selling out the rye—or to recover the ground lost when he had made Wilhelm angry by hints about the neurotic character? Or did he have no purpose except to talk?

"I think you worry a lot too much about what your wife and your father will say. Do they matter so much?"

Wilhelm replied, "A person can become tired of looking himself over and trying to fix himself up. You can spend the entire second half of your life recovering from the mistakes of the first half."

"I believe your dad told me he had some money to leave you."

"He probably does have something."

"A lot?"

"Who can tell," said Wilhelm guardedly.

"You ought to think over what you'll do with it."

"I may be too feeble to do anything by the time I get it. If I get anything."

"A thing like this you ought to plan out carefully. Invest it properly." He began to unfold the schemes whereby you bought bonds, and used the bonds as security to buy something else and thereby earned twelve per cent safely on your money. Wilhelm failed to follow the details. Tamkin said, "If he made you a gift now, you wouldn't have to pay the inheritance taxes."

Bitterly, Wilhelm told him, "My father's death blots out all other considerations from his mind. He forces me to think about it, too. Then he hates me because he succeeds. When I get desperate—of course I think about money. But I don't want anything to happen to him. I certainly don't want him to die." Tamkin's brown eyes glittered shrewdly at him. "You don't believe it. Maybe it's not psychological. But on my word of honor. A joke is a joke, but I don't want to joke about stuff like this. When he dies, I'll be robbed, like. I'll have no more father."

"You love your old man?"

Wilhelm grasped at this. "Of course, of course I love him. My father. My mother—" As he said this there was a great pull at the very center of his soul. When a fish strikes the line you feel the live force in your hand. A mysterious being beneath the water, driven by hunger, has taken the hook and rushes away and fights, writhing. Wilhelm never identified what struck within him. It did not reveal itself. It got away.

And Tamkin, the confuser of the imagination, began to tell, or to fabricate, the strange history of *his* father. "He was a great singer," he said. "He left us five kids because he fell in love with an opera soprano. I never held it against him, but admired the way he followed the life-principle. I wanted to do the same. Because of unhappiness at a certain age, the brain starts to die back." (True, true! thought Wilhelm.) "Twenty years later I was doing experiments in Eastman Kodak, Rochester, and I found the old fellow. He had five more children." (False, false!) "He wept; he was ashamed. I had nothing against him. I naturally felt strange."

"My dad is something of a stranger to me, too," said Wilhelm, and he began to muse. Where is the familiar person he used to be? Or I used to be? Catherine—she won't even talk to any more, my own sister. It may not be so much my trouble that Papa turns his back on as my confusion. It's too much. The ruins of life, and on top of that confusion—chaos and old night. Is it an easier farewell for Dad if we don't part friends? He should maybe do it angrily—"Blast you with my curse!" And why, Wilhelm further asked, should he or anybody else pity me; or why should I be pitied sooner than another fellow? It is my childish mind that thinks people are ready to give it just because you need it.

Then Wilhelm began to think about his own two sons and to wonder how he appeared to them, and what they would think of him. Right now he had an advantage through baseball. When he went to fetch them, to go to Ebbets Field, though, he was not himself. He put on a front but he felt as if he had swallowed a fistful of sand. The strange, familiar house, horribly awkward; the dog, Scissors, rolled over on his back and barked and whined. Wilhelm acted as if there were nothing irregular, but a weary heaviness came over him. On the way to Flatbush he would think up anecdotes about old Pigtown and Charlie Ebbets for the boys and reminiscences of the old stars, but it was very heavy going. They did not know how much he cared for them. No. It hurt him greatly and he blamed Margaret for turning them against him. She wanted to ruin him, while she wore the mask of kindness. Up in Roxbury he had to go and explain to the priest, who was not sympathetic. They don't care about individuals, their rules come first. Olive said she would marry him outside the Church when he was divorced. But Margaret would not let go. Olive's father was a pretty decent old guy, an osteopath, and he understood what it was all about. Finally he said, "See here, I have to advise Olive. She is asking me. I am mostly a freethinker myself, but the girl has to live in this town." And by now Wilhelm and Olive had had a great many troubles and she was beginning to dread his days in Roxbury, she said. He trembled at offending this small, pretty, dark girl whom he adored. When she would get up late on Sunday morning she would wake him almost in tears at being late for Mass. He would try to help her hitch her garters and smooth out her slip and dress and even put on her hat with shaky hands; then he would rush her to church and drive in second gear in his forgetful way, trying to apologize and to calm her. She got out a block from church to avoid gossip. Even so she loved him, and she would have married him if he had obtained the divorce. But Margaret must have sensed this. Margaret would tell him he did not really want a divorce; he was afraid of it. He cried, "Take everything I've got, Margaret. Let me go to Reno. Don't you want to marry again?" No. She went out with other men, but took his money. She lived in order to punish him.

Dr. Tamkin told Wilhelm, "Your dad is jealous of you."

Wilhelm smiled. "Of *me?* That's rich."

"Sure. People are always jealous of a man who leaves his wife."

"Oh," said Wilhelm scornfully. "When it comes to wives he wouldn't have to envy me."

"Yes, and your wife envies you, too. She thinks, He's free and goes with young women. Is she getting old?"

"Not exactly old," said Wilhelm, whom the mention of his wife made sad. Twenty years ago, in a neat blue wool suit, in a soft hat made of the same cloth—he could plainly see her. He stooped his yellow head and looked under the hat at her clear, simple face, her living eyes moving, her straight small nose, her jaw beautifully, painfully clear in its form. It was a cool day, but he smelled the odor of pines in the sun, in the granite canyon. Just south of Santa Barbara, this was.

"She's forty-some years old," he said.

"I was married to a lush," said Tamkin. "A painful alcoholic. I couldn't take her out to dinner because she'd say she was going to the ladies' toilet and disappear into the bar. I'd ask the bartenders they shouldn't serve her. But I loved her deeply. She was the most spiritual woman of my entire experience."

"Where is she now?"

"Drowned," said Tamkin. "At Provincetown, Cape Cod. It must have been a suicide. She was that way—suicidal. I tried everything in my power to cure her. Because," said Tamkin, "my real calling is to be a healer. I get wounded. I suffer from it. I would like to escape from the sicknesses of others, but I can't. I am only on loan to myself, so to speak. I belong to humanity."

Liar! Wilhelm inwardly called him. Nasty lies. He invented a woman and killed her off and then called himself a healer, and made himself so earnest he looked like a bad-natured sheep. He's a puffed-up little bogus and humbug with smelly feet. A doctor! A doctor would wash himself. He believes he's making a terrific impression, and he practically invites you to take off your hat when he talks about himself; and he thinks he has an imagination, but he hasn't, neither is he smart.

Then what am I doing with him here, and why did I give him the seven hundred dollars? thought Wilhelm.

Oh, this was a day of reckoning. It was a day, he thought, on which, willing or not, he would take a good close look at the truth. He breathed hard and his misshapen hat came low upon his congested dark blond face. A rude look. Tamkin was a charlatan, and furthermore he was desperate. And furthermore, Wilhelm had always known this about him. But he appeared to have worked it out at the back of his mind that Tamkin for thirty or forty years had gotten through many a tight place, that he would get through this crisis too and bring him, Wilhelm, to safety also. And Wilhelm realized that he was on Tamkin's back. It made him feel that he had virtually left the ground and was riding upon the other man. He was in the air. It was for Tamkin to take the steps.

The doctor, if he was a doctor, did not look anxious. But then his face did not have much variety. Talking always about spontaneous emotion and open receptors and free impulses, he was about as expressive as a pin-cushion. When his hypnotic spell failed, his big underlip made him look weak-minded. Fear stared from his eyes, sometimes, so humble as to make you sorry for him. Once or twice Wilhelm had seen that look. Like a dog, he thought. Perhaps he didn't look it now, but he was very nervous. Wilhelm knew, but he could not afford to recognize this too openly. The doctor needed a little room, a little time. He should not be pressed now. So Tamkin went on, telling his tales.

Wilhelm said to himself, I am on his back—his back. I gambled seven hundred bucks, so I must take this ride. I have to go along with him. It's too late. I can't get off.

"You know," Tamkin said, "that blind old man Rappaport—he's pretty close to totally blind—is one of the most interesting personalities around here. If you could only get him to tell his true story. It's fascinating. This is what he told me. You often hear about bigamists with a secret life. But this old man never hid anything from anybody. He's a regular patriarch. Now, I'll tell you what he did. He had two families, separate and apart, one in Williamsburg and the other in the Bronx. The two wives knew about each other. The wife in the Bronx was younger; she's close to seventy now. When he got sore at one wife he went to live with the other one. Meanwhile he ran his chicken business in New Jersey. By one wife he had four kids, and by the other six. They're all grown, but they never have met their half-brothers and sisters and don't want to. The whole bunch of them are listed in the telephone book."

"I can't believe it," said Wilhelm.

"He told me this himself. And do you know what else? While he had his eyesight he used to read a lot, but the only books he would read were by Theodore Roosevelt. He had a set in each of the places where he lived, and he brought his kids up on those books."

"Please," said Wilhelm, "don't feed me any more of this stuff, will you? Kindly do not—"

"In telling you this," said Tamkin with one of his hypnotic subtleties, "I do have a motive. I want you to see how some people free themselves from morbid guilt feelings and follow their instincts. Innately, the female knows how to cripple by sickening a man with guilt. It is a very special *destruct*, and she sends her curse to make a fellow impotent. As if she says, 'Unless I allow it, you will never more be a man.' But men like my old dad or Mr. Rappaport answer, 'Woman, what art thou to me?' You can't do that yet. You're a halfway case. You want to follow your instinct, but you're too worried still. For instance, about your kids—"

"Now look here," said Wilhelm, stamping his feet. "One thing! Don't bring up my boys. Just lay off."

"I was only going to say that they are better off than with conflicts in the home."

"I'm deprived of my children." Wilhelm bit his lip. It was too late to turn away. The anguish struck him. "I pay and pay. I never see them. They grow up without me. She makes them like herself. She'll bring them up to be my enemies. Please let's not talk about this."

But Tamkin said. "Why do you let her make you suffer so? It defeats the original object in leaving her. Don't play her game. Now, Wilhelm, I'm trying to do you some good. I want to tell you, don't marry suffering. Some people do. They get married to it, and sleep and eat together, just as husband and wife. If they go with joy they think it's adultery."

When Wilhelm heard this he had, in spite of himself, to admit that there was a great deal in Tamkin's words. Yes, thought Wilhelm, suffering is the only kind of life they are sure they can have, and if they quit suffering they're afraid they'll have nothing. He knows it. This time the faker knows what he's talking about.

Looking at Tamkin he believed he saw all this confessed from his usually barren face. Yes, yes, he too. One hundred falsehoods, but at last one truth. Howling like a wolf from the city window. No one can bear it any more. Everyone is so full of it that at last everybody must proclaim it. It! It!

Then suddenly Wilhelm rose and said, "That's enough of this. Tamkin, let's go back to the market."

"I haven't finished my melon."

"Never mind that. You've had enough to eat. I want to go back."

Dr. Tamkin slid the two checks across the table. "Who paid yesterday? It's your turn, I think."

It was not until they were leaving the cafeteria that Wilhelm remembered definitely that he had paid yesterday too. But it wasn't worth arguing about.

Tamkin kept repeating as they walked down the street that there were many who were dedicated to suffering. But he told Wilhelm, "I'm optimistic in your case, and I have seen a world of maladjustment. There's hope for you. You don't really want to destroy yourself. You're trying hard to keep your feelings open, Wilhelm. I can see it. Seven per cent of this country is committing suicide by alcohol. Another three, maybe, narcotics. Another sixty just fading away into dust by boredom. Twenty more who have sold their souls to the Devil. Then there's a small percentage of those who want to live. That's the only significant thing in the whole world of today. Those are the only two classes of people there are. Some want to live, but the great majority don't." This fantastic Tamkin began to surpass himself. "They don't. Or else, why these wars? I'll tell you more," he said. "The love of the dying amounts to one thing; they want you to die with them. It's because they love you. Make no mistake."

True, true! thought Wilhelm, profoundly moved by these revelations.

How does he know these things? How can he be such a jerk, and even perhaps an operator, a swindler, and understand so well what gives? I believe what he says. It simplifies much—everything. People are dropping like flies. I am trying to stay alive and work too hard at it. That's what's turning my brains. This working hard defeats its own end. At what point should I start over? Let me go back a ways and try once more.

Only a few hundred yards separated the cafeteria from the broker's, and within that short space Wilhelm turned again, in measurable degrees, from these wide considerations to the problems of the moment. The closer he approached to the market, the more Wilhelm had to think about money.

They passed the newsreel theater where the ragged shoeshine kids called after them. The same old bearded man with his bandaged beggar face and his tiny ragged feet and the old press clipping on his fiddle case to prove he had once been a concert violinist, pointed his bow at Wilhelm, saying, "You!" Wilhelm went by with worried eyes, bent on crossing Seventy-second Street. In full tumult the great afternoon current raced for Columbus Circle, where the mouth of midtown stood open and the skyscrapers gave back the yellow fire of the sun.

As they approached the polished stone front of the new office building, Dr. Tamkin said, "Well, isn't that old Rappaport by the door? I think he should carry a white cane, but he will never admit there's a single thing the matter with his eyes."

Mr. Rappaport did not stand well; his knees were sunk, while his pelvis only half filled his trousers. His suspenders held them, gaping.

He stopped Wilhelm with an extended hand, having somehow recognized him. In his deep voice he commanded him, "Take me to the cigar store."

"You want me—? Tamkin!" Wilhelm whispered, "You take him."

Tamkin shook his head. "He wants you. Don't refuse the old gentleman." Significantly he said in a lower voice. "This minute is another instance of the 'here-and-now.' You have to live in this very minute, and you don't want to. A man asks you for help. Don't think of the market. It won't run away. Show your respect to the old boy. Go ahead. That may be more valuable."

"Take me," said the old chicken merchant again.

Greatly annoyed, Wilhelm wrinkled his face at Tamkin. He took the old man's big but light elbow at the bone. "Well, let's step on it," he said. "Or wait—I want to have a look at the board first to see how we're doing."

But Tamkin had already started Mr. Rappaport forward. He was walking, and he scolded Wilhelm, saying, "Don't leave me standing in the middle of the sidewalk. I'm afraid to get knocked over."

"Let's get a move on. Come." Wilhelm urged him as Tamkin went into the broker's.

The traffic seemed to come down Broadway out of the sky, where the hot spokes of the sun rolled from the south. Hot, stony odors rose from the subway grating in the street.

"These teen-age hoodlums worry me. I'm scared of these Puerto Rican kids, and these young characters who take dope," said Mr. Rappaport. "They go around all hopped up."

"Hoodlums?" said Wilhelm. "I went to the cemetery and my mother's stone bench was split. I could have broken somebody's neck for that. Which store do you go to?"

"Across Broadway. That La Magnita sign next door to the Automat."

"What's the matter with this store here on this side?"

"They don't carry my brand, that's what's the matter."

Wilhelm cursed, but checked the words.

"What are you talking?"

"Those damn taxis," said Wilhelm. "They want to run everybody down."

They entered the cool, odorous shop. Mr. Rappaport put away his large cigars with great care in various pockets while Wilhelm muttered, "Come on, you old creeper. What a poky old character! The whole world waits on him." Rappaport did not offer Wilhelm a cigar, but, holding one up, he asked, "What do you say at the size of these, huh? They're Churchill-type cigars."

He barely crawls along, thought Wilhelm. His pants are dropping off because he hasn't got enough flesh for them to stick to. He's almost blind, and covered with spots, but this old man still makes money in the market. Is loaded with dough, probably. And I bet he doesn't give his children any. Some of them must be in their fifties. This is what keeps middle-aged men as children. He's master over the dough. Think—just think! Who controls everything? Old men of this type. Without needs. They don't need therefore they have. I need, therefore I don't have. That would be too easy.

"I'm older even than Churchill," said Rappaport.

Now he wanted to talk! But if you asked him a question in the market, he couldn't be bothered to answer.

"I bet you are," said Wilhelm. "Come, let's get going."

"I was a fighter, too, like Churchill," said the old man. "When we licked Spain I went into the Navy. Yes, I was a gob that time. What did I have to lose? Nothing. After the battle of San Juan Hill, Teddy Roosevelt kicked me off the beach."

"Come, watch the curb," said Wilhelm.

"I was curious and wanted to see what went on. I didn't have no business there, but I took a boat and rowed myself to the beach. Two of our guys was dead, layin' under the American flag to keep the flies off. So I says to the guy on duty, there, who was the sentry, 'Let's have a look at these guys. I want to see what went on here,' and he says, 'Naw,' but I talked him into it. So he took off the flag and there were these two tall guys, both gentlemen, lying in their boots. They was very tall. The two of them had long mustaches. They were high-society boys. I think one of them was called Fish, from up the Hudson, a big-shot family. When I looked up, there was Teddy Roosevelt, with his hat off, and he was looking at these fellows, the only ones who got killed there. Then he says to me, 'What's the Navy want here? Have you got orders?' 'No, sir,' I says to him. 'Well, get the hell off the beach, then.' "

Old Rappaport was very proud of this memory. "Everything he said had such snap, such class. Man! I love that Teddy Roosevelt," he said, "I love him!"

Ah, what people are! He is almost not with us, and his life is nearly gone, but T. R. once yelled at him, so he loves him. I guess it is love, too. Wilhelm smiled. So maybe the rest of Tamkin's story was true, about the ten children and the wives and the telephone directory.

He said, "Come on, come on, Mr. Rappaport," and hurried the old man back by the large hollow elbow; he gripped it through the thin cotton cloth. Re-entering the brokerage office where under the lights the tumblers were speeding with the clack of drumsticks upon wooden blocks, more than ever resembling a Chinese theater, Wilhelm strained his eyes to see the board.

The lard figures were unfamiliar. That amount couldn't be lard! They must have put the figures in the wrong slot. He traced the line back to the margin. It was down to .19, and had dropped twenty points since noon. And what about the contract of rye? It had sunk back to its earlier position, and they had lost their chance to sell.

Old Mr. Rappaport said to Wilhelm, "Read me my wheat figure."

"Oh, leave me alone for a minute," he said, and positively hid his face from the old man behind one hand. He looked for Tamkin, Tamkin's bald head, or Tamkin with his gray straw and the cocoa-colored band. He couldn't see him. Where was he? The seats next to Rowland were taken by strangers. He thrust himself over the one on the aisle. Mr. Rappaport's former place, and pushed at the back of the chair until the new occupant, a red-head man with a thin, determined face, leaned forward to get out of his way but would not surrender the seat. "Where's Tamkin?" Wilhelm asked Rowland.

"Gee, I don't know. Is anything wrong?"

"You must have seen him. He came in a while back."

"No, but I didn't."

Wilhelm fumbled out a pencil from the top pocket of his coat and began to make calculations. His very fingers were numb, and in his agitation he was afraid he made mistakes with the decimal points and went over the subtraction and multiplication like a schoolboy at an exam. His heart, accustomed to many sorts of crisis, was now in a new panic. And, as he had dreaded, he was wiped out. It was unnecessary to ask the German manager. He could see for himself that the electronic bookkeeping device must have closed him out. The manager probably had known that Tamkin wasn't to be trusted, and on that first day he might have warned him. But you couldn't expect him to interfere.

"You get hit?" said Mr. Rowland.

And Wilhelm, quite coolly, said, "Oh, it could have been worse, I guess." He put the piece of paper into his pocket with its cigarette butts and packets of pills. The lie helped him out—although, for a moment, he was afraid he would cry. But he hardened himself. The hardening effort made a violent, vertical pain go through his chest, like that caused by a pocket of air under the collar bones. To the old chicken millionaire, who by this time had become acquainted with the drop in rye and lard, he also denied that anything serious had happened. "It's just one of those temporary slumps. Nothing to be scared about," he said, and remained in possession of himself. His need to cry, like someone in a crowd, pushed and jostled and abused him from behind, and Wilhelm did not dare turn. He said to himself, I will not cry in front of these people. I'll be damned if I'll break down in front of them like a kid, even though I never expect to see them again. No! No! And yet his unshed tears rose and rose and he looked like a man about to drown. But when they talked to him, he answered very distinctly. He tried to speak proudly.

". . . going away?" he heard Rowland ask.

"What?"

"I thought you might be going away too. Tamkin said he was going to Maine this summer for his vacation."

"Oh, going away?"

Wilhelm broke off and went to look for Tamkin in the men's toilet. Across the corridor was the room where the machinery of the board was housed. It hummed and whirred like mechanical birds, and the tubes glittered in the dark. A couple of businessmen with cigarettes in their fingers were having a conversation in the lavatory. At the top of the closet door sat a gray straw hat with a cocoa-colored band. "Tamkin," said Wilhelm. He tried to identify the feet below the door. "Are you in there, Doctor Tamkin?" he said with stifled anger. "Answer me. It's Wilhelm."

The hat was taken down, the latch lifted, and a stranger came out who looked at him with annoyance.

"You waiting?" said one of the businessmen. He was warning Wilhelm that he was out of turn.

"Me? Not me," said Wilhelm. "I'm looking for a fellow."

Bitterly angry, he said to himself that Tamkin would pay him the two hundred dollars at least, his share of the original deposit. "And before he takes the train to Maine, too. Before he spends a penny on vacation—that liar! We went into this as equal partners."

VII

I was the man beneath; Tamkin was on my back, and I thought I was on his. He made me carry him, too, besides Margaret. Like this they ride on me with hoofs and claws. Tear me to pieces, stamp on me and break my bones.

Once more the hoary old fiddler pointed his bow at Wilhelm as he hurried by. Wilhelm rejected his begging and denied the omen. He dodged heavily through traffic and with his quick, small steps ran up the lower stairway of the Gloriana Hotel with its dark-tinted mirrors, kind to people's defects. From the lobby he phoned Tamkin's room, and when no one answered he took the elevator up. A rouged woman in her fifties with a mink stole led three tiny dogs on a leash, high-strung creatures with prominent black eyes, like dwarf deer, and legs like twigs. This was the eccentric Estonian lady who had been moved with her pets to the twelfth floor.

She identified Wilhelm. "You are Doctor Adler's son," she said.

Formally, he nodded.

"I am a dear friend of your father."

He stood in the corner and would not meet her glance, and she thought he was snubbing her and made a mental note to speak of it to the doctor.

The linen-wagon stood at Tamkin's door, and the chambermaid's key with its big brass tongue was in the lock.

"Has Doctor Tamkin been here?" he asked her.

"No, I haven't seen him."

Wilhelm came in, however, to look around. He examined the photos on the desk, trying to connect the faces with the strange people in Tamkin's stories. Big, heavy volumes were stacked under the double-pronged TV aerial. *Science and Sanity,* he read, and there were several books of poetry. The *Wall Street Journal* hung in separate sheets from the bed-table under the weight of the silver water jug. A bathrobe with lightning streaks of red and white was laid across the foot of the bed with a pair of expensive batik pajamas. It was a box of a room, but from the windows you saw the river as far uptown as the bridge, as far downtown as Hoboken. What lay between was deep, azure, dirty, complex, crystal, rusty, with the red bones of new apartments rising on the bluffs of New Jersey, and huge liners in their berths, the tugs with matted beards of cordage. Even the brackish tidal river smell rose this high, like the smell of mop water. From every side he heard pianos, and the voices of men and women singing scales and opera, all mixed, and the sounds of pigeons on the ledges.

Again Wilhelm took the phone. "Can you locate Doctor Tamkin in the lobby for me?" he asked. And when the operator reported that she could not, Wilhelm gave the number of his father's room, but Dr. Adler was not in either. "Well, please give me the masseur. I say the massage room. Don't you understand me? The men's health club. Yes, Max Schilper's—how am I supposed to know the name of it?"

There a strange voice said, "Toktor Adler?" It was the old Czech prize-fighter with the deformed nose and ears who was attendant down there and gave out soap, sheets, and sandals. He went away. A hollow endless silence followed. Wilhelm flickered the receiver with his nails, whistled into it, but could not summon either the attendant or the operator.

The maid saw him examining the bottles of pills on Tamkin's table and seemed suspicious of him. He was running low on Phenaphen pills and was looking for something else. But he swallowed one of his own tablets and went out and rang again for the elevator. He went down to the health club. Through the steamy windows, when he emerged, he saw the reflection of the swimming pool swirling green at the bottom of the lowest stairway. He went through the locker-room curtains. Two men wrapped in towels were playing Ping-pong. They were awkward and the ball bounded high. The Negro in the toilet was shining shoes. He did not know Dr. Adler by name, and Wilhelm descended to the massage room. On the tables naked men were lying. It was not a brightly lighted place, and it was very hot, and under the white faint moons of the ceiling shone pale skins. Calendar pictures of pretty girls dressed in tiny fringes were pinned on the wall. On the first table, eyes deeply shut in heavy silent luxury lay a man with a full square beard and short legs, stocky and black-haired. He might have been an orthodox Russian. Wrapped in a sheet, waiting, the man beside him was newly shaved and red from the steambath. He had a big happy face and was dreaming. And after him was an athlete, strikingly muscled, powerful and young, with a strong white curve to his genital and a half-angry smile on his mouth. Dr. Adler was on the fourth table, and Wilhelm stood over his father's pale, slight body. His ribs were narrow and small, his belly round, white, and high. It had its own being, like something separate. His thighs were weak, the muscles of his arms had fallen, his throat was creased.

The masseur in his undershirt bent and whispered in his ear, "It's your son," and Dr. Adler opened his eyes into Wilhelm's face. At once he saw the trouble in it, and by an instantaneous reflex he removed himself from the danger of contagion, and he said serenely, "Well, have you taken my advice, Wilky?"

"Oh, Dad," said Wilhelm.

"To take a swim and get a massage?"

"Did you get my note?" said Wilhelm.

"Yes, but I'm afraid you'll have to ask somebody else, because I can't. I had no idea you were so low on funds. How did you let it happen? Didn't you lay anything aside?"

"Oh, please, Dad," said Wilhelm, almost bringing his hands together in a clasp.

"I'm sorry," said the doctor. "I really am. But I have set up a rule. I've thought about it, I believe it is a good rule, and I don't want to change it. You haven't acted wisely. What's the matter?"

"Everything. Just everything. What isn't? I did have a little, but I haven't been very smart."

"You took some gamble? You lost it? Was it Tamkin? I told you, Wilky, not to build on that Tamkin. Did you? I suspect—"

"Yes, Dad, I'm afraid I trusted him."

Dr. Adler surrendered his arm to the masseur, who was using winter-green oil.

"Trusted! And got taken?"

"I'm afraid I kind of—" Wilhelm glanced at the masseur but he was absorbed in his work. He probably did not listen to conversations. "I did. I might as well say it. I should have listened to you."

"Well, I won't remind you how often I warned you. It must be very painful.

"Yes, Father, it is "

"I don't know how many times you have to be burned in order to learn something. The same mistakes, over and over."

"I couldn't agree with you more," said Wilhelm with a face of despair. "You're so right, Father. It's the same mistakes, and I get burned again and again. I can't seem to—I'm stupid, Dad, I just can't breathe. My chest is all up—I feel choked. I just simply can't catch my breath."

He stared at his father's nakedness. Presently he became aware that Dr. Adler was making an effort to keep his temper. He was on the verge of an explosion. Wilhelm hung his face and said, "Nobody likes bad luck, eh Dad?"

"So! It's bad luck, now. A minute ago it was stupidity."

"It is stupidity—it's some of both. It's true that I can't learn. But I—"

"I don't want to listen to the details," said his father. "And I want you to understand that I'm too old to take on new burdens. I'm just too old to do it. And people who will just wait for help—must *wait* for help. They have got to stop waiting."

"It isn't all a question of money—there are other things a father can give to a son." He lifted up his gray eyes and his nostrils grew wide with a look of suffering appeal that stirred his father even more deeply against him.

He warningly said to him, "Look out, Wilky, you're tiring my patience very much."

"I try not to. But one word from you, just a word, would go a long way. I've never asked you for very much But you are not a kind man, Father. You don't give the little bit I beg you for."

He recognized that his father was now furiously angry. Dr. Adler started to say something, and then raised himself and gathered the sheet over him as he did so. His mouth opened, wide, dark, twisted, and he said to Wilhelm, "You want to make yourself into my cross. But I am not going to pick up a cross. I'll see you dead, Wilky, by Christ, before I let you do that to me."

"Father, listen! Listen!"

"Go away from me now. It's torture for me to look at you, you slob!" cried Dr. Adler.

Wilhelm's blood rose up madly, in anger equal to his father's, but then it sank down and left him helplessly captive to misery. He said stiffly, and with a strange sort of formality, "Okay, Dad. That'll be enough. That's about all we should say." And he stalked out heavily by the door adjacent to the swimming pool and the steam room, and labored up two long flights from the basement. Once more he took the elevator to the lobby on the mezzanine.

He inquired at the desk for Dr. Tamkin.

The clerk said, "No, I haven't seen him. But I think there's something in the box for you."

"Me? Give it here," said Wilhelm and opened a telephone message from his wife. It read, "Please phone Mrs. Wilhelm on return. Urgent."

Whenever he received an urgent message from his wife he was always thrown into a great fear for the children. He ran to the phone booth, spilled out the change from his pockets onto the little curved steel shelf under the telephone, and dialed the Digby number.

"Yes?" said his wife. Scissors barked in the parlor.

"Margaret?"

"Yes, hello." They never exchanged any other greeting. She instantly knew his voice.

"The boys all right?"

"They're out on their bicycles. Why shouldn't they be all right? Scissors, quiet!"

"Your message scared me," he said. "I wish you wouldn't make 'urgent' so common."

"I had something to tell you."

Her familiar unbending voice awakened in him a kind of hungry longing, not for Margaret but for the peace he had once known.

"You sent me a postdated check," she said. "I can't allow that. It's already five days past the first. You dated your check for the twelfth "

"Well, I have no money. I haven't got it. You can't send me to prison for that. I'll be lucky if I can raise it by the twelfth."

She answered, "You better get it, Tommy."

"Yes? What for?" he said. "Tell me. For the sake of what? To tell lies about me to everyone? You—"

She cut him off. "You know what for. I've got the boys to bring up."

Wilhelm in the narrow booth broke into a heavy sweat. He dropped his head and shrugged while with his fingers he arranged nickels, dimes, and quarters in rows. "I'm doing my best," he said. "I've had some bad luck. As a matter of fact, it's been so bad that I don't know where I am. I couldn't tell you what day of the week this is. I can't think straight. I'd better not even try. This has been one of those days, Margaret. May I never live to go through another like it. I mean that with all my heart. So I'm not going to try to do any thinking today. Tomorrow I'm going to see some guys. One is a sales manager. The other is in television. But not to act," he hastily added. "On the business end."

"That's just some more of your talk, Tommy," she said. "You ought to patch things up with Rojax Corporation. They'd take you back. You've got to stop thinking like a youngster."

"What do you mean?"

"Well," she said, measured and unbending, remorselessly unbending, "you still think like a youngster. But you can't do that any more. Every other day you want to make a new start. But in eighteen years you'll be eligible for retirement. Nobody wants to hire a new man of your age."

"I know. But listen, you don't have to sound so hard. I can't get on my knees to them. And really you don't have to sound so hard. I haven't done you so much harm."

"Tommy, I have to chase you and ask you for money that you owe us, and I hate it."

She hated also to be told that her voice was hard.

"I'm making an effort to control myself," she told him.

He could picture her, her graying bangs cut with strict fixity above her pretty, decisive face. She prided herself on being fair-minded. We could not bear, he thought, to know what we do. Even though blood is spilled. Even though the breath of life is taken from someone's nostrils. This is the way of the weak; quiet and fair. And then smash! They smash!

"Rojax take me back? I'd have to crawl back. They don't need me. After so many years I should have got stock in the firm. How can I support the three of you, and live myself, on half the territory? And why should I even try when you won't lift a finger to help? I sent you back to school, didn't I? At that time you said—"

His voice was rising. She did not like that and intercepted him. "You misunderstood me," she said.

"You must realize you're killing me. You can't be as blind as all that. Thou shalt not kill! Don't you remember that?"

She said, "You're just raving now. When you calm down it'll be different. I have great confidence in your earning ability."

"Margaret, you don't grasp the situation. You'll have to get a job."

"Absolutely not. I'm not going to have two young children running loose."

"They're not babies," Wilhelm said. "Tommy is fourteen. Paulie is going to be ten."

"Look," Margaret said in her deliberate manner. "We can't continue this conversation if you're going to yell so, Tommy. They're at a dangerous age. There are teen-aged gangs—the parents working, or the families broken up."

Once again she was reminding him that it was he who had left her. She had the bringing up of the children as her burden, while he must expect to pay the price of his freedom.

Freedom! he thought with consuming bitterness. Ashes in his mouth, not freedom. Give me my children. For they are mine too.

Can you be the woman I lived with? he started to say. Have you forgotten that we slept so long together? Must you now deal with me like this, and have no mercy?

He would be better off with Margaret again than he was today. This was what she wanted to make him feel, and she drove it home. "Are you in misery?" she was saying. "But you have deserved it." And he could not return to her any more than he could beg Rojax to take him back. If it costs him his life, he could not. Margaret had ruined him with Olive. She hit him and hit him, beat him, battered him, wanted to beat the very life out of him.

"Margaret, I want you please to reconsider about work. You have that degree now. Why did I pay your tuition?"

"Because it seemed practical. But it isn't. Growing boys need parental authority and a home."

He begged her, "Margaret, go easy on me. You ought to. I'm at the end of my rope and feel that I'm suffocating. You don't want to be responsible for a person's destruction. You've got to let up. I feel I'm about to burst." His face had expanded. He struck a blow upon the tin and wood and nails of the wall of the booth. "You've got to let me breathe. If I should keel over, what then? And it's something I can never understand about you. How you can treat someone like this whom you lived with so long. Who gave you the best of himself. Who tried. Who loved you." Merely to pronounce the word "love" made him tremble.

"Ah," she said with a sharp breath. "Now we're coming to it. How did you imagine it was going to be—big shot? Everything made smooth for you? I thought you were leading up to this."

She had not, perhaps, intended to reply as harshly as she did, but she brooded a great deal and now she could not forbear to punish him and make him feel pains like those she had to undergo.

He struck the wall again, this time with his knuckles, and he had scarcely enough air in his lungs to speak in a whisper, because his heart pushed upward with a frightful pressure. He got up and stamped his feet in the narrow enclosure.

"Haven't I always done my best?" he yelled, though his voice sounded weak and thin to his own ears. "Everything comes from me and nothing back again to me. There's no law that'll punish this, but you are committing a crime against me. Before God—and that's no joke. I mean that. Before God! Sooner or later the boys will know it."

In a firm tone, levelly, Margaret said to him, "I won't stand to be howled at. When you can speak normally and have something sensible to say I'll listen. But not to this." She hung up.

Wilhelm tried to tear the apparatus from the wall. He ground his teeth and seized the black box with insane digging fingers and made a stifled cry and pulled. Then he saw an elderly lady staring through the glass door, utterly appalled by him, and he ran from the booth, leaving a large amount of change on the shelf. He hurried down the stairs and into the street.

On Broadway it was still bright afternoon and the gassy air was almost motionless under the leaden spokes of sunlight, and sawdust footprints lay about the doorways of butcher shops and fruit stores. And the great, great crowd, the inexhaustible current of millions of every race and kind pouring out, pressing round, of every age, of every genius, possessors of every human secret, antique and future, in every face the refinement of one particular motive or essence—*I labor, I spend, I strive, I design, I love, I cling, I uphold, I give way, I envy, I long, I scorn, I die, I hide, I want.* Faster, much faster than any man could make the tally. The sidewalks were wider than any causeway; the street itself was immense, and it quaked and gleamed and it seemed to Wilhelm to throb at the last limit of endurance. And although the sunlight appeared like a broad tissue, its actual weight made him feel like a drunkard.

"I'll get a divorce if it's the last thing I do," he swore. "As for Dad— As for Dad—I'll have to sell the car for junk and pay the hotel. I'll have to go on my knees to Olive and say, 'Stand by me a while. Don't let her win. Olive!' " And he thought, I'll try to start again with Olive. In fact, I must. Olive loves me. Olive—

Beside a row of limousines near the curb he thought he saw Dr. Tamkin. Of course he had been mistaken before about the hat with the cocoa-colored band and didn't want to make the same mistake twice. But wasn't that Tamkin who was speaking so earnestly, with pointed shoulders, to someone under the canopy of the funeral parlor? For this was a huge funeral. He looked for the singular face under the dark gray, fashionable hatbrim. There were two open cars filled with flowers, and a policeman tried to keep a path open to pedestrians. Right at the canopy-pole, now wasn't that that damned Tamkin talking away with a solemn face, gesticulating with an open hand?

"Tamkin!" shouted Wilhelm, going forward. But he was pushed to the side by a policeman clutching his nightstick at both ends, like a rolling pin. Wilhelm was even farther from Tamkin now, and swore under his breath at the cop who continued to press him back, back, belly and ribs, saying, "Keep it moving there, please," his face red with impatient sweat, his brows like red fur. Wilhelm said to him haughtily, "You shouldn't push people like this."

The policeman, however, was not really to blame. He had been ordered to keep a way clear. Wilhelm was moved forward by the pressure of the crowd.

He cried, "Tamkin!"

But Tamkin was gone. Or rather, it was he himself who was carried from the street into the chapel. The pressure ended inside, where it was dark and cool. The flow of fan-driven air dried his face, which he wiped

hard with his handkerchief to stop the slight salt itch. He gave a sigh when
he heard the organ notes that stirred and breathed from the pipes and he
saw people in the pews. Men in formal clothes and black homburgs strode
softly back and forth on the cork floor, up and down the center aisle. The
white of the stained glass was like mother-of-pearl, the blue of the Star of
David like velvet ribbon.

Well, thought Wilhelm, if that was Tamkin outside I might as well wait
for him here where it's cool. Funny, he never mentioned he had a funeral
to go to today. But that's just like the guy.

But within a few minutes he had forgotten Tamkin. He stood along the
wall with others and looked toward the coffin and the slow line that was
moving past it, gazing at the face of the dead. Presently he too was in this
line, and slowly, slowly, foot by foot, the beating of his heart anxious,
thick, frightening, but somehow also rich, he neared the coffin and paused
for his turn, and gazed down. He caught his breath when he looked at the
corpse, and his face swelled, his eyes shone hugely with instant tears.

The dead man was gray-haired. He had two large waves of gray hair at
the front. But he was not old. His face was long, and he had a bony nose,
slightly, delicately twisted. His brows were raised as though he had sunk
into the final thought. Now at last he was with it, after the end of all distractions, and when his flesh was no longer flesh. And by this meditative
look Wilhelm was so struck that he could not go away. In spite of the tinge
of horror, and then the splash of heartsickness that he felt, he could not go.
He stepped out of line and remained beside the coffin; his eyes filled
silently and through his still tears he studied the man as the line of visitors
moved with veiled looks past the satin coffin toward the standing bank of
lilies, lilacs, roses. With great stifling sorrow, almost admiration, Wilhelm
nodded and nodded. On the surface, the dead man with his formal shirt
and his tie and silk lapels and his powdered skin looked so proper; only a
little beneath so—black, Wilhelm thought, so fallen in the eyes.

Standing a little apart, Wilhelm began to cry. He cried at first softly and
from sentiment, but soon from deeper feeling. He sobbed loudly and his
face grew distorted and hot, and the tears stung his skin. A man—another
human creature, was what first went through his thoughts, but other and
different things were torn from him. What'll I do? I'm stripped and kicked
out. . . . Oh, Father, what do I ask of you? What'll I do about the kids—
Tommy, Paul? My children. And Olive? My dear! Why, why, why—you
must protect me against that devil who wants my life. If you want it, then
kill me. Take, take it, take it from me.

Soon he was past words, past reason, coherence. He could not stop. The
source of all his tears had suddenly sprung open within him, black, deep,
and hot, and they were pouring out and convulsed his body, bending his
stubborn head, bowing his shoulders, twisting his face, crippling the very
hands with which he held the handkerchief. His efforts to collect himself

were useless. The great knot of ill and grief in his throat swelled upward and he gave in utterly and held his face and wept. He cried with all his heart.

He, alone of all the people in the chapel, was sobbing. No one knew who he was.

One woman said, "Is that perhaps the cousin from New Orleans they were expecting?"

"It must be somebody real close to carry on so."

"Oh my, oh my! To be mourned like that," said one man and looked at Wilhelm's heavy shaken shoulders, his clutched face and whitened fair hair, with wide, glinting, jealous eyes.

"The man's brother, maybe?"

"Oh, I doubt that very much," said another bystander. "They're not alike at all. Night and day."

The flowers and lights fused ecstatically in Wilhelm's blind, wet eyes; the heavy sea-like music came up to his ears. It poured into him where he had hidden himself in the center of a crowd by the great and happy oblivion of tears. He heard it and sank deeper than sorrow, through torn sobs and cries toward the consummation of his heart's ultimate need.

HERMAN MELVILLE
(1819-1891)

Some of Herman Melville's later concern with themes of good and evil can be traced back to the Presbyterianism of his father and the Dutch Reformed views of his mother. Both parents came from distinguished families. The Melvilles moved to Albany after their prosperous merchant business failed in New York City during the depression of 1826. Herman's father, Allan Melville, strove courageously to recoup his losses, but he died bankrupt and embittered in 1832, leaving the family close to poverty. Their financial condition worsened under Mrs. Melville's mismanagement. After only four years of formal education, Herman tried his hand at various jobs, including school teaching in Pittsfield, Massachusetts. Driven from home by need and, as he claimed later, by his mother's coldness toward him, he shipped as a cabin boy on a freighter bound for Liverpool when he was seventeen. The voyage wedded his spirit to the sea. His next berth, aboard the whale-ship *Acushnet,* took him to the South Seas and initiated a series of rare and youthful adventures which supplied the imaginative stuff of his fiction for years to come. Deserting the *Acushnet* because of its brutal discipline, he lived in pleasant captivity among the cannibalistic Typee islanders for four months. He escaped aboard an Australian whaler, jumped ship again in Papeete, lived as a beachcomber and pin-spotter in Hawaii, joined the U.S. Navy there, and finally reached America as a seaman of the U.S.S. *United States* by way of Cape Horn in October of 1844.

Melville had little anticipation of a literary career as he began to write of his exotic experiences. The fact was that he did not know what else to do: he was untrained for any occupation on land. The appearance of *Typee: A Peep at Polynesian Life* (1846) and its sequel *Omoo* (1847) made him famous as "the man who had lived among cannibals." His works went through numerous editions, and he was lionized in New York literary circles as a promising young author. In 1847 he married Elizabeth Shaw, daughter of the Chief Justice of Massachusetts. She was staunch in her devotion to Melville although she proved to be quite incapable of understanding his artist's soul. Their two sons died in childhood; one daughter outlived her parents.

Mardi (1849) presaged Melville's shift from the fiction of romantic adventure to the complex treatment of allegorical symbolism and theme. *Mardi* was an extremely complicated novel, burdened with themes of sin and guilt, politics, ethics, and metaphysics. Unfortunately the novel was not a good one, partly because Melville's ability to fuse fact and imagination was not yet mature, and for the first time he knew the sour taste of literary failure. Because he sorely needed money, he reverted to variations of his earlier fiction of adventure in *Redburn: His First Voyage* (1849) and *White Jacket; or, The World in a Man-of-War* (1850). His trip to Liverpool supplied background for the first work, and he drew on his experiences in the Navy for the second. Beneath the adventurous surface of both novels, vestiges of symbolic meaning persisted.

Melville's creative powers were forever engendered and revived by the sea. After crossing the Atlantic to negotiate the publication of *White Jacket* in London, he moved his family from New York City to "Arrowhead," a farm in Pittsfield, and began work on *Moby Dick; or, The White Whale.* In need of money as always, he planned to please his readers with a light-hearted, nonmetaphysical tale of whaling, packed with adventure and realistic detail. The story began in that way, but before long Melville found himself enmeshed in a work of great complexity. Genial comedy alternated with scenes of demonic terror, and metaphysical speculation proliferated. Melville knew, when *Moby Dick* was finished in 1851, that the story of Captain Ahab's search for the white whale was an epic of modern man: man's technological passion, his social alienation, his fallen morality and religious thirst for redemption. Writing the novel was a spiritual effort that exhausted Melville. He was never quite the same man again. To his grief, *Moby Dick* was badly reviewed and the public ignored it. He was by nature an exuberant man, with a deep vein of irony that usually allowed him to mock his disappointments, but his following novels reveal that something inside him had broken. Desperate for recognition as he was, he turned away from his popular audience and from the world, and retreated into the dark ambiguities of his own mysticism. *Pierre; or, The Ambiguities* (1852) was a powerful melodrama of incest, pessimism, and misanthropy, reflecting Melville's descent into the turmoil of self. *Bartleby the Scrivener* appeared during this period, in 1855. *Israel Potter* (1855) and *The Confidence Man* (1857) both manifest his vision of the United States as a land corrupted by hypocrisy; the second novel especially writhes with repressed cynicism and fury.

His family, fearing that his anxiety might lead to madness or death, scraped up the money to send him on a curative voyage to Palestine via Constantinople. In Liverpool he spent an afternoon talking with his misunderstood old friend, Nathaniel Hawthorne. On his return he attempted to make a living by lecturing. Failing in that, he moved back to New York City and for twenty years supported himself as a customs inspector—a task of deadly boredom, but one which kept the life-giving sea within his view. Hollow-eyed and heavily bearded, he spoke with no one, and lived "reconciled to annihilation." In these late years he wrote several volumes of poetry, but little of it was good. He had fallen into such complete obscurity that local papers did not even note his death in September, 1891.

FEDOR DOSTOEVSKY
(1821-1881)

"That is truth in art. . . . The truth has been revealed and announced to you as an artist, it has been brought as a gift; value this gift and remain faithful to it, and you will be a great writer," said the famous literary critic Vissarion Belinsky upon reading Dostoevsky's first novel, *Poor Folk*. At the age of twenty-five Dostoevsky was launched upon a tumultuous, haunted, brilliant career.

He had grown up in a family of eight children within the dingy confines of a Moscow hospital where his father was chief surgeon. Family life was dominated by the patriarchal strictness of Mikhail Andreevich Dostoevsky, who despite his religious fervor was drunken, avaricious, and cruel. He undoubtedly sowed the seeds of Fedor's later obsessions with themes of irrational violence, punishment by authority, and father-murder. At thirteen Dostoevsky went to board at a private school in Moscow. Two years later his mother died. In 1839, when he was studying at the Military Engineers School of St. Petersburg, his father was murdered by serfs in his own village of Darovo. Fedor became qualified as a military engineer in 1843, but after a year he resigned from the Engineers Corps to become a writer.

Short and heavily built, he was described at the age of twenty-two as "very fair with a rounded face and slightly upturned nose . . . under the high forehead and sparse eyebrows were hidden the small, rather deeply-set gray eyes: the cheeks were pale and covered with freckles; the color of the face was sickly, pallid, the lips thick." After his success with *Poor Folk* he went on to write a short novel, *The Double*. This remarkable study of paranoia, spiritually akin to the later *Notes from Underground,* reveals how a wretched government clerk is driven into madness by his own devilish psychological double. Dostoevsky was already working with the idea that strictly rational society, without compassion for the irrational, is itself a kind of madness. *The Double* and Dostoevsky's succeeding stories were poorly received and the influential critics now dismissed him as a failure. Frustrated to the point of illness, he retreated from his literary friends and began to attend Friday gatherings at the house of Mikhail Petrashevsky, where he partook in discussions about Utopian Socialism and plans to promote a revolution among the serfs. The Tsar's government, riddled with suspicion in that age of political turmoil, arrested the Petrashevsky group. After eight months' imprisonment, Dostoevsky and twenty of his comrades were condemned to be shot. On a cold December morning in 1849 they witnessed all the preliminaries of their own execution, only to be reprieved at the last second by the Tsar. Nicholas I had planned the entire execution scenario as a ritual torture. Dostoevsky was so tormented by the ordeal that ever afterward he suffered from a form of epilepsy later diagnosed by Freud as extreme hysteria.

For his "crimes" of political discussion, he spent five years in a Siberian prison camp and another five in the lowest ranks of the army. He began his imprisonment as a radical and unbeliever. He emerged as a new man, with a mystical faith in Christ and a surprising respect for the government which had punished him. He also brought from Siberia a new compassion for the suffering prisoners he had known there; to him, they were the soul of Russia. While a soldier in the Siberian town of Semipalatinsk, he married

Marya Isaeva, a pretty but rather hysterical widow. Their relationship was not a happy one, but he was now able to read and write with relative freedom once again. In December of 1859 he was allowed to return to his beloved St. Petersburg, a free man.

His next two novels met with success. In 1861 he joined with his brother Mikhail to edit *Time,* a literary magazine. At around this time he pursued a ruinous love affair with a beautiful and intellectual woman named Polina Suslova. He also published a highly acclaimed novel based on his prison experiences, *The House of the Dead,* and in the following year he left the magazine and his sick wife in Mikhail's hands to pursue his long-cherished dream of touring western Europe. Appalled by what he saw in Paris and London, he returned more convinced than ever that Russia's destiny was to lead depraved Europe to spiritual salvation. Another trip to Europe in 1863 saw him fall prey to his compulsion for gambling. He lost continually and engaged in another unsuccessful love affair with Suslova. It was common for Dostoevsky to write at his best after just such ruinous escapades, presumably because they psychologically justified the irrational sense of guilt that plagued him. True to this pattern, he began the serial publication of *Notes from Underground* in his magazine, now called *Epoch,* after an interlude of government suppression due to an "unpatriotic" article. Part of his motivation in writing was political: he was understandably anxious to convince the government of *Epoch*'s newly reformed conservatism. In Part I he ridicules activists like N. G. Chernyshevsky who were then advocating a new, utopian state based on thoroughgoing rationalism. But the political theme of *Notes from Underground* comprises only one dimension of its meaning, and a relatively superficial one.

Dostoevsky's wife Marya and his brother Mikhail died in quick succession, and *Epoch* folded, leaving him with his stepson and his brother's family to support on his uncertain income. He was harassed by debts, and by epileptic seizures. In 1866 a particularly threatening contract deadline forced him to gain time by dictating *The Gambler* to a stenographer. The young lady, Anna Gregorevna Snitkina, proved to be so congenial to his temperament that despite the twenty-five-year difference in their ages, they soon married. Together they escaped Fedor's financial burdens by fleeing to Europe. Of their four children, one son and one daughter survived. Despite his continued gambling, his fits of irrationality, and the resumption of his affair with Suslova, Anna's devotion remained a source of enduring strength to him. This combination of genuine love and chronic suffering must have contributed substantially to the creation of his four master-novels within fifteen years: *Crime and Punishment* (begun in 1865 before his marriage, finished in 1867); *The Idiot* (1868); *The Possessed* (1871–1872); and his supreme achievement, *The Brothers Karamazov* (1879–1880). The Dostoevskys returned to Russia in 1871. His last years were his best and most prosperous. His death in 1881 was a national event, and his colossal stature as a writer and religious visionary was acclaimed.

HENRY JAMES
(1843-1916)

Henry James was born in New York City a year after his brother William, who was destined for fame in the realms of psychology and philosophy. The James family, which grew to include two younger boys and a daughter, was lively, intense, competitive, travel-prone, and independently wealthy. Henry James Sr. had declined rule of his father's three-million-dollar business empire, preferring instead to devote himself to enthusiastic but inconsequential philosophizing. Owing to their father's yearning for changes of scene, the James children's education became a geographical adventure. Henry was provided with quality tutors or classes in New York, Albany, Geneva, Paris, Boulogne, Newport (Rhode Island), again in Geneva, and Bonn.

While serving as a volunteer fireman in Newport at age seventeen, Henry received a back injury, recorded in his memoirs as "a horrid even if obscure hurt." The injury strangely echoed his father's loss of a leg while fighting a fire in his own childhood. "Horrid" or not, his injury kept him from action in the Civil War and more importantly provided him with an excuse to retreat from physical and sexual aggressiveness. He spent a year in Harvard Law School but he had little interest in the law and was soon publishing stories and reviews. William Dean Howells, novelist and editor of the *Atlantic Monthly,* encouraged him warmly at this time and through much of James's career. Two visits to Europe instilled in him a passionate desire to live there. His move to Paris in 1875 may have been spurred by uncertainty about his place within the family—a place made even less comfortable by his father's demands that he marry and settle down. Marriage was never a serious question for James. His one deep affection for a woman had been a medieval worship of his cousin, Minny Temple, whose death in 1870 had enshrined her in his memory.

In Paris he became acquainted with Flaubert, Zola, and Turgenev before leaving in 1876 to live in London. The following five years occasioned his publication of six extensive works, including *Daisy Miller: A Study* (1879) and one of his finest novels, *The Portrait of a Lady* (1881). The appearance of *Daisy Miller* created a *cause célèbre,* and made James famous. Before and after *Daisy Miller* he lived London's refined social life to the hilt. His revelation that in 1879 he "dined out 107 times" during the season has become the epigraph of his social success. Social intercourse, travel, and his perpetual recourse to writing consumed his days. Although his fame persisted through the 1880's, his popularity as a writer declined, and with it his income, so that he was led to delve into playwriting for about six years. In January, 1895, his participation in the theater ended sadly when his play *Guy Domville* was hooted on its first night. Shaken but stoic, James intuited that he had forsaken novel-writing for too long. "Produce again . . . better than ever, and all will yet be well," was the self-exhortation he intimated to Howells.

He moved from London to a small estate in Sussex and began writing fiction once again. The best of this later work is the triad of *The Wings of the Dove* (1902), *The Ambassadors* (1903), and *The Golden Bowl* (1904). In these novels James left behind the mellow voice of his middle period and created the most intense and complex art of his career. In 1905 he paid an extended visit to the United States, traveling from coast to coast and lecturing. The coming of the war in 1914 shocked him, as it did almost all socially perceptive artists. Although he was an old man of seventy-one when the fighting began, he busied himself energetically with war charities. Partly out of indignation at the United States' hesitancy to enter the conflict, he became a British subject in 1915. He received the Order of Merit before his death in the following year. His ashes were buried in the family plot in Cambridge, Massachusetts.

LEO TOLSTOY
(1828-1910)

"Who would have dared to invent him? No scheme holds so outrageous a man, certainly none of his own schemes. Not even *War and Peace* would be big enough to hold him," says George P. Elliott of the remarkable vitality which confronts today's reader as the preeminent fact of Tolstoy's existence. Leo Tolstoy was born on his parents' large estate, Yasnaya Polyana, about a hundred miles south of Moscow. His father had bolstered the family's fortune by marrying a wealthy noblewoman, who unfortunately died two years after Leo's birth. As his father survived only another seven years, the children were finally relegated to the care of an aunt in Kazan. Leo, always physically strong from youth onward, developed an enduring love for bodily exercise and the outdoors. A mediocre student due to lack of interest, he was good-natured, eager for affection, and inclined to show off. At sixteen he enrolled to study Oriental languages at the Kazan University, but after being expelled for poor work he changed to the law curriculum for two years. Finally he quit to return to Yasnaya Polyana. As a college student and afterward, Tolstoy revealed himself as a sexually passionate young man with an eye for easy women.

After two years spent aiding the serfs on his estate he enrolled in university courses once again, but this time the lure of army life took him and his brother Nicholas to the Caucasus. There he found time to write three autobiographical volumes which, upon publication, aroused widespread interest

In the unknown young author. Participation in the Crimean War occasioned his three *Sevastopol Sketches* (1855-1856), vivid accounts of the war's realities. In between writing he was a good soldier. His courage under fire drew praise from a general, and he had been promoted to lieutenant by the time of his resignation in 1856. In St. Petersburg, Turgenev introduced him to the influential literary world. The following year he left to tour western Europe, where he studied culture and educational systems, and expressed disappointment at the flourishing materialism he found.

At his estate he founded a school for peasant children, putting into practice some of Rousseau's libertarian theories. He even became involved in teaching and at a later date wrote an educational text. Growing dissatisfaction with his own libertine ways led him to search for a wife. In 1862 he married Sofya Andreyevna Bers, an eighteen-year-old woman of noble birth, pretty, cultured, but at times aloof and insecure. Eight of their thirteen children survived to maturity. Despite quarrels, their early marriage was happy. During the next seven years Tolstoy's talents flourished in the creating of *War and Peace*. This massive novel, considered by many the world's greatest, involves the lives of two aristocratic families during Napoleon's invasion of Russia in 1812. The panorama of its action, the intimacy of its focus on diverse but normal humanity, and the range of its ideas give it a startling impact as a whole and self-contained vision of life. Seven years later Tolstoy completed his second epic novel, *Anna Karenina* (1876). Again he chronicled aristocratic Russian life, but now with a sense of urgency deepened by his own impending crisis. Like his fictional hero Levin, who reflects him, Tolstoy had reached a point where his essentially secular values, based on instinct, humanism, and art, threatened him with spiritual bankruptcy. His dilemma came to a climax in the late 1870's. He evolved a quasi-religious philosophy which denied Christ's divinity but looked to Christ as the model for man. Literature, he now claimed, was valueless except for its moral teaching. On these grounds he repudiated his novels, and even attacked Shakespeare. Private property, capitalism, social divisions, all violence, and all power based on violence were wrong. The ideal life was a primitive agrarianism, in which men lived close to the earth and provided for all their own needs. He envisioned humility and brotherly love as key virtues, and he held that assertion of the ego was the most radical evil.

Driven by his immense fury to live and by an equally terrifying presence of death, he adopted the life of a moral reformer. He immersed himself in the life of the peasants, dressing as one of them and even making his own boots. Among the moral tracts which he wrote to popularize his beliefs, *My Confession* (1879) and *On Life* (1887) particularly mirror the ideas of *The Death of Ivan Ilych* (1886). The compassion of Tolstoy's teaching and the rigor of the man himself won disciples throughout the world. Tolstoyan communes sprang up. The young Mahatma Gandhi was greatly influenced by correspondence with him, and Maxim Gorki said, "One looks at him and it is frightfully pleasant to feel that one is also a man, to realize that man can be such as Leo Tolstoy." Famous men frequented his estate, and even though Tolstoy's message embraced anarchy, the government respected his freedom. His wife, however, was more difficult. Bewildered by her husband's transformation from artist into preacher, she flailed at him with a hysterical possessiveness. Because of his deviant religious teachings, the Orthodox Church excommunicated him in 1901.

Maddened by life at home and anxious to fulfill his own ideal of poverty, Tolstoy fled from his estate with a loyal daughter at the age of eighty-three. Less than a month later he was removed from a train at a remote railstop and died of nervous exhaustion in the station-master's bed. He was buried at Yasnaya Polyana, in a wooded area where his favorite brother, Nicholas, had claimed in boyhood to have buried a green stick inscribed with a message which would bring love and peace to the world.

THOMAS MANN
(1875-1955)

Thomas Mann grew up in the ancient town of Lübeck, near the Baltic coast of northernmost Germany. His father was a most dignified man, a descendant of an influential family of businessmen, politicians, and intellectuals. Twice Mayor and once Senator of the city, Johann Mann was nevertheless unconventional enough to marry Julia Da Silva-Bruhns, a part-Portuguese-Creole beauty of romantic passion and intensely musical sensibility. Scholars have frequently remarked, as did Thomas Mann himself, that his art was deeply influenced by the contrasting strains of his parentage: the earnest, hard-working, mercantile northern character, and the passionate, dreamy, vital traits of the south. As a child Mann thrived in the warmth and security of upper-middle-class German life. He described the family's summer vacations on the Baltic as "undoubtedly the happiest days of my life."

The tranquillity of his early years was disturbed by school. He was a lackadaisical student at the *Gymnasium*, and he looked upon its Prussian strictness with mocking, literary detachment. Several colleagues joined him in establishing a short-lived school newspaper, in which he published poems and plays. When Johann Mann died in 1890, the family's declining, 100-year old grain business went into liquidation, and the spacious home in Lübeck was sold. Leaving Thomas to finish his schooling, Julia Mann moved south to the more genial life of Munich with her two daughters (who later committed suicide) and her two other sons. Thomas joined them four years later, worked for a year in an insurance office, quit to take university courses, then moved to Rome with his older brother, Heinrich. The brothers spent two years in Italy, Heinrich practicing to become a painter and Thomas writing stories and poetry. The aspiring novelist was rewarded by the publication of a volume of short stories, *Little Herr Friedemann,* in 1898.

He returned to Munich with the thick and still-growing manuscript of *Buddenbrooks.* His publisher was at first reluctant to venture money on such a bulky first novel by a little-known writer, only twenty-six years old. But the work appeared late in 1900 and the German literary world gradually realized that this was no ordinary first novel. It was a highly complex psychological study, fully mature in both craftsmanship and wisdom. Probing darkly into Europe's deepening spiritual crisis, Mann transformed much of his own family history into a story of a German business dynasty and its decline from vitality into entropy. Here, as elsewhere in his work, he perceives the dilemma of civilized man in terms of the subtle interplay between the mercantile ethos, with its brisk, controlled mentality, and the more compassionate, self-conscious energy of the artistic mind. *Buddenbrooks* was deeply influenced by Mann's current fascination with the ideas of Schopenhauer and Nietzsche, even though he rejected Nietzsche's ethics.

In the glow of his brilliant success, Mann took Munich's cultured society by storm. During this period he published *Tonio Kröger,* his favorite work, in a volume of short novels entitled *Tristan.* In 1905 he married Katja Pringsheim, the only daughter of a distinguished German-Jewish family. The couple shared a devoted relationship and lived prosperously in a fine house in Munich. Katja bore Mann six children, whom he raised with great affection. He was sought after throughout western Europe to lecture and read from his works. In 1913 appeared *Death in Venice,* acclaimed as one of the best novels ever written.

World War I inflicted Mann with anxiety especially because his insight revealed the conflict to him as a symptom of terrifying cultural evil. From 1913 to 1924, while raising his large family and meeting a heavy schedule of activities, he wrote his second master-novel, *The Magic Mountain.* His sense of the macabre is powerful in this work, which envisioned a mountain-top sanatorium as a symbol of Europe's imprisonment within its own dilemma. In a central moment of insight the novel's hero, Hans Castorp, realizes that salvation lies in maintaining an intimate knowledge of death without succumbing to the morbidity of that knowledge.

Between the wars, Mann continued to produce expertly crafted shorter works, among them the symbolic study of dictatorship, *Mario and the Magician* (1930). In 1926 Mann's attention was drawn to the Biblical story of Joseph and he became fascinated with the tale as a vehicle for expressing a complex of mythic themes. He studied the legends meticulously, making research trips to Egypt and Palestine. Begun on a small scale, *Joseph and His Brothers* burgeoned into a tetralogy, not to be finished until 1942. Mann was fortunately lecturing in Holland when Hitler burned the *Reichstag.* In a coded telegram his daughters warned him not to return because the housecleaning would be too much for him.

Mann knew, as well, that his name was already on the Nazis' list of intellectual traitors. After a pensive interval, he renounced Hitler's Third Reich as the tragedy of Germany and as the enemy of civilization. The Nazis burned his books and in 1936 deprived him of German citizenship. He moved from Switzerland to Princeton, New Jersey, in 1941, then to Santa Monica, California, in 1944. *Dr. Faustus,* the fourth and last of his major novels, appeared in 1947. A modern recasting of the Faust legend, the story reveals Mann's talent at its most ironic: dimensions of hope and despair tangle inseparably in this analysis of the tragic German spirit and the artist's impossible search for integrity. Although his exile was by no means a harsh one, his truly European spirit led him back to live in Zürich and to lecture in both zones of Germany, where enthusiastic crowds affirmed his continued popularity. Among the honors bestowed on Mann were the Nobel Prize in 1929 and the Goethe Prize in 1949. He died in Zürich on August 12, 1955.

JOSEPH CONRAD
(1857-1924)

After Conrad's death in 1924, his friend John Galsworthy recalled, "My memory is of a dark-haired man, short but extremely graceful in his numerous gestures, with brilliant eyes, now narrowed and penetrating, now soft and warm, with a manner alert yet caressing, whose speech was ingratiating, guarded and brusque in turn. I had never seen before a man so masculinely keen yet so femininely sensitive. . . ."

Conrad was born at Berdichev, in a Polish-Ukrainian province left under Russian rule by political partition in the late eighteenth century. He was christened Jozef Teodor Nalecz Korzeniowski, the only son of an aristocratic, landed family. His father, Apollo Nalecz Korzeniowski, was a writer, translator, Polish patriot, and nationalist. Because of his activities in the secret Polish National Committee Apollo Korzeniowski was arrested in 1862 and sentenced to deportation to Russia. He settled his family into miserable exile first in northern Russia, then farther south, in Tchernickow, north of Moscow, where his wife died. In 1869 Conrad's father also died, leaving him an orphan in the guardianship of his maternal uncle, Tadeusz Bobrowski. Conrad attended high school in Cracow and later studied with a tutor from the University of Cracow, to whom he confided that his greatest desire was to go to sea.

By 1873 he had persuaded his uncle to approve of his plan. He hastened to Marseille by train and for the next five years engaged in youthful love involvements, political intrigue, and sea voyages under the flag of the French merchant marine. He sailed to the West Indies and Martinique. With his professed "sea-daddy," the colorful, experienced Corsican, Dom-

Inle Cervoni, he bought a small vessel, apparently to smuggle arms for political activists who were seeking to restore Don Carlos as king of Spain. He also became involved in such serious debts and other personal difficulties that his life in France ended in disaster. Under the burden of merciless self-recrimination he attempted suicide, but the bullet missed his heart. When he found himself wounded, deserted by his embarrassed friends, and confronted with the censure of his uncle Tadeusz who had hurried from Poland to see his disgraced ward, Conrad determined to redeem himself through unquestionable success as a sailor. To him this meant becoming an English seaman; he wrote in *A Personal Record*, "If I was to be a seaman, I would be an English Seaman and no other." He first reached England in June, 1878, as a crewman on the steamer *Mavis*. As yet he knew little English. Polish was of course his mother tongue, and he knew French well. So it happened that mastery of English and mastery of seamanship befell Conrad as simultaneous challanges while he came of age as a man among men. During the following sixteen years merchant voyages took him to Australia, India, Malaya, Java, Borneo, China, and Indo-China. His advance toward authority was steady. He acquired third-mate status in 1880, first-mate papers in 1883, and his master's papers in 1886. At Bangkok in 1888 he inherited his first command, the *Otago,* from a dead captain—a circumstance reflected in *The Secret Sharer.* To the company's regret he resigned his command a year later to make a fateful journey up the Congo for a Belgian commercial organization. There he suffered disease and mental stress from which he never entirely recovered. After one further voyage he found himself in London in 1894, and although he tried for another six years to return to the sea, the more exacting vocation of writing was to claim him from then until his death.

The acceptance and publication of his first attempted novel (*Almayer's Folly*, 1895) remained a matter of perpetual surprise to him. Shortly after its appearance he married Jessie George, daughter of a London bookseller; they had two sons. Life did not become easy for Conrad. He worked prodigiously, producing a steady stream of novels and tales. Even so, his family endured financial stress, which was not substantially alleviated until 1910, when a Civil List pension of £100 per year was granted him until his death twelve years later.

FRANZ KAFKA
(1883-1924)

Franz Kafka was born in Prague, the eldest of six children in a prosperous family of Czech Jews. His two younger brothers died as children, leaving him at an early age with an intimate sense of loss through death and making him the sole male child among three hostile females. His mother was an intelligent woman, entirely devoted to her husband, a self-made man who after years of difficulty had succeeded in consolidating a whole-sale business in luxury goods. Franz's relationship with his father was a crucial one. Hermann Kafka naturally hoped for a capable business heir in his eldest son, especially after the loss of his other sons. Franz idolized, feared, and resented his father, and his unsuitedness for business intensi-fied his shattering self-image of worthlessness and failure. Much of his upbringing was entrusted to a young French governess; she tutored him in preparation for school, and secretly introduced him to sex. After graduat-ing from a strict, competitive, German-run *Gymnasium* (high school), he studied law in a Prague university, receiving a doctorate in jurisprudence in 1906.

Inwardly, he had already chosen literature in preference to a legal career. To support himself with a minimum of time and effort, he sought perfunc-tory bureaucratic jobs, first with an Italian insurance company, then in a government office as an insurance assessor. The psychological alienation engendered by family life was compounded by ethnic tensions. Kafka was a Jew in a city where Jews had been forbidden not long before, and among Jews his unconventional ways made him suspect. In addition, he had been raised to speak German, whereas most of his countrymen spoke Czech. To counter his growing isolation he studied the Czech language and attended nationalist cultural meetings. Yet he continued to drift into introspection, tormented by headaches and anxiety. He experimented with spiritual disci-plines—vegetarianism, theosophy, the Cabala. His studies included the works of Pascal and Kierkegaard, two of the few writers to have significant influence on his later work. During this time he began to make important contacts in the literary world, among them Franz Werfel and the Zionist writer-publisher, Max Brod.

1912 proved to be the year of Kafka's breakthrough as a novelist of great promise. In August he met a young woman ("F.B.") at Brod's house in Prague. Over the succeeding five years his anguished love for her inspired him to frenzies of creativity, and more often, bouts of extreme depression. On September 22–23 he wrote the story *The Judgment* in a single all-night session, and by the end of November he had completed *The Metamorphosis,* working "with incredible ecstasy." His ruinous love affair with F.B. ended when she married someone else, a circumstance which was both a cause and effect of Kafka's deteriorating health.

Because of his government position Kafka was exempt from military service when the First World War broke out, but shortages of food and coal, and other austerities of the war, further worsened his sickness. Never-theless he worked steadily on *The Trial* during the winter of 1916–1917. He refused to go to a sanatorium as his friends urged, although he did retreat to a country estate managed by his youngest sister. In 1918 he returned for a time to his insurance work. In order to stave off death he was soon forced to flee from one sanatorium to another. A teenaged girl named

Dora Dymant came into his life when he was forty. Their relationship during his last year was the nearest to fulfillment in love he ever came. They attempted to settle in Prague, where Kafka lay ill with high fever between Christmas and New Year of 1923. Afterward they continued searching desperately for a suitable hospital. He died of tuberculosis at a sanatorium in Klosterneuberg, Austria, on June 3, 1924.

D. H. (DAVID HERBERT) LAWRENCE (1885-1930)

D. H. Lawrence grew up in the coal-mining town of Eastwood, Nottinghamshire, an industry-marred region of the English midlands legendary as the former haunt of Robin Hood. The turbulent relationship of his parents played an unusually large role in the formation of his creativity. His mother, the capable and resilient daughter of a dockyard engineer, had attained considerable culture as a school teacher. She married an uneducated coal miner, partly because of his burly, vital charm, and partly because she had been disappointed in a courtship nearer to her own level of refinement. John Arthur Lawrence accepted lower-class life as inevitable. He looked upon his five children as future coal miners and housemaids, he relished good times with his friends at the pub, and when drunk often treated his wife brutally. She came to despise the colliery town's low life, longing desperately for the betterment of all her children, but especially David, who was fiercely devoted to her. Although he showed early promise of exceptional intelligence, he was physically weak. An early attack of pneumonia initiated the tubercular onslaughts (although tuberculosis was never diagnosed until 1925) which made much of his life a rhythm of sickness and recovery.

With his mother's encouragement he sought education aggressively, pursuing his studies as far as a college degree in teaching. At twenty he won a position as a biology teacher in an elementary school near London. His first break as a writer came when Jessie Chambers, with whom he shared a formative intellectual companionship for ten years, sent a number of his poems to the *English Review*. His subsequent acquaintance with Ford Maddox Hueffer led to the publication of his first novel, *The White Peacock,* in 1911. This success convinced him to seek his fortune as a writer, although at the time he was deeply shaken by his mother's death. He resigned from his teaching post, where he had done well. In April of 1912 he visited his former French professor to inquire about a lectureship in Europe, and fell in love with the professor's wife at first sight. Frieda von Richthofen Weekley was an intensely vital woman; thirty-one years old and mother of three children, she was frustrated in a marriage with a man fourteen years older. Lawrence convinced her that their flight would be jus tified by their mutual passion and his potential genius. They fled to Europe and sought out her father, commander of the German military garrison at Metz, who gave Lawrence such a chilly welcome that he was forced to stay away. For the next two years they led the kind of austere, itinerant existence that was to become their dominant life style. They stayed in Austria, Italy, and Germany, living on the meager income from a second novel, *The Trespasser*. Frieda was unaccustomed to poverty, and Lawrence himself did most of the cooking and housekeeping. Despite the strong fulfillment they found in each other, their relationship was not surprisingly punctuated by heated quarrels. Lawrence despised her longing for her children (she was to have none by him), and she complained bitterly then and later that his real passion was for his mother, not herself. Nevertheless they married immediately when Frieda's divorce became final in 1914.

World War I seemed to herald misfortune of every kind. After returning to London late in 1915, they retreated to a cottage in a remote region of Cornwall. They were hounded by the authorities because of their unconventionality and foolish indiscretions, and because of Frieda's German ancestry—a situation made worse by the aerial exploits of her famous cousin, the (Red) Baron Manfred von Richthofen. The police ordered them out of Cornwall; at the same time, their requests for emigration were turned down. Lawrence had some success in gaining intimacy with London's intellectual set: Middleton Murry, Katherine Mansfield, Bertrand Russell, John Maynard Keynes, and others. As was so often the case in his friendships, philosophical differences led to personal acrimony. Russell and Keynes, among others, vehemently put down Lawrence's stormy ideas as irresponsible. Worst of all during these years was the condemnation of *The Rainbow* as obscene. For half a decade he had lavished his best talent on the novel, and he badly needed the income from it. In 1916 he said bitterly, "I wish one could be a pirate or a highwayman in these days. But my way of shooting them with noiseless bullets that explode in their souls, these social people of today, perhaps is more satisfying." Possibly because of his frustrations, he wrote prolifically during the war years, turning out a volume of stories, two volumes of verse, and his finest novel, *Women in Love,* which was also long suppressed by censorship.

When peace came in 1919 the Lawrences went abroad immediately, never to live in England again except for brief periods. In Italy and Sicily, he summarized the esoteric, highly imaginative theory of his art in two volumes: *Psychoanalysis and the Unconscious* (1921) and *Fantasia of the Unconscious* (1922). Their next journey took them to Taos, New Mexico, by way of Ceylon, the Antipodes, Australia, New Zealand, Tahiti, and San Francisco. Mabel Dodge Luhan had invited them to her ranch high in the Rockies, promising Lawrence that the climate would bolster his health. He envisioned New Mexico as a place where he might fulfill his dream of forming a remote community of artistic souls who would live together in peace and creativity. The vistas and brilliant sun of the Southwest, as well as the ritualized life of the New Mexico Indians, did provide him with new health, peace, and inspiration. Again Lorenzo (as he was always called) and Frieda quarreled. She refused to take his communitarian dreams seriously, perhaps because she realized that his extraordinarily stubborn, dominant nature could never exist within a close community. When she returned to England and became intimate with John Middleton Murry, Lawrence hastened after her, on the verge of insanity, to bring her back to New Mexico. After two more years in the Southwest, failing health made him forsake his dogged quest for an intellectual community. They returned to Italy, where he wrote *Lady Chatterley's Lover* in 1926. Continued restlessness and illness drove him to Switzerland, to Mallorca, and back to Florence. For several years he had been painting as well as writing. When he exhibited his work in London in 1928, police raided the gallery on an immorality charge. In 1930 Lawrence died of tuberculosis at Vence, France. His ashes are buried in the Taos mountains.

KATHERINE ANNE PORTER
(1890?-   )

Katherine Anne Porter has been reticent about the facts of her past, so uncertainty lingers even over many of the details scholars agree on. She was probably born on April 15, 1890 (but 1894 persists), in Indian Creek, near San Antonio, Texas. Her mother died two years later and the family moved to Kyle, Texas, where the five children were cared for by their paternal grandmother until her death in 1901. Miss Porter claims that her formal education took place "in small southern convent schools. I was precocious, nervous, rebellious, unteachable, and made life very uncomfortable for myself and I suppose for those around me." She began writing literature early in girlhood, destroying manuscripts "literally by the trunkful," while reading "a grand sweep of all English and translated classics from the beginning up to about 1800." Her fierce independence was always a dominant trait. It led her to elopement at sixteen and divorce by nineteen. In 1911 she moved to Chicago, working as a reporter. Her attractiveness, which had something of movie-star glamour, also helped her attain minor film roles. From 1914 until 1917 she traveled throughout Texas and Louisiana as a cabaret singer of Scottish ballads. Afterward she worked for a year on a Fort Worth newspaper. Then in Denver she became a reporter for *The Rocky Mountain News*. Sometime during this period, which provided the background of *Pale Horse, Pale Rider* (1939), she suffered a near-fatal case of influenza which profoundly altered her sense of self. In a *Paris Review* interview of 1963, she said, "I had what the Christians call the 'beatific vision,' and the Greeks called the 'happy day,' the happy vision just before death. Now if you have had that, and survived it . . . you are no longer like other people, and there's no use deceiving yourself that you are."

After a year of freelance writing in New York City, her travels took her to Mexico for much of the next ten years. The culture of Mexico had always fascinated her, and she was now afforded a close look at the country's revolutionary struggle. She may have played a small part in it. Her experiences there were reflected in her first published book of fiction, *Flowering Judas, and Other Stories* (1930) which won her a Guggenheim Fellowship. Following a disillusioning confrontation with her friend Hart Crane, who accosted her with obscene language in one of his drunken rages, she sailed for Germany in August, 1931. Her journal notes from this voyage formed the basis for her most ambitious work, *Ship of Fools* (1962).

She stayed in Europe for about six years. In Berlin she met Hitler, Goering, and Goebbels, whom she later described as "detestable and dangerous." In 1933 she married Eugene Pressly of the American Foreign Service. Her first genuinely popular literary success came when her story *Noon Wine* was granted the Book of the Month Club award in 1937. Back in the United States, divorced from Pressly, she married Elbert Erskine, Jr., a literature professor at Louisiana State University. A third divorce in 1942 was followed by the publication of *The Leaning Tower, and Other Stories* (1944). During the next dozen years she held numerous writer-in-residence positions in American universities, and she became a sought-after speaker at writers' conferences and literary symposia.

The appearance of the long-awaited *Ship of Fools* in 1962 was by far her greatest popular success. The novel was an immediate best-seller and became a popular movie. Miss Porter was awarded the Pulitzer Prize and the National Book Award for fiction in 1966. Her collected essays were published in 1970. Undaunted by age, she claimed in 1973 that she still had three books to write.

RICHARD WRIGHT
(1908-1960)

Richard Wright was born in the Deep South, the son of a sharecropper on a cotton plantation near Natchez, Mississippi. He was five when his father deserted the family after repeated crop failures. His mother, a trained school teacher, tried to support her two sons by working as a housemaid. Plagued by illness and poverty, and angered by Richard's constitutional rebelliousness, she beat him severely. For a crucial portion of his childhood the family lived with his grandmother in Jackson, Mississippi. A fanatical Seventh-Day Adventist, she forbade non-religious books, baseball, and marble-playing, and reduced their already meager diet with dogmatic restrictions. In school, Richard came under the tutelage of an equally strict aunt. He shrugged off the crippling demands for submissiveness that came at him from every direction, refusing to smile and mumble before whites, or to join in protective solidarity with acquiescent Southern Negroes. When he was fifteen, the local Negro newspaper printed one of his adventure stories, "The Voodoo of Hell's Half-Acre." He graduated first in his grade school class without having spent a full year of schooling in any one place.

Survival, he knew, meant flight. Memphis was a waystop on his journey north. There he saved money from odd jobs, and spirited H. L. Mencken's works from the public library with a forged note: "Dear Madam: Will you please let this nigger boy have some books by H. L. Mencken?" Mencken's invective opened a new world to him; Dreiser and Sinclair Lewis revealed the fictional uses of environment as imagery and influence.

In the winter of 1927 he moved to Chicago with his brother and crippled mother. The Depression cost him his job as a postal clerk, forcing him back to menial work again. Still he read avidly, devouring massive sociological studies from the University of Chicago library. Despite hardships, the city's quick pace and toughness enlivened him. He joined the Communist Party in 1932 and began to publish numerous poems, stories, and essays in leftist periodicals. 1937 found him in New York, working as the Harlem editor of the Communist *Daily Worker.* The following year *Story* magazine awarded him a $500 prize for his first book, four stories collected under the title *Uncle Tom's Children.* A Guggenheim Fellowship helped him find time to finish *Native Son* (1940), which became a best-seller and a Broadway play. *Native Son,* a case study of a black man who can find identity only through violent crime, achieves literary power through the force of its prophecy. In a way that was prophetic for both American society and Wright himself, the novel foretold a dilemma of choice between love and the demonic, between selective acceptance of tradition and destructive alienation. In the end Bigger Thomas chooses a tortured self-affirmation through violence, exclaiming, "What I killed for, I am!"

In 1941 Wright divorced his wife of two years to marry Ellen Poplar, a Communist Party organizer from Brooklyn. The NAACP honored his writing achievement with its coveted Spingarn Medal. *The Man Who Lived Underground* appeared in 1942, followed by the autobiographical novel, *Black Boy: A Record of Childhood and Youth* in 1945. The public impact of *Black Boy* exceeded that of *Native Son,* and the work has endured as Wright's best full-length novel. In it he suppressed his occasional impulse to preach and used a picaresque series of encounters as a vehicle for self-revelation and scourging social comment.

Successive visits to Paris in 1946–1947 convinced him to live there. In 1949 a second daughter was born to him. He immersed himself in the vibrant cultural life of France and became acquainted with the circle of French Existentialists led by Jean Paul Sartre. In Europe he enjoyed a fame he had never known before. Lecture invitations and famous visitors converged on his Left Bank apartment. He traveled to Spain, England, and Africa. During the fifties he published three more novels, and more importantly, a series of political commentaries dealing especially with the politics of new African nations. In the collected lectures of *White Man, Listen* (1957) he emphasized the world-wide importance of Black Africa, defending the right of African nations to develop without colonial restraint. At age fifty-two he died in Paris of a heart attack.

CARSON McCULLERS
(1917-1967)

Carson McCullers was born Lula Carson Smith in Columbus, Georgia. She was a shy, precocious, bitter girl, and gave evidence of unusual talent at an early age. Economically her family was lower-middle-class, but her parents warmly encouraged her abilities. When she revealed her interest in music as a five-year-old, her father bought her a piano. When she began to write plays and stories at fifteen, he brought home a typewriter. Her sister recalls "intense dramas written as vehicles for herself to star in (with minor roles for unwilling siblings), to be mounted in the parlor before perplexed parents and whatever relatives and neighbors could be corralled." Carson adds that during her teens she also "dashed off . . . a novel, and some rather queer poetry that nobody could make out, including the author."

At seventeen she left home to study piano in New York at the Juilliard School of Music, supported by money from the sale of a valued family ring. But a girl friend from Columbus, with whom Carson was to have roomed in Manhattan, claimed to have lost all the tuition money on the subway their second day in the city. Instead of studying music, Carson had to work at part-time jobs, but she managed to take creative writing courses at Columbia and New York University. Just before her twentieth birthday she published her first story, "Wunderkind," in *Story* magazine. That same winter a severe attack of rheumatic fever exposed her already frail health to successive attacks of pneumonia, heart disease, and paralytic strokes during the remaining thirty years of her life.

In 1937 she married J. Reeves McCullers, a charming young Georgian with literary aspirations. Her poor health forced them to move south. They settled in Charlotte, North Carolina, where Reeves worked as a credit manager and she wrote her first novel, *The Heart Is a Lonely Hunter* (1940). Set in a dreary southern town, the work tells a strange tale of a deaf mute who ironically becomes an object of adoration to a group of misfits. Despite its structural looseness and other faults, the novel was recognized for its intense, compassionate characterization. For an author only twenty-two years old, it was an extremely promising beginning. Her second novel came quickly. *Reflections in a Golden Eye* (1941) deals with infidelity, murder, and perversion on a peace-time army base in the South. The predominant critical reaction was hostile. Critics charged that the neurotic horrors of the story were not balanced by an adequate background of human normalcy.

Her disappointment was compounded by domestic turmoil. She and her husband agreed to a divorce, and she spent most of the following five years in a Brooklyn commune of artists, an illustrious group which at times included W. H. Auden, Richard Wright, Christopher Isherwood, and Gypsy Rose Lee. During the war she again began exchanging letters with Reeves, who was wounded while overseas. In 1945 they were married for a second time. The following year saw publication of her best novel, *The Member of the Wedding,* about an adolescent girl's struggle to find her place in society and to reconcile her creative vision with reality. Rewritten as a play, *A Member of the Wedding* became an award-winning Broadway hit in 1950. *The Ballad of the Sad Café,* the most expertly crafted of all her works, appeared in 1951.

She and her husband bought a house near Paris, where they lived for about two years. But after Reeves fell prey to bouts of violence fueled by alcohol and drugs, Carson fled desperately to her mother's house in Nyack, New York, only to learn that Reeves had committed suicide in Paris. By this time her own disastrous ill health had made her a semi-invalid. Nevertheless she struggled to complete one last novel, *Clock Without Hands* (1961). After a tumultuous and varied series of health complications, she succumbed to a stroke on September 29, 1967.

SAUL BELLOW
(1915-   )

Saul Bellow, often acknowledged as the most distinguished American novelist of his generation, was born in an industrial suburb of Montreal. It was a polyglot neighborhood, he recalls, "of Sicilians, Ukrainians, Scots, Croats, and Indians." He says in a *Time* magazine interview with characteristic humor, "I had an Iroquois nurse who chewed meat before feeding it to me. I'm sure it did me good." He was the fourth and youngest child of Orthodox Jewish parents who had emigrated from Russia in 1913. After the family moved to the Division Street section of Chicago in 1924, Bellow spent much of his time in libraries, but he also nourished his imagination on the city's garrulous and colorful street life. Financial struggle was a problem throughout his youth. His father, a businessman with a penchant ror risks, failed in a series of enterprises. The whole family, Bellow claims, worked for years to pay off debts when one of his uninsured coal trucks had a fatal accident. His mother wanted him to become a Talmudic scholar in the family tradition; his father wanted him to enter a profession and make money. The bitter disaffection of his father was a part of the price he paid for rejecting all parental demands and following his own pursuits. After high school he studied at the University of Chicago, but was unhappy there and transferred to Northwestern, earning a bachelor's degree in anthropology and sociology with honors in 1937.

He enrolled at the University of Wisconsin at Madison but quit a few months later to get married. For a time he worked in Chicago for the WPA writers' project, composing biographical pamphlets on "Middle Western authors," of which he remarks, "I'm glad to say they've all disappeared." He was an editorial staff writer for the *Encyclopaedia Britannica* when his first novel, *Dangling Man,* appeared in 1944. After a brief war-time duty in the Maritime Service, his second novel, *The Victim* (1947), brought him a Guggenheim Fellowship to live in Paris and Rome. For much of the next fifteen years his home was New York City, although he also spent intervals in Puerto Rico and Nevada. He forsook New York in the early sixties because, he says, "I knew intuitively that it was going to go mad. It did go mad." He has resided since in Chicago. Married and divorced three times, he lives in a bachelor's flat on the South Side and teaches literature at the University of Chicago, where he is also a member of the prestigious Committee on Social Thought.

His later novels are *The Adventures of Augie March* (1954), *Seize the Day* (1956), *Henderson the Rain King* (1959), *Herzog* (1964), and *Mr. Sammler's Planet* (1970). Among the many honors awarded Bellow have been two Guggenheim Fellowships, the International Literature Prize, and three National Book Awards.

Index